The Color of Light

The Color of Light

HELEN MARYLES SHANKMAN

Text copyright © 2013 Helen Maryles Shankman

ISBN-13: 9781490473246

To every English teacher I ever had.
To anyone who ever told me a story.
To all my vampires, alive and dead.

But most of all,
To Jon.

When I'm asleep, dreaming and drowsed and warm,
They come, the homeless ones, the noiseless dead.
While the dim and charging breakers of the storm
Rumble and drone and bellow overhead,
Out of the gloom they gather about my bed.
They whisper to my heart; their thoughts are mine.
—*Siegfried Sassoon*

Prologue

New York City, 1992.

It was late, but the blond girl he had seen panhandling earlier in the afternoon was still there, sharing a cigarette with another junkie in the doorway of a store for rent at the corner of Broadway and 8th Street.

"One hundred dollars." he said to her.

"Okay," she said, and handed the cigarette to her companion. The boy, skeletally thin beneath his dirty Rush t-shirt, leaned over and whispered something to her. Clearly, he didn't like the looks of him. He could hear her murmur something back, and then the boy looked at him with cold, hard eyes, took another drag of the cigarette, and headed off in the direction of St. Mark's Place.

She got to her feet, dusting off her pants. "What do you want me to do?"

She was young, so young that her cheeks still looked downy and round, like a child's. Her hair was shiny, bouncy, with a good cut. She was probably a recent runaway; she seemed unsure of herself, almost innocent.

He came closer to her, and now she could see him better in the yellow glow of the streetlight. He had a long, aristocratic face, high sculptured cheekbones like you'd see on a statue, full sensual lips.

Beautiful eyes. She couldn't stop looking at his eyes.

"Why don't we get you fixed up first?" And a voice like a priest.

"Wow," she said, a little girl getting a new toy. "Thanks, mister."

He followed her to a club on the Bowery, where he paid the guy who worked the door for a tiny glassine envelope. She led him around the corner onto a narrow, dimly lit street, to a dark doorway, away from the crowd and the noise and the bright lights of the club. She opened the envelope with shaking hands and hungrily sniffed its powdery contents up her pert little nose.

With a deep sigh, she leaned against the rusting, steel-gated door. It squealed in protest. An ocean of peaceful easy feeling washed over her. "Okay, mister," she murmured. "Let's go."

He drew near her, put gentle hands on her body, turned her to face the wall. She twisted her fingers in the gate to keep herself from falling down. As he came up behind her, swept the hair from her neck, touched his lips to her shoulder, she took in a cacophony of smells. Vanilla. Something green, like distant fields. Musk. Sandalwood.

The last thing she would remember as she coasted down into a druggy trance was the prick of his teeth as they pressed into her throat.

Part One

1

$\mathcal{W}$e're late," said Raphael Sinclair, as he ran up the long flight of stairs to the Cast Hall. "That idiot Turner will already have them all riled up."

"I had a little trouble getting here," the man beside him said mildly. "A car caught fire on the West Side Highway. It's backed up all the way to the bridge." Levon Penfield, the Dean of Admissions, glanced over at his companion, amused. "Sometimes even I believe what they say about you. What are you doing in a hat and overcoat? It's 83 degrees out there."

Rafe didn't answer. They reached the second floor landing. He held open the fire door for his companion.

But Levon wasn't there. "I have to check on my transfer students," he called down as he continued up the stairs, two at a time. Rafe cursed, slammed the door shut and followed the echo of his footsteps up to the fourth floor.

"Good God," he said as the door closed behind him.

As part of the school's expansion plan, a huge lofty space with white-washed walls thirty feet high had been converted to studios. Windows soared from floor to ceiling. Ten large rooms took up either side of the floor, made from moveable white walls and white drapes, with a wide aisle down the middle. Dozens of fluorescent lamps tricked out with reflectors and full-spectrum bulbs filled the room with light the color of the sun. Rafe closed his eyes and inhaled deeply, the scent of turpentine and linseed oil intoxicating him.

Hearing Levon's deep voice, he moved slowly down the aisle, peering into each studio. Picture postcards of paintings by Michelangelo, Leonardo,

Raphael, Rubens, Rembrandt, Titian, Botticelli, Velasquez and Vermeer, were tacked up on the homosote walls alongside life drawings, grocery lists, phone numbers and thumbnail sketches. Canvases were stacked in corners, easels held today's wet work.

He found Levon in the second studio on the right, talking with a delectable pastry of a girl standing at the top of a ladder. She was wearing a very short plaid skirt that made her look like a naughty Catholic school-girl. She reminded him of a cannoli, a voluptuous vanilla cream filling stuffed into a soft golden crust.

Levon spun around to introduce him, his eyes shining, as if he were the host at a wonderful party. "There you are, Rafe! This is Graciela. She's new here this year. Look how beautifully she draws!"

Rafe crossed over to the piece she was working on. She did, indeed, draw beautifully. It was a life-sized charcoal drawing of herself naked, making love to a good looking, well-endowed young fellow. "It's my boyfriend," she said giggling, tossing her bronze-colored hair. "It's for his birthday."

"You're very talented," he agreed, then turned to look at the other things on the wall.

"Do you work from photographs or from life?" he heard Levon ask.

"I did his thing from memory," he heard her reply, but Rafe was no longer listening. She really did draw beautifully. Each mark on her figures was precisely placed, with a satisfying variation of thick and thin lines, describing the way a leg turned, or the expression in a face.

Curious to see what she used for inspiration, he noticed a postcard of his favorite Madonna and Child on the opposite wall. Next to it was a small pencil sketch. Something about it drew him closer.

With a nod to the Renaissance painter Raphael, it was a mother holding a child. Every shadow was delicately rendered, creating form, revealing features, or hiding them in shadow. They were dressed in clothing from the 1930s, the mother covering the little boy's eyes with her hand.

Now he was so close he was almost touching it.

Her face was a mask of horror. Flames leaped in her eyes. At her feet was a suitcase with a name printed on it.

Wizotsky.

Rafe heeled around and stared deliberately into Graciela's amber eyes. "What made you do this drawing?" he said, pointing at the tiny sketch on the wall. His voice was light and gentle, but there was an underlying current of something else.

It took her a moment to answer, transfixed by his gaze. When she saw which one he meant, she broke into peals of laughter. "Oh, *that* one!"

He smiled politely, not understanding.

"That's not mine. I just share a studio with her. Isn't it scary and depressing?"

He stared at the drawing for another moment, then dropped his gaze. "Yes. Of course. Scary and depressing. Well—good luck, then."

He ducked under the curtain draped over the doorway and disappeared. Levon followed close behind.

Their footsteps echoed off the shadowy purple walls as they swept past statues of Greek wrestlers, the *Dying Gaul,* the head of Michelangelo's *David.* A Roman beauty in carved drapery gazed at them with empty eyes. A Rodin hand implored them from a block of raw marble.

Two rows of folding chairs were set up at the end of the Cast Hall. A table was arranged with little petits fours and a coffee urn. Board members and instructors turned around to smile hello.

"Glad you could join us, Levon, Rafe." Whit Turner was standing at the front holding a clipboard, not looking glad at all. "We're just talking about the focus of the school this year. We thought we'd get a jump on it this time, steer it in the right direction from the beginning."

Levon took a seat, glanced over to Harvey Glaser, the sculpting teacher. Harvey shook his head. *Not good.*

"We're talking about bringing on board some artists who belong to the postmodern discipline, but who bring the human figure into their work. Some of us think that would put the school on a more contemporary track, make the art world take us a little more seriously."

"It seems like a good idea," agreed Blesser, the school's chief financial officer. "Might get us more endowments, if they see us as a serious art school."

There was a silence, a collective intake of breath.

"A *serious* art school?"

"Don't, Rafe," muttered Levon. "He's trying to provoke you."

"So... you don't think what we do here is serious."

Turner sighed, waited.

"No other school in the entire world is teaching these skills. Parsons, Pratt, even the École des Beaux-Arts—they've all abandoned it." His voice flowed over them like a caress, a siren's song. "How to draw like Raphael. How to paint like da Vinci. How to sculpt like Michelangelo. How to create works of art that one may appreciate without reading a handout that explains what you're looking at, and what you should be feeling.

"The methods of the old masters are being lost in the mists of time. And you don't think that's *serious?*"

Rafe leaned against the table with the little cakes on it with his arms crossed, his strange eyes burning into Whit Turner, filling him with dread. *I swear,* Turner would tell his friends, his voice cracking a little. *There's something that's just not right about that guy, something that makes your blood freeze when he looks your way. And if you disagree with him...well, you lock your windows at night.*

But today Turner stood his ground, turned his blocky body and his square head to face his adversary down. "Of course I think it's serious. But I also know what they call us out in the art world. Remedial art school. Art School 101. Art School for Dummies."

He paused, looking from one face to the next as he let it sink in. "They say we're obsessed with skills that passed into redundancy around the time of the invention of the camera. And if we want to attract serious patrons, and serious money, we have to look like a serious art school. And that means we need some big name artists teaching here, even if they don't know how to draw."

Late afternoon sun slanted in through the windows, the kind of light that only comes in early autumn, falling in golden bars across the two men.

"No. Never." Rafe said quietly. "Please excuse me." He strode away, his coat billowing out behind him, and vanished through a back exit.

There was an audible feeling of relief, even from his supporters.

"Anybody else smell smoke?" muttered Blesser.

"I've been working here for four years, and I didn't know there was an exit back there. Did you?" said the chairman of the drawing department, nervously patting her forehead with a paper napkin.

"Can't we just discuss fundraising for once, you know, parties, like other boards?" the Dean of Student Affairs said plaintively.

"Hey, I know he founded the school, and I'm on his side, but every time he catches my eye, I want to run home and hide under my bed," said the anatomy instructor, who had once worked as a butcher.

Cautiously, Turner looked all around the room, peered as far down the darkened Cast Hall as he could. When he had satisfied himself that the school's founder was not lurking anywhere in the shadows, he wiped the perspiration from his brow and continued.

"You all know my work. I'm a classical painter. I do guys in Renaissance drapery on marble staircases in two-point perspective. However…" Turner went on, confidentially lowering his voice, "this is about our careers, too. Do you want to be known as a teacher from that funny little art school that lives in the past? Or do you want to be a professor at a boutique art school to rival Yale, Parsons, Rhode Island School of Design, the Chicago Art Institute?"

There was an uncomfortable silence.

"I'll make some inquiries," he said and made some notes on his clipboard, signifying that the meeting was over. Chairs scraped on wood floors. People drifted to the table with the coffee.

"You know," Levon said. Inwardly, Whit groaned. "Have you asked the students what they think?"

The conversation that had started up after the meeting died back down. Levon continued in his affable voice.

"They come from the far corners of the earth to be here, at this school. There's a student here from frigging *Norway* this year. Every day I get these calls. 'Are you really a classical art school? Can you really teach me how to paint like Rembrandt?'

"Okay, maybe the guy is eccentric, but hey, he's British. Raphael Sinclair sought out each person in this room to create this place. He knew our backgrounds, and experience, and our work. He went to Russia to recruit Mischa when it was still the Soviet Union. He went to Paris to persuade Ted. He found Inga in East Germany, and Geoff in Glasgow and Langley in Pasadena. Tony, I don't know where the hell he found you." Scattered titters.

"There are a hundred schools that teach kids how to use video cameras and make art out of stuff they find in dumpsters. But there's only one Academy."

The instructors looked at one another and then down at their plates. Levon looked at his watch, rose to his feet. "I've got to go. I've got a kid coming in from Wisconsin for an interview. Good meeting, Whit." And he set off through the Cast Hall, leaving them to the coffee and petits fours.

In the stairwell, Rafe leaned against the steel door, counted to ten, took deep cleansing breaths in an attempt to control his blinding fury.

Originally, he had planned to be there for the length of the meeting. He chose to remove himself when tearing Turner's head off began to seem like a workable solution. Also, there was the matter of the sun streaming into the room.

He leaned over, put his hands on his knees, trying to bring his rage down to something more human and manageable. There was a pay phone in the hallway on the third floor landing. One side of a disembodied conversation floated down the stairs.

"I'm not working tonight. I'll be over later." It was a girl. A pause as whoever was on the other end of the phone replied. "Oh." A world of pain in that two-letter word. "Where were you last night? I thought your meetings were on Sundays." Another pause. The voice was becoming sadder. "Some of the guys? Okay. Well...maybe tomorrow." The click of the pay phone being hung back up. A moment of silence, followed by the awful, clanging cacophony of the phone being smashed furiously against the box, magnified a hundred times by the cinderblock and steel in the enclosed space. Finally, the sound of stifled weeping echoed through the stairway, and a steel door opened and closed.

Ah, art students. Come for the talent, stay for the tears.

He straightened up, rolled his shoulders. The rage was subsiding. Halfway down the stairs, he thought he'd see if the cannoli would come out with him for a drink. He straightened his tie and headed back up to the fourth floor.

The staircase he'd taken opened into the sculptors' studio. Though it was only the beginning of the school year, everything was already covered with a fine white coating of plaster dust. Armatures and clay figures jostled each other for space on bookshelves and windowsills. Some of the students had begun working on ideas for their thesis projects, ghostly contorted figures rising up from clay-spattered turntables, covered in damp rags to keep them from drying out.

The floor seemed abandoned. And then, from the direction of the girl's studio, Mozart's *Requiem* began to play.

Softly, softly, he began to walk towards the music.

It was coming from behind the curtain that draped the cannoli's doorway. He stopped, stood perfectly still, closed his eyes, breathed in the scent.

He could catch the thinnest glimpse of a girl in the sliver of air between the curtain and the partition. She was small, dressed in art school standard-issue basic black, with an ass like an upside-down heart. But her hair. Oh, her hair. It cascaded in a fall of loose curls down her back, not red, not blonde, not brown, and yet all of them mixed together, trailing off at her waist. With a pang, he imagined the colors he would have used to paint it, in the years when he could still paint; golden ochre, terra rossa, raw sienna.

She was bending over, setting down two space heaters and a reflector lamp. When she straightened up, her gaze wandered to the sketch of the mother and child he had seen earlier. She stood there, perfectly still, absorbed in her thoughts. Then he realized that she was looking past the sketch, at a drawing tacked up beside it, done in sanguine and charcoal.

A naked woman sat at the edge of a rumpled bed, yearning with her whole body toward a man leaning against the wall next to an open door. The man was dressed in a tuxedo, ready to go out. His face was expressionless, lost in shadow.

The girl in the room seemed to sense Rafe's presence. She turned her head toward the doorway, just enough for him to see fear wash over her like a tide.

A strange sensation of vertigo came over him. He rested his hand on the wall as if he could touch what was behind it. And then he moved on, quicker now, almost running, until he reached the door at the other end of the hall.

The girl blinked, wondering what had come over her. It had been something more than being female and alone on a deserted floor. Something ancient. Primeval.

At that moment, a door clanged open. Heavy footsteps treaded through the back where the sculptors' studio was. She heard scraping noises. Something thrown heavily onto the floor. The sound of chairs being moved.

"Damn! Missed the blackboard!" someone exploded. The Simpsons theme music blasted through the vast hall. The girl let out her breath; she hadn't realized she was holding it in. Just the sculptors gathering around the TV for their nightly ritual. She smiled in relief, feeling silly. It had only been someone late for an evening class. And yet…

She shrugged the feeling off, went back to staring at her drawing.

Midtown, a nondescript limestone and brick building like a hundred other buildings on Forty-fourth and Madison.

He passed the information desk, the newsstand, went straight into a waiting elevator. Three other people were in the car; one woman in a serious black suit and a short blunt haircut, a man wearing a red paisley shirt with ruffled sleeves and pinstriped polyester bellbottoms, and one tall, frighteningly thin young girl with a blank, pretty face.

They all got off at twenty-two. The reception area was papered with gold leaf. A sign in three-foot-high block letters announced, ANASTASIA. The man in bellbottoms nodded politely at Rafe as he breezed past, the woman in black hurried down a staircase to another floor. He waited with the model until the receptionist whispered, "She can see you now."

Rafe walked down the corridor past empty desks and offices. Most of the editors and assistants had already left for the night. Computers winked quietly into the dusk. At the end of the passageway, a severe little Englishwoman peered disapprovingly over her glasses at him and said, "Go on in, then."

A small plaque on the door read, *Anastasia deCroix, Editor in Chief.* He knocked twice, let himself in. A tiger-skin rug covered the floor. Orchids in pots were scattered tastefully around the surfaces and corners. At the center of the room was a round table and five chairs with sleekly twisted, brushed aluminum legs, upholstered in a silky, lipstick-red fabric. At the opposite end of the office was a desk with a Tizio lamp and a computer. A leopard-spotted daybed lounged discreetly in the shadows.

Though it was a corner office, with floor to ceiling windows on two sides, the shades were always drawn. Anastasia deCroix's aversion to sun was well documented. The door opened, and Anastasia herself stalked through it, talking to someone unseen.

"I don't care what she told Italian *Vogue,*" she snapped in French-accented English. "If she can't be at the lingerie shoot on Friday, she won't be on the cover next month. Tell *that* to Elite Models. Hello, my darling," she said as she strode past him to the table, laid out with grainy gray photographs of pretty people apparently having sex.

Rafe picked up a picture, scrutinized it. "What's this for?" A headless female torso bent over backwards, nipples erect.

"The December orgasm story. We have one every month. You like this one?" She plucked it from his fingers, surveyed it thoughtfully. "Anthea!" she called sharply. The severe woman poked her head around the door. "Take this to the art department right away, please. Tell Ram, 'Orgasm.' Now, what is it, my darling? You have five minutes before I have to rush off. My car is already waiting downstairs. Tell me while I change." She picked up a garment bag and shut herself behind a door marked *Private.*

"Why? Where are you off to?" A photograph on the table caught his eye. Though the couple in the picture was joined at the hips, their silvery bodies were arcing away from each other and their eyes were closed in passion. "Were they really making love?"

"A child could see they are pretending. Look. They are not even sweating. Jean-Paul is throwing a party for his new fragrance at the Puck Building."

The door opened. She stepped out in a tight burgundy dress with a plunging neckline shaped like an inverted heart. She leaned over to pull on black stilettos, revealing a generous sweep of cleavage, then straightened back up, flipping back her short dark hair. "How do I look?"

Nobody knew how old Anastasia deCroix really was, or where she had come from. The columnists put her age at anywhere from thirty-five to fifty-five. As editor-in-chief of the eponymous *Anastasia,* the most influential women's magazine in the United States, she was both revered and feared in the fashion industry. It was said that one day, Leo Lubitsch had flown her in from Buenos Aires and given her an office. The next day, *Anastasia's* sales numbers had overtaken *Vogue, InStyle, Elle,* and *Marie Claire.*

"Terrible," he said. "Like an old skank."

She smiled at him. Her lips were stained dragon red, in a discontinued Chanel color that they still made just for her. "So, what is it today? Is that horrible little man still trying to take your school away from you? Is the entire faculty still sleeping with the students?" She selected a round brush from a chromed caddy, began fluffing her hair.

"Funny you should ask." He related the story of going to the girl's studio, the drawing on the wall.

"Wizotsky? Like your little girlfriend from school?" The irises of her eyes gleamed ruby red, not quite human. Her pupils narrowed and dilated voraciously, the real reason she wore her signature dark glasses night and day. "Are you sure?"

"Same spelling, anyway."

"Come, we'll talk in the elevator." She put the glasses back on, took her bag, a jeweled box that was made to look like a wrapped present, raced ahead of him down the corridor.

"Have you met her, this girl?"

"God, no. I can't even bring myself to say hello."

"Hm." She swished on face powder, put the compact back in her bag. They were zipping down in the elevator now. "Perhaps it's a different Wizotsky," she suggested in a soothing voice. "It was such a long time ago."

They were walking through the lobby now. Rafe had to lengthen his stride to keep up with her. She smiled at the old German couple who ran the magazine stand, hurried through the revolving door. "Why don't you accompany me, my darling? Maybe we'll meet someone…nice." Her lips stretched in a rapacious smile as she slid into the limo. "Join us. We could have dinner together." She patted the seat next to her. "Come. Leo will be happy to see you."

He got in. The car slid away from the curb, headed downtown. "How is Leo? Not dead yet?"

"No, my darling. But he is getting old. He shakes now. And Margaux…" she sighed. "Poor Margaux. She was always so chic. Remember, during the war, in Paris? They were adorable. She was always wearing some little hat that she had just made, and he was charming and dapper, every inch the Russian aristocrat, so courtly and ruthless. They were more—how can I put it—like us, than anyone I have ever met."

For a moment, he was silent, remembering. "Funny that he never asked to be changed."

She responded with a Gallic shrug. "I offered it to him once. When Brodov died, after suffering a long illness. You know, they had this big rivalry going on when they first came to America, Leo with *Femme*, Brodov with *Bella*. It was in the papers all the time how they were stealing each other's ideas, photographers, models. Wives. Anyway, he said he didn't want to outlive his times. Can you imagine?" A short, sharp laugh.

They were shooting down Fifth Avenue at Twenty-fourth street, past old Madison Square. The Flatiron building reared up before them. A derelict was standing in front of the Civil War monument holding up a sign that read, *Lost job, please help.*

"I like his jacket," she said, tapping on the glass. "Look at those buttons."

They rode in silence for a while. Below Twenty-third, the look on the street changed. Thin couples headed for the trendy new restaurants grouped around Union Square. Pale, tattooed girls with long dark hair streaked magenta, or electric blue, lugging huge portfolios. Flocks of the young and the hip, dressed all in black, flowing steadily towards the Village, Soho, Tribeca.

"Perhaps she has a friend you could ask," she suggested. "She must be friendly with the other girl in her studio, what did you call her? The cannoli."

"I don't think so." he replied, remembering the astonishing accuracy of Graciela's anatomical drawing. "Their interests seem to be very different."

"They are girls." Anastasia said emphatically. "If they are sharing a studio, they will become intimates. You will see. Befriend the cannoli, and you will learn all the scary depressing one's secrets."

He was looking out the window. A boy and a girl were strolling down Fifth Avenue looking in shop windows, her arm circled around his hips, his thumb hooked into a belt loop on her jeans. They stopped in front of an antique toy store on Sixteenth Street to kiss. He turned away.

"The flames in her eyes," he whispered. "It made me feel…"

She touched his arm. "My poor Raphael. You suffer so beautifully." Taking his face in her long, pale, manicured hands, she kissed him avariciously on the mouth, undulating her voluptuous body against his chest. It took him a moment to respond, but he did, reluctantly.

"Come." Anastasia's warm words poured over him. "Let us go to this opening, and we will drink horrid white wine, and we will make polite, boring conversation, and then we will sneak out and grab something for dinner and forget all about these…*feelings.*"

The arch at Washington Square Park loomed suddenly before them, lighted for the evening, abruptly invoking Paris. They were at Eighth Street now. There was still an orange glow behind the buildings on Sixth Avenue, but over his head, and to the east, stretched night. "Let me off here," he said, and got out.

The window hummed down. "Leo will be so disappointed," she said, and slipped her dark glasses back on. The limo pulled away from the curb, leaving him alone under the arch.

Washington Square was almost deserted at night. Lights were coming on in the windows of the brownstones and apartment buildings surrounding the park, making it seem colder and darker by contrast. A couple of brave souls, ex-cons, or refugees of Soviet Russia, afraid of nothing, were still playing chess at the concrete tables in the southwest corner. A boy and a girl, NYU students, made slow circles on the swings in the playground.

"If you perform an altruistic act that benefits you as well," the girl was saying urgently, "is it still altruism?"

He thrust his hands in his pockets, turned under the coffered arch, followed the walkway to the dry fountain at the heart of the park.

Legend had it that there was an old hanging tree somewhere on the grounds. Bodies of the victims of the Great 1849 cholera epidemic lay buried under its grass. The strumming of a faraway guitar wafted by on a breeze, as did a smoky, herbaceous whiff of marijuana. Shadowy figures moved in the golden windows of the brownstones and apartments and NYU dorm rooms all around him, preparing dinner, dressing to go out, or to study, or go to work. To fight, or to make love, or perhaps only to buy groceries.

"Sess, sess," muttered a dealer lingering near the fountain. Autumn's first fallen leaves swirled around Rafe's Italian leather loafers as he passed. He slowed to watch a lone artist packing up his gear, folding up the workings of a French easel as complicated as an origami swan.

He'd been this way for more than half a century now. Though technically, at eighty-three he was a year older than Leo, he had stopped aging at thirty, the year he drew his last breath on the cold paving stones of a narrow London alley.

For fifty-three years he'd been apart from the world, a world whose pursuits and desires pushed on all around him. He would never know the breathless excitement of courtship and marriage, the milestones of a career, fatherhood, a child's tottering first steps, birthday parties with piñatas and clowns, gray hairs, grandchildren, retirement, the headlong rush towards mortality.

For him, there had been other, darker milestones. His own death. The unlucky soul who had served as his first meal. Europe in the 1940s, awash with blood. Sofia.

Sofia Wizotsky, with her black curling hair and her black fiery eyes. Translucent skin the color of skim milk. Red red lips turned up to kiss him, to beat back the darkness in the cattle car. Isaiah's soft round cheek pressed to his face, so light in his arms.

He stopped, brought his hand to his cheek as if he could still feel it there. A torrent of grief welled up inside him, roiled into his throat, burst out in an anguished cry under the yellow moon.

"Sess?" the dealer repeated dubiously.

With a roar of rage, Rafe bounded over a bench, buried his fangs in his throat. The dealer got off one strangulated bellow before being struck to the ground.

He was a big man, and strong, but still Rafe held him down with ease, ferociously took what he wanted. When he'd finished, he staggered to his feet, wiping his mouth. The magnitude of what he'd done hit him with full force. Washington Square Park, for God's sake. Why not Times Square? It would be on the cover of the *New York Post* by morning, though the *Times* would probably bury it in the Metro Section.

Behind him, the dealer began shaking uncontrollably, going into shock. If he didn't receive emergency medical attention, he would die.

Rafe dragged him to a grassy area under a tree, stripped off his overcoat, laid it over the shuddering body. And then he fled into the warm night, cursing himself for letting his passions overtake his reason, stopping only long enough to put in a quick 911 call at a pay phone on Fourth Avenue.

2

"No, that's not right," said Turner from behind.

He put his hand out for the brush. Tessa stepped away from her easel. It was late afternoon in fall, the last class of the day, and the room was already dark. The only light came from the lamp focused on the model.

"You got into the details too quickly. Remember; get the big shapes right first; big lights, big darks." His hand moved quickly and surely, wiping out the details she had spent all afternoon creating. Using her brush, he glazed over the dark areas, eliding them with the shadow under the model.

The effect was magical. A man's torso emerged from the shadows on the canvas. The instructor handed back her brush and moved on to the next student. Tessa saw Portia's body go rigid; she hated when teachers worked on her paintings.

"You've got the big lights and darks down," he was saying to her, "but you're going to have to put in details some day." He put his hand out for the brush.

Tessa smiled to herself, wiped her brush clean on a rag. She wasn't going to be doing anything more on her painting today, she might as well start cleaning up. She was supposed to meet Lucian at his loft at seven. If she hurried, she would still have time to wash the turpentine aroma out of her hair.

This was her favorite time of day. Something about the painting studio at dusk put a damper on conversation, invoked a reverential silence. The dark gathering in the corners made the room feel like a cave, as if they were primitives painting in Lascaux, perhaps an austere order of monks creating art for cathedrals.

From somewhere in the dark, Turner said, "All right, that's it. Everybody bring your paintings to the front. Would someone hit the lights?"

They blinked like raccoons caught in car headlamps. The model stepped down from the stand, pulled on his robe, went off into a corner to change.

Turner strolled slowly past their canvases, considering each one. He stopped in front of a figure made from dirty oranges, taffy browns, olive greens, subdued purples.

"Wow," he said. "DJ, right? Look at the way he planted the feet on the floor plane. Feel the weight of that. And look at the way he painted the light, from the top of the head, all the way down to the shadow on the model stand. It's just right, in color, tone, hue and value. Nice work, DJ, can I borrow it? I want to put it in the display case. Okay, everybody, see you on Friday."

Now came the clatter of palettes being scraped down, easels being pushed apart to make room to pass, the rattle of brushes being dumped in the sink for washing, the sound of water running through antiquated pipes.

"We should just work on the same canvas," Portia said in a low voice as she stirred her brushes in turpentine. "I'll do the big lights and the big darks, and you can come in for the details."

"He still wouldn't like it," said Tessa as she retrieved the damask fabric swathing the stage. "We're not boys."

"Hey. He doesn't like my work either, and I'm a boy," said David, on the other side of Portia.

"Yes, well, he feels threatened by you." Portia said kindly. "You're better at color than he'll ever be. He finds that intimidating."

"He never says anything nice about my paintings, either," offered Ben, behind Tessa. "I think maybe it's a racial thing." His umber skin glistened under the fluorescent lights.

"I think maybe it's a sculptor thing. No one expects you to be able to hold a brush."

"He likes my paintings," said Gracie breezily. "Look. I really nailed the color of the penis this time."

DJ, sitting in front of them doodling a head, giggled. "You said 'nailed.'"

Gracie picked up her art case and her canvas and went to sit next to him.

"Doesn't she have a boyfriend?" said David. "You should know. You're her roommate."

"I am not her roommate," said Tessa pointedly. "We share a space. And yes, she does. His name is Nick. Nicky. Nicky-boy. Nick-arino. He's from Queens, he does car detailing, drives a '67 Dodge Camaro. He's currently appearing naked on the wall of my studio, if you want to know more."

"Hey, did you hear? There was an attack in Washington Square Park last night." Portia's eyes went big and round. She'd just moved from Boston to New York.

"Wow," said Tessa. "That's, like, a block away from your apartment."

David's eyes were on his brushes. "Say, Tessa. What are you doing later?"

Portia brightened. "Yes, we're going out for Indian food, as long as David walks me home. Why don't you join us?"

"I can't, I'm meeting Lucian after this."

There was a silence as Portia wiped her brushes clean on paper towels, and David busied himself rubbing his palette down with mineral spirits.

"What?"

"Nothing," said Portia.

"The guy's a jerk," said David.

"What do you mean?" Tessa said uneasily.

"*Nothing.*" Portia glared at David. "See you tomorrow. But if you change your mind, we'll be at Madras Palace."

"Is there something you want to tell me?" Tessa tried to catch David's eye, but he was concentrating on getting every last trace of paint off of his palette.

"No. Have fun." he said shortly. His knife made a horrible screeching sound as it scraped on the glass.

"He's just jealous," Portia said soothingly. "Have a great time tonight."

Tessa took her paint box in one hand, her wet canvas in the other, and headed out into the hall. She stopped to look at the new paintings in the display case, then went on to the office, where she dropped off the space heaters and the drapes. Having discharged her monitorial duties for the evening, she went through the fire door that led to the stairway.

It came to her, as she ran lightly up the steps, that she was completely happy. She realized, also, that she had never felt this way before, had never been completely happy in her entire life.

The exact moment Tessa knew she was an artist was a memory crystallized like one of those prehistoric insects preserved in a drop of amber. She'd been sitting on the kitchen floor of her parents' house, begging her mother for a pony.

"She wants a pony?" said her grandmother, having a cup of tea at the kitchen table. "I'll giff her a pony." After a few fluid strokes with a plain yellow pencil, she'd handed her a stallion with a flowing mane. Which Tessa had, at the age of four, copied perfectly in every detail.

There were lessons, the same lessons given to many little girls whose mothers think they have talent. But Tessa was not like other little girls. From the moment she could draw, she was concerned with unusual details, like getting the light right as it played across the features of a face. Her drawings and paintings had an air of loneliness to them, disquieting in the work of a child. Viewing a velvety black-and-white charcoal rendering of a girl looking out of an empty window, one of her teachers wondered aloud how a seven-year-old girl came to make such mournful drawings, then thought the better of asking a child such questions, and put a comforting hand on her shoulder.

Her grandfather, and by extension, her father's side of the family, viewed the pursuit of art as the worst kind of foolishness, an assault on morality. There had been a real war when she decided to go to art school. Her family valued marriage and children above all else. *Narishkeit!* her grandfather had thundered. *Nakkeda nekayvas!*

Foolishness and naked ladies. Her mother rolled her eyes, made her swear not to tell anybody.

"Loosen up," was the advice she heard most often from her instructors. "Have fun with it." But Tessa didn't want to loosen up. She had a gift; she could draw anything that was put in front of her. What she wanted was technique. She wanted to paint like a Renaissance old master. She wanted to know what color Titian tinted his canvas before he started working on it. She wanted to know what colors Caravaggio mixed to make his lights. She wanted to know exactly which pigments Rubens utilized to achieve those juicy flesh tones, what brown Rembrandt used in his shadows, what combination of oils and resins went into Vermeer's painting medium. She wanted someone to show her how to make Raphael's line and Michelangelo's muscle masses. She wanted to know what made a good composition, and what made a bad one. She wanted to *know*.

After six months in the prestigious graduate program at Parsons School of Design, Tessa knew she didn't belong. Her fellow students were strewing dirt and found objects in corners of rooms; she wanted to paint the human figure. Seeking to transfer, she made the rounds of local art schools. One after another, their admissions counselors stared at her blankly as she explained what she was hoping to find. They had floors devoted to video and computer departments, but only the most rudimentary instruction in craft. The admissions guy at Yale actually laughed, adding snarkily that if she were looking for a school that was mired in the past, she should look up the American Academy.

So she did.

She'd stood for a moment before the glass-fronted entrance on Lafayette Street, afraid to go in, afraid to be disappointed again. A banner billowing in the cold March wind advertised that she was at the American Academy of Classical Art. A painting was on display in a case in the window that she took to be a Madonna and Child by Raphael. A small plaque nested next to it identified the artist as Josephine Whitby, one of the professors.

That year, the artists' studios were still in the basement, reachable only by freight elevator. The doors slid open on what looked like an entire floor of drying laundry; curtains zigzagging every which way, rigged precariously on clotheslines. She stood still for a moment, warily contemplating the sight; the other schools she had visited had pristine white walls, natural light from many windows, state of the art ventilation systems, well-lit studios arranged around open central areas with couches and plants. This was more like a shelter built by the homeless under a bridge.

As she pushed drapes aside on her tour through the improvised warren of studios, she saw dozens of canvases at various stages of finish; some were in grisaille, the gray first layer utilized by classical painters like Titian and Vermeer. Some were sketchy underpaintings in earth tones of umber, sienna and ochre. There were studies of faces and hands, dramatic portraits of a single nude body standing in the light, small figurines worked out in clay as preparations for final compositions. Things she had only read about in books about secrets of the old masters. In awe, she went from one crazy space to the next, confirming over and over again that she had finally found what she'd been searching for.

At the fourth floor, she elbowed open the door. There was a hum of activity, music, voices shouting to be heard. The sounds of the end of the day and the beginning of evening, happy sounds. Tessa pushed aside the curtain and entered her studio. She leaned her canvas against a stack of other figure studies, arranged her wet brushes in a mason jar on the windowsill, set her paint box on the floor near the radiator. Her eyes fell on the drawing of the naked woman on the bed turning toward the man in the tuxedo. She stood in front of it and gazed upon her work, her eyes half shut, in a kind of trance.

Absorbed in the contemplation of her drawing, she paid no notice when the curtain lifted and dropped again. She heard the sound of Gracie's voice, and a deeper, richer voice answering her; the boom of motorcycle boots on the wooden floors; the sound of Gracie throwing her things in a pile in the corner, then rushing out again.

It was early in the semester. Gradually, voices and music and footsteps died off as people put their supplies away, propped their work up somewhere safe, and headed out to whatever they had planned for the evening. Still Tessa stood there, absorbed by her drawing and her thoughts. The floor was empty now, silent but for the sounds of the street outside.

"Hello," said a voice behind her.

Tessa gasped, jerked around, took an involuntary step away from the voice, tripped over her paint box and knocked over a week's worth of work drying against the radiator.

A man was sitting in a folding chair on Gracie's side of the studio. He wore a wide-brimmed fedora and a light overcoat over an immaculately tailored, double-breasted charcoal gray suit. His legs were casually crossed, as if he had been sitting there for some time.

"Sorry," he apologized sincerely, but there was a bemused look on his handsome face. "I was actually trying *not* to startle you. Let me help you with that."

He uncrossed his legs, preparing to rise. "No," she said quickly, her heart pounding. She had been so lost in her own thoughts, he might as well have yelled *Boo*. "You'll be covered in paint. Don't move. I'll take care of it."

Gingerly handling the wet paintings by their sides, she inspected for damage, setting them one by one back against the radiator. Four of them were unharmed. She viewed the fifth with chagrin. A particularly deft three-quarters profile of a male model, on a very nice piece of oil-primed linen canvas she had bought for a song at New York Central Art Supply because it was in the remainder bin, had sustained a long white scratch across the groin. She sighed.

"That's got to hurt," the man behind her commented mildly.

Tessa turned to glare at him.

"I really am sorry," he apologized again, this time looking like he meant it. "It's a nice piece of work. You're very talented."

"Thanks," she replied. She wondered who he was, unmindfully sitting there amidst the messy detritus of art, in his impeccable suit, with his plummy British accent, under the giant drawing of Gracie having sex with her boyfriend. He didn't seem like someone her studio partner would know.

"I'm waiting for Graciela," he explained, as if he was following her thoughts. "She's on the student liaison committee."

"Oh," she said, turning back to her damaged painting. "Are you a teacher here?"

"No. I'm on the board."

"Oh," she said again. "What's a board?"

His eyebrows shot up, and his lips—full, sensuous lips, she noticed—curved in a smile. He unfolded his legs, stood, brushed himself off. She saw now that he was tall, more than a head taller than she was. He came closer, put out his hand.

"I'm Raphael Sinclair."

Tessa put her hand in his, a little unwillingly. "Tessa Moss." His hand closed around hers. It was cool and dry. Powerful.

He was standing very close to her, and she felt something like an electric current running through her body as he held onto her hand. She looked up into his face; long and narrow, except for those cheekbones jutting out of it. Wide, almond-shaped eyes, as pretty as a girl's. They were a shifting, indefinable hue, the color of smoke and shadows.

He was not looking at her, but past her, at the drawings on her wall. The skin around his eyes tightened, and he looked as if he wanted to say something. And then Gracie was back, her heels clacking across the floor.

"Sorry it took so long," she explained breathlessly. "I had to make a call."

"Oh my God, Lucian!" Tessa slipped her hand out of his, whipped off her apron, hung it on her easel. Took off the kerchief tying back her hair, shook it out. There would be no time to wash it now. Well, Lucian was an artist, too; presumably, he was used to the smell of turpentine.

Gracie had changed out of her painting clothes. For her meeting, she had donned a translucent white blouse with a black silky thing clearly visible underneath. Instead of her usual short skirt, she had on a pair of zebra-striped pants.

"Feel these," she said, guiding the stranger's hand to her thigh. "They're really tactile."

There was silence behind her. Tessa made lots of noise throwing her lipstick, Walkman and sketchbook into her bag, wished she were somewhere else.

"You look ravishing." she heard him say. "Honestly. Good enough to eat."

She executed her signature giggle. While he held her leather jacket up for her to slip into, she tossed her curls around to make them dance and shimmer. He held the curtain aside for her to pass. He glanced back at Tessa and said, "I'm sorry about your painting," and then they were gone.

Odd. Graciela seemed to genuinely care for Nick. They'd just moved in together somewhere in Little Italy. It didn't make sense. Then again, Gracie flirted with DJ and David and Turner, and while she was on the subject, everybody in the whole school. Maybe this wasn't what it looked like. Maybe they really did have student liaison committee matters to discuss.

Tessa looked at her watch, and realized that she was supposed to meet Lucian downtown in five minutes. She threw her knapsack over her shoulder and ran.

As she dashed up the two and a half very long flights to Lucian's loft, Tessa felt the butterflies take flight in her stomach. Every time she went to see him, it was like the first time, her heart pounding from exhilaration and the climb. She reached the landing, knocked on the heavy door and hauled it open, feeling like her heart would burst with excitement.

"Hallo, dahling," said Lucian, doing his best Michael Caine. He was standing over the antique refectory table, scribbling something onto a yellow pad, movie-star handsome in the faded olive green J. Peterman sweater she'd gotten for his birthday that was exactly the color of his eyes.

He finished with a flourish, came towards her and gave her a kiss, smiling brightly. His brown hair flopped boyishly over his forehead, and he raked his fingers through it trying to get it to behave.

Tessa had met Lucian a year earlier, after attending a guest lecture he gave at Parsons. A week later, when she worked up the courage to call him to volunteer her services as an unpaid slave, he'd invited her up to his loft for a drink. To her great good fortune, one of his stable of assistants had just left, and a position was open. At the end of the evening he made a discreet pass at her, which she politely sidestepped, which was never mentioned again.

The Eighties had been good to Lucian Swain. He cleaned up with his giant canvases of climactic moments from classic movies, doodling ironic little commentaries on top. With his dashing good looks, savvy socializing and pitiless British wit, he was an art star, the king of Wall Street and West Broadway. Recently matriculated MBAs, brokers, investment bankers with vast expanses of exposed-brick to cover and bonus money to burn outbid one another to own his next creation. Coincidentally or not, he also had an uncanny knack for sleeping with women who could advance him to the next level; art buyers, gallery owners, collectors. Women fell into his bed, if the stories were to be believed, by the dozen. He'd lost count of the actual number years ago.

Tessa went to Pearl Paint for art supplies. She answered the phone. She lied to his gallery. She lied to the women. She took his daughter to the playground in Washington Square Park. She totted up his shoebox full of receipts and delivered them to his accountant. She picked up milk. She picked up lunch. She picked up his super-cool movie editor girlfriend's dry-cleaning.

Though he was almost twenty years older than she was, Tessa had nursed a secret crush on him; she thought he was warm, charming, brilliant, and funny. She had never met anyone like him before, coming from her little suburban corner of Chicago.

But she had arrived on the scene late; the Eighties were over. In 1990, the recession hit the arts hard. The go-go investment bankers lost their jobs, sold their lofts at a loss, went back to school to become lawyers. And stopped buying art.

Commissions dwindled, sales went flat. And every morning, there were two empty wine bottles on the table.

To save money, he said, he quit drinking; the wines he preferred were all pricey. The super-cool film editor girlfriend left him. The assistants were let go, one by one, till there was only Tessa. Whatever money trickled in went to a first wife in England and child support in California, and after that, to overhead.

The day after his gallery dropped him, he tried to take his own life, swallowing a bottle of prescription sleeping pills. Arriving at her usual time, she found him collapsed on the floor near his bed, unintelligible. An ambulance had rushed him to St. Vincent's, where emergency room doctors pumped his stomach and kept him overnight for observation.

She got him home and into bed, where he stayed for the rest of the day, crying. The days became a week, the weeks, a month. She spent her hours reassuring him that he was an important painter, persuading him to eat, fielding calls from worried friends. He told her that he loved her, that he realized now that he had always loved her. He asked her to move in with him. He asked her if she would marry him.

His therapist thought he was finally experiencing feelings of loss he had repressed about his mother. His ex-wife in England thought he was just feeling sorry for himself. His ex-wife in California thought he was faking it to avoid paying child support. His current ex-girlfriend thought he was having a nervous breakdown because she'd left him. Tessa didn't know what to think. She stayed at his side and held his hand.

One of his old friends at *New York* magazine suggested Alcoholics Anonymous. Tessa found the nearest meeting, got him out of bed and dressed in something clean, walked him there herself. An older man with white hair and clear blue eyes found them seats, and said gently, "Welcome. There's a lot of recovery in this room."

Tessa left him there, went to Balducci's to buy a pound of Kona coffee and pick up a toothbrush, returning an hour later. He was waiting among a group of men with Astor Place haircuts and carefully manicured facial hair; soul patches, goatees, Elvis sideburns. Artists. He smiled when he saw her. "I think I'm in the right place," he said.

And slowly, as late winter turned to early spring, he had gotten better. One day, after a couple of weeks had gone by, she found him at his drawing table, sketching. The week after that, she found him in the studio with some of his new AA artist friends, building a ten-foot canvas. The phone rang all day. His sponsor, women he'd met at meetings. He began staying out later and later. The rakish smile returned to his face. He didn't need her to hold his hand anymore. Or to stay over. Or to marry him.

"Hey, Lucian. Sorry I'm late." She put her knapsack down on the table.

"Have you eaten?" He was cheerfully rubbing his hands together.

"No. I'm starving."

"Well, then..." his brow furrowed dramatically. "I think there's some salad niçoise left over from lunch...also, some Chinese food from the veggie place on Mott Street. Help yourself to whatever you find in the fridge. Now, come take a butcher's at this."

By habit, Tessa followed him obediently through the doorway to his studio. Black-and-white movie stills were scattered across every work surface in the large, airy room. He picked up some quick pencil sketches on plain white paper that were lying on his drawing table. "First, I thought I could do *The Wizard of Oz*. You know, icon of American culture, stay in your own backyard, don't mess with the order of things, blah, blah, blah."

"I thought *The Wizard of Oz* was about looking inside yourself to find happiness."

He patted her shoulder patronizingly. "Tessa, Tessa, Tessa, sometimes you are so naive. You've got to get above 14th Street once in a while. It's about the class system. Keeping the little people exactly where they belong. Find me something big and iconic that I can swoosh all over with ironic little doodles, we get into the Whitney Biennial, and Bob's your uncle."

He moved some pencils around on his drawing board, as if the next thing he was going to say was difficult for him. "Then, I thought, I'm always doing classic movies," and here he took a deep breath, "why not something from a classic *naughty* movie? You know, *Deep Throat,* or *The Devil and Miss Jones."* He put the pencils down. "So, what do you think?"

Tessa was still trying to grasp the notion that he had summoned her to work. She thought he had asked her to dinner.

"I think…" she said slowly.

A woman sauntered into the studio, dressed to go out in a mannish white shirt and fitted black pants, all sleek dark hair and red lipstick. She sidled up to Lucian and twined her arm around his.

"I think it's a wonderful idea, don't you? I think a little porn will really get our boy here to loosen up."

To his credit, Lucian looked embarrassed, maybe even a little pained. "Tessa, this is April Huffman."

Tessa knew the name. She was an artist best known for making paintings of blowjobs in the style of the impressionists, using car paint.

"This is the assistant that I was telling you about. My Tess."

April put her hand out, shook firmly and confidently. "I've heard a lot about you," she exclaimed enthusiastically. "The way Lucian tells it, you saved his life! I wish my assistants were that loyal."

"Why don't you wait in the other room," he said to her. "I just need to tell Tessa what to work on while we're at our meeting."

"Really, help yourself." said April, slinking back through the doorway. "The veggie Chinese food was delicious. Who would have thought."

Lucian's eyes followed her as she glided out. "Mm, mm, mm," he murmured. "Is there anything sexier on a woman than dark hair, red lipstick, and a white shirt?"

Tessa felt herself go numb with shock.

Lucian noticed her expression. "Oh, come on," he chuckled. "You know I'm not allowed to get into a relationship during the first year. She's just someone I know from my Monday meeting." He ran his hand over his hair, rubbed the back of his neck. "She comes on a little strong, but she's all right. She's been sober two years. I hope you get to know her. You'd like her."

"I guess I'm a little confused," she said slowly. "I thought we were going out for your birthday tonight."

The look on his face told her all that needed to be said. It was like someone kicking the chair she was standing on out from under her.

"You know I have to get to a meeting every night," he reminded her. "We're trying a new one over at Saint-Martin's-in-the-Fields. April says there's a lot of recovery in that room."

Tessa struggled desperately on. "How about after the meeting? A meeting is what, an hour and a half? I could work till then, and then we could have dinner."

"Sorry, sweetheart, sometimes the gang goes out for coffee afterwards." He was saying no as gently as he knew how. He thought for a moment, brightened up. "I know. How's about you take me to the Cupping Room tomorrow morning?"

A storm of tears was weltering behind her eyelids. She didn't want to cry in front of him, so she nodded her head.

He gave her instructions; she was to sort through his picture files and movie books and see if he had anything useful from *The Wizard of Oz*. *Deep Throat* and *The Devil and Miss Jones* would have to be ordered from an agency. And there were some dishes in the sink.

"Right then." He clapped her on the shoulder, gave her a smile. "See you in the morning."

"Lucian," she said to his departing back. "Is that what you tell people about me? That I'm your assistant?"

"Only the greatest assistant in the world!" He answered with cheerful belligerence, as if someone were challenging her standing.

"Is that all I am to you?" she went on huskily.

"Of course not." he said quietly. "You know that. I don't know what I'd do without you. And someday, a year from now, or two, things may be different."

She nodded, furtively wiped away a tear. It would have to do. Suddenly, she remembered. "Wait. I can't make breakfast. I have class in the mornings."

"Oh, come on. How important is class?" He gave her a dazzling smile, seducing her. "Come to the Cupping Room with me."

"Sorry. I'm working this one."

"All right then, I owe you one breakfast. Hold me to it. I'm a man of my word."

She heard the door slam, heard him charming April all the way down the stairs. He was using his date voice. She recognized it, because he used to use it when he was with her.

3

$\mathcal{M}$ay I take your coat, sir?"

The man in 5A flicked his eyes up at her and smiled. "I'm rather chilly. I think I'll keep it on."

He was disgracefully handsome, the flight attendant decided, with the kind of face you saw in old black-and-white Hollywood movies. And, oh, that British accent! Even better. Nadia loved British accents. He was so courteous, such a gentleman, that she wondered if he might somehow be connected to the royal family. Just thinking about it made her *pizda* tingle. "Then perhaps I can fetch you a blanket."

"A glass of wine, if you have it."

"Of course, sir. Red or white?"

"Always red."

Rafe watched the shapely bottom swing pertly away toward the galley. With blue baby-doll eyes and wide pouty lips, she was an adolescent wet dream of a sexy stewardess, long-legged and busty, extravagantly curvy in all the right places under the snug red Aeroflot uniform.

He was seated in an otherwise empty row on the redeye from St. Petersburg to Frankfurt. Except for him, the passengers scattered sparsely around the first-class cabin were asleep. Outside his window the world rushed by, cold and black but for a glittery network of fairy lights outlining streets, farms, factories, refineries, roads.

He'd informed Turner that he was flying to St. Petersburg to interview an instructor at the Repin Institute of Arts, and that was partly true, but the real purpose of this trip was to chase down a promising new lead. Miraculously, one of Sofia's drawings had turned up at a museum in Israel.

God knows where they'd gotten it, but surely they would have information about the artist Sofia Wizotsky, who for a short while in 1939, lived and worked in Paris.

The exhibition was called "Art of the Holocaust." In the small pen and ink sketch, barely larger than a cocktail napkin, a solemn little boy sat on his mother's lap, the figures modeled on a Raphael Holy Family that hung in the Louvre. "Sofia Wizotsky," read the plaque. "Last known location, Poland, 1942. Artist's fate, unknown." He'd stood before the drawing for a long, long time, switching his hat from one hand to the other and resisting the overwhelming desire to reach up and stroke the black lines. When he finally worked up the courage to query the pretty young thing staffing the visitors' desk for more information, she shook her head. It had come in as part of a collection. That was all she knew.

Alone in his hotel room overlooking the old walled city of Jerusalem, he grieved. The following day, he continued with his mission to St. Petersburg. The professor at the Repin didn't speak English, but Rafe was fairly certain he'd engaged his services for the fall semester.

The flight attendant returned with his drink. Leaning over to set it on his tray table, she spilled a few drops on his shirt. Apologizing effusively, her lips twisted into a rueful red shape as she dabbed at the stain with a towel. For a prolonged moment, her breast pressed against his arm. Could it have been an accident? But then the hand wielding the towel slid delicately into his lap.

When he glanced up at her, the glint in her eye was unambiguous. "Clumsy me," she apologized in her sultry Russian burr. "Turbulence, you see. The seat belt light has been turned on. But if you just follow me back to the galley, I can take care of you with greater efficiency."

He checked his watch. Still an hour before they landed in Frankfurt. Plenty of time. He rose from his seat and padded after her. In the dark, he counted ten or twelve passengers stretched across empty seats, sleeping. Even the flight attendants were napping, their heads bobbing in unison with the movements of the plane.

Right there, in the greenish light of the galley she pounced. After exchanging a frenzy of kisses, she skipped her fingers down his chest, then down the front of his trousers.

Rafe fitted his hands around her ass and hoisted her up onto the narrow counter. Skimming his hands under the tight fabric of her uniform, he shimmied her skirt up to expose long white thighs, sliding his fingers between them until she opened for him like the pages of a book.

He undid her uniform one button at a time. "Yes, oh yes," she exhaled, adding a string of Russian endearments, or perhaps they were only dirty words. Whisking the thick chestnut hair from her neck, he tightened his arms around her, pressing his lips here, and then there, along the length of her white throat. Her mouth opened and her eyes closed. As she flexed back in pleasure, his fangs locked around her larynx.

Between his jaws, he could feel her trying to form a scream, but it was too late for that. Her feet drummed against the stainless steel cabinets, the bulkhead, but this sound, like the others, was drowned out by the steady roar of the engines. However, this concerned him. Going by his vast catalogue of human experience, she should have lost consciousness by now. But Russian girls were tough. The way she fought and churned in his arms, it almost felt like love.

He detached himself just long enough to look into her face. She couldn't talk anymore—he had seen to that—but the wide baby-doll eyes were bewildered and clouded with pain.

He smoothed the hair back from her forehead. "Don't fight it," he said gently. The sympathy in his voice was genuine. "It only hurts more when you fight."

Then he fastened his teeth in her throat a second time. Her long red nails scrabbled uselessly against his chest, his back. It didn't matter. Nothing mattered but her bright briny blood pumping down his throat, filling him with life.

Under his teeth, he felt something give. The flight attendant—the pin on her uniform said, "Hello, my name is Nadia"—shuddered violently and slumped into his arms. He pulled her body into his, wanting to feel her last heartbeats vibrate against his sternum, her last breath warm his cheek.

Beneath the belly of the plane, he felt the landing gear shift and whine. He was running out of time. Levering up a ceiling panel, he maneuvered her long, lovely limbs into the empty space above the galley. Before returning to his seat, he remembered to wash her blood from the corners of his mouth.

It would be a full day before the flight attendant's body was discovered by a traumatized cleaning crew. By then, Raphael Sinclair was striding through passport control at JFK, humming snatches of Mozart's *Requiem*. He had a board meeting at noon.

4

osephine was late to class. She was often late, which would not have been such a big deal if she weren't the teacher.

Tessa liked Josephine. She was a broad hipped, long-legged woman, with honey blond hair and a honey smooth Texas accent, who, not surprisingly, called everyone "honey."

She was teaching them grisaille. They had begun by making monochromatic gray paintings. In the next step, they would be glazed over with translucent layers of bright colors. Artworks created in this way had a glow to them, as if they were lit from within.

This was Day One of color. The easels were in a semicircle around the small stage, the canvases dry and ready, paint tubes lined up on work tables. Tessa hung the drapery, posed and lit the model. And then the students sat down to wait. And wait. And wait some more.

After forty-five minutes passed, Tessa went down to the office and made a call to the instructor's home. The voice on the answering machine assured her that no one was available to take her call, but that they would return it as soon as possible. Tessa shrugged her shoulders, returned to class, reported that she was on her way.

Just as she was about to call it a day, Josephine blew in like a hurricane, bellowing instructions before she was fully through the door. "Sorry," she muttered as she threw her coat and bag down on a chair behind her. "Kid's sick. Had to wait for the babysitter. F train took forever."

It took only five minutes for Tessa to realize that she had found her painting style. The brush glided over the surface of the canvas, the sable hairs leaving delicate marks in the Naples yellow, letting light shine through from underneath. The color slipped on like a veil over the grisaille, revealing just enough gray to make it look like flesh. "I think I'm having an orgasm," she heard David whisper to Portia.

At the end of the day, when they propped their paintings up on the model stand for the critique, a hush fell over the classroom. All around them, the gray figures on the canvases had sprung to three-dimensional life.

"It's like magic," Tessa said in wonder.

"It *is* magic." Josephine corrected her. "Secrets of the Old Masters, honey. Remember, you saw it here first."

"I think I'm going to ask her to be my adviser." said Tessa later, as they cleaned their brushes in the trough sink.

"I don't know. She's been late an awful lot."

"I've been looking for this all of my life. Plus, she's a woman. She'll take me seriously as an artist."

Portia sounded doubtful. "All I'm saying is, look around a little first. You want someone you can depend on."

"I'll be your adviser," David offered as he reshaped the ends of his sable brushes into points. "I have all kinds of useful advice. Like, right now I advise you to change into something low-cut and black for tonight."

"Hey, that reminds me," exclaimed Portia. "How's it going with Lucian?"

Tessa had managed not to think about it all day. An awful queasiness gnawed at her insides. She looked down at her brushes. "Um...fine."

Portia and David exchanged a private look.

"Uh...I have to get this stuff to the office. You know. My job." She gathered up the drapes and the space heaters, hurried out of the room.

"I can't stand it," he said between gritted teeth. "She doesn't deserve this."

"It can't be true," whispered Portia fiercely. "After all she's done for him? What if you're wrong? Maybe it was just someone who just *looked* like Lucian Swain."

"With a British accent. Who's a painter. At a downtown AA meeting. Who said, 'Hello, my name is Lucian.'"

"I bet that describes ten different guys. Come on. Until you know for sure."

Tessa was back, spilling her brushes and paints into her art box. "Going to the new student thing tonight?" said David.

"I don't know. Lucian might need me."

This was met with a lengthy and uncomfortable silence. "You know what—I'll come back for my stuff later." She snatched up her bag and escaped to the stairwell.

Up two flights of stairs and down the corridor she ran, seeking refuge in the privacy of her studio. On the other side of the curtain, she dropped to her knees and rested her forehead on the cold floor.

She'd stayed at Lucian's till eleven the previous night, hoping he might come home early, maybe go out for a bite. For three long hours, she had looked out of his windows onto the streets below, watching all the hip and happy couples head arm in arm down Church to Odeon, or up across Canal Street to LaGamelle or Lucky Strike.

Slowly, it had dawned on her. He didn't really need her to work at night, he just wanted to impress his new girlfriend. And if she didn't want to be hurt, she should get the hell out of there before he returned. So she had hurried home, afraid of what she might see, feeling like a fool.

Gracie was perched at the top of her ladder, putting the finishing touches on the giant drawing of her own ass.

"Are you all right?" she called from ten feet off the ground. "What's the matter?"

"Oh, I'm just tired." Tessa said, embarrassed, getting to her feet, brushing off her knees. She had to remember not to do that again; the floors were really dirty. "I worked late last night."

"Me too!" exclaimed Gracie. "The coolest thing happened!" She put down her charcoal pencil and climbed down, her eyes glistening. "I waitress at Ferrara's, you know it, down on Mulberry Street? It's a nice night, lots of people out on dates, leaving big tips. Guess who walks in and sits at one of my tables. Lucian Swain!"

"Really." Tessa tore off a sheet of Bounty, rubbed dust off of her forehead where she had pressed it to the floor.

"He's pretty hot for an older guy. Not as hot as Nicky, but you know, that British accent. I told him that I was an artist, too, and he left me a twenty-dollar tip for two cannolis."

"Wow." She turned around, looking for somewhere to throw the used paper towel, made a mental note that she needed to bring a garbage bag from home. Gracie's words registered. Two cannolis? He was supposed to be watching his weight, now that he had stopped drinking.

"I think he was just trying to impress the chick he was with. She must be a new girlfriend, because they were all over each other. I was, like, get a room!" Something jogged her memory. "Hey! Isn't he the artist you work for?"

No answer. Gracie looked up from putting away her charcoal pencils to find her studio partner staring at her. Every feature on her face was trembling.

"Yes," she said in a faraway voice. "I guess that is what I do. I work for him."

Gracie took another look at Tessa and left the studio.

Tessa sat carefully down in a folding chair, across from the drawing of the naked girl and the man in the tuxedo. She pulled it off of the wall, took the pushpins out of the corners. Looked at it for a long moment.

Portia strode into the room, with Gracie trailing behind her. "I'm so sorry," she said softly, putting her long arms around her in a hug.

"I feel like an idiot." said Gracie apologetically.

"No, no. The only idiot here is me."

"Listen," Gracie said earnestly, her golden cat's eyes filled with sympathy. "I'm working the new student party tonight. All I have to do is put out a bunch of folding chairs and tidy up when it's over. I couldn't get anybody to help. You're work-study. Why don't you come?"

"I can't," she said, hating herself for what she was going to say next. "What if Lucian needs me?"

"He'll survive without you for one night." said Portia.

"Come on, it'll be cool." Gracie urged her. "It's at this board member's townhouse on Gramercy Park." She brightened up, waggled her eyebrows at her. "They say he's a vampire, you know."

"Okay, okay." She sighed, rolled her shoulders, swiped at her eyes with a clean paper towel. "But he'd better be a real vampire, or I'm going to be very disappointed."

They split a taxi going north on Lafayette Street; it was too late to walk the ten blocks to Gramercy Park. Clouds were gathering overhead, the sky deepening to the transparent dusky blue of evening.

They got out at Irving Place and Twentieth Street and walked the rest of the way. The park was an oasis of emerald lawn, carefully tended flowerbeds and gravel paths, surrounded by a high iron fence that ended in sharp golden spikes. Oxidized bronze urns emerged from moody groves of rhododendrons and pachysandra. A neoclassical statue of some forgotten nineteenth-century figure stood sentry from his pedestal at the heart of the park, casting his beneficent gaze over all who passed.

A cat was sitting on the grass soaking up the moonlight. At their approach, it melted into the shadows under a copse of cherry trees. The townhouses around the park dated from Victorian times, with fanlights, leaded windows, and elaborate wrought iron galleries. Windowpanes shimmered with age, slatted shutters were pinned back against gracefully crumbling brick. Gargoyles grinned down from downspouts, window boxes spilled flowers and vinca vine down from the upper floors. Gaslight lamps flickered wanly in small gardens, casting shadows over stairways leading down to cellar apartments. The crouching trees spreading their branches around the square must have tapped into the sewer system, because they grew lush and high here, blocking out the light from the streetlamps, making it seem darker.

"Which one is it?"

Gracie pointed to a mansion at the southeastern corner. It was almost hidden by a trio of London plane trees, their mottled gray and silver trunks looking like bleached bones in the moonlight. A dense thicket of wisteria grew in knotty gnarled bundles over the mullioned windows and colonnaded portico, almost completely cloaking the chiseled facade of the brownstone. Behind a decorative iron gate was a heavy old door with long brass hinges that splayed over the grooved oak like scythes.

"Okay, that's kind of spooky," conceded Tessa.

"See? Vampire."

The iron gate was bolted open. Gracie rang the doorbell, pushed open the door. Inside, the walls were a deep Moroccan red. A fire was burning in a huge marble fireplace, big enough to stand in, with fat putti sculptured in relief on either end of the mantle.

Over the fireplace hung a small drawing of a serene, smiling Madonna and a laughing baby in a wide, ornately carved gold frame. Tessa approached it, studied its impossibly graceful lines. "Is that a real Raphael?" she asked, dumbfounded.

There was a statue of a winged angel, gazing beatifically down at them from a pedestal, her cool white arms open in welcome. Behind her, two intricately carved Gothic stairways circled gracefully up to another level.

"This way," said Gracie, and led her up the stairs.

5

Sofia was sitting on top of him, rocking. His eyes closed, he thrust upwards, cried out her name, tangled his fingers in her hair, pulled her face down to his. She ground a kiss from his lips, lashed up, fell back down upon him, exhausted.

He held her close, kissed her again. Her hair brushed against his face. Morning light was streaming in the windows, warming his skin.

She straightened back up, rested her hands on his chest, smiled at him with eyes full of love, the sun behind her making the outlines of her hair blaze red.

Rafe slid his hands from her back down to her hips. He gazed at her, wanting to keep her there forever. "I love you," he told her again.

She raised her arms high over her head, stretching, the straps of her silky white slip falling down her shoulders, her upturned breasts bouncing jauntily.

He closed his eyes. *Happy. So happy.*

She plunged a stake into his heart.

He gasped, his eyes opened wide, searching for explanation.

"They asked me to give you this," she said. "Everybody wanted to say thanks."

Rafe jolted awake. Next to him, a woman slept on, clad only in the black garter belt and stockings she had on from last night. He swung his feet onto the floor, sat at the edge of the mattress, passed his fingers through his hair. His throat felt sore and parched. *Just a dream. Just another damn dream.* He didn't recall much of last night. His guest, wearing a skinny black thong with a pink bow on the back that made her beautiful ass look like a present. Something else, slippery and wet.

She stretched like a lazy cat, pointing her toes and arching her body.

"Wakey, wakey, eggs and bakey."

Her reply was muffled by pillows.

"How do you feel?" he said, reaching for his robe.

"Fine," she yawned, rolling over onto her side, tracing circles on his back with one long nail. "What's your hurry? I could use a bite."

Janina, he remembered. *Her name is Janina.* "Sorry, darling. I've got a thing."

"Yes, I know all about your *thing.*" She gave him a sleepy secret smile. He stood, pulled on a brocaded silk robe with burgundy satin lapels. Janina flicked her lustrous dark hair back, exposing the graceful curve from her neck to her shoulder, pouted.

"Not even one teensy bite?"

The smell rising off of her long, languid body was potent, irresistible, inebriating. He brought his face close to her neck, inhaled her musky scent. The call for blood went thundering through his chest, rising up to his brain.

Her skin, the color of milk, fractions of an inch from his mouth. He brushed his lips softly against the arc of her neck. She sucked in her breath, waiting. He touched his tongue to the spot where it was pulsating. *Salty.* He bared his fangs, sharp and triangular, pressed them to her skin. She gasped, buried her hands in his hair as if she were going to pull him close or force him away, and then he bore down, driving them into her throat. She gave out a strangulated cry and thrust her hips into the air. He clasped her naked body to his bare chest to feel her heart racing, *ba-boom, ba-boom, ba-boom,* pounding inside of him, making it feel as though he had a heartbeat. Hot, living blood spilled down his throat. Heat radiated through him, warmed him, lulled the throbbing beast that had overtaken his brain. Made him feel alive.

And then he let go.

"Are you all right?" he asked gently.

She opened her eyes, blinked, looked at him hazily. Slurred something in Ukrainian.

He laid her back down on the bed, wrapped the covers around her. Pulling on his robe, he went to the kitchen to get her some orange juice and cookies, as if she had just given at a blood drive.

The caterer was already there, busily loading trays of hors d'ouevres into the hulking old Viking range. Two uniformed waitresses were billowing a black and gold damask tablecloth over what would be a buffet table.

"How's it going?" he asked rhetorically. The caterer uttered something dire about prosciutto and melon balls and something compensatory about goat cheese and endive in rapidfire Irish brogue. He nodded politely and headed back up to the girl in his bedroom. The guests would be arriving within the hour. He had to get the girl into a cab, then shower and dress.

Janina was lying where he had left her, eyes closed. The marks on her neck were blackening into a hematoma. "Hey," he said, sitting at the edge of the bed. "Here you go. Bottoms up, now."

She opened her eyes, sat up. "Orange juice." she wrinkled her nose in distaste. "Cookies. Don't you have anything for grownups? A Bellini, perhaps?"

"This is better for you after you've...lost blood."

She shrugged, took the glass, tossed it down. Picked up a cookie, nibbled at it because he was watching.

Apologetically, he said, "I'm sorry, but I'm in a bit of a hurry."

"Oh, I see." She rose to her feet. Last night he hadn't noticed, but now he could see that she was nearly six feet tall, built like a dancer. "May I call my agency?"

"I've already called them."

They would send a cab. While she scrounged for her clothes, he wrote her a check, which she tucked in a small satin bag. Then he handed her a folded bill. "And this is for you." She unfolded it, smiled at him, tucked it behind the lace of her black brassiere. Sauntered over to him, slid her hand beneath his lapel.

"I will see you again sometime? You will tell the agency I make you happy?" Between her long, lacquered fingernails was a business card. It smelled of jasmine.

"Very happy."

She slipped on her stilettos, stuffed the tiny dress she had worn to his house the night before into the bag with the check, threw her coat on over her underthings. The coat was a luxuriant, floor-sweeping black fox, with a wide shawl collar that she flipped up to hide the bite marks.

He led her down the medieval staircase, past the open-mouthed caterer holding a tray of bruschetta, past the black-clad waitresses stealing a smoke. She strode by them like a model on a runway, fur flying open to expose her magnificent body. He smiled at her audacity. She showed them everything but the holes in the side of her neck.

Her heels clicked across the floor of the foyer, laid with white marble veined in black. Unlocking the front door, he swung open the ornate iron gate twisted with wisteria vines. "I will wait outside," she announced. Only then did she wrap her fur around herself and swish out, leaving him alone.

Now he would have to hurry. Leaving the front door unbolted so that his guests could let themselves in, he went back past the aghast caterer and the waitstaff and up to his room. He untied his robe, let it drop to the floor, walked naked into the bathroom. Turning the knobs in the shower, he watched the steam rise and cloud over the mirror, obscuring the image of the white-tiled walls, the pristine porcelain toilet, the potted orchid, the claw-footed tub, the old-fashioned brass shower fixtures. No matter how many times he'd seen it before, it was jarring not to find himself reflected in the mirror. From time to time he would catch a glimpse of himself in the polished blade of a knife, or a jagged shard of glass. But only a tantalizing fragment, as if he had just passed.

The water beat on his chest, made him feel warm for a while. He was always cold. One of the lesser-known curses of being a vampire. Unless, of course, he had just fed, or was, like now, under a hot shower.

Finished, he stepped out, toweled off, patted cologne on his face, ran a comb through his hair. He stood before his closet, chose a chalk-striped charcoal gray double-breasted suit with a bright crimson lining, the best materials and tailoring New York City had to offer. The buttonholes on the sleeves actually worked.

The girl. She was coming tonight.

Tonight was the annual welcome party for new students. They would wander through his brownstone fondling the statues and getting too close to the paintings, exclaiming anew over each object they found that they had seen somewhere before in an art history textbook. They would gape at the Raphael drawing and crowd around the Botticelli, the Vermeer, the Rembrandt and the Klimt. They would sit on his antique furniture and Persian carpets and eat canapés and play the old Steinway that had belonged to the movie star from the Twenties who had lived in the townhouse on Gramercy Park before him.

In his capacity as Dean of Admissions, Levon would give a little how-we-doing-so-far talk. Giselle Warburg, the Dean of Student Affairs, would tell them about upcoming parties, guest lectures, and demonstrations by famous artists whose work she collected. Turner had some news he wanted to share with them as well, though he was keeping it very hush hush. And Rafe would say something about the history of the school.

Two work-study students were coming early to help out. One of the work-study volunteers would be pretty Graciela. He had seen to that.

So far, his meetings with the cannoli had brought no new information about the elusive studio partner. Apparently, they shared a space, nothing more. Surprisingly, she had proved to be a passionate and articulate advocate for her fellow art students. There were two other tidbits on the liaison committee; a boy Gracie's age, and a young man with a spectacular Roman profile who went by the improbable name of Clayton El Greco. The boy sat there doodling, and the young man with the profile spun tall tales about his Southern boyhood in a deep Mississippi drawl, while Graciela argued for better ventilation and lighting in the classrooms.

Rafe smoothed the collar of his cream-colored shirt, clipped on his tie bar, straightened his gold silk tie, secured onyx cufflinks through the buttonholes in his cuffs, made sure no more than a quarter of an inch of cuff was showing. Buttoning his suit jacket, he glanced at the clock. Six-thirty. A flutter of nervous anticipation in the pit of his stomach.

The doorbell rang. He was ready.

6

Tessa swiped a wine glass off of the Stickley sideboard before it could leave a ring, then pulled a smoldering cigarette out of a very old looking green urn. "Harker!" she hissed. "Use an ashtray! Not antiquities."

Graciela passed by with a tray of spinach puffs. Harker Miller, balancing a battered electric guitar on his lap, pushed his lanky hair back behind his ears, crossed his long legs, commenced rolling another cigarette. He stuck it between his lips, lit it. *"Bella, bella,"* he mumbled in Texas-flavored Italian.

"Tutta bella," said DJ, sprawled over an Arts and Crafts leather recliner, absently drawing Clayton's dramatic profile.

"Bella luna." said Ben.

"Molto bella," added David. He'd gotten a fresh haircut on his way over, which somehow made his eyes look very blue.

"Bela Lugosi," drawled Clayton. "I *vant* to *suck* your *bloooooood*. Could you roll me one, my brother?"

"Shhh," said Portia. Her long body was stretched out on an elaborately patterned signed Isfahan rug. "That's not very gracious, Clayton," she said softly. "I'll bet he doesn't find those rumors so funny."

Clayton had wrestled in college, and now he shifted his formidable body on the couch, crossed his legs, tipped his head, acknowledged her sensitivity. "Sorry, Sister Portia. You know, I don't know why people are so afraid of making enemies. It keeps life interesting. Hey, did y'all see the Botticelli nude?" he went on, reclining with one arm behind his head and making kissing noises. *"Grazie,* buddy," he saluted Harker, who handed him a hand rolled cigarette. "Say, what's up with the leather pants?"

Harker blew smoke rings into the air over his head. "Got a gig later. Everyone's invited, naturally. Some hole on Houston. There's no cover, but there is a two beer minimum."

Clayton tried to float smoke rings through Harker's. "All's I'm saying is, if he really is a vampire, where's he getting all the money from? This is a pretty nice place. And if that drawing downstairs is a bona fide Raphael, he's got to have some righteous bucks. Where do you suppose he sleeps? Think there's a coffin here somewhere filled with dirt from the motherland? My theory, if you want to know, is he cozies up to rich orphaned heiresses, makes them his demon brides, then takes over their bank accounts." He took a thoughtful drag on his cigarette, let it slowly drift out. "It's a good plan."

"Are you done with that?" Tessa indicated Clayton's wine glass, sweating on an inlaid ebony and mother-of-pearl chess table.

"Yes, darlin', I believe I am. Would you mind getting me a refill? There's something extra in it for you." He winked.

She took his glass, headed to the table that served as the bar. For the hundredth time, she wondered if Lucian had called her, if he was sitting alone in his loft trying desperately to reach her. It was so quiet and lonesome at night. *I should find a phone. At least I can check my answering machine.*

Gracie was filling wineglasses, white on the right, red on the left, as fast as she could. There were also tumblers filled with Diet Coke, but they didn't seem to be moving.

"Red. It's for Clayton, and I think he's had more than enough, so only halfway."

Levon was leaning against the bar. He gave Tessa a big happy smile through his grizzled beard. "Look at that, my two favorite people in the whole wide world. Hey, Tessa, how you doing? Glad you could make it. You decide on an adviser yet?"

"Yes." Reluctantly, she tore herself away from thoughts of Lucian. "I'm going to ask Josephine. I really like her style."

Levon opened his mouth as if he were about to say something, then changed his mind. He looked at her speculatively. "I think that's a great idea," he said thoughtfully. "You can learn a lot from her."

A dark figure in a tailored suit materialized at the other end of the room, slender and tall, with wide shoulders. His neatly clipped hair came to a peak over his forehead, and in the low light his eyes were hidden in shadow. With a sharp little thrill, Tessa recognized the man who'd been waiting in her studio.

He lingered at the edge of the scene, surveying the crowd. He seemed to be looking for someone. When his gaze fell upon her, she felt a sudden flush of heat, as if someone had breathed on her neck. She stood rooted to the spot, unable to move, as he came straight towards her, shouldering through the throng of people milling around the bar. And then he went right past her, greeted Levon like an old friend, took his arm and steered him away. The spell was broken. Tessa swung around and headed back with Clayton's wine.

Ben, David, Harker and Clayton were hunched forward conspiratorially, their heads almost touching. "He's not drinking. I told you so." Clayton stated triumphantly.

"Who are we looking at?"

"The vampire! Look, he's the only person in the room without a glass."

Clayton was pointing at the man in the suit. Portia, still stretched out on the rug, was rolling her eyes.

"Him? He's not a vampire. He's just the founder of this whole school."

They were too far away to eavesdrop on any conversation. The alleged vampire spoke earnestly to Levon. Listened thoughtfully as Levon responded and rested a hand on his shoulder. Vampire, very passionate about something. Levon, the voice of reason, even if they couldn't hear him. Finally, they came to some kind of agreement and Levon moved off, carrying a single glass of white wine. The man in the suit turned to Gracie, smiled, said something. She nodded, stepped back. He reached around her, pulled out a green glass bottle that had been hidden under the table. He handed it to her. She uncorked it, poured out something red into a wine glass, which he drank down and set back on the bar.

"Blood." Clayton whispered.

"Definitely."

"Oh yeah, it's gotta be blood."

Gracie returned, shoehorned herself in between Clayton and David on the weathered leather couch. "Ooh." she said, wiggling her luscious tush just a little. "Comfy."

"So tell us, Graciela," said Harker, brushing ash off of his black leather pants, "what was in that bottle."

Cautiously, she peered around, then hissed, "Blood, just like you guys thought."

"I knew it!" said Clayton, striking his fist on his knee.

"I'm kidding," she said, settling back into the kilim pillows. "Some fancy wine. A nice Chianti, I think."

"Hey, Portia," said David. "Auden coming down for a visit any time soon?"

She propped herself up on her elbows. "Yeah. He's going to be here for the Halloween Ball. It's a Friday night, so we get a whole weekend together." Auden was Portia's boyfriend, finishing a graduate degree in art history in Philadelphia.

"I guess we won't be seeing much of you that weekend," said Clayton, giving her a wink.

"No, you won't." she said emphatically. "David, how about Sara? When are we going to meet her?"

"I plan to keep her away from you people for as long as I can," he replied. "I can barely stand you myself."

"Tessa," said Harker, picking tobacco off of his lower lip, "I hear you work for Lucian Swain."

"Yes, I do." Her mind had been wandering back to the loft on Walker Street.

"I hear some girl rang his bell once, and when he answered the door, she ripped open her shirt to show him his initials, painted on her breasts."

It had, in fact, happened twice. She smiled, remembering his face when he told her the story over darts at the Brewery. "The Eighties were rock star time for artists."

Harker played the signature riff from *Smoke On the Water*. Since he was toting an electric guitar, it didn't sound like much. "Does he get as much poontang as they say he does? I mean, he's only one man. If he's done as many ladies as they say, where did he find the time to paint?"

Before she could answer, David said, "I hear his assistants do most of his work." He looked straight at Tessa. "My mom works for the Thoroughgood Gallery. She hears a lot of things."

"Well...she heard wrong. I just pull the pictures together and sketch it out on the canvas and do the underpainting."

There were raised eyebrows all around.

"Here's to having an assistant like Tessa," Clayton said solemnly. They clinked their glasses together and drank them down.

Rafe stood apart from the art students spilling through his Great Room, scanning the crowd for Levon.

It had come as something of a shock that Gracie brought Tessa to help her set up. Unnerved, he'd made himself busy in the room he used as an office until more people arrived.

Behind him, someone said, "I want to do both of them together."

"Yeah, the contrast is fantastic. Look at her hair! I'm thinking Venetian red. Some golden ochre. Burnt sienna."

"Who said anything about paint? I want to die with it wrapped around my naked body."

He turned to see who was talking. First-year students under the influence of his wine, slavering like hungry dogs at Tessa and Graciela. *Levon, where was Levon?*

He found him at the bar. To his dismay, the girl was standing right next to him. She had a coffee-colored glass bead strung on a brown leather thong tied around her neck, looking for all the world like a sucking candy. And though she was meeting Levon's eyes and nodding in agreement, she was somewhere else, somewhere deep inside herself.

She must have felt his gaze upon her, because suddenly she was looking at him. A flash of heat sicced his body like the onset of fever. For a brief moment, he considered taking the coward's way out, escaping to the loft until everyone was gone.

Just as he was about to cut into the crowd, a thin girl with long dark hair stepped into his path, blocking his way. Though it was a chilly evening in the middle of October, her shoulders were bare. She was attended by a pair of young men, each eyeing him warily, obviously hoping she would go home with them tonight. She stopped him with a hand on his arm. "Hey, I love your house! Is that a real Raphael downstairs?" She had a wide helpless mouth and grasping, needy eyes. She put a bony hand out. "Allison."

He gave it a polite, generic shake. "Yes, it is. Lovely, isn't it?" He gazed fondly at the claret silk walls, hung with art he had collected over the past six decades, the rich wood paneling, the high coffered ceiling, the genteelly threadbare velvet curtain he had acquired from the old Ziegfeld Theater drawn over the soaring three-storey window. "I like my house, too. It took me a long time to get it just right."

When he glanced back down at her, she was giving him a trembling smile, one that offered all the wrong solutions to her own problems. "Have you tried the smoked salmon? Help yourself to some more wine," he said, and eased away from her.

Just a little further. He moved through the last dozen people between himself and Levon. With a sidelong glance at the girl, Rafe steered Levon away from the bar.

"Hey, Rafe, you decided to show up."

"I was in the middle of something. Personal business."

"Hell of a place you have here."

"Haven't you been here before?"

"No, last year we did this in the Cast Hall. This is my first time."

"Oh." Rafe liked Levon. He was the only person on the Academy staff who didn't treat him as if he were...well, as if he were a vampire. "I should have you and..." he knew Levon was married, but he didn't know her name.

"Hallie."

"...Hallie over for dinner sometime."

Levon chuckled and his eyebrows went up. "Yeah, let's do that. So. What's up?"

"Do you know what Turner's big surprise is?"

"Yeah. He filled that open studio painting position."

"I didn't hear anything about that," he said, pulling closer to him, his eyebrows drawing together. "I'm supposed to be notified when there's a new hire."

"Well, this woman's an adjunct. Temporary. She's here for the semester. If we're happy, she gets to come on board full time, with your blessings, of course. If not, *vaya con Dios,* we look for somebody else. We're in a bind. The semester's well along, and we're still short an instructor. It's hard to find people who teach the kind of stuff we do."

Rafe shook his head, bewildered. "Why don't we just hire one of our graduates?"

Levon put up his hands. "Not my policy. Whit thinks it's too incestuous."

He nodded, stifling his impatience. "All right. Where did she train? What's her experience?"

Involuntarily, Levon rubbed the back of his neck. "Um...she has an MFA in painting from Yale."

"Well, then. We know she can *talk* about painting."

"She has lots of experience. She taught at NYU and exhibited all through the Eighties. You've probably heard of her. April Huffman."

Rafe was incredulous. "The same April Huffman who does blow jobs in car paint? She's going to be teaching at my Academy?"

"Whit wanted a name."

"They're not even very good blow jobs. She can barely draw. We're betraying the students. Tell me, Levon. Are we that desperate?"

There was real anguish in his eyes. Levon rested his hand on his shoulder. "Hey. I know this school is your baby. You know, the monitor will set up the model, and she'll walk around giving them suggestions. Which they can take or leave. It's Painting 101, very basic stuff. It's not like she's teaching Anatomy. The chairman of painting at NYU gave her a big thumbs up. And she seems really excited about teaching here."

Rafe was furious. Turner had, as promised, brought an artist on board who could hardly draw. The men and women filling his townhouse today had come to the Academy to learn how to paint like Rubens and Rembrandt. Most of them were already better than April Huffman. He could think of nothing she could add to their skills. He felt as if he were putting one over on the students. On *his* students.

Levon changed the subject. Rafe had a crazy look in his eyes. "Say, how are the student committee meetings going?"

"Graciela had some good suggestions. The two young men, well..."

He let his restless gaze sift through the hundred or so people drinking wine, talking art and hitting on each other throughout his Great Room, thinking of Gracie's amber skin glowing through the translucent material of her blouse. A month ago he would have had her without giving it a second's thought. But after she guided his hand to her thigh to feel the fabric of her stretch pants—and they were indeed tactile, just as promised—he hadn't so much as touched her. It was the girl. She wandered through his thoughts like a crooked river, filling him with fear and wonder.

At this moment Graciela was refilling wineglasses at the bar at a furious rate. Clayton, the loquacious Southerner with the Roman profile, was holding forth to a cadre of painters and sculpting students staked out on a couch he'd had shipped from a shuttered Parisian café. The girl circled around them collecting empty glasses, her long titian curls glimmering in the warm yellow light cast by dozens of candles placed around the room.

"Beautiful, isn't she."

Rafe agreed. "Yes. She is."

"Gracie is more exotic, but I've always had a soft spot for redheads. I'm a happily married man, and I still want to die in that hair. She making you just a wee bit sorry you passed that bylaw about dating students?"

He smiled politely, said nothing.

"Her name is Tessa Moss. She works for Lucian Swain." Levon lowered his voice before he went on. "He says she saved his life."

Rafe turned to him, intrigued. "That's the girl?"

"Last year he had some kind of breakdown. He lost everything when the market crashed. When yuppies stopped ordering paintings to go over their sofas, he lost his house in Amagansett, his assistants, his gallery, his girlfriend. Even the art magazines were slamming him. People said he tried to kill himself. She kissed his boo-boos, got him into rehab, took care of business, got him back on his feet. He called her his angel."

They watched her glide around, removing glasses, furtively wiping wet rings from his furniture and retrieving cigarette butts from Chinese porcelain. "And now?"

"I hear he's screwed his way through the Soho AA meeting and now he's working his way through the West Village."

"Good God. After all that."

Levon nodded. "After all that."

"How do you know this?"

Levon sighed. "Ten years sober, baby. But I still go to meetings once a week." He was silent for a while. "Lucian Swain," he mused. "That was me. When I was using, I nailed anything with two legs. My wife threw me out, my kids hated me, I lost my job at the advertising agency. When I got sober, things changed. I realized I didn't want to design ads for cars anymore, I wanted to go back to being an artist. So I got a job teaching at the Art Students League. I married Hallie a year later. I've never slipped, not once. I don't mean with drugs. There was a joint at a Muddy Waters concert in '84, and the occasional glass of wine. Gives me something to talk about in meetings. But Hallie...she saw me at my worst and she loved me anyway. There's never been another woman. But...that's me." He lightened his tone. "How about you? The papers are always putting you together with Anastasia deCroix."

The expression on his face was partly a grimace, partly a smile. "Let's just say we've been many different things to one another over time."

There was a flash of scarlet as he raised his arm to smooth his hair, a nervous gesture. "Hey," Levon said. "Is that jacket lined in *red*? Let me see."

Rafe complied. Levon rolled the scarlet silk between his fingers. "Now, that is a fine suit. Where did you get it? No, don't tell me. Look who I'm asking. Savile Row."

He gave him a self-effacing smile. "Barney's, actually."

"I'm a sweater guy, myself, but if I was looking to buy a suit, it would be this one. Anyway, about half an hour ago, Inga asked me to fight my way through the crowd and bring her back a white wine." He turned to go.

"The girl," said Rafe.

"Tessa." Levon corrected him.

"There's a drawing on her wall." He spoke very deliberately, as if it hurt him to get the words out. "A woman holding a child. Clothing from the thirties or forties. A suitcase. Do you know what it might be about?"

Levon studied Rafe's expression, shook his head no. Thought for a moment, shrugged his shoulders up and down. "I can look into her file. Maybe her essay will give us some insight." He plucked a potato pancake topped with crème fraîche and salmon roe from a silver tray carried by a petite waitress in black and white with shapely calves who was also one of the school's regular models. "Hi, Sivan. These any good?"

She tilted her hand back and forth. *Comme ci, comme ça.*

"Don't worry about April Huffman. I'm sure it will work out just fine. And I'll look into that thing for you. I'm going to find a seat. It was nice talking with you." And he looked him squarely in the eye, grinned. "Really."

He wouldn't allow himself to dwell on what Levon had just told him, not now. Heading for the bar, he reached behind it for the '87 Rothschild Bordeaux he had secreted earlier.

"Is anybody drinking the wine?" he said dryly to the lovely Graciela.

She laughed her merry laugh. "Allow me. I actually used to work as a bartender." He handed her the bottle, and with one fluid move she deftly pulled the cork and poured it into his glass.

He downed it all at once. It coursed through him, giving him fleeting warmth and taking the edge off of his emotions. Not as powerful as the hit from living blood, but there were times it got the job done.

He started to make his way to the focal point of the room, a massive fireplace with an Art Nouveau mantle, rescued from some defunct tycoon's Roaring Twenties North Shore palace, all chubby angels and nymphs and grapevines. On impulse, he changed directions, headed for his office. He would be the second to speak tonight, right after Giselle. But before he went on, he needed to make a phone call.

"Hi, guys."

Giselle Warburg was the heiress to a banking fortune, and she looked it, every inch the aristocrat, with her long thoroughbred body, her casually expensive clothing, her narrow patrician face, the easy confidence in her throaty voice. Right now, she was standing in front of the central fireplace, trying to get their attention. "Guys, if you could find a seat."

Gracie and Tessa had set out all the folding chairs in the closet, but there weren't nearly enough. Some students perched on the carved staircase leading to the second floor. Others leaned against anything upright, the squared oak columns, the lacquered walls, the display cases, the piano.

"On behalf of the board, I just want to tell you how proud we are of you. Just from the stuff we've been seeing in your studios and the things in the cases, I want you to know, everybody is very impressed. You're the most talented group of students we've had at the Academy to date. I can see it's going to be very hard to choose a winner of the Prix de Paris this year."

There was thunderous applause. She smoothed a strand of straight ash-blond hair back behind her ear and glanced at her notes before she went on.

"The Naked Masquerade is in two weeks. For you first-years, that's the annual American Academy Halloween party. There will be prizes for the most creative costumes, so get cracking. On the job front, Dreamland mural studio is looking for painters. And Clarice Runyon, some of you know her work, is looking for an assistant to answer phones and do light office work. Come see me if you're interested."

"Now, I want to introduce you to the man throwing this party, the man whose home you are trashing and whose wine you are guzzling. The man with the vision. The man who founded this school. I give you Raphael Sinclair."

There was a surge of murmuring as Giselle stepped back out of the spotlight. *The vampire, it's the vampire! Did you notice any mirrors in this whole house? Did you see him eat anything? Don't let him look you in the eye! So why does he wear that hat all the time?*

I hear he's a vampire.

The area in front of the fireplace remained empty. The restless muttering grew louder. Giselle's expression grew puzzled, then concerned.

And then, there he was.

Somewhere, someone must have opened a window or a door, or perhaps it was only the evening breeze wafting in, because suddenly the curtain draping the window gusted in and then out again. The candles flickered and guttered, sending a series of shadows rippling across his face. There was a wagon wheel chandelier over their heads, studded with twelve white pillar candles, and the light from above threw his eyes into deep shadow. From somewhere outside, they could hear the sound of chimes ride in on the wind.

He stood there with his hands in his pockets, gazing down at the floor, collecting his thoughts. When he finally glanced up, there was an audible intake of breath.

"Hello," he said. "I'm Raphael Sinclair. Welcome to my home."

The pitch of the murmuring rose, then died away.

"The other day, someone said to me, 'What's a board member?'" There was a flutter of laughter. "And I thought, yes, what is a board member? What do we do? What do we create?"

Rafe looked around the room as he spoke, his eyes alighting briefly on one face and then another. Those under his thrall felt a shiver of warmth followed by the hairs prickling up on their neck, though they could not say why.

"The first and more pedestrian thing we do is make money. It is our job to bring in the funds that pay the instructors, pay the water company, pay for electricity and garbage pickup and stopped-up sinks and leaky roofs and broken window panes and the broken boiler and repainting the walls and changing the light bulbs and the custodians and the bookkeeper and the secretary and the scholarships. And we bring in that money by leaning on our rich friends, throwing parties, and courting wealthy patrons. Giselle is actually in speaks right now with a member of the royal family who likes to dabble in painting." He arched his eyebrows meaningfully. A buzz of whispered speculation. He raised a pale hand, wagged a finger. "No, no, I can't say who it is. That would be telling, and a gentleman never tells. But he is a very civil fellow married to a very pretty girl who may be in a position of great power someday if his mother ever gives him the chance."

Excited oohing and ahhing. He waited for it to quiet down.

"Our second, and far more important task, is to spearhead the direction of the school. Whether you are here to pursue your demons or to exorcise them, our aim is to give you the tools you need to bring them to life. Every time we consider a new instructor, we debate whether he or she will bring you a missing piece of the puzzle. When modernism triumphed after World War II, the world rejected realism. Too many associations with Third Reich art and architecture. So many skills were lost. Finding a teacher with the old knowledge is like a treasure hunt. It's slow and time-consuming and sometimes we go up blind alleyways."

His voice was irresistible, gentle and forceful all at the same time. It held out the sincere promise that he was completely on your side and would never, ever, lie to you. It whispered in your ear other, darker promises. The students, the faculty, the alumni and the other members of the board listened, hypnotized, enraptured.

"There are artists out there who call themselves realists. They put a photograph in a projector and trace it onto a canvas. Or they snap a picture and hand it to their assistants to draw up. The poseurs, the pretenders, the usurpers of figurative art. They are not welcome here. We seek only those who can tell you how to build a painting from the inside out, not those who are out to sell you cheap shortcuts to the Whitney Biennial.

"It is we who are responsible for the soul of the school. Our goal is nothing less than to take back art from the hands of the twentieth century. Welcome to the American Academy of Classical Art."

This time, the applause was deafening. The room rocked to its feet, clapping and stomping and hooting its unequivocal approval. Behind him, Giselle threw her clipboard on the floor and clapped.

Rafe took a step back, taken by surprise at the vehemence of their response. He smiled nervously, then blissfully, reveling in their support.

Leaning against the back wall with Bernard Blesser, Whit Turner grimly watched Raphael Sinclair basking in his moment. *Ha, ha, Sinclair. You got me.*

"That bastard." said Blesser incredulously. "Is he trying to sabotage you?"

Turner compressed his lips. He should have known Rafe wouldn't go down without a fight. Maybe he could put off his announcement to a time when the students would be more receptive.

Still clapping, Giselle stepped forward and shouted over the din, "Thank you, Mr. Sinclair, for that stirring call to arms, and for reminding us why we're all here. And now, with some exciting news, the head of the painting department, Whit Turner."

Damn. Too late. Sinclair, you bastard, you set me up.

Turner pushed awkwardly through the crush of people, hating the feeling of their bodies fumbling against his. Rafe was trying to make his way out, but his progress was slowed by students stopping him to shake his hand and slap his back. The two men almost touched, brushing past each other in the throng. Rafe let a sly, surreptitious smile lift the corner of his lips. As he moved towards the other end of the floor, he heard Whit's even voice rise over the din.

It was common knowledge that the school was short a painting teacher. For the past six weeks there had been wild, speculative rumors circulating. Virtually everyone who was anyone in the pantheon of contemporary figurative painting had been discussed. Supposedly Whit was in secret talks with Julian Schnabel, Eric Fischl, David Salle, Wayne Thiebaud, Lucian Swain. Or perhaps some unknown master from the art academies deep in the former Soviet Union.

"Quiet, quiet everybody. Settle down. First things first. At this point, you should all have a pretty good idea of who you want as your adviser. Ask them before their dance card gets filled, or you could end up shut out. Okay, here's the news you've all been waiting for. As you all know, we're short a painting teacher. We've interviewed a lot of people, because we were searching for an artist who could bring you something new, skills nobody else can give you."

There was an excited burst of chattering, then a hush. Turner waited a few seconds, let the momentum build, then launched his news. "April Huffman has agreed to teach painting this semester."

There were audible gasps around the room. Over the noise, Whit continued. "April has an international reputation. She has a Masters in Fine Arts from Yale, where she studied under William Beckman. She showed at O.K. Solomon all through the Eighties. Until recently, she was teaching at NYU."

Silence. For one crazy moment, Whit thought, *They're going for it.*

A hand went up in the crowd. "Yes, do you have a question?"

Someone with a deep Southern accent said, "Thank you, sir. Excuse me, sir, but isn't she that artist who does blow jobs in car paint?"

He kept his voice level. "Her content is controversial, but I think you guys are mature enough to handle it. She's a successful contemporary realist with a lot of real-world experience."

The silence was broken by angry babbling that gathered into a threatening roar.

"Settle down, settle down, everybody..."

Rafe smiled triumphantly to himself as he ascended the stairs to the loft.

Safe to come out now.

The dark-haired girl he'd spoken with earlier had offered to stay and help straighten up. She tried to catch his eye, to signify that she was willing, but he had pretended not to notice, and she and her gargantuan neediness went out, unsatisfied, into the night.

All hell had broken loose after Whit made his announcement, instantly polarizing the artists into vehemently pro-April or savagely anti-April. With the able assistance of several drunken sculptors, the discussion got very heated, very quickly.

The wine was all gone, down to the last bottle. The damask tablecloth covering the bar had been cleared off, leaving a bare folding table in its stead. He found the Rothschild buried behind some books, turned it over. Not a drop.

Rafe removed a cigarette butt from a potted orchid on a Moroccan coffee table, examined it. Hand-rolled. He ran it under his nose, expecting marijuana, but it was plain loose tobacco. Artists. They liked to craft things, even something as simple as a cigarette.

He could hear the caterer piling her sheet pans on top of one another and the chink of glasses being placed on the counter in the kitchen. He wondered if the cannoli was still around. Perhaps she needed a hand.

There was a noise in the telephone alcove near the stairs, the smallest of sounds, the rustling of fabric, a sigh. Click of the phone being placed back on the receiver. The acrid scent of disappointment rolled over him before he knew who it belonged to, calling him, followed immediately by another scent, her scent, blackberries and musk.

Just a little closer.

A mane of red-gold hair came into view. Faded jeans, a macramé shirt. The girl, Tessa, standing in a circle of light. She was studying a small sculpture displayed beside the stark black rotary phone, a clique of feminine figures carved from a single block of watery green stone. The little women, perhaps eight inches high, were huddled together in a corner, heads almost touching, whispering, conspiring. As he watched, she reached out to run her fingers over the lustrous surfaces, to stroke their small perfect bodies.

"It's called *The Gossips,*" he said.

The girl jerked back, choked out an exclamation of surprise, and snatched her hand away from the sculpture. The wineglass she was holding dropped out of her hand, smashed to pieces and skittered with a silvery sound across the polished floor. The stem and part of the bottom rolled to a rest near his shoe.

"Camille Claudel," he continued, smiling wryly. "She worked in Rodin's studio as one of his vast army of assistants, then became his lover." He stooped to pick up a piece of glass. "It drove her mad. Those women were probably whispering about her."

She was holding her hand to her chest, trying to catch her breath. He indulged himself in the small pleasure of watching her breasts go up and down inside her macramé sweater, allowed his eyes to dwell on the glass bead cosseted in the hollow of her throat.

"Holy cow, how do you do that?"

"My fault. I should have made more noise, let you know I was nearby." He smiled again. "Dropped a glass or something."

"I'm so sorry. I'll take care of it," she said quickly, and embarrassed, she went down on her knees before him, gingerly picking up the pieces and putting them on a tray of dirty glasses that she was collecting.

"Where's Graciela?"

"She had to leave early. She waitresses at Ferrara's. Someone didn't show up tonight and they called her."

He took another step forward, into the light. "It's Tessa, isn't it?" Then, casually, "What a lovely name. How did you come by it?"

"Old family name," she said, tantalizing him.

"You're Lucian Swain's assistant, aren't you," It was a statement, not a question. "You're the one who saved his life."

She gave a self-deprecating little lift of the shoulders. "I was there. It could have been anybody. "

"You don't really believe that. There were others. Everyone else left."

She was pretending to be cool about it. "Okay, it could have been anybody who actually cared about him."

"He's better now, I hear. Back to painting. Back to himself." She was nodding, gingerly picking up broken glass. "He must be incredibly grateful. Probably needs you now more than ever." It was cruel, he knew. He wanted her reaction.

A small, involuntary sigh. Her shoulders folded like cards, she pressed her hands flat on his gleaming floor.

He could physically feel the lacerations Swain was opening inside of her; the ache of her pain, the weight of her anxiety, the relentless gnawing of self-doubt. It filled him with delicious excitement and exquisite sorrow, all at the same time.

Gently now. "You know, Giselle hears about jobs all the time. Maybe something interesting will come up."

Angels must have voices like his, she thought dully, as soothing as a mother's lullaby, like a warm hand on your cheek. She reached for a shard of glass under the telephone console.

He heard her gasp. She sat back on her knees, holding up her right hand. White skin, blue veins. A thin red line snaked across her wrist. He stared at it, mesmerized, as a streak of blood skidded down her arm.

The smell was intoxicating, rich and salty and winey, galloping through his brain, arousing a tidal surge of desire. Didn't she know? Hadn't she heard the rumors? Did it cross her mind that she was in an isolated alcove in the vampire's lair, bleeding at his feet? Was it some sort of trick?

Three moves, that's all it would take, three simple moves. Lift her up, the blood skipping down her pale flesh his appetizer. Bury his face in her hair. Find her throat. Feel her struggle.

Just be human now.

"Are." He licked his lips, swallowed. "Are you all right?"

She lifted her head, looked up at him for help. For the first time, he found himself staring directly into Tessa's eyes, and all the rest of what he was going to say blew right out of his head.

Sofia's eyes, accusing him across half a century, staring at him from a stranger's face.

His lips parted, showing even white teeth. He took a shaky step backward. "Oh my God," he whispered. "It's not possible."

"No, no," she said, misunderstanding. "I'm okay."

"It's not okay," he said. "It will never be okay."

She looked at him strangely. He gazed stupidly down at her, still on her knees.

Pull yourself together. With visible effort, he composed himself. "God, I'm sorry. I, uh, have a thing about blood. Let me have a look."

He helped her to her feet, took her hand in his, turned it over. "It's not deep. It's just long," he informed her after examining her injured wrist. "Fortunately, there's no glass in there. Let's get you sorted out."

He led her to the kitchen, where he opened a cabinet to find an empty Band-Aid box. He whipped open a drawer and took out several white linen napkins. Carefully, he wound the napkins around her hand, then secured them with masking tape. She was close enough to breathe in his cologne, sandalwood, smell of distant seas.

"Which hand do you draw with?"

"This one," she said. Blood seeped through the linen, staining it red.

"You have to press on it for awhile, that will stop the bleeding. Like this." He took her hand in his, laid his palm across her wrist, bore down. The beat of her pulse shook him, pounded through him like hoof beats.

A twinge of desire coiled through her as he closed his hand around hers. While he held her hand, she could see the muscles working under his well-cut suit, and she wondered what he was built like under his fine white shirt. Her mouth opened with the surprise of it, and she stared up at his face, as cool and as beautiful as the marble angel in his foyer, as they stood there together in his immaculate kitchen.

The caterer was finished. She approached them hesitantly, spoke in rapid Irish brogue. He directed her towards an envelope on the counter. She bid them goodbye, at least Tessa thought it sounded like goodbye. One of the waitresses threw her a look as she followed her friends out the door.

They were alone. Suddenly, Tessa felt uneasy.

"I should go. I've done enough damage for one evening."

His eyes penetrated her, held her motionless. She felt something clandestine bloom inside her, like one of those flowers that only opens at night. He lowered his gaze, let go of her arm.

"I think it's stopped bleeding." He took a tactful step back. "Let me call you a car."

"No, no. I live just a few blocks away. I'll be fine."

"It's nearly midnight," he said with finality. "You never know what's prowling around out there this late at night. Take the car." He disappeared. She heard his voice speaking to a dispatcher, and then he was back. "They'll be here in a few minutes."

"Well—thanks," she said. "I think I got all the glasses. Sorry about the mess." He waved it away.

He followed her down the stairs and through the foyer to the entryway. She halted in front of the drawing of the Madonna and Child just as the last log in the fireplace popped, crumbled into ashes with a whoosh.

"Is it a real Raphael?"

He looked at her speculatively, then shook his head. "No. It's a copy. Done a long time ago by someone very dear to me."

"It's incredible." She stepped closer to it, regarded the perfectly placed pen lines in the crosshatching, the confident draughtsmanship, the delicate rendering in the shadows. He watched her hair tremble like a living thing, the dying fire outlining it in gold.

There was a soft honk outside.

"Thanks for everything, Mr. Sinclair," she said, "it was a swell party."

"No, thank you. You did a first-rate job with those folding chairs." He found himself trying to keep her there a little longer. "Hey! Starving artist! Do you want any leftover hors d'ouevres? There's a refrigerator full of them."

She smiled at his offer, shook her head. The door clicked closed behind her.

He collapsed into one of the handsome Morris chairs facing each other in front of the fire. Good God, that had been a multiple choice test written in hell. There's a pretty and vulnerable girl bleeding copiously in your apartment. You're a vampire. Do you: A. Ravish her. B. Ravish her and drink her blood. C. Bandage her up, offer her snacks, put her in a car and send her home. D. All of the above.

An ember had rolled against the fire screen, and using the poker, he knocked it deeper into the fireplace. He gazed up at the Madonna and Child, the loving sparkle in the mother's eyes, the capering of the sweet baby boy.

Pressed against the rough wooden wall, feverishly hiking up her skirt with both hands. Her soft red lips everywhere, as if I were a new continent they were eager to explore. The heat of her hands on my skin. The rhythmic clackety-clack, clackety-clack of the train calling the cadence for our lovemaking like a metronome. Isaiah, asleep in the corner in the bed I made for him with my coat.

There was a tentative knock at the door. That would be Anastasia. He glanced at his watch. They had arranged to meet at ten, but this would be uncharacteristically early for her. Perhaps she had somewhere to go afterwards.

"You're early," he said as he undid the deadbolt, pulled it open. "You must be really intrigued."

It was Tessa, her upturned face white in the lamplight under the portico. A black town car waited behind her. "You were amazing," she said breathlessly. "That speech you gave earlier. It was like a manifesto. They should put it on the first page of the catalogue. I didn't want to leave without telling you."

And then she stepped out of the warmth of his foyer, ran lightly down his front steps into the night.

7

Rachel—that was the model's name—sat on a high stool in front of the classroom as students trickled in, dragged easels into a circle around the model stand, and mixed paint alongside their coffee and bagels.

She was a beauty, with coltish legs, hips like a lyre. High round breasts, high Yankee cheekbones, aquiline nose, satiny brown hair.

Tessa asked her to twist her torso so that the pose was more dynamic, directed her to put one hand on her thigh, the other on her hip. She clipped a reflector lamp onto a stand and aimed it so that it was lighting the model's left side, throwing her right flank into dramatic shadow. She rearranged the long swath of fabric working as a backdrop so that it swagged farther down. She laid down masking tape where the model's feet touched the stage so that she'd be able to recreate the pose after her breaks. Then she circled slowly around the set-up, checking to see that the pose was interesting from all angles.

Not all models were this great looking; usually they ranged from average to downright scary. So it came as a surprise to find the entire male faction of the class whispering together in a corner of the room, very much not looking in her direction.

Tessa went over to them, did her duty. "Uh, guys," she said. "Beautiful naked girl over here. And get this—she's naked."

Disregarding her, Clayton continued enthusiastically, "–and then he says, 'yeah, but are you still the master of your domain?'" They broke into shrieks of laughter.

Tessa went back to her easel, got down to work. She laid out her paint in an order that was rigid to the point of fanaticism, starting at the top left corner, where she left a pile of flake white. Next, she squeezed out yellow ochre, red ochre, burnt umber, raw umber, and stirred together a black and yellow puddle that stood in for green. Last on the palette was ivory black, a pigment made from burnt bones. Then she went around again, mixing a dab of each color with a dash of white. By the time she was finished, the edges of the palette were rimmed with two rows of color. She wiped her knife clean on a carefully folded pad of Bounty paper towels and waited for the teacher to arrive.

Gracie dropped her things at a paint stand behind Tessa. "Hey," she said, leaning forward and depositing a Ferrara's bag in her lap. "Brought you a little present. Sorry I had to leave you with all that work last night."

Tessa reached into the bag, drew out a cannoli. "I should be thanking you," she said earnestly. "Not for breakfast. For making me go to the party."

"What time did you get out of there?" She opened up her art box, dumped out her paints.

"I was done by ten. However, there was an incident." Waggishly, she brandished her bandaged wrist.

Gracie gasped. "Ohmigod! What happened?" The golden eyes went big and round. "So it's true?"

The room hushed, went quiet. The boys in the corner, drifting back, gaped at Tessa's hand. She felt herself blush, and her voice suddenly sounded very loud as she went on with her story. "No, no. I'm kidding. I was round-ing up the last glasses, and I was looking at this little green sculpture next to the phone—"

"Camille Claudel," said Ben.

"That's what he said."

"Who?"

"Mr. Sinclair. I didn't even hear him come up behind me. When he spoke, I guess it kind of spooked me and I dropped a wineglass. I opened up my wrist on a piece of broken glass while I was cleaning it up."

Gracie's mouth fell open. Harker's eyebrows shot up. David looked concerned. Suddenly Clayton was too close, leaning his wrestler's bulk over Tessa's chair.

"Were you two alone?"

"No. The caterer was still there. Somewhere. Loading up her stuff, I think. Oh, come on, Clayton."

"Okay, let me get this straight." His blue eyes bored into her. "You, a beautiful girl, were alone with the vampire. In his lair. In the dark of night. During a full moon. Bleeding."

"Sorry, boys, you've got it all wrong." She put her hands out, pushed Clayton back a few inches. "If anything, I think he's a little freaked out by blood. He almost fainted when he saw me dripping all over his floor."

"So, nothing happened?" Portia wanted to make sure.

Privately, Tessa remembered the shiver of emotion she had experienced when he took her hand. "Perfect gentleman. Bandaged it up for me. Used some very expensive-looking linen napkins, too. Linen, Clayton. None of your cheap polyester blends." She held out her hand with a flourish. In the fluorescent light of the classroom, she noticed an embroidered monogram, R with an S twined through it.

"So, are you, like, the evil dead now?" Harker was genuinely curious.

"Did he lick the blood off the floor with his tongue?" said Gracie eagerly. There was a pause as they all turned to stare at her, appalled. "Over the line, huh?"

Clayton spoke very slowly, enunciating carefully. "Tessa. Try to remember. Did he drink any of your blood? You know, maybe while you were looking the other way." He dropped his voice, made it whispery, insinuating. "Now, this is very important. Did he turn you into one of his demon brides?" He looked to their classmates for affirmation. "You can tell us. We're all friends here."

"I'm not your friend," said Ben.

"I don't like either of you," said David.

"There was no exchange of fluids," said Tessa, clearly uncomfortable with being the topic of conversation. "Fluids of any kind. Really. Now, can we talk about something else? Hey, look over there! A girl with no clothes on!"

Portia moved forward, put herself between Tessa and the boys, waved her arms in a wide circle. "Remember that talk we had, Clayton. Personal space."

"Are you talking about Raphael Sinclair?" inquired a student Tessa barely knew, Graham McSomething—McKay? Macavoy?—in a bored Midwestern accent. Rumor had it that he'd been a professor of art history at some Ivy League college. Right now, he was leafing slowly through a newspaper. "I hate to be the one to break it to you people. Did you check out his suit? His beautifully manicured nails? The mathematical precision of his haircut? His cologne? If those things happened to escape you, perhaps you noticed his exquisite taste in Mission furniture. Trust me. He's just a great big Mary."

"Show us your neck," Clayton commanded.

"I think there's a sexual harassment issue here I could pursue," said Tessa.

"Oh, baby," confirmed Portia.

Tessa pushed back her heavy tresses to reveal her neck. The skin was unbroken, as smooth and white as a whale's belly, protected from the rays of the sun by the sheer mass of her hair. "Vampire," she snorted. "Even if it wasn't totally idiotic, it would still be the least of my problems." She released her hair, letting it fall around her face. "And what would you do if it was true? Drive a stake through his heart? What is it with you and vampires, anyway? He founded this whole damn school. Aren't you happy here?"

Clayton sauntered back to his easel, started mixing paint. "I'm just messing with y'all," he admitted genially. "Actually, I think it would be kinda cool. I mean, aren't we all vampires, in a metaphorical kind of way?"

"Um...qué?" queried Harker.

"Half-human, half something else raw and primitive that the rest of the world doesn't get. Artists are in touch with something out of the common man's reach, something godly. And that scares people. Look at us sculptors. We create figures from the dust of the earth. The way God created Adam."

"That's poetic, Clayton," said Portia, surprised.

Turner hurried into the room, carrying his clipboard. He reviewed his notes, scribbled something down. "As you know, I've been filling in until we found a new painting instructor. Starting today, April Huffman will be teaching your section of Studio Painting. As I told you last night, she's a very successful figurative painter. You can all learn a lot from her. Enjoy, guys."

He scurried out again, not sticking around for a reaction. Had he looked up from his clipboard, he might have noticed Tessa blanch a whiter shade of pale.

April made her much-ballyhooed entrance, wearing sunglasses, dressed in a white men's shirt and slim black pants. She carried a huge pocketbook, a black leather jacket, a sheaf of papers, and a *New York Times* under her arm.

"Hi, class." Still wearing her sunglasses, she consulted the roster, surveyed their faces. Her gaze stopped on Tessa.

"I know you. You're Lucian's assistant." She smiled. "You're my monitor, right? Give me a hand."

Reluctantly, Tessa set her coffee down next to her palette, rose out of her chair. April thrust her handbag and jacket into her arms. "Can you find a place for this that's out of the way? I have to pose the model."

"I already took care of that." Tessa carried April's things to a safe corner of the room, far from paint and turpentine, deposited them on a clean chair.

"Well, it's atrocious. Too classical. Too pretty. I *hate* pretty. And what's with all this drapery? Uch." She was wrinkling her nose as if something smelled bad. She whipped the fabric off of the model stand, balled it up and stuffed it on a shelf behind her. "Do something more confrontational," she instructed the model.

"Like what?" Rachel said.

"I don't know." She looked at her for a moment, her brow furrowed. "Open your legs wide. Wider, as far as you can. Yes, like that. Can you hold that for twenty minutes? Good. Hmmmm, that's nice." The men in the class stared, then looked away, suddenly uncomfortable. The model was no longer nude. She was exposed.

April noticed, adapted. "Maybe it's too out there for you guys." She replaced the stool with a folding chair. "Okay. Slide your ass forward. Uh huh. Lean back. Now cross your legs. No, more open. More. More. Good. Hook your arms behind the chair. Great. Now let's move the lamp over here." She hung the lamp squarely over the model's head, bathing her in flat, unflattering light.

Tessa saw David looking at her. She averted her gaze, bent to her work, trying to decide what color to start with. She chose a sable brush, stirred it in turpentine to wet it, then dipped it in burnt umber.

"Hey Tess," April was standing behind her. "Would you get me a cup of coffee? Not that sludge in the office. Is Dean and Deluca's too far? Okay, then. From the deli next door. No sugar, skim. Not too light. Also, a bagel with a shmear of low-fat cream cheese. Thanks." She drew a hundred dollar bill from her Coach wallet. Tessa looked longingly at the other students already painting, took the money, and headed down the hallway.

By the time she returned, something was different, a definite shift in the atmosphere. Something had happened while she was out getting April's coffee.

"Thanks, you can leave it right there. My change?" Tessa let it slide into her palm. April settled into a chair in a corner, unwrapped her breakfast, unfolded her *Times.*

Tessa went back to her easel. Confronting the white canvas, she picked up her brush and squinted at the model, shutting out everything else. She began by sketching an outline of Rachel's body in the center of the canvas. Swishing her brush clean in the can of turpentine, she contemplated the setup, analyzing the color of the light. On the far side of the room, April was commenting on someone's piece. It was met with an edgy retort. Already steeped in her work, the disturbance took place somewhere far in the distance.

She dipped her brush into a yellow-white, then into a pink-white. *Too hot,* she thought, *too bright.* She added a brush-tip of raw umber to tone it down. Now the combination of colors was just right; it looked exactly like morning sun falling on flesh. She covered the canvas with a transparent veil of burnt sienna and began massing in the lights.

When the bell rang two hours later, it was almost a relief. There was commotion as fifteen artists rose as one, dropped their brushes in turpentine and brought their canvases to the stage. Standing back with their arms folded, they waited for her to speak.

April took a moment to don her black Wayfarers, then paced slowly back and forth in front of the paintings. Halting at one, she peered closely at it, muttering to herself, before moving to the next. She repeated the performance, with killing suspense, in front of each canvas. Finally, she stopped, resolutely shaking her head.

"This is a disaster," she announced. "A dis-*as*-ter."

In the blink of an eye, Tessa realized that the disaster under discussion belonged to Portia.

"I'm sorry?" said Portia, not sure she understood correctly.

"Your painting," April repeated. "It's a disaster. You've got this ghostly figure here, and this blue fog in the background. I don't know what this is about. Where's your composition? Where's your structure?"

She could tell Portia was taken aback by her choice of words. "I like to concentrate on the big relationships first, the big lights, the big darks." Ever the diplomat, she was trying to explain her working philosophy.

"I don't want to hear your excuses. It's not even drawn well. I taught at NYU. They're undergrad, and let me tell you, every one of them is farther along than you are."

Tessa could almost hear her friend struggling with the situation. Perhaps the new teacher misunderstood. "This is figure painting," Portia reminded her gently. "We kind of focus on the figure."

April's voice rose sharply. "Don't tell me what class I'm in," she snapped. "I know *exactly* what class I'm in. I have a show opening at O.K. Solomon in a month. Do you? Stop questioning my methods or learn how to type, because if you keep painting like this, you're going to need it."

There was an awkward, disbelieving silence.

"So...when you say, 'get the background in,' you mean, you want us to include the junk on the shelves?" David said slowly. "The easels? Coffee cups? People's coats? The garbage can?"

"Or make something up, I don't care. Just get something down." She moved on.

Tessa turned around to sympathize with Portia, but she couldn't, or wouldn't, meet her gaze. She wore a dazed expression and her cheeks were highly colored, as if she had just been slapped.

"Portia," she whispered fiercely. "Don't listen to her. She's a monster."

She threw her brush down and walked quickly out of the room. Tessa looked to David, but he just lifted his hands into the air. *I don't know what to do either.*

Tessa followed her out to the hallway, but she had vanished. Reluctantly, she returned to class as if it were a prison sentence, waited for her turn to be pilloried.

"All right, kids." April was saying. Several of the students in their class were over thirty, but it seemed to be her favored expression for addressing them. "Now you know what I expect from you. I'm not going to continue critiquing today's' work, because as far as I can tell, it's all one big brown mess. Let's dethrone 'The Figure.' I don't want you to treat the model any differently than the walls, or the coat hooks, or a Snapple bottle, or the sink. Go look at the work of Edwin Dickinson to see what I mean. See you next week."

Class was dismissed. The shuffle of feet, chairs scraping the floor. The sound of knives scraping down palettes, turpentine cans snapped closed, rattle of brushes dropped in the sink for cleaning.

April beckoned to Tessa in the far corner of the room where she had stowed her gear. "That was a little rough," she conceded, stuffing her papers into her bag and slipping on her supple, expensive-looking jacket. "Sometimes you have to be cruel to be kind. Like an intervention. They might not appreciate it now, but in time it will make them better artists. You'll see." She gave her a bright smile, patted her shoulder. "I can't believe you're my monitor! I'm going to call Lucian right now to tell him."

Tessa managed a fake smile, nodded. Why didn't she go already? She was still there, looking at her thoughtfully. "Are you working tonight? Because, if you're not, I could really use your help. I'm always on the lookout for good assistants. And we're going to a show uptown tonight, we wouldn't even be in your way."

There was a sick feeling in her stomach. No, no, a thousand times no. She would starve first. "Sorry," she said. "I have plans."

"Oh, well." April said, throwing her pocketbook over her shoulder. "Another time. This is going to be so much fun!" And then she was gone, leaving a cloud of Calvin Klein's *Obsession* in her wake.

There was a moment of silence.

"That is one crazy bitch," stated Graham. "And I should know. I've dated a lot of crazy bitches."

"She's not a teacher, she's a bully," said Harker, with a kind of awe. "She uses words the way other people use knives. How do you know her, Tess?"

"Friend of my boss," she replied grimly.

"Did you find Portia?" said David.

"No. She was already gone."

"Maybe she went back to the studio."

Rachel was dressed in street clothes, leaving for the day. She sought out Tessa. "I'm going to the office to tell them I don't want to model for her," she said matter-of-factly. "I can live with the pornographic poses. It's the negative energy she's putting out that makes me uncomfortable. Sorry."

Like a whirlwind, Portia was back, picking up her supplies. Her long, narrow face was impossibly pink. Even her hair seemed furious, blond hairs snapping loose from her tight bun. As she slammed her paints into her box, she appeared to be holding back turbulent emotions with great difficulty.

"I'm sorry." said Tessa, touching her arm. "So sorry."

"Why?" Uncharacteristically biting off the words. "You didn't do anything wrong."

"I didn't do anything at all," she said regretfully. "I should have told her she couldn't talk to you that way."

Portia stopped throwing her things into her art box. "Tessa," she said. "Don't blame yourself. She took us all by surprise. Anyway, she's right. I do need to focus more on composition. She just said it in a jaw-droppingly inappropriate, unacceptable, inexcusable way. So I went to the office and transferred out of her class."

"You can do that?" said one of the sculptors. "Out of my way."

There was a hasty exodus to the office. In an instant the room emptied out. A handful of students remained. "Why are you still here?" demanded Portia. "Go, now. If we all walk out of her class together, we make a powerful statement about who we are and what we want from this school."

Ben shrugged. "I'm a sculptor. What do I care what she says about my composition? I just need a body in front of me."

But in Clayton's pale eyes burned the fire of a zealot, and he gave Portia a dazzling smile when he replied, "You know, I think I'll do just fine here, thank you."

"Tessa." But Tessa wouldn't meet her gaze, she was focusing her attention on wiping paint off of her brushes. "What are you doing here? Run, do not walk, to the office and transfer to Geoff Anderson's class. There are a few openings left."

"I can't," she said abruptly. "I can't transfer. I'm the monitor. I need the work-study hours. Also," she hung her head, ashamed even as she formed the words, "April is Lucian's new best friend. What would he think if I transferred out after the first day?"

Portia didn't give a damn what Lucian thought. "I really don't think this is a good idea," she said carefully.

"I'll be fine. She has to make nice to me if she wants to stay in Lucian's good graces."

"What about you, David?"

David was wiping his palette down with turpentine. "Nah, I think I'll stick around for the Clayton and April fireworks extravaganza," he said. "Even if it is detrimental to both my education and my self-esteem."

"Should be good," Graham said. "I'm in."

"You people are insane," said Portia firmly as she lifted her bucket of paints to her shoulder. "I will not be responsible for repairing any damage, emotional or otherwise. Tessa, are we still on for tonight?"

"Is today Friday?" In the turmoil of the past week, she had lost track.

"Yeah." said David. "Can you still whip up lamb tagine with your arm bandaged up like that?"

Tessa flexed her wrist up and down. It felt tight, the skin stretched to the limit. "Maybe we should make it next week."

Groans of disappointment all around. "Aw, Tessa. It's not Friday night without your challah," said Ben.

"I can't get through the week without your *kreplach*," added David.

"You are not the first man to tell me that."

"Please?" Clayton pleaded. "I'll pick up the Manishewitz."

"I'm going over to the Green Market in Union Square. I'll bring fruit," Portia volunteered.

"All right." Tessa gave in. She liked having friends over for Shabbos dinner. "See you at seven. But no Manishewitz, Clayton. I'm not kidding. And if I hear one more obsessive crack about vampires, you go home."

She picked up the space heaters and headed for the office. It was already twelve o'clock. She was going to have to hurry if her bread was going to be baked before sundown.

8

$\mathcal{T}$he challahs were warm and doughy, the lamb fell off the bone. Tessa made *kiddush* over a very nice George Duboeuf Clayton picked out that came highly recommended by the knowledgeable fellow at Crossroads on 14th Street. The artists filed into her kitchen to wash hands, then waited respectfully for her to make the blessing over the bread before they tore it to pieces and washed it down with Clayton's Beaujolais.

The tagine, scented with cinnamon and cardamom, fell apart at the touch of a spoon. Tessa's current roommate, a French Moroccan NYU business student, pressed her slice of challah to her nose to savor the aroma before devouring it. She kissed her fingers, flicked them in the air. *"Magnifique,"* she told her. "Better than in Paris."

The men followed her every move as she shoveled food into her mouth with shameless pleasure, licking her fingers, oohing and ahhing and mmming with gustatory abandon.

She pulled a last piece of challah off of the loaf, swiped it across her plate and swallowed it. *"Bon,"* she announced, pushing away from the table and embracing Tessa on both cheeks. "Good *Shabbat.* I am going to see Daniel. I will see you later." She smoothed her glossy hair behind her ear, tossed her leather knapsack and tennis racquet over her shoulder and bounded off like a panther, slamming the door behind her.

"You can stop drooling now," said Tessa. "She won't be back till tomorrow."

"Is this one a keeper?" asked Portia. "How long has it been?"

"Six weeks," said Tessa. "She seems nice. What do you think, guys, does she seem nice to you?"

"I think I speak for everybody when I say, very very nice." Ben said.

Harker fished a packet of Zig-Zag out of his breast pocket. The scent of tobacco perfumed the room.

"Hey Tess." Harker frowned as he licked the edge of the rolling paper, twisted the cigarette tight. "I thought Jews weren't allowed to make graven images. That's what my Daddy said." Harker's father was a minister. "Isn't it in the bible somewhere?"

"I think I'm squeaking by on a technicality," she replied. "I'm not actually praying to the graven images."

"I don't think I'm allowed to, either," added Ben. "Witnesses are pretty strict about that sort of thing."

"You're a Witness, huh? The door-to-door kind?" Harker flipped a hand-rolled cigarette into the corner of his mouth, a neat trick that made everybody go, "Ooooh," in an admiring sort of way.

"That's right. In Indianapolis, I used to go every Sunday with my mother and my auntie until I was big enough to say no."

"How do they feel about your career choice?"

"Well...it's not exactly a choice, is it." Ben rubbed the stubble accumulating on his chin. "If they weren't Witnesses, I think they'd be proud. But as it is, they don't ask and I don't tell."

"So, you've never had a birthday party." said David.

He shook his head matter-of-factly.

"Never dressed up like Superman for Halloween. Never been trick or treating." said Harker.

"Never got a present on Christmas?" said Clayton. "I respect all religions, my brother, but that is harsh."

"Would you raise your children the same way?" Tessa was curious. Ben chuckled, shaking his head. "I'm not looking to get married."

"Why not?"

"Art is my mistress. And she is a jealous, demanding, hellbitch of a mistress."

"Gee," said Graham. "I've never actually heard anybody put it that way before. That's kind of beautiful."

"Look. You fall in love, you get married. Before you know it, you have a kid. If you're a man, you have to support a family. You fellas know what

I'm talking about. So, you get a job. Nothing too grueling, maybe painting murals for Dreamland Studios, or freelance graphic design. You can still do your thing at night, on weekends. Then your wife says she's tired of pushing the stroller around junkies passed out in doorways and using the hall closet for a second bedroom. She's ready for a house in the burbs. So you get a better job, the kind that requires you to wear a suit and put in long hours. Before you know it, art is a hobby on weekends, slipped in there between raking the lawn, fixing the leaky faucet, fourth grade homework and little league. You tell yourself that someday you'll get back to it."

"That's cheery," said David. "I think I'll just go into the bathroom and slit my wrists."

Ben shrugged. "That's just how it is. Unless you have a trust fund."

"Hey," said Portia. "Leave my trust fund out of it."

Tessa poured herself more wine. "I thought only people in movies had trust funds."

Portia leaned her willowy body back in her chair, crossed her long legs, held her glass out for a refill. "Everybody I went to school with had a trust fund. After high school they all just quit. They didn't feel like going to college. They didn't have to work. They waste their lives hanging out at the club, going to parties and talking about other parties they're going to later."

Graham said, "Where do I sign up?"

"I was in school with kids like that," said David. "Some of them were pretty messed up."

"So how come you're not messed up?" Harker asked Portia.

"I just have a small trust fund."

"Speaking of messed up," said David. "How about that April Huffman."

"Tessa, you're her monitor. Did you happen to notice three sixes tattooed anywhere on her person?" Clayton was completely serious.

"Who can we tell?" asked Portia gloomily. "Who would believe us?"

"The student liaison committee," said Tessa, lifting herself up from the table to get dessert. A little unsteady on two glasses of wine, she swayed into the small galley kitchen, returned with a pan of brownies. "They can tell Mr. Sinclair. He'd want to know."

"I don't think he can do anything about it," said Graham morosely.

"Why not? It's his damn school."

"The board and the teachers are separate but equal," he explained. "Turner's the chairman of the painting department. He's supposed to be independent of the board's influence. This April Huffman snafu is his baby."

"I'll talk to him," Portia said. "I'm sure he'll tell her to tone it down."

"I wouldn't be so sure," replied Graham.

"What do you mean?"

"The ivory towers of academia are filled with personalities who have supersize egos and happy meal paychecks. They fill the gap with petty bickering and backstabbing. I've heard some things."

"What kind of things?" said Portia, leaning forward, elbows on the table, her eyes narrowing.

"That Raphael Sinclair and Whit Turner hate each other. That Turner is trying to wrest control of the school away from Sinclair. That Turner is shopping around for names, not talent. Famous artists who might sprinkle a little magic fairy dust on our quaint school. Even if they don't know how to draw Binky."

"He can't do that," protested Tessa angrily. "We're the only classical art school in the country. It's right there in the catalogue. If I wanted to paint like April Huffman, I would have stayed at Parsons."

"Gentlemen," said Graham, lifting his glass. "Arm yourselves. I think we are about to be witness to a holy war over the soul of this school."

"Bring it on," said Clayton, a peculiar joy lighting up his face. "I love being on the side of the righteous."

They carried their dinner plates into the kitchen and scraped them into the garbage, piled them up next to the sink. Tessa arranged Portia's apples in an Armenian pottery bowl and set it on the table.

With the cigarette still dangling from his lips, Harker reached for an apple. "Say, Portia. What's that sketch in your studio supposed to mean? The one with the kid in footsie pajamas, and the bald guy holding up a feather."

"Oh," she smiled bashfully. "I don't know yet. Sometimes ideas just come to me, and I get them down as fast as I can. The meaning comes later."

Graham was brushing crumbs from his lap. "As long as we're on the subject. I've been wondering about a sketch I saw on your wall, Tessa. By the way, did you make these brownies? I'd eat the whole pan, but it would go straight to my hips."

"Which sketch?"

"The woman covering a child's eyes."

"Oh." She was relieved she wasn't going to have to explain the one with the naked girl on the bed. "It's about the Holocaust. My grandparents are survivors. Their families died in the camps."

The table fell silent.

"This month's *Cosmo* says that bringing up Auschwitz is a great way to jump start conversation at a dinner party," Graham finally said.

"I had a friend whose father was in a concentration camp," said Portia, ignoring him. "He never talked about it. But whenever we had sleepovers, I'd hear him having these awful nightmares in the middle of the night, calling out in German."

Tessa nodded. "My grandfather never talks about it either. He came from this really big family. They all died. After the war he moved to Chicago. And that's all I know." She picked out an apple, began to take off the peel in one long ribbon. "I've been wondering ever since I was a little girl. What he had to do to survive. Who he lost. What life in his town was like before the war. What happens to you when you lose everybody you ever knew, every-body you ever cared about? How do you survive that? How do you go on?"

"You have a right to know," said Portia. "It's your story, too."

"It's like a hole in the world," she murmured pensively. "The past is a blank canvas."

"You should tell him that it's for history's sake. Everyone should hear these stories."

Tessa pictured her grandfather, eating soup like he was afraid someone was going to steal it from him, her grandmother hovering nearby in case he needed anything.

"I don't think that's ever going to happen," she said quietly. "Sorry, guys. I'm drunk. More brownies, anybody?"

After the third bottle of wine was gone, Harker got up from the table, stretched, patted his flat belly. "Well, folks. I hate to eat and run, but I got a gig in a dive on the Lower East Side tonight. Thanks for the eats, Tessa."

THE COLOR OF LIGHT

"Did you choose your adviser yet?" Graham asked him, picking at the remains of the brownies.

"Yeah. Turner." They glared at him accusingly. "Hey, the man's a good teacher."

"I'm going to go, too," said Graham. "If I run, I can still catch *Breakfast at Tiffany's* at Film Forum."

"I'm going to a party at NYU," said Clayton. "Come with me, Ben, otherwise I'll look like I'm all by myself and no one will talk to me."

"If I go with you, you have to model for me tomorrow. I need a male figure for my thesis project."

"Who am I?"

Ben smiled. "The devil, of course."

Harker and Graham left with the sculptors, engaged in arguing about whether Clayton had to pose clothed or nude.

"I have to go too," David said. "If I don't call by ten on Friday night, Sara thinks I'm out with another girl."

He really was very handsome, Tessa realized. He had dark hair that he kept cut short over laughing blue eyes. A chin that jutted just enough. Cheekbones out to here. Straight narrow nose. A bemused mouth. Nice shoulders, slim hips.

She walked him to the door. "Where's Lucian tonight?" he said deliberately. "Doesn't he ever come to your Friday night dinners?"

"He has these meetings," she started to explain, then faltered and fell silent. David, seeing something cringe inside her eyes, was instantly sorry he had said anything.

"Good night, Tessa." he said, his eyes seeking and meeting hers. "Can't get through the week without your *kreplach.*"

He held her gaze longer than was considered polite, and she knew that he'd stay if she asked him to. "Good night," she said. "See you on Monday."

He turned, walked the short distance down her hallway and rounded the corner. She heard the door to the building squeal open and closed.

"I told you he liked you," said Portia when she returned to the table.

"He has a girlfriend."

"My mother says it's not over till there's a ring on the finger."

"Hey," muttered Tessa. "Kind of involved here. There's this famous artist. Saved his life once."

"Tessa," said Portia, then stopped, after three glasses of wine unsure of the right combination of words. "You deserve better. Someone who is there for you."

"I don't want better," she said mournfully. "I want him."

9

*L*evon."

Levon jumped out of his chair. Bernard Blesser, standing next to him, clapped his hand to his throat. The founder of the school was framed in the doorway, the brim of his fedora pulled low over his eyes.

"Damn it, Rafe! You could say something."

Rafe smiled, enjoying his little parlor trick. He came into the room, flopped carelessly down in a chair in front of Levon's desk. With one gorgeous gesture he swept his hat off and held it restlessly in his lap. "Sorry. Listen, I was just passing through, and I saw Blesser in here with you. How is it looking, Bernard? Are we going to be able to afford to put in that ventilation system this year?"

Blesser held up his hand, indicating that he needed another moment to catch his breath, then rapped his white knuckles on Levon's desk. "Knock on wood, if the furnace holds up for one more winter."

Rafe nodded. Good. Gracie was right, the students were getting stoned on turpentine fumes. He leaned in closer. "Have we heard from the Rockwell Foundation?"

He skimmed his fingers over the pale wood of Levon's desk. "Yes," he admitted.

"Well, what did they say?"

Blesser wouldn't meet his eye. His fingertips traced loops and whorls on the glossy surface. "Well, there's good news and bad news. The good news is they're very interested in our school, in what we're teaching here. They've been thoroughly vetting us, and they think we're perfectly positioned to ride the backlash against modernism. They think we're going to train the next generation of artists who make history."

Rafe nodded impatiently. "And?"

"The bad news is, they want to see more recognizable names on the faculty page of our catalogue. Art stars. As insurance. You know, there are some big people nowadays working with the figure, Rafe. If we just—"

"No," he said smoothly, brushing a speck of dust off of the gray felt on the crown.

Turner hustled through the doorway, frowning at a paper on his clipboard. By habit, he stopped just short of Levon's desk, laid two papers in his inbox.

"Whit," Rafe said civilly.

Turner started and grabbed the desk for support, dropping his clipboard to the floor with a loud clatter.

"God, I hate when you do that." He straightened back up, trying to regain his dignity.

"I was just telling Raphael that we've heard from Rockwell," said Blesser cautiously.

"And I was telling Bernard to find another rich family that's desperately trying to give away their money," said Rafe, looking Turner in the eye.

"Well, we're going to have to do something," Turner burst out angrily. "You can't go on supporting us forever. Some rich, eccentric British guy underwriting an entire school. We look ridiculous. Or try this scenario. What if something happens to you? What if you run out of money? Someday it's going to have to fly on its own, Rafe."

Turner wheeled and stalked back out. Blesser shut the accounting ledger that was open on Levon's desk, gathered it under his arm and scurried after him.

"You know he's right," said Levon.

Rafe expelled a sigh, leaned forward, ran a hand through his hair. "I know, I know. Find another way, Levon. More parties. More patrons. More publicity. More foundations."

"We're trying. But they're all saying the same thing. You have to try, too. April Huffman is a good start. We just need a couple more like her."

He shook his sleek head. "It's a slippery slide. I'm worried about diluting our message."

Levon said mildly, "If something doesn't change soon, there might be no message to dilute. Turner's right. What if something happened to you? We could lose the school."

"Is that why Blesser was here?"

"We walk a thin line. He wanted to show me how thin."

There was an awkward silence between them for a moment. Levon shuffled some papers on his desk. "So," he said, changing the subject. "Coming to the Naked Masquerade?"

Rafe was relieved. "Yes. Anastasia's never been."

"Hallie's first time, too. We're going as Frida Kahlo and Diego Rivera. Are you dressing up? You know, admission is free to everyone who shows up nude."

He smiled. "Anastasia's coming as Ingres' *Odalisque.*"

Levon frowned. "Doesn't that mean she's going to be naked except for a towel around her head?"

"Worth the price of admission, I should think."

There was another awkward silence. Restlessly, Rafe drummed his fingers on his knee. "About that other thing," he said, feigning carelessness.

"Right," he said, turning to take a manila folder from a table behind him. "I remember. Tessa Moss. Nice girl. Good artist. Got her file right here." He thumbed through it, holding the sheaf of typewriter paper at arms length, squinting. "These days, my arms can't get long enough." He read rapidly through her application essay, his eyes moving at a measured pace back and forth, his lips pursed. In the silence, Rafe could hear the buzz of a fly beating its wings against the glass, trying desperately to find a way into the red slash of light on the horizon visible through the window.

Levon was bobbing his head up and down. "Oh, yeah, I remember now. Originally from Chicago, transferred from Parsons, got a job working for Lucian Swain, you know that much. Hmm, this is interesting. Grandparents are Holocaust survivors, lost their families in World War II. She plans to do her thesis project around the Holocaust. Here. You can look for yourself." He turned the typewritten sheet around and slid it across the desk to Rafe.

"Does it say where they came from?" The paper remained on the desk where Levon had left it. Rafe sounded detached.

Levon picked up the paper, scanned it. "Here it is. Poland. Town I've never heard of. Can't even pronounce it. Wi-li-doh-wah? I can't read those names. All consonants, no vowels. You'll have to ask her."

Rafe seized the paper, scanned the neatly typed pages, found the right paragraph. *No, no, anything but that.*

"Wlodawa," he said in a distant, toneless voice, pushing the application away. "It's pronounced, Vluh-duh-vuh." The founder of the school suddenly looked tired, and he was rubbing his long fingers across his eyes as if they pained him.

"You okay, Rafe? You don't look so hot. I was just on my way out to meet Hallie. We're headed over to Curry Hill for Indian food. Why don't you join us?"

He shook his head, unfolded himself from the armchair, stood up. "That's very kind of you. It's nothing. Too many meetings. It's been a long day."

Levon nodded his head, believing him. "So, did it answer your question? You said something about the drawing on her wall. That's why you wanted me to look at her essay."

He swept his hat back onto his head, adjusted it just so. "It opens the door to more questions."

"Like what?" Levon opened his drawer, dropped the file back in.

"About someone I used to know a long time ago."

"Ooh," he chuckled. "Well, keep me posted." He turned his attention to neatening a scattered pile of papers on the table behind his desk. "Just... be careful."

Rafe drew closer, stared at him from beneath the brim of his hat in a way that made Levon uneasy. "What do you mean?"

"I mean, she's a very pretty girl. And vulnerable. You're on the board, Rafe. Also, you're a well-known man-about-town sort of guy. Your interest could look inappropriate. And this year, we need all the votes we can get."

Rafe felt a flush of anger. "My *interest* is my own business, Levon." With that, he turned and stalked out of the office, his coattails billowing behind him.

Levon sighed, straightened out a pile of grant applications knocked askew when Raphael surprised him earlier.

"Don't worry," Rafe's voice came floating back as his footsteps echoed down the hall. "I promise not to sleep with her until after graduation."

10

*H*alloween morning dawned a raw, leaden gray. Wind and rain lashed the yellow leaves off the trees and beat remorselessly at the nineteenth-century windowpanes. It howled down the deserted downtown canyons, snaked itself around the old buildings and whistled disconsolately through cracks in windows and doors. The few stalwart pedestrians that could be seen on Lafayette Street were harried down the debris-strewn sidewalks by furious gusts of wind. Passersby huddled under umbrellas looked up to find their shelters blown inside out. Masking tape crisscrossed windows, making huge X's in building facades up and down the street, like a crazy game of tic tac toe.

The weatherman on 1010 WINS called it a nor'easter first, and then the Halloween Storm. Later on that night it came to be known as the Storm of the Century. But at the American Academy of Classical Art, it was just another Halloween. The skeleton in the anatomy room wore a pirate hat cocked at a jaunty angle. A petrified parrot was wired onto his bony clavicle, the cigarette still clamped between his yellowy teeth. Someone had broken into the case that held the cat and the dog skeletons and dressed them as a bride and groom. A furry black and orange spider zipped up and down a wire suspended from the ceiling near the office, vibrating and emitting spooky electronic moans. First-year students swooped in and out of studios wearing capes and vampire teeth. Michelangelo's *David* wore a Rastafarian cap and a mass of dreadlocks.

The Naked Masquerade was held in the Great Hall, at street level, where they kept the Michelangelos. Party guests encountered *The Dying*

Slave in the foyer as they entered the double doors leading in from Lafayette Street. For today, the statue sported a sequined gold Speedo.

Inside, a row of fluted Doric columns marched along the borders of the cavernous space. Hundreds of yards of cream-colored fabric gathered in pleats across the ceiling and plunged in deep swags behind the massive statues. A full-scale replica of the *Pietà* was the focal point of the room, occupying its own coffered niche. Replicas of the recumbent figures decorating the tombs of the Medicis, *Dusk, Dawn, Night* and *Day*, were arranged in the four corners of the enormous hall.

All day long, vans pulled up to the curb with deliveries for the Halloween Ball. Uniformed drivers, bent almost double in the driving rain, conveyed saran-wrapped platters of painstakingly styled hors d'ouevres, artisanal breads, meats, crudités, sushi, cheeses, fruits and pastries, then departed, their place at the curb taken almost immediately by the next van.

Waiters and waitresses glided through the crowd, invisibly whisking away lipstick-kissed glasses and replacing empty platters. The men, hired for their physiques as much as their abilities, were stripped bare from the waist up. The waitresses wore bodystockings adorned with a few well-placed feathers and sequins, but as they hurried by hoisting platters over their heads, they looked as naked as artists' models.

Accustomed to seeing nudes on a daily basis, the students ignored the waiters and gathered in clumps to ooh and aah over the food. A table staggered under the weight of a giant brown sugar glazed turkey and a leg of prosciutto di Parma. Next to the prosciutto, a silver tureen filled with ice was topped with a crystal bowl of smoky gray caviar and all its customary accompaniments, chopped egg, chives, crème fraîche. Silver trays bore battalions of amuse-bouche, each bite an edible art object; a tiny cube of smoked salmon on a tiny cube of black bread, a strip of grilled chicken threaded in an S shape onto a bamboo skewer. One of the sculptors had spent all day carving the centerpiece, a tall pumpkin that glowed from within like a fiery furnace, bearing the skull-like face from Munch's *Scream*.

"I'm faced with having to choose between caviar with toast points and Kraft macaroni and cheese for dinner tonight," said Graham, looking wise and inebriated under his wreath of laurel leaves. He was Bacchus. A bed sheet toga was slipping off one shoulder. "It's one of those times when you just have to say, 'What would Jesus do?' Holy jet beads, Portia, did you rob the Costume Institute at the Met?"

Portia was wearing a vintage Victorian dress with a striped skirt that swept the floor, a tight corseted bodice, and a long, low, scooped neckline that made her neck look as if it had a couple of extra vertebrae. Her hair was pulled back and piled up into a nineteenth-century bun, held together with jeweled combs. Auden was outfitted as John Singer Sargent, in a dark brown three-piece suit and beard, wearing a straw hat from a questionable time period. He was carrying around Portia's palette and brushes for authenticity.

"There are a million trunks in my grandfather's attic," she said abashedly. "We've got these great old clothes from my grandparents and my great-grandparents."

"To misquote Woody Allen," Graham said dryly, "my Grammy would have saved me all of her museum-quality designer clothing too, but she was too busy being raped by Cossacks."

"Who are you supposed to be?" Harker asked curiously. David and Sara were wearing street clothes, toting glasses of white wine.

"We're dressed as a couple of art teachers from a small college upstate. Sara doesn't like costume parties," he added apologetically.

There was a stir of activity, a flurry of commotion, at the front of the room. The party grew a little brighter, a little more frenetic. A statuesque voluptuary of a woman came gliding through the doorway, ostensibly naked but for an ankle bracelet, a gold turban, and a pair of dark glasses. Behind her was Raphael Sinclair.

"Oh my Lord," said Graham.

"Who is that?" breathed Portia.

They turned to see Giselle Warburg hurrying towards the door in a high, powdered wig and a sky-blue satin gown, voluminous petticoats flouncing behind her. She looked like a portrait by Gainsborough. "Anastasia!" she was calling in her throaty voice, and the woman stopped, embraced her on both cheeks.

"That, children, is Anastasia deCroix, editor of *Anastasia* magazine. Perhaps you've heard of her," said Graham, reverently.

"Wow," breathed Portia. "Tessa should be here. Has anyone seen her?"

"I think I just bumped into Madonna!" said Gracie excitedly. Nobody had noticed her arrival, which said something about the power of Anastasia's magnificent body, considering that their classmate was painted blue from her head down to her toes.

Ben whistled. "Damn, girl. How did you do that?"

"Poster paint," she explained matter-of-factly. "And a body suit. Nicky helped me with all the hard-to-reach places."

"I would have helped you," said Harker. "Hell, we all would've helped you."

"Are the Sonic Death Monkeys ready to rock?" said Portia hastily, changing the subject. Harker's band had been hired to play the Halloween Ball.

He pushed his hair back behind his ears. "Oh, yeah. We've got a whole Halloween party playlist worked out. Should be righteous."

Alone, unnoticed, Tessa came through the door.

In the subdued light, the chandeliers sparkled like jeweled necklaces, the draped ceiling rippled with shadows. A random shaft of light would catch the side of a face and immortalize it before it turned away, or reveal a sculptured female back, turning it into a scene from an old black-and-white movie. Tessa stood at the entrance to the enormous hall filled with happy strangers, and for a fleeting moment, considered fighting her way back home through the storm and spending the night in bed with a good book.

"Hey, there, girlfriend, I didn't think you were going to make it!" Portia yelled at her. In a floor-length silk dress, with her hair swept off of her long, lean face, she was transformed, looking every inch the consummate American aristocrat, like the painting Sargent had made of her great-grandmother when she was an art student in Paris before the turn of the century. "So does this mean we're finally going to meet Lucian tonight?"

No, he's going to Cape Cod with his new girlfriend. "He couldn't make it." she said abruptly. "Some other time."

"Who are you supposed to be?"

She touched the brim of her hat, a swooping black velvet cap with a slouchy satin crown and an ostrich plume that quavered tremulously in the updraft. The hat had been an impulse buy, weeks ago, at an open air market in Soho. The very full, very stiff, black crinoline petticoat, she had picked up for five dollars at the Sixth Avenue flea market. The camisole, all black lace and ribbons, was leftover from a time when Lucian...well, from Lucian.

"I kind of hoped it would make me look like I'm from a Rembrandt painting. What do you think?"

"I think it makes you look like a Flemish hooker," said Graham. "I don't know if any of Rembrandt's hooker paintings survived."

David was staring at her. With candlelight illuminating the right side of his face, he looked devastatingly romantic. "Hey," he said shyly. "I, um." And he stood looking blankly at her, as if he had forgotten why he was there.

Tessa didn't know the blond woman with the short haircut and the neat sweater set who was standing next to him, sticking her hand out to shake. "Hi," she said. "I'm Sara."

At that moment, she sensed, more than felt, something like a hot breath on the back of her neck. She turned around, just in time to see Anastasia deCroix striding by with the languid gait of a leopard on the savannah, slow and majestic.

Anastasia inclined her head to look at her. Lowered her sunglasses. Smiled. The hairs on the back of Tessa's neck tingled, stood up at attention.

The editor was encircled by an intimidating cortege of young women, pale and cruelly thin, dressed in various shades of black. Following close behind was Raphael Sinclair. He wore a shawl-collared dinner jacket that looked like it had been sewed onto him, expressing the sensuality of his body in the strength of the shoulders and the narrowness of his hips. He smiled as he passed and she caught a whiff of sandalwood; her heartbeat quickened, went *thump thump thump thump thump;* then he turned his attention to someone else.

"I'm thirsty," she said abruptly. "Anybody else want a drink?"

"I'll come with you," said Portia. Leaving Auden to bond with David and Sara, they drifted into the crowd.

Harker's band took the stage. The lead singer shouted, "Two, three, four," and they charged into *The Monster Mash*. At the bar, a big black cauldron sat on a fake fire, boiling out clouds of steam. It was just punch and dry ice, but the waitress behind the table wore a pointy hat and insisted on calling it witches' brew.

Levon waved at them from the dessert table and came over to greet them, carrying a tiny tart filled with a dot of mascarpone and one perfect raspberry. "Hey, girls! Wow, Portia." He whistled. "That's amazing. You look just like that Sargent portrait in the Met."

"Well, it *is* the same dress," she said.

Tessa recognized Inga, the head of the drawing department, engaged in conversation with a dark-haired, pale-skinned woman wearing a colorful Mexican dress, her black hair braided and pinned up on top of her head. With a marker, she had drawn on a single thick eyebrow and the suggestion of a faint mustache.

"Is that Hallie?" she asked.

"Yeah," said Levon, turning to look. He burst out laughing. "I'm really digging on the mustache."

Tessa studied Levon's clothing. He was in a baggy three-piece suit and a Panama hat. "You're Frida Kahlo and Diego Rivera," she guessed.

Still chuckling, he nodded confirmation. "Say, Tessa. Long as I have you here. Have you met with Josephine about your thesis project yet?"

A flush of guilt. "No. I was supposed to meet with her last week, but there was some crisis with her babysitter and she couldn't make it." She shrugged. "Just as well. I've been so busy that I don't have anything new to show her."

"Don't let her get away with it," he advised her. "You'd better get started. You don't want to fall behind."

She nodded. He turned his attention back to Portia. "And just so you know, Ballard, because I know that's what you're going to ask me, we're going to put exhaust fans in all the studios. Well...I've got to be getting back to Hallie. See you later, girls." He popped the pastry in his mouth and moved off in the direction of the bar.

"Is he all right?" Portia frowned. "He's walking kind of funny."

Tessa squinted after him, but there were too many people for her to get a good look. They located Auden talking with Ben and David. He was easy to find, standing next to Gracie. Graham was nearby, shoveling hors d'ouevres onto his plate with both hands.

Clayton ambled over, beaming. Next to him was a fragile, birdlike girl. He looked slightly dazed, as if he couldn't believe his luck. "This is Gioia. She's in art history at NYU. Doesn't speaka da English, but luckily, I am fluent in the mother tongue."

"I thought you were coming as Dracula," said Graham.

Clayton fished something out of his pocket, put it in his mouth, then growled, showing off dimestore glow-in-the-dark vampire teeth.

"You're not even trying." David said.

"Hey. Who says vampires have to wear capes and dinner jackets? I think if Dracula was here today, he might look just like anybody else. Even you, David."

A flawless Jackie O went by in a pink and black Chanel suit with a pillbox hat, sporting a somewhat incongruous five o'clock shadow. Suddenly, Gracie darted away from them, disappearing in the flow of costumed party guests. The crowd parted for a moment, and they could see her with Raphael Sinclair in a pocket of space between the churning waves of humanity.

"Hey, Mr. Sinclair!" Clayton hollered to the founder of the school. "How are you, sir? May I say what a lovely party this is," and here he hollered even louder for Tessa and Portia's benefit, "—and I want to personally thank you for creating this place. There's nothing else like it in the entire U S of A, God bless it, and I think I speak for everybody when I say we've all been looking for this art school our whole lives."

The founder of the school's eyebrows shot up, and he smiled his gorgeous smile, encompassing them all.

"Hi," said Portia, extending her hand. "I'm Portia Ballard. I don't think we've met."

"Portia," he said, his voice smooth as silk, taking her hand. "What a beautiful name."

His hand was so cold she almost gasped. His eyes were a strange color, she thought, looking directly into them. Gray? Brown? Green? Blue? Indefinable, like the color of a shadow. With a guilty flutter, she realized that she found him shockingly attractive. He exuded a varnished sexuality, promising that whatever price she paid for her weakness, he was worth it. He was remarkable to look at, high cheekbones angling out of his handsome face, soft-looking sensuous lips. Impossible to guess his age, thirty or forty. His skin was youthful and smooth, but the lines that formed around his mouth when he smiled went deep. His eyes looked as if they knew every last one of her secrets, everything she thought, everything she feared. They looked as if they knew what she had in her underwear drawer, as if they knew what she looked like without her clothes on, and what she liked for breakfast. Portia couldn't stop staring into them.

"Ballard?" he inquired courteously. "I used to know a Ballard. Where are your people from?"

"Boston," she said. She thought she saw him flinch, though she couldn't be sure.

"Her grandfather is Sawyer Ballard," added a young man who wasn't in costume. "You know. Head honcho at the Met." He seemed to be giving her a sly prod, for she broke her gaze to give him an annoyed look.

"Is that true?"

"Yes," she smiled abashedly, clearly embarrassed. "You can't pick your family, huh?"

Tessa was standing slightly apart from them, dressed in a fetching beribboned camisole and layers of crinoline, like a black wedding cake. Her glorious hair, not red, not blond, not brown, spilled down from a slouchy velvet hat with a feather in it.

"Hello, Tessa," he said.

"Hi, Mr. Sinclair." she said.

Later, whoever was there would remember the way he had stood there looking at her, and she at him; but with the low lighting, with the noise and music and commotion floating like physical entities through the air, it went unremarked.

"And who's this?" he said to Clayton, stirring himself.

"Oh, I'm sorry. This is Gioia."

At this, the girl exploded into impassioned Italian, her voice taking on a frantic beseeching tone. Clayton's eyebrows knotted together with his efforts to follow her rapid colloquial dialect.

"Well..." Raphael touched Gracie on her blue shoulder, took a step backwards out of their circle. "I've got to be going. This is a work night for me. Have fun." He rejoined the current of costumed revelers flowing towards the back of the room, disappeared.

Words were still pouring out of Gioia. Clayton was shaking his head, not understanding. Finally she lifted her right hand, made a fist with her pinky and forefinger raised into horns. She thrust it in the air, brandished it in the general direction of the founder of the school.

There was an excited burst of noise from the door, another flurry of activity.

"Oh my stars and garters, we must really rate. It's Lucian Swain." said Graham, excitement stirring his laconic voice.

Tessa's heart turned over like a car engine, knocked hard against her chest. "Where?" she said in an offhanded way.

"Over there. He *is* cute."

She followed the direction of his pointing finger. He was lingering at the edge of the dance floor, looking a little lost and out of place, wearing the sweater she had given him for his birthday. He had come after all. Maybe it was over with April. Maybe he did love her. A smile lifted the corners of her lips.

She dived into the crowd, her excitement mounting. Frantically, she fought her way through the undulating masses, losing sight of him, finding him again, then losing him once more. Finally she was standing at the pool of light where she had first seen him; but he was nowhere to be found, and her shoulders drooped in dejection.

"Hullo," he said, tapping her shoulder.

Startled, she spun around. He was behind her, grinning waggishly.

"Lucian!" Weightless with joy, she launched herself into his arms. "I can't believe it!"

"Thought I'd come see this school of yours." He gave her a little hug, grinned jovially, gently but surely letting her back down.

"Come," she said, reaching for his hand. "Let me introduce you to everyone."

"Tessa!" April appeared from behind him, where she had been conversing with a man with his head in a cage made out of light bulbs. She took Lucian's hand, confidently twined her fingers through his. "Wow, the place looks amazing! Are you working here tonight?"

"Flights are all cancelled." Lucian explained. "Just as well. Storm unleashed hell all over the Cape."

"So here we are!" exclaimed April, smiling brightly. "Eric Fischl says this is the best party of the year!"

Tessa stood still, a stony smile pasted to her lips.

"Ooh, honey, Julian's over there." April exclaimed, looking to the left over Tessa's shoulder, in the direction of the crepe table. "Come on, baby, let's dance."

Lucian waggled his eyebrows at Tessa. "Don't do anything I wouldn't do," he said cheerily, and followed April around and past his assistant.

Across the room, floating in Anastasia's wake, Raphael Sinclair turned around, feeling a seismic rift in the atmosphere. He let his eyes roam over the crowd, but it was useless; there were already hundreds of people, and more were arriving every minute. Bernard would have good news for them Monday morning after he'd totted up the receipts.

His pulse, or whatever he had instead of a pulse, was slowing now to whatever it did normally. Seeing the girl attired like that had roused a gush of emotion that left him shaking.

The dreams were coming on almost every night now. Last night he'd been with Sofia again. It had begun as pure pleasure; she was on top of him, slowly rocking; but suddenly he was sinking, sucked into the feather mattress. The bed was swallowing him, and he was falling down, down, down, clawing for purchase. When he finally slowed, came to a stop, he was surrounded by bodies, buried alive in an undulating mountain of corpses.

Anastasia stopped and turned around, her eyes gleaming. "What a fantastic crowd! I should have come last year. Look at that girl painted blue. She is so fabulous, I want to eat her all up. Has Leo ever come to your little Halloween fete?"

"No, of course not. He's a diehard modernist. He thinks we're a collection of reactionary realists."

Rafe was restless, his eyes roving over the partygoers. Something was in the air, something he couldn't quite get a grip on, but he could sense it, like a water moccasin snaking through murky water. "I'll catch up with you later," Rafe told her. "I have to go chat up the paying customers."

He moved out into the crowd. Pretty girls like fireflies brushed up against him unselfconsciously as they flitted to their friends, to the bar, to the sushi. Something inside him thrummed at their touch. He was buffeted by their exhilaration, their expectations, their disappointments, their desperation, sharp as an insect's sting.

The room looked well, he was happy to see. The chandeliers he'd dragged back from a ruined *fin-de-siècle* café in Budapest were studded with tiny orange string lights and wrapped in gauze. Dozens of burning pillar candles pooled wax on every free surface. Forests of tapers occupied entire tables. Votive candles cupped in copper mesh were wedged anywhere there was space. Fake medieval torches mounted along the walls rippled fake flames. The design firm he hired had done a bang-up job of balancing Halloween kitsch with downtown sophistication.

A girl detached herself from a circle of young men and trotted alongside, matching his stride. "Hey!" she said, trying to catch his eye. "Remember me?"

"Of course," he replied, slowing down, searching for a name. *Damn.* The girl with the greedy eyes at the newcomer's party. "Ann? Andrea?"

"Allison," she said helpfully. "You can call me Ally. Well, what do you think?"

She was in a floor-length red satin dress that was threatening to slip off her thin shoulders. Long black opera gloves ruched up her bony arms. Her exposed skin was coated in heavy white makeup, except for her lost-looking mouth, which was painted a deep, dark crimson and outlined in black. Two drops of cosmetic blood dribbled out of one side of her mouth. "Look," she said, showing off plastic fangs. "Vampire teeth."

"Very authentic," he told her politely.

The synthesizer knocked out honkytonk chords. People were dancing now, in a circle of light in front of the stage. A woman with a crystal chandelier on her head did the Monkey with a man wearing a duckling costume made from real yellow feathers. There were excited exclamations from one side of the room, and the student Rafe knew as Clayton, the one with the Roman face, pumped his fist in the air and shouted, "Sonic Death Monkeys *rock!*" A blue girl broke through the crowd in front of the band and started to dance. Rafe recognized Gracie, and a smile broke over his face in appreciation of her nerve.

"You look happy," said someone behind him. "Hey, Allison."

Rafe glanced around, found Levon making his way through the throng.

"Oh. Hi, Mr. Penfield." She flashed him an unhappy smile, disappointed at the intrusion. "Wow, you look really great. Van Gogh, right?"

He planted himself next to Rafe. "Love your costume, honey. Why don't you go help yourself to some caviar? Rafe's paying."

The girl looked torn, unwilling to give up. "Go on," Levon urged her. "Don't feel bad. He's loaded."

Her shoulders slumped. She raised woeful eyes to him. "I guess I'll see you later, Mr. Sinclair." She slinked away into the sea of humanity herding towards the dance floor.

Levon chuckled. "Van Gogh. I've been getting that a lot. I think it's the beard."

Rafe smiled, relieved. "Thanks for the save."

He shrugged. *"De nada.* She's a nice girl, but she comes on a little..." he searched for the appropriate word. "Pathetic." Levon looked him up and down. "Okay, I give up. What are you supposed to be?"

Rafe gave him a sly smile. "A vampire, of course."

Levon threw his head back and laughed.

"Place looks great."

"Robbins and Weill did a nice job."

Together, they surveyed the room. Suddenly, Levon did a double take. "Is that Anastasia?"

Rafe followed his gaze. Sure enough, Anastasia was on the dance floor. She was dancing with a pretty boy in a tuxedo. He was imitating her, move for move. She pulled him to her, and now they were cheek to cheek, their bodies glued together. Suddenly, she was kissing him, bending him over backwards in a graceful curve. Then they broke apart, laughing.

Levon glanced at him, too shocked to say anything.

"Look again," he said, enjoying his discomfort.

The boy was too short, his body too rounded, feminine. It was a girl, her short shining hair slicked back against her head.

"So...at the risk of you punching me in the face; what's the deal? Did she have to pay to get in?"

Rafe raised his eyebrows, smiled, replied, "No. She's my guest."

"Damn!" Levon said to himself. Then, "I gotta know, man. Is that a costume? Or is she in the altogether?"

"She's covered in paint from head to toe. She had three airbrush artists with her all day. Not a centimeter of skin is showing."

"Wow. You weren't kidding. Worth the price of admission."

The band downshifted into a slower beat. The singer moved to the front of the stage, planted his legs apart and leaned back, his hips jutting forward. His voice dropped, became sultry and insinuating as the band slewed into a new song. Couples on the dance floor now parted or moved closer together for a slow dance. The cocktail chatter ebbed away. The music swelled louder, the singer's voice throbbed with passion.

Dangerous things that love will make you do,
My heart was on fire, and all I saw was you.
Fate and desire, breaking my heart in two...

At the opposite end of the room, Auden pulled a protesting Portia by the hand onto the dance floor. Sargent and his subject slipped their arms around each other and began to sway in time to the music. Near the stage, Gracie laid her blue head on Nick's shoulder and slipped her fingers into the back pockets of his jeans. David coaxed a reluctant Sara into the edge of the crowd. In another part of the room, Clayton was dancing in front of Gioia, a joyful little two-step of sheer happiness.

Alone, Tessa remained rooted to the spot near the dance floor, her arms wrapped around herself as if that were the only thing keeping her from falling to pieces. Auden and Portia swayed in place, barely moving, their foreheads touching. Giselle twirled by with her husband, her sky-blue skirts billowing out like a bell as they glided by.

Just for a moment, the swathes of costumed revelers parted, revealing Lucian and April. His hands rested surely on her waist, her arms were hooked around his neck. They were gazing into each other's eyes, sharing an intimate smile. Her fingers played with the hair on the back of his neck as they moved slowly back and forth in time to the beat.

Tessa clapped her hands over her eyes to shut out the sight. A hot flush of shock and humiliation crept across her face. Opening her eyes just a crack, unable to tear her gaze away, she fixed on Lucian's hands, so familiar to her that she could almost feel their heat. Hands she had held so faithfully, and for so long, as she had reassured him day after day of her love and of his importance in the art-world firmament. Those same hands slid down April's hips, cupped her trim ass.

"Oh, get a room." she heard Graham mutter. He had come to stand next to her. Lucian slid his arms around April's shoulders, bowed his head a little lower, and then they were kissing. She took his handsome face in her hands, the long manicured fingernails like claws against his skin.

...why did you let me fall for you?
You swore you felt the same.
Why did you let me dream of you?
Part of your twisted game.

Gracie looked up from Nick's shoulder to find Lucian Swain and April Huffman right in front of her. She prodded his chest. "Look! It's Lucian Swain!" she told him excitedly. Her delight was followed by a plummeting feeling in her stomach. "Oh my God!" she said, covering her mouth with her hand. "Where's Tessa?"

On the other side of the dance floor, something made Portia turn her head. To her left, a well-dressed middle-aged man was embracing a younger woman as they danced, their gym-toned bodies pressed close together. The man was in his forties, but still held onto the cocksure good looks of his youth. The woman looked familiar. Out of context, it took her a moment to recognize them.

"Oh no," she whispered as the final notes of the song sounded through the room. "Where's Tess?"

Halfway across the room, making small talk with an aeronautics heiress wearing her mother's coming-out dress and a beehive hairdo, Raphael Sinclair felt it like a physical blow. He turned around in mid-sentence, his eyes searching the room, anguish calling to him like a beacon.

It was Tessa, alone at the edge of the dance floor. Her hands were folded over her heart, her face pale as parchment. She was staring at something, her gaze fixed and unblinking, and he followed it to where Lucian Swain was fielding a passionate clinch with the new painting teacher, April Huffman, artist of impressionist blow jobs.

Rafe plunged into the crowd, leaving the heiress open-mouthed and speechless. "Tango," he commanded the lead singer as he strode past the stage, pulling a discarded Mardi Gras mask over his eyes. The band halted halfway through the first chorus of *Bad Moon Rising.*

Too far away to stop him, Levon saw Rafe moving single-mindedly across the Great Hall, shouldering aside the very people they were there to court. Frantically scanning the room for the cause, he spotted Tessa, and almost immediately afterwards, Lucian Swain, making out with the new painting instructor on the dance floor.

"Don't do it, Rafe," he muttered to himself. "Don't give it to them. Don't give them what they're looking for."

"May I have this dance?" said a voice with a graceful British accent. A man in a mask was standing in front of her, tall and slim in a tailored tuxedo, extending his hand.

She was looking down, shaking her head. *Go away, can't you see I'm dying here?*

"Tessa," he said gently. She glanced up, her eyes blurred with tears. Behind the mask, the gray eyes were kind, filled with compassion.

"Look into my eyes," he said. "Keep looking into my eyes."

She raised her head, fixed her gaze on him like he was a lifeline. Hesitantly, she put her hand in his, and he drew her out onto the dance floor.

With one swift movement, he pulled her close. Arranging her body as if she were a doll, he placed her left hand on his upper arm just above his bicep, pushed her elbows up till they were parallel with the floor. He turned her so that they were both facing the same direction, his cheek just touching the top of her hair. Finally, he rested her palm lightly against his.

The band, consulting furiously with each other in hushed whispers, seemed to agree on something. The music began, an edgy minor key melody. Suddenly, he lunged forward, driving her back. The steps had a slinky staccato beat. Slow slow, *quick* slow. Slow, slow, *quick* slow. She could feel his other hand between her shoulder blades as he spirited her around the floor.

> *The streetlamps on Bleecker light my way,*
> *As the moon casts its cold glow on the day.*
> *Gazing up at her windows I yearn until morning,*
> *And then I slink home again, until evening comes dawning.*

They made a striking couple, the slender, elegant masked man and the pale girl with the pre-Raphaelite hair. Other dancers fell away as they glided around the pool of light in front of the stage.

Lucian and April were still swaying slowly back and forth in their own private world near the corner of the stage. As he pivoted Tessa past them, Rafe's elbow just nicked Lucian's shirt. He looked up to see who had sideswiped him just as they whirled past. His mouth fell open.

"What is it, baby?" April asked, touching his arm.

"Nothing." he said, giving her an artificial smile. "I just need a bit of a breather."

"Then let's go find a place where you can..." and here she paused with a naughty smile, *"breathe."*

"No," he said, and tucked himself into the crowd that had formed around the dance floor. "Let's just watch for a while."

At the dessert table, someone tapped David on the shoulder. "Have you seen Tessa?" Portia was asking urgently.

"No," he said, trying to seem casual. Sara was hotly jealous of his female friends. "Why?"

"Because Lucian and April are on the dance floor now, and it looks like he dropped something down her throat and he's trying to find it with his tongue."

"Whoa." Concerned now, he craned his neck, searched the crowd. There was a seething mass of onlookers over by the dance floor.

"I know that song," said Portia, frowning. "What is it?" The bass line ran counter to the synthesizer, carrying the melody, a wistfully seductive tune.

Trailing Nick, Gracie joined them now, looking worried. "Have you guys seen Tessa?"

"I've seen Tessa," said Ben, looking a little stunned. "Come on."

Through his jacket, through his shirt, he could feel her heart knocking against his chest, booming through his body.

It was a long time since he had danced the tango. Paris, 1939. The body never forgets.

He'd been unable to suppress a gasp of desire as his fingers touched the bare skin between her shoulder blades. The warmth of her palm in his hand sent shudders along every nerve pathway.

Tessa's feet hardly touched the ground. He pivoted her around his knee, maneuvering her backwards or forwards or sideways, deftly guiding her with the pressure of his hand on her back, or his hip against hers. Arms outstretched, he advanced on her, sweeping her clear across the floor with predatory ferocity; then they reversed positions, she the aggressor, he retreating sinuously backwards to the plaintive cry of the melody.

He'd told her to look in his eyes, and she obeyed, gazing up at him as if her life depended on it. Her eyes were dark like Sofia's, yes. Those extraordinary eyebrows, without a doubt, also Sofia's. But the rest was her own; the unruly lion's mane of titian hair, the sweet expression of faith and trust.

He swept her past Lucian Swain. There was an indefinable look on his face, caught somewhere between admiration and envy, like a little boy who sees someone else playing with a toy he has put aside.

Rafe twirled her around one last time, then slid his arm down to the small of her back, arching her over backwards till she was almost touching the floor. Tessa flung her head back, let her arms drop, her fingertips brushing the floorboards. Her hair cascaded to the ground like a waterfall, the ambient light turning it to a river of gold. There were exclamations of stunned admiration from the audience that had formed around them, breaking into spontaneous applause.

Rafe watched an ecstatic smile bloom across her raspberry lips. His arms still around her, he could feel her chest heaving up and down, feel her warm breath. Her lips parted, and he could see the pink tip of her tongue behind her teeth. As the last haunting bass notes sounded, he realized he wanted her, wanted her in the most achingly human way.

The entire student body hooted their approval. The crowd around them clapped harder, calling for more.

Tessa looked up into his extraordinary face. Soft, sensual mouth. Eyes the color of shadows and fog. She thought she saw something clear inside them, like storm clouds drifting apart. Gazing up at him, a scant few inches from her face, she felt her suffering lift, take flight.

Portia clapped so hard her hair started coming loose from her bun. Gracie shouted, "You go, girl!"

Lucian Swain stood with his hands at his sides, emotions flitting across his face like ghosts. Watching him, April Huffman finally understood the real extent of the relationship between the artist and his assistant.

Helplessly rooted to the spot where he stood with his longtime girlfriend, David Atwood watched Raphael Sinclair bend over Tessa Moss, and felt a guilty stab of envy and desire.

Standing near the cheese table with Bernard Blesser, Whit Turner noticed the intensity with which the founder of the school was regarding his work-study student and slowly, emphatically, nodded his head up and down.

Rafe held her a moment longer than was necessary. A hush came over the crowd, followed by whispers. *What's going on? I can't see. Is he going to kiss her?*

And then slowly, gracefully as a cat, he straightened, returned her to her feet.

The crowd exploded into applause. Tessa was laughing, her cheeks pink with exhilaration and exertion. Rafe bowed deeply, backed away, gestured at his partner. Tessa flounced a clumsy little curtsy, made more charming by the yards of crinoline.

And then, just like that, it was over. The band plunged into *Don't Fear the Reaper.* The crowd dissolved, moved towards the tables or back onto the dance floor.

Portia fought her way through the last circle of party guests between her and her friend.

A man, apparently in a rush to reach the dance floor, bumped her, glanced frantically around, cursed, hurried off in another direction. With a start, Portia realized it was Lucian Swain.

Suddenly, she recognized the song Harker's band had played during Rafe and Tessa's sultry dance. The words leapt out at her.

> *With the face of an angel and the hands of a Beast,*
> *My love is a poison, there is no release.*
> *As the moon casts its cold glow on the day.*
> *The streetlamps on Bleecker light my way,*
> *As my footsteps draw closer, you'd better pray.*
> *While the moon sinks behind Bleecker Street.*

Standing on her tiptoes, craning her neck, she searched the Great Hall. The room was thick with tall, aristocratic-looking men, but none of them was Raphael Sinclair. Fear stirred in her heart. Tessa was gone.

11

_T_hank you," she said. In the confusion after the dance ended, he had grasped her hand and made a dash for the back stairs. They ran up all four flights to the studio floor and threw themselves on an ugly crushed-velvet couch one of the students had dragged in from the street and laughed with sheer exhilaration.

"For what?" he said lightly. "For dancing with the most beautiful girl at the party? I should thank *you.*"

They drifted through the darkened studio floor, the only light an orange glow coming from the Exit sign in the sculptors' studio.

"What was that tune the band was playing?" he said curiously. "I asked them for a tango."

"Oh." she said, smiling. "I don't think I should tell you."

"Oh, but now you have to tell me."

They wandered on a little further down the center aisle as she mulled it over.

"Moonlight on Bleecker Street." He shook his head, not recognizing it. "It's about a vampire," she added sheepishly.

He stared at her. Then his eyes grew merry; he threw his head back and laughed at the joke. She laughed too, relieved that he wasn't offended.

Pushing aside the curtain over her doorway, she entered her studio. By habit, she stopped in front of her drawing, the one with the naked girl and the man in the shadows.

"It's Lucian, isn't it." he said.

She bobbed her head up and down once, with finality. The excitement of the moment was wearing off; affliction was stealing slowly over her features, transforming her lovely face back into a mask of sorrow.

"How did you two meet?"

She told him about the guest lecture at Parsons, offering herself as an assistant, her crush, his breakdown, rushing into the breach when no one else was left. It was an old story, an art world cliché. From such innocent beginnings had many similar calamities of the heart taken shape.

"Are you all right?" he asked gently. He reached out to touch her, to comfort her. But he didn't dare; instead, he busied himself straightening a crooked postcard on her wall.

"I'm nothing," she said, wanly.

"Nothing?" he repeated, perplexed.

"Not his girlfriend. Not his lover. Not a colleague. Not his friend. Just a nobody from nowhere who does his work for him." She turned away from her drawing. "I thought we were going to be together forever."

"Tessa," he said. His voice was like an adagio in a minor key, melodic and sad. "You won't believe me when I tell you this. No one ever does. But I've been to the same cold and lonely region of the damned. You think it's the end of the world. You think you'll never get past feeling this bloody awful. Get up. Go to class. Cry with your friends. Make art. Break some hearts. Soon, an hour will go by where you don't think of him. A week. A month. I promise you. It will pass."

This is the part where I maneuver her over to that niche by the door...I push the heavy curtain of hair from her neck and take the life running through her veins.

"You'll see," he said.

She had lost her hat, and her hair was an ocean of shimmering waves in the dark. Her bare shoulders glowed like marble, the summery scent of blackberries rising off of her like steam. There was a gnawing in his belly, the wrong kind.

He turned to Gracie's side of the studio. A long sheet of butcher paper was tacked up on her wall, spanning the entire height of the divider. She had begun sketching out a floor-to-ceiling column of nudes, crones, women, children, all intertwined, rising up into the air.

"She draws like an angel."

"She does." Tessa agreed. She touched a chubby baby cheek with one finger.

Isaiah's cheek. So pink and round. I'd never touched anything that soft.

"So...are you, like...dating her?" she blurted out.

"Dating her? Gracie?" he barked out a short, sharp laugh. "Good God, no. What makes you say that?"

She was fumbling awkwardly for words now. "That time you came to pick her up for a meeting, you...she...it seemed like...I thought...Oh God, I'm sorry."

"We're just on a committee together. Though I will confess, she certainly is fun to look at."

Even in the dark he could tell she was blushing furiously. Tendrils of her miraculous hair were quivering. It was altogether charming. "Have your friends started working on their thesis projects yet?" he asked her, changing the subject.

"I don't know," she admitted.

"Well then," he said, "Let's have a look."

Directly across the aisle was the small space Graham shared with DJ. His wall was papered with dozens of heads, hands, feet, drawn with pen on notebook paper, napkins, envelopes, brown paper bags. Small clay figurines stood on a table made from sawhorses and an old door. Big, confident paintings were stacked against the wall, solid figures standing in contrapasto or reclining on pillows and drapery, blocked out in masses of glorious color.

"So, what are you looking for, Tessa Moss?" he mused. His voice traveled up and down like a musical instrument, lovely and melancholy. "The usual thing? Fame, fortune, beautiful lovers?"

"What am I looking for." She pondered his question. "It would be nice not to worry about money...I could afford to buy that tube of genuine Old Holland Cerulean blue instead of the cheap imitation stuff. Maybe even get some Isabey Kolinsky sable brushes in the same trip. As for beautiful lovers," she gave him a rueful look. "I just need one."

She fell silent, absorbed in her own thoughts. Abruptly, she turned to him. "How did you know about me? Who told you? Does everybody know?" She put a hand to her head. "This is so embarrassing. I feel like an idiot."

"Lucian and I have a mutual friend," he said hastily. "Anastasia deCroix." He paused, then said mildly, "No one thinks you're an idiot."

"I'm okay, you know. You can get back to the party now. They must be looking for you."

"I'm sure they can do without me for a little while longer."

She looked wistfully at one of Graham's pen and ink drawings, a sketch of a model's back. The anatomy was flawless; not one extraneous mark, not one line out of place. "Fame," she mused, returning to his question. "I've been around fame. It leads to strangers showing up at your door with your name painted on their breasts."

It made her absurdly happy to see him stop and laugh, she couldn't have said why. "It's not like I want to labor for years in obscurity," she added. "I'm not a martyr. I want people to see my work. I'd like if it made them feel something, or if it made someone think a new thought, or see things in a different way."

This had the heavy ring of truth. "That's it," she said as they meandered into the aisle. "I want something I make to make a difference to somebody." She rolled her eyes. "I sound so pretentious."

"I don't think you're pretentious," he said.

They drifted from studio to studio. Tessa stole a glance at the man beside her, felt herself responding to the grace with which he moved, the way his clothes fit his lean, muscular body. She felt like she was under a spell, a thrill of enchantment, as if she had discovered a room in her apartment that hadn't been there before.

In the sculptors' studio, they were confronted by a doleful, empty-eyed female figure. Small, contorted human bodies writhed from the contours of her skirt.

"Ben," she said. "I think it's for a competition. A slavery monument somewhere."

He studied the plaster cast. "Right. He came to us from some dreary technical school in Indiana."

They moved on to David and Portia's studio. David's wall was neatly hung with figure studies, flawlessly executed in paint, charcoal, pen and ink.

"He's good," Rafe commented.

"Yes." she said in a way that made him glance at her, "Really good."

Portia's side was stacked with her studio paintings of nude models. They had a lyrical, haunting quality to them, owing to the delicacy of her line and the way she handled her paint.

"Lovely," he said, inspecting them closely. "Filled with light."

"Why did you do it?" she said curiously. "Pull me out onto the floor, dance with me. Why?"

Yes. Why? His heart was a riot of confusion. He had no business being alone with her, no business making a scene, no business skipping out on the party when hundreds of wealthy lovelies were downstairs, waiting for his attentions, begging to be convinced that the Academy was exactly the right institution at which to throw their money. This could bring nothing but disaster, after all the years he had spent sculpting his persona as a society fixture and cultivating the reputation of his school.

He prowled restlessly through the room to the empty student lounge at the front of the building. She was following him; he could hear her stiff skirts swishing somewhere in the dark behind him.

The windows facing the street had been crisscrossed with huge masking tape X's, and they threw eerie rippling patterns on the studio walls. He rested his palms on the cool glass. "You called to me." he finally answered. "I can't explain it." And then suddenly, with a rush of feeling, "I've felt connected to you since the moment I first laid eyes on you. Don't you know? Can't you feel it?"

Tessa was astonished. It was as if a character in a movie she was watching had walked off the screen, found her in the theater, and delivered the lines from the big love scene.

He looked up at the ceiling, where workmen had already begun installing the new ventilation system. "But I'm a thousand lifetimes older than you. And I'm on the board. I'd be kicked right out if anyone suspected anything. And then we all lose."

The wind started up again. It whistled mournfully through chinks in the buildings armor, sent plastic grocery bags tumbling end over end and paper cups skidding down the sidewalk on the street below.

"Listen," he went on, in a tense, low voice. "I know you're in love with Lucian Swain. And, for what it's worth, I think he loves you, too. Not as much as he loves his dick, of course. But...he is what he is. And he's not fit to touch the hem of your skirt." The neon sign on the Astor Place Theatre advertising Blue Man Group flashed on and off, staining his face blue and yellow by turn. The blue light heightened the angles of his handsome face, made him look almost dangerous. A muscle in his jaw flexed; and then he added, "And neither am I."

Tessa studied her image in the dark window.

Oh, dear God, she can see that I have no reflection.

He heard the rustle of her petticoats, felt the warm aura of her presence tickling the hairs on the back of his neck. She was standing beside him, looking out over the rooftops of Greenwich Village through windows dotted with raindrops.

"Thank you," she said softly. "Thank you for all of it. The dance, the school...the things you said. Everything." Her breath made a foggy patch on the glass. She traced a heart with an arrow through it. "You know, this is my turf," she said forlornly. "What's he doing here, anyway?" She expelled a deep, shaky sigh. "I always imagine this block is mine," she explained apologetically. "I feel safe here. Silly, huh?"

He registered a surprising flutter of pleasure. "No," he said. "Not silly at all."

Take her. Take her now. No one else is around. She wants it. She's waiting for you.

"Look," he said, against his better judgment. "Would you like to go out for a drink?"

She shook her head no. "I'm sorry. I have to get home. It's Friday night."

"Friday night?" he repeated, not understanding.

Shy, embarrassed. "It's a long story. I'm usually home on Friday nights... my Sabbath...I didn't want to miss the Halloween Party."

Sofia's hands describing circles in the air as she lit the Shabbos candles. Isaiah covering his eyes with his baby fists, imitating her.

"Do you mean...Shabbos?" he said, the syllables rusty on his tongue.

Tessa's mouth dropped open. "How do you know that word?" she asked slowly.

I want to tell her.

Don't be an idiot.

There was a burst of noise over in the sculptors' studio; a bump, a crash, a whispered oath, shh-shhing. Drunken party guests looking for a place to consummate their excitement, knocking over someone's hard work.

The spell was broken. "I'd better go."

"Stay," he said. She shook her head no. He could feel her withdrawing, backing away from the intimacy of the moment. "Let me walk with you, then."

A ghostly figure in a red dress materialized from the gloom. "Mr. Sinclair? Is that you?"

It was Allison, accompanied by one of the first-year students, a boy from Germany. Exasperated, he turned to her. "Yes?"

"Giselle is looking for you. She thought she saw you come up here."

Damn. "I'll be right down. He turned back to Tessa. "Will you wait for me?"

"I can't." She was receding from him, irretrievably called back to her life, the world of light, the land of the living.

Allison, from the shadows. "Mr. Sinclair?"

"Tell Giselle I'll be there in a minute," he commanded her. "Now, go." He could hear her muffled giggles as she fled through the studio floor with her new friend, the staccato clatter of their tread echoing down the stairs.

"Tessa?" he said, his voice soft and low, trying to win her back again.

Her eyes, her eyes. They looked at you the way you had always wanted someone to look at you. They believed every tale you ever told and took your side. They roused him, made him restless, made him want to protect her, pursue her, hunt her down, keep her safe.

"Yes," she said quietly. "I feel it too."

And then she was backing away, letting herself be swallowed up by the darkness. He heard the steel door slam; the sound of her footsteps running down the stairs was drowned out by the noise of Harker's band playing *Rock Lobster.*

A fiery ball mounted in his chest, rising to his brain. Her bare flesh under his hands, under his control as he forced her backwards around the dance floor. The swell of her breasts over the lace as she arced back in a dip. Her long white neck. His head throbbed. He pressed his fists against his temples.

Go. The party. Remember? Giselle. Biggest fundraiser of the year.

Halloween. A million people dressed as someone else on the streets of Greenwich Village tonight looking for a good time. Some looking for that special someone. Others looking for trouble. Odds were good that some would find both.

Tessa, by herself, on a night like this, in the path of someone like me.

Now he hurried, racing down the stairs to the service entrance at the back of the building.

In the middle of Lafayette Street, he stood still. He closed his eyes, inhaled, concentrating. Due to the storm, tonight New York was a confusing jumble of unfamiliar odors, full of questionable smells blown in from faraway places. The stench of wet garbage; the burnt-rubber stink of asphalt; the overpowering odor of the homeless blowing up from the subway vents. The omnipresent scent of dry cleaning chemicals; the sharp reek of sweat and vinyl raincoats; the smoky musk of burning wood; cooking smells from the Korean deli; the unmistakable cold tang of winter.

There it was, a whiff of summer, the scent of blackberries trailing off in the direction of Astor Place. He headed north on Lafayette, then west on Eighth Street, circumnavigating a bevy of NYU students, their hair spray-painted purple, blue, ruby, emerald.

Despite the storm of the century, the streets of the village were packed. He lost her scent as he passed through a platoon of transvestite Marilyn Monroes, catching it again at Fifth Avenue. The crowds leaving the parade route along Sixth Avenue made way for him, a striking but slightly sinister man in a tuxedo stalking down Fifth Avenue, focused on a single object somewhere ahead of him.

Crowds were flowing down all the major avenues, converging on Union Square, the end of the parade route. A man strode past him wearing nothing but blue body glitter, a codpiece and a pair of white feathered wings. A couple of Chers, a couple of Lizas, several different versions of Judy Garland from various eras. A pair of hippies. Leather-legged punk rockers sporting hair shaved and shaped into neon-green mohawks. A couple outfitted as condoms. Scattered rubbery George Bush masks. One diehard Nixon.

There she was, crossing Ninth Street, heading uptown. He would have recognized her anywhere, her hair hanging almost to her waist, the curls jouncing with each step.

There were girls dressed as cats, girls dressed as witches, girls dressed as Elvira, girls dressed as Playboy bunnies, girls dressed as hookers. Posses of young men in flannel shirts and jeans, redolent of Corona and Sam Adams, come down from the East Side, or Columbia, or the boros, or Jersey, for one wild night in New York City. A unicorn, resplendent in a sparkling transparent body stocking, shimmery lavender tail and an iridescent horn glued to his forehead. A hooded Grim Reaper, ten feet tall, sweeping by on stilts, tapping on an oversized watch as he passed.

Expertly, Tessa navigated her way through the lanes of foot traffic moving along the sidewalks with a native's feel for the natural rhythm of the street. Rafe watched young men glance covetously over their shoulders for a second look at her luminous face, one slamming with an audible *oof* into the person walking just ahead of him.

At Sixteenth Street, in front of Armani Express, she turned left, a single diminutive figure fighting the hordes surging east. A skeleton the size of a Macy's Thanksgiving Day parade balloon hovered over the throng, in the wake of a samba band trying to find its way to Union Square. The giant skull bobbled left and right with a wicked grin, and the staring empty eye sockets seemed to be searching for someone in the crowd. Tessa hugged the buildings, squeezing past a stoop with an Anarchy symbol spray-painted on it, just avoiding the reach of its skeletal fingers.

Near the end of the block she reached in her pocket for a key, pulled open the glass fronted door of a building and entered. Rafe sprinted forward, getting there just in time to see her pass the elevator, turn right, and disappear from view.

There was a row of wide, high, street-level windows, and he peered into them through a chink in the dirty venetian blinds. Here, between the slats, he could plainly see a long narrow room with a door at the end of it. Ubiquitous New York City exposed brick walls. A staircase, a sagging corduroy couch, a wooden table, a lamp, a TV, a coffee table. Tessa, throwing her coat down on the couch.

"Hey!" a sharp male voice behind reprimanded him. "We don't do that here."

Rafe turned his head. A clean-cut young man in a suit and trench coat, Wall Street type, or a lawyer, doing the right thing. At any other time, he would have applauded his civic responsibility, but now he fixed him with a hard, baleful glare. The young man sucked in his breath, jerked away like he'd been stung, then hurried off down the street, fearfully glancing back to see if he was being followed.

By the time he turned back, Tessa was gone. He straightened up, noted the location. 43 West 16th Street, her awning said, between Fifth and Sixth Avenues.

He had left the party without his coat, and now he felt the chill biting into him. A bitter cold front was riding in on the tail of the storm. There was a phone booth in front of the Korean deli on the opposite corner. He trotted across the street, pulled a business card from his wallet, dropped a quarter into the slot with shaky hands. Fumbled the number. Cursed himself. Found another quarter, dialed again.

"Drohobych Import Export," answered a bored Russian operator.

"This is Mr. Sinclair," he said urgently. "Janina, please. Now. The usual place."

"Yes, sir. We know there are many other import export businesses in the city. We appreciate your patronage," she droned, and cut the connection.

He placed the phone back on the receiver. His eyes fell on the dim glow of her window. For a fleeting moment he felt warmed just by being in her corner of the city.

He was shivering now, and the hunger made it worse. He pulled up the collar of his tuxedo jacket in a fruitless attempt to keep out the cutting wind. Luckily, an empty taxi turned down Sixteenth Street.

Go back to the party. It's not too late.

"Gramercy Park," he told the driver. "Northeast corner."

"This could take awhile," the cabdriver told him. "Faster to walk."

"That's all right," Rafe said. As the cab nosed its way through the crowds, he settled back into the scarred leather seat and closed his eyes, letting fatigue overtake him.

12

April Huffman held a makeup class at eight a.m. the following Monday.

Over the weekend, the temperature plummeted. Heavy snowstorms and frigid conditions blanketed the Midwest, a parting gift from the perfect storm. The classroom was cold. David, Clayton and Graham were huddled in their winter jackets mixing paint and blowing on their fingers when Portia stuck her head in the doorway.

"You're not in this class anymore, you sissy," said David.

"Yeah," said Graham. "This class is only for real men." They made hooting caveman noises.

"Tessa here yet?" she asked, trying to sound casual.

"No," said Clayton, putting down his palette knife. "Why?"

"Oh, you know. Just wanted to say hi." Portia hadn't heard from Tessa all weekend, and she was concerned. Not that she heard from her any other weekend.

"Are you worried that she's been turned into a vampire?" he said, lowering his voice.

"Clayton," said Portia, putting her hands on her hips. "I thought we were over that."

"Hey," he said defensively. "I *was* over it. It's Gioia. That's what she was saying at the party. She was talking so fast I couldn't understand her. She kept saying, '*vampiro, vampiro, vampiro.*' She wouldn't shut up about it. So now I can't help thinking Tessa got turned into the evil undead over the weekend."

"Hey, guys." said Tessa, lugging in her load of paints and space heaters. "Evil undead monitor, coming through."

"Tessa!" Portia pounced on her joyfully. "Where did you learn how to dance like that! You should have seen the look on Lucian's face!"

"Those were some sexy moves, Tess," David said. "Why don't you give us a little show right now?"

"That's the thing," she said. "I can't. I can't move like that. I can't do the hokey pokey. It was all him. Anyway...nothing happened. We went up to the studios. We talked, that's all. He's nice."

Clayton groaned. Ben shook his head sadly.

"No, no, no." David said firmly. "We don't want to hear any of that 'he's nice' crap. Many things have been said about Raphael Sinclair. No one has ever said he was nice. Let's hear it, Tessa. What really happened up there?"

"He knows about me and Lucian. He was trying to make me feel better."

More head shaking from the men. "I'm sorry," said Graham, "But recent polls indicate that nobody believes you. Come on, Tessa. We saw the way he was looking at you."

"He wanted to see what everybody is working on for their thesis projects. I took him around the studios."

David, Clayton, Graham and Ben were like a wall; they crossed their arms expectantly, waiting patiently.

She sighed, set down the heaters. "Okay," she said, lowering her voice. "I never thought it would happen to me. First, I said, 'You have really beautiful eyes,' and I asked him if he would pose for me. He said he didn't want to, but I could tell he really did want to. So then I said, 'Hey, Mr. Sinclair, you look uncomfortable, why don't you take off your jacket?' So he takes off his jacket, and stands there just kind of looking at me, like you're doing right now. And then, I say, 'I paint better when I'm nude, is it okay if I take my clothes off?' And he says, 'Okay, I guess that's all right.' So I take my clothes off, and then he says, 'My pants are really chafing me, would you mind if I removed them?' And I say, 'Sure.' And then the cleaning lady comes in, and she sees us, and she asks if she can..."

David cut her off. "Come on, Tessa. The guy's a major hound. He's boffed half the women on the Upper East Side. You can't expect us to believe that nothing happened."

"Hey, I want to hear the rest of the story." Ben protested.

"Nothing happened," she repeated, thinking of Raphael Sinclair's eyes, his voice, feeling a little flutter of warmth.

"I know this sounds crazy," said Portia hesitantly. "Look...I'm incredibly grateful to him, for what he's done for us, for this school...nobody appreciates it more than me. But when I looked in his eyes, when he shook my hand, I felt...*violated*. You have to trust me on this, Tessa. I have a nose for these things."

"He was so kind." Tessa said, in a voice filled with wonder. "I don't know how he knew, don't know how he found me...when Lucian came in with April...and then later, when I saw them making out on the dance floor...well, for me, it was like the end of the world. I've been with him through so much, and for so long, I don't even know what I am anymore, besides Lucian Swain's assistant. When I looked in his eyes, when he touched me, suddenly none of it mattered. He said—"

Portia never got to hear the rest of what Rafe said, because at that moment, April Huffman blew in like a cold front. Without a word, she closed the door in Portia's face.

"Monitor, where are the heaters?" April demanded. "Where are my lights?"

"I'm sorry," Tessa apologized swiftly. "Here you go." Hurriedly, she clipped the lights to scaffolding on the ceiling and distributed the heaters. In the meantime, April posed the model. She put a stool on the stage next to her, then added a coffee cup and a trashcan to the composition. As an afterthought, she placed her leather bag next to her feet.

For a while there was quiet, nothing but the sound of bristles scratching on canvas as they roughed out their compositions. The trouble began after the second break.

"Awful," April ejaculated. "Just awful."

She was standing behind Ben. Tessa heard him murmur something in reply, and it grew quiet again.

Come on, Tessa, focus. She frowned at her canvas. Normally, she concentrated on the figure, getting the anatomy right, trying to paint the progression of light as it moved and changed across the body, but April wasn't interested in that. She scraped in some lines to describe the pose, then drew the bag, the coffee cup, and the trashcan. Squinting to eliminate unnecessary detail, she began painting in Sivan's torso.

April's loud voice broke the silence. "I want everyone's attention," she announced. "Look over here."

She held up Graham's canvas. "This," she declared, "is a disaster. The composition is static. The drawing is clumsy. The colors are muddy." Her words cut clear across the classroom. "I'd say it's ugly, but it's worse than ugly. It's *boring.*"

She handed the painting back to Graham. "Painting is seduction, boys and girls. Seduce me."

And then she turned to Tessa.

"Hey there," she said brightly, with a big artificial smile. "Great party, huh?" Her candy-apple-red lipstick made her look vaguely wolfish. "I had no idea you could move like that. You were *hot,* girly."

"It was all Mr. Sinclair," she responded politely. "My talents lie elsewhere."

"No, kiddo. It was you. You were sizzling."

There was a moment of silence. Tessa thought she was studying her composition, but apparently, the painting instructor had other things on her mind.

"It was a bummer about the Cape," she continued affably, as if they were friends. "It's so romantic there, especially during a storm...you should go there sometime, when you have a boyfriend. After the party, Lucian wanted to drive out to Coney Island to hear the waves crashing on the beach... you know Lucian, he's such a romantic. Then we picked up Chinese food and went back to his place and played Strip Trivial Pursuit. I let him think he won." Her voice dropped to a conspiratorial whisper. "Get this! Four times in one night...I could barely walk the next day. Someone should have warned me. Anyway, I was just cleaning out some drawers over at his place. Are these your things?" She slipped a Balducci's bag under the easel.

"Okay. Let's have a look." April stepped back to view her work. Her lips drew together as she shook her head. "Oh, no. This is a disaster. A dis-*as*-ter."

Tessa looked at her painting, confounded. "What's wrong with it?"

"What's right with it, you mean." She took a wad of paper towels and wiped everything on the canvas into a greasy brown smear. Then she moved on to the next student.

Tessa stared at the ruined canvas in disbelief. She felt like she'd been assaulted. Putting down her brush, she retrieved the bag April had left under her easel. Inside were a couple of back issues of *Vanity Fair,* a dried up Maybelline Great Lash mascara that could have belonged to anybody, an old toothbrush, a half-empty bottle of Crabtree and Evelyn almond massage oil. Her nightgown, balled up like a rag at the bottom of the bag. A single Polaroid picture.

Curiously, she pulled it out and turned it over. There she was, kneeling on the floor of Lucian's studio in a black teddy and cowboy boots, trying to look sexy. A black-and-white self-portrait taken six months ago. She ran her fingers over her miniature image. She had sent it to Lucian when he was away in rehab, along with extra socks. Scrawled on the bottom were the words, *This is waiting for you. Come home.*

She looked furtively to the right, then left. Her heart pounding like a hammer, she slipped the photo into her art box.

When it was time for the critique at the end of class, Tessa was the last to come forward. She propped her canvas up next to Clayton's, and melted into the back row, trying to hide behind the burlier sculptors.

April put on a pair of glasses and stepped up to the stage to survey the day's work. She moved slowly, from left to right, as if she were reading. At Clayton's painting, she came to a stop. There was the model, sensitively drawn, richly painted. Everything was lovingly, exquisitely rendered, except for one thing.

"Whose is this?" April demanded.

"That one's mine, Miz Huffman." Clayton said.

She consulted her clipboard. "You are..."

"Clayton El Greco, ma'am." he said, stepping forward with a dazzling bad-boy smile. Tessa glanced at him. With his shirt tucked in and his hair combed back, he looked just like Elvis.

"That's quite a name to live up to," she said, smiling back at him, putting her clipboard down. "Any relation to the painter?"

"That is what they say, ma'am." he said, disarming her with his raspy Mississippi drawl and winning smile.

"Traitor," Ben whispered to him.

She peered at her clipboard. "It says here…you're a sculptor."

"That's right, ma'am. Please go easy on me."

"No, no," she said encouragingly. "It's very good. Don't sell yourself short." She turned her attention back to the painting. "So, Clayton El Greco…what happened?"

He frowned. "What do you mean, Miz Huffman?"

April gestured at his canvas. "The model. When I saw this painting earlier, it was pretty much finished. Then you scraped off her ass. What happened?"

He rubbed his chin. "Huh. You might say…I dis-*assed*-her. Get it? Disaster? Dis-assed-her?"

The room exploded in raucous laughter. April Huffman's smile froze on her face. Without another word, she grabbed her bag off of the model stand and stormed out of the studio. Hilarious laughter followed her, echoing wildly down the hall.

"Okay," said Graham, when he was sure that she had gone. "Is there anybody in this room who didn't hear how many times she came on Friday night?"

Tessa glanced at Clayton. He grinned at her, patted her shoulder. "I didn't like the way she was treating you."

"I hope you don't get in trouble for this."

He shrugged. "It seemed like the right thing to do," he said authoritatively. "I don't know why folks are so worried about pissing off other folks."

Harker moseyed over to them, holding a can of Colt 45. "That was totally uncalled for," he agreed.

"Are you drinking beer before noon?" Graham asked him.

"Are you drinking in school?" David said incredulously.

"Nah." Harker flipped his long black hair back behind his ears. "It's for my chewin' tobaccy. I'm using it for a spittoon."

They all took a step back.

Clayton followed Tessa around like a puppy as she gathered up the heaters. "Why don't you transfer to another class? I know people like April. She's not gonna give up until one of you is dead."

"She can't," said Graham, rubbing down his palette with turpentine. "She's on work study. All the monitor positions have already been assigned. If she's not working, she loses her scholarship."

For a moment her classmates halted in their activities, considering her predicament.

"Here. Let me help you with that." Clayton offered, taking the heaters.

"I'll do the lights," said David. "Why don't you just take your stuff and go?"

There were six more weeks of painting with April before the fall semester was over. Tessa wanted to run all the way home and bury herself under the covers. But she had to work; she had another class in an hour. She gathered up her coat, her palette, her brushes and her canvas. Mournfully, she weaved her way through the easels and paint stands.

On the way out the door, she stopped just long enough to stuff her painting in the trashcan.

13

The phone was ringing. Rafe opened his eyes, slammed his hand down upon it before he was fully awake.

"I had forgotten what a thing of beauty it is to see you at work, my darling," purred Anastasia. "Your little tango has the knickers of *tout le monde* in a tangle! The passion! The drama! Everyone is calling."

Rafe stifled a yawn, rolled over, squinted at the clock. "What time is it?"

"Three o'clock in the afternoon. I have a meeting in a few minutes, but I just had to know."

"Know what?" He jogged the hump in the bed next to him. "Wakey wakey," he whispered to Janina, covering the phone with his other hand.

"What happened after you left, of course."

"Nothing." He swung his legs out of bed and onto the kilim rug next to his bed. Janina yawned and stretched, pointing her toes like a ballet dancer. "We went up to her studio and talked. She was in a bad way after that Lucian Swain thing. Art students are like hothouse flowers. I gave her the benefit of my experience and then I made sure she got home safely." Janina rolled over and nipped playfully at his back, baring her teeth, making little growling noises.

"I've had the benefit of your experience, my darling. Talking had nothing to do with it."

"Not with this one." He pushed Janina away.

"Really! Not even a taste? A lick?"

"No." he said shortly.

"Raphael, Raphael." He could visualize her red lips, turned down with disappointment. "So bourgeois, with all your fine, delicate feelings. No one is going to believe your noble story. I'm going to have to make something up."

"She's one of my students, Anastasia. If there's even a whiff of hanky panky, I'll be thrown off the board of my own school. I've got to be as pure as the driven snow." Naked, he went to the dresser, found his wallet and fished out a hundred dollar bill. He waved it at Janina, silently gesturing to her to go. She looked offended.

"Watching you dance with her...I thought you were going to bite her at any moment. Every time you drove her backwards around the floor, when you did that *quebrada*...the suspense! The anticipation! I really thought you were going to do it, and just make it look like it was part of the dance. That deep dip at the end, right down to the floor...the way you were looking at her neck with such hunger..." she was almost whispering. "It felt like the old days. Back in Europe."

Rafe was taken aback. Was he that transparent? "I've got to go."

"Are you alone?"

"No." He pressed the heels of his hands into his eyes. He'd gotten to sleep at daybreak. "Isn't it Saturday? Why are you at work?"

"You are the only person in New York City who doesn't know it's Fashion Week. Things are crazy. I am zigzagging from party to party, from one runway to the next. That Giselle woman, she was looking for you all night. You are going to have to do some fancy footwork to dance yourself out of this one. Luckily, there is that party at the Guggenheim tonight. Perhaps you can make it up to her."

Rafe massaged the back of his neck and rolled his head. He had forgotten about that. "How do you stay up all day? Why aren't you tired?"

She laughed. "You forget, I'm much older than you. I barely need any sleep at all. Listen. I have some information for you. I received a tearful phone call from Lucian Swain. He is beside himself. He wants his little assistant to stay right where she is. He's terrified that she's going to go off with you."

"Good," he said, scrounging through his drawers for a cigarette. Funny. He hadn't smoked in years. "Then it worked."

"It gets better, my darling. You won't believe it. Lucian says our girl is a virgin. She's religious or something. I know, I know, it is impossible. A virgin in New York! A virgin with Lucian Swain! He says that she is kind, faithful, trusting, loyal. The kind of girl you marry." She sniffed contemptuously, as if it were in bad taste. "I can't wait to see what happens next."

Janina wasn't leaving. She threw back the covers to show off her underwear-model's body, still in the black rubberized bustier from last night.

"So, did you ask her? You had the perfect opportunity."

"Ask her what?" He found a cigarette, lit it, inhaled deeply.

"Whether she knows what happened to your little friend from school."

Janina wanted the cigarette. He passed it to her. "No. I still can't bring myself to do it. I don't know whether I want the answer to be yes or no."

There was commotion at the other end of the line. Her tone of voice changed; he heard her issuing icy commands to someone in her office. Then she was back, warm throaty words pouring into his ear. "I have to go, my darling. I will see you later. *Au revoir.*"

He hung up the phone, took the cigarette back from Janina, who had rolled over on her stomach and was waving her legs around in the air like a school girl.

"You are in love with one of your students, eh? Someone you should not touch?" she said. "What are you, a teacher?"

"Yes," he said. "No. I'm not a teacher. The student. I don't know. I can't stop thinking about her."

"Does she like you?"

"She's with somebody else. Someone who's not good for her."

Janina burst out laughing. He looked over at her, his eyebrows raised.

"I'm sorry," she apologized, not looking sorry at all. "I don't mean to laugh at you, but it's funny to hear someone like you say that."

Rafe sat back down on the edge of the bed and sighed. "You know what I am."

She took the cigarette, rolled over on her back, clenched it between her teeth. "Yes."

"A long time ago, before I was this way, there was this woman. We were in school together in Paris, right before the war. I'm pretty sure she...I'm pretty sure she died. But all these years, there's always been this lingering shadow of a doubt. Ridiculous, really." He took the cigarette from her. "It's impossible, I know. There were no survivors from her family. Still, I can't stop myself from feeling they must be connected. I could ask her. Then I'd know for sure. Though…" he inhaled, drawing warming smoke into his lungs. His eyes narrowed ruminatively behind the glowing tip of the cigarette. "There are parts of the story that are best not held up to the light of day."

Janina nodded. "That was a bad time. My grandmother says that one day, the Nazis came and rounded up all the intelligentsia. The teachers, the doctors, the town officials, the professors. They took them to the forest and shot them."

"Where are you from?"

"Ukraine," she replied. "But my grandmother was from Lublin, in Poland. Right outside of town, there was a concentration camp. Maybe you heard of it, Majdanek. My grandmother says she used to go up to the fence when guards weren't looking and give the prisoners food."

"Really," he said, thinking of the impenetrable double walls of electrified barbed wire, the guard towers. "She must have been a very brave woman."

"Yes," Janina agreed. "She was very surprised when the Russians liberated the camp. She says the people in the town had no idea what was going on in there."

He remembered the unmistakable stench that had permeated clothing, hair, everything it touched, the greasy ash that had to be washed off the car windows every morning. "Of course not."

She came to sit next to him, rolling on her stockings, her knee not quite accidentally touching his. He slid his hand up her thigh. "Very nice," he said, stubbing out the cigarette.

"Do the Jews still use the blood of Christian children for their holidays?" she asked him as she pulled her hair back into a ponytail.

"What?" he said, staring at her in disbelief. "Good God, no. Where did you hear that?"

"From my grandmother," she said, surprised at his reaction. "Everyone knows."

"It's not true," he said, his face hardening. "It was never true. It's a stupid peasant superstition." He removed his hand from her thigh.

"Oh, look," she said, genuinely contrite, pulling a sad face. "I have upset you with my silly questions. Let me make it up to you." From an array of small colored bottles on the nightstand, she chose three, one blue, one brown, one chartreuse. Her long fingers made smooth, lazy circles over his body, starting with his chest, expanding to his back and shoulders. Despite himself, he found himself yielding, letting her skilled hands assuage his anger.

"Mmm," he said. "What are you using?"

"Sweet orange, ginger and ylang ylang for stimulation," she said, following the convex curve of his lower back. "Eucalyptus and rose for relaxation," she slid to her knees on the floor in front of him. "Jasmine and vanilla for sensuality."

She touched her scarlet lips to his throat, his chest, his flat belly, working her way down. "What's this?" she asked, touching the inch-long scar near the center of his chest.

"Old war wound," he said, gently removing her hand.

As she went to work, he leaned back on the bed, visualizing Tessa as she had looked at the Naked Masquerade last night. Lightly, he rested his hand on his chest, picturing a tumbled mass of red-gold curls a man could get lost in. It was Tessa's hands massaging scented lotions over his body, Tessa's skin the color of a peeled twig under the laces of her black camisole, Tessa calling out his name as she arched her back beneath him.

And then Janina did something with her mouth that drove all such visions from his head, and he closed his eyes and fell into a deep but uneasy sleep, where he dreamed that Tessa hid under the floorboards in Sofia's kitchen as he forced the door shut to keep out the Nazis, while Janina offered them lotions from outside the kitchen window.

14

The clocks had been turned back to daylight savings time the previous Saturday night. White Street was dark and deserted, with deep, shadowed doorways that made Tessa stay a safe distance away from the buildings.

Perspective 101 wasn't going well. One-point perspective was a revelation, the way it made furniture and buildings recede believably into an imaginary vanishing point; but today Whit had introduced Brunelleschi's system of transferring a plotted floor plan to elevations and two point perspective by a confusing system of rays and vators, and the math, never Tessa's favorite subject, was becoming more complex. Whit had been annoyed by her request to go through the calculations again. Everyone else seemed to get it the first time around.

Tessa ascended the three flights of stairs up to Lucian's loft as if she were going to her execution, sending a little prayer up into the stratosphere; *Please, Lord, let them be at a meeting or something. Anywhere but here.*

She pushed open the heavy door. It was blessedly silent. Relieved, she dumped her knapsack on the table and went into the studio.

"Hullo, Tess," said Lucian.

He was alone, hunched over the drawing table. His pencil made a scritch-scratching sound as he sketched away, magnified by the echoey silence in the studio. Tessa went to her customary place, a tatty mustard-colored hydraulic chair clawed to shreds by his cat, at a long work table covered with piles of photos and magazine clippings.

"What's all this?" asked Tessa, rolling up her sleeves.

"*Wizard of Oz, Behind the Green Door.* There's an envelope of snaps in there somewhere as well. I rented *The Devil and Miss Jones* and took some pictures. Very educational. Say, have you seen my August *Vanity Fair?* You know, the one with Demi Moore preggers on the cover. April keeps rearranging my stuff and I can't find a bloody thing."

"I think I know where it is," she said. "How about if I sort these out?"

"That would be great." he said absently.

Half an hour later, he stretched, yawned, left the studio. She heard him on the phone in his bedroom, making one call, then another. He returned to his drawing table, picked up his pencil again. "Ordered us some din din from that veggie Chinese place. Got you the oysters. Closest to real oysters you'll ever get, eh?"

He was wearing a sweater in a faded denim color that went perfectly with his eyes, making him look rather dashing. It occurred to her that he was being unusually solicitous.

"Meeting tonight?"

"No." he said. "Come over here. Take a butcher's at this."

Tessa went around to the other side of the drawing table and stood next to him. The top of her head was even with the line of his shoulder. She breathed in his scent. He smelled of wood and lime.

"It's from *Behind the Green Door,*" he said. "What do you think?"

She could see the silhouette of a woman's head and something like psychedelic fireworks shooting off all around it. It took her a moment to figure out what she was looking at. She swallowed hard and looked away.

"Um...interesting." she said gamely. She was desperate not to come off as provincial. April wasn't provincial. "What images are you thinking of putting on it?"

"I don't know," he admitted. "April wants me to do this porn thing. I want to paint *The Wizard of Oz.*" He sighed.

Tessa went back to her piles, Lucian returned to his drawing. For a while, the only sound was the scratching of the pencil and the rustle of paper. The radio was tuned to NPR, providing a hum of background noise. Tessa could hear the dry whisper of Garrison Keillor's Lake Wobegon program.

"Hell of a party," he said casually, breaking the silence. "You had a lovely time with Raphael Sinclair, eh?"

Surprised, she turned to face him. Emotions struggled for dominance across his guarded features; fear, worry, envy, resentment, all overshadowed by a childlike fear of being left alone. Lucian was jealous.

"He asked me to dance," she said.

"You were the most beautiful thing in the room," he said.

Tessa watched him draw. She loved watching his hand move over the paper. Huge paintings of *The Godfather* or *Easy Rider* or funny faces he made when he was doodling, it was all the same to her. She still couldn't believe that the paintings she saw hanging in galleries and reprinted in books came from his fingers.

"How long have you known him?" There was a bitter edge to his voice. "Do you like him?"

She kept her eyes on her work, sorting Judy Garland from Marilyn Chambers, pulling pictures she thought might make an interesting painting and putting them in a separate file. "Ooh, this is a good one. She's clicking her heels together."

"I saw the way he was looking at you. There are things you don't know."

"Oh, really. Like what?" Lucian looked troubled, as if he were wondering whether he should take his chances and tell her a secret he was sworn to keep. "You're not going to tell me he's a vampire, are you? Because I've already heard that one."

"Have you ever looked in his eyes, Tess?" His voice was suddenly harsh. "They're flat. Like there's no life behind them. Hey, this is New York City. People have a right to be any bloody thing they want to be. But I've got a bad feeling about that one. You know he's Anastasia deCroix's sweetheart, don't you? Well, Anastasia's a mate of mine. Let's just say he makes me look like a choirboy."

The moment passed. He got hold of himself, passed a hand through his spiky hair. "Sorry for barking at you," he went on in a husky voice. "Bit of a rough weekend. I've been trying to wrap my head around the idea that you're going to leave me one of these days."

She raised her eyes from the pile of pictures. He looked stricken. Coming up behind him where he sat sketching in his chair, she slid her arms around his chest. "I don't want to leave you, Lucian," she said into his shoulder. He put the pencil down, laid his hand over hers.

"No one knows me like you do, Tess," he said with feeling. "Don't know what I'd do without you." His pencil went scritch scritch scritch. "You know, April was after me all weekend to fire you. She thinks it would be for your own good, time for you to move on. I said no, of course. 'Tessa is not negotiable,' I said. I might have to cut her loose. She's driving me mad."

The buzzer rang. The food had arrived. Tessa took money out of Lucian's wallet, ran down the three long flights of stairs, paid the delivery boy, came back up with the bags. She opened the bright red containers and set them on the table while Lucian disappeared into the stainless steel galley kitchen, returning with a bottle of wine and two stemmed glasses. Tessa couldn't remember the last time they'd had dinner together. It was just like the old days.

"Non-alcoholic. Not half bad. Try it," he said. Deftly, he poured for her, then for himself. They clinked glasses. "To the greatest assistant in the world," he toasted her.

She took one sip, staved off a grimace. It was horrible. "It's good!" she managed brightly. "Nice woody floral overtones. With an earthy aftertaste, something about green peppers."

"Liar," he said, grinning boyishly at her. "Note to self. Wine a big failure, Tess a poor liar. All right, try this, then. I discovered it last week. If you take a bit of the bean threads together with the Szechuan wheat gluten, and you add just a bit of so-called eel…" He stirred them together and pinched it up with his chopsticks. "Open up, that's a good girl."

Obediently, she opened her mouth. He deposited it on her tongue. She chewed, swallowed, considered, while he waited expectantly.

"You're right," she agreed. "They are better together. If this art thing doesn't work out for you, you can always go to work for a vegetarian Chinese restaurant."

"I might have to, if my spring show doesn't sell," he said grimly.

"What spring show?"

"Didn't I tell you? Mary Boone called. They want to take me on." He gave her a wintry smile.

She dashed around the table to give him a hug. "It'll sell," she promised. "Your paintings always sell."

He sighed, gazed moodily off into the distance. With a single practiced gesture he lit a cigarette, cupping it in his hand till it glowed red, then leaned back in his chair to blow a stream of smoke off to the side, showing off the picture-perfect profile that almost got him a movie deal a couple of years back.

"Tell me about the time you met the Rolling Stones," she said, propping her elbow on the table and resting her face in the palm of her hand.

"Oh, not that one again. You've heard it a hundred times." he said.

"I love the way you tell it. Please, Lucian." she begged.

So he told the story about the time Mick Jagger asked him to do an album cover. He did all the voices with Cockney accents, did the funny thing with his hands, the silly faces, the goofy walk, the UK slang that made her laugh. Then he told her the one about the time Steve Martin flew him out to spend the weekend after he bought one of his pieces, the one about the portrait he did for Dennis Hopper and the one about Annie Lebovitz shooting him for a spread in *Vanity Fair.*

"I remember the first time you came to see me," he said, leaning forward and flicking the ash off his cigarette. His words rolled over her like a tropical swell, washing her back to the coast of his island. "You were wearing that macramé shirt."

"You remember what I had on?"

"Of course I remember, you silly girl. I asked you to the Brewery, bought you a pint."

She smiled. "I let you win at darts, just because I wanted the job."

"Let me win? Hardly." He dragged on his cigarette. "I laid it on thick. Regaled you with sad tales of me Gran raising me all alone in Portsmouth, my sordid youth in Swinging London. By the time I got to the one about my knee being blown up in that IRA bus bombing, I had you. Then, when I asked you to stay you made up some ridiculous story about having to check your answering machine.

"I told you a space had opened up…it opened up because I fired some poor bastard the next day. I knew I had to have you in here. Never told you that, did I." He exhaled a stream of smoke into the air directly overhead.

And then he leaned forward and took her hand, looking at her with the same expression as the night he told her that he wanted to marry her.

After they had cleared the plates away and Tessa had done the dishes, Lucian stretched and said, "You know, I don't feel like working any more tonight."

"All right," she said, getting up, looking around for her bag. She still had to analyze a painting for History of Composition the next morning.

"You don't have to go, you know." He was standing at the door with his hands in his pockets, looking beautiful and vulnerable, a dangerous combination. "We can watch a movie. I've got *Stairway to Heaven*. Michael Powell, you know. Greatest movie ever made. Or perhaps you feel like letting me trounce you at a game of Trivial Pursuit."

Tessa looked at her watch. It was already nine o'clock. "I really should—"

"Don't leave me, Tess," he said in a low, choking voice, looking down at the floor. "Please. I'm not ready for that yet."

And then his arms went around her, and he pulled her to himself as if he wanted to climb inside her, and she kissed his injured-looking eyes and the place where his hair came down over his craggy forehead and held him tight.

Come on, Lucian. Lift me up now and carry me to your big bed behind the wall over there, teach me how to make love to you. Only say you want me, and I'll be your slave forever.

But he released her, slipped his hands back into his pockets. "Go on, then. I suppose you've made plans with all your new school chums. Don't mind about poor old Lucian."

She lingered, feeling guilty. It was cold out. "Maybe I'll just stay a little longer."

"Great!" he said enthusiastically, perking right up. "Why don't you get that packet of snaps from the studio? The ones of *The Devil and Miss Jones*. I haven't gone through them yet. Maybe something will inspire me." He pulled a face. Clearly, this was some kind of an assignment from April.

The envelope from the one-hour-photo place on Canal Street lay by itself on the table. Tessa opened the package and flipped through it. Many pictures of an ordinary-looking woman in her thirties with laughably bad Seventies hair and unaugmented breasts. In some shots she was reclining naked on a bed eating fruit. In others, she was sandwiched between two men. In the last few she was sharing what appeared to be a large tuna wrap with a similarly nude woman. Photographed from Lucian's television screen, the image was grainy and blurry. Tessa squinted at it, then gasped. It was not a tuna wrap.

She returned the pictures to the envelope. As she did, one slipped out, swooshed down to the floor face down. She stooped to pick it up.

Just another naked lady, lolling across an Indian print bedspread. Tessa frowned. Though the picture was dark and yellowy, there was something familiar about the setting; she recognized the blue glass Art Deco airplane lamp on the nightstand, the framed Cassandre poster behind the bed. April, sprawled languorously across Lucian's big double bed, knees open wide, looking directly into the camera.

Tessa's heart kicked into high gear. A cold sweat broke out across her forehead. With a sense of shame, she took the photograph and shoved it deep into her knapsack.

"There you are," Lucian said, poking his head into the studio. "Well, what do you think?"

"I think I have to go," she said hurriedly. She threw her bag over her shoulder and scooped up her coat, running for the door.

"What?" Lucian said, bewildered. "What happened? I thought we were going to—"

But she was already down the stairs and striding down Church Street. She broke into a run, not stopping until she had crossed Canal, where it turned into Sixth Avenue. And then, under the cold light of the moon, she put her face into her hands and waited to break into sobs.

Nothing happened. Tessa straightened up, panting, her breath rising in clouds of frozen vapor in the frigid air. *Why aren't I crying?* In the past two months she had wept over Lucian on every subway line in the city.

Puzzled, she hugged her coat tighter around herself. A platoon of taxis shot by, all taken. She pulled the lapels close around her neck and let the wind chase her up Avenue of the Americas towards home.

15

he weeks between Halloween and Thanksgiving went by quickly, as they always do. The witches, skeletons and spider webs in store windows disappeared, to be replaced with turkeys and pilgrims and horns of plenty.

The next time April's Friday painting class met, Turner showed up and gave them a stern talking to on the subject of how important it was to make the brand-name artist welcome at the school. When Graham tried to tell him about her questionable teaching methods, Whit got a faraway look in his eyes and walked out without another word.

April continued to act like a feral cat staking out territory. Whenever she came around to Tessa's easel, she regaled her with tales of double dates they went on with other famous artists, the weekend at the Cape they finally rescheduled, a house they were looking at together in Sag Harbor. She began sending her on time-consuming errands: she wanted coffee, but only from faraway Dean and Deluca's. She sent her to the office to make handouts advertising her upcoming gallery opening, or to break a hundred dollar bill into singles in a neighborhood without a single bank. After three weeks of April's special attention, Tessa was willing to look for alternatives. Geoff Andersen's monitor was willing to trade positions with her, but when she went to Whit to finalize the transfer, he told her that he wouldn't allow it this far along in the semester.

For his part, Clayton continued to torment April Huffman at every opportunity. One week he filled his canvas with the silhouette of Graham's back, insisting it was all he could see from where he was standing. The next week, when the pose was particularly explicit, he painted April's head onto the nude on his canvas. And on the day she came in with her hair dyed red,

Clayton, leafing idly through the paper, expressed his doubts to David that the carpet in the ad he was looking at matched the drapes.

Fortunately, the school was able to recoup the money lost the evening of the Halloween party. Rafe attended the Guggenheim benefit on Anastasia's glamorous arm, easily seducing the majority of Giselle's friends and relations into taking out their checkbooks. By the end of the evening she said she had forgiven him, but he could tell she was still miffed, and rightfully so.

On Monday, visiting Blesser's office for a scheduled meeting, he found Whit sitting on the corner of the chief financial officer's desk, his arms folded, the smile on his face making him look vaguely demonic. Though he didn't say anything, he gloated as if he were in possession of a wonderful secret.

Levon was there too, glaring at him. After the financials were done with, he casually asked him into his office, where he spent the next half-hour enduring a well-earned tongue-lashing on the subject of his steamy little tango with a student and his inexcusable disappearing act on the most important fundraising night of the year, at a time when the school's existence itself was in danger.

Tessa really did try to meet with her adviser to discuss her end-of-year thesis project, but Josephine broke every appointment she made. It seemed like a child was always sick, or that her newest babysitter had just called to say she was going back to Honduras.

On the first Monday following the Halloween Party, she found a gift left on the work table in her studio; a tube of genuine Old Holland Cerulean blue, made by the same venerated supplier Van Gogh had bought his paint from. It was accompanied by a note, written in a beautiful cursive hand on a sheet of heavy, cream-colored paper. *Make something that matters,* it read. Under it, an R twined through an S.

She turned it over and over again in her hands. That one tube cost fifty dollars, her paint budget for the entire semester. She weighed it, thinking of Raphael Sinclair's eyes when he asked her to dance, remembering the cool pressure of his fingers between her shoulder blades, the roller-coaster thrill-ride sensation of being swept backwards around the room.

In class or alone in her studio, she would feel a dizzying surge of unexplained heat, and she would glance up to see his coattails billowing past as he swept through the hallway. Once, in sculpture class, she looked up from her turntable just in time to catch his eye as he strode towards the office, and he smiled hello, turning her insides to jelly. Thinking back on the night of the Naked Masquerade, a secret smile would creep across her features as she bent back to her work.

As she doodled in the margins of her notebook during an art history lecture, she was struck forcefully by a clear vision. Men, women and children, dressed in World War II era clothing, carrying suitcases, books, violins, sucked into a whirlwind, carried upward, where they dissolved into gray smoke. Hastily, she had scribbled it down, then stared at it in surprise. She hadn't had an original idea since she had been consumed by the Lucian/April morass.

Since Halloween, something had come to flower inside her; ideas began to spring up like mushrooms out of the earth. Later that same week, she scribbled a rough outline of a landscape, train tracks running parallel to the picture plane in front of a darkened forest. Almost lost in the lengthening shadows, she drew a long line of boxcars, human arms reaching out from air slats located high up the sides. It had come to her during the model's break in sculpture class; she'd wiped clay off of her hands on a wet rag and reached for her new sketchbook, getting it down as quickly as she could, before the image in her mind's eye could disappear.

Dissection Day was scheduled for the Wednesday afternoon before Thanksgiving. As part of their Anatomy studies, they would be visiting the pathology lab at Bellevue. First there would be a lecture, and then the art students would see for themselves the bones and muscles they had been copying in plasticene for their écorché figures. The expectation of what she would see filled Tessa with dread. She didn't know from where she was going to summon the fortitude to be in the same room with death, let alone the courage to touch a cadaver.

The following morning, she would be flying home for Thanksgiving. There was a big celebratory dinner with all the cousins planned in honor of her grandfather's eightieth birthday. Tessa didn't look forward to going home. Her mother would be in the kitchen the entire time with her grandmother and aunts, her father would be waving his arms and jumping through hoops in a futile effort to get her grandfather's attention. As usual, Zaydie would all but ignore him, bestowing the lion's share of his consideration on his two other sons and their children. No one would ask Tessa anything about her opinions, her friends, her life, her work. All they ever wanted to know was if she was any closer to getting married. It was the same at every family get-together. It was as predictable as an after-school special. She consoled herself with the knowledge that it would, at least, be brief.

The building was uncharacteristically quiet. Wednesday night before Thanksgiving was the busiest travel night of the year.

Outside the wall of windows, the sun was setting in bands of purple and red over the water tanks and rooftops of the West Village. As Tessa made her way through the lounge area and down the aisle, her footsteps sounded unnaturally loud on the wooden floor. She was completely alone. Even the sculptors' grotto was empty.

As the day drew to a close, the old building was full of strange noises; yawing creaks, thumps, the skittering of small things running past. The hairs prickled up on the back of her neck. She flung aside the curtain to her studio and stepped inside, coming face to face with Raphael Sinclair.

Choking back an exclamation, she reared back, knocking over a turntable Gracie had borrowed from the sculptors' studio to support her écorché. He dived forward, righting it before any damage could be done.

"Sorry," he smiled his wry smile. "That happens a lot."

"Hi, Mr. Sinclair," she said.

"Hello, Tessa." he said.

In his overcoat and fedora, he looked like a character in a 1940s film noir, someone gliding through Rick's in Casablanca. She was taken again by his extraordinary beauty, the strange-colored eyes ringed by a halo of dark lashes, the sensual mouth, those luxuriant lips. A mouth you wanted to kiss for a very long time. Tessa shook it off. Founder of the school, for God's sake. She lowered her eyes, took her coat off, hung it on her easel.

They had not spoken since Halloween, though she had been very much on his mind. She looked fetching, as always, even in that horrible shaggy coat she wore over her customary black leggings and shirt. Today she was adorably disheveled, her cheeks pink, her curls in disarray, as if she had just gotten out of bed.

"I like to come up here and look around sometimes," he said.

She plopped her knapsack down on the floor. On cue, the sketchbook slipped out onto the floor. Hurriedly, she picked it up, lovingly brushing crumbs of dried clay from the velvety calfskin cover. "Thank you for the Cerulean blue," she said. "And the sketchbook. You really didn't have to do that."

"You needed a sketchbook," he said.

She picked up a spice-colored Indian scarf shot through with silver, twisted it into a rope and threaded it behind her neck. Surreptitiously, he watched her breasts lift and fall as she tied back her heavy hair, revealing her smooth white forehead, those sharply angled eyebrows that made him ache, a squarely determined jaw line he had not noticed before. There was a small mirror in the corner. She furtively peeked in it now to check her look.

"How have you been?" he said.

"Fine. Busy. And you?"

"Good, good. Also busy."

She fiddled with the radio, looking for a song. A melancholy voice wailed that it was losing its religion.

"Say, wasn't this Dissection Day?" he asked, as if he hadn't made a special trip up to her studio just to see how she was handling it. "How did it go?"

She hesitated in tying her apron, just for a tick, then finished with a flourish. "It was fine."

"Oh," he said. "Did you find it helpful?"

Her face clouded. "It was terrible," she confessed.

"Really." he said, moving closer. "Why?"

She reached for her hair, stretching a single curly lock around her finger. "The cadavers. They were so..." she was frowning at something on her wall, but her eyes were very far away. *"...dead."*

"Yes. Well. If you're going to dissect them, they're better off that way, really."

She flashed him a resentful look, making him feel sorry he had been flip. "Have you ever lost anyone you loved?" he asked gently, trying to make up for it.

"No," she said. "Well...my grandparents." His heart fluttered. "But I was just a little girl, I barely remember them. That's not it."

"I think they're alcoholics, mostly," he said. "Donated their bodies to science. It's a nice way to make up for a wasted life. There's a symmetry to it, don't you think?"

"She was wearing pink nail polish," she said. He looked at her blankly. "The cadaver, I mean." She crossed her arms, hugging herself. "Where was her family? Where were her children? Didn't anybody care about her? Why were they allowing her to be cut up into little pieces by art students?"

Rafe took off his gloves, drawing closer. "Don't feel too sorry for them. If they could feel anything at all, I'm sure they would feel glad that they're finally able to contribute something useful to society. The medical students learn healing from studying their diseased bodies, and then you art students take what you need to make your figures come to life. It's a kind of alchemy."

"What happens when you die?" she burst out, bewildered. "Where does life go when it leaves? Is that all that's left after all our rushing around and bill-paying and clothes-shopping and apartment-hunting and staying on the straight and narrow is done with? Is that all there is?"

Now he understood. She had come face to face with mortality. "Everybody dies, Tessa," he said, in a voice that was a sad but lovely song. "You have many years to live and many lives to touch. She had nothing but her body to leave to the world. You, on the other hand, will leave a body of beautiful work. Don't be sad, Tessa. She's not you."

She sighed. He wanted to put his arms around her and lay his cheek on top of her shining head, rest upon that river of tawny hair. But of course he couldn't; she was as forbidden to him as those special tubes of paint they kept locked up in the case at Pearl Paint. He moved away from her, away from temptation. There were new sketches tacked up around her space, new postcards, notes to herself. Several small canvases, stacked with their backs facing out, stored in a dark corner.

"Why are they in the corner? Have they been naughty?"

She smiled at that. "Those are from April Huffman's painting class."

He turned to stare at her. "You're in her class? That must be awkward."

Tessa sighed again. So many unexpressed emotions in a single sound.

"Why don't you transfer to another section?"

"I need the work study hours. That's the only monitor position available."

"Why don't you switch with another monitor?"

"Whit won't let me."

"Whit won't...*what?*" he said incredulously. His eyes narrowed, glittering. His nostrils flared. A muscle in his jaw flexed and hardened. She couldn't have explained why, but at that moment, he looked fully capable of killing someone. For the first time, Tessa found his presence intimidating. She took an involuntary step backwards, towards the door.

With obvious difficulty, he suppressed his rage. "Sorry," he said. He gestured at the paintings. "May I?"

There were three of them, sloppy, amateurish affairs. The models were baldly posed and badly lit. In their blatant sexuality, they were neither erotic, nor sensual. In the unflattering light, the models looked as if they were being shot for a low-budget porn video.

He moved away from her, over to Gracie's side of the room. The giant self-portrait of the artist astride her boyfriend was gone, presently occupying the wall above the bed in their apartment in Little Italy. There were new drawings taking its place; a tapestry of fat babies evolving into three sensual young women, who evolved further into a withered crone. A studio painting of a seated male nude with six-pack abs. A life-size charcoal drawing of a belly dancer.

"What's old Lucian up to these days, anyway?" he said casually.

Unconsciously, her shoulders bent into a curve, as if she were protecting herself. "Oh. He's all right. Mary Boone took him on. He's set for a show in the spring. April's trying to get him to paint a scene from a porno flick. She says it will get him to loosen up."

"I think Lucian's always been pretty loose," he said dryly.

He turned from her to study her wall. She had been busy. There was a flurry of new compositions, hastily scribbled on the backs of envelopes, a phone bill, a class handout. A swirling mass of bodies spiraled upwards into a whirlwind. A landscape with a train, arms waving out of airholes in the sides. Three small figures on a train platform, overshadowed by a wall of flame.

Tessa studied him from the corner of her eye. He was wearing an over-coat the color of bittersweet chocolate. It swooped and swirled around him with a careless elegance as he moved through her space, reaching out a hand to caress one of Gracie's sculptures, straightening a crooked postcard pinned to a wall, bending to prop up a canvas slipping forward onto the floor. She was torn between enjoying the beauty of his movements and wanting to warn him that he was going to get oil paint all over his nice coat.

"So, why are you still here?" he said, turning to her. "Why haven't you taken off for parts unknown like everyone else?"

"Couldn't get a flight until tomorrow."

Another half-truth. "Your family must be very proud of you," he said, probing.

They'd be prouder if I was popping out grandchildren. "Yes, they must be," she said.

There was a couch, a tufted and fringed kidney-shaped red velvet affair that would not have been out of place in a Storyville bordello. Gracie had discovered it at the curb across the street and managed to persuade Clayton and Ben to shlep it upstairs for her. Rafe dropped into it, removing his hat and crossing his long legs with the leisurely grace of a cat. "My father wanted me to go into finance," he offered. "He said art was no business for a grown man."

"You went to art school?" She was taking out her sketchbook, opening it, smoothing the pages.

"Yes. In Paris. At the École des Beaux-Arts."

"Paris! That must have been amazing." She was doodling with a yellow number two pencil. Eyes, hands, shoes. Warm-up exercises.

"Yes, well...we drew from plaster casts for a whole year before they let us get near a live model. That was a bit excessive. But that's what I've been trying to do; I want to recreate the classical training I received, here at the Academy."

"So what happened?" she said curiously. "Why don't you paint anymore?"

He turned his head towards the window. The last red rays of sunset filtered in through the curtains, outlining his profile in gold. The details of the left side of his body were lost in velvety chiaroscuro darkness.

She sucked in her breath with the drama of it. "Don't move," she said.

The face she turned to him now was strong, calculating, confident, as if someone else had stepped into her body. She was looking at him with an artist's eye, evaluating the pattern of light and shadow falling across his face, his clothing, his hands. Her eyes narrowed, eliminating, he knew, extraneous detail, flicking impartially from his face to the paper.

With a few lines, she described the stresses and folds of his suit, the way one leg balanced lightly across his knee, the sensitivity of his fingers and hands. With the lightest of touches, she rendered the line of his nose, the bow of his lips, the angle of his cheekbones. A tremor ran through his body. It was like she was touching him.

She cocked her head, critically viewing her drawing. "Uch. It's all wrong."

"May I see it?"

"No. It's terrible."

She closed the sketchbook and tossed it with feigned casualness onto a red Chinese altar table she had bagged from a dumpster on Greene Street. Rafe smiled pleasantly at her. At the same time, they both lunged for the sketchbook.

She was too slow; he had it in his grasp. Though he had seen himself in photographs, the immediacy of the drawing was undeniable. She had captured him emerging from the shadows of the couch, the vee of his white shirt a bright patch in the dark drawing, gazing like a visionary into the distance. The image was a tone poem, tender, beautiful, a romanticized vision of himself, suggestive too of reserves of power and strength.

Another drawing came to mind, a drawing pressed flat in a sketchbook more than half a century ago. *Ah, Tessa. If you knew the things I've done.*

Abruptly, he got to his feet and paced around the space as if it were too small.

"That sketch," he said, his back turned to her. "The one of the mother and child."

"Yes."

"Tell me about it."

"They're getting off the train at Auschwitz," she said. "I'm doing a series of paintings on the Holocaust."

"Oh," he said. His back was turned to her. "How did you happen to choose the Holocaust?"

"My grandparents are survivors."

"I see. From where?"

"Poland."

"Where in Poland?"

This struck her as an odd question, and she looked at him questioningly as she answered, "Wlodawa."

She pronounced it just as Sofia had, *Vluh-duh-vuh.* He crossed his arms to keep them from shaking. Keeping his voice deliberately casual, he said, "Where did you come by the name on the suitcase?"

"Wizotsky?" She pronounced it with the W sounding like a V. "It's my grandmother's maiden name."

"Does she talk about it much? The war, I mean."

She shook her head regretfully. "Not at all. Whatever happened must have been terrible. She lost everybody."

He gave her back the sketchbook. Tessa closed it with a snap and tucked it into her knapsack. His questions seemed weirdly out of place, inconsistent with his wealthy playboy image.

"I'm sure it was dreadful. What do you know of her story?"

"Only that she came from this huge, wealthy family, and then the Germans came and took them all away. Really. That's everything."

"Does she." His voice failed him. He tried again. "Does she talk about her life before the war?"

Something stirred in her memory. "There was a family business. A tea company."

"Wizotsky," he said. "The Tzar of Teas."

She looked at him with a dawning sense of unease.

"Tessa." he said, drawing closer. His voice dropped to a whisper. "Is your grandmother's name...Sofia?"

"No," she said. "It's Freyda."

He had been so completely certain of her answer, that for a moment afterwards he actually thought he had heard her say yes.

"Freyda?" he repeated stupidly. "Are you sure?"

"Yes." She was looking at him curiously.

"But I was so sure," he protested weakly.

His eyes had turned opaque, remote. He had been holding on to something, some kind of a hope, and with that one word, that name, she had utterly dashed it. "I'm sorry if that's not what you wanted to hear," she said apologetically.

He reached out and took her hand, as natural as breathing. "Truthfully, I'm not sure what I wanted to hear," he said.

Tessa's hand was honest and square, the nails filed short and neat for working purposes. The blue veins in her wrist were like rivers on a map of the world, her skin the color of parchment. Hands made for creation. But not Sofia's hands.

On impulse, he kissed her upturned pink palm. The heat from his touch seared up through her arm, burned like a lit fuse throughout her body, settling in the pit of her belly.

Somewhere behind them, the steel door slammed, admitting a burst of conversation. Several sets of resounding footsteps echoed past them, stumping to the sculptors' studio.

He released her, stepping away to a discreet distance. "I should be going," he said, smoothing the brim of his hat. "Big reception at the MoMA tonight. Opening of the Matisse retrospective. Lots of wealthy women there who need to be persuaded to give freely."

"Say hello to Lucian," she said. "That's where he's going, too."

He pulled on his kid leather gloves, flexing his fingers. "I will."

Still, he lingered, unwilling to leave the warmth of her studio. Yellow light from a 1950s vintage lamp spilled over the cracked leather cushions of a pair of Danish modern chairs reclaimed from a curb on Tenth Street, across a threadbare Persian rug, illuminating the accidental collages that unfurled across the walls like vines.

The velvety plush of the couch beckoned to him. He surveyed the room with obvious regret. "I've never liked Matisse," he confessed. "Oh, it feels so good to say that."

"I don't like him either. Makes a nice thank-you card, though."

That earned her a smile. "Come back soon, Tessa Moss," he said, his voice a caress, lean and as limber as a whippet. And then he was gone, the curtain swishing closed behind him.

It came out of nowhere, the image that rose up before her mind's eye. A crooked old woman in a babushka bowed over a table swaying under the weight of a hundred flickering *yahrzeit* candles. She dug out her sketchbook, hurriedly scribbled it down.

There. She had five sketches to show Josephine on Monday. Now she could go home. She untied her apron and slipped it over the easel, shrugged into her coat. She turned around one last time, reluctant to leave the inviting space, the art-covered walls. With her hand on the switch, she hung back, hesitated. But she had to be up at four to make it to the airport on time, and she still had to pack.

"Goodbye, art," she murmured as she turned out the light. "See you on Monday."

16

"I'm sorry, my darling," said Anastasia. "You really thought it was her, didn't you."

He barely nodded. His eyes were dark, grieving.

"Raphael," she said gently. "Why are you doing this to yourself? Sofia died a long time ago."

"Fifty years ago this winter. But I never actually saw her..." and here he stopped.

"You never saw her body." She finished the sentence for him.

He nodded.

"Let it go, Raphael," she advised. "Let her rest in peace." Emotions juddered off of him in waves, delectable, invigorating. Behind her dark glasses, her eyes glowed red, drinking it in. "She must be some kind of a cousin. It's still something."

He didn't answer, swished the ice in his drink in slow circles while his eyes roamed over the crowd. They were at the Museum of Modern Art, standing at the epicenter of a slowly revolving organism of celebrated New Yorkers, the apex of the worlds of art, fashion, and society. Anna Wintour wandered through a roomful of frolicking blue swimmers with Muccia Prada. Tim Robbins and Susan Sarandon were deep in conversation with Annie Lebovitz and Susan Sontag. Lucian Swain was laughing in a loose confederacy that included David Salle, Julian Schnabel and a dark-haired woman he didn't recognize.

Slim waiters in black and white whisked around clusters of chattering celebrities and socialites, bearing silver trays of Moroccan mezze and Spanish tapas. The dresses of the women were outshone by the paintings the way the sun outshines the stars, blazing with crayon-bright color, laid out side by side on new-painted walls around the third floor of the museum.

He had been sure, so sure that he had built up a whole scenario of how it would go, with Tessa replying yes, anticipating the conflicting sensations of pleasure and pain that would wash over and around him, the questions that would follow. How did she do it? How had Sofia survived where so many others had not? Other, more selfish questions; did she ever think of him? And if she did, was it with love or hate that he lived on in her memory? Tessa would have questions of her own, questions he would be forced to answer.

Tessa. That would change, too, the proprietary way he would feel towards her, not just his student now, but his responsibility. What if she came to hate him? What if she heard his story and felt only terror, or revulsion, as any decent person would? Rafe smoothed his hair back, unconscious of the nervous gesture. He didn't think he could bear that; he liked being welcome in her studio, liked being on the periphery of her world. In the end, of course, it hadn't mattered. She had never heard of Sofia. Wizotsky was just a name on a distant branch of a family tree. There was no connection after all. Perhaps this was why he had avoided asking her for three months. He meant nothing to her. And Sofia was dead all over again.

Rest in peace? Please, God, no. Haunt me, Sofia. You said you'd haunt me.

"Sinclair," came a cordial voice with a slight European accent at his elbow.

"Leo," he replied without enthusiasm to the elderly, silver-haired man beside him. This June it would be fifty-one years that Leo Lubitsch had been editorial director of *Anastasia* and the eight other magazines that made up the roster at Agha Publishing, since the day he had arrived from Paris at the height of World War II to oversee the creation of *Femme*. At eighty-two, he was still dashing, even a bit rakish. Rafe remembered when Leo was the talk of all of chic Paris, when he dressed to compete with the Prince of Wales. These days he was always seen in an inconspicuous gray glen-plaid suit, notable only if you appreciated the finer details of tailoring and a Savile Row provenance. Leo said he didn't like to outshine the art.

"How are you?" he continued in that smooth, continental voice. "Still heading up that quaint little school?"

"You should come by. I'll have one of the students give you a tour. I'll find you a pretty one."

Leo gave a polite smile. "Yes, yes, of course."

"Leo." Anastasia darted forward, kissed him on both cheeks.

"Anastasia." He smiled with delight. She was wearing a flouncy black silk taffeta affair, with a low round décolletage, a cinched waist and big, brightly colored polka dots. *"Merveilleux, mon cherie. Qui ce fait cette chemise?"*

"Lacroix," she replied. "Isn't it fabulous?"

He chuckled. *"Tu est XXX,"* he said, and they both laughed.

"How's Margaux?" Rafe said bitterly. "Do give her my best."

Leo looked resigned, suddenly old. Anastasia gave him a stern look, then turned back to Leo. "We have a mystery," she said lightly, changing the subject. "Raphael has a *jeune fille* enrolled at his *petite academie* who may be somehow related to an old girlfriend."

Leo's mournful expression changed. "You can't mean...Sofia?"

"Yes! He says the eyes are just the same."

"But that's impossible," said Leo. "Didn't she..."

"Yes." said Rafe shortly. "That's why it's impossible. Anyway, the names are different...a distant cousin at best..." he could feel himself backing away from the conversation. It was too private a matter to be airing with Leo Lubitsch at a gala reception for a blockbuster Matisse show.

Leo was looking at him in surprise, completely nonplussed. For a moment, he looked younger, more like the dapper young artist he used to be in 1939, the only son of a Soviet functionary and an actress; and then his face collapsed, realigned itself in wrinkles, the Morse code of old age.

"Sofia Wizotsky," he said, shaking his gray head. His eyes were moist, his thin moustache quivering. "Such a lovely girl. Caught on the cusp between innocence and revelation. What a loss. You didn't know her, did you, my dear."

"Not really," replied Anastasia, scanning the crowd.

Leo sighed, gazed with an old man's melancholy at the painting before him. *"La Danse,"* he said meditatively. "From the Hermitage. Before the Revolution, it belonged to my uncle." He took a pair of glasses out of his breast pocket, took his time unfolding them. Anastasia was right. His hands shook, a barely perceptible but continual tremor. It took a moment for him to get them on correctly. The process of aging was full of small, unexpected everyday indignities.

Out of the corner of his eye, Rafe saw Giselle at the other end of the gallery, drifting past the deep russet of *The Red Studio* with a tall, skinny, severely fashionable older woman he had bedded back in the early 1950s, when she was still a debutante. Her husband, a pioneering television executive at CBS, had died a year ago, leaving her with bags of money. She had just donated the contents of her closet, a veritable timeline of twentieth-century couture fashion, to the Costume Institute at the Met. Perhaps, with just a bit of encouragement, she could be induced to open up her Judith Lieber handbag and endow a scholarship.

"Excuse me," he said to Leo and Anastasia, and he cut into the crowd.

The circles had shifted. Alexander Liberman and S.I. Newhouse had joined Anna Wintour and Tina Brown. Catching his eye, Tina smiled at him like the schoolgirl she had been when he first met her, working as a lackey at the *Tatler*. Nearby, in front of *Bathers in a River*, Sawyer Ballard, six foot four in his Gucci loafers, was going on about some show scheduled for the end of the year. Rafe felt his hands tighten into fists. *Steady now.* He was with Lucian Swain and the dark-haired woman from before. It struck him that this must be April Huffman.

"Every artist should take Dissection," she was saying brightly. "I brought along a film crew, part of a documentary I'm making. It's going to be running on public television around the time of my gallery show."

The sensible thing would be to give them wide berth. But some other force was at work inside him tonight, and as he glided past them on his way to Giselle, he brushed lightly against the other man's elbow, jostling him. Lucian leaped back, cursing. Rafe was gratified to see tomato juice dripping down his nice white shirtfront.

"Bugger!" he rasped, his shaggy eyebrows lowering into a knot.

"So clumsy of me," said Rafe apologetically. "Please. Send me the bill. May I get you another drink? What was it, a Shirley Temple?"

Lucian was dabbing at the stain on his shirt. "I'll get seltzer," April said, glaring at him, and disappeared into the crowd.

Sawyer unfolded his long arms to enthusiastically pump his hand up and down. "Sinclair! God, you look more like your old man every time I see you. It's uncanny."

Rafe smiled politely. *Sawyer, you bastard.* He knew him from his art student days in Paris. He hadn't liked him much then, either. His hair had stopped thinning, but in the intervening years, had turned from dirty blond to iron gray. Rafe still pictured him in the same little round wire-rimmed glasses, though contact lenses had replaced them years earlier. The first time he ran into him in New York, it was the 1960s. It was simpler to tell him that he was his own son, from the wrong side of the sheets, than to tell him the truth.

"Your father hated Matisse. Said he couldn't draw. Can you imagine?" He was shaking his patrician head, laughing.

"Freud, eh?" said Lucian. "I thought you only showed dead artists at the Met."

Sawyer grinned. "It does seem that way sometimes...but this fellow, he's blown the lid off of figure painting. There's nothing like him out there. Are you familiar with his work?" He was addressing Rafe.

"Not really."

"Well, after this, he's going to be a household name. Fantastic stuff. Huge, fleshy, bodies. No pretensions, no sugar coating. Incredibly textural. Comes right off the canvas at you."

"I'll have to look him up."

The boyish enthusiasm faded. His face grew opaque, inscrutable. Rafe followed his gaze to a painting across the way. A woman with short dark hair gazed moodily into a fishbowl, resting her chin on her arms, crossed on the table in front of her. The colors were uncharacteristically muted for Matisse, a palette of subdued blues and greens, the drawing more finished than typical for him.

"There was this girl," Sawyer said. He smiled at Rafe. "Your father and I actually came to blows over her. In La Coupole, no less." He shook his head. "I haven't thought about that in years."

"What was her name?" said Rafe.

"Sofia," he answered without hesitation. "Sofia...something Polish, I forget now. She was at the Academie Julian with us for a little while, right before the war. Your father had a real thing for her. Always following her around. Completely doomed, of course."

"I never heard this story," Rafe said, coming closer. "What was doomed about it?"

"Oh...she wasn't interested in him. Didn't stop him from trying, though. He was completely obsessed."

"Really," he said. "What happened to her, anyway?"

"Lost in the war." Sawyer looked reflective. He was silent for a little while, staring at the painting of the girl, rubbing his chin. "I should have done more," he mused. "We all should have done more." He raised his wiry eyebrows ruefully. "Anyway. Enough ancient history. How's your little *atelier* coming along?"

A slim young man in a blue blazer slipped up to him, whispered in his ear. The older man had to bend over to hear the message. He listened, nodding, then straightened back up and made his apologies. "They find me everywhere. There's a problem with a painting we're borrowing from Japan." He moved stiffly off, leaving him alone with Lucian.

Rafe made as if he were continuing on his way, then turned back as if he had suddenly remembered something. "I'm just coming from your assistant's studio," he remarked. "Thought she could use a bit of company, all alone up there on the fourth floor."

From beneath half-lowered eyelids, Rafe watched Lucian's face grow purple. He dropped his voice now, made it sultry, insinuating. "She asked me to pose for her. Spur of the moment, you know how that goes. I happened to be there, the lighting was just right. Very talented girl. Beautiful, too."

April was back with a bottle of seltzer, pouring it onto a napkin and holding it to the juice stain. "Really?" Lucian said, feigning carelessness, but he raked his fingers through his stylishly spiky brown hair, belligerently shifted his stance, betraying messy emotions. "She's got a new boyfriend now, I understand. Some boy from her class."

He was lying. Why? Tessa was as loyal to him as ever. Ah, yes. Jealous girlfriend. He jumped on it. "No, I don't think so. I'm on a committee with her studio mate. I would have heard. No, no boyfriend."

Lucian's handsome face colored, his expression darkening to resemble a sullen little boy. They were interrupted by a comely waitress, who lowered her tray of hors d'ouevres for their inspection, fat orange beads of salmon caviar rolled into tiny blini. Rafe took one, smiling at her, making her weak in the knees.

He turned his attention to April, letting his eyes roam over her body, blatantly evaluating her. She was attractive, a dark-eyed, pale-skinned woman of forty-one or forty-two, self-assured, with a glib sense of entitlement that comes from success early in life. She wore a sheen of glossy sophistication on her trim shoulders, a forward-facing confidence, along with a worldly sexuality that was not part of Tessa's makeup. He knew the type. He'd slept with a hundred women just like her in every era since the 1940s.

Looking her straight in the eye, he placed the blini on his tongue, swallowed it down in one rapacious bite. "I don't believe we've met," he said, extending his hand. "Raphael Sinclair."

She must not have heard the rumors, or perhaps she was just trying to prove something, because she looked right back at him. He saw a hunger for recognition, a hard-edged ambition. Fear, too; fear of aging past desirability, of growing old alone. Fear of missing her time, of bungling the fifteen minutes when she was the next big thing, the exact moment that she must seize her opportunity or forever be relegated to the art-history ranks of almost-was, might-have-beens. He dialed up the volume of his preternatural allure, letting a dirty smile sneak across his lips.

She was responding; he could see her wanting him, in the way she played with her hair, the way her body relaxed and realigned itself in an unconscious responsive rhythm. He applied just enough pressure to her hand to make her sigh.

Lucian's face was a study in bottled British rage. Rafe could feel his fangs begin to lower, his eyes shifting to a predatory icy clarity.

"There you are," said Anastasia. She stepped up to Lucian, kissing him, then April, on both cheeks. "What happened to your shirt? Love your blouse, my darling. Vera Wang?" She slid her hand through Rafe's arm, leaned her sleek head on his shoulder.

"Sorry about the shirt, old man," he said to Lucian. "I mean it, though. Send me the bill."

Arm in arm, they turned as a unit, drifting towards an eight-foot canvas of primitive scarlet figures scattered around a bright blue and green background. Guiltily, Rafe glanced at the entrance to the exhibition where he had spotted Giselle earlier, but it was too late; she was gone.

"Why are you tormenting poor Lucian?" said Anastasia. She picked a glass of red wine off of a passing tray, smiling at the waiter. "He's going to start drinking again if you keep this up. Then your little art student will never leave him."

"Come on. Admit it. He can barely draw."

He meant Matisse. They were standing in front of *Carmelina,* a studio painting of a heavy-featured woman seated on a red-draped table, unpretty, unposed, rendered in shades of orange and brown.

"How charming," she said. "It makes you sound provincial *and* academic. Is it possible that you, an artist, are not transported by the ecstasy of the colors? What was the point of mindlessly rendering boring details in those years after the invention of the camera? He was a revolutionary, a sophisticated primitive, a *fauve.*"

"There's nothing mindless about what we do," Rafe disagreed, his temper rising.

She gestured around the room. "None of these speak to you? How about the goldfish? You wouldn't believe what John had to promise the Pushkin to borrow that one."

He dismissed it with a shrug. "Makes a lovely poster for a Barnard dorm room."

"And the *Blue Nude?* What about that one?" she demanded, pointing to a reclining female figure.

"The worst student at my school can do better than that on a bad day. And that one. Poor Madame Matisse, with that green stripe down her face. Who deserves to be remembered like that? *The Piano Lesson?* God-awful, those mingy grays, that unfinished thingy floating around the background."

She was bemused. "You sound like a doting daddy when you talk about your students," she said.

They drifted forward. Rafe smiled at women who smiled at him, ladies he had already slept with, the ones he had not slept with yet. Ram swooped down on them to peck hello on Anastasia's cheeks and to announce that the February issue had shipped. The art director of *Anastasia* was dressed for cocktails in another era, in an aqua dinner jacket with wide padded shoulders and huge lapels that swashed downward and pinched at the waist. His hair was close-cropped to the point of stubble, skinny sideburns jutting to a cruel point halfway across his cheek. The lyrics to *Relax* by Frankie Goes To Hollywood were block-printed in red and black on a white gavotte, tied just so around his neck.

"*R-r-raphael*," said Ram, rolling the name off of his tongue with an exaggerated Spanish inflection, "*Love* your apartment. The pie safe next to your kitchen? Fabulous. Has Anastasia figured out yet that you're just a great big homo?"

Rafe turned to Anastasia, raised his eyebrows. She gave him a small, dismissive shrug. "I left my pocketbook at your place. I sent him to retrieve it."

"He was in my house? By himself?"

Her eyes were scanning the crowd. "I really like that pocketbook."

Rafe watched Anastasia in profile, the edges of her brunette bob just brushing the edge of her jawline, eyes hidden as always behind enormous dark glasses. Wherever she went, she was deluged with enthusiastic endorsements of improbable hole-in-the-wall boutiques just visited in Brooklyn, marvelous new hair salons on the wrong side of Soho, fitness trends observed in Los Angeles. There were those, too, that kept their distance; they hovered just beyond the edge of his vision, staring, whispering to each other the rumors they had heard. She didn't care. She had never cared. She was famously intimidating, and proud of it; she rather liked frightening away the ones who lacked the courage to step into her orbit.

She came to a dead stop in front of a large red painting, so suddenly that he bumped into her bare shoulder. A woman dressed in black, blond hair caught up over her head in an old-fashioned bun, leaned over a red table in the middle of a red room, setting a silver tureen filled with fruit and flowers on a red tablecloth. A pattern of blue flowers and vines swarmed up the tablecloth and onto the walls.

"This one," said Anastasia. "It reminds me of..." She snatched off her dark glasses to better view the painting. The fires in her eyes danced, reflecting the red lacquered background. She gazed at it for a long moment before fitting the glasses back onto her polished porcelain face. "My mother had a tablecloth like that," she said in a faraway voice, but Rafe didn't hear her. He was back in 1943, Sofia was lighting the Shabbos candles, and it felt like home.

When she spoke again, her voice was brisk, practical. "Listen. I'm going to say hello to Alex Liberman and the rest of the Condé Nast Mafia, and then I am leaving with..." she scanned the crowd. "...that one." She indicated a tall, slender young man with hollow cheeks and curly black hair, slouching attractively in a simple but very good black sweater and black jeans. Ralph Lauren, with a twist of Tribeca. "Up and coming designer. I'm trying to get him a place in the House of Lanvin."

"Pretty," Rafe admitted. "Isn't he gay?"

"That is very politically incorrect of you," she instructed him sternly. "I would say he is omnisexual. Anyway, he is adorable. So handsome. So sweet. So talented."

"You sound happy. Congratulations."

"He is thinking about becoming one of us."

His voice betrayed an edge of alarm. "Anastasia. Don't do it."

"Why not?"

"Look," he said. "What you do behind that door with your interns, your assistants, your little pet projects, it's your business. But whatever you want to call it, whatever you think you're doing, the reality of the matter is, you're damning him. Forget God, forget hell, forget right or wrong. That hunger, a hunger that rages night and day, a hunger you can never slake or satisfy, forever. How can you wish that upon someone you say you care for?"

"My dear Raphael. So provincial. You need to get out there and hunt." She glared at him. "Calling in girls from that agency, like ordering Chinese food. You are getting to be like one of those fat politicians who pays to shoot tame animals at a game farm." She dismissed his protests with an impatient gesture. "What about the rest of it, my darling? The extraordinary gifts? The events you have witnessed. The sights you have seen. The personalities we have known." Her voice dropped a notch, became intimate. "Remember Sighisoara, my darling? The rocks sticking up out of the mountains like teeth. The vermillion of the clouds at dawn."

"The peasants and their pitchforks," he said.

"The stars over the ruins of Constantin's castle," she countered. "The sharpened senses. The sharpened wits. The textures. The flavors. Would you trade those away so quickly?" She tilted her head, arched her eyebrows. "Wouldn't you wish immortality on someone you cared for? Your little girlfriend, for instance. Sofia. Come on. Tell me you never thought of it."

A jolt of pain. To disguise it, he turned from her, gazed into the crowd. Of course he'd thought of it. He had dismissed it almost immediately. Everything he loved about her would have been changed.

She took his arm. "Come with us," she purred, seducing him. "I promise I will make it worth your while."

"Thanks," he said. "I still have to work the room. Can't go home until I've coaxed a new heating system out of someone."

"Again with your art school," she said. "So mercenary." She gave him a French peck on the cheek and headed into the crowd.

A young woman in a white halter dress was standing by herself near the entrance to the room, gazing up at *La Danse,* pretending she hadn't been staring at him. She had upturned almond shaped eyes in an oval face, a ripple of shining chestnut-colored hair, smooth brown shoulders. There was a drop of something exotic in her genetic pool, though he couldn't tell what it was. She glanced at him as he approached.

"I thought this was in the Barnes Foundation," she said. She had a Texas twang in her voice.

"It is," he replied. "Matisse did several of these. This one belongs to the Hermitage, in St. Petersburg. Actually, I think this one is nicer than the one at the Barnes."

She smiled at him, flashing perfect white teeth that matched the string of pearls around her neck. Two girls with straight blond hair drifted close behind him, giggling meaningfully. Friends of hers.

"I love your purse," one of them said. "Who made it?"

She angled it up, the better for them to admire the plain black nylon in the shape of an envelope. "Kate Spade," she said. "Isn't it cute?"

"Where did you get it? I've got to have one." They glanced at him, then back at her, telegraphing their approval, made plans to meet on Sunday for brunch, then drifted in the direction of the entrance to the exhibition.

"My parents have one like this, but smaller," she said. She was referring to *La Danse.* "I think it's a study." She turned to him. "I know who you are." She was still smiling, coquettishly now. "You're Raphael Sinclair. I went to that Naked Masquerade Ball at your school on Halloween. Are you really a vampire?"

He came closer, his eyes gleaming. "And if I was? Would it make a difference?"

She flicked a stream of ebony hair behind her shoulder with a coy flip of her hand. "That depends," she said. "Are you going to make me do your evil bidding?"

"Very likely," he said.

"Can we go somewhere for a drink?" she said. Modern girls. They didn't wait for invitations.

"I know a place," he said.

They went to a clubby, crowded singles bar called Dorrian's on Eighty Fourth and Second. The room was long and narrow, the lighting low and warm, the music loud and pulsating. Pretty girls clustered at the bar and tossed their heads back when they laughed, glancing sideways to see if anyone was watching them. Young men with moussed hair and pressed jeans, smelling of cologne and breath mints, clung to their friends and drank beer for courage.

Rafe found them a table at the back. She ordered a Cosmopolitan. "So you're a vampire," she said.

"Suppose I am," he said. His eyes locked on hers, and her face went a little blurry for a second.

She shook her head and laughed. "My mom used to watch *Dark Shadows*," she said. She leaned forward across the table, giving him a peek down the front of her dress. "Honestly, I think my stepmother is a vampire. She sleeps all day and parties all night. Sucks men dry and then moves on. Come to think of it, I never see her eat anything, either."

"That's a fallacy," he admitted. "We can. We just don't."

"What about the garlic?"

"Its power is limited."

She had finished her first drink. She leaned her elbow on the table, stirred her ice. "And the holy water? The sign of the cross?"

He shrugged.

"Sunlight?"

"Well, now. That packs a wallop." he said, gesturing to the barman for another margarita.

"Really?" She touched the pointed tip of her tongue to the grains of salt mounted around the rim of the glass. "Would you really, like, burst into flames?" Without waiting for an answer, she kicked her Manolo Blahniks off, ran her toes up inside his pants leg. Under the table, he slid his hand under her dress and ran it along her firm tanned thigh, wiggling his fingers under the elastic of her panties. She gasped, then closed her eyes and straightened up very suddenly, her mouth open, quivering. He whispered something in her ear that made her arch her back. She leapt up from the table and headed for the door. He followed her out through a gauntlet of girls in halter tops staring at them with naked envy.

In the taxi, he slipped his hand under her dress and continued his ministrations, watching her, the expressions flitting across her face. They got out somewhere in the Seventies, at a nondescript postwar doorman building between Park and Madison. Rafe followed her into a cool, understated lobby, and when the elevator doors closed behind them, he pressed her against the Brazilian rosewood paneled interior, opening her mouth with his tongue.

The elevator went up, up, up, stopped somewhere near the top floor. She pulled herself away from him long enough to wobble out, turn the key in the lock, open the door. High above the Upper East Side, New York City sparkled with a hundred million lights, filling a wall of windows at the far side of her apartment.

She entered, her stiletto heels clicking on the marble floor, set her purse down on a table. She turned around to look for him. Seeing him waiting at the door, she laughed. "Oh, I forgot. Vampire." She put her arm out, bowing in a theatrical gesture of welcome. "Please come in."

Mesmerized by the view, he moved to the windows. By night, the buildings fell away, replaced by a dream landscape, starry constellations in the shapes of skyscrapers. The headlamps from the cars surging along Park and Madison Avenues turned the streets into rivers of gold and red. Further south, he could see the outlines of the Williamsburg and Brooklyn Bridges twinkling in the distance like spiderwebs spun from Christmas bulbs, their scallops of cable like strings of pearls. Just beyond the glow of Manhattan occurred an abrupt absence of color and light, a long and winding tributary of deep and utter blackness that was the East River, and beyond it, the faint, glimmering lights of Brooklyn.

"Nice," he said.

"I know," she said. "Some view, huh." She was looking at him.

He turned from the view of the city lights to the girl. "What's your name?" he said, walking slowly towards her.

She lunged at him, suckering her mouth to his. He peeled off his coat and jacket, propelled backwards through a doorway into another room and onto a bed. He pushed her skirt up to her waist with both hands, pulled down a black thong, and then her hands were on his head, pushing him downward, and he lowered himself between her thighs.

Later, after she had moaned out her approval again and again, he made his way up to her pleasured face. He kissed her, and she smiled at him, propping her head up on her elbow.

"You sure know what a girl likes," she said.

"I'm gifted that way," he said.

She was fumbling around in a side table drawer. A moment later, she was offering him a round pink pill. A heart with an arrow through it was stamped into its surface.

"Ecstasy," she said.

He politely declined, explaining that drugs had no effect on him. Her face clouded over. He took one to make her happy. She downed hers without water, and then she climbed on top of him, settling to the right, to the left, as if she were testing out a saddle. She smoothed her hands over his chest and down his abdominal muscles, dusted with a shadow of curling hair.

"Wow," she said. "You're really ripped. Where do you work out?" She slid down his body to the end of the bed, her shining hair a puddle of silk slipping across his flesh. The things she did with her hands and mouth banished all tangible thought from his mind, and he grasped the sheets and wound them into ropes, forgetting for a little while the events of the day. He could feel his muscles tightening, the storm gathering in his belly, in his quadriceps, mounting, and then the dizzying, explosive unleashing of pressure. Then came the long spiral down into sleep.

When his eyes fluttered open again, it was still dark. She was on her side, watching him. It took him a moment to remember who she was, how he got there.

"I want it," she said, tracing a pattern on his chest with one finger. "I want you to bite me."

"Oh," he said, sliding one hand over her hip and down her thigh. The shadowy, indefinite color of his irises began to change, growing lighter, lighter still, until they were the blue-white of pond ice. His voice rolled over her, voluptuous, impassioned, dark. "Daddy's little girl wants to know how it feels to be sucked by a big bad vampire? Is that it? Is that what you want?"

She smiled flirtily at him, smoothed her hair back behind her ear, turning her head just a little, exposing her neck. "Will it hurt?"

"Oh, yes." He nuzzled the unprotected skin of her throat. His jaw muscles began to swell, his fangs descending. He worked his way down her body, tonguing the base of her throat, moving his lips across her flat brown nipples, flicking his tongue into the dip of her navel. He rolled her over and kissed the cleft of her ass, and moving down, kissed her belly above the dark thatch of her symphysis pubis. He wrapped his arms around her waist and pulled her to him.

"Tell me you want it," he said roughly. "Tell me you want me to suck your blood."

"I want it," she groaned. "I want you to suck me."

He folded one of her legs into an inverted vee, skimming his fingers delicately along the smooth skin of her calves, brushed his lips against the soft skin of her inner thigh. She trembled with fear and anticipation. He hesitated for a moment longer, just barely dimpling her flesh with his teeth, waiting, waiting, heightening her apprehension, her arousal. Without warning, he bit down. Blood welled up, spilled into his mouth. She flinched, kneading handfuls of Frette sheets, then arced up in narcotized frenzy as he sucked hard and deep from the blue artery inside her thigh.

Her name was Oleander Haier. This he learned when Bernard Blesser read him the name she signed on the check that arrived in the mail the following week. Also, that she was the daughter of a rubber tire baron, newly arrived in New York, ostensibly to go to NYU business school.

At five in the morning he arose from her bed, regarding her sleeping body for a moment before dressing hurriedly and taking the elevator down to the main floor.

The lobby was empty, the doorman missing, probably asleep in a back room somewhere. The streets were deserted, with the curious silence the city develops on holiday mornings. He found a taxi at once, sank back into the seat and closed his eyes as it hummed down the empty streets to Gramercy Park.

At the intersection of Thirty-fourth Street, Broadway, and the Avenue of the Americas, the car rumbled over steel plates, past ghostly teams of high-school marching bands from Wisconsin and girls from Oklahoma in short cheerleader dresses and cowboy boots stamping their feet in the frigid hours before dawn, already in position, waiting for the Macy's Thanksgiving Day parade to begin. Underneath Sixth Avenue, Tessa Moss stepped aboard the subway train that would whisk her to Kennedy Airport.

17

*J*s that the nicest thing you have to wear?" her mother hissed. "It's a *shmatta*. You look like a gypsy. Go upstairs and change." Shaking her head, she continued past her to the kitchen.

Tessa, caught midway down the stairs, glanced down at the chocolate-colored cotton and velvet dress she had bought at a flea market in Soho, embroidered all over with Klimt-like swirls and patterns. She thought it was beautiful. The doorbell rang. Too late to change now. She went to get the door of her parents' house, a 1960s derivation of a Prairie style bi-level. It was her uncle Bernie and his wife Barbara, her married cousins Cilla and Alex and their children. The kids ducked under her arm and raced to the den to turn on the television.

"What an interesting dress!" Auntie Barbara exclaimed. She was holding a Pyrex casserole covered in tin foil, containing, Tessa knew, her famous zucchini kugel. "Where did you find such an interesting dress?"

"Hey! How's art school?" said Uncle Bernie. "Do you really draw nudes?"

She gave him a sheepish smile. "Yes. We really do. So often you don't even notice they're naked."

He laughed. "Maybe I'll audit your class. You know, I could have gone to art school. You've seen my portrait of JFK, right?"

Tessa nodded. "I sure did. It's good." And in truth, it was pretty good. But Uncle Bernie had also been interested in baseball cards and tropical fish, followed by slot car racing and his stereo system, and in the end, he had gone to work in the family import-export business.

"You should settle down," he suggested. Then, lowering his voice, he said, "You're not getting any younger, you know. Zaydie's worried about you."

"Don't mind him," said Auntie Barbara, rolling her eyes. "He just wants to see you settled, like everybody else."

"Pa!" Uncle Bernie veered off into the living room to greet her grandfather, already ensconced on the sofa. Her aunt went to the kitchen to put her casserole in the oven. Tessa closed the door, her face burning. The doorbell rang again, and it was Uncle Allen and Aunt Eva with cousin Goldie and her husband Josh. Their kids scooted around her to join the other children in front of the TV.

"You need a haircut," Uncle Allen growled. "Wearing your hair that way makes a statement."

Auntie Eva shook her head, nonplussed. "Don't listen to him," she whispered as he went to join his father on the couch. "He's grouchy today. He wanted the dinner to be at our house. Maybe if you put it in a ponytail. You must be hot with it around your face all the time."

"No, I like it this way," she said. "It's all right. Really."

But Auntie Eva was determined. She dug around the bottom of her purse, found a rubber band, bundled Tessa's tresses into a ponytail. "See?" she said, steering her to the mirrored door of the bathroom. "Doesn't that feel much better?"

Tessa looked at her reflection. Her hair was spread out in a huge puffball.

"I think you look funny," said Suri, Cilla's oldest daughter. She had freckles and carroty orange curls cut short around her head.

"I think so, too," she agreed, tugging on the rubber band. It was stuck. She would have to use scissors to get it out. "Thanks anyway, Auntie Eva."

She shrugged. "Suit yourself." She went to drop off an aluminum foil pan covered with more foil in the kitchen.

"Will you draw me a horsie?" Suri addressed her hopefully.

"Sure." Tessa said, playing with her irresistible orange curls. "Later."

"I want to grow it long, like yours," the little girl confided. "Mommy won't let me. She says it's messy."

"My mommy wouldn't let me grow it long, either." she whispered. "Wait till you're older. Then you can do anything you want. You can even dye it blue."

Suri laughed and laughed at the idea of blue hair and ran off to tell her cousins the funny thing Aunt Tessa said.

She found Usher sneaking out of the living room. Tessa's brother stood a full head taller than anyone else in the family, a big, rangy guy with a reddish-gold goatee and a reckless grin that made him look faintly like the devil. He worked as a sous chef in an Italian restaurant downtown known for the freshness of its seafood and its mob connections, something of a family scandal. Not because of the mob connections; because the restaurant was not kosher.

"I've already kissed the ring," he said. "You're up."

"Uncle Allen says my hair makes a statement," she said.

"It does," Usher agreed. "It states that you are a smoking hot babe. That seems to make old Uncle Allen uncomfortable."

"What's going on in the living room?"

"Nothing good," he said. "We're doing everything wrong. Allen doesn't like Mom's stuffing. He says Eva's is better. Also, that Rosie lets Maya get away with murder, and that she could learn something from the way Cilla is raising her kids. He also mentioned that you look wild and that he wouldn't have let you move to New York if you were his kid."

"What's Dad doing?"

"Nodding. He agrees with everything they're saying."

Tessa sighed. Her sister Rosie had her hands full setting the table while keeping an eye on her toddler, Maya. At the glorious height of her terrible twos, she was hell-bent on flushing down the toilet anything she could get her chubby little fists on. Tessa could see Zaydie looking their way and shaking his head.

As usual, her dad was blissfully oblivious, in the honored position of sitting at his father's right hand. Tessa knew how devoted he was to his beloved Pa, anticipating and attending to his every need.

It would have been understandable, forgivable even, if only Zaydie returned his devotion. No matter how hard he tried to be the perfect son, Zaydie reserved the bulk of his affections for his younger brothers. For them, Zaydie always had a warm smile. When he turned his gaze on Tessa and her siblings, he always seemed vaguely disappointed.

His disapproval extended to Rosie's choice of a husband and Usher's choice of a career. But the real throwdown was reserved for Tessa. He nearly had a heart attack when he found out she was going to art school.

Nakkeda nekayvas! he exploded. Why are you letting her draw *nakkeda nekayvas?*

Her parents were nonplussed at his vitriol. Even her father thought he was overreacting. In the end, they decided not to discuss it with him any further, telling him instead that she had exhausted the dating possibilities in Chicago and was moving to New York to expand the pool of available nice Jewish boys. That explanation, he accepted.

Irritated with herself, Tessa shook it off. Ancient history. He'd been through the Holocaust, for God's sake. Lost his parents, countless aunts and uncles and cousins. She could forgive him a few eccentricities.

Zaydie was seated in the middle of her mother's couch, a frail, pious old man with a full white beard. He was nodding and smiling as one of the little girls presented him with a posterboard. Taking it into his palsied hands, he sat back deeper into the couch, shaking his head and stroking his beard. Tessa could see him push his glasses down his nose, running his fingers along the poster, his lips moving.

Curious, she moved closer. The posterboard was covered with glitter and glue, carefully ruled lines, photographs cut into the shapes of little boxes or ovals, names scrawled in magic marker in spidery little girl handwriting. Tessa recognized a family tree, going back several generations.

"Wow," she said. "I thought he didn't talk about anything from the war."

"You don't know about this?" Usher said, surprised. "Zaydie helped her with it. All these names he's never mentioned before."

"Really." Now she was interested, moving closer, squinting to decipher the childish curlicues. But then dinner was called, and the poster was quickly rolled up and put away.

The women drifted into the kitchen. "What a pretty dress," said her cousin Cilla. Cilla had big green eyes, just like Eva.

"Thanks," said Tessa. "How do you stay so thin?"

She patted her flat stomach. "You call this thin? I'm a big fatso. Look at this belly. I don't fit into any of my old clothes." Tessa nodded politely. Cilla was as thin as a fence post.

"Did you hear?" Eva said. "Cilla's pregnant again."

Tessa received a bowl of vegetable soup from her mother and carried it out to Zaydie, sitting at the head of the table, in her father's place. He looked older than the last time she had seen him, more wizened, more shrunken, more vulnerable, but his eyes were as piercing as ever. In elementary school, the teachers had all remarked on the Moss children's extraordinary eyes.

"How is New York?" he asked, as he picked up his spoon. "You meet some nice boys?"

"Still looking, Zaydie," she replied. The conversation was over, he was busy blowing on his soup.

Back in the kitchen, her mother set her to peeling cucumbers for the salad. "How's Lucian?" Usher said, dicing onions into perfect little quarter-inch squares.

"Oh—he's fine. We have a big show opening in the spring."

There was a queasy feeling in the pit of her stomach. Tessa had never told anyone in her family the truth about her involvement with her employer. She looked around the kitchen now, at her mother ladling out soup, at the parade of cousins carrying bowls out to the men seated in the dining room, at her grandmother setting squares of kugel onto serving platters, at Auntie Barbara peeling aluminum foil off of a tin pan of stuffed cabbage. She couldn't picture Lucian here, dressed in his colorful Paul Smith shirts, his funky trousers with the corduroy running the wrong way, circulating among the people in this room, joking with her aunts in his self-assured British accent. He belonged to a different world, her other life. She would tell them someday, she thought. When the time was right. For now, it was better to wait, to keep it to herself, until...

Until what? Until he stops screwing around? Until he marries you? Come on, Tessa. Is that ever in a million years really going to happen?

A wave of nausea washed over her. She put her palms down on the counter to steady herself. Absorbed in his mounting pile of onions, Usher didn't notice.

Who am I? she wondered. *Where do I belong?*

It came to her suddenly, an epiphany. "I'm going to show Zaydie my sketchbook," she said.

"Don't do it." Usher said without hesitation.

"Maybe he'll appreciate it," she said urgently. "My paintings are about the Holocaust, our family history. Maybe he's changing, maybe he's ready to open up about it. Look how excited he is about a fourth-grade family tree!"

Usher shook his head. "Don't even think about it. He really has a weird thing about art. To him, it's all *nakkeda nekayvas.*"

Tessa ran upstairs to her room, drew her sketchbook out of her knapsack. The black leather gleamed dully in the light. She put it to her nose, inhaling the fragrance of the Italian calfskin, and suddenly she felt Raphael Sinclair's cool hand between her shoulder blades, propelling her backwards around the Cast Hall. Opening the sketchbook to her drawing of him, she turned her head, viewed it critically. It wasn't as bad as she'd first thought. She had captured the beauty of his face, the drama of his gesture. She ran her finger around the contours of his figure, a smile playing on her lips, thinking of Raphael Sinclair prowling restlessly around her studio, Raphael Sinclair sprawling photogenically onto the red velvet couch that belonged properly in a bordello, kissing her upturned hand. The voices drifting up from downstairs intruded on her reverie. She snapped the sketchbook shut and headed downstairs.

Zaydie was eating his soup. Her father, at his right hand, barely noticed she was there. She stood behind him for a moment, hesitating. She could still withdraw, beat a hasty retreat. She firmed her resolve, stepped forward.

"Look, Zaydie," she said, her voice trembling. "I want to show you what I've been doing in New York." She opened her sketchbook and drew out the drawings for her thesis project, laying them carefully side by side. The mother and child, the landscape with the boxcar, the family on the train siding, the whirlwind of bodies, her grandmother stooped over the table covered with memorial candles.

"It's about the war," she said shyly. "It's about us." She drew back, waiting for his reaction.

Abe Moss put down his soup spoon. He looked to the drawings, then at his granddaughter, then back to the drawings again. His right hand rose from the table, faltering, the skin jaundiced and spotted with age. He slammed it down again with so much force that the plates jumped off of the white cloth.

"This...is...*NOTHING!*" he roared. His face turned red and then purple, mottled with rage.

There was dead silence. All eyes were riveted on Tessa. She felt her face burning. Now, his voice softened, tender, he stretched forth his arm indicating the three tables packed with family, traversing the dining room from the kitchen door all the way to the other end of the living room, his gesture taking them all in.

"This..." he continued in a sonorous voice. *"This...is something."*

Then he turned his attention to her father, his fierce eyebrows lowering. "Sender. Why do you let her fill her head with this *narishkeit*? And Usher. Why do you let him live in that *goyishe* neighborhood downtown? Why aren't they married? All my other grandchildren are married. What's the matter with you, Sender? *What did you do wrong?"*

Her father sat like a stone, his face white. Uncle Allen and Uncle Bernie glared at her, shaking their heads. Her face burning, Tessa slunk off to the den.

She had been hugging her sketchbook to her chest. As she unwound her fingers from it, placed it on the desk, she saw that her hands were shaking. Usher was right. It had been a bad idea.

The posterboard covered with glitter glue and little girl's curlicued handwriting lay on the desk. Tessa skipped her fingers along the generations, finding herself and her cousins, tracing the magic-marker lines back to her grandparents' pictures. There, in a balloon next to a photograph of a smiling Zaydie, was a group of names she had never seen before. *Sarah Tessa. Usher Zelig. Cilla Bracha. Aryeh Lev. Rifka Maya. Rosa Dina. Noah Ezra.* Underneath each of them was scrawled *Died, 1942.*

No lines, no descendants, extended from these names. This branch of the family tree was shriveled and dried up like dead branches. A line connected them to her grandfather. Tessa stared at it, confused.

Rosie came in, ushering Maya ahead of her. She stuck a tape in the VCR. The Sesame Street overture played.

"I think I ruined Zaydie's birthday dinner." said Tessa.

"Mom and Dad are really pissed. What were you thinking?"

"I guess I thought it would inspire him to tell me something about our history. You know, I'm doing my master's thesis on the Holocaust. It's ironic, isn't it? Our grandparents are survivors, and I don't know anything that I didn't read in a book. Don't you want to know?"

Rosie rolled her eyes. "Always with the Holocaust. Can't you just forget about it? Why can't you paint happy things?"

Instead of answering, she ran her finger along the line connecting her grandfather's picture to the unfamiliar names. "Do you know who these people are?"

"Sure. Zaydie's parents. Also, his wife and children. The ones who died in the war."

Tessa stared at her, not comprehending. "Zaydie had another family?" "You didn't know?"

She shook her head, mute with astonishment.

"Four children." Rosie shivered. "I can't imagine it, can you?" She turned to look at Maya, mesmerized by Cookie Monster singing that sometimes the moon looks like a cookie, but you can't eat that.

Her finger stopped over her own name, Tessa pondered. Were they, the children of survivors, and the children of the children of survivors, supposed to replace loved ones that had been lost in the war? Was Zaydie's disappointment so much greater because of the expectation that they would somehow fill out dear lives that had been cut short?

Thoughtful now, she returned to the kitchen. Her mother was alone, critically confronting a huge brown turkey while the others finished their soup. Looking at it, Tessa was reminded of Dissection Day, and she winced. Glaring at her, her mother handed her a serving bowl and started scooping stuffing out of the turkey's cavity. Tessa loved her mother's stuffing, made from leftover challah, spiked with celery, scallions, and mushrooms.

"What's the matter with you?" her mother said, angrily plopping stuffing into the bowl, "You're going to give him a heart attack."

"Sorry," she said humbly. "I really thought he might appreciate them."

"Did it have to be today? At our house? At his own party? Your father is...." she left the sentence unfinished.

"Don't you want to know?" Tessa said plaintively. "Don't you ever wonder what happened?"

"I know what happened," said her mother, pushing hair off of her forehead. Her face was shiny with steam. She'd been preparing for this dinner party since Sunday. "They all went up the chimney at Sobibor. My parents didn't talk about it either. Why do you need to know the details? Did you ever think that maybe it hurts him too much to think about it? Some things are better left alone."

"Mom," she said. "How come I never heard that Zaydie had a family before the war?"

"You lived twenty-five years in this house and you didn't know?" She arranged a serving spoon in the bowl. "Go put this in front of your father."

Tessa, in disgrace, did as she was told. She set the stuffing down on the table, not quite brave enough to meet her father's eyes as Uncle Allen glared daggers at her.

"When do you think we'll be old enough to sit at the grown-up table?" she muttered to Usher, as she elbowed her way in beside her brother.

"When you're married with children," he said. "And by the way, I told you so."

Suri was at her elbow now, holding a pencil and a not-too-clean paper napkin. "Can you draw me a picture now?" she lisped.

"Sure, sweetie." She drew a horse with a flowing mane and tail.

The little girl regarded it critically. "It needs wings," she instructed.

Obediently, Tessa gave the horse wings. Suri beamed, and leaned her head against Tessa's shoulder as she viewed her prize. "We think you should go to the Wailing Wall in Jerusalem and pray for a husband," she confided before running back to her seat.

"She told me I should pray for a better job," said Usher.

The stuffing landed fortuitously on their table. Tessa scraped some onto her plate and passed it on. "Hey, did you know that Zaydie had a family that died in the war?"

Usher helped himself to salad. "I think I did know that. I heard it at a Shabbos lunch once."

"Oh, good," she said grimly. "So I'm the last one to know."

"No, no, you're not the last one to know," he corrected her. He turned to his right. "Hey. Suri. Did you know that Zaydie had a different family before the war?"

"What?" Suri said, engaged in shooting peas at her sister Rifkie.

"There," said Usher. "Now Suri is the last one to know. You're in the clear." He passed her a bowl of pasta. She sniffed it suspiciously. She detected sweet Italian sausages, penne pasta, broccoli rabe, tomatoes, red peppers.

"This is not traditional Moss Thanksgiving food, unless Auntie Barbara is trying something different with her zucchini kugel," she said.

"This is my contribution, courtesy of my *goyishe* gourmet education," said Usher. "And may I say, to die for." Tessa tried the pasta, swooned. It was, indeed, to die for.

The turkey made its entrance. Her mother had taken it off the bone, sliced it up, and put it back together again, a feat of mind-boggling skill. The platter was passed around for everybody to admire before it was placed before Zaydie. On the table were gefilte fish, stuffed cabbage, fried rice with onions, sweet potatoes with marshmallows, green bean casserole with mushroom soup and fried onions, challah stuffing, the aforementioned zucchini kugel, and cranberry sauce from a can. Tessa tried everything except for the zucchini kugel.

At seven o'clock, Zaydie lifted himself from the table. "Where are you going?" Sender said swiftly. "Do you need something? Can I get it for you?"

"No, no. Just going to take my pills." He waved off Sender's help. "I'm fine." He pushed up onto his cane, steadied himself, and disappeared into the kitchen.

For a moment, there was silence. And then Allen said, "Sender. What's the matter with her? Does she have to rile him up? He's an old man. She should have some pity."

Her father sank further down into his seat.

"Hey," said Bernie. "Don't be so quick to criticize. Pa can come down really hard sometimes. Remember when you came back from yeshiva in Israel and told him you wanted to be a rabbi?"

Allen smiled. "Oh, yeah...he didn't think that was such a good idea."

"He called you an idiot."

Uncle Allen, Auntie Eva, Uncle Bernie and Auntie Barbara all laughed. Sender smiled.

"Sender. Remember when you wanted that Lionel train set," Allen said. "Your friend Hershel had one. With the really heavy cars, and the metal tracks. You spent a whole week washing dishes, taking out garbage and making your bed. And when you finally worked up the courage to ask him, Pa said, 'I had enough of trains on my way to Auschwitz.'" The adult table erupted in shrieks of laughter. The tension in the room dispersed.

Zaydie hobbled back in and took his seat at the head of the table. Tessa's mother came to the doorway between the kitchen and the dining room, holding an enormous sheet cake covered in silver white frosting. Everyone oohed and aahed. Someone turned the lights down. Zaydie was beaming. Sender didn't take his eyes from his father's face, basking in his reflected happiness. Bernie got his camera ready.

She set the cake down in front of the old man. Suri and her sister Rifkie ran to sit in Zaydie's lap. He leaned forward on his cane to inspect it through lenses like the bottoms of Coke bottles. "Beautiful, Marta," he said to Tessa's mother, delighted. "Beautiful."

All together, the three tables sang *Happy Birthday*. "Come on *shay-falehs*," he said to the little girls, stroking their hair. "Help me blow out the candles."

Together, they blew out the flames. Tessa's mother cut the cake into squares and passed them around. Rosie poured coffee and tea. The littlest cousins sang a song they had made up about Zaydie to the tune of *The Anniversary Waltz*. Cilla played piano. Usher juggled. Bernie took pictures. Suri chased Rifkie around the living room, knocking over a crystal vase. Ari pulled Maya's hair. The party was winding down.

Bubbie, a tiny, wizened wisp of an old lady, finally sat down in the chair to Zaydie's left. Tessa's grandmother barely spoke English. Mostly she smiled bashfully at them, her children, grandchildren and great-grandchildren. She showed her love in other, more concrete ways; her apartment was always redolent with the smell of chocolate cake in the oven, sugar cookies in a jar on the counter.

Suddenly, Tessa remembered the name Raphael Sinclair had given her. "Bubbie," she said, leaning forward. "Did you ever know a Sofia Wizotsky?"

As if they were on strings, all the heads at the adult table jerked around to stare at her in unison. But nothing was more extraordinary than the change that came over Zaydie.

"What did she say?" said the old man.

"Nothing, Pop," said Bernie swiftly. "Nothing."

Sender was watching his father anxiously. "You okay, Pa? Can I get you something?"

"Sofia Wizotsky?" The old man's voice began to rise, crackling and popping like an old radio. His breathing became harsh, ragged as sandpaper. *"Tell me, did she say Sofia Wizotsky?"* He was struggling to rise, staggering to his feet, staring at her with an ugly expression that looked like hatred. His face went white, then red, then purple, then white again. And then, as if someone had flicked a light switch, his eyes closed and he went limp, keeling over onto the carpet.

Bedlam. The adult children leaped out of their chairs, knocking them to the floor. Someone called 911. The smaller children pushed in for a closer look. Maya was crying. Tessa's heart was hammering. She could feel Usher's hand on her shoulder, pushing her back into the living room, hear him saying, *it's not your fault, it's not your fault.* And as the paramedics rushed in and performed CPR, and as they loaded him into the ambulance and sped him to the hospital with sirens wailing, as she stayed up through the long November night waiting for the phone to ring with news, any news, she knew only one thing was for certain; they would never, ever forgive her.

18

$\mathcal{H}$e didn't really say that," said Portia with a kind of hushed awe.
"He would." Tessa confirmed. "He did."

"Wow," said David.

It was a week after Thanksgiving. The second-year students of the American Academy of Classical Art were out celebrating Tessa's birthday, clutching beers and sitting on barstools in Burritoville, where the food was, a sign advertised, Mexellent. Tessa hung onto the neck of a Dos Equis like she was holding onto life.

"No big deal," she said, and closed her eyes. She was feeling a little woozy on one margarita and half a bottle of beer.

A waiter reported that their table was ready. They got unsteadily to their feet and eased around the other customers to an empty table in the crowded restaurant. Tessa sank into the peaceful reverie afforded by the warm glow of alcohol, letting the conversation flow over and around her.

It was official, Zaydie had had a heart attack. Tessa spent the rest of the weekend under a cloud of shame and disbelief. The little time her parents weren't at the hospital, they were either sleeping or running out the door.

The flight from O'Hare to JFK was flat, uneventful, drawing a numbing veil over the disastrous weekend, and she settled back into her seat and closed her eyes. A little over an hour later she was jolted awake by the plane's slow descent, the bump and grind of the unfolding landing gear. As always, there was an excited tingle in the pit of her stomach at the thought of returning to New York City, and she leaned forward for her first glimpse of the twinkling lights, unfurling over the many miles like a magic carpet.

Monday morning, she finally had her first appointment with her adviser. Josephine was predictably late, blowing in with the November wind, her cheeks apple red. She had raced over after a meeting, she told Tessa as she heaved her coat and bag onto the couch, of faculty, staff and board members. There had been a heated exchange over bringing in additional celebrity teachers, an idea embraced in some corners of the faculty and vociferously rejected by others. Harvey and Tony lashed out against hiring instructors with modernist backgrounds, warning that they were ill-equipped to teach classical technique, while Turner, Blesser and April smiled smugly and Levon tried to keep the discourse at a professional level. All the while, Raphael Sinclair had audited the proceedings from a corner, half hidden in the shadow of *Night.* Or *Dawn,* Josephine could never remember which one of those Medici tomb sculptures was which.

"What do you think?" Tessa wanted to know.

"Keep your friends close and your enemies closer, I always say," said Josephine, checking her lipstick in Tessa's mirror. "Also, we could bask in the reflected glory of having some of those big names around. Lend us the sheen of relevancy. And then my paycheck might get larger. Let me tell you, honey, life as an artist is expensive, with a couple of children, a mortgage, and a Guatemalan housekeeper."

Finally Josephine turned to Tessa's sketches. She immediately dismissed the mother and child, the drawing of the family on the railroad siding, and the landscape with the boxcars, calling them "too illustration-ey." On the other hand, the sketch of her grandmother with the *yahrzeit* candles made Josephine positively green with envy. "Wish I'd done that," she told Tessa admiringly. "I don't know what the hell's going on. But I can't stop looking at it."

Tessa fought for the mother and child, protesting that it was the central image of her projected series. Tilting her head this way and that, Josephine frowned at the little drawing, leaving her with, "I don't know. I'm still not convinced. Make it better."

She had other questions, as she thumbed through Tessa's sketchbook. How big are you planning to make them? How many will there be? Are they a triptych, or are they just three paintings with the same theme? What will you do for models? When do you plan to start? Tessa struggled for answers. Truthfully, she hadn't thought that far ahead.

The sketchbook fell open to the drawing of Raphael Sinclair on the couch. Josephine surveyed it for a long moment before speaking, and then her voice was serious, devoid of its usual homey folksiness. "Honey," she said. "I don't like to interfere with my students' love lives. I think every experience is valuable. But I gotta say here, I don't think this is such a good idea."

"I'm not—it's not like that," said Tessa, blushing.

Josephine looked at her curiously as she handed her back her sketch-book. "All right," she said, shouldering her purse. "All right, honey. Say. Do you really work for Lucian Swain?"

After her meeting, Tessa went in search of Portia, but found only David at work in their shared studio. He was standing over his work table, the sleeves of his denim shirt carefully rolled up, a waiter's apron tied around his hips, meticulously mixing colors for a studio painting class at noon, while Harker idly picked at his electric guitar, black cowboy boots propped up on Portia's table.

He glanced up when she came in, used a rag to wipe the paint off of his palette knife. David's palette was an object of art in itself, dabs of perfectly modulated color set at perfectly regular intervals all around the edges of the glass surface.

"Portia around?"

"I haven't seen her yet."

David already knew what he was doing for his thesis project, a series of still lifes. Tessa was puzzled. They were at a school of figurative art, after all. Figurative implied, well, *figures.*

"Still lifes aren't necessarily about fruit and flowers," he explained. "It's all about metaphors. A skull is a symbol for mortality. So are all those dead rabbits and decaying fruit. A pomegranate implies fertility. An apple is an allegory of temptation." His words were measured, his gaze steady, but something in his look was asking questions, suggesting possibilities.

"You sound like a teacher."

"That's what I plan to do after I finish here. Well, that and paint. Sara will put in a good word for me at SUNY."

Like everyone else, David had postcards pinned to his walls, hung in neat rows of five, the edges meeting seamlessly. Finely-detailed Flemish compositions with tulips, hares and rotting fruit. Bowls of Fantin-Latour's rapturous roses, the color of lingerie, petals splayed promiscuously across the canvas. Platoons of Cezanne apples standing at attention on ice blue tables.

There was a new postcard, separate from the others. A woman with upswept honey-colored hair set a silver bowl of fruit down on a cherry red tablecloth. Cobalt blue vines swam across the cloth, climbed up the walls painted in the same vibrant hue as the table.

"Who did this?"

He came to stand beside her. "Matisse. It's called *Harmony in Red*. I just saw the exhibition yesterday."

"It's beautiful," she said. "It makes me feel…" she hesitated, searching for the right words. "like I've come home."

"Me, too," he said. "And I'm not a big Matisse fan."

A shaft of weak winter sun found its way through the dirty window and washed her hair gold. Suddenly he understood that the painting reminded him of her Friday night dinners, Tessa with her bright hair setting the table with a colorful patterned tablecloth, her apartment warm and welcoming, full of good smells and promises of good company and lively conversation.

The same beam of light illuminated his eyes, already the blue of a Bellini sky. Once again she realized how attractive he was. It occurred to her that David was exactly the kind of man she should be dating, smart, sensitive, articulate, steady. She knew he would make an excellent teacher, just as she was sure he was a considerate and thoughtful lover.

He smiled at her, and she knew he was correctly guessing at what she was thinking. She had turned to study a framed painting on his wall, a knobbly branch of apple blossoms set against a jade-colored background. The rendering of the pink and white petals was exquisite, with subtle gradations of transparency and opacity, mixed in minute titrations of hue and saturation. It was deeper and richer than a photograph, lovelier even than real apple blossoms. In small red letters at the bottom, were two sets of initials. *BC* and *SD, 1991*.

"Who's SD?"

"Sara," said David. "We work on the same painting sometimes. Our styles are similar."

"Wow," Harker said, looking up from his guitar. "That's pretty intimate, isn't it?"

David had leveled his gaze at Tessa. It was clear to her that this was not the direction he wanted this conversation to go. And just then, Portia had come in through the curtain.

But the big story upon her return from Chicago involved Lucian. Half a dozen calls awaited her on the answering machine, all saying the same thing; he had broken up with April, he was in a bad way, would she meet him for dinner. Still in her coat, she had stabbed his number into the phone before the second message spooled to an end.

He'd greeted her at the door looking strained, distant, a little sad. "You're the only one who really understands me, Tessa," he said as he took her hand, slid it over his belly and down the front of his jeans.

"I love you," she whispered afterwards in his bed, laying her head on his chest. He grunted, already falling asleep.

Tessa sat up beside him for a long while, staring at the famous artist cradled in the crumpled sheets, his skin colored blue and gold in the lamplight, reflexively taking note of the shadows and highlights as they chased each other across his sleeping figure. For the first time, she noticed the lines around his eyes, the flesh just beginning to sag under his jaw. And though he was fit, working out at a gym downtown twice a week, his was still the body of a middle-aged man.

Raphael Sinclair's lean physique, prowling through her studio, stretched out on her couch, flickered before her mind's eye. Feeling disloyal, she had pushed the thought away. She loved Lucian, none of that mattered. Still, something had been left unsaid in the dark; something was not wrong, and yet not right.

"How about you?" the waitress was saying.

Tessa stared at her blankly. "I'm sorry. I was thinking about something else."

"Do you need another minute?"

Tessa shook her head no, she was ready, she got the same thing every time anyway, the bean and cheese burrito. The beer had softened the edges of everything, making the room feel warmer. David, on her right, leaned over to reach for a napkin, brushing against her shoulder, and it left a pleasant tingle.

"Whit says we have to go to the Matisse show," said Graham morosely. "He wants me to see *Carmelina* up close and personal."

"You don't like Matisse?" said Harker.

"Most overrated artist on the planet."

"I went last Saturday," said David. *"Carmelina's* not so bad in person. But the crowds! I haven't seen anything like it since the Van Gogh exhibitions in the Eighties."

"I thought it was only open to members over the weekend," said Graham.

"My mom's a docent."

"Well, la-di-dah," replied Graham without conviction, paging through a *New York Post* that lay open on the table.

"How was your Thanksgiving?" Portia asked him.

Graham grimaced. "Oh, the usual. I pretended to be straight. They pretended to believe me."

"Your family's been here so long they were probably at the first Thanksgiving." David said to Portia. "Do you do anything different than the rest of us mortals?"

"We have a big family get together with the cousins at my grandfather's house, just like anyone else."

"Sounds like fun."

Her lips were compressed into a thin line. "Well, it's not. My grandfather makes a big deal about inspecting my work. He leafs slowly through my portfolio, drawing by drawing. Big sighs at each page. Then he tells the whole table how artists were so much more talented when he was in art school. My grandmother favors my cousin India and her brothers more than me and my brothers. India reminds me yet again that her family has a bigger house, faster cars, better connections and more money. One of the younger cousins breaks a cherished antique handed down from my great-grandmother. My uncle drinks too much. We pretend it is fine. I'm sure the same stuff happens in your family."

"My parents are divorced," David said. "My grandparents are dead."

"Lucky." Portia muttered.

"So, who's going to be our next president?" Harker said, changing the subject, stretching his legs out under the table.

"Oh, please Lord, anybody but Bush." said Graham. "Not a day goes by that I don't worry that someone's going to shoot him and make that moron Quayle our President."

"I like Clinton," Clayton said. "My daddy says he's the smartest man he's ever met. Also, it would be nice to have a fellow without an accent in the White House."

"How can you read that crap?" asked David, indicating the *Post*.

Graham fixed him with a disapproving glare. "Excuse me, but this newspaper has been the source of some of the finest writing in the history of journalism. I am speaking, of course, of the greatest headline of all time, *Headless Body found in Topless Bar*. Also, I need to know what Princess Di is up to at all times."

"Say, Tessa," said David, working on his second Corona. "How's it going with old Lucian?"

She knew she shouldn't say anything, but the beer coursing through her system did all the talking. "He broke up with April." she said, and a smile, shy at first, then dazzling, broke across her face.

"Must've been after this picture was taken, then," said Graham, tapping on the newspaper. Tessa leaned forward. Lucian and April, shoulder to shoulder, smiling brightly for the Page Six photographer. She shrugged, though her confidence stumbled a little. She remembered the photograph of April, still in her knapsack, and felt guilty.

"And looky here, if it isn't the founder of our school." Graham turned the tabloid around and pushed it into the middle of the table. Raphael Sinclair, caught in the harsh light of a photographer's flash, wearing a dinner jacket, was cozied up next to a dark-skinned girl in a white halter dress. They were both smiling.

Harker read the caption out loud. "Photographed at the opening of the new Matisse Exhibition at the Met, Raphael Sinclair and a friend."

She was surprised by the sharp pang of emotion. Immediately, she reprimanded herself. Of course he was at a party with a beautiful girl. He could have anyone he chose. Despite the week's commotion, she had still had the presence of mind to notice that he hadn't stopped by her studio.

"Hey, Tessa. What did the great Lucian Swain give you for your birthday?" said Gracie, with a wink.

"Yeah, girlfriend!" Portia laughed. "Anything you can show us?"

She smiled tentatively. Lucian had forgotten her birthday. "No, nothing I can show you."

Amidst the hooting, Clayton looked concerned. "Tessa, please," he said. "Whatever's going on between you and Lucian Swain, just don't get Mr. Sinclair angry. You know. Vampire and all."

Tapping Page Six, she said, "I don't think we need to worry about that."

The food came. To her vast relief, the subject of conversation turned to other things; plans for the holidays, meetings with advisers, galleries they had visited, breakthroughs in their work. In the storm of events that had followed her catastrophic visit to Chicago, she had forgotten the peculiar conversation in her studio last Wednesday night. She leaned forward and opened her mouth to tell them, but as the words formed on her lips she thought the better of it. She was beginning to feel sleepy. It was very warm in the room. And then the waiter was wading through the tables, carrying a jiggling flan with a candle in it and singing *Happy Birthday,* and the whole restaurant joined in. Somehow, David ended up walking her home on his way to the subway, and in the warm amber glow of the beer, his eyes met hers, and his hands lit on her shoulders as he pulled her towards him for a kiss.

19

essa was late to class the next day. For the first time in her life, she had a hangover; that morning, as she got out of bed, she staggered, gripping the side of her dresser for support. She had to sit back down until her room stopped revolving.

As she walked the three-quarters of a mile from her apartment to school, gusts of December wind threatened to loft her canvas into the wind like a kite at every street corner. Her head pounded with every jarring step. Maybe someone in the office would have Advil. Guiltily, she remembered kissing David last night under the awning of her building. What had she been thinking?

She hurried down the hall towards the classroom, burdened with the lamps and heaters. Her heart gave a little twitch when she remembered whose class she was headed for. She dreaded confronting April after the events of this week.

A first-year student stared at her as she passed, a tall, gangly printmaker with blond dreadlocks. Self-consciously, she raised her hand to her head, wondering if something had blown into her hair on the way over.

A group of sculptors lounging on the couches near the office followed her with their eyes as she hustled past them towards the classroom. A pair of first-year painters who had been chattering near the display case fell silent at her approach. Puzzled, she checked her reflection in a glass case before she swung into the classroom. Nothing out of the ordinary. Just the usual unruly hair. Maybe her eyes were a little puffy .

The room was dark. No one had thought to open the shades. The class skeleton, swaying gently on his stand in a dusty corner, had a cigar stub clenched jauntily between his teeth. Today he was also wearing a sporty-looking driving cap, a mordant caricature of Levon.

The model was leaning against the stool on the low stage, reading a newspaper, still dressed in his robe. She dropped her bag on a painting stand next to Graham. It was the spot nearest to the door, belonging to the easel with the worst view. She was the last one to arrive. The rest of the class was already there, bent over their palettes.

A few minutes went by before she realized that it was unnaturally silent, devoid of the usual back and forth of classroom chatter. Something big had blown through before she arrived. Her pulse quickening, she wondered if it was possible that someone had seen her kissing David. He was on the other side of the room, making a point of not looking at her, carefully mixing his paints. Even Ben was studiously avoiding her glance, taking a great interest in arranging his tubes of paint. Harker had his earphones on, deep in his music. But Clayton lifted his head to meet her gaze, and there was an unfamiliar look on his face, something like desire, and hunger, and a kind of surrealistic awe.

Graham leaned over to her and whispered, "You've been outed."

Clayton put down his palette knife and came to hover near her, his hands jammed in the pockets of his jeans. For the first time since she had known him, he seemed tongue-tied, searching for the right words.

"Tessa," he said in his soft Southern accent. "When the time comes, I hope you'll consider me. I respect you so much, as an artist, and as a woman. It would be an honor."

"Shut up, Clayton," said Ben.

Tessa swung around, looked to Graham in confusion.

"April's been here already," he said, his lip curled. "And, boy howdy, is she pissed. She filled us in about her painful but necessary breakup with her precious Lucian Swain. Incidentally, it seems that all the rumors about his legendary equipage are true."

He cleared his throat before he went on. "More of interest to you," he continued mildly, "she mentioned, shall we say, the state of your maidenhood. I believe her exact words were, 'Tessa's a *virgin!* Can you believe it? What is *up* with that, anyway?'"

"People were staring at me in the hallway," she whispered.

"Well. The door was open. And she was pretty loud. Whatever medication she's on, they need to jigger the dose."

Tessa was dumb with shock. She knew what every man in the room was thinking, imagining, picturing, even if they had never thought of her in that way before.

"Her last words as she left the classroom were, 'Now they can finally have each other.'"

Tessa reached inside her knapsack and pulled out the photograph of April spread-eagled on Lucian's bed. Without a word, she walked over to Clayton and handed it to him. Then she left the classroom, her head ducked down inside the collar of her coat, not looking up until she was safely inside her apartment.

It was late on Friday afternoon. The sun had made a great show of setting among stacks of fluffy purple evening clouds. Levon was just putting away his files when there was a soft knock at his door. "Come on in," he called, slipping the last one into a cabinet behind his desk.

When he turned back around, Raphael Sinclair was in his office, watching him. At six foot two and two hundred and fifty pounds, Levon Penfield didn't startle easily, but he took an involuntary step back into a cardboard box full of office supplies.

"Man!" he said, shaking his head and grinning. "Gets me every time. Where've you been? I haven't seen you since Monday's meeting."

"Prague," he replied, removing his fedora and picking a speck of city soot from the crown. "Flew over to talk to an artist out there. Got back at five o'clock this morning."

"Phew. You must be tired. Was it worth it?"

"Regretfully, no."

"I hear Prague is beautiful," said Levon. "All that Art Nouveau and crazy Gothic architecture."

"It is," he agreed. "It's changed a lot. Lots of cafés, tourists, students. You should go sometime."

"Sounds like you've been there before. Were you there when it was still under communism?"

"Something like that."

He'd been to Prague, yes, but it was to chase down a lead, not an art teacher. For years after the war ended, he'd checked the Red Cross lists, looking for a Sofia Wizotsky, a Sofia Weiss. He'd even been vain enough to seek a Sofia Sinclair. A private detective he paid to look for just this sort of thing found one in Prague. She was even an artist this time. He'd spent the better part of the past weekend lurking outside a wildly ornate apartment building on Parizska Street in the old Jewish Quarter, wondering what he would say when he saw her. Unfortunately—or fortunately, depending on which way he chose to look at it—Sofia Sinclair turned out to be an expatriate art student from the UK, with a spiky blond updo and an East End accent.

"Did I miss anything while I was away?"

"I don't know if you heard out there in Prague, Lucian Swain and April Huffman broke up over the weekend."

"Pity," said Rafe, smiling slightly.

Levon lifted his glasses, rubbed his eyes. "We lost another teacher. Inga has been hired away by RISDI."

That was a blow. Inga was the head of the drawing department. "She was so excited about what we're doing. Did she say why?"

Levon shrugged. "Benefits. More money. Better connections. Looks grander on her resume. Take your pick."

He sighed. Art teachers were a dime a dozen. Finding one with Inga's inborn ability to draw like an Old Master...well, that was something else.

A gust of wind rattled the window, a draft penetrating the old sash, blowing a couple of typewritten pages across Levon's desk.

"We should look at hiring one of our graduating students," he said, thinking of Gracie's column of figures. "A number of them would fit the job description nicely."

Levon grimaced. "You know Whit's policy on hiring ex-students."

"Yes, yes," he said irritably. "I really should do something about that."

They were both quiet for a minute. Reflexively, Levon straightened the objects on his desk, adjusting his stapler, Rolodex, memo pad, ruler and photographs of his children so that they were at right angles to each other.

"Oh, yeah," Levon said. "Whit finally clued us in on who he picked for guest instructor over Intersession."

Rafe drew closer, his eyebrows lifting. "And?"

"It's Wylie Slaughter."

A thunderstorm threatened to break across his even visage. "Slaughter? The progenitor of all those poorly-drawn saucy suburban housewives and school boys?"

Levon put his hands up in surrender. "I know. I know. What can I say? He's another name brand artist. He says he loves what we're doing here. He'll attract lots of media attention, which is what we're looking for. Also, I think it's only fair to tell you, I kind of like those paintings of saucy suburban housewives."

Rafe threw himself down in a chair. "Has anyone told the students?" he said gloomily.

Levon shook his head no. "Giselle is announcing it on Monday." He pursed his lips, ran his fingers along the surface of the desk. "Listen. A monitor walked out on a class this morning."

"Really," said Rafe. "Whose class?"

He hesitated before continuing. "April Huffman."

The strange eyes sharpened, held him. "What happened?"

He rubbed the back of his neck, as if it was sore. "Well...April's been inappropriate. Abusing personal knowledge. It's been an ongoing problem."

"Personal? Like what?"

"Well...she told the entire class that the monitor is a virgin."

Rafe unfolded himself from his chair, got slowly to his feet. "Is Tessa all right?"

"She walked out at the break. Hasn't been seen since. Left her paints and everything. Some of her friends were going to check up on her."

With one gorgeous motion, a fluid sweep of his arm, Rafe settled his hat back on his head. There was a murderous gleam in his eye.

"I'm just on my way out," said Levon. "Do you mind handing me my cane?"

"That's new. Everything all right?" There was a knobbly, walnut-colored walking stick in the umbrella stand. He handed it across the desk to Levon, who was already on his feet, pulling on his coat.

"Oh, yeah. Fine. Old sports injury's been acting up. I ought to see a doctor about it, but you know how that goes."

"Track, wasn't it?"

"You remember. I'm touched. The joys of getting old. Well, I guess it's better than the alternative." He shut the lights and closed the door behind them. The two men walked down the semi-darkened hallway, plaster busts of Roman emperors glowering at them in the gloom from behind blank eyes.

"How long has this been going on?" Rafe said.

"Since her very first day," he admitted grudgingly. "April's been whispering in her ear all kinds of nasty about whatever it is she does with Lucian Swain, sending her out of the building on all sorts of errands that have nothing to do with lights and heaters. I said something to her, but... well, you can see how well that worked."

They took the elevator. On the sidewalk below, a biting wind blew a tumbling newspaper against Levon's legs as he put his arm out to flag down a taxi. "Where are you headed?" he said as a yellow cab screeched to a stop beside them.

"Holiday party for *Anastasia*," Rafe said, looking at his watch. "I should be getting over there now."

"I still remember reading about those naked waiters. What's she got planned this time?"

He smiled faintly. "All I know is that it's at the Convent of the Sacred Heart."

"Ooh," said Levon, from the warm interior of the taxi. "Sounds naughty. I'll be looking forward to hearing about that. Can I offer you a ride?"

"No, thank you. Look after that leg, will you?"

He shut the door on the cab. It wheeled back into traffic. He pulled his collar up around his neck, pulled the brim of his hat down against the cold and started striding purposefully uptown.

All his instincts told him that he should head straight for wherever it was that April lived and tear her throat out. The thought of Tessa showing up for class every Friday to be tormented by one of his teachers made him physically ill. He felt responsible; after all, his signature was at the bottom of every one of April's paychecks.

He turned up Broadway, gliding past the Gothic spires of Grace Church on 10th Street. Though Tessa had not held the answers to his questions, though she had not proved to be the direct link to Sofia that he had hoped for and dreaded, he couldn't stop thinking about her. She was always on his mind, drifting in and out like background music. His thoughts returned to her again and again, caressing the memory of their moments together like a smooth beach stone some men might carry in their pocket to remind them of a pleasant vacation.

Prague had been strangely cheerful, vibrant, a medieval town come to bustling life. Light and music spilling out of café doors. Drunken Scandinavian students with steins of beer. Sleek, dark-haired girls with portfolios under their arms hurrying to meet lovers in Old Town Square. The last time he'd been there, he'd purchased a Klimt from a furtive little man who was selling all his earthly possessions for next to nothing so that he could get himself and his family out of Nazi-occupied Czechoslovakia.

He turned onto Sixth Avenue, the cold wind hustling him forward. Now his mind turned to the information Levon had given him. So Lucian Swain had broken up with April Huffman. Rafe didn't give a blessed damn. All it meant was that Lucian was back on the prowl again, looking for that next special girl, at a guest lecture, or a restaurant, or a club, or a meeting, but to Tessa, sweet, trusting, faithful Tessa, it would mean that he was coming back to her. And knowing Lucian, he would not be averse to letting her have another taste of his charms, his much vaunted and much practiced talents, to keep her trailing in his wake a little while longer.

He tried to tell himself that she was just another student, well off bounds and entitled to her own mistakes, but it was useless, he felt the muscles in his jaw swelling, the fangs breaking through the gums and descending. Something was changing in his eyes, too; he could feel his pupils dilating, his vision growing more acute.

He was crossing Herald Square now. Macy's windows had been changed over to cheerful tableaus of merry Victorian winter scenes. Christmas shoppers laden with shiny red bags hurried along the wide promenades of Thirty-fourth Street and Broadway. Rafe stalked through the throngs, causing a dozen women to move aside with a little gasp, the hair along the back of their necks prickling straight up.

At the garment district, he slowed. The crowd was thinner here, the lights dimmer, the skyscrapers older, the streets dirtier. His eyes raked east and west, searching out women lingering in subway exits or alone at bus stops, waiting for the right aura to strike him as he swept past.

There. A woman sat in a gray Toyota, parked halfway up Thirty-eighth Street, turning the key again and again on an engine that would not start. The buttons and trimmings stores were all closed now, their gates and shutters locked down for the night. He could feel her desperation grow as she sat there wondering what to do; how to get home, where to find someone to tow the car, what her husband would say. Her fear at being alone, stranded on this little-traveled street at night.

The door squealed as she emerged cautiously from the safety of her car. She was peering fearfully towards Broadway, hoping to spot a phone booth. Rafe glided soundlessly alongside her.

He smelled wool and sweat, a dimestore imitation of Chanel No. 5. Gently, so gently she almost didn't notice it, he swept the hair away from her neck. By the time she heeled around, choked out an exclamation, he was ready. He drove his fangs into her throat.

She gasped, struggled, made noise. He clapped his hand over her mouth and dragged her into a lightless loading dock between the buildings.

Pinning her against a sign that advertised ribbons of all colors and widths, to the trade only, please, he sucked voraciously at the jagged hole he'd ripped in her flesh. She tore at him with her nails, but he just forced himself harder against her, hearing bones crack. It made no difference to him; he grew warmer, more alive, by the minute.

Her body began to slide through his arms. Insatiable, he held on, fastened his teeth in a new place. He caught her just as her legs gave out, lowering her onto a bundle of flattened cardboard boxes.

Whatever had made her human was gone; it was like looking at a broken department store mannequin. Her blouse was open, hiked up, and her skirt was twisted round the wrong way. One of her shoes had fallen off and was lying at some distance, kicked there during the struggle. Her eyes were partly open, staring at him.

A police car squealed down the avenue, *whee-oo, whee-ooh, whee-ooh.* He searched his pockets for a cigarette, put it between his lips, doubled over with dry heaves. And then he sprinted down the street toward Broadway.

The next day, Page Six would report breathlessly on the decaying lime-stone beauty of the old Otto Kahn mansion, the marble floors and coffered ceiling of the ballroom, the cherubs carved in the rococo moldings, the red velvet banisters and the stained glass skylight. They would mention the hard-bodied waiters, naked but for little white wings and glittering white thongs, their trays of chicken satay skewers held aloft. There would be a photograph of a smiling Anastasia deCroix wearing a stunning silk satin halter-top gown made for her by her good friend Gianni Versace, ruched enthusiastically up past her hips, shirred provocatively over her breasts.

When the students in Harvey Glaser's sculpture class looked closely at Graham's paper on Monday, they could see Raphael Sinclair, looking preoccupied, standing in the background behind her.

20

$\mathcal{A}$ll day Monday, Tessa drew curious stares. Every man in the lounge, every teacher, every student, seemed to turn around to look at her, to judge her, to undress her with their eyes as she walked by.

By Tuesday, no one gave her a second glance.

"How?" Portia had asked on Friday night, bewildered. "You've been with Lucian Swain. I just assumed...how did you two..." she lapsed into silence, too discreet to finish the sentence.

Tessa raised guilty eyes to her. "There are things you can do," she said, a little abashed, a little defensive. "Lots of things."

"Why, Tessa?" asked Gracie, mystified. "That's what I want to know. *Why* are you still a virgin?"

Of all people, it was Clayton who came to her rescue. "Cause she's religious," he explained patiently.

She considered unburdening herself to Levon about April's unrelenting barrage of harassment. In the end, she left things as they were. She had won, after all; Lucian was hers; April was just hurt and jealous, and the semester was almost over, anyway.

If Tessa had hoped for a resumption of the time when she and Lucian had spent every waking moment together holding hands, she was disappointed. Life went on as it had before, which meant days spent in class, evenings spent working in the studio. Sometimes he was there, sometimes he was absent, off at AA meetings while she scraped away on his giant canvases or straightened up the apartment. He had not asked her to stay over since the night she had returned from Chicago.

Christmas vacation drew nearer, and with it, the month long Intersession. The special guest instructor was announced, Wylie Slaughter, a painter famous for his shocking scenes of schoolboys being seduced by women twice their age. Tessa had met him once, out for lunch with Lucian.

In infrequent phone calls, her mother reported that Zaydie was better, back in his own home. They had installed a new adjustable hospital bed, and there was a nurse looking after him around the clock. He tired easily, sleeping frequently, his rest interrupted by wild dreams.

Tessa struggled with her guilt. After all, she alone had been responsible for his illness. She tried to push it away, burying her fears under the mountain of work due before the end of the fall semester. Most worrisome of all was a complicated project for Whit's Perspective class that involved multiple figures and structures seen from three different angles, including but not restricted to a cone, a sphere, a cube, and a pyramid, gridded out in an architectural elevation map, then rendered with appropriate lights and shadows. It counted for a third of her grade.

Clayton never brought up the photograph. Perhaps he didn't know who was in it; perhaps he had more tact than she gave him credit for. More disturbingly, perhaps he thought it was her. In any case, Tessa was so embarrassed that she couldn't ask for it back.

By the end of the week, she had not seen Raphael Sinclair outside of the society column in the *Post*. She found that she missed his unexpected visits, his gifts, the notes he left in his flowery handwriting on heavy laid paper. Perhaps his infatuation with her had ended. Though her feelings were wrapped up with Lucian, she still noticed, and regretted the loss.

Tessa reached school with scarcely enough time to pick up the lights and heaters. The lobby was wallpapered with an impromptu tapestry of new flyers, in magenta, cyan and yellow, doubtlessly advertising a band someone's boyfriend played for. She rode up the creaky old elevator, mentally urging it to hurry, too worried about being late to read the colorful photocopies lining the walls. She stopped in the office to pick up equipment. Burdened with the lights and heaters, she hurried down the hallway, the flyers on the display cases dancing in the breeze from her passing. A flurry of xeroxes covered the wall near the elevator banks. Flyers were taped to the white marble buttocks of the statues in the hallway. Flyers covered the window in the door to the classroom, one in every color.

Her hand on the knob, Tessa finally glanced at one of the photocopies. Her jaw dropped slowly open as she realized what she was looking at: April Huffman's naked body, splayed over hundreds of printed flyers, fluttering from every surface in the building.

I have a show opening at O.K. Solomon in a week, boasted the words above the grainy picture. *Do you?*

Frantically, she spun around, her hand clapped to her mouth as the enormity of the event registered. April's cooch winked out at her from flyers in lavender, in periwinkle, in pink, in chartreuse, in neon orange and canary yellow. Flyers papered every surface; every window, every cabinet, every display case, every column, every door, every wall. Tessa ran to the stairs, slammed open the steel door; flyers were taped neatly up and down the stairwells as far as the eye could see.

Slowly, she walked back to the classroom, picked up the heaters, and opened the door.

Bedlam. Everyone was talking at once. Tessa's heart was pounding, her mouth dry. She dropped the heaters near the stage, threw her bag on a table.

"David saw the whole thing," Portia insisted. "Let him tell it."

At eight forty-five, April had gotten off the elevator and started down the hall towards the classroom, her high heels clacking loudly on the wooden floor. David, who had arrived early to mix his palette, happened to be in the lounge at the exact moment that her eyes flicked up at the solid wall of colorful copies, rustling in the rush of air from the descending elevator.

At first she'd peered closely, frowning. Fumbling in her bag for her glasses, she slipped them on and brought her face within an inch of a flyer printed on fluorescent pink paper. David said he'd heard a choked-off exclamation, then saw her rear back, almost falling off her heels, after which she'd gone tearing off towards the office. Watching through the glass, he saw her tell the secretary, her hands jerking hysterically through the air, and then she steamed back out and stomped off down the hall, tearing copies off the wall as she went along.

Back inside the classroom, she seemed to pull herself together. The model was already on the stand, reading the paper. She addressed his back, asking him to disrobe so that she could pose him. He turned around and flung off his robe, wearing nothing but a wide, friendly grin.

"That was when she screamed at the top of her lungs and left the room." David explained.

"Clayton was really thorough," said Ben. "He registered with the modeling office and everything."

"Oh Lord," breathed Tessa, feeling triumphant, feeling ill. "Was he naked?"

"Boy howdy," said Harker.

"Like a Greek god," added Graham.

"Where is he now?"

"Levon's office," said Ben.

"You should have been here," said Graham, taking off his earphones. "It was epic in both scope and vision."

"What should we do now?" said Gracie.

They turned to her expectantly, waiting for an answer. With no teacher, the monitor was in charge of leading the class. "I think we should draw," said Tessa. "We'll all take turns modeling."

"Me first," Gracie volunteered. She pulled her short, pleated plaid jumper up over her head, unconcerned with appearing before them in a short white belly shirt and black leggings. Part of a tattoo peeked out of the waistband just above her round bottom, an angel's wing. She lay down on the model stand, crossing her arms behind her head and opening her knees in a conscious imitation of April's photograph.

The room fell silent. Tessa thought she could hear the sound of the men breathing as they evaluated her voluptuous body. One by one, they dipped their brushes in their turpentine and began to paint.

April never returned to class, but Whit showed up with his clipboard, his square, heavy body stiff with suppressed rage. In clipped, furious tones, he accused them of harassment, spitting out in no uncertain terms that they were all responsible for her departure, and they had damn well better find a way to apologize, fast. They could start by taking down the flyers. As they filed out of the room, he bent a ferocious glare on Tessa. She stared back at him, ashamed but unrepentant.

She was alone in the classroom, taking down the lights, when Levon stuck his head in the doorway. She stumped across the wooden floor, feeling like she was on the way to her own execution.

"Tessa," he said in a low voice, once she had joined him out in the hallway. "Clayton swears up and down that this was completely his idea, that you had nothing to do with it. Is that true?"

Half-heartedly, she nodded her head up and down. A flyer they had missed accused her from the side of the display case.

His voice dropped another notch. "April says this photograph came from Lucian Swain's studio, that it had to have come from you."

She couldn't look at his kind face. She stared wordlessly at the toes of her boots, white with plaster dust.

"Clayton claims he found this picture in a girlie magazine."

She didn't answer, didn't move. She could have been laughing or crying; her hair was a curtain shielding her from his scrutiny.

"Come to my office," he said.

She trailed after him. Levon's was the third door down the corridor, on the left. He closed the door behind her, indicated the seat in front of his desk. Raphael Sinclair was there, too, leaning against the cabinets, looking out the window at a dull gray sky scudded over with low-hanging pewter-colored clouds. Now she was embarrassed, a high, scarlet flush flaming across her face.

"Clayton is in a lot of trouble." said Levon, lowering himself into the seat behind his desk. He was as serious as she had ever seen him. "He's been suspended. April just left. She wants me to call the police."

Her heart squeezed itself down into a tight ball inside her chest. She was incredibly guilty. There was nothing she could say. Certain that she was going to be expelled, a tear slipped down her cheek. It all seemed terribly unfair.

Levon leaned forward on his desk. "I know what's been going on," he said gently. "For what it's worth, I think April deserves it. Matter of fact, I think it was brilliant. But..." and here he sighed, "We are talking publicity disaster here. Look. I know you care about this school, and that's why I'm talking to you. I'm going to let you in on a little secret. The Academy is running out of money. There are grants out there that will only look in our direction if April teaches here. Whit wants her to be happy, no matter how bad an instructor she is. So, he's out for blood."

Tessa blanched as white as a sheet of Arches watercolor paper.

"However," he continued matter-of-factly, "She can't do anything to you without exposing her own bad behavior. So you're in the clear."

A great rush of relief flooded her body, leaving her weak. She stumbled to her feet, found her way to the door.

"On the other hand, Clayton's daddy is getting on a plane right about now, coming to take him home."

Tessa stopped, her hand on the doorknob. "What?" she said slowly. "Isn't Clayton, like, thirty?"

"Well. Twenty-nine," he said. Then, mildly. "I don't know if he's ever told you. He spent several months in a psychiatric institution."

She stared at him, stupefied. "His father had him committed." he went on calmly. "Apparently, he's got some trouble with authority figures. Also, he exhibits a certain amount of dangerously reckless judgment. As you can see."

Tessa stood rooted to the spot. She felt as if someone had told her the past three months had been a dream.

"Okay. Your hand has been officially slapped. You can go."

She was dismissed. Rafe was looking at her now. He gave her a small, reassuring smile.

Chastened, she shouldered her bag, slipped out the door. As it clicked closed behind her, she heard Levon call out, "Hey! You have a good Shabbos, now."

The phone started ringing at nine. Deep in sleep, he had ignored it the first three times. The fourth time, he struggled up out of the depths of a dream, slammed his hand on the receiver and put it to his ear.

"You'd better get down here," Levon had said in a level voice.

Though he'd gotten to bed only a few hours earlier, Rafe had risen and come straightaway. As he entered the building, he noticed a flourish of colorful flyers lining the lobby, the walls of the elevator, fluttering all down the corridor to Levon's office.

"Terrible, just terrible," he had murmured, hiding a smile as he listened to the charges.

The celebrated Ms. Huffman was pacing furiously back and forth across Levon's office, her voice shrill, demanding a full police investigation. Nothing less than having Clayton arrested would satisfy her. And she knew exactly who that photograph had come from.

"What can we do to make it up to you?" Levon had said soothingly, spreading his hands wide, palms facing up in apology. "We value the balance you bring to our program. How can we make you feel comfortable again?"

April had stopped pacing and stared at him, her eyes hard and glittering. She knew what she wanted; Tessa shamed, humiliated and expelled. Something about her reminded Rafe of a mean dog guarding a bone. With her greedy red mouth, her smooth auburn hair, her lithe, toned body and her emotional volatility, Rafe could well understand how Lucian would want to bang her. But there was something ugly walled up in there, a venomous streak a mile wide. He couldn't believe he had chosen her over Tessa.

Levon was sympathetic, penitent, regretful, conciliatory, inferring that it might be difficult to make a charge of indecent exposure stick in an art school where full frontal nudity was an everyday affair. He apologized profusely and sincerely for the students' behavior, reminding her that they were, after all, students, not criminals.

In the end, April had to be content with Clayton's immediate suspension. Slinging her oversized bag over her shoulder, she grabbed her black leather jacket and stalked out of the office, muttering that she had some calls to make. And with that, the disaster was over.

"Whatever they're paying you here," Rafe said to Levon, "it's not enough."

"If anything like that happens again," Turner said flatly, "they're out. No questions asked."

"C'mon, Whit," said Levon. "She was asking for it."

Rafe dropped into the chair in front of Levon's desk. "What happened, Whit?" he asked, honestly curious, dusting off a knife-pleated pants leg so blue it was almost black. "Remember when you first started here? There were seven students in that first class. You were working out of that hole on Rivington, heroin addicts shooting up in the entryway. You were beside yourself when I found you. A classical art school teaching Renaissance technique! You couldn't wait to get started. You called it *historic*. Now that we're attracting better students, getting some positive notice, you can't wait to take an axe to it. Why?" He leaned forward, his eyes taking on an unnatural blue-white glow. "Is it the money? Is it the prestige? Or are you just tired of waiting for fame and fortune?"

"What do you mean, when *I* first started here?" Whit snapped. "You wrote the checks, all right. But I pulled together the first teachers, the staff, the catalogue, the freaking *office machines*. This is my school as much as it is yours. Bernard is in touch with people he knows in the NEA, the Krasner Foundation," he held up his hands, ticking them off on his fingers. "—the Kellogg Institute, the Warhol Center, the Forbes Foundation—all eager to support us if we just add a few big names to the faculty roster. So they can't draw! So what? They have great connections. They need assistants. At the very least, they can teach the students how to *sound* like successful artists."

"The students don't want to be postmodernists, Whit," said Levon in a reasonable voice. "They came here because they want to be Rembrandt."

"Don't you get it?" Whit's face was red, the veins standing out in his neck. "We could be really big. *And you are holding us back.*"

"Whit." Rafe's voice was cajoling; strong, soft, inviting, an irresistible melody. "We are a small boutique art school, dedicated to the giving over of classical technique. After two very short years here, our graduates scatter to the ends of the earth. In time, they will pass on what they learn from us to their own students. Every course counts."

"Save the sales pitch for the debutantes," Whit snarled. "I've already heard it."

Rafe had never seen him angry before; his chin was trembling in outrage. For the first time, he noticed a gold cross hung on a filigreed chain around the Chairman of the Painting Department's neck. He was certain he hadn't seen it before. He leaned in for a closer look.

"Never knew you were Romanian Orthodox, Whit," he said quietly.

The two men confronted each other across Levon's desk. Turner's face was livid, a meaty purple. By contrast, the founder's expression was calm, clear-eyed, almost tranquil.

There was a soft knock. Bernard Blesser put his head around the door, looking for Whit. Upon seeing Rafe, he swallowed, blanched, almost backed out.

"Hello, Bernard," said Levon. "No, it's all right, we're finished here." Whit glared at Rafe one last time, wheeled and stomped out of the office.

The two men sat in silence for a moment.

"Well, we got it under control," said Levon. "That's the important thing."

"Yes, yes, of course." Rafe agreed.

At precisely the same moment, they burst into laughter.

"Can you believe Clayton? The sheer organization—the scope of the operation—he's a *genius.*"

"He couldn't have done it by himself."

"And Whit...his nose is so far up her ass—"

"—I thought his brain was going to *explode.*" They erupted in fresh laughter, Rafe bent over double, Levon pounding the desk and wiping away tears.

Eventually their laughter slowed to a stop, and the two men sat in silence, considering the consequences of the morning's events. Rafe picked up one of the picture frames on Levon's desk. Two teenagers with braces on their teeth smiled at him. The boy looked just like his father.

"How old are they?"

"Eliot is seventeen. Sharon is twenty-one."

"You never talk about them."

Levon steepled his fingers together, leaned back in his chair. "I didn't leave their mother on such good terms," he said. "I'm still trying to convince them that I'm not that guy anymore."

Rafe turned his gaze to him, observing his kind, creased face, the grizzled beard, the comfortable but very good sweater, the black felt driving cap that he knew covered a bald spot, the wire-rimmed glasses, the smile waiting to break into a guffaw. "It's hard to imagine you as anything other than Mr. Nice Guy."

"People change," said Levon. "It's hard to imagine you being friendly with Whit."

"We were never chummy. We had a common interest. I wanted to start an art school. And, as he rather heatedly pointed out, he knew who to call."

"Where did you meet him? I don't see you two frequenting the same circles, somehow."

A black-haired girl in a black tank top and black lipstick, blue tattoos of snakes coiled around her arms from elbow to shoulder swam into his memory, then receded back into the 80s. "We had a mutual acquaintance. One of his students. She was a tattoo artist, of all things. That was why she wanted classical training."

"Why doesn't April just quit?" Levon finally said, frowning. "She's got to know she isn't wanted."

"Her kind doesn't quit," Rafe said. "They conquer, kill everything that's still living, level the trees and buildings, then walk away, salting the earth behind them."

"Poor Tessa," said Levon, shaking his head. "Imagine being on the other side of that." Then he broke into a grin. "Nice, sweet Tessa! Who would have thought?"

A slight smile turned up the corners of Rafe's mouth. "Yes," he said. "Who would have thought."

21

$\mathcal{S}$ aturday night, and Harker was throwing a Christmas party. He lived with Katie in a grimy ground floor apartment in a narrow pocket of the East Village that had so far escaped gentrification, on Second Street, near First Avenue. Graham, David, Ben, Portia, Gracie and Nick were all well into their second beers by the time Tessa arrived, pink-cheeked and out of breath.

The music was deafening. Strings of colored lights crisscrossed the dim, low-ceilinged room. Tessa squinted through the haze of cigarette smoke; she didn't recognize anybody. The small apartment was packed with people who looked like they were in the music business, thin even by New York standards, dressed in black, long-haired, tattooed. Something made her look down. A large cockroach, the size of a man's thumb, was lumbering past her shoe. It had been sprayed with orange glow-in-the-dark paint. She could see another one making its way towards the kitchen, fluorescing a neon green.

David appeared at her side, and she smiled, happy to see him. She could smell his aftershave over the odors of sweat and beer. "We're out here," he said. Lightly, he took her elbow, guided her through the crowd to the yard. The Academy students had laid claim to the patio, where they were sitting in lawn chairs looking up at the stars.

Whatever light there was reflected on Graham's high white forehead, making him look wise. Tessa wondered why Gracie wasn't freezing her butt off in a box-pleated plaid skirt that was even shorter than usual. Portia was stretched out on a rusty chaise lounge, legs crossed at the ankle, hands shoved deep in the pockets of her navy pea coat for warmth.

"I thought you weren't going to show," shouted Portia over the music. "Aren't you supposed to be with Lucian tonight?"

"He had a meeting," said Tessa. "I'm going over there later." There was a startled look on her face, as if she had received an important piece of unexpected news she hadn't quite processed yet. Portia was about to ask her about it when Harker appeared. He looked lankier than usual in a pair of black stovepipe pants. Tonight he was wearing black horn-rimmed Buddy Holly glasses, making him look a bit like a Sixties campus radical. He kissed Tessa on the side of her cheek, thrust a Corona into her hand, balancing one of his hand-rolled cigarettes in the corner of his mouth.

"Welcome to Casa Miller," he said, gesturing out into the dark recesses of the yard. "Have you met the neighbors?"

The yard behind the apartment ran for some distance, stopping momentarily at an antiquated wrought iron gate, then rolled on into the darkness. Tessa made out one stationery shape in the near distance, and then another, and another.

"Are those...headstones?"

Harker chortled in delight, the cigarette bobbing up and down. "Yeah. Our place backs up to Marble Cemetery. Founded 1831. Ain't it creepy?"

A lean, dark-haired girl came outside looking for him, hugging her thin arms around herself to ward off the cold.

"Your daddy's really a preacher?" Ben said.

"Yeah. So is Katie's," he said, slinging his arm around his girlfriend and giving her a squeeze. She smiled at him, gathered up some empty glasses, headed back inside where it was warm.

"And he's okay with you two living together?" asked Graham, curious.

"Insisted on it," said Harker. "He figured she was safer that way." He pushed his hair back behind one ear. "Gotta see to the guests inside, man. There's an agent in there somewhere. Sonic Death Monkeys are rocking out CBGB's later tonight."

"Go get him, tiger," said Graham.

Tessa lowered herself gingerly into a shredding 1970s era webbed lawn chair. Happily, it held. "Hear anything from Clayton?" she asked Ben, who was reclining on the next lounge with his hands folded over his chest.

He shook his head no. His umber skin rendered him barely visible in the darkness of the backyard. "He'll be all right," he said. "He's been through worse."

She leaned in closer. "Levon told me he spent some time in an institution."

He sighed, a deep, troubled sound. "Clayton's father is in construction. And when I say he's in construction, I mean he built half the buildings in Jackson, Mississippi. Old South, a World War II veteran, saw half his buddies blown away on Omaha Beach, fondly remembers when black folks rode in the back of the bus. He wasn't really happy about his only son wanting to be an artist. That's how it is down South. God first, then football. He told him art was for faggots, boys play sports. Well, you know Clayton. There were daily battles all through his school years, real knockdown, drag-out, take-no-prisoners affairs.

"He told me he tried sports; freshman year he did a half-assed job playing baseball, sophomore year a half-assed job wrestling, but at night, in the privacy of his own room, he was sculpting little clay figures when he should have been doing homework. When his daddy found out—a maid found them under the bed and brought it to his attention—he went ballistic. Smashed them to bits. Put him in a nut house, kept him there for six months."

"Wow," she said, shocked. "I had no idea."

The talk drifted on to a discussion of the upcoming Christmas vacation. The lawn chair was deceptively comfortable. It was one of those mild December nights you get sometimes in the city, the air fresh and smelling of fallen leaves, earth and wood smoke. Tessa burrowed deep into her scarf, leaving only her eyes visible. Resting her head against the frayed webbing of her chair, she gazed up at the sky, colored a murky reddish purple by the lights of Manhattan, and let the conversation eddy on without her.

Zaydie was in the emergency room again. During lunch at Uncle Allen's house, his head went down and he slumped over on the table. It was only for a moment—he had revived seconds later, said ach, it was nothing—but Allen called an ambulance and rushed him to the hospital.

Hesitantly, her mother had added, "There's something else, Tessa." And proceeded to tell her that her grandfather's name was not Abe Moss, but Yechezkel Wizotsky.

Reeling in shock, Tessa had barely comprehended the rest of the story. In the summer of 1944, after the Soviets liberated Wlodawa, they'd drafted him into the Red Army. For the price of a bottle of vodka, he was able to bribe a guard to smuggle him out of their encampment, dressed in women's clothing. To confound the agents who would surely come after deserters, he changed Wizotsky to Moscowicz, his mother's maiden name. Later on, when the immigration officer at Ellis Island couldn't pronounce the Hebrew name Yechezkel, he said, "Okay, Abie," and inscribed the simpler Abraham Moskowitz onto his papers. Zaydie, eager to leave the ashes of Europe behind him, signed on the dotted line. A couple of years later, when he saw his suppliers struggling with the name Moskowitz, he shortened it to Moss.

"Don't tell anyone," her mother warned her. "Zaydie's still afraid the KGB is coming to get him. He's only telling us now because he thinks he's going to die."

Her father's voice in the background. They were leaving for the hospital. Her mother said a harried goodbye and hung up the phone.

Someone was talking to her. Portia was looking at her curiously. She had just asked her for the second time if she had plans for Christmas.

She forced herself back to the present. "I'll be here. No plans to go back to Chicago anytime soon."

"What about Lucian?"

"Always goes to England for the week. His old school chum made it big in television over there, he has some grand manor house on the River Tweed or something."

"So you'll join us!" Portia said gleefully. For the seven days between Christmas and New Years, her parents would be at the villa of an Italian noble they had met while sailing to Turkey. Graham needed to save money, he was sticking around to work on his thesis. Harker's band was signed for gigs all through Christmas week. And Witnesses didn't celebrate Christmas, so Ben would be staying on in New York.

"I could always go to my grandfather's place in the city," she admitted. "But I think I'd rather be in Newport. I'm inviting everybody who can't be with family. Come on, it'll be fun!"

"Newport?"

"Rhode Island. My family has a place there, a cottage."

"Um. Okay," she agreed, envisioning the lot of them crammed together into a thatched hut, something from *Snow White and the Seven Dwarfs*.

The music changed. It was Dee Lite and *Groove is in the Heart* now. Gracie and Nick got up to dance. David looked over at Tessa, smiling, raising his eyebrows, an invitation. For a moment, she thought of Lucian. Not for the first time, she wondered if April had called him to cry on his shoulder over Friday's prank, and a pang of remorse stole into her heart. Then she smiled back at David and got up to dance.

Later that night, they all ended up at CBGB's to see Harker's band. As expected, the Sonic Death Monkeys rocked the house. It was packed, the walls resonating with heavy bass vibrations and pre-holiday excitement. The art students drank, danced, sweated, shouted until they were hoarse, pumped their fists into the air along with the rest of the downtown creatures of the night, and at two in the morning they emerged from the club, spent, sweaty, deafened, steam rising off of their overheated bodies in the cold air.

The weather had changed in the few hours that they had been inside the club. The sky had cleared and the temperature had dropped twenty degrees, a sharp wind penetrating their damp clothing. For a few moments they huddled together before breaking off into smaller groups and heading off into different directions, and it was in that moment that Tessa felt someone watching her. Turning around, she was sure she saw something, a glimpse of billowing coattails, disappearing around the corner into a dim and gritty side street. Curious, she waited for a figure to cross the puddle of light under the streetlamp.

But the sidewalk was empty. A homeless man was sleeping on a pile of flattened cardboard boxes in a doorway; this was the Bowery, after all, the wide boulevard lined with SRO's and shelters. After a moment she shrugged and turned back to her friends, attributing the mirage to the lateness of the hour and the beer.

22

*T*he first flyer was spotted a few days before Christmas, fluttering from a telephone pole at Spring Street and West Broadway.

I have a show opening at OK Solomon, it said under the by-now familiar photograph of April spread-legged on Lucian's bed. *New Paintings, by April Huffman.*

By lunchtime, they had been sighted all over downtown. Legions of them were pasted in long rows along the temporary scaffolding used as informal kiosks all over the city. Hundreds more papered the sides of buildings, stapled over posters for movies and upcoming concerts. The flyers had sprung up overnight, defacing every lamp and telephone pole between Broadway and the Hudson River. It was all anyone could talk about.

"Well," said Graham. "She's a genius at marketing herself. You've got to give her props."

"Are we going?" David asked Portia.

"Are you kidding? When's the opening?"

"Thursday night," said Tessa, the steel door that led in from the stairway shutting behind her. Sculpture had just ended, and she was hauling a small statuette of a woman standing in contrapasto, hands linked fetchingly behind her back, surprisingly heavy for its size. It was the product of a six week pose with the model named Sivan, petite but well-proportioned, a back like a cello, a pear-shaped bottom, slim cylindrical arms, long curly hair. Tessa was considering using Sivan as a model for her thesis project.

"What do you reckon she's done this time?" said Harker. "I mean, how many impressionist blow job paintings can you sell?"

"Maybe she's tried a new medium this time," said David.

"Decoupage," suggested Graham. "Or maybe she's doing portraits now. You know. From the waist down."

There was a commotion in the back of the room. Clayton had materialized in front of the sculptors' studio, where he was grabbing a thrashing Gracie around the waist and throwing himself backwards onto the floor. His big body broke her fall. "Come on, show me some love!" he was bellowing.

"What about you, Tessa?" David prodded her. "Are you going?"

Tessa made a sad face. "Gee, I have to work Thursday night. So sorry."

"Come on, Tessa," he coaxed. "One hour, one lousy hour. Free white wine. It's bound to be terrible. Aren't you even a little bit curious?"

In final days before winter break, Tessa had already handed in her History of Composition report, using up a dozen sheets of tracing paper to analyze the horizontal, vertical and diagonal movements in Hopper's *Nighthawks*. She wasn't through with Whit's Perspective assignment yet, it was taking longer than she had expected. Tomorrow was the due date, no exceptions, so she would be working late into the night.

By now, they were supposed to be well along in their thesis projects. Ben was steadily working on a huge slab of gray clay, to which he continually fastened small, writhing forms. When Tessa peered closer, she could see the figures were all trapped, desperately struggling to escape. She'd looked to him for explanation.

"It's my *Gates of Hell*," he said, referring to Rodin's famous doors. "We're all trying to get away from something."

Portia had decided on a series of paintings with the theme of childhood. Her sketches had a delicately unbalanced Diane Arbus quality to them, as if the children who populated them were negotiating through an unsafe world. Harker was making portraits of people he knew in the East Village; a waitress at Veselka, a Halal butcher, a club kid who said she was a vampire.

Graham was doing biblical art. "Aren't they a little, um, *too* classical?" Tessa asked cautiously, looking at the sketches on his wall. "I mean, we're supposed to be fighting this image of being stuck in the past."

Leafing through a Rembrandt book, he shrugged, bored with the argument. "What do I care what people think? If I want to paint Saint

Sebastian, the sexiest saint, or Sergius and Bacchus, martyred for the love that dares not speak its name, I will. Why do I have to get the art establishment's Good Housekeeping Seal of Approval first?"

The only student who seemed completely up in the air was Clayton. Upon returning from his two-week suspension, he'd mocked up a table full of clay figurines, all genders and subject matters. There was a Minotaur, holding its huge horned head as if it had a headache. To this he had added a pair of wrestlers, a rearing horse, two women embracing, a bust of his own head.

There was also a ghostly winged figure spreading its arms in welcome, a skeletal face hidden by a cloak, ragged drapery suspended behind it like it was whipped by the wind. When she asked him what it meant, he wrapped his arms around her waist and flew backwards into the air. Tessa experienced a momentary feeling of weightlessness before bouncing onto Clayton's hard abdomen. She'd struggled to her feet, feeling confused and a little embarrassed while the first-year students who were gathered around brayed with laughter and he grinned like a devil, or a fool.

Late one night, as they lay sprawled across the beat-up couches in the lounge area near the windows, finished with their work but too exhausted to go home, she finally related the convoluted history of her family name.

"Holy cow," Ben said. "So technically, you're Tessa Wizotsky."

She'd shaken her head, at a loss for words. There had been a moment of silence that stretched on and on, a bit too long for comfort. Perhaps it was too unimaginably foreign for them, the children and grandchildren and great-grandchildren of Americans, longtime citizens of nice, safe, US of A.

"Atwood wasn't my family's original name either," David offered. "It was Blumenfrucht."

Portia and Gracie tried to pronounce it, tripping on the guttural *ch* sound. Graham had gotten closer than the others, though it still sounded like he had something caught in his throat. "It's *beautiful*," he insisted, laughing.

"It's a very pretty name." David said, with great dignity. "It means fruit blossom, in German." Which only made them laugh harder.

She remembered that David was still looking at her, hoping she would join them later. Throwing her backpack over her shoulder, she shifted the dead weight of her sculpture to her other arm. "Sorry, guys," she apologized. "Can't make it. Got to get to my studio. Lots of work to do before the night is out. Lucian doesn't want to go to April's opening. He scheduled his flight at the same time as her stupid show, just out of spite. You'll just have to manage without me."

The last student, a sculptor, left at 11:45. She heard his footsteps echo down the aisle, and the boom of the steel door as it closed behind him.

Tessa was on her knees on the floor of her studio, sheets of 18" x 24" paper spread out all around her. She held her weary head in her hands, exhausted, out of ideas.

Perspective hated her. Perspective wanted her to fail, wanted to break her, bite her in the ass, wanted to bring her down.

The long and short of it was, her plan was not working. The buildings looked all right, simple rectangles grouped around a fountain in a plaza, but the obelisk was slanted in a funny way. The cone she had plotted at the top of a tower was tilting over, undeniably wrong. Something had to be missing; the flat, graphed, two-dimensional plan, transferred by a series of lines and angles called vators into a fully three-dimensional drawing, was off somewhere.

Tessa dug her hands into her hair and squeezed as if it would extract the formula that would save her drawing. Desperate for a distraction, she turned the tape over in her boom box, pressed down the forward key.

Dies irae! Dies illa! Solvet saeclum in favilla...teste David cum Sybilla....

The choir shrieked out its warning, the music thundered up the empty aisle and across the deserted floor. Raphael Sinclair stood framed in the doorway.

Something like, fear, or excitement, took hold deep in the pit of her belly. For the first time, she wasn't startled, though her heart still knocked a tattoo against her chest, *boom boom boom boom boom boom,* he could almost feel it in the close air of the studio.

He stared at her, not smiling. She couldn't read his expression, and a feeling of shame crept over her as she began to wonder if he was there to tell her how disappointed he was with her for the April Huffman fiasco, how much damage she had done to his school. Perhaps he had waited till everyone else had left to save her the embarrassment.

"Look, I'm sorry," she said hurriedly. "I'm sorry about the April Huffman thing. I never meant to harm anyone. I would never do anything to hurt the school. I don't know what came over me. Please don't ask me to leave. I belong here."

It was his turn to be startled. "You're sorry?" he said in amazement. "I'm the one who's sorry, Tessa. That you felt you must...that you were driven to..." His lovely, lulling voice was colored with regret. "You were placed in an impossible position. I'm sorry we didn't protect you."

"It's not your fault," she said. "How could you have known?"

He saw that she was trying to comfort him, and he was touched. "I should have known," he said, looking directly at her with those extraordinary eyes, bright, like beams of light.

"I've missed you," he said, surprising both of them.

It was cold. At night the thermostat was turned down to save money, and it was particularly chilly in the studios, where the wind easily found the gaps in the old window frames. He noticed that Tessa had taken to wearing gloves with the fingers cut off to keep warm as she worked.

"I haven't seen you in a while," she said.

If anything, her studio was even more inviting at night, the light from a rusted vintage 1930s torchiere suffusing it with an orange hue, like an old photograph, or a memory. A flurry of new postcards were tacked up on her wall. A single house silhouetted against the sky, blue with lengthening evening shadows, crouched before a railroad track. Preternatural black-and-white photographs of children with angels' wings. *Nighthawks,* by Edward Hopper. A long time ago, he had wanted to paint just like Hopper, scenes filled with raw light and his own loneliness.

She watched him, privately enjoying the way his body bowed and flexed as he reached out to straighten a postcard, swooped down to peer behind a portfolio.

"You're working late," he said.

"Perspective assignment," she said grimly. "Not my best subject."

"Let's have a look," he said. "I used to be pretty good at Perspective." Unbelievably, he crouched down in his spotless trench coat, sweeping the gritty floor with his coattails. After a moment, she squatted down, joining him.

"Oh, yes. That tower's not right, is it." He frowned, concentrating, scanning the drawings. His eyes moved from one paper to the next, following the lines on the graph to their terminus. One finger slid slowly down a ray, then stopped.

"There. That one."

She squinted at it, trying to see what he meant. Then she saw it; she had made a tick mark one-sixteenth of an inch too low. She went for a yellow pencil, carefully erased the tower, moved the tick mark, redrew the tower. It was definitively better.

"Thanks," she said with obvious relief. "Now I can start on my self-portrait for Ted. And my sketches for Josephine."

He looked at her in disbelief. "Do you have any idea what time it is?" He tapped the face of his expensive-looking watch. Both hands pointed to midnight. "Go home."

"I'm meeting with her tomorrow," she said wanly, rubbing her eyes. "I have to be ready."

"How is that going?" He stood back up, brushing off his coat.

"She threw out two of my sketches. She wants me to lose the mother and child, too, but I told her I would make it work."

His face registered surprise. The sketch was tacked up on the wall in front of him, the suitcase reading *Wizotsky* like a reprimand from the grave. A pencil drawing was tacked up beside it, an old woman in a babushka surrounded by a hundred burning memorial candles. "I haven't seen this one," he said.

"It's my grandmother," she said. "Every holiday she lights these memorial candles. One for every member of her family that was lost. It drives Zaydie crazy," she added, smiling. "He tells her she should just light one, she's going to burn the whole house down."

So warm, so intimate, the crimson couch, the orange light, the Persian rug, the girl. There was a new addition, a fretted hexagonal coffee table painted Venetian red, somebody's souvenir of a long-ago college trip to Morocco. A small wooden crate of clementines sat on the table's patterned surface, filling the room with its fragrance. He never wanted to leave.

His eyes fell on her sculpture. With its round bottom and nipped-in waist, the little clay figure reminded him of her. He touched it, ran his fingers over its curves. Tessa thought she could feel the warmth of his hand.

"How was your Thanksgiving?" he said. "Home to the heartland, wasn't it?"

She made a smile that was more of a grimace. "Best not mentioned."

"Why is that?"

"I don't know," she said. Then, a confessional rush of words. "That's a lie. I do know. My grandfather had a heart attack at Thanksgiving dinner."

"How awful," he said, drawing closer.

"I showed him my sketches. I thought he would be proud of me." Her voice was couched in remorse. "I should have known better."

"I'm sure he's very proud of you," Rafe said gently.

She sighed. Like a flash of light illuminating something hidden in a drawer, or under a bed, he understood that he was mistaken, she was entirely correct, her family wasn't proud of her at all.

"My grandfather thinks art is a waste of time," she said. Then, with a maturity that was poignant in someone so young, she explained, "I'm not exactly what my family had in mind."

"I wasn't exactly what my parents had in mind, either," he said.

He wanted to reach out, touch the tangle of curls on her shoulder, but of course he couldn't. She was tying on her black waiter's apron now, taking the brown-paper wrapping off of a creamy white sheet of Bristol board. He roamed through the small space, dodging stacks of canvases, inspecting her most recent work.

It was clear that Tessa's talent had grown over the course of the semester. Her drawing had become more fluid, assured, her compositions more sophisticated. Her paintings, even ordinary studio poses, filled him with yearning, he could not explain why. Seeing her progress thrilled him. The program he had created was working; she had already surpassed some of her teachers.

She was dragging an old oak office chair before a small mirror. She clipped the paper to her drawing board, and balanced it on her lap.

"Is it true?" she asked, concentrating on her image in the mirror. "That we're running out of money?"

"Yes," he said, uneasily eyeing the mirror.

"Is there anything we can do? I mean, the students."

He sighed, lifted his hat, raked his fingers through his hair. When he raised his arm she caught a glimpse of the lining of his suit, a brilliant crimson. "Whit's right," he admitted. "We really do need to attract support from big foundations. But they all want us to have famous names on our faculty roster. And there aren't many art stars with classical backgrounds. Lucian Swain, for instance. Where did he go to art school?"

She frowned, trying to remember. "Some local college near Portsmouth, I think. They taught commercial art. How to draw soup cans, fashion illustration. Then he went to Slade."

"Slade," he pronounced it as if it were an obscenity. "You're already better than he is. What can he possibly teach you?"

It wasn't the shape of his eyes, she thought, or their size, or the shifting color behind the fringe of dark lashes. He looked like he could see right through her, into the darkest corners, her squirmiest secrets, and whatever those might be, he accepted it, took her side, understood completely.

"Um. Well, he taught me a lot of things."

"Really." He was circling the small room, his back to her. "Like what?"

He smelled of sandalwood. It wafted through the studio as he moved, a sweet counterpoint to the odor of turpentine. *Concentrate.* "Like how to talk to someone at a gallery," she replied, with some difficulty. "How to present my work. How to come off like a professional." *How to make tea the British way, steeping the leaves in a brown ceramic pot. That Kona coffee beans from Balducci's are the best and need to be ground just so. How to twirl a whisk in the Cadbury's drinking chocolate so that it gets all foamy at the top, just the way he likes it. How to hold hands with someone who's dying. How to pretend that everything is fine when the whole world is falling down around my head.*

He turned, smiled at her. "Those *are* useful things to know. Maybe I've been wrong about these post-modernist blokes."

He had purposely stayed away from her since Thanksgiving. It was just too risky. Being near her made him throb with all kinds of hunger, made him want to throw her on the tufted couch and pull off her clothes. He filled his nights with balls and benefits, and the women who attended them.

He caught a glimpse of her outside CBGB's late Saturday night, where he had come after one thing or another at the Museum of Contemporary Art. He melted into a doorway before she could get a good look, but she saw him, he knew it; she stared his way for a long moment before turning back to her friends. He'd drawn deeper into the shadows until she moved on, his hand over the mouth of a pink-haired girl who was dozing off to a drug-enhanced sleep on his shoulder, just to be safe.

With the night growing colder, and a sharp wind biting through the flaps of his overcoat, he had tried to puzzle it out. Over the decades, he'd known hundreds of women. Women more beautiful than Tessa, more educated, more experienced, more accomplished, more exotic. And yet she was all he could think of, all he could see when he closed his eyes. Making mindless small talk at endless cocktail parties, he smiled down at poised and polished faces and wondered if she was working late in her studio. He couldn't explain it; something about the girl felt like home.

She was frowning at her own face in the mirror, her head tipped to one side. He glanced at her drawing. On paper, she was unsmiling, her expression apprehensive, doubtful.

"You're prettier than that," he said.

She smiled politely. He could tell she thought that he was trying to be nice. She turned the charcoal stick lengthways to lay in a shadow for the side of her face.

"We saw you in the *Post,*" she said. "There were pictures of you on Page Six. The opening of the Matisse Exhibition. You were with a girl in a white dress."

"Oh, yes. Oleander Haier."

"She's beautiful." Meaning. *Is she your girlfriend?*

"She's a big donor."

She erased a smudge. "Oh, I see," she said.

"Tessa," he said.

She turned, looked up at him. He leaned down and kissed her pink lips, her raspberry mouth, his hand resting lightly on the side of her face, and it was just as he knew it would be, a blurry rush of warmth and light. The part of him that had once been an ordinary man, with ordinary hopes of coming home at night to a pretty girl who looked at him as if he could change the world stirred, came roaring back to life.

He pulled away, retreated to a safe distance. She was staring at him, her mouth slightly ajar.

"I'm sorry," he said quickly. "I shouldn't have done that."

"I," she said shakily, then lapsed into mortified silence. Not because he had kissed her, but because she had liked it, she wanted it to go on and on, she wanted to take his face in her hands and kiss him back.

"I'm—it's just that..."

"I know," he put his hands up, stopped her. "I know. I'm sorry. It won't happen again."

"No, you don't know," she said helplessly, her eyes wide and stunned. "I wanted you to. I liked it. I liked it a lot. Too much. It's just that I...Lucian..."

He nodded vigorously. So good, so devoted, so loyal. If only Lucian Swain deserved it. "I understand. Really. You don't have to explain yourself. I don't know what came over me."

"I should go home," she said.

"Yes, of course," he said automatically. "Let me put you in a cab."

He held her coat for her, a ratty, tatty heathered thing that smelled like a goat and looked like she had gotten it off a dead man. As she raised her hair up over the collar, there was a flash of white neck, a whiff of her blackberry scent, and he closed his eyes, shuddering with the wanting of her.

She reached up, turned off the reflector lamps. "Oh, Mr. Sinclair. I meant to tell you. I asked my grandmother whether she ever knew a Sofia Wizotsky."

"What did she say?"

"That was when my grandfather had his heart attack."

"God. I'm sorry to have had any part in that."

She shouldered her backpack. "Turns out my grandfather is not Abe Moss, after all. He changed his name during the war to escape being drafted into the Russian army. His real name is Wizotsky."

Rafe stood rooted to the spot. "I'm sorry," he said, very slowly, and very deliberately. "Could you repeat that, please?"

"My grandfather's last name is Wizotsky," she said, staring at him.

"That can't be," he protested. "It can't be. They all died in the war. I checked the lists for years. There were no survivors." Suddenly, he needed a smoke. Panicking, he patted himself down, ransacking his pockets until he found a stale cigarette jammed in a lining. Clenching it between his lips, he put an arm out to steady himself.

"Let me get you a chair," she said quickly, turning to grab her shabby office chair.

With the lights off, the floor-to-ceiling windows became mirrors, reflecting the objects in the room in their black depths like some evil alternate reality. She frowned at the reflection in the window. Something wasn't right. True, the hour was late, the lighting was poor, and she was very tired. She closed her eyes, then looked again. *Trick of the light,* she told herself. *I'm in the wrong spot. It's the angle.*

She could see herself as clearly as if she were looking into a mirror, shadows under her eyes, hair frizzed out to there. She could make out Gracie's drawings, the lamps, the couch, the new table. But Raphael Sinclair, standing right behind her—well, *he just wasn't there.*

The truth came to her all at once. As she backed away from him, she knocked her shin against the chair. It rotated in lazy circles behind her.

"What *are* you?" she whispered.

Rafe snapped back to the present. Tessa's eyes were darting from his face to the window, then back again, and with a sickening swiftness, he understood. *The windows. I forgot about the bleeding windows.* With a dizzying sensation of overwhelming inevitability, he understood that the game was up, the part of the story where he was a harmless visiting benefactor was over, and the next chapter already begun.

"I think you know exactly what I am," he said, crushing the cigarette beneath his shoe. "Come on, Tessa. You must have heard the rumors."

He walked slowly towards her, feeling the rising tide of her fear as she backed away. "Is that what this has been about all along? You just want to..." She blanched a deathly white.

He stopped a safe distance away. "To drink your blood? No. I'm not going to hurt you. I'm a wealthy man. This is New York. I can buy anything I need."

She drew a ragged breath, not believing him.

"Come on, Tessa. If I was going to harm you, it would have already happened by now. God knows, I've had plenty of opportunity."

She mulled that over. Curiously, now. "So...you're really a vampire?"

"Yes," he said.

"And you have to drink blood to live."

"Yes."

"Aren't you afraid I'm going to give away your secret?"

"No," he said. "Not really."

"Why not? Aren't you afraid of what people would say? Of what people would do?"

"This is New York City. Here, you can be anyone you want to be."

She thought about that for a while. "Does anyone else know?"

"A few people."

"Is Levon one of them?"

"No."

"Whit?"

"I don't think so. Though he has his suspicions."

She scoured her memory for all the vampire lore she had ever heard. "Are you really afraid of the cross?"

"No, not particularly."

"What about garlic?"

"A mild deterrent."

"Holy water?"

He rolled his eyes.

A thought occurred to her. "Are you really immortal?"

"Yes. Well, to a point. I can still die. Stake through the heart, sunlight and all that."

"I don't like sunlight either," she confessed. "If I'm in the sun for more than thirty seconds, I burn."

He smiled. The color was returning to her face. She was already accepting it.

"Do you have to sleep in a coffin filled with dirt from your homeland?"

"I sleep on a very nice, very thick, extra-soft pillow-top Stearns and Foster mattress, thank you very much."

"Do you have demon brides and evil minions? Clayton wanted to know."

"No. At least, none that I know of."

"Have you ever hurt anyone?"

He hesitated, nodded.

"Killed anyone?"

He nodded again, slower this time. That shook her. She went white again.

"But I don't do that anymore," he added hastily. "I have to drink blood. I don't have to be a killer."

"Oh," she said.

Her eyes were wide and terrified. Terrified of *him*. It made him ache to see it. He wished things could be back the way they were five minutes ago, when he was the mysterious and very sexy founder of the school paying her a private late night visit instead of a vicious killer promising not to hurt her. The thrall. He would use the thrall.

"Look at me, Tessa," he said softly. "Look in my eyes." *Forget everything you've seen, everything you've heard.*

But she was watching him closely, her eyebrows knitting together, flying apart, alive with questions, afraid of the answers. With a sigh, he gave up. It went that way once in a while; some people were just immune to it.

Well, he thought grimly. *In for a penny, in for a pound. No way out but through.*

"You must have more questions," he said. "Go on."

"Is it true that you don't have a heartbeat?"

He reached for her hand. She didn't try to pull away. He peeled off the glove, slipped her fingers under his jacket, laid her hand over his heart and held it there. Her eyes clouded with horrified wonder, then, affectingly, tears.

"How did you... when did you become a..."

He fixed his gaze on her, so full of unrelenting sorrow, that despite her worst fears, her heart fluttered, just a little.

"I was in art school in Paris," he said. "There was this marvelous girl. She was kind and gifted and beautiful, from a town on the far eastern border of Poland, where her family had a tea importing company. On the night she married another man, I went out to drown my sorrows. I picked up the wrong girl. She left me dead on the cobblestones outside a bloody bucket called The Lamb and Jackal in the center of London. The date was August 23, 1939."

"Which one was she?" she asked. "Sofia, I mean. The marvelous girl or the vampire?"

"The marvelous girl," he said.

"What happened to her?" she said. "To Sofia."

Somehow, he had not been prepared for this. He turned his head away; she saw him swallow hard, saw a muscle in his jaw jump. "She died, I think. In Auschwitz. In the winter of 1943."

"Oh my God," she whispered.

"You remind me of her," he said to her reflection in the window. "Every day. Since the first time I saw you."

Across the street, the lights at the Astor Theatre advertising Blue Man Group flickered and went out. Four storeys below, the metal shutters clanked and rattled as the Korean deli closed down for the night. Goth girls in high heels laughed together as they clacked past the school and on down Lafayette Street towards the clubs. On the fourth floor of the American Academy of Classical Art, it was quiet enough to hear the ticking of a clock on the wall in the sculptors' studio, quiet enough to hear the creaks of the old factory building settling further into the bedrock underlying Manhattan.

She picked up her drawing board and tucked it under her arm, bringing him with a wrench back to the present. He glanced at his watch. One o'clock. "Let me put you in a taxi," he said.

He followed behind her to the end of the floor, her bright curls bouncing with every step. In the elevator, he was careful not to crowd her. When they reached the ground floor, she scurried though the lobby and out to the street, hungry for the safety of public spaces. The whorls of her hair whipped and churned as if they were in torment, making her look like an anguished Medusa.

He could see that her tatty coat was no defense against the sharp wind, and it made him want to put his arms around her. Instead, he stepped out into the street, put out his hand. A taxi crossed three lanes, screeched to a stop beside them.

He turned to her. He had not stopped to close his coat, and it flapped and billowed in the icy wind. His arms opened wide, in unconscious imitation of the marble angel that stood at the foot of the double staircase in his townhouse. "Tessa," he said. "It doesn't define me. It's not who I am."

She nodded, her face half-hidden in her scarf.

He opened the cab door for her. She slid onto the leather seat. He knocked on the driver's window, handed him some bills, told him where to go. Then he closed the door and stepped back onto the curb.

She rolled down her window. "Say," she said abruptly. "Are you going to the April Huffman opening on Thursday night?"

"I don't know," he said. "Why?"

"Bite her for me, will you?" she said.

He stared at her in surprise as the taxi pulled away into traffic, then began to laugh. He watched until it rounded Astor Square, where it shot up Fourth Street and out of sight.

23

*J*osephine never showed up for their meeting the next day. Perhaps it was a misunderstanding, perhaps it was a babysitting conflict. At any rate, four o'clock came and went with no word from her advisor. At five o'clock, Tessa packed up her gear and headed downtown.

She was driving Lucian to JFK for a seven-thirty flight. Then she was supposed to return his old green Citroen to the parking garage for the week, after which time she would take it to the airport to pick him up.

Tessa reached his loft at 5:15 p.m. At the top of the stairs, she knocked, then pushed the door open. She dropped her knapsack on a chair. His bags were packed and waiting on the refectory table, alongside an empty bottle of non-alcoholic wine and a couple of smudgy glasses, a stack of bills, a list of AA meetings in London, today's *Times.*

She called his name. But the apartment was empty; he must be taking in a last AA meeting before his trip, she decided. There would be massive drinking, on a UK level, all week long at Stephen's place in the country, there always was, and he had told her he was worried about slipping.

She went into the studio. A pile of photographs on her table needed to be filed away, and she took care it, putting them neatly in color coded folders with stickers marked *Men Walking, Women Seated, Bill Clinton, Judy Garland,* and two hundred other categories he might need on any given day. She slipped the folders in alphabetical order onto the shelves, where they would reside until they were needed again.

From the studio, she went to the kitchen, where there were dishes and a frying pan left in the sink. She washed them, left them to dry on a dishtowel, then sat down on the le Corbusier couch to wait.

At six-thirty, he still had not returned. She looked at the clock, did the calculations. If there was no traffic, she would get him there at the very earliest, seven, half an hour before his flight, still worth a run for the gate. But there would be traffic; it was high rush hour, on the busiest travel day of the year. The Van Wyck would be crawling, at best. They should have left an hour ago. He had already missed his flight.

Perhaps there was a note. She looked under the bags, under the table. In the studio, she searched her desk and his drawing table, finding nothing more significant than some doodles on a lined yellow pad.

By seven o'clock, she understood that his plans had changed. Something must have come up. As a last resort, she thought to check her answering machine. But there was only a message from Portia, telling her they were meeting at April's gallery on West Broadway at seven.

There was nothing else to do. Before she locked up, she wrote Lucian a note; she wanted him to know she had been there, she had left, and that he could find her at home. *I love you,* she signed it. *Tessa.* She anchored it under his bag, took one last look around, and closed the door behind her.

It had warmed up since the day before. The sky was clear and glittered with stars, the air crisp and full of possibilities. She could smell wood smoke and the agreeable odor of grilling steak coming from just up ahead. Her stomach growled; she hadn't eaten since noon. She sprinted across the rush hour traffic snarling the length of Canal Street, passed the cherry red facade of Pearl Paint, and turned up Greene Street.

The sidewalks of Soho were clogged with pink-cheeked shoppers, all in a hurry to be somewhere else. Passersby smiled holiday greetings as they scurried past one another with their shopping bags. The storefronts had an enticing yellow warmth to them in the holiday dusk, their windows overflowing with beautiful things that nobody needed.

Automatically, she turned left at Spring Street, then right at West Broadway. Her legs carried her forward, having formulated a plan her mind had not yet agreed upon. OK Solomon lay straight ahead, before the intersection with Prince Street.

She would meet Portia and David at April's opening after all. Perhaps there would be hors d'ouevres, at the very least, free white wine. She could use a laugh. She looked at her watch. It was already 7:30. She picked up the pace, hoping she hadn't missed them.

There was a crowd gathered on the wide pavement outside the gallery, five deep. A few steps closer, she saw why.

The gallery's windows displayed a tableau of six men and women. A model stood with his arms at his sides, his weight supported by his right leg, in a classic contrapasto position. A light-haired Adonis reclined on a sculptor's stand, revolving in slow circles. An auburn-haired beauty straddled the back of an Eames chair, the vee between her thighs both masked and echoed by the curvilinear design. Three women stood with their arms twined around each other, like Graces.

They were, of course, completely naked. Even Tessa, used to looking at bare flesh for as long as six hours a day, was taken aback. Seeing them displayed in the windows as if they were merchandise made it deliberately sexual. Maybe it was the way they were staring confrontationally back at the viewers on the sidewalk, heavy-lidded with postmodernist irony.

New Works by April Huffman, said the white letters printed in Futura on the window. Tessa walked up the two steps, and went in through the frosted glass door.

She stopped just inside. To the right was a table of plastic tumblers, filled halfway with white wine. To the left was another table bearing Camembert and crackers. Hung at even distances around the walls were a dozen paintings in April's signature style.

April with her legs twined around the head of a dark-haired male figure. April on her knees, her eyes closed and her mouth open. A close up of April with her head in an anonymous male lap. April tongue-kissing a German Shepherd. An interesting composition that appeared to be the view of an erect penis as seen from between April's legs.

Tessa circled around a statuette displayed on a pedestal in the center of the room. A naked ceramic April on all fours, being serviced from behind. Apparently, she had taken up sculpting. Harvey would have given her a C.

In another corner, a screening area played the documentary film she made on Dissection Day over and over again in a continuous loop. April looking faintly demonic, waving a scalpel around and slicing into a helpless cadaver. Behind her, Graham could be seen ducking out of the way.

Tessa moved between throngs of people who all seemed to know one another, massed in circles large and small, all dressed in varying shades and textures of black and nearly black. The conversational level was just below the level of a roar.

"This is new for her. Look at her surfaces!" she heard someone exclaim. "Her study of anatomy has really moved her work forward," someone answered. "The way she uses color!" said a skeletal man with a shaved head and a Teutonic accent. "Her audacity!" said a petite, dark-haired woman who seemed to know.

Finally, bathed in the spotlight being cast by a video camera, Tessa saw the artist herself. She was framed by an enormous painting that took up the entire back wall of the gallery, dressed in a mannish white shirt and fitted black pants, all sleek hair and red lipstick. She had dyed her hair brown again, Tessa noticed, and she was talking animatedly into a mike being held by a television reporter.

Behind her, standing a little way out of the spotlight, was Lucian, his arms folded, looking proud and happy.

Now Tessa looked at the painting. It was very large, perhaps ten feet wide and six feet tall. As she focused on it, the background grew familiar; she knew that Indian print bedspread, she knew the blue glow of that particular 1930s airplane lamp. With a great heaviness, a feeling of gravity that threatened to pull her down to the floor, she slowly, reluctantly, let her eyes drift to the figures.

April Huffman's pale-skinned back, her straight dark hair, her bony knees, her small flat ass, her legs straddling her partner's sides as she mounted him, the famous painter Lucian Swain.

The interview must have ended, because the cameraman turned off his spotlight and moved away. April turned to Lucian, who smiled brightly and folded her into an ecstatic embrace.

There was a tightness in Tessa's chest. The babbling noise in the room grew louder, the voices garishly high-pitched. Darkness swelled around her, beating the air like a murder of crows taking to the sky. The voices inside the gallery rose to the level of a shriek.

It was intolerably hot inside the crowded space; when did it get so hot? She could feel her face burning. She turned and tried to make her way to the door, but there were too many people. The exit seemed very far away.

"Hey there, girlfriend!" exclaimed Portia, pushing the door open.

"You're here!" said David with a surprised smile. "Is it as bad as we thought?"

She groped past them into the night. Outside, with the breeze fanning her skin, she stopped for a moment, blowing out gusts of white vapor. Seeing her, a passerby might have thought she was uncertain about in which direction she should be heading.

And then tears began streaking down her face. She swiped at them with the back of her hand and started moving, stepping heedlessly into traffic, weaving through the cars coming down West Broadway. At Prince Street, she broke into a run, disappearing into the yellow night.

In a taxi coming down West Broadway, Raphael Sinclair felt a massive jolt in the atmosphere, followed by a sudden vertigo. He reached for the side of the car to steady himself.

"You all right?" said Levon, concerned.

"Yes, I'm fine. Headache," he forced a smile, rubbing his fingertips in a slow circle on his temple.

Levon struggled with his cane as Rafe paid the driver. "Knee's really bothering me tonight," he puffed as Rafe gave him a hand.

"You really should see a doctor."

"You and Hallie," he groused. And then they were gaping at the nude models in the window, along with the rest of the crowd on the sidewalk.

"Shall we?" said Rafe. He pushed open the door. "Allow me."

"Holy cow," said Levon.

Rafe arched his eyebrows, wordlessly taking in the texture and variety of April's carnal experiences.

Levon paused before one of the sculptures. "Damn," he said. "Wish I'd known her when I was younger."

"It's not too late," said Rafe. "I hear she's available."

Sawyer Ballard's granddaughter and the young man who was always hanging around Tessa's studio were standing at the front of the gallery, clearly agitated. Other graduate students from her year were threading towards them through the crowd.

"Excuse me, Mr. Sinclair," Portia said, then turned away from him, urgently addressing Levon.

Anastasia was at the back of the room. Waving, she called to him, her cheeks colored with excitement. She was chattering away with the artist, who looked strangely diminished with her clothes on. Rafe gazed impersonally at the art on the walls. The paintings really were shocking. Her lack of basic anatomy was appalling.

He glided through the throng of black-clad guests, his overcoat floating behind him like a shroud. Crowds parted in his path. Women in short cocktail dresses put their hands to their throats and turned to find what made them feel simultaneously so frightened and so aroused.

Anastasia stepped away from a circle of people to greet him. She was wearing a voluminous golden orange silk faille evening coat with enormous balloon sleeves, the hem dragging along the floor behind her. Her ebony hair was as smooth as satin, cut into a severe bob that ended at her jaw. Balancing a glass of red wine in one hand, she stooped to kiss him on both cheeks, taller than he was tonight in patent leather stilettos.

"You just missed your little art student," she said, her eyes sparkling behind her sunglasses.

"Tessa was here?" he repeated, puzzled. In the circle of black-clad well-wishers, he saw Whit, sweating profusely, clearly overjoyed to be in such elevated company. Next to him stood Lucian Swain, holding a glass of tomato juice and looking a little tipsy.

"...the inspiration for this whole show," April was saying to Jeff Koons. She turned from her conversation to take Lucian's hand. His face split with a bashful grin. Only then did Rafe focus on the enormous painting behind them. He stepped back from the ten-foot canvas, the better to survey the giant, pixilated image.

At the other end of the gallery, Portia's gaze happened to fall on him at the moment he stood back from the canvas. She saw his shoulders jerk slightly, saw him raise his hand to his mouth. Inexplicably, she shivered.

"Isn't it delicious, my darling?" Anastasia's warm voice poured over him, inviting him to share in the cosmic comedy of the situation. "Come, join us. You know everybody."

Rafe wheeled around, went stalking back through the gallery.

"I think we should split up and look for her," Levon was saying. "Where do you think she would go?"

"I'll try her studio," offered Ben.

"David and I will take her apartment," said Portia.

"Come on, guys, think. Where else?" said Levon impatiently. "Is there somewhere she likes to go, a coffee shop, a favorite park bench?"

The students looked helplessly at each other, then back to Levon. "Well, there's Lucian's place," Graham said dryly.

"All right, let's go," Levon said. "Call me when you find her."

The students raced out the door and split up, the two groups going in different directions.

"You don't think she'd do anything stupid, do you?" he said when they were gone.

Rafe shook his head slowly. "Artists," he said. "We live and die by our passions."

Levon watched him toying with his hat, absently running his fingers over the wide gray brim. Suddenly, he came to some kind of decision; he set the fedora back on his head, tilting it down with a snap.

"I've seen enough." he said curtly. "Call me at home when you hear something."

"Where are you going?" Levon said. There was a yellow light, proceed-with-caution tone to his voice.

"To find her," he said.

Rafe pushed through the frosted double doors, planted both feet on the pavement. He closed his eyes and inhaled, tasting the air on his tongue.

The temperature had grown milder as the sun went down, one of those balmy December evenings that makes New Yorkers think of spring. Windows were open. The clinking of glasses and plates, the convivial roar of people gathered in bars and restaurants spilled out onto the sidewalks. Smells unfurled across the cool night air. He detected the twin spices of ginger and garlic wafting from a restaurant a few doors down, and the odor of a condom warmed inside someone's leather wallet. The sour smell of the subway blowing up from the grates. A cacophony of expensive fragrances whenever anyone entered or exited the gallery.

A faint trace of blackberries lingered on the pavement near the glass doors. Rafe set off at a trot across the street, continuing on West Broadway to where it met Prince, then turned the corner. She was headed west.

Rafe followed the scent to Sixth Avenue. She had traveled briefly on the Avenue of Americas, then made a left at Bleecker. She stayed on the south side of the street for a few blocks, hurrying past Carmine and Mulberry, the cafés, the bakeries, the t-shirt and poster shops, and then he lost her. He felt a stab of panic as he stood there, catching up with her scent again a few steps further, in front of a hip home goods place with the unpronounceable name of Mxplyzk.

Where Bleecker met up with Christopher Street, he stopped, lifted his head, tested the air. It was busy this time of evening, dozens of gay and straight couples ambling up and down the quaint Village street, last minute Christmas shopping, dining with friends, ogling the leather fetish clothing in the windows. Now he quickened his pace, spurred on by fear. Tessa was heading directly for the river.

The West Side Highway is the farthest west you can go on the island of Manhattan, a lonely strip of gravel and cracked pavement abutting the mighty Hudson River. At this point in New York history, it was home to hookers, strip clubs, parking lots and pornographic video stores.

Just across the highway was an abandoned pier, thrusting out into the river, sixty feet of cracked concrete and twisted iron rebar. A chain with a heavy padlock hung from one side of the entrance to the other, a half-hearted attempt at keeping trespassers away.

A transvestite prostitute and his client scattered at Rafe's approach. Two men strolled past, shoulder to shoulder, hands thrust deep in each other's back pockets.

At the end of the pier, he could see a small figure leaning over the cable that served as a flimsy railing, looking down at the black water. Rafe stepped over the chain, slowly approached the apparition, stopping when he was about twenty feet away.

"Hello, Tessa," he said.

She turned towards him. In the dark, he couldn't clearly see her features. The river gurgled and sucked at the pilings.

"Are you all right?" he asked, taking a step closer.

"We used to come here sometimes after meetings," she said. "We'd hold hands and talk about how it would be when he got better."

She turned her head away from him, looking down the river to the Wall Street skyline, at the World Trade Center lit up like towering twin Christmas trees. "Did you go to April's show?"

He took a few cautious steps closer. "Yes."

There was a tear sliding down her face. "I think I already knew," she said. "I think I've always known." Savagely, she wiped it away with the back of her wrist. Her voice filled like a sail, billowing with despair, and as lovers have done since the beginning of the world, she cried out at the starry night, "Why? What for? What did I do wrong?"

"Oh, Tessa," he said, in a voice that rose and fell like the river. "When things went bad, he clung to you like a lifeboat. When things went back to normal, he became the same thoughtless, narcissistic, self-serving egotistical bastard he's always been. It's not your fault, Tessa. You didn't do anything wrong."

She sighed, a wet, ragged little sound. There was nothing he could say, other than the obvious.

"You are everything that is clean and good and right with this world. And if it was me, if you had saved my life—if you were mine, I would never let you go."

They were both quiet for a while, listening to sound of the water lapping against the pier. He had just told her that he loved her.

"I've been lying to myself for a long time," she said.

She wriggled out of her coat, letting it slip from her shoulders. It fell in a pile around her feet. The water bucked and shimmered, the moon broken to pieces on its dark and shining surface. Fearing that she was about to leap, he took another step closer, readying himself to grab her if that was what he had to do.

And then she was breaking down, like the little girl that she still was, and he could see her cheeks glistened with tears. He opened his arms wide to receive her, and she ran to him, slipping her arms inside his coat and pressing her face against his shirt. Something was dying inside of her, a dream, in a slow, thrashing struggle, a butterfly impaled on a pin.

He held her, stroked her hair, whispered her name. Her face was warm against his chest. He could barely contain his joy at her touch. And then she put her hands around his face and pulled him down to her, kissing him with a combination of ferocity, inexperience and passion that was a revelation, made him weak with need, made him want to tear her clothes off and take her right then and there on the cracked pavement and broken beer bottles littering the pier. He hooked his finger in the bandanna around her hair, pulled it out, all the while knowing he shouldn't, he mustn't, it was the worst idea in the world, it was madness, it was an irreversible mistake. The mass of curls sprang loose, fell around her face, down her back. Slowly, he kissed her eyes, then her lips, opening her mouth with his tongue, and as he did, the inside of his head filled with radiant light.

"I won't do anything unless you want me to," he whispered to her.

He needn't have been so cautious, they were alone at the end of a condemned pier in the middle of the Hudson River, but somehow he felt himself to be under the watchful eyes of God, and he wanted to get it right.

"I want you to touch me," she whispered back, her voice shaking.

She was wearing the macramé shirt she had worn the night of the party in his townhouse, and he slid his hands over it, rubbing his fingertips over the cotton fabric covering her breasts. She made a sound, a sharp intake of breath. He slipped his hands underneath, his fingers moving over the silky material of her underthings, feeling her nipples stiffen and rise to his touch. He pulled her shirt over her head, let it drop from his fingers, stood back to look.

She was all light and shadow in the moonlight, like a marble statue shaped by the hand of Rodin. Her breasts were small but full, with upturned pink nipples exactly the size and shape of a silver dollar. He moved his hands down the long valley of her spine, feeling the prickle of goosebumps in the chilly air, taking pleasure in the tensile fluidity of her skin. She took a shuddery breath, undulating under his touch. Standing on tiptoe, she put her arms around his neck.

Bending down, he cupped one of her breasts, marveling at the way it fit perfectly in his hand. He tickled the pearly tip with his tongue, then drew it between his lips.

With a surprised gasp, she sucked in her breath, bit down on her lip, cried out. Her legs buckled beneath her, and she collapsed. She would have fallen if he hadn't caught her.

"Are you all right?" he said quickly. "Did I hurt you?"

"What," she said when she could talk. "What was that?"

He smoothed the hair away from her face. "What was what?"

She was breathing hard. Her eyes were half-closed, dreaming. "I was teetering on the edge of this cliff, this...precipice. And I had a choice. I could back away, or I could go over the top."

"Did you just...come?" he asked her, incredulous.

"Is that what that was?" She looked at him drowsily, unfocused. She was holding onto him for support. "Wow."

"Didn't Lucian ever...didn't he ever, ah, do anything nice for you?" he said, phrasing it as delicately as he knew how.

She didn't answer. He put the folds of his coat around her like wings. When he kissed her again, her soft pink mouth opened for him at the touch of his tongue. He was lost in the innocence of it, after all the women he had known, the games he had played, the strange places he had been, it was as if he were being made new again, starting all over from the beginning.

He could feel her body tremble, with desire, or the cold, maybe both. "Are you cold?" he asked her. Tightening his arms around her, he rested his cheek on her shining hair.

Wrapped in his coat, they watched the lights play on the water. An old lightship was moored nearby, the words *Frying Pan* painted by hand on her rusty hull. The crests of small waves gleamed silver as they rose up against it on their way downstream. Over and over again, the moon dashed itself against the pier, shattering to pieces, then gathered itself together for another try.

He wanted to stay there forever, her warm smooth body pressed against his shirt. Maybe if he remained perfectly still, she would let him. But she stirred, restless. He knew how that song went. She had to keep moving, stay ahead of the pain.

Regretfully, he let her go, stooped down for her shirt. She turned away from him to dress, a charming nod to modesty. He watched the muscles of her back ripple and stretch as she pulled it over her head, shrugged it on, held her ratty coat for her as she slipped into the sleeves. She hoisted her backpack over her shoulder. Fully dressed, she was his art student again.

"Look, would you like to go somewhere, get something to eat?" he asked her.

But she wasn't hungry, she didn't think she'd ever be hungry again. She shook her head, the tendrils trembling.

"Shall we walk, then?"

Yes, she would like to walk. Side by side, they picked their way across the old pier, through the cigarette butts, used condoms and broken glass. As they approached the West Side Highway, she reached for his hand. His fingers closed around hers.

Through the narrow, winding streets of Greenwich Village they walked, past handsome brownstones ornamented with great swags of evergreen and red velvet ribbon, past small glowing storefronts displaying candles and creams and soaps and books and greeting cards and all manner of cheerful gifty things. Turning on Greenwich, they passed a restaurant called Tea and Sympathy, where a homesick Brit could order shepherd's pie, bangers and mash, Lucozade, treacle pudding. Further on was a shop that repaired and blocked men's hats, the last one in the city. A watchmaker occupied a tiny storefront nearby, the window filled with antique silver pocketwatches. The traces of ghostly advertisements painted onto the sides of buildings along Sixth Avenue exhorted them to buy from extinct neighborhood businesses: a carriage maker, corsets, men's opera hats and gloves.

They walked slowly, dawdling, suddenly shy with their new knowledge of each other. All the way from Christopher Street to Sixteenth Street they went, then halfway across the diameter of Manhattan Island to Sixth Avenue. All the while, Rafe thought of how some things don't change all that much in fifty years, and how good her hand felt in his, how right and just, and how remarkable it was after all this time to be back at the beginning, deliriously happy to be holding hands with the girl of his dreams.

They were waiting for the light to change at the corner of Sixteenth and Sixth when he realized that someone might see them, and he used the lame excuse of having to look at his watch to reluctantly let go of her hand. By the dim yellow light of the streetlamp, it was two-thirty a.m.

"I need a new job," she said suddenly. "I can't go back there."

"I know someone who might be able to help," he said.

They came to a stop under her awning. He glanced across the street, to the church, where homeless men slept in huddled piles on the limestone steps.

"Do they ever bother you?"

"No," she said. She shivered. "Poor creatures. By morning, they're gone."

In the light, he could see that her mascara had run, making dark circles under her eyes. He smiled. She looked like she was dressed up as a vampire for Halloween. Her eyes weren't precisely brown, he realized. There was a ring of green around the pupil, easy to miss if you weren't paying close attention. An image floated in the lovely, liquid depths of her iris, the reflection of a man in an overcoat with the collar turned up, wearing a fedora, silhouetted against the stained glass rose window of the church across the street.

"Oh God," he whispered. "I can see myself in your eyes."

She stared at him. And then they were surrounded, circled by a cloud of her friends, pouring out of the lobby of her building, all talking at once.

Luscious Graciela hugged her from top to bottom. Sawyer Ballard's granddaughter put her long arms around her shoulders and squeezed. Clayton lifted her up off of her feet in a bear hug. The good-looking young man who was always in her studio gazed at her in a particular way that was not the way friends ordinarily look at other friends.

Rafe took a step out of their circle, then another. Tessa belonged to them now, and he was again relegated to the position of mysterious and untouchable founder of the school.

"You found her!" exclaimed Portia, grinning. She resembled her grandfather, tall, lean, patrician, blond. "On an abandoned pier? Wow! How did you know?"

"Just luck, really." he said.

Now they fell silent, looking at him curiously. He put his gloves back on, just to give himself something to do. He wanted to go inside with her, undress her, draw her a warm bath, get into bed with her, make love to her until she fell asleep, but clearly, that was not going to happen tonight.

And then they turned back to her, in the center of their circle, asking a hundred different questions at once, deriding April's motives, her exhibitionism, her composition, her color, her technique, and while they were at it, Lucian Swain's entire *oeuvre* of work as well.

He cast one last look at Tessa, sheltered by the protective shield of her friends. Though her eyes were still achingly sad, something in her demeanor was clearly changed.

He extended his arm, grasped her shoulder. "I've got to be going," he said.

"Oh," she said, and for a minute she looked lost again. Then she remembered herself, managed a wan smile.

He backed away, keeping her in his sights for just a moment longer. Then he turned and crossed the street, disappearing into the long shadows that fell around St. Xavier.

24

*Y*ou're going down, son," said Harker, crouched over a blue plastic top, his cheek parallel with the floor.

"I'm going to hit you so hard, they'll only find little bitty pieces of you over the state line," Ben replied.

The tension in the room was palpable. The two men were kneeling on the polished oak floor in the formal dining room of the Ballard's cottage, each of them wielding a colored plastic dreidel with Hebrew letters embossed on the sides.

"Gentleman. Battle stations, please. Man your dreidels," droned Graham. "On my mark. One. Two. Three."

The tops spun in tight circles, knocking lightly together, as if testing each other's mettle. Then, so quickly that nobody saw exactly how it happened, Harker's blue dreidel whacked Ben's red dreidel out of the ring. It spun out, skittering over the floor and across a Persian carpet before coming to rest under a Chippendale chair. In triumph, Harker threw his arms in the air, yodeled out a victory yell.

"Not so fast," cautioned Graham. "Judges?"

Portia inspected Harker's dreidel first. "This one's a *hey.*" She crawled over the carpet on her hands and knees to where Ben's top lay under the chair, inspected it by the light of the candles burning in her great-grandmother's candelabras. "Sorry, Harker. Ben has a *gimmel.*"

Ben punched his fists into the air. "In your face, Miller! In your *face!*" He put his hands around the pile of chocolate coins in the middle of the floor.

"A little competitive?" said Portia.

The cottage, it turned out, was a massive gray stone-faced Norman chateau, with fifteen bedrooms, a banquet dining room, a nursery, a library, various foyers, sitting rooms, and parlors. There was an enormous kitchen with a long plank table, a hulking old Viking stove and a silver vault. A breakfast room, a painting studio, a music room, and a cracked old swimming pavilion that was closed for repairs. Connecting the rooms were numerous hallways, mysterious back passages and hidden stairways. Miles of coffered wood paneling the color of aged cognac ran throughout the house, the warm burnished glow the result of many anonymous hands polishing with beeswax over many decades. Separate quarters were built over a nineteenth-century carriage house to house the complement of thirty-three servants who once worked there.

Parklands rolled as far as the eye could see, the centerpiece of which were formal gardens laid out by Frederick Olmstead. There were walls of manicured hedges, a formal rose garden with arbors and a gazebo, a goldfish pond with a Monet bridge, a playhouse that was an exact replica of the cottage, built for Portia's grandfather when he was a little boy. Behind the house was a colonnaded veranda and a wide swath of lawn that ran down to a rocky beach fronting the harbor. An L-shaped dock rose from the beach, the end lost in the fog.

Tessa was led through two sets of grillwork gates, past fierce black wrought iron lamps and Baccarat crystal chandeliers, past leather couches and great green marble fireplaces. Gazing at her reflection in silver mirrors oxidized with age, she tiptoed across acres of oriental carpets and gaped at the deeply beamed and coffered ceilings. She was shown to her room by an efficient Portuguese housekeeper named Irma.

"You're in the Red Room," Irma informed her, indicating a door to the right. It opened onto a large bedroom papered over with yellow and blue stripes. At its center stood a four-poster bed with a high, arched canopy. The fabric on the bedspread and the fabric on the ruffled canopy were in the same pattern as the wallpaper.

"Why is this called the Red Room?" she wanted to know.

Irma shrugged. "It used to be red," she answered.

Tessa dropped her bag and went to look out her window. There was a dense, low-hanging mist, obscuring all but the closest details, but she could make a red brick patio and the lawn running down to the water. If not for the fog, she would have a view of the harbor and the Jamestown Bridge.

"Hey, Tessa," said David. He was leaning against the doorway behind her, his hands tucked in the pockets of his jeans.

"Hi." She turned back to the window, where the fog rolled and churned. "I didn't know you were coming. Where's Sara?"

"Couldn't get away until Sunday night."

Tessa nodded. She was tired; she hadn't gotten to bed until well past three. After that, she had slept fitfully, her grief remembering to wake her up every hour or so.

He crossed the threshold, joined her at the window. "How are you doing?" His aftershave was sweet, green, woodsy, with an undertone of musk. *Aramis,* she thought with a pang. Lucian wore *Aramis.* She could see it as clearly as if it were happening in front of her right now; the painting on the wall, Lucian embracing April Huffman. She put her hands over her eyes as if that would block the pictures out.

"Tessa," he said gently, touching her shoulder. "I'm so sorry." His hand moved in slow circles over her back.

A tan and white Jack Russell terrier scooted into the room on short legs, galloped in happy circles around the carpet. "Hey, girlfriend!" Portia swooped in for a hug. "You made it!"

Tessa smiled. "So this is what you people call a cottage?"

Portia grinned. "This one isn't that big. My great-grandmother was just a local girl. The really grand places are over on Bellevue Avenue. Rosecliff, the Breakers. Don't you need to light your Hannukah candles before sundown?"

She led her to a doorway set flush with the wall, almost invisible in a field of striped wallpaper, then down a narrow winding stairway to a scarred, low-ceilinged passageway where she opened one of many cupboards. The dog, whose name was Ringo, bounded ahead.

"This is where we keep the candlesticks," she said.

Tessa caught her breath. Here were candelabra from every era, starting in the eighteenth century. Pewter, silver, brass, cut crystal, delicate china cherubs. Like a display in a museum, she thought. There was no time to gawk, however, after the sun went down it would be Sabbath and she would not be able to light a fire. She picked out plain brass candlesticks, thinking they looked sturdy.

"Oh, those," said Portia. "Those are *really* old."

Portia led her to a large sitting room. A Christmas tree twinkled in a corner, festooned with tiny white lights. Tessa placed her candles in the window looking over the harbor. The fog lifted for a moment as she sang the blessings and lit the flames, revealing the ghostly image of the Jamestown Bridge; then it slowly disappeared into the mist again.

"Happy Hannukah, Tessa Moss."

"Happy Christmas, Portia Ballard, of the Boston Ballards."

Just then, there was a tremendous boom, a sound that rattled the walls. Instinctively, Tessa ducked.

"The Yacht Club fires off their cannon every night at sundown. It's officially time to start drinking." Portia explained.

"Thanks for inviting me," said Tessa. "But I don't think I'm going to be very good company this weekend."

"Oh, Tessa," Portia said earnestly. "We love you the way you are. You don't have to entertain us."

Beyond the curtain was a narrow, utilitarian hallway that led to the kitchen. There they found the rest of their party, assembled around the wide plank table. Dinner was already laid out, a motley collection of plastic spoons inserted in aluminum foil baking dishes and Tupperware containers. Paper plates were set around the bare table. For atmosphere, two candles were jammed into empty wine bottles.

Portia stood with her hands on her hips, regarding the bounty. "You know," she said thoughtfully. "Why don't we do this right."

She strode to the other side of the kitchen, swung open a thick, heavy metal door recessed into a niche in the wall. She returned with a box of ornate silver flatware and serving pieces, some shaped so oddly that Tessa couldn't immediately identify their function.

"Asparagus server," said Portia patiently as she pointed to each one. "Butter pick. Five o'clock spoon. Ice cream fork. Tomato server. Toast fork."

Then she led them into the chipped green hallway, turning keys to open cupboards and cabinets along the way. One closet held table linens;

banquet sized tablecloths, napkins by the hundred. A dozen sets of china stood at attention in cylindrical stacks, filling two separate cupboards. The rounded edges of silver trays, buckets, bowls, serving platters, teapots, tureens, gleamed in the low light. Stemware in every shape and color sparkled from a cupboard with a light inside it, rimmed with gold, or cut in geometric patterns, crafted to hold every liquid the nineteenth century had to offer.

"Okay," said Portia. "Let's set the table."

The dining room was painted a muted forest green, the dentil work moldings a soft antique white. The stain on the table and chairs was so dark it was almost black. Another oriental carpet lay under their feet. There were framed prints on the wall, flowers, birds, a painting of a sailing ship.

They set the dishes on a heavy burgundy damask cloth, dramatized with a gold runner with tassels at either end. The china had rims shimmering with undulating lines of real gold. Beside the plates were gold linen napkins, pulled through rings covered in gold leaf.

"The Meissen," said Portia matter-of-factly. "My great-grandmother's wedding china."

The pattern on the stemware swirled like so many fragile glass tornados. The silver was fantastic; an Art Nouveau nymph, her drapery falling away from her body, arching ecstatically at the end of each handle, vines and cupids peeking around her sides.

"Looks like she's having a happy," said Harker.

"Well," said Portia. "Shall we eat?"

Though it was Christmas Eve, it was also Friday night. Tessa, caught up in her own misery, had forgotten to bring wine and challah for the Sabbath. Another reason to be angry with herself. Right on cue, Ben said, "Hey, isn't it Friday night?"

"Oh, no," said Portia, concerned.

"It's okay," said Tessa. "I forgot. It's all right."

Portia turned, went through the green curtain. David went in the other direction, came back moments later with two dinner rolls. "Can you use these?" he said.

Touched, Tessa said, "Really, guys. Please don't go to any trouble."

Portia reappeared, holding a green bottle. "This was in a little wine place across the street from the Touro Synagogue. I was saving it for later, but now seems like a good time."

Bartenura Asti Spumante, it said. Kosher champagne. Tessa covered her face, deeply moved. In this one moment, her friends and classmates had shown her more consideration than Lucian had during their entire year together.

David popped the cork, poured it into her glass. Tessa could feel his eyes on her as she chanted the Friday night *kiddush* and the blessings over the challah.

And then they tore into the food. Tessa watched as it passed her on its way around the table. None of it was even remotely kosher. Clayton, who had been entrusted with the appetizer course, apologized again and again. She waved it off. She didn't have much of an appetite, anyway. "I'll just have some of these," she said, reaching into a bowl of crackers.

He reached out and grabbed her wrist before she could put them in her mouth. "Grandpa's secret recipe for beaten biscuits," he told her ruefully. "Secret is, they're made with lard."

Graham was complimented on his five-can bean dip, David on his gazpacho. "It's nothing," he said, shrugging modestly. "Throw a bunch of stuff in the blender and turn it on." Casually. "Oh, by the way, Tessa, it's completely vegetarian."

There was more champagne. The salad was tossed in a footed trifle bowl. Portia presented a roasted turkey set on a Rosenthal platter trimmed with pine boughs. Tessa's latkes were arranged over a pair of eighteenth-century lovers frolicking on a gold-rimmed Limoges serving plate. Harker and Katie served their red beans and rice in a colonial era punch bowl. Ben's cake drew oohs and ahs, a mile high and festooned with shredded coconut and swags of snowy frosting. He sliced it up with what looked like a giant detangling comb, a strange silver implement that Portia insisted was a cake server.

"You'd better leave this with me," Clayton said solemnly to Tessa, confiscating her plate. "This frosting's full of lard. I can tell."

From the other side of the room, Ben said. "There's no lard, Tessa. He just wants your cake. Give it back to her, Clayton."

"A toast!" Harker proclaimed, tapping his glass with a fork. "To Portia Ballard. For being a fine painter. A fine hostess. A fine figure of a woman. And to the senior Ballards, past and present, for letting us pillage their ancestral home."

"Here, here," said Graham, pleasantly soused.

"Let's sit on the veranda," said Portia. "Bring your glasses."

She pushed aside a green velvet curtain, wiggled through a claustrophobic butler's pantry. The others picked up their glasses and followed her, emerging in a parlor crowded with Victorian furniture. Accent tables from many eras displayed photographs gone sepia with age. From there, they passed through the sitting room where Tessa had lit her candles. Portia levered open a set of French doors overlooking the harbor.

Outside, a salty tang hung in the air, the smell of the tide and the sea. A circle of wooden rocking chairs awaited them in the mist.

"Nice night," said David.

"It is," agreed Portia, folding her long body into a chair. "It's always warmer here by the water. Sometimes you can see sea lions sunning themselves out on the rocks."

Ringo struggled into her lap, turned a few circles before settling down with his head on her knee. She leaned back and closed her eyes. She looked serene, at peace. Portia belonged here, Tessa realized, as much a part of the house and the town as the rocks jutting up out of the harbor, in a way she herself had never belonged anywhere, until she had come to New York.

Clayton had had three flutes of champagne, and was waving his glass at Graham for a refill. "All right. Listen up, y'all. I've got one for you. Does art have a purpose? Discuss."

"Who says art has to have a purpose?" countered David.

"Everything has a purpose," said Graham.

"How about evil?" said Ben. "Does evil have a purpose?"

"Sure it does," said Graham dourly, buried deep in his coat. "It keeps us home at night; it keeps us from wandering, keeps us in line, makes us appreciate what we have. It serves as a dark mirror for us all to look inside and say, 'At least I don't do *that*.'"

"Whoa there, son," said Harker, rolling a cigarette. "Before you go all Psyche 101 on our asses. There's enough hardcore evil to go around. Hitler was evil. Stalin was evil. This guy Saddam Hussein is evil. I don't know what purpose they serve."

"It's not just the big bad," said David. "Hannah Arendt wrote about 'the banality of evil.' You know, Eichmann didn't hate anyone. He just followed orders, handed in the paperwork, made sure the trains ran on time."

"Hey," said Clayton. "I just wanted to talk about art. If we're going to be discussing the banality of evil, I'm gonna need another beer." Unsteadily, he got to his feet, went back into the house.

Tessa was lulled by the rhythm of the runners rocking on the slatted floor of the veranda. Beyond the end of the porch, the fog rolled itself slowly into indefinable shapes, clearing briefly to reveal the lighthouse and the piers of the Jamestown Bridge before closing up ranks again. The only sound was the mournful lowing of the foghorn.

"Do you think it's possible for someone to change?" she said suddenly. "Someone who's done...*really* bad things."

"Hitler, Stalin, those guys were psychopaths," said David. "I think that kind of evil is hardwired."

"People change," said Harker. "I was a different guy in high school. Skipped class, stole stuff, smoked a lot of weed, blew off anyone who tried to help me. That was before I got into music."

"Is that when you got all those tattoos?" Portia asked. Thorny vines climbed up Harker's arms, from his wrists up to his shoulders. Skulls and roses bloomed in the thicket of canes and leaves.

"Nah. That was later." His guitar lay across his lap, and he picked it up now, strumming out the opening chords for God Rest Ye Merry Gentlemen.

"Hey," Portia said. "If you could ask God one question. What would it be?"

"I'd have to think about that," said Harker. "Wait. I got it. I want to know about the Resurrection. Like, do you have to come back in the body you died in? I mean, what if you were old and sick?"

"Maybe you get a choice," suggested Katie.

Harker shivered. "I'd hate to come back as me back then. All that cow-tipping and setting stuff on fire. And I'd have to learn to play guitar all over again."

"I would want to know if my father is proud of me." said Ben. "He died when I was eleven."

"I'm sorry," said Portia wistfully.

He shrugged his big shoulders. "He worked on the first nuclear submarines, before anybody knew asbestos was bad for you. What about you, Portia?" he said, turning the conversation away from himself. "What would your question be?"

Portia stroked the dog's silky head. "I would ask why there has to be so much suffering in the world."

"How about you, Graham?" said Harker, his hands busy with the guitar.

"Well," Graham drawled. "If I believed in God, which I don't, I would ask Him this. When animals die, do they go to Heaven? Also, after the Resurrection, will the pets come back too? I had this shepherd mix named Blue."

"You're not taking this very seriously." Portia said, smiling.

"I'm with Graham," David admitted. "I'm kind of an agnostic. You know. Prove it to me. But if He really exists, I'd ask Him how long I've got."

"Really?" asked Tessa curiously. "I don't think I want to know."

"Also, how I go. That way, I can plan for it."

There was a heavy tread on the floorboards of the veranda. Clayton was back. "What'd I miss?" he huffed, opening a Sam Adams.

"Oh, you know. If you could ask God one question."

"That's easy," he answered immediately. "If time travel exists, and if there are travelers among us now."

Ben said, "Come on, Clayton. You must have a question."

He put the beer to his lips, then wiped his mouth. "All right. I guess I'd want to know what I should do for my thesis project."

There was a lull in the conversation, smoothed over by the water lapping against the shore. The foghorn groaned again. A buoy clanged from somewhere out in the harbor.

"I know I already said the thing about the pets," said Graham pensively. "But I guess if I could, I'd ask if there was someone out there for me. I'm always falling for straight guys, hoping they'll have this epiphany that they've really been gay all along. Did I really just say that out loud," he mumbled, covering his eyes. "I must be completely hammered."

Tessa turned to look at Graham, slumped down in his rocking chair, his sallow face floating like a ghost over the upturned collar of his raincoat. She leaned over and touched his hand. "There's someone out there for you, Graham," she said earnestly. "There's someone out there for all of us."

"Even Clayton," said Ben.

"I really love you guys," Clayton blubbered sloppily. Then he put on a wolfish grin, treating them to his best Elvis sneer. "Seriously, though. I'm really glad to know y'all. I didn't know a soul when I moved to New York. You're like family to me. Only, you know, without any of the hurting."

"I didn't know anybody either," said Ben. "I'm glad I met you, too."

"Us, too." said Harker. "All right, that's not strictly true. I already knew a lot of people here, and Katie's got some cousins. But still. You guys are all right."

"That goes for me, too," David agreed. But he was looking at Tessa.

Tessa leaned back in her chair, stared down into her glass. "I couldn't have gotten through this year without all of you," she murmured.

"I think we're all incredibly blessed to have found one other," Portia said softly.

"Say," Harker said. "Getting back to Clayton's question. Does art have a purpose?"

"Sure," said David. "It elevates whoever is looking at it."

"To enlighten," said Portia. "To inspire."

"To educate," said Ben.

"To the class of '93," said Graham, solemnly raising his glass. "May we be blessed with the ability to create works of art that elevate, that enlighten, that educate, that inspire." The students rose to their feet and clinked glasses.

"To art that matters."

"Those are good answers," said Harker, taking out his sketchbook, another cigarette jiggling up and down in the corner of his mouth. "I'm going to write them down."

Which was followed by the marathon dreidel battle. It began genteelly enough. An hour later, when Portia and Tessa quit, the boys were still at it, hurling terrible invective at each other, imprecating each other's integrity, manhood, the sorry state of their mothers' virtue.

Tessa and Portia cleared the table, brought the dishes to the kitchen. Irma washed up in the old apron-front sink. Tessa carefully wiped the china dry with soft dishcloths while Portia counted the silver and returned it to the vault. By the time they were finished, it was ten-thirty. Tessa needed to keep busy. Left on her own, her mind kept returning to scenes from the night before. Portia must have sensed it; when the last dish was put away, she turned to her friend and said, "You know, it's still early. Come on. I'll show you the grounds."

The floor in the grand hallway was checkered with black and white marble, just like in glossy magazine spreads of fancy homes in *Architectural Digest*. Just inside the foyer stood a bust on a fluted marble pedestal. Tessa thought it looked vaguely like Portia. She was searching for an identifying plaque when she remembered that she was in a private home.

"It's by Rodin," Portia said, hiding a smile. She knew what Tessa had been doing. "He made it when my great-grandmother was studying in Paris. I found it in a cupboard in the attic. When I asked my mom why it wasn't on display, she said, 'It never really looked like her.' After I was done genuflecting in front of it, I said, 'Mom. *Rodin.*'"

"She kind of looks like you," said Tessa.

Portia tilted her head. "Really? You think so?"

Tessa took in the long lovely face, the calm eyes, the strong chin, the hair piled up in a bun on top of her head. By coincidence, Portia was wearing her hair in a bun tonight. The resemblance was uncanny.

"What was her name?"

"Rose. Rose Sawyer Ballard. I never met her, she died before I was born. From what I can gather, she was a remarkable woman. It was a real scandal when she went to art school. People would cross to the other side of the street to avoid her. Well-bred girls just didn't do that back then, draw naked men."

They left Ringo in the house; he whined pitifully, dancing on impatient white paws, but Portia wanted to avoid a repeat encounter with a family of skunks that wandered the grounds at night. They descended the wide stone steps, crossed the circular Belgian block driveway. Tessa followed Portia down a flagstone walk that vanished into a shifting wall of fog. As visibility diminished, Tessa grew uneasy; she hesitated, looking back at the house, its squared-off edges already lost in the fog.

"I love it when it's like this," she heard Portia say from somewhere up ahead. "It's like being in a ghost story."

Well. If Portia wasn't going to be afraid, she wasn't either. They followed the walkway as far as it went. At its end, they turned onto a path that meandered to the left, gravel crunching under their feet.

Ahead of them was the Monet bridge spanning a goldfish pond in the Japanese style. Ghostly images of trees materialized around them, one, then another, veiled in mist. A structure loomed up at them, twenty feet ahead; Portia stopped.

"Want to see the playhouse?"

"Sure."

They crossed the little bridge, the fog muffling the sound of their footsteps. "My grandmother had these Italian craftsmen make replicas of furniture from the big house," Portia explained. "Little armchairs, little Persian rugs. I used to love being out here away from the grownups. My brother and I played house all the time. I haven't been inside in years."

She tried the knob. It wouldn't yield. She frowned, put her hands on her hips. "When did they start locking it?"

The little house must have been handsome once, but now it looked as if it had fallen upon hard times. Located under the trees, its stucco was turning green with moss. The hipped roof was sticky with sap, under a blanket of pine needles. Frustrated, Portia tried to sweep them off with her coat sleeve, quickly giving up. She looked glum.

"That's all right," said Tessa, comfortingly. "We'll come back another time."

"I really should come out here sometime and clean this up," she said. Her face brightened. "Wait a minute," she said. She pulled out the keyring she had used to open the china cupboards, sorted through the various blackened skeleton keys, trying them in the lock one by one until finally, with a satisfying click, Portia exclaimed, "Open Sesame!" and pushed open the door.

It was empty. A lone folding chair was left in the middle of the room. Portia was crestfallen. "Oh," she said wistfully. "He must have given the furniture away." She dropped down into the chair. It gave out a puff of dust. A frightened vole trundled away along the baseboard. "My grandfather is always doing that, giving stuff to museums. They love him."

"I'm sorry," Tessa said, wanting to comfort her friend. Even in the dark, she could make out the dovetailed joints, the carved moldings around the window, and she turned around in a circle, awestruck by the exacting nineteenth-century craftsmanship. "It's still amazing. How often do you see coffered ceilings in a child's playhouse?"

Portia didn't answer. Her face was occluded, far away.

"It's not going to be in the family much longer. None of us will be able to afford it. My grandfather is talking about selling it. The Yacht Club is interested."

Tessa hugged her arms around herself for warmth. The yellow windbreaker she had borrowed from the front closet on her way out the door was made for summer squalls, not a night in December, even a mild one.

"When I was fifteen," Portia said absently, staring out of the child-sized mullioned windows. "My cousin Caroline got married out on the lawn."

"That must have been fun."

"Mm," Portia agreed. "My grandfather put up a big white tent, right over there, in front of the house. I was a bridesmaid. I had never been in a wedding before. I had a new dress that Caroline had picked out, and someone was coming to do all the girls' hair and makeup.

"Caroline was much older than I was, and I thought, so sophisticated. She worked as an editor at a magazine in New York. She was so pretty, and so confident. She had this throaty laugh. I adored her.

"There was this big luncheon, a kind of meet-the-families thing, planned for the day before the wedding. It was the end of May. The sky was blue, it was a cool, brisk morning. There were whitecaps on the water, and you could hear the sound of the banners and flags snapping on the ends of their poles. I was in the art studio, trying to capture it all on paper, when Caroline's fiancée poked his head around the door.

"Drew Foster. I had this mad crush on him. He was tall and smart and funny, with these really broad shoulders—he played football in high school—and a smile that made me feel all jumpy and nervous and excited inside. He had just graduated from Harvard, and he was starting law school in the fall. He asked if it was all right if he came in. I said, sure. I was so flattered. The day before his wedding, and he wanted to spend time with me! Anyway. He came in, closed the door. He came up behind me to see what I was doing. 'Wow,' he said. 'You're really good.'

"My heart was beating about a hundred miles a minute. 'You're so talented,' he said. Then, 'Of all Caroline's cousins, I think you're the prettiest.'

"I loved him for that. Even then, I was a head taller than all my classmates. I didn't feel pretty. I felt awkward and clumsy and shy. He came closer. Too close. I could feel his breath on my hair. And then he kissed me.

"I was shocked. 'But you're marrying Caroline tomorrow,' I said.

"He gave me one of those winning smiles, you know, the kind that makes you feel all oogly, like your insides are made out of chewing gum, and he said, 'Come on, Portia. We're practically family.'

"So I let him kiss me. And then he was opening his mouth, and touching me, and I was saying no, no, no, and pushing him away, and he was holding me too hard and forcing me down onto the floor, and..." Portia stopped. Her long face was furrowed with an old grief. She shivered. "Let's get out of here."

They left the playhouse behind, ducking through the child-sized door. There were more trees now, trunks appearing out of the mist, the scent of crushed pine needles pleasantly reminiscent of turpentine. They had to watch where they were going; here under the trees, knotty roots heaved themselves up out of the earth. The ground under their feet grew soft, spongy, emitting a faint marshy odor of decay. The fog thinned for a moment, letting in moonlight, revealing a small clearing in the woods.

"Where are we?" said Tessa.

"The pet cemetery," said Portia. Tessa ran her fingers along a bench. *Kermit, a St. Bernard. He Was A Good Dog 1913* was engraved in spidery capital letters on one of the weathered gray slats.

"Look. This is where I buried my cat." At Portia's feet was a lichen-covered stone with the name Alice inscribed in it, and the year 1979. "There's a horse under here somewhere, too."

"What happened?" said Tessa cautiously. "Drew. Did they call off the wedding?"

She looked down at the ground, studying the pitted, mossy stones. "No. Nothing like that." She shoved her hands deep in her pockets. The breeze stirred the tails of her coat. "Drew said that if I told anybody, he would swear that I was a liar, that I came on to him, that I made it all up because he turned me down. I believed him. I was fifteen, you know? Years later, I understood. He picked me because I was young, and shy, and vulnerable.

"I told my mother that I couldn't go to the wedding, I was sick. My aunt was furious. My grandfather came stomping up to my room to give me a piece of his mind. Act like a Ballard, damn it. Couldn't I just grit my teeth, walk down the aisle and puke later? I stayed in bed with the lights off for three days."

"Did you ever tell anybody?"

"When I was eighteen, I told my mother. She was horrified. It couldn't be *possible*. He was from such a *nice* family. Was I sure I hadn't *imagined* it. Maybe he was just *horsing around*. Then she got angry. What had I done to make him think I wanted it? Of course, by then, it didn't matter. Everyone knew he was cheating on Caroline.

"No one ever said anything. It just got swept under the carpet with all the other bits and pieces of stuff that was never discussed in my family. My grandfather leaving my grandmother. My mother, firing every nanny who ever got close to me. My parents, sending us off to boarding school so that we wouldn't interfere with their party plans. Portia's *feelings.*" Her shoulders trembled with unexpressed rage. "So *untidy.*"

She squatted down, moodily picked a piece of moss off of the cat's headstone. "Anyway. I didn't pick up a paintbrush for the next eight years. Until I met Auden." At the mention of his name, the soft, serene expression returned to her face.

Tessa shifted from one foot to the other. "Portia," she began. What could she possibly say that wouldn't sound trivial or banal?

Portia turned a smile to her, gracious as always. "You don't have to say anything," she said, getting to her feet, brushing pine needles from the tails of her coat. "I shouldn't have burdened you with all of this."

"The terrible things that happen to us," Tessa said slowly. "What we do with them...I think that's what makes us artists. Your paintings are filled with grace. With light. With air. With forgiveness. I don't know how you do it. But somehow, you transform your pain into a world, a universe of beauty."

It was a moment before she spoke again. "Thank you, Tessa," she said. "Thank you for that."

They sat in silence for a moment. *Mowgli, a mischievous Spider Monkey, 1927,* Tessa read. *Eloise, a beloved Pekinese, 1952.*

"You know, you haven't mentioned Lucian once."

"Mm." She didn't want to talk about Lucian anymore. She wanted to forget about him forever.

"What happened Thursday night?"

"I was supposed to drive him to the airport. He wasn't there. I waited. He didn't show. I was walking home. Somehow, I ended up at April's gallery. I saw the painting. I saw him kiss her. I left."

Portia was kicking the moss off of a small gravestone so pitted with age that the writing on it was illegible. "How did Mr. Sinclair find you?"

"Oh. That." She wondered, too. Was it a vampire thing? "I don't know," she admitted. "I may have mentioned to him that I used to go there with Lucian."

Portia nodded. "I like the way he appreciates you," she said. "And for all the right reasons. You're smart. You're talented. You're beautiful. Of course he's attracted to you. And him, well...I get it. That face, that body. That voice. But Tessa...remember what he is."

Tessa felt a small tremor go through her body. What did Portia know?

"He's the founder of the school, yes. But he's also, well...he has kind of a reputation." She sighed. "Look. I have a confession to make. I told you that story for a reason. Remember, the day after the Halloween Party, I tried to tell you. I have a sensitivity for these things. When I looked in his eyes, when he shook my hand, I felt..." She looked meaningfully at her friend, took a deep breath. "I don't think this is going to end well."

A pair of headlights came searching through the fog, turning in through the gate and into the driveway, stopping in front of the house.

"Who's that?" Portia frowned. "There's a bed and breakfast up the road. Sometimes tourists pull in here by mistake." She glanced apologetically at Tessa. "I'll be right back." She marched off through the woods towards the house.

The night was getting colder; Tessa could see her breath. She wrapped her arms around herself, rubbing them for warmth. The layers of fog separated just enough for her to have a sightline to the house. A man was getting out of the back of a taxi, paying the driver. Tessa heard the little dog yapping, saw Portia slow, then break into a run. As she reached the car, she launched herself into the passenger's arms. He caught her, swinging her around in a joyful circle. Auden. He must have come up early to surprise her.

"Tessa! It's Auden!" Portia's voice confirmed it, sounding very far away through the fog. "We're coming back for you!"

"That's all right," she hollered back, not wanting to intrude on their moment. They hadn't seen each other since Thanksgiving, she knew. "I'm okay. Go on ahead."

Portia waved, turned back to Auden. Tessa watched the lovers mount the wide stone steps, their arms around each other's waists. The fog drew around them like a curtain.

Tessa shivered, her bravado fled. The sad little graveyard would have been spooky enough at any time, but at midnight, thick with winding sheets of mist, it was monster-movie scary. She could hardly see her hand in front of her face. She moved forward, towards the house, she hoped. After her third step, she snagged her shoe on an unseen obstacle, nearly falling flat on her ass on the boggy ground. She looked to see what had tripped her up. *Tessa, A Persian Cat Died 1945.* Wonderful, she thought.

She heard twigs snap and crackle, something moving towards her. Now she felt real fear. The hairs stood up at the back of her neck, the flesh of her arms prickled into goosebumps. She strained for a sound, any sound, in the dead quiet of the fog. At last, she heard an angry whir, a scuffle, taking place in the bushes nearby. Moments later a red fox trotted across the clearing, a few feet in front of her.

Tessa froze, holding her breath; she had never been this close to a wild animal before. The fox was carrying something in its jaws, the outstretched feathers of a wing stretched stiffly between its teeth. It stopped and glanced at her before trotting off, the white tip of his brushy tail disappearing into the fog.

She exhaled, pulled her arms a little tighter around herself. Finally, she allowed herself to think back on the events of last night.

Had she really been that stupid? Was she, nice, law-abiding Tessa Moss capable of doing something as dangerous as walking out onto a dark, deserted pier at midnight, then throwing herself at a stranger who was, by his own admission, a vampire?

The clouds seethed and parted, revealing the silhouette of a man in a hat and overcoat standing between the trees. Just as quickly, the image was gone, the fog churning in the space under the boughs.

Last night, blind with pain, she'd fled up Bleecker Street, tears streaking down her face. Couples and crowds separated around her and stared as she stormed by. She knew exactly where she was going. Sepia-toned memories of sitting on the pier for hours, the sun warming her back, holding Lucian's hand as the water lapped up against the pilings and he told her how much he needed her.

She'd stared at the broken surface of the water, watching the moon gather itself up and shatter, like her heart, over and over again. She knew now she could never have him, would never have him, if she waited as long as she lived. If she changed her face, her name, her shape, her religion, the color of her hair. She was not the one he wanted. She was not what he was looking for.

I'm nothing, she'd realized. *Not his girlfriend, not his lover, not his colleague, not his friend.* The words clumped together, stopping her throat. She'd given so much of herself, and for so long, that there was nothing left. She was empty. Resting one foot on the steel cable, looking down at the river eddying by, she imagined the cold water closing over her head. Holding her breath until it escaped in a great gush of bubbles, her lungs filling with water. Darkness, expanding as far as the horizon, floating forever.

And then he was there, Raphael Sinclair, standing on the cracked and broken pier in his Savile Row coat and handmade shoes, calling her name. He always knew when she was in trouble. He always knew where to find her.

She remembered her desire for obliteration as she pulled his face down to hers, grabbing at him like she was drowning, the tightness in her chest as she tried to breath with his arms locked around her waist. The sound of his voice like the rustle of bare skin on cool sheets.

Fog coiled around her like a cocoon. She closed her eyes, remembering how right it had felt to be half-naked, enveloped in the warmth of his overcoat. She brought her fingertips up to her mouth, wanting to feel the imprint of his lips. Spreading out her fingers, she followed the course his hands had taken down her body. The line of her jaw, under her hair. The back of her neck. Gliding down her flanks. His shadowy eyes watching her in the darkness. The feel of his thick hair falling between her fingers. His hands pulling on her hips, sliding under her shirt. Her breast in the cup he made with his hand. His soft, sensuous mouth tugging at her, over her heart.

Alone in the graveyard, wisps of fog gliding around her like spirits, she felt a dizzying rush between her legs, and collapsed forward onto her hands and knees.

Tessa pressed her forehead against the damp earth, breathing hard. And began to laugh. She had come again, this time just thinking about him.

It had been happening all semester, long before she walked into April Huffman's exhibition last night. Raphael Sinclair, with his beautiful face, his stopped heart and his sorrowful story. One man, defying the establishment, trying to change the course of art history with his brave little art school. He might be a vampire, but he was twice the man Lucian would ever be.

To her right was a large rock, almost a boulder, that said, *Michael, A Golden Retriever*. Steadying herself on it, she climbed to her feet. "Good dog," she said.

Looking up at the sky, she could make out a star or two, a crescent moon appearing in a hazy halo through the pine boughs overhead. The fog was dissipating as the night grew colder. The house swam into view, a monument to a vanishing world.

She heaved a sigh, squared her shoulders. Breathing in the salty air, she thought about the week to come. She had to look for a job. Build the canvases for her thesis project. Start drawing. If she had extra time this week, she would paint her apartment, make the kitchen red. That would be cheery.

The gravel path was clear now, shining with a rime of new frost that glittered like diamonds under the pale moonlight. Hugging her arms around herself, she made a mad dash for the house.

It was ten o'clock on Sunday evening by the time Clayton's car eased up in front of her building. Ben popped the trunk. David got out of the car, handed Tessa her bag. He lingered, not wanting to say goodbye.

"Maybe I'll see you."

"Sure."With Sara in town, she knew he wouldn't. "I'll be in my studio."

He struggled to keep her a moment longer. "Look, if you need to talk. I mean, about the Lucian thing. Call."

"I will."

There was no longer any reason to stay. He leaned forward to give her a kiss, lightly touching her shoulder. Clayton rolled down his window, yelled, "Get a room!" He gave her a last look, got back into the car. Clayton stepped on the gas, and the Datsun roared down Sixteenth Street.

He was already beside her, shouldering her bag, a dark shape separating from the shadowed doorway of the brownstone next door.

"Hello, Tessa."

"Hello, Mr. Sinclair."

They stood beneath the canopy to her building. Inside, the lobby looked bright and inviting.

"About Thursday night," she said hurriedly. "I was...I don't know what I was thinking. I was out of my mind, throwing myself at you like that."

He smiled down at her. She was so young. He took her face in both hands, kissed her lips, once, twice.

"Would you like to get something to eat?"

Her smile warmed him like the sun. "I've been living on cereal and milk since Friday."

They started down Sixteenth Street. As they waited for the light on the corner of Sixteenth Street and Fifth Avenue, he took her hand.

25

She must have been starving, but she took her time looking up and down the menu before ordering the cheapest item on it, a tuna fish sandwich on toasted rye, with pickle.

He urged her to order some protein, a steak. She demurred, insisted that what she really wanted was the tuna fish. Then he remembered that she had lost her job. Tuna was probably the only thing she could afford.

He leaned closer so that only she could hear. "Come on, Tessa. I'm buying."

She protested. She was proud, she wouldn't have him paying. Rafe ordered the tuna and a Romanian tenderloin, rare. When the food came, her sandwich and a long, dense, charcoal-broiled strip of skirt steak buried under a heap of caramelized onions, he pushed it all over to her side of the table and said, "Eat."

She shook her head, resolutely reached for the sandwich.

"It's just going to go to waste," he said, cajoling. "I'm not hungry."

She frowned at him—*okay, this time*—cut off a slice and took a bite. "Mmmm," she said, almost a purr, closing her eyes, savoring. It occurred to him that as an art student on a tight budget, her diet must consist of quite a lot of tuna. She had probably not encountered a slab of meat like this in a long time.

She wanted to share her pleasure with him. For her, he choked down a bite or two. Then she ate it all, down to the last bloody bite. She offered him that last piece, charred on the outside, red and glistening on the inside. The earthy, primal aroma of grilled meat rolled over him, made his mouth water. God, he missed steak.

This time, he declined, explaining that food had no real taste for him. Tessa stopped in mid-chew, stricken. "I'm sorry," she said, her pity mingled with embarrassment. "This must be a terrible tease for you."

"I do miss it," he said. "But I can still smell it. And I enjoy watching you eat. Really. I do."

She liked the deep lines that formed at the sides of his mouth when he smiled, the crinkles at the corners of his eyes. He was wearing a charcoal gray suit, with peaked lapels and wide chalk stripes, set off by a shirt exactly the color of heavy cream, and a silk tie in a subdued violet. His cuffs shot a precise quarter of an inch past the ends of his sleeves. His light-colored hair was combed off of his forehead and back along the sides, shining in the light of the overhead lamps. One leg was balanced lightly, casually, over the other, the crease in his trousers like the edge of a knife. Against the backdrop of dark woodwork and white tile, he looked like a Bruce Weber photo shoot for Calvin Klein. Tessa smiled, amused by the idea of him sitting across from her in the comfortable familiarity of a kosher deli.

He noticed she was looking at him, glanced down at his hands, playing with a matchbook. They were in the East Village, crowded in among the other diners at the Second Avenue Deli, the air alive with the peppery essence of Romanian pastrami and the ebulliently cheery sounds of dishes crashing in the kitchen. She was wearing a faded brown shirt with embroidery at the neck and sleeves, the sort of thing you might buy on a trip to India, or a souk in the Middle East. Around her neck she wore the coffee-colored glass bead on a leather thong that reminded him of sucking candy. Innocent, happy, her cheeks pink from the walk, her hair blown in messy curls all around her lovely face.

"Dessert?"

"God, no. I'm going to be full for a week."

"Here, take this home with you." He signaled for the waitress to wrap up the tuna sandwich, untouched on the white china plate.

"How was Newport?"

"I've never been in a house like that. It was like being dropped into *Brideshead Revisited.*"

He was nervous, desperate for a cigarette, thought about asking someone at the next table, decided against it. "What did you do out there?"

Tessa took a paper napkin, idly started sketching. "Oh, you know. Ate too much. Drank too much. Strolled around the grounds. Discussed the meaning of life. Thought about my thesis project. Decided to paint my kitchen." She looked down at her drawing. "Thought about you."

"I thought about you, too. Are you...all right?"

"Yes. I'm fine." She folded the paper in three, concealing her drawing, pushed it over to his side of the table. With a feeling in his stomach like an airplane plummeting to earth, he understood it was his turn.

"Do you know how to play?"

Yes, I know how to play.

She was looking into his eyes. Sofia's eyes, gazing at him through the moist air of a smoky restaurant, another time, another place.

He got to his feet. The waitress nodded at him, came over with the bill. Tessa looked around for her knapsack to pay for her share, but he was too fast for her, she was already gone with his credit card. Tessa frowned at him. "You'll get it next time," he promised. "Come on. Let me put you in a cab."

"Let's walk," she said.

He carried her bag through a drab if well-lit foyer, past a wall of mailboxes and a mirror that stretched up to the ceiling. Tessa didn't even glance at it, but he did. According to the mirror, she was alone.

He followed her past the elevator bank. Hers was the first door in a small hallway on the right. She inserted the key in the lock, pushed it open, walked in.

The apartment was clean, but not too clean, neat but not too neat. Directly before him was a long narrow space, a wide corridor, really, with a couch on one side and a dining room table on the other. A few posters hung on the wall. Klimt's golden *Kiss,* a voluptuous Titian nude, Hopper's *Nighthawks.*

She plopped her bag on the table, hung her coat on a coat tree in the corner. She realized that he was still standing before the doorway, and she looked at him questioningly.

"You have to invite me in," he said.

"Oh," she said, and regarded him for a long moment. She looked sad, he wasn't sure why. "Won't you please come in," she said.

He stepped across the threshold. She was gathering up a heap of laundry left on the couch, straightening a tipped pile of newspapers, snatching at a plate on the table. "Place is a mess," she muttered under her breath, and he realized that what he had taken for doubt was embarrassment at the state of her living quarters.

"Stop," he said firmly. "Stop cleaning up for me." He took hold of her arm, meaning only to stop her from fussing, but then he swung her around and pulled her close and he was kissing her, his hands sliding up her arms to the sides of her face.

His hands were cool on her face, even his lips were cool, and it excited her, the temperature of his touch, the difference between him and other men. His hands held her arms at first, gently but surely, and then they slid around to rest on the ridges of her back and then down to her waist, bringing her body against his. There was a quick intake of breath, a hiss of air sucked between her teeth, as they came together.

"I want to be with you," he whispered into her hair. "I'm sorry, I know it's wrong, I'm not supposed to, but I can't help it, I do."

She slipped her arms inside his coat, laid her cheek against his shirt. He could feel her all along the length of him, some part of her was touching him all the way from his chest down through his legs. He leaned over to kiss her, and her face turned up to him in the semi-darkness of her apartment. So soft, so ready, so willing to give herself to him, and as if he were watching from outside himself, knowing who he was and what he was capable of, he felt a pang of fear for her, for what he might do given just the right circumstances.

He loosened his hold, stepped back. "This is a terrible idea," he said, forcing his hands deep into his pockets. "I should go." He wheeled around, swept towards the door.

"Rafe," she said.

It was the first time he had heard her say his name. He stopped. When he turned around again, he said. "Listen. I just want you to know. You've probably heard things about me."

"No, no, of course not."

"As I've heard things about you."

She fell silent.

"Here's the thing. About me, the things they say. They're all true. All of them. Tessa...if we start something...I'm afraid I won't be able to stop myself. I may look like a man. But I am what I am. And I'm afraid I might hurt you."

Tessa came closer, then closer still. Took his hand, kissed it, laid it on the side of her cheek. Moved it under her jaw, to the side of her neck, where he could feel her jugular pulse under the palm of his hand.

Rafe closed his eyes. Came to a decision. Opened them again.

"All right, then. Here's how it's going to be. I'm not going to try anything on you, Tessa. You're in charge. You're going to take the lead."

One eye gleamed at her from the deep shadow on his face cast by the brim of his hat. The single light from the kitchen turned the color of his coat to rich chocolate, the shadows in the folds to crisp black. She could smell him, the sandalwood note of his cologne cutting through the stale air of the apartment, and she felt excitement mingled with fear, wanted to feel his lips on her, his hands on her, moving, applying pressure.

She reached forward, took his hands, pulling him forward across the threshold. "Come on," she said, smiling, seducing him. "Let's draw."

She set up her easel near the window, plugged in the reflector lamp and aimed it at him. "Take off your coat," she told him.

"Where shall I put it?"

"The bed is fine."

He folded it carefully, placed it on her bed, covered with an old but clean chenille spread. He glanced up. "High ceilings here."

"It used to be a warehouse, I think." She was attaching a sheet of creamy white paper to a drawing board, whittling a charcoal pencil into a fine point.

"Nice space. How did you come by it?"

"Oh, you know. The usual New York story. Sublet it from someone who sublet it from someone who's subletting it from someone."

"Do you live alone?"

"I have a roommate, Anna. She has the loft."

They were in her room. Unlike her studio, which was lush with found objects, her bedroom was bare, spartan. A window. White walls. A twin bed.

An old wooden dresser, doubtlessly rescued from the street. A bookcase made from cinder blocks and wooden planks. A drawing table. An easel. A chair.

There was a mirror hung over the dresser. Photographs and picture postcards were stuck at intervals between the frame and the glass. He moved closer. A girl at a café stared dreamily into the distance, Manet's *The Plum*. Tessa, her arms around a tall, red-haired young man with a goatee. A Bouguereau *Birth of Venus*. Tessa posing beside a dark-haired girl in a wedding dress, both of them smiling. A sexy black-and-white snapshot of a long-haired girl in lingerie and cowboy boots. On closer inspection, he realized it was her.

She pressed down the button on her tape player. A cool, dry voice rasped through the air, silk and sandpaper.

As the moon casts its cold glow on the day.
The streetlamps on Bleecker light my way,
As my footsteps draw closer, you'd better pray.
While the moon sinks behind Bleecker Street.

She turned to him. It was a different Tessa now, Tessa with confidence, Tessa with a purpose. She surveyed him analytically, her head tilted.

"Stand straight," she commanded him. "Hands in your pockets."

He straightened up, did as she told him. The pose made the vee of his shoulders seem wider, his waist narrower as the tails of his jacket flared. The lamp she positioned at his right threw dramatic shadows along his left flank, from his head down to his shoes.

"I'm thinking of that Eakins at the Met. You know, the big portrait in the American Wing."

"Oh, yes. I know the one."

"Legs apart. Look down."

He obeyed.

"That's too much, I can't see your eyes. Up a little, just a little. Good."

He liked it, the way she was directing him, telling him what to do. She frowned, aimed her pencil at him, held it vertically, then horizontally. He knew she was measuring the height and width of his stance. Soon he heard the familiar scritching of pencil against paper, the acrid smell of charcoal released into the air. Instructed to stare at the floor near her feet, he couldn't see her face, but he could feel her eyes on him, studying him, roving over his body.

"Okay," she said briskly. "Jacket off."

Just like that, no "Please," no "Would you mind," just "Jacket off." He did as he was told. There was a flash of violet satin as he folded it, placed it carefully on top of his coat.

She posed him, taking hold of his arms, his shoulders, turning him towards the light. "Contrapasto," she said. He shifted his weight to one leg.

This time, he watched her while she drew. A line formed between her eyebrows as she worked to get the contrasting planes of his chest and pelvis, the stresses and folds of his white shirt, the contour lines his braces made running over his chest.

She clipped another sheet of paper to the drawing board. He could see she was hesitating, wanting to ask him something. Ah, he thought. Understanding, he pulled his shirttails out from the waistband of his trousers, unbuttoned his shirt, laid it on top of his jacket.

"Suspenders," she said.

He pulled them down. They hung around his knees. He stood before her in his trousers and a sleeveless white undershirt. He lifted his arm to remove his hat.

"Leave the hat," she said tersely. "Hands in your pockets. Relax your body. Slouch. Head down more. Good. Now. Turn toward me."

He did as he was told. Tessa shut off the overhead lamp. The brim of his hat threw a deep shadow over his face. Hot white light washed down his body, starting at his shoulders, picking out the sinewy strength of his arms, crossing the rise of his pectorals, skimming over the ridges of his abdominal muscles. One eye gleamed, the edge of a cheekbone caught the lamplight. The rest of him was cloaked in shadow. Her breath caught in her throat.

She whipped the drawing board off of her easel, reached for a canvas. Holding a pencil in her hand as if it were a sword, she stared at him for a moment. Then she dropped her gaze to the blank white surface and started to sketch.

Her eyes were black, burning with fierce energy. He watched her mark each detail, bringing him to life. It was as if she were running her hands over him from across the room, and he grew flushed, heated, feeling his body begin to respond.

Yes, she thought. *Now.* She threw down the pencil and reached for her paints. The sharp resinous tang of turpentine impregnated the air. With a large bristle brush, she laid in a dark, transparent background. Choosing a different brush, she modeled the creases of his trousers, the swags of his suspenders. Next, she reached for a soft rag, balling it up to rub clean areas of light. A figure began to emerge from the gloom on the canvas.

Using the tip of the brush the way someone else would use a pencil, she traced the fine line of his profile, the mass of his upper body, bringing them forward from the shadowy background. Abandoning tools altogether, she used her fingers to blend the edges around his hips, his legs, merging them with the darkness.

She stepped back from the easel. It was all there, in the tilt of the hat, the U-shaped neckline of the undershirt, the corresponding curve where it tucked into the waistband of his trousers. The insouciant slant of his shoulders. The way his hip bones jutted forward. She had captured him more truthfully than any camera could; the beauty, the sensuality, the razor's edge of danger.

She eased back into her chair, exhausted. Leaning her elbow on one of the padded armrests, she closed her eyes, just for a minute.

It was too quiet. He broke out of the pose, glanced behind the canvas. There she was, her chin resting in the palm of her hand, asleep in her chair. He smiled, turned to look at her painting. The pain in his heart took him by surprise. Another girl, another time, another drawing of him in his undershirt and braces.

He touched her shoulder. "Tessa."

She started to her feet. She blinked at the light, looking confused, rumpled, adorable. There was a smear of paint along the line of her jaw.

"What time is it?"

He looked at his watch. "It's four-thirty."

Maybe it was the time, maybe it was the amount of turpentine dissolved in the air of the small room. She was swaying on her feet. He moved to catch her. He pulled her up into his arms, carried her to the bed, shoved his coat aside.

The raw sexuality of him, so close to her. Nothing more between them than his ribbed cotton undershirt. The smoothness of his skin, the play of hard muscles under the skin. Words swam into her head, stung her lips. She couldn't believe she wanted to say them. She fought them back down.

Holding her, he felt a dizzying sensation. He wanted to pull her against his chest, to feel the rhythm of her heart pound through his body again. He wanted to climb into bed with her, part her knees, pour himself out into her.

He steadied himself, kissed her slowly, luxuriously. There was nowhere to go, nowhere he had to be. They had all the time in the world.

"Tell me," he whispered. "Where did you get that photograph that you gave to Clayton?"

He could feel her smiling against his lips. "Who wants to know? Raphael Sinclair, the founder of the school? Or Raphael Sinclair, in my room without his shirt on?"

"That one."

"Lucian's loft."

"You are a naughty, naughty girl."

"I know. I feel just terrible about it."

Now she saw it, a thin gold chain around his neck. From it hung a gold ring, plain, cylindrical in shape, like a small yellow machine part. It caught the light from the reflector lamp as it revolved slowly in a circle.

Self-consciously, his hand curled over the ring. He looked down into her pale, serious face, grave brown eyes full of questions she was afraid to ask.

In the semi-darkness, he took her right hand, the one she used for drawing. Kissed the fingers one by one, placed them over his heart.

"Tessa," he said quietly. "There's no one but you."

He kissed her then, the brim of his hat blotting out the light.

That week, everywhere Tessa went, Raphael Sinclair was already there.

At Pearl Paint, where she went searching for General's charcoal pencils, he was drifting towards her through Fine Papers. At Elephant and Castle, where she ordered coffee and toast, he was already seated at a table in a lightless corner with the Times. At Porto Rico Coffee Roasters on Bleecker Street, where he suggested she try Peter's Blend. At Sherwin Williams, where she was hovering indecisively near the paint chips trying to decide what color to paint her kitchen, he helped her choose between Moroccan Red and a glossy Merlot.

At the MoMA, she wandered through the Matisse exhibition, rolling her eyes at crayon-colored paintings of fruit and women that looked like they had been dashed off between lunch and dinner, and wondered what the world saw in them. He was there, of course, standing before an enormous red painting, hands clasped behind his back. He smiled at her approach.

"Fancy meeting you here," he said.

She joined him, turned her gaze to the canvas. A golden-haired woman was setting down a bowl of apples on a carmine-covered table in a carmine-painted room. Cobalt blue vines seemed to climb from the tablecloth to the walls. To the left, a dream landscape, seen through a window. It seemed eerily familiar, and then she remembered she had seen it on a postcard, tacked up on David's wall.

"I like this one," she said.

Surprisingly, he reached for her hand. Her heart gave a little flutter.

Friday night, New Year's Eve, 1992.

Though he had plans with Anastasia later that evening, Rafe found himself heading towards Sixteenth Street, as he did most nights, to take his place on the steps of St. Xavier, to watch over her.

He approached her window, peered through the chink in the blinds. There she was, wearing an orchid-colored jalabiya shot through with gold threads, her hair hanging down her back in damp curls. One plate, one wine glass. He tapped on the glass. She turned her head towards the window. When she saw who it was, she smiled blissfully, as happy as a little girl.

"Happy New Year, Tessa Moss," he said through the glass.

"Happy New Year, Mr. Sinclair."

She let him in. The hand-painted plate on the table, blue vines winding across a white background, held the remains of her dinner. Chicken bones, lemon peel, a few olive pits. Sweet, sour, savory, salty. Rafe identified the aromatics of coriander, cumin, saffron, olives, preserved lemon.

Marrakech, 1944. A man muttering his last bitter words in a foreign language, sinking against blue shutters in an alleyway, Rafe's teeth tearing open his throat.

"Moroccan chicken," he said. "Where did you learn how to cook like this?"

"My roommate," she said. "French Moroccan. From Paris."

She took his coat. To his surprise, she buried her nose in its folds. She smiled. "Mmm," she said. "Smells like you."

"Let me show you something else that smells like me," he said, pulling her to him. He kissed her, then, her mouth, her hair, perfumed with memory.

Outside, New York City accelerated in its orgy of preparatory celebration as the temperature dropped to twenty degrees. The clatter of pedestrian footsteps echoed down the street in a continual parade out of the subway. The hale shouts of friends meeting on the corner before heading up to the madness at Times Square rang through the frigid air. But inside her apartment, the TV was off, the radio silent. The *Times* lay open on the table. A paperback novel awaited her attention on the arm of the sofa. An otherworldly quiet.

"Not watching the ball drop?"

"It's Friday night," she explained. "Sabbath. I don't turn anything electrical on and off until tomorrow night."

"Shabbos," he said.

"Yes," she said, her eyebrows coming together, "You never told me. How did you know that?"

He looked at her, said nothing. She saw a nameless sorrow pass over his face. He turned away. Took an extra moment to balance his hat on top of the coat tree. When he turned around again, the expression was gone.

He flopped onto her couch. "Looking forward to Intersession?"

She came to sit next to him, curled her legs under her, cat-like. "I guess. Do you know Wylie Slaughter?"

He shrugged. "No. Whit recruited him."

She moved, playfully straddling his lap. Raising herself up on her knees, she laid her hands on his chest and kissed him.

"Are you allowed to do this on Shabbos?"

"It's actually encouraged," she said. "Well. If you're married."

He leaned back on the couch, rested his hands on her thighs. "And why aren't you married, Tessa Moss?" he murmured. "A nice Jewish girl like you."

She lowered her gaze, fingered his tie. "You know, I've been out with dozens of boys," she said. "Back home, in Chicago. Doctors. Lawyers. Businessmen. I would sit across from them at some restaurant, thinking, what's wrong with me? They were all perfectly nice, perfectly eligible... something was missing. Something was always missing. Maybe it was missing in me.

"Late at night, alone in my bed, I'd hear the train whistle, on its way from somewhere to somewhere else." She smiled apologetically. "I know. Oldest cliché in the world. But I'd say to myself, someday..."

"...someday, I'm going to be on that train." He finished the sentence for her, then kissed her, thinking of ten-year-old Titian leaving his small alpine village for Venice, of seventeen-year-old Raphael Sanzio leaving Urbino for the big city of Florence, of a beautiful black-haired girl leaving a forgotten town on the far edge of the Polish border for the City of Light. He whispered into her hair, "It's always been that way for people like us."

She pulled his shirttails up out of his trousers, tentatively slipped her hands under his white undershirt. He made himself perfectly still as she explored, moving her fingers over his abdominals, his ribs, following the line of hair that ran down from his chest like an arrow to his groin. He had no breath, but something made him gasp when she leaned over and kissed his belly.

He was charmed, amazed, that the simple act of pushing up his shirt was all it took to arouse him. With Tessa, the smallest gesture returned intense pleasure. He was alternately thrilled and fearful of the way she made him feel; hungry, naked, unsure of himself, vulnerable.

He trapped her face in his hands. He didn't want her doing things for him. On the contrary. She was owed.

She rose up on her knees. She was above him now; he could feel the tips of her hair tickling his face, the unevenness of her breath on his forehead. Her nipples, taut under the thin cotton of her dress. He brushed them with his lips, reached out with his tongue. He felt her back stiffen, heard the hiss of her breath.

She pulled his head close, dug her fingers into his hair. He could hear her heart beat double time, *boomboomboomboomboom* and he found it curiously moving; he hesitated, wanting just for a moment to hold her, to be held by her.

The labored sounds of her breathing excited him. He slid his hands under her dress, wrapped his arms around the smooth skin of her bare bottom, crushed the length of her body against his. Her breathing quickened, grew rough. He reached for her hair, her face, her mouth.

That night, Anastasia's party forgotten, they walked to Central Park, where a steadfast group of runners in fancy dress gathered for the annual 5K run. One intrepid athlete was dressed as a sumo wrestler. Another wore the flowing saffron robes of a Buddhist monk. A third came as Yosemite Sam. And one wore a dark suit and a rubber Bill Clinton mask.

At the sound of the starting pistol, the crowd gathered in the cold cheered. Lovers embraced. The waiters at Tavern on the Green handed out paper cups of champagne. A man in a pink bunny suit took the lead.

Rafe slipped his arms around Tessa and kissed her, as red and gold and green fireworks arced overhead through the starry sky.

26

*T*essa put down her brush, stepped respectfully away from her easel. Wylie Slaughter plowed his fingers through his signature shock of coal-black hair, put on a pair of glasses with black plastic frames, and came in for a closer look.

On Monday, the students had gathered in the Cast Hall, straining in their folding chairs for a better view of the famous artist. He stood at the front, holding a blue Ty Nant bottled water, pacing slowly back and forth in front of Michelangelo's *Pietà*, laconic to the point of comedy.

"Why," he finally said, "In this time of cameras and instant photography, do we still paint the human body?" The students settled down, quieted, waiting for his answer. Minutes ticked by. None was forthcoming. "Your assignment," he continued, "will be to give me the answer."

They were to give him a scene taken from a dream. The students participating in the Intersession project were to expect a visit from the great man once a week, in their studios. Due to understandable time constraints on his part, they would not know when these meetings were to take place. It was in their best interest to be in their studios as much as possible between the hours of ten-thirty and five, Mondays through Thursdays.

Tessa was already halfway done. The canvas showed her hiding under a bed, staring at a pair of highly polished jackboots.

"My grandparents are Holocaust survivors," she explained. "I have these recurring dreams that I'm being chased by Nazis."

He nodded sagely, tilted his head. "Well. Who hasn't had that one. Got anything else?"

She opened her sketchbook. He took it from her, began flipping through it.

Tessa rubbed her eyes. She was tired. At four in the morning, she had been sitting on a stool at the counter at Lox Around the Clock, listening dreamily to the up-and-down notes of Rafe's supple voice as he told her a story from his student days in Paris, something about trying to concoct Vermeer's legendary lost painting medium, a complicated recipe that included melting beeswax into Venice turpentine. When he'd tried to cook it on an electric burner, the whole thing caught fire.

She must have nodded off, because the next thing she remembered was his amused face close to hers, trying to wake her without startling her into falling off the stool. In that brief lapse of time, she had had a short, vivid dream. A family, sitting around a table, holding hands, their eyes closed. A spotlight shone down on them from above. In the background, shadows. She had reached for her sketchbook, scribbled it down.

Slaughter studied it now, tapped it with his finger. "Yeah. What's *that* about?" He plowed back his hair, tapped on her sketchbook. "Definitely this one."

"Really?" She was surprised.

"Really." He stepped back from the canvas. He glanced at her, then looked again, more closely this time. Here it comes, she thought. "Say," he said. "Aren't you Lucian Swain's assistant?"

Suddenly it was hard to breathe. "I was," she managed to say. "Not anymore."

He leaned over, peered closely at the sanguine and charcoal drawing of the naked girl turned towards the man in the shadows on the wall behind her. "He's seeing April Huffman now, I hear."

She sighed. He raised his eyebrows, *Oh, I get it.*

His arms crossed, he made a circuit of the room, taking in the postcards and sketches on the wall. He paused before a particularly fine studio nude, a woman seated on a chair, simple, well lit and sensitively rendered.

"Wow," he said. "You guys are really good. I should sit in on some classes. Could you do this before you came here?"

She dropped her brush into turpentine. "Before I came here," she said. "I could draw. What I've learned here, made me an artist."

He stopped in front of her écorché, studied the muscles. "Wish they'd had a place like this when I was going to school. Course, it was the Sixties. We didn't even have a drawing teacher. Mostly, we got stoned and slept around with other students."

He stopped one last time to study the sketches for her thesis project, tacked in a little block of four on her wall. When he reached the curtain that served as the door, he said, "You know, you're very talented. I'd take you on myself, but I already have an assistant. I could ask around."

"Thanks, I'd appreciate that," she said.

It was Monday, midway into the Intersession project. Two weeks before winter semester would start. Two weeks since she had realized she was in love with Raphael Sinclair. Tessa knew she was getting in too deep, too soon. Portia, had she been around, would have told her she had jumped from the frying pan into the fire. She didn't care. She felt utterly complete, as if a missing piece of herself had been restored to her, in a way that was very messy and complicated and regrettable and made no sense at all if you held it up to the light for too long.

Now they had to be discreet. With the holiday season over, he had returned to work, which for him meant meetings at school, the board, various committees. Tessa became adept at coming up with reasons to wander down the hallway that led to the offices of the Deans, developing a sudden interest in the work in the nearby display cases, a ruse that had paid off yesterday, when Rafe emerged from Giselle's office, a too-skinny first-year student named Allison clinging to his side. As she bubbled animatedly away about an upcoming committee meeting, he had breezed smartly past Tessa, smiling politely while managing to brush his fingertips against her hand. The hairs had stood up at the back of her neck, and an electric current hummed up and down the entire length of her body for the rest of the day.

What she really needed was to find a job, and she made a lackluster stab at it, dutifully calling a few listings she saw in the back of the *Times*, mentioning casually to Giselle that she could use some assistant work. Truthfully, she wasn't trying very hard. A job would have meant being less available for Rafe, and if she didn't mind living on macaroni, and met the minimum payments on all of her bills, she could stretch out her money, just a little bit longer.

"Tell me something about yourself," she said.

"All right," he said agreeably.

"Where are you from?"

It was midnight. They were sitting across from each other at a small table in Florent, a funky little all-night bistro in the Meatpacking District, a seedy, nineteenth-century neighborhood of low buildings and cobblestoned streets on the far west side of Manhattan that even smelled dangerous. At some point she noticed that all the other customers seemed to be club kids or transvestites.

He ordered the *mousse au chocolat,* just so that he could watch her lick it off the tip of a spoon. "How is it?"

"Incredible."

"Tell me."

She closed her eyes. "The texture. It's light and fluffy." Another taste of what was on the spoon. "Dense and silky. All at the same time." She thought some more. "Bittersweet chocolate. Not too sweet. And the aroma...I wish you could taste it."

He leaned forward, licked a trace of mousse from her upper lip. "Lovely," he murmured. He slid his fingers across the table until they touched hers. "Cambridge," he said. "Originally. Then I spent some years in a boarding school in East Anglia. Moved to London in my teens."

"Where is East Anglia?"

"Northeast of London. Very rural."

"It sounds pretty."

"Yes, it does."

She smiled. "I wish we could have been in art school together. That would have been fun."

"Oh, yes."

"Do you think you would have been attracted to me?"

"I would have to be dead not to find you attractive." He frowned. "Technically, I *am* dead."

"I think I would have opened with, 'Wow, you have beautiful eyes. Would you pose for me sometime?'"

His smile deepened. "I would have said yes."

"I'd start off very professional. Do a few quick sketches. And then I'd ask you to take your shirt off."

Now he laughed. "I would have said yes to that as well."

"I'd have the studio next to yours. I'd keep coming over, asking for your opinion."

"There would have been a lot of late nights." He reached under the table, rested his hands on her legs, just above her knees. "One day, we would be riding the elevator to the fourth floor. As the other students stepped out, and the doors closed, I'd press you up against the wall and have my wicked way with you."

She laughed with delight. They were quiet for a moment, happy together. She sought out his eyes. He found he could not meet her gaze for long; he glanced away. She reached out, took his face in her hands. "Hey. I was looking at those."

He tried, stared down into her lovely brown eyes for a moment. Flecks of green. Faith and trust. A man in a fedora.

She took out her sketchbook, began to draw. He tried to peek, but she covered it with her hand. Finally, she tore out the page, folded it in three. Pushed it across the table.

"Your turn," she said.

He stared at it as if it were a dead thing. Picked up the pencil, put it to the paper, then put it back down again.

"I can't," he said.

She was surprised. "What do you mean? I thought you were an artist. You said you went to art school."

"I can't draw," he said abruptly. "I lost the ability, the talent, whatever you want to call it, when I, ah, when I." He fell silent.

"Oh, God." she said awkwardly. "I'm so sorry."

Beautiful Tessa Moss, a remnant of Sofia's blood running through her veins, her extraordinary eyes sad on his account. Under the table, he took her hands, laced his fingers through hers. "Come on," he said. "Let's walk."

The school building was darkened, empty. She turned on the reflector light in her studio as Rafe stopped short, staring at the painting on her easel. She whisked it away, replacing it with what looked vaguely like a family saying grace. "Wylie likes this one."

Good. The image of Tessa, hiding under a bed, Nazi bootheels inches from her head, had shaken him.

"So, how is it going with the great Wylie Slaughter?"

"You know, for a postmodernist, he's not such a bad guy. He really likes what we're doing here."

"Hm. What else did he say?"

"He said I'm very talented."

"Did he now." He sat down on the frivolous red velvet couch, patted the tufted cushion next to him, beckoned with one finger. She sat, instead, across his lap, leaned her head on his shoulder, closed her eyes. He enclosed her in the circle of his arms.

"Tired," she said.

"You should get to bed earlier."

"I should."

Leaning his cheek on her hair, he let his gaze play over the maze of images on her wall. Her studio stirred up memories of his own student days. When he was with her, they were pleasant, not painful.

"Have you done anything more on your thesis project?"

"Who wants to know," she said, her eyes still closed. "Raphael Sinclair, the founder of the school? Or Raphael Sinclair who comes knocking on my window every night?"

"The first one."

"Then, the answer is, you bet." She yawned.

"Really. Tessa. What about canvases? Have you started building your canvases?"

"I still haven't gotten Josephine's final OK on my sketches. She never showed up for our last meeting."

"What?"

She felt guilty, now, for getting Josephine in trouble. Her eyes fluttered open. "She has two kids. She's busy. Sometimes her babysitter doesn't show up. Or the kids get sick. Or the subway gets stuck."

"Look," he said. "I'm taking over as your adviser now. Three paintings." He ticked them off on his fingers. "The grandmother lighting the candles. The whirlwind of bodies. The mother and child." On the last one, his voice may have faltered slightly. "All right?"

"All right."

The fingers of one small white hand came to rest in his lap, making it hard to concentrate. He settled back into the couch, closed his eyes. Suddenly, his eyes flew open, he caught her wrist.

"Tessa. You don't have to...I don't want you to..."

She bent a beatific gaze on him. Smiled lasciviously.

His lower lip caught between his teeth.

She reached up and turned out the light.

Afterwards, she stood up, stretched. It was cold in the studio. She wrapped herself in a length of cloth she kept for draping models and eased away from him, over to her easel, turned the reflector light back on.

Drawn in by the world she had created, she picked up a scarf and absentmindedly tied back her hair. Her eyes narrowed; in a kind of trance, she picked up a bristle brush, daubed it in a pile of burnt umber left on her palette. Unnoticed, the drape slipped to the floor, as she began to fill in the background.

Drowsily, Rafe opened his eyes, looked at his watch. Five a.m. Outside her window, the sky was still a deep, wintery blue. Fluffy flakes of new snow were falling, gathering on the windowsill. He had dozed off; soon he would have to dress, brave the snow, get home before daylight. Tessa was standing in front of her canvas, wearing only a skimpy camisole and jeans. He came to stand behind her, watched her paint, inhaled the turpentine as if it were air. His hands lit on her hips. She paused for a moment, went back to work.

"How did you find out you couldn't draw anymore?"

"I was on the *terrasse* of a restaurant in Antibes, the south of France...I asked the waiter for a pencil. I was going to draw the couple at the next table, the sea...the woman I was with. The pencil came. I held it between my fingers, just as I always had, every day since I was five. I knew exactly where to start, what to do."

He brought his hands close to his face to scrutinize them in the low light, turning them over to look at the palms, the slender fingers, as if the answer were still to be found there. *"Phhht.* Gone. Whatever small talent I had died with the man I used to be."

Tessa took his right hand, kissed it. Holding his hand in hers, she chose a brush. "Closer," she murmured, turning to her easel.

He moved behind her. She raised the brush to the canvas, then, their fingers grasping it together.

Together, they drew the sable tip across the surface, as delicately as a skater gliding across a pond. Their hands swooped and soared. They moved across vast open expanses of snowy canvas, the hairs of the brush leaving marks in the thick paint. He could feel the liquid viscosity of the varnish under his fingertips, and thrilled to the smooth sensation of the brush glissading over the paint. Holding her hand, he made gestures small and large, edges soft and sharp. He felt the bones and tendons in her fingers jump and dance as they lingered tenderly over the features of a boy's face, scumbled light falling over the mother's hair, glazed a shadow over the father's eyes.

A mixture of smells and textures, freedom and discipline, just as he remembered it. He yanked her around to face him. He kissed her, ferociously, rapaciously. The brush dropped to the floor.

She tore at his shirt, pulling it free of his trousers and up over his head. He slipped down the straps of her camisole, then kissed her breasts. She pushed him down on the couch. He reached for one bare arm, pulled her between his knees.

"Tell me what you want," he whispered.

"I want you," she whispered back. "In my studio. Just like this. For always."

She knelt on the floor between his legs, touched her tongue to the arrow of hair that ran down his abdomen and disappeared under the waistband of his trousers. He felt his muscles twitch, aroused.

"How many girls have drawn you, over the years?" she said.

"Just two."

She rose up through his knees to kiss the ridges of his stomach muscles, the finger-like projections of his serratus, the smooth rise and fall of his pectorals. He lay back on the couch, dug his fingernails into the tufted cushions. Warmed by the pressure of her breasts against his skin, he caught her face between his hands, kissed her. She bent her head to the tender and vulnerable hollow formed by the clavicles and the tendons at the base of his throat.

"What is this?" There was a small, raised welt of white flesh to the left of his sternum, over his heart, about an inch in length. She touched it with a finger.

"Don't," he said, capturing her hand in his.

She put her tongue to it, then her mouth. Sucked lightly.

Unexpectedly, he gasped, shuddered, cried out her name, clasped her to him.

A great swell of emotions welled up, broke over her, penetrating her through and through. With some deeper feminine instinct, she knew. This was not the grasp of a lover, but the clutch of a drowning man.

In one of those moments of perfect clarity that comes along perhaps once or twice in a life, she suddenly understood that she would give herself to him completely; love him, fight for him, cling to him, protect him with her life, if that was what it took.

"I love you," she breathed in his ear.

He stopped, gripped her face in his hands, stared into her eyes. Immediately, she wished she could take it back. Portia had tried to warn her. This was Raphael Sinclair, wealthy bachelor, man-about-town, notorious cocksman. How many Lucians would there have to be before she learned her lesson?

"Oh, thank God," he said. "At last. Thank God."

On the last Thursday afternoon in January, Rafe received a disturbing phone call from Giselle, demanding to know why he had missed the party at the International Center for Photography the previous evening. The truth was, he had blown it off in favor of a nighttime visit to Tessa's studio.

Giselle went on to mention that April would continue as a painting instructor in the coming semester, and that Turner was about to hire one of her friends to fill an empty drawing instructor slot. When he tried to question her further, she suggested that he try coming to the meetings.

Janina, who couldn't help but hear the tone of Giselle's voice as she lay next to him in bed, silently mimed. *Tsk tsk tsk.*

That evening, as the sun set in her window, and Tessa put the finishing touches on her dream painting, the curtain was shouldered aside, and David Atwood stood there.

Over the past month, she had forgotten how good-looking he was. He shoved his hands in his pockets and strolled casually forward.

"Nice," he said, looking at the canvas on her easel. "Look at those tones. This is different for you."

She warmed to him, happy for the praise. She put her brush to the canvas, whittling the edge of a shadow. "What are you doing here? I thought you'd be having one last glorious weekend together before Sara goes back upstate."

"She went back early," he said. He came closer, stopping just a short distance away from her. Close enough for her to see him breathing, to smell his aftershave, close enough for her to admire the clear china blue of his eyes. "Tess," he said. "I can't stop thinking about you."

Tessa never heard the conclusion of what was actually the opening volley of a carefully prepared speech, because at that moment, the curtain moved aside again, and Raphael Sinclair stood there.

He looked at her, and she at him, and instantly, David Atwood knew exactly what else Tessa had been up to during Intersession, and his mouth dropped open in shock.

"Excuse me," said the founder of the school, and vanished through the curtain. It swished soundlessly closed behind him.

She turned to him and smiled, but now every nerve in her body was humming, he could feel the heat, standing a foot away from her in the confines of the studio. He could see it slowly come to her, the meaning of his words, and as the heat around her faded to a faint warm glow, he thought she had never been lovelier or more desirable.

"Oh, no," he said earnestly. "Not him."

"What do you mean?" she said, but he could tell she knew exactly what he meant, and she found a reason to break eye contact, putting one final streak of paint to a lock of hair falling over the older daughter's forehead.

"So...I guess it's over with Lucian Swain. You don't still work for him, do you?"

She laughed. "No. Know anybody who needs an assistant?"

"Tess," he said again, then fell silent. She focused on his hands, nice hands, his skin a deeper shade of ochre, the nails square and neat. Hands capable of creating subtle tones of color richer than in real life. She herself would never be able to mix color like that, it was a gift, like a photographic memory, or an intrinsic ability with math. She should have met him years ago, she thought, before Lucian. Life was funny like that.

They chatted for a few more moments, about this and that, the news, the weather, the progress of her thesis project, and then, tactfully, he was bowing himself out.

At the curtain, he hesitated, half-turned to her. "I really think we could have something," he said quietly. "Whatever happens. I want you to know. I'm there for you."

In the darkened studio next to hers, with the curtains drawn, Rafe listened to the entire conversation. He could find no flaw in Tessa's responses or in her behavior, yet he felt an underlying unease.

Later that night, as he fed from a barely-conscious club kid of indeterminate gender before heading over to her apartment, he realized what had made him uneasy. David Atwood was a good man and a good painter. And he, Raphael Sinclair, was a blood-sucking vampire.

Alone in his office, Turner cursed. Luckily, it was too late to do anything about April—she had already signed a contract—but Raphael Sinclair had just stopped in to chew him out, icily informing him that he would not be rubber-stamping the hire of the new drawing teacher, an emerging artist April had suggested. Her contract sat in front of him now, awaiting only her signature. True, she worked in photo collage, but she had an MFA from SVA, she was equipped to teach Life Drawing 101, for God's sake. He sat at his desk and fumed. He had been hoping that Rafe would be too busy sneaking around with his hot little art student to notice the hire of a new teacher. He reached for the black office phone, dialed Blesser's extension.

"Hiring her would be a step in the right direction," Bernard agreed cautiously. "I hate to be the one to say this, but...is there any way around him?"

Arletta, the front office secretary, swept through, dropped a pile of old-fashioned computer printout paper, the kind that was connected by perforated folds, into his inbox. "Grades are in," she called back over her shoulder as she hurried out.

Whit lifted the heavy sheaf of paper, set it in front of him. Flipped through the pages. Stopped somewhere in the middle, ran his index finger across the page. Tapped a letter in the third column. Smiled.

Rafe strode up Sixteenth Street towards Tessa's apartment, letting the anticipation of the evening ahead slowly overtake him. One by one, the muscles in his lower belly tensed or tightened as he thought of certain places on her body; the small dip above her clavicle; the color of her skin, pink and cream, like the edges of rose petals; the valley of her spine where it deepened and disappeared under the waistband of her jeans; the place between the cups of her breasts when she wore a particular black lace bra. The white of her neck when he pushed away her hair.

It was not yet dark. He could have rung her doorbell, but he preferred the familiar intimacy of knocking on her window. In his jacket pocket was a plane ticket, the redeye to Italy. Late in the afternoon, he had received a call that there was an instructor at the Accademia di San Luca who could draw like Da Vinci. He doubted anything would come of it, but he felt duty bound to chase down every lead. He wished he'd had the forethought to buy a ticket for Tessa; he would have liked to show her Rome, the Sistine Chapel, the ruins of the Forum, the Colosseum, the Arch of Titus. Another leap of the muscles in his belly. *Someday.*

The sun was not yet down, she buzzed him in. He swept through the doors, ignoring the mirrors in the entryway, made the turn to her apartment.

He could smell her cooking before he reached her door; fresh bread, ginger, olives, saffron, chicken. Oh, the things she could make. A pity he could not taste them, but he could still find pleasure in the way they perfumed the air.

She was on the phone when he came in. She had already showered, he could see; her wet hair hung heavily down her back, staining the orchid jalabiya a darker purple. She turned to face him, and now he was jolted out of his happy reverie. Her eyes were dark and stricken, something was up. Probably the grandfather. The old man must have died. He looked at her sympathetically. After the call, she would run to him, he would hold her. *Whatever this is, we can get through it.*

She was nodding, nodding, funny, because the person on the other end of the line couldn't hear her response. Her eyes fastened on him, wide and wild, as if she wanted to remember him this way forever. Finally she said her goodbyes, put down the phone, and then she was his. He waited expectantly.

The phone call came at six, as she was toweling off after her shower. Frowning, she pulled on her robe and ran to answer it, wondering who would be calling her this late on a Friday, so close to Shabbos.

Usher's voice on the other end of the line sounded tight. There was an unfamiliar note to it, suppressed rage. She braced herself for what would surely be bad news.

"It's Zaydie," he said.

"Is he..." she couldn't bring herself to say the words.

"He's fine," Usher said shortly. "He was really shaken by the heart attack. Apparently, he and Bubbie have been talking it over, that's what he said, anyway, and they decided to give their jewelry away to their children. They don't want to wait until after they're gone. They want to see the family enjoy their gifts."

"Very big of Zaydie to give away Bubbie's jewelry."

"Let me finish. Eva gets Bubbie's diamond engagement ring. Bernie gets a gold watch. Auntie Barbara gets Bubbie's diamond wedding ring. Allen gets the other gold watch. Cilla gets a pearl necklace. Suri gets a diamond broach. Rifkie gets emerald earrings. And *Dad, gets nothing.*"

Tessa was stunned. "Nothing?"

"Nada."

"What did he say?"

"You know Dad. He'd never say anything that might upset his beloved Pa. A week goes by, maybe two. He invites Zaydie over for a Shabbos lunch. Finally, he comes around to asking him why. And you know what he says?"

At that moment, there was a rap at the window. Rafe, in all likelihood. She buzzed him in.

"He says, '*Because of your Tessa.*'"

She put her hands flat on the table to steady herself. Her head was swimming, she found she couldn't breathe. There was a small click at the door as Rafe let himself in.

Rapidly, Usher sketched out the rest of the story. Zaydie had a sister, he never talked about her. She was trouble. An *artiste!* There was a *shonda,* she had drawn her friends, children in the village, her own brother, without their clothes on. *Naked.* Disgusting! No one in all of Poland would have her for a wife. Just before the war, the family sent her to Paris, maybe there she would find someone more modern. She went wild there, running around with some *shaygetz.*

"'It was a disease, a sickness! And I can see your Tessa is traveling down the exact same road! I'm giving you one warning, Sender. Stop her! Or you're not my son anymore. You'll be a stranger to me.'"

Numb with shock, Tessa didn't really hear what Usher said after that. Somehow she got through the rest of the conversation, wished her brother a good Shabbos, and hung up the phone.

She turned to look at Rafe. He was standing near the kitchen, and the left side of his face was cast in warm yellow light. As she stood there, with her grandfather's harsh words singing in her ears, he smiled reassuringly.

"What is it?" he said.

She slipped her arms inside his coat, buried her face in his chest. His arms went around her, and he rested his head on her hair.

"Tell me," he whispered into her ear. He waited for the tears, the guilt, the recriminations. He thought of all the comforting things he would say to her. Thought of other, softer, fleshier ways he would comfort her.

Angry tears flooded up, surprising her, scalding her cheeks. She swiped at them with her fingers. "Zaydie had a sister. An artist. She drew her friends, children in the village, her own brother, naked. He says it was a *disease,* a *sickness.* And I'm just like her."

Rafe blinked at her, staggered back a step, as if she had shot him.

Suddenly the walls were closing in on him, history was closing in on him, he had to get out of there. Easing away from her, he groped blindly for the doorknob. He tried not to look at her small hurt figure as the door slammed shut behind him.

That night, she slept poorly. She leapt out of bed at every sound, thinking it was Rafe, knocking on the window. But she was mistaken. He was gone.

On Saturday afternoon, feeling like she was trespassing, she walked to Gramercy Park and knocked on the intimidating oak door of his townhouse. Of course, no one answered. A well-dressed little boy being guarded by a uniformed nanny with a face like a bulldog stared at her through the sharp rungs of the park fence. It was cold. She wrapped her coat tighter around herself and walked back home.

Sunday morning dawned a clear, cold gray. She awoke to a stuffy nose and achy limbs. Still, tomorrow was the first day of the new term, and she had promised the founder of the school that she would begin building her canvases. *Rafe.* A throb in her heart. She turned over and went back to sleep.

After lunch, she pulled on leggings and an old sweater, headed off to school. The studio floor was empty and cold. People were still away, returning to the city later today, or tonight. She put on the news. More hand-wringing over the Bill Clinton and Gennifer Flowers affair. Some dumb story about a Hillary Clinton/Barbara Bush cookie bake-off. Background noise.

At work in her studio, she felt better. She went through her paints and threw away tubes that were dried up or empty. She took inventory of her supplies and noted what she would need for the upcoming semester. Took down the three thesis sketches and worked out the measurements. Kicked herself for not trying harder to find a job. For the first time in a month, she wondered what Lucian was doing.

At dinnertime, footsteps echoed down the corridor. The footsteps headed up towards the sculptors' grotto, bypassing her, stopping at Graham's studio. Tessa heard Turner's voice, Graham's voice, Turner's voice again. The back and forth of a meeting with an adviser. After twenty minutes or so, it was over. The footsteps headed back up the corridor, stopped outside her studio.

Turner was dressed in a light blue button-down shirt with a thin tan stripe, khakis. He was holding, as usual, his clipboard.

"You're here on the last Sunday night of Intersession? Very dedicated."

"I'm a little behind on my thesis project," she admitted.

There was a smirky little half-smile on his pale, doughy face. "Josephine's your adviser, isn't she?" He put the clipboard behind his back, strolled around her space. "How's that going?"

"She's great. It's just that, well...she doesn't have a lot of spare time."

He was looking appreciatively at Gracie's drawings. "Well, you know. That's how it goes with women artists sometimes. They get married, they have a couple of kids, art goes *poof.*" He turned to face her, clipboard in hand. "So, these are your thesis sketches? Mind if I have a look?"

She was perspiring. Was it warm in the studio? He parked his squat body in front of her wall, looked from one to the next, then back again.

"Hmmm. Kind of illustration-ey, aren't they," he mused. "You know what the problem is, Moss," he confided, turning towards her. "They're too generic. Anybody could have done this. You're not bringing anything new to the table."

She stared fearfully at her drawings. He was right. Anyone could have done them. Suddenly, her face was burning, she felt sick to her stomach.

"But that's not why I'm here," he said. He consulted his clipboard. "I have your grades from last semester." He hesitated, tapping it with a pen. "It looks like you got a C in Studio Painting."

"I did?" She was sweating, the world was spinning. She brushed her hand across her forehead. *So hot.* "But that was with April. You can't count that."

"Well, maybe." He checked his clipboard again as if he didn't already know what was there, looked at her with all sympathy. "But there was also this C+ in Perspective. I'm sorry, Tessa."

Baffled, she looked at him, not understanding.

"Your scholarship. You have to keep up a B average, or you lose your scholarship," he explained.

"But...but I didn't know that."

"You should have. It was in the contract you signed." He thumbed through a xeroxed form. There was her signature, on an application she'd filled out last June. "See?"

Slowly it dawned on her, the import of what he was saying.

"Of course, if you can pay for this semester up front," and he spread his arms out, as if to say it was no big deal. "That will be seven and a half thousand dollars."

"I don't have any money," she said.

"What about your family?" he asked helpfully.

Her heart was hammering. "No."

"Friends? Grandparents? A favorite aunt?" Wordlessly, she shook her head, kept shaking it.

"Well," he said, sounding genuinely contrite. "I'm sorry to be the one to say this. You're going to have to clear out your studio."

She wondered if it were possible for her heart to stop inside her body, for her to die right in front of him.

He glanced around the crowded room. He actually felt excited. "Take all the time you need," he insisted. "It doesn't have to be tonight. Tomorrow is fine." Her face was very white, she was standing perfectly still. With satisfaction, he noted a faint sheen of perspiration over her forehead. "Now, listen," he said firmly. "Don't take this too hard. You'll find the money somewhere, it'll just take a little time. You can always reapply next year."

His job here was done. He pushed aside the curtain, paused on the threshold, turned back as if he had just remembered something. "Oh, hey," he said conversationally. "How about April Huffman and Lucian Swain getting married at City Hall on Friday? Who saw *that* coming? Took us all by surprise." A faint predatory smile, and then he was gone.

She was very cold and very hot at the same time. She maneuvered herself into a chair, trapped her freezing hands between her knees. God, it was so hot. Was it always this hot in the studios? She pushed open the window. Frigid air rushed in. She doubled over, put her head between her knees, tried to breathe.

I'm nothing. I'm nothing. I'm nothing.

Alone in her studio, she bent her head into her hands. She couldn't bear the thought of showing up tomorrow morning, clearing out her things with all her friends surrounding her, pitying her, trying to help. She would do it right now. Where to start? She cast her unseeing gaze around the room, taking in the bordello couch, the Moroccan table, the Persian rug, the accoutrements of art. So warm. So inviting.

The wall. She would start with the wall. Slowly, she started unpinning the postcards and sketches, the Exquisite Corpse games she'd saved because they were so funny. One by one, she put them on the work table, dropping the pushpins into an empty coffee cup. Faster and faster she worked. In a frenzy, she made one pile, then another, and another. The first pile tipped over, taking the others with it. She took no notice when they spilled onto the floor. She would get it later.

Next, she turned to her canvases. There was one for every day of school so far, and class had commenced way back in September. She laid the first canvas on the floor—a real beauty, Sivan, laying on her side on the model stand, the light following the curves of her languorous figure—then laid another flat on top of it. In this way, she made three precarious heaps in the middle of the dusty floor. The stacks teetered over the top of the makeshift wall separating the studios.

Well. She couldn't take them all home, not like that. *So hot.* She brushed her arm across her forehead, went to the studio one over, the studio across the way, opened those windows as well. *There.* Returning to her work table, she selected an xacto knife out of a coffee can. The light glinted off of the razor-like blade.

She took a canvas from the top of the pile. With four measured strokes, she cut it out of the stretchers. It lay like a corpse on the dusty floor. And then she selected another. And another. And another.

Hours later, she had flayed every canvas free of its wooden supports. They lay around her like fallen leaves. The joints in her fingers ached. Her back throbbed, her knees were sore from kneeling on the hard wooden planks. For the first time, she wondered if she was coming down with something. She went to the window to cool her burning face, watched her breath disappear into the night as gusts of frozen vapor. Glancing at her watch, she saw the hands pointing to three in the morning. Morning creeping up on her, and still so much to do.

Morning. What would she do the next morning? And the next day? And the day after that, and the day after that, and the day after that? The thought of classes starting tomorrow without her, the thought of walking out the front door never to return, was a knife in her heart. Worse; with no money and no job prospects in sight, would she have to give up her apartment? Go back to Chicago? She knew what they would say to her upon her return. Enough with the art *narishkeit.* Settle down already.

April Huffman's pale-skinned back, her straight dark hair, her bony knees, her small flat ass, her legs straddling her partner's sides as she mounted him, the famous painter Lucian Swain.

The pain exploded inside of her then.

I'm nothing. I'm nothing. I'm nothing. I'm nothing. I'm nothing.

Her gaze fell on the last item on her wall, now a sea of white. The finely textured charcoal drawing of a naked woman seated at the edge of a bed, her whole body yearning towards a man hidden in the shadows.

The temperature in the studio had dropped precipitously; she could see her breath as she stepped over the canvases littering the floor, and pulled out the four pushpins in the corners of the paper.

Savagely, she ripped the drawing in half, then in half again. Again and again, into smaller and smaller pieces, until it was nothing but tiny bits of very expensive imported four-ply confetti, scattered across the floor.

She was dizzy. Swaying on her feet, she put her hand across her eyes until the sensation passed. *I should lie down for a little while,* she thought to herself. But the couch was so far away. *You know, right here is good. Just for a few minutes.* She went down on her knees then, folded herself over until her head touched the floor. Her last conscious thought was that it felt good on her burning forehead. And then she passed out.

At eight-thirty Monday morning, Levon walked out of the elevator on the second floor with the *Times* under his arm, waved hello at Arletta, continued down the corridor to his office.

The lounge was packed with students, the comfortable jumble of backpacks and portfolios, dozing on the makeshift couches, or excitedly exchanging news of the winter break. It was good to have them back. He found Intersession lonely, with its deserted classrooms and empty halls.

He unlocked his door, placed his cane in the umbrella stand, took off his coat. Just as he was about to sit, a first-year student burst through the door with urgent news.

Levon ran down the hall, flew up the stairs two steps at a time, the pain in his knee be damned.

The first thing he noticed was the temperature. It was so cold he could see his breath. A crowd was gathered around the second studio from the front, and he made his way down the corridor, pushing through the curious onlookers.

He shouldered aside the curtain. And there he stopped.

Some catastrophe had occurred during the night. Scattered around the floor were a tangle of distended stretcher bars bent at odd angles, picture postcards, drawings, drifts of studio paintings hacked free of their supports, all dusted over with a blizzard of torn paper. In the middle of it all, Tessa Moss, huddled in a heap on the floor.

He looked to her friends, David, Ben, Clayton, Portia, Gracie. They all wore the same pale, frightened expression. "Go get Raphael Sinclair," he said.

But he was already there.

Conversation ceased as if it had been shut off with a switch. He stood framed in the doorway, his voluminous coat stirred by the cold breeze blowing in through the open windows, calmly taking in the situation. And then he strode into the studio.

He squatted down beside the motionless girl, tilted his head to hers. She whispered. He listened. For a minute, nothing happened. Then he swooped her up in his arms, turned, and swept out of the studio, his coattails billowing out behind him. A path opened up for him, then closed after he passed. No one said a word.

Portia caught his gaze as he went by. For a moment, their eyes locked. Her blood ran cold. For suddenly she knew, without a doubt, felt it in the marrow of her bones, that the rumors were true, he was exactly what Clayton had said he was. A vampire.

27

*T*essa dreamed. She was flying, swooping up and down above the narrow twisting streets of lower Manhattan, above the fire escapes, the water towers, the chimney pots. Coming slowly back down to earth, she floated through the colonnaded portico of a townhouse on the corner of a pretty little square. Strong arms carried her up a flight of stairs. Ghostly figures passed back and forth, touching her and whispering. She had vague recollections of being undressed, a warm bath. A voice like a lullaby. The world's softest bed, and then sinking down into deep, dreamless sleep.

She woke up in a strange bedroom. She had no idea where she was; what time it was, what day of the week, or for that matter, whether it was night or day. The walls were painted a glossy brown, the moldings a contrasting creamy white. The room contained a desk, a lamp, a bed, a bureau, all Mission, all very good. There were blush-colored roses in a green Depression-era urn, set in front of an antique mirror oxidizing with age. A door that might lead to a bathroom. Floor length velvet curtains suggested a terrace. Pillar candles splashed the surfaces all around with yellow light.

Raphael Sinclair was in the armchair next to the bed. He leaned forward, took her hand in both of his.

"My sweet girl."

"Where am I?"

"My home," he said. "My bedroom, actually. Your friends found you on the floor of your studio Monday morning. You passed out. "

Oh, yes. Two C's. Lost my scholarship. Kicked out of school. Lucian and April. Her whole body crumpled with the impact of the memory.

"Listen," he said quickly. "Yesterday, a new scholarship was endowed. The Sofia Wizotsky Memorial Scholarship, to be awarded annually to a gifted student. You are the first recipient. I should have done it years ago." She opened her mouth to protest. He put up his hand to stop her; *not yet.* "Secondly. Levon will be your new adviser. Josephine is a wonderful painter, but it sounds like she has a bit much on her palette right now. Third. I've spoken with a friend of mine. You can start working at *Anastasia* as soon as you're ready."

"What day is it?"

"Wednesday," he said. "Three in the afternoon."

Her mouth dropped open. "I've been asleep for *three days?* What happened?"

"A virus, accompanied by high fever. A touch of whatever's going around." He leaned closer. "I'm so sorry," he said earnestly. "Sorry I wasn't there for you."

For three days she'd laid in his bed, small and white and vulnerable. Outside of a few hours spent making arrangements, he'd hovered over her, holding her hand, watching her breathe, reliving the moments of his life that had brought him to this point, this girl.

He turned it over in his head a hundred different ways, but always, it came down to this: *she has been returned to me.* And also this. How could he. How *dare* he. And this. *Run away. Run as fast as you can.*

Still... Tessa's bare skin by the light of the moon. Tessa smiling down on him, a Pre-Raphaelite apparition. Her raspberry lips, her lithe, little, welcoming body. The informed innocence of her touch.

The doctor had clocked her temperature at 104 degrees, then scribbled a prescription. Keep her cool, he said. Give her this, twice a day. Soup. Tea. Let her sleep. After he left, Rafe stood over her motionless body and thought. *You can suck the life out of someone without ever touching a drop of their blood.*

During dreams where she panted like she was running from someone, where she whimpered and wept, he held onto her, fearing that in her delirium she would launch herself from the bed and injure herself coursing blindly through the unfamiliar house. At times he gathered her in his arms, wanting to feel the reassurance of her heart beating against his chest.

Thinking about what he would tell her when she awoke. Wondering how he would live without her, for she would surely leave him after the tale he had to tell.

There was a sick feeling at the pit of his stomach. He rested his forehead on the crisp white sheets. He felt her hand on the back of his neck, her fingers in his hair. She forgave him. Of course she did.

"How?" he asked her, honestly bewildered. "How?"

But she was almost asleep again, her breath returning to steady, rhythmic waves. He stood over her, regarding her. A small flutter of pleasure at the sight of her hair spread over his pillow. A small flutter of grief. After tomorrow, she would be gone.

"Sleep, sweet girl," he said, kissing her forehead. "I'll take care of everything. Now sleep."

The next time she awoke, it was evening. The curtains had been drawn open to reveal a view of the park. There was a smear of red in the western sky. She was alone. She pushed aside the duvet. She was wearing a clean white tank top and white silk shorts, not hers.

She swung her legs over the side of the bed, and stood. A little shaky, yes, but manageable. She shuffled off to the bathroom, admired the white porcelain fixtures, the polished brass knobs, the subway tiles, a huge white magnolia blossom floating in a glass bowl.

There was a painting hanging over the quarter-sawn oak headboard. A pair of lovers, tangled in a froth of white sheets. The man hoisted himself up over the woman, gazing down at her lovely face, her black hair tousled across the pillow, her arms around his neck. The lines were bold and confident, but the feeling was unmistakably tender. Klimt? Schiele? She couldn't tell which.

She moved to the bureau. There was a grooming set on a mirrored tray, silver and tortoiseshell, monogrammed with the initials RS. She picked up an oval hairbrush, stroked it delightedly against her curls.

Next to the tray was a sketchbook. It was bound in smooth black calfskin, like the one he had given her. She opened it, flipped through it. The pages were good heavy paper, yellowing now around the edges, bristling with drawings in every medium, charcoal, pencil, pen and ink.

There were quick studies of people at café tables, parks, restaurants. The way the light fell across this table, across that face. Mothers pushing baby carriages. Soldiers in uniforms. Still lifes, half-empty wine glasses, half-eaten baguettes. Unfinished love poems. Dates jotted down; times, places, mysterious meetings with long-ago comrades.

The drawings were beautiful; there was a wistful stillness to them, a stark loneliness that reminded her of Edward Hopper's *Nighthawks* hanging on the wall of her apartment.

A paper fell out, fluttered to the floor. She picked it up. Yellowed and cracked at the folds, it appeared to be a game of Exquisite Corpse. The head of a young man, the body of a Roman statue, the wings of an angel. With a start, she recognized Raphael Sinclair. She wondered who had drawn it, and when. Carefully, she folded it and slipped it back in the sketchbook, replaced it on the bureau. And turned around.

Rafe was standing behind her, hands in his pockets.

"Hello, Tessa."

"Hello, Mr. Sinclair."

"I see you've found my sketchbook." As if he hadn't left it out where she would find it.

"You're very good," she said.

"Thank you," he said. "I like to think I was." He smiled at her, a sad, rueful sort of smile, but a smile just the same. "You must be famished."

"Well. Maybe a little."

"Why don't you come downstairs, and let's see what we can find."

He bundled her into his robe, carried her downstairs, installed her in a corner of the Stickley couch, swathed her in a silk shawl from Kashmir. He unfolded a tray table that he found in a closet, then disappeared into the kitchen. Moments later, he returned with a toile tray, trimmed in gold, bearing a footed soup bowl in white porcelain, with lions' heads for handles.

Tessa picked up the spoon, then hesitated, poised over the bowl.

"It's from Bernstein's," he said. "Don't worry, it's kosher. Eat." He pulled up a chair opposite the couch, watched her, inhaled the herbal bouquet of parsley, bay leaf and dill. When she was finished, he brought her another.

"How do you feel?"

"Better now."

She lay back on the couch, gazed around the Great Room, at his furnishings, the woodwork, the red lacquered walls, the hanging lamps from Morocco, the masterpieces of art history.

"Do you like it here?" he asked.

"I love it here," she replied, running her hand over the lustrous velvet nap of the couch cushions.

"I'm so glad," he said, meaning, *I love you.*

He sat back in his chair, passed his hand across his forehead. "Forgive me," he said quietly. "But this...this brings back the worst memories in the world."

"I know," she said. "I'm sorry."

"Oh, Tessa," he said. "Don't ever apologize to me."

Rafe took her hand in both of his, turned it over, tracing the lines in her palm with his fingers. "What did your grandfather—Yechezkel—tell you about her?" His voice tripped a little. "About Sofia."

Anguished. "He said she was trouble. There was some scandal."

"A *shonda,*" he said.

"Yes," she agreed. "It must have been serious. They were a well-to-do family, and they couldn't find anyone in all of Poland who would marry her."

"Oh, Yechezkel. You're still such an asshole." he muttered. "What else did he say?"

She spoke in a muffled voice, barely audible. "She went wild in Paris, always hanging around with some *shaygetz.*"

Rafe angled his head sharply away from her. Though his expression was lost in shadow, she saw him swallow hard, blink something away.

"That's so cruel," he said in a low voice. "So cruel."

He got up, began to move restlessly around the room. His pace altered, lengthening, until it resembled the stride of a jungle cat stalking prey. He prowled through the floor, in and out of nooks and shadows, opening and shutting drawers until he found what he was looking for, a cigarette. He leaned against a table, lit it with a tortoiseshell lighter, blew out a stream of smoke.

"I didn't know you smoked."

"I don't," he said. "For years now."

It was a few minutes before he spoke again. "I have something to tell you," he said.

A shiver went up the back of her neck. His eyes. They were changing. The irises first, growing lighter and lighter until they were a shade of blue so pale it was almost white, until she could almost see through them, like pond ice. His pupils changed too, the smooth black borders rapidly contracting and expanding, almost to the edge of the iris. Simultaneously, the whites of his eyes flamed a fierce, bloody red.

"Tell me you love me," he said. "Tell me again, before I begin. Because, by the end of the night, you will want to run from me. And I want to hear you say it, just one more time."

She got to her feet. The robe fell to the floor. She stood over him, looked directly into the strange, wolfish eyes.

"I love you, Raphael Sinclair." she said.

He stared back at her. And then his arms went around her, and he pulled her close, burying his face in the wilds of her hair, whispering something she couldn't hear. Then he dressed her in his robe as if she were a little girl, settled her back on the couch again, spread the shawl over her knees.

"I have a story for you, Tessa Moss." he said. "A story of light and dark, of good and evil. Of love and art, of wrong and right. And the blurred lines in between."

Part Two

$\mathcal{I}$ was born in Cambridge, England in 1909, the product of a May Fair fling that went too far. My father, a physics student at the university, and my mother, a local girl hoping to improve her station, knew straight off that it would be a mistake to marry, but marry they did, and seven months later, I was born.

They split up when I was two. Since I was in the way of Mother's compulsive partying, and Father went on to hook up with a proper social equal, they agreed to send me off to a dismal boarding school in East Anglia.

I don't remember much from the early years. Bad food. Cold rooms. Hateful teachers. Mean older boys. Holidays with my mother, who had married a pilot, drinking too much and asking tearfully if I forgave her for giving me away. Rare meetings with Father, who could barely bring himself to look at me. Only one thing saved me. I could draw. I copied the funny papers, the comics. I covered the pages of my schoolbooks with drawings of trains, fighter planes, automobiles. Caricatures of the masters, the boy sitting in front of me.

When I was thirteen, my father asked me to come live with him in London. He had been knighted while I was away at school; he'd invented something in the tinning industry that helped feed our boys in Flanders, and now he was a Sir. He had a house in Bloomsbury near the British Museum, a stone-faced Georgian townhouse as cold and as gray as he was. I showed him my drawings. I thought they would make him proud of me. The kids at school used to ask me if they could keep them. He told me art was no profession for a man.

When I came into my majority, I left for Paris. I attended the Academie Julian, where we painted from models in the morning and went off to copy old masters in the Louvre in the afternoon. I wanted to be the next Hopper, creating soulful landscapes of loneliness and alienation. In the evenings I would meet my friends at La Coupole or Café de Flore and try to talk the French women and American expatriates into bed. It was 1939, and I thought I was the luckiest man alive.

I remember everything about that day. It was a Tuesday, a sunny January morning. The model was Lulu, a bored brunette with a nice behind. I may have slept with her once or twice. Sofia was late. She was wearing a pea-green dress, and she was a little flustered, which made it harder for her to remember her French conjunctives. She apologized to the master in very bad French, and he pointed to an empty spot a little ahead of me to the right. The light had changed, and the monitor went to roll up the shade a little more. Just as she took her seat, a single shaft of sun beamed in, cutting through the haze of cigarette smoke, bathing her in a brilliant white light. Like God's flashlight. Everybody turned to stare. She looked like an angel.

That morning, I drew very badly. I couldn't keep my eyes off of the new girl. I finally gave up on trying to draw the model and satisfied myself with drawing Sofia's lovely profile. In my head, I practiced what I was going to say to her. *Bonjour, je m'appelle Raphael Sinclair. Guten Tag,* something something Raphael Sinclair. You haven't seen Paris till you've seen it with an Englishman with a limited command of French. Hey, my dad's a knight! Please allow me to introduce myself, Raphael Sinclair, I think I love you.

Finally, the monitor dismissed the model. I put my drawing board under my arm, screwed up my courage, leaned over and said, *"Excusez-moi,"* to her shoulder.

She turned around, looked up at me from under a velvety fringe of thick black lashes, and said, "Yes?" in heavily-accented English.

I stared down into the wild tragic depths of her eyes, and whatever clever thing I was going to say was lost forever.

Just then, a big blond American fellow slid over to her, and said breezily, "Care to join me for lunch? Just heading over to Brasserie Lipp."

Without turning her gaze from mine, she said, "No, thank you."

"I'm sorry," he apologized with a winning smile, extending his hand. "I'm Sawyer Ballard. Of Boston, Massachusetts and Newport, Rhode Island. I know we haven't been introduced, but we're all pretty informal here. I promise I won't bite. Unless you're a *croque monsieur*. Come on, it'll be fun. I'm meeting some other artists there. You too, Sinclair, you can bring your girl."

There was someone I saw sometimes, and she was not my girlfriend, but Sofia didn't know that, and I saw her face fall; only for a moment, but there was no mistaking it.

"All right," she agreed, and began to gather up her things. Sawyer caught my eye, gave me a sly smile, shrugged. *All's fair,* he was saying.

Already, I had lost. Any man with an ounce of self-respect would have picked up his marbles and gone home. Me, I followed them to Brasserie Lipp.

A clutch of artists I knew from Beaux-Arts and Academie Julian were already at a table inside. They rose when we approached, waved, made room, called for more chairs. Sawyer introduced Sofia around the table. She smiled bashfully, making every manly heart beat faster.

We were an artistic League of Nations. There was Mlotek, a Romanian Communist who only painted religious tableaux. Max Erlichmann, a German newspaper photographer, and his Czech journalist girlfriend, Beata Grunzweig. Colby, a fellow Brit, wondrous at watercolor, and the closest thing I had to a best friend.

He pulled out a chair for her next to someone I knew only peripherally, Leo Lubitsch. Yes, that Leo Lubitsch, the one who publishes all the fashion magazines. At the time, he was working as the graphic designer for *Vous,* an arty little magazine we all admired. He knew everybody. I was always seeing him with someone famous; Picasso, Kandinsky, Gary Cooper, Jean-Paul Sartre. Hemingway, once. Today he was there with Margaux DuBois, which was rather scandalous, considering that she was already married to somebody else.

He nodded pleasantly to me, smiled at Sofia like she was the first day of spring. We all took our seats. Sofia and I were separated by Sawyer's large frame. I took out my sketchbook and a pen as I always did.

"Your girl meeting you here, Sinclair?" said Sawyer, carelessly running his hand through his thin hair and adjusting his little round glasses. If I were a dog, I would have growled. Rumor had it that he kept a woman in an apartment somewhere. "Smoke?" He took out a silver cigarette case, offered it to Sofia. Gingerly, she took one, placed it between her pillowy red lips. He bent close to her face to light it, winning the envy of every man at the table. The match flared, glinting off his wire-rimmed glasses and casting a golden glow over her features.

It was obvious that she had never smoked before. She inhaled deeply, coughed, tried to cover it up, and her eyes went watery.

A waiter bent over Sawyer, whispering. He threw down his napkin and pushed away from the table. "I have a call. Be right back."

I had tipped the waiter well to lure him away. This was my chance. My heart was knocking so hard I was sure she could hear it. I had already made a lame first impression. What could I possibly say to undo it?

"Pardon," someone was saying. "Excuse me..."

What if I told her how I felt? That her eyes made me want to save her? Or that I was already thinking about what paints I would mix to get the exact color of her white skin? I looked down at my sketchbook, at the quick caricatures of café patrons drinking coffee, reading the paper, posturing, smoking. My fingers gripped the pen so tightly it hurt.

"Excuse me, English?"

I raised my eyes, and there she was, leaning towards me, trying to get my attention in the noisy bistro.

"Yes?" I wondered if she could hear my voice shaking.

"Please, I did not get your name." she said apologetically. From her accent I guessed she was from somewhere in Eastern Europe.

I introduced myself, stuttering over the syllables. "But you can call me English if you like."

"Raphael." Her voice was low and husky in the din of the busy lunchtime café, and I had to lean close to hear her. "The angel of healing."

"I liked your drawing today," I told her. "There was something about it...there's a real wallop to your line."

Her eyebrows drew together. They were thick and black, arching up to a peak and then sharply down again. It was a look which was not in fashion then, but they set off her eyes perfectly. "I do not understand, but it sounds like you think it was good."

"Yes. I meant that it was good."

That made her happy. She gave me a shy smile, as if she were not used to being praised.

"Where are you from?"

"Poland."

"Oh, really. Warsaw?"

"No. I come from town you never heard of." The forgotten cigarette was smoldering to ash dangerously close to her fingers. With an exclamation, she dropped it in on her bread plate and put her burned finger in her mouth. I handed her my glass. She dipped her injured finger into the cold water. "That is my hand I use to draw," she murmured. Then she raised her eyes to mine, transfixing my heart once again.

"You speak English very well," I said, unable to come up with anything more clever.

"I study it with teacher," she replied, and suddenly she looked away as if she had thought of something unspeakably sad.

There was a terrible grief in her eyes that made me want to know her better, made me want to take it away whatever it cost me, but I could think of nothing to say. And then Sawyer was back, wedging his big rangy body between us like a barrier, grumbling about the waiter calling him away for nothing.

The waiter came, we ordered. God, I can smell it now; sausages in wine and onions, bouillabaisse, pork with red cabbage, raw oysters, snails drowned in butter. Mysteriously, Sofia would only have coffee. Only later would I come to understand. This was her way of keeping the kosher laws.

"Anybody up for a round of Exquisite Corpse?" said Leo. "Sinclair, may we borrow a page from your sketchbook?"

I thought for a moment, then scribbled furiously, folded it over, passed it to Sawyer. He bent close over the paper, took his time. When he was done, he folded it over and passed it to Sofia. She smoothed the paper, sat contemplating for a moment. I watched thoughts flit over her face, taking in the curve of her neck when she shifted positions. Finally, she smiled and began to draw.

Only children play it now, but Exquisite Corpse is an old Dada bar game. You know. The first person draws a head, folds the paper over to cover it, and passes it to the next player, who begins where the last person left off. And so on.

It fell to Leo to finish the feet. He smoothed open the paper, folded like a fan, studied it as we waited. Then he looked at me, his eyebrows raised.

It was a crazy amalgam of different creatures and styles. Along the way it had acquired huge breasts, sea lion flippers, donned a Nazi uniform, arms tattooed with snakes. Long tentacles wriggled out of the bottom of a sultry black evening gown. But crowning the top of the fantastic beast was a perfect portrait of Sofia.

After that, I saw her almost every day. I grew to know every detail of her body from behind, the way her head bowed over her drawing board, the graceful line of her back, her thin shoulders, the way her hair parted along her neck.

Together with us, her new friends, she would laugh at jokes, listen to jazz, watch a movie, debate the political situation. But there was something she wasn't saying, a secret she wasn't sharing. She could be helpless with laughter, and her eyes still wise with sorrow.

As for me, I was completely besotted. My sketchbook, previously filled with quick drawings of café patrons and old men sitting on park benches, suddenly began to sprout passionate love poems.

I was obsessed and unfulfilled; I wanted to possess her, to rescue her from the mysterious sealed fate her eyes predicted, but something about the way she held herself kept me from even speaking to her.

"What was she like? As an artist, I mean." Tessa didn't know why it should matter to her, but it did.

He closed his eyes, remembering Sofia's bold lines, shading so fine he couldn't see pencil strokes. Copies of Raphaels and Caravaggios she had made at the Louvre, propped up against an old wooden steamer trunk in her room. Grave Madonnas on the escritoire. Holy Families on the vanity. A single *Pietà,* lovingly rendered in crow-quill pen on the mantle.

Models with plump thighs and round bottoms. Models with skinny legs and flat asses. Models with thick necks and sculptured torsos. Models with scars, models with moustaches, models with stockings and garter belts, models in corsets and high heels, framed and lovingly arranged on the peeling papered walls of her sitting room.

His voice broke with a despairing awe. "Extraordinary. I've never seen anything like it. There was a swaggering sexuality to her work, it was always there, didn't matter whether the model was fat, ugly, naked, or asleep...something about the thick black lines describing the figure gave me goosebumps."

A Klimt hung on the wall over the piano. His eyes flicked upward to study it, the portrait of a heavy-lidded, dark-haired beauty, in a gown that was a shimmering tower of swirling gold pattern. "Oh, my love," he muttered. "My sweet, sweet love."

Tessa felt the flesh on her arms prickle. He wasn't talking to her. He was talking to Sofia.

Now he turned to her. "There was a time when a box of Wizotsky tea could be found in virtually every home in Eastern Europe, did you know that? The Tzar of Teas, they called it."

The story came swiftly, like a precious object he'd been keeping for someone else, and the time had finally come to unshoulder the burden and pass it on.

The first Monday in February, she didn't show up to class. Neither was she at the Louvre in the afternoon, nor any of our usual haunts that evening.

Tuesday found her absent again. My eye, trained to glance up at regular intervals to rest on her slight figure, kept returning to her empty seat, like a tongue running over the space where a tooth has been pulled.

What if she was sick? What if she needed help? Worse, what if she had returned to Poland? I resolved to visit her apartment that evening. How I would find her apartment, I had no idea.

After a dismal painting session at the Louvre where I ruined a week's worth of progress with sloppy brushwork, I went to La Coupole for dinner. By the time I arrived, the party was going full swing, hundreds of people ordering hundreds of meals, drinking gallons of wine and having a wonderful time.

As I walked in, I bumped into Leo, who was just leaving with Margaux. It was all over town that she had left her husband to move in with him. They were accompanied by another woman, tall, with long legs and wide hips, high round breasts. She had bright intelligent eyes that made promises of carnal adventure, and scarlet lips that curved into a greedy smile when Leo introduced us.

We made the smallest of small talk. I felt a hot poker of desire flare inside my gut. Margaux murmured that she was an old friend, did something in fashion, they would be at Le Dôme later in the evening. We said our *au revoirs,* and they moved languorously on to whatever was next on their full social calendar.

I found an empty table, ordered something, took out my sketchbook and pencil. I felt someone's eyes upon me, so I glanced up, and there she was.

Sofia was alone at a table by the wall. There was a forgotten plum in a glass compote sitting in front of her. Next to it lay an open letter. And though it seemed as if she was looking at me, she was a million miles away.

I waved at her and broke the spell; she blinked and gave me a small smile of recognition. I picked up my sketchbook and went to say hello. She gestured to the seat across from her. *Sit.* So I did. Our saga together had begun.

"Where have you been?" I asked her. "We've been worried. It's all anyone can talk about. I thought Sawyer was going to call the police."

She smiled at my joke. I felt tingly all over.

"Hello, English." Her perfume rolled over me, blending with the smell of coffee. Lilac. "My brother was visiting. Better he doesn't know I go to art school."

The letter lay on the table between us, written in a spidery foreign hand. "Letter from home?"

She nodded.

"Money, I hope." I joked, trying to keep it light, and she smiled a little smile, then burst into tears.

Oh, God, my first moments alone with the woman I craved, and I had made her cry. Not good. I fished in my pockets for a handkerchief, and not finding one, gave her my napkin.

"I'm sorry, I didn't mean to..." It wasn't my moment after all. "I'm sorry. Why don't I go."

She shook her head no, wiped at her eyes with my napkin. Her red lips were even more captivating now, all soft and puffy and quivering, paralyzing me. She wiped her nose, exhorting me not to watch. And then she began to talk, the words gushing out of her like water from a broken main.

Sofia's story began in a place called Wlodawa, a city of seven thousand souls in the far southeast corner of Poland. She grew up in a white Baroque villa on the edge of town, set amidst trees and gardens, attended by servants, with electricity, running water and indoor plumbing, great luxuries in that place in that time. There were party dresses and a pony, holidays in the spa town of Rapkha, sleigh rides in winter behind horses with bells on their harnesses, feasts on the Sabbath and Jewish holidays. People rang their bell all day long looking for charity, and her pretty mother would come to the front door, always a few zlotys for anybody in need. Her family didn't call her Sofia; she was *Shayfaleh,* little lamb, or *Shayna maidel,* pretty girl.

Every Saturday morning, she would put on her nicest dress, buckle on a pair of shoes that were just for this purpose, and go to *shul* with her family. She could see the synagogue from her house, a grand white edifice with gold onion domes. On New Years and the Day of Atonement, two thousand people filled the seats. High up in the gallery, she would hold open her silver-clad prayerbook and listen to a superstar cantor from Lodz sing the prayers in a sobbing, operatic voice.

A fairy-tale upbringing.

One day, when she was six or seven, she found a little bird dead in the front yard. She ran inside for a pencil and paper and spent the next hour drawing it in great detail. When she was finished, she brought it in to show her mother, who accused her of making up stories. She was sure her older brother Yechezkel had done it; it was far too sophisticated for someone so young.

The next day, she showed her mother a drawing of Yechezkel in the bathtub. For this, Sofia received a spanking. She had drawn him naked, and nice Orthodox girls were never to see boys in the altogether until they were safely married.

After that, she drew everything in sight; her father, her mother, the cook, the driver, the furniture in her room. The horses that pulled the carriage, the flat Polish landscape. In the mornings, the teacher at school scolded her for drawing on the cover of her grammar book. In the afternoons, the rabbi scolded her for drawing in the margins of her prayer book.

Her father smiled wistfully at her, told her how talented she was, arranged for her to receive lessons from someone in town. His sister had been artistic. She had died before the first world war, of a disease she could only name in Polish.

On her twelfth birthday, she looked at herself in the mirror as she was getting ready for her bath and noticed that her body was changing. Fascinated, she drew herself. She had gotten in trouble once for drawing a naked boy. Nobody had said anything about naked girls.

She became obsessed with the human body. Furtively, she studied her brother when he dressed, the housekeeper as she bent over the beds, the children playing by the pump in the village. When her friends took off their clothes to go swimming, she observed the details of their anatomy and recorded it on paper, which she naively stashed in her writing desk.

One day, when she came home from school, she found her mother waiting for her, holding an armful of her drawings. *Nakedda nekayvas,* she spat out as she shook them in her face. Sick in the head! Something must be wrong with you to make you want to draw these things!

Her mother threw the drawings into the kitchen fire. The flames licked the pictures of her family and friends, then consumed them.

She took away Sofia's pencils, told her if she ever caught her drawing again, she would put her fingers in the fire. When she looked to her father for help, he avoided her gaze. Then he took off his belt.

Poor Sofia. They never looked at her the same way again, not really. The belt was applied regularly and with conviction if she so much as doodled on the corner of a newspaper. They made her pray three times a day to be released from the demons that must have possessed her to make those pictures.

Though they tried to keep it hush hush, somehow it got around that the Wizotsky girl was sex-crazed. *Nakkeda nekayvas!* Maybe it was the help, maybe it was Yechezkel, but everyone in town heard the story. When she went to synagogue the following Shabbos, people turned around to stare. When she walked through town, people whispered, and women hid their children behind their skirts. It was a *shonda,* the kind of scandal that ruins a family's reputation.

The *shonda* reflected badly on all of them, but her parents' fortune eased the pain, and her brother was married off anyway. Grandchildren followed shortly thereafter. One year went by, then another, but there were no takers for the Wizotskys' damaged flower. Though Sofia was accomplished, intelligent and beautiful, nobody in the Orthodox world wanted to have the girl who drew *nakkeda nekayvas* for their daughter-in-law. The story of the *shonda* floated through the Polish Jewish world like feathers from an opened pillow.

This suited Sofia just fine. She didn't want to marry those boys in black coats and black hats anyway.

At twenty-two, she was practically an old maid. Her parents worried for their unmarried daughter, with war threatening and no husband to protect her, so in the winter of 1939, they packed her off to Paris. She would be safe there while their search continued, someone perhaps more *modernishe,* or with lower standards. They had a friend with a house in the Pletzel, the old Jewish neighborhood in the Marais. There was a flat on the top floor Sofia could rent while the landlord's wife kept a sharp eye on her.

Her father was busy directing the movers when he came across a drawing, hidden behind her bed. Angrily, he yanked it out, ready to be outraged. But it was an innocuous landscape, massive gray storm clouds rolling over a patchwork of plowed fields. He stared at it for a long time. Perhaps he was thinking of his dead sister. Finally, he sighed and murmured, "So beautiful. So talented. What will become of you, my *shayna maidel?*"

They sent Jewish suitors for her consideration; a widower in his fifties, bald, bearded and fat. The one with the crippling limp, one leg a full foot shorter than the other. A hunchback with a profound speech impediment. The one who was terribly scarred.

She rejected them all. For the first time since she was twelve, Sofia was truly happy. She was on her own in a city that was, in itself, a work of art. Men and women strolled casually down the boulevards with portable easels under their arms, as if it were the most natural thing in the world. The Louvre, filled with the world's masterpieces, was open every day. She would get so close to the paintings that she made the guards nervous. She took the money her mother gave her to buy pretty dresses and spent it all on art classes.

There were caveats. She had to be back in her room by nine o'clock every night. She was allowed no visitors, male or female. If her landlady thought her dress was immodest or too alluring, she would send her back upstairs to change. She was supposed to take all her meals with the family she lived with, but she flouted that particular rule, posing as a vegetarian at the cafés and restaurants she frequented with her artist friends.

Every day, she prayed to God that her parents would never find that suitable match for her, the man who would take her away from the life she loved. Each time she opened a letter from home, her hands shook and her heart pounded with fear as she raced through her mother's longhand, searching for the words that told her she was still free.

Sofia had run out of words. We sat in silence. A table of people near us exploded into uproarious laughter. The sounds of cutlery scraping plates and the babble of conversation went on all around us.

I wanted to take her in my arms and hold her and stroke her hair and kiss her eyes until there was no sorrow left in them. I wanted to take her back to my flat and make sweaty, reckless pornographic love to her till she was washed clean of everything sad that had ever happened to her.

She made me swear not to tell anyone a single detail. Bewildered, I asked her why.

"I just want to be Sofia," she murmured as she lit a cigarette. Her face became blurry, lost in a haze of blue smoke. "Just Sofia Wizotsky, for a little while longer."

She tapped my sketchbook. "Forget everything I told you. Let's play."

I tore out a page and passed it to her. She borrowed my pencil, looked at me sharply, bent to her task.

I told her a few tasty bits of my own history; my parents' abandonment, my bleak childhood, how Art had carried me in her hands, saved me from it all. And while I talked on, her black eyes filled with emotion, her eyebrows acting as punctuation marks; swooping fiercely up and down, asking questions, expressing sorrow, outrage or pity.

I never told anyone the things I told her. The act of shaping it into words for her caused me physical anguish, as if it were happening all over again. At the end of it, I was bent over the table, exhausted, spent.

Her small white hand glided over mine, alighting as gently as a butterfly. "We are just the same," she said softly.

My fingers curled around hers.

In the course of a single evening, I had fallen truly, madly, deeply in love, and found that the woman of my dreams could never be mine. I knew now, beyond the shadow of a doubt, that I could never walk her home, that she would never invite me in, that we could never be seen kissing on Paris street corners. I should have been distraught. Instead, I felt that something important had passed between us, something had changed.

Slowly, regretfully, she slipped her hand out of mine.

"Here. You open it." She pushed the drawing across the marble topped table.

"Ladies first." I pushed it back.

She unfolded it. Her face broke into a dazzling smile, and then she giggled, clapping her hand over her mouth, as if she were afraid to be caught being happy. She turned it around to show me.

Sofia had drawn my head, a perfect miniature likeness. Beneath it, I had drawn a longshoreman's torso, with huge muscles and washboard abs, feathery white wings. At the bottom, she had drawn a clawfoot bathtub full of bubbles. I burst out laughing.

Now she noticed the time. "Oh! I'll be late!" She gestured for the waiter. "Good night, English. See you tomorrow." She pulled her collar up around her face and went out into the night.

Waiting for my change, I smoothed out the drawing, pressed it flat. In her hands, I was smoldering, sensuous, sexualized. I ran my fingertips over her lines, feeling the grooves in the paper. Was that really how she saw me, or did she just draw me the way she drew everything else?

That night, I started on a painting of Sofia as I found her that evening, alone at a table by the wall in La Coupole, letter in hand, the plum in the glass, the thousand-mile stare. The next day, after class, I would ask her to pose for me in my studio in the green dress she had worn the first time I laid eyes on her. And after a moment of hesitation, she would say yes.

Our innocent little trysts went on for another six blissful weeks.

By March, the background of my painting was already roughed in. I had been to La Coupole so often I could paint it in my sleep. Sofia's skin was the color of skim milk, almost blue-white. I was using zinc white for its transparent bluish properties, mixing it with lead white for creaminess. Her lips were a holy matrimony of cadmium red scarlet and alizarin crimson. On breaks, we gazed dreamily into each other's eyes over cigarettes while I told her how well it was going and pondered what it might be like to kiss her cushiony lips.

Under the discreet cover of a crowd, we were always together. Strolling together through the barren Tuileries, lagging behind a group of classmates on their way to the Louvre, she told me a song she heard on the radio had made her weep; I told her a new Balthus painting I had glimpsed in a gallery made me wretched with jealousy. She whispered guiltily that she disliked Picasso; I assured her he was overrated. She cried her eyes out during *Wuthering Heights;* I laughed at her. She told me she was tired of the dreary Parisian winter; I told her I had already used up three tubes of Payne's grey and it was only February. She griped that the master kept telling her that she was rushing, she should get the big relationships in the painting down first; I told her that since she had started, the master hardly noticed anyone but her.

On March 16th, Hitler rolled over Czechoslovakia, and we finally knew that war was imminent.

That night, we met at La Coupole, as we often did, under cover of acquaintances from school and the expatriate artist community. I arrived before Sofia. At the table were Leo and Margaux. Salvador Dali with his beloved Gala. One of the lesser Surrealists. Colby. Erlichmann and his girlfriend Beata. Sawyer Ballard.

I took out my sketchbook and pencil, waited for something to catch my eye, but the truth is I was watching the door, my heart already pounding, living for the moment she would walk through it and smile just for me, illuminating the room like the sun.

Sawyer got up, came around the table to me, leaned over to shake hands. Despite the fact that Sofia politely declined his advances, he'd kept right on trying, some kind of belligerent American can-do, go-getter attitude at work there, as if he thought she ought to say yes out of gratitude.

"What do you say, Sinclair?"

"Evening, Sawyer. How's that landscape coming along?"

"Oh, you know. Nothing I haven't done already ten times over. I'm thinking of going back to Boston. There are too many uniforms in this place. Things are about to get hairy, and if war comes, I want to be back home." Absently, I nodded agreement, only half listening.

Just then, Sofia came through the door. She slowed, scanning the vast crowded eating hall. She looked stricken.

"Looks like she picked you," Sawyer said enviously. I had already forgotten him. "You win."

"What do you mean?" Not taking my eyes off of her, I tried to look as if I didn't know what he was talking about.

"Oh, come on. She chose you. Must be that ripping accent you Brits have," he groused. "Completely unfair advantage. Well, congratulations. I hear those Jew girls are wildcats in the sack. I guess I don't have to tell *you* that."

Before I had time to think, I struck him full on the mouth. He staggered and went down, knocking over chairs, falling against a table full of Hungarians.

I threw myself onto him, punched his smug face two more times before someone pulled me up from behind, pinned my arms back.

"Sinclair!" Angrily. It was Colby. "What the hell are you doing?"

Sawyer propped himself up on his elbow, put his hand to his mouth. He rolled over, spat out blood.

We were instantly surrounded by a swarm of curious onlookers. This was La Coupole, after all, where a fistfight over a woman was part of the floor show along with celebrity spotting. I was unreasonably happy to see

Sawyer bleeding like a pig. Someone retrieved his glasses from a bowl of bouillabaisse and passed them to him. Colby gave him some clean napkins. He wiped his mouth, grimacing at the sight of his own blood. Rejecting offers of help, he got to his feet. He put his glasses back on, carefully winding the gold wires around his ears. The fight was obviously over. Disappointed restaurant patrons went reluctantly back to their own altercations.

"So it's that way," he said, dipping a napkin in soda water and brushing at the bloodstains on his white shirt. "You're in love with her. You're crazy, Sinclair. What are you going to do, bring her home to meet your mother? *Marry* her?"

Suddenly, I realized Sofia was there, aghast at the sight of us both spattered with blood.

"What is this about?"

I looked at her, then away, ashamed, not knowing what to say.

"This is about me?" she said, her face pale.

"Hey, Sinclair," said Sawyer. I turned to him, and he socked me on the jaw, sent me sprawling over a table and onto the floor.

I lay there for a minute, the taste of blood filling my mouth. Sofia was on her knees beside me, cupping my face in her small white hands. A *garçon* came over, gesticulating furiously, jabbering in French to the tune of *you must leave now.*

"Raphael, Raphael, my angel of healing," she whispered, "What have I done to you?"

"You're going to have a hell of a mark." Colby frowned at me, folded some ice into a napkin, squatted down and held it on my jaw. I winced and pushed him away.

"What's gotten into you, Sinclair? Sawyer's a prick. You know that. You've known it for five years."

Slowly, I pulled myself up off the floor, rubbing my jaw. I needed to talk to her, tell her to forget everything she had heard. I needed to tell her that Sawyer was wrong, that he didn't know anything about it, that she was too damn good for my so-called family. But she had disappeared during the confusion in the noisy restaurant.

My sketchbook had fallen to the floor when Sawyer hit me. Looking around, I spotted it under our table, between Erlichmann and Beata. I apologized for disturbing their evening. He waved it off. "Love is a messy undertaking," he advised me in his morose German accent. "Enter at your own risk."

I bent to retrieve it from between the legs of Beata's chair. "Don't go to her," she instructed me in a low voice. Her gray eyes were serious and sad. "There is something you don't know."

I clenched my jaw. It hurt. "I know I love her," I replied. I pulled my collar up and went out into the misty night.

I had only one thought. She was going to cut me out of her life without another word. I looked up and down the street, but it was empty of passersby. Taxis stopped in front of the restaurants and bars and cafés, spilled out their loads of laughing passengers, zoomed off again to pick up their next fares. I hailed one, instructed the driver to take me to the Fourth Arrondissement, Rue des Rosiers, and there's an extra franc for you if you step on it.

When he squealed to a stop, I threw the driver his money and got out. The street was deserted. The rain was making a tremendous racket, beating a tattoo on the roofs and garbage cans and gurgling down the drainpipes. I looked up, wondering which window might be hers, but water ran down my face and into my eyes, making it impossible to see more than five feet ahead. Too late, I remembered her rules. *No visitors, male or female.* Without a plan, I splashed across the flooded gutters to her door.

And there she was, hatless, completely drenched. She was standing before the gate to the courtyard, key in hand, as if she were about to open it when she had become absorbed in thinking about something else.

I wanted to put my arms around her, protect her forever from idiots like Sawyer. Instead, I came up behind her, hands safely in my pockets.

"I'm sorry, Sofia." I repeated helplessly. "I'm sorry."

She acknowledged me, imperceptibly nodding her head, as if she had decided something.

"Let's go," she said abruptly. "Let's get away from here."

I waved my arms, flagging down the taxi I had just left. Once inside, I directed the driver to take us to nearby Place de Bastille. Here were the kind of places where the lowest rungs of society came to dance, to argue, to fight, to drink, where sailors and day-laborers came to negotiate a price for services rendered in small rooms nearby. Places where nobody would recognize Sofia or me.

We took a small, scarred table in the back of an odiferous joint on the Rue de Lappe, smelling suggestively of urine, beer and sweat. She shrugged off her coat, left it dripping on the back of a chair. I looked across the table at her, glowing in the poor light of the squalid bar. Bits of blue-black hair clung to the sides of her face.

"Have you got a cigarette?"

I did. She placed it between her lips and leaned forward for a light, our faces almost touching, so close that I could feel warmth emanating from her skin. She leaned back in her seat, held her cigarette aloft. Gray smoke rose in a lazy line towards the ceiling.

"Tell me, English," she said. Her voice was low, melancholy, thrilling. "Tell me what you are going to do when you are finished with your studies."

Here, I was on solid ground. I told her I was going to stay in Paris forever, painting lonely landscapes and alienated apartment dwellers. There was a gallery showing some interest in my work, and I hoped they would take me on. I told her I wanted to buy a little place in Provence, something charming, surrounded by picturesque Van Gogh fields full of picturesque Monet haystacks. I told her she should visit England someday, that I could take her to see the sights, maybe the places where I grew up.

She listened to me drone on and on, resting her chin in her hand, looking at me through drowsy half-closed eyes. I think she just wanted to hear the sound of my voice rising and falling, telling stories, weaving dreams. They must have been her dreams, too.

The music changed to jazz. "I want to dance," she said suddenly. "Let's dance."

I rose to my feet and followed her obediently onto the small, close dance floor. She turned to face me. I stood as awkwardly as a schoolboy, my arms dangling at my sides.

"Go on," she said. "I want you to."

I slid my hand around her tiny waist. She curved her hand over my shoulder, placed her other hand lightly in mine.

I had been with women before, dozens of women, oceans of women, straddling, you might say, the entire spectrum of the social strata. Models, actresses, society girls, hat check girls. American art students with more money than talent. Once, a sword swallower from a troupe that was performing at the Place du Tertre, and her sister the fire-eater. I didn't care what color they were or what language they spoke or how much money their daddies made. All I ever asked for was a good time.

This burned.

Burned with an incandescence that consumed, lit me up from within like a house on fire. With every lunge forward, with every step back, with every brush of her body against mine, the flames leapt higher. I burned for her.

The dance floor became packed with unwashed bodies touching us as they swayed in time to the music, the air thick with smoke. The band grew louder and more insistent, the saxophone lamenting over the piano and the violin. From time to time, there were bursts of raucous laughter, or shouted indignation, threats of violence. The tobacco-stained walls beaded over with droplets of humidity. Nine o'clock came and went. When I pointed out the hour, Sofia acknowledged me with a nod, bowed her lovely head, and delicately rested her cheek on my chest. I hardly dared to move. I feared that any sudden movement would frighten her away.

This was it, then. This was love, blinding, selfish, unassailable, deathless love. Yes, I did want to marry her, bring her home to meet my mother, then take her away and spend the rest of my life erasing the memories of everything that had come before. This was the last woman I ever wanted to make love to, the only face I ever wanted to see in the morning when I opened my eyes to the new day.

At two in the morning, damp from the exertion and the humidity, we found our table, collapsed into our seats. Sofia fanned herself. I ordered drinks.

"Sofia," I said. She turned to me expectantly.

"I love you. I love you more than anything in this world or the next. I love the kindness in your voice, the passion in your eyes. I want to be the only man to ever see you naked, the only man to ever lay his hands on your porcelain skin. I want to make love to you every night before we fall asleep, then wake up in the morning and do it again. I don't know if I believe in God, but I believe in the salvation of your love. Marry me."

But I never said it, never said any of it. I don't know why. I couldn't get the words out, as much as I yearned to say them. Maybe my parents' marriage put me off the whole institution. Maybe it was the hand of God. Or maybe Sawyer's words got to me, after all.

She waited for a moment, then tilted her head, reading me, taking it in. Then she smiled a sad little smile, the corners of her mouth turned down instead of up, her black eyes telegraphing the tragedy still to come, if only I had been paying attention.

"Let's play," I said, and I tore out a page out of my sketchbook, hurriedly drew a picture, folded it over, slid it across the table.

She scanned the room, searching for inspiration. Her hair was longer than was fashionable, and the rain had turned it curly; it hung in tight ringlets around her head. I watched her as she drew. I loved looking at her hand grasping the pencil, her small tapered fingers like some kind of Italian cookie rolled in powdered sugar.

She squinted at her drawing, folded it and passed it back to me.

My turn. I hesitated, staring at the blank paper. I scribbled something down, slid it across the table to her.

"Go on," I said. "Open it."

She lifted the top flap, unfolded the bottom. When she saw what was inside, she sat back in shock, then clapped her hand over her mouth as if she were afraid something would fly out, something she could never take back.

Sofia had made a mermaid in the centerfold, a beautiful female torso with a long, shimmering tail. Bubbles rose to an imaginary surface. A shark glided in the distance behind her.

But at the top, looking like it belonged to another picture, was a couple embracing. The woman had dark curling hair, a small pointed nose, her rosebud mouth pressed to her lover's lips in an eternal kiss. The man lay across her body, concealing it, his arms clasped around her slight shoulders. His hair was clipped close in the back, coming to a peak as it fell over his forehead.

Under the mermaid, abandoning the game, I had scrawled the words *I love you.*

She took a good, long time looking at it, smoothing out the creases in the paper, tracing her fingers along the lines I had made. An artist's caress.

"Raphael," she finally murmured. "One more dance."

The band was playing a scratchy tango, *Una Por Cabeza,* passionate even for a tango, and this time there was no hesitation when I put my arm around her waist and she settled her hand upon my shoulder.

For just a little longer Sofia upheld the imaginary space between us, like a student at a proper dance academy; but in the final wistful minutes of the night before daylight begins to send feelers out into the darkness, the entire length of her body dissolved into mine, and the lilac perfume of her scent filled my senses when I rested my cheek against her hair, and her pale face was luminous in the smoky haze when she turned it up to mine.

Her hand moved to the back of my neck. I shuddered at her touch. Now, on the edge of the precipice I hesitated, knowing with certainty that after this, nothing could be the same. For just one more moment I held back, measuring the full weight of its meaning, for her, for me, for ever, after this night.

But when I felt her soft red mouth on my eyes, felt her soft white hands on my face, a chasm opened under me; all rational thought fell down and down into its shadowy depths. I closed my eyes and gave myself over to her completely.

When they threw us out of the place at closing time, it was three or four in the morning. We emerged from the fetid air of the bar to find it had stopped raining. There was a thin rime of ice on the cobblestones and the sky had cleared to a brilliant Prussian blue, littered with an anorexic sliver of a moon and cold white stars.

Sofia had had two pastis, just enough to affect her ability to walk a straight line. Lightly, she rested her hand on my shoulder as I maneuvered her into a taxi, slid in next to her.

Now I remembered the expression on her face as she searched for me in La Coupole earlier this evening, a hundred years ago.

"Sofia," I said, just loud enough so her eyes would flicker open. "Last night. You looked like the world was coming to an end. Is everything all right?"

A deep, heartfelt sigh. "It doesn't matter anymore," she muttered, her eyelids fluttering down like shutters. She yawned charmingly, covering her mouth with her gloved hand. "Tell me, English," she murmured. "I didn't see the paper this morning. Tell me something funny that the monitor said today." And she closed her eyes and leaned her dark head against my shoulder.

Now I wished I had taken her someplace farther away; we were in front of Sofia's apartment in a matter of minutes. I touched her arm. She stirred, cried out anxiously in a foreign language. A brief bad dream.

"Look," I said gently. "We're here." She sat up rubbing her eyes, adorably disheveled, stared dully out the window at the chipped plaster and rusted wrought iron balcony of her building. I put my hand on the door handle, meaning to go round the car to open the door for her.

"No," she said, laying her hand on mine. "Better you stay here." We sat in the back seat with the car running for a little while longer, hip to hip through the layers of clothing, touching but not touching, until the windows of the taxi fogged over with our breath and the heat rising from our bodies.

Obediently, I let her slide out of the taxi, watched her walk on unsteady legs to the door and take her key from her bag. She put it in the lock, turned it till it clicked. The metal gate swung open. For one more moment she was in my sight, framed by the darkness of the courtyard beyond. And then she was gone.

It came from nowhere, a torrent of sickening, gut-wrenching panic. Flinging myself out the car door, I caught the gate before it could clang closed, then seized her, pulling her into my embrace, as if by doing so, I could lock her up inside of me.

I can still feel the heavy silk of her dress sliding through my fingers, her body yielding, melting into mine, the sweet, sweaty, intimate smell of her skin, the salty taste of her mouth. And when she crept her arms around my neck and shyly gave me what I knew to be the first kisses she had ever given any man, shining visions of a new life opened up before my eyes; and in my heart, I was wedded for eternity to her unforeseeable fate.

I couldn't sleep anymore than night; I told the taxi driver to take me to my studio, then gave him all the money I had in my pockets.

I felt burdened by new responsibilities and light-headed with happiness. By the leaden light of dawn, I finished my painting of Sofia. Every stroke of the brush was a caress; every daub of cadmium red on her lips a kiss.

By seven-thirty it was done, and I meant to go out and have coffee at the café round the corner before class. Instead, I promptly collapsed onto my couch and slept till noon.

When I awoke, the sun had slipped past the midpoint in the sky. It was a hard, bright afternoon, one of those late-winter days that you can actually smell spring. I had missed my morning classes hours ago.

For the remainder of the day I roamed the streets of Paris, plotting out our lives together. We would keep separate apartments to satisfy her family. But every morning would find us at the same café. From there, we would go to class, spend the early part of the day working, then break for lunch. There, we would stare hungrily into each other's eyes as we nibbled on our midday meal. Then we'd tear ourselves away from one another, go to our respective studios and paint until dark. As evening fell, we would meet at one of the restaurants in the Fifth for dinner, and from there we would go to the theater, or a concert, or stroll the boulevards, it didn't matter so long as she was by my side, her arm safely tucked under mine.

We would become one of those art couples you envied in art history books, like Frida Kahlo and Diego Rivera, or Georgia O'Keefe and Alfred Stieglitz. I would paint her again and again, with and without her clothes on. She was the only model I would ever need, like Edward Hopper with his Josephine.

We would end each night falling into each other's arms, and here, I really embellished. Afterwards, exhausted, spent, sleep would find us, our bodies twined together in the blue moonlight sneaking through the blinds.

I would heal every wound her family had inflicted on her soul. She would be all the home I ever needed.

I was crossing over the Pont de l'Archevêché as the sun dipped low in the west. Above me, the sky was deepening to ultramarine. At the same time, lights were blinking on all over Paris, sparkling across the city like a diamond necklace. A pink neon sunset seared the horizon, turning Notre Dame's array of soaring Gothic windows into mirrors, shattering the restless face of the Seine into glassy shards of brilliant color.

When the last garish hues had faded regretfully to gray, I checked my watch. Seven-thirty. Dinner time. The boulevards would be awakening, blazing with light and music and bright chatter and steamy good smells.

Time to head back to Montparnasse. Sofia was waiting.

I found them at Brasserie Lipp. Under the undulating ceiling paintings of African scenes, Colby was rubbing shoulders with a leggy blonde, an American student I had met before. Havasi was with a man I didn't know, arguing in Mlotek and smacking a newspaper laying open on the table. Sawyer was looking very natty, wearing one of his better jackets and a bowtie. Margaux was surrounded by a coterie of brilliantly attired fashionistas, chattering excitedly in French. Leo was hovering behind her, speaking with a heavyset Russian diplomat who kept running his fingers through a pomaded shock of dark hair. Erlichmann looked festive, his round face scrubbed and pink. He leaned across the table, shouted to me above the noise, "Sinclair, you have missed everything!"

I pulled out a chair next to Colby. "What did I miss?"

"Margaux and Leo got married this afternoon."

I leaped up, extended my hand across the table. Leo, beaming, pumped my hand up and down enthusiastically, if politely. He even seemed a little tipsy, which was for him, unheard of.

I wished Margaux well, kissed her on both cheeks. She accepted my congratulations, looking at me from beneath hooded eyelids with that speculative gaze of hers.

"Good luck," I told her, meaning it. I was genuinely happy for them. It seemed like a good omen. I sat back down, took out my sketchbook. I always took a seat facing the door so that I could see Sofia the moment she arrived. A waiter set a glass in front of me, filled it with champagne, topped off the other glasses, and disappeared in the crowd.

Greta Garbo made an appearance. Marlene Dietrich came and went. Coco Chanel stopped by, embraced Margaux like a sister. Elsa Schiaparelli swept up to the table in a gloriously silly hat shaped like a shoe. The three of them hugged and kissed, conferring a glittery aura of glamour upon our little party.

Checking my watch for the hundredth time, I waited for Sofia to make her appearance. It was already nine o'clock. Beata noticed my impatience. She lost her festive expression and shot me a look of compassion, just before she leaned over the table to Leo and Margaux.

"I'm sorry, I completely forgot to tell you!" she exclaimed. "Sofia couldn't be here tonight. But she wanted me to tell you how thrilled she is for both of you. She says she has never seen two people so perfect for each other."

"Where is she?" asked Leo pleasantly.

"She has a visitor from the United States," she told them. Then, her lips curved up in a delighted smile. "Her fiancée."

I didn't make it to class the next morning. Nor the next day, nor the day after that. Art, the blessing that had raised me from the grim monotony of my sad beginnings, ceased to hold any interest for me. I remained closeted in my flat, unshaven, undressed, unbalanced.

A week went by, then a month. Towards the end of April, I received a phone call.

The furtive female voice on the other end had an Eastern European accent, and for a moment my heart leapt at the possibility that Sofia was calling. But it was Beata. Sofia wanted to see me, she said. I could imagine her delicate lady-like features, the corners of her mouth turned down, her grave gray eyes distinctly disapproving. She gave me a time and a place. Café de Flore, the upstairs room, four o'clock sharp. If I wasn't there by four-fifteen, she would leave. Then she hung up.

Frantically, I raked a comb across my hair, slapped on scent, pulled on a clean shirt and tie. Outside my flat, I waved down a cab. My watch ticked off the last minute as we screeched to a stop and I threw the driver too much money. Sprinting out, I bulled through the front door and took the steps two at a time to the second level, where only foreign tourists and the unfashionably dressed were seated.

She was still there, wearing a little green hat and pulling on her oyster-colored gloves, getting ready to leave.

"Hello, Sofia," I said.

She startled, looked up. "Hello, English," she said softly.

I took a seat opposite her. I noticed she had a chic new haircut. "You look lovely." I tried to sound casual as I struggled to bottle up my emotions; despair, rage, betrayal, desire. "Really. Smashing." My hands were shaking. I folded them in my lap. "Have you ordered?"

"I only have a little while. I have to catch a train."

Her eyes were moving over my face, her dramatic eyebrows drawn together. She was looking at me the way only lovers do before embarking on a long journey. I didn't know it then, but I think she was trying to memorize my features.

"So, you're engaged. What's the lucky fellow's name?"

"Arthur. Arthur Weiss. His friends call him Skip."

"Wonderful! What's he do, this Skip?"

"His family owns a poultry processing company. In Toledo, Ohio." She pronounced the unfamiliar names carefully.

"Poultry processing! But that's *brilliant!* When's the big day?"

She dropped her eyes. "Soon. A few more weeks."

"Well then! Let's have some champagne. We should celebrate."

She ignored the savagery in my voice. Or perhaps she didn't hear it. "I wanted to...I have something I want to give you. Have you got a cigarette?"

I patted down my pockets till I found one, then handed it to her. She put it between her lips and leaned forward as I struck a match, held it till the tip of the cigarette glowed red. She inhaled deeply, then leaned back and let a stream of smoke drift into the air over her shoulder. I got the feeling that she didn't smoke around her precious fiancée.

"Come on, Raphael. One more game of Exquisite Corpse."

I had not carried my sketchbook since that awful night. I flagged down a passing waiter who brought us some writing paper.

Pencil in hand, she bent over the paper, giving me the chance to observe her. There was no mistaking it. Sofia was transformed. She looked happy. Of course she was happy. So much to look forward to. With a husband, she would be back in her family's good graces, and I was just a last stop on her way to a life of luxury in the United States.

I wanted her to hurt as much as I did. "What does Skip think of your drawings?" I said offhandedly.

She took her time answering. "He thinks they're very…nice." She finished the top, folded it over and passed it across the table.

I sketched quickly and forcefully, passed it back. She frowned, curling and uncurling a ringlet of hair while she thought, then smiled and began to draw. I watched the sure way she clasped the pencil, watched the point bite into the paper, watched her pretty white fingers make strong, sure lines, as natural to her as breathing.

"You open it," she said, sliding it forward. I unfolded the paper and glanced at it. Sofia had drawn a soldier wearing a helmet and a look of grim determination, to which I had attached a nude female torso. She had given it the legs of a tightrope walker, slippered feet sliding along a rope suspended over a precipice. She laughed nervously.

"You haven't shown him your work, have you." I said.

"No." she said shortly. She opened her bag, fished around inside and took out a set of keys, which she slid across the table. "These are the keys to my apartment."

I stared down at the keys.

"I left some things there. Things I will have no use for in America. My paints, my brushes, my easel…my drawings."

I nodded, unable to speak. It hit me like a fist. She was really leaving me. I bowed my head, unable to continue this charade of civility. She reached across the table and took my hand. "Raphael," she said softly.

I pulled my hand away as if her touch burned. I couldn't stand it any longer. "How could you do it to me, Sofia? Not a word of explanation, not a hint of goodbye." I could feel my voice rising out of control. In another moment, I'd be crying. "You'll have to forgive me, Sofia, because after that night, that splendid rainy night…the night I punched Sawyer in his stupid mouth, the night we danced until they threw us out, the night you kissed me…that was it for me, Sofia. I thought we were going to be one of those old couples you see doddering down the boulevard, still holding hands. You should have seen my expression when Beata told me you were engaged. Too bad you missed it. I'm sure it was hilarious."

"I was going to tell you," she said. "But when Sawyer hit you…and I saw your face, your beautiful face…I couldn't do it. I could not make myself say the words."

Then she grew angry. "What did you think, English? That I would stay in Paris forever, playing our little game? This was always temporary, like a dream.

"All of my life, I have thought there is something wrong with me. That I deserved to be punished for what I did. For the way I see. For the pictures I make with my hands. I thought, 'No one will ever love a low creature like me. I will be alone forever, and I must get used to it.' You have shown me that I am...how do I say this...worthy of the love of a good man. You see, Raphael, you are my angel of healing."

Her eyes were wet now, her eyelashes clumping together, long and black like spiders' legs against her cheeks. "I am sorry, terribly sorry that you are suffering. But my family is back east, waiting in Wlodawa. I cannot just turn my back on them." She put her head into her hands. "How did this happen? I just wanted to paint."

"You mean the same people who beat you with a belt for drawing kids playing at a pump? The people who hid their children from you? The people who offered you their cripples? *Those* people?"

Her eyes were blazing with emotion. "When I'm with Arthur, none of that matters. You understand? It's like all those bad things never happened. Like when I was a little girl."

She dropped her gaze, stirred her hot cocoa. "Anyway..." she said ruminatively. "Terrible things are happening in Germany. War is coming any day now. We're leaving for America right after we..." and here, words failed her. She pushed a strand of hair that had fallen in her eyes back behind her ear. She murmured almost to herself. "In America, I can be whatever I want to be."

"Oh, really?" I lashed back. "I know you, Sofia. I've seen your drawings. They scream, they *writhe* with sexuality. What do you think they'll make of *that* in Toledo, Ohio?" I slammed my hand down on hers, pinning it to the table, leaned forward till our heads were almost touching. "I love you," I said between gritted teeth. "Did you think I would just keep quiet? That I would just let you go? I've been in love with you since the moment I met you. The first time I looked into your eyes, I saw a story being written there, Sofia. A fairy tale, with monsters, goblins, ghosts, a beautiful maiden. And I always thought I would be the happy ending to that story."

Her face blurred with anguish. She leapt to her feet, knocking over her cup, spilling cocoa over our silly drawing and spattering my shirt. As she flew down the steps, out of the café and onto the street, I lunged after her.

"I wish I had died that night," I shouted at her back, following along like a dog at her heels. "Died in your doorway. Because without you, all I have to look forward to is a vast, empty landscape; empty arms, empty bed, empty hours till the day I die."

Suddenly she spun around. She flung her arm out like a policeman, stopped me with a hand to my chest.

"There is something you can do, Raphael." she said in a steely voice. "And we can forget all this. We live together happily ever after, like in your fairy tale. Marry me."

I stopped dead in my tracks.

"Just one little thing. You must become Jewish. That's all! Such a small thing. And we get married tonight."

She waited expectantly. I wavered under the warmth of her hand. Gazing into the depths of my beloved's eyes, I was torn apart by what I found inside them, one last time.

I bowed my head. And said nothing.

"That is what I thought," she said simply.

She gave out a small sigh, her shoulders rising and falling just once. "Have a good life, Raphael Sinclair. You are a great painter. Your work will be in museums one day. You are in Paris. Find a beautiful girl. Fall in love. Forget me. Be happy."

The spring air was soft and fine and smelled of lilacs. On an evening like this, I should have been strolling down the boulevard with my lover. Instead, I watched her walk away from me into the gathering clouds of evening.

And suddenly, with a rush, she was back, her hat gone, her hair in wild disarray. My heart lifted like a bird in flight, and my arms went around her, and she held my face in both her hands and pressed her lips to mine.

Her black eyes bored into me. "I lied," she whispered fiercely. "Don't forget me. The Sofia Wizotsky who lived in Paris and was, for a little while, an artist. I want to haunt you, Raphael Sinclair. Let me haunt you."

Paris was dead for me after that.

Everywhere I went, a black-and-white movie reel of a smiling Sofia spooled through my memory. I tortured myself with images of Sofia and her handsome new beau kissing on every romantic corner. I imagined him taking her arm on a stroll along the quays. I saw him leaning over to steal a kiss in a cab ride through the Bois de Boulogne, his hands all over her body. Then I started withdrawing from people; classmates, my circle of friends, casual acquaintances. Getting together with them only magnified the size of the hole she had left inside me.

Without hope of seeing her each day, the City of Light seemed dull and foolish. I slipped away one warm and lovely night, saying no goodbyes, leaving my scruffy bachelor flat exactly the way it was. Back in London, my father asked no questions, merely ruffled his *Times* and gave me a courteous little smile of acknowledgement at the breakfast table the next morning.

Some men drown their sorrow in drink or narcotics, others in violence. I prowled the streets of London, seeking relief from the relentless loop of images cycling through my brain. I drifted like a ghost among the laughing throngs of theatergoers around Covent Garden. I trolled Soho, taking comfort from the streetwalkers there, following dark-eyed, dark-haired girls down shady alleyways, calling out Sofia's name as I expelled my frustration upon them. I walked alongside the thirsty waters of the Thames, and sanely considered the cold arms of a watery death.

The morning of August 15th—well, morning for me, but it was actually rather late in the afternoon—there was a knock at my door. My father's man, telling me there was a call for me from Paris. Gentleman, name of Colby.

"Sinclair, old boy," he was almost shouting. There was a lot of background noise. Colby didn't have a telephone in his apartment, he used the pay phone at Café de Flore whenever he needed one. "There you are! Been looking for you! Wanted to see how you were doing!"

I lied, as men do in these situations, told him everything was brilliant, I'd gotten a bit nervous about the war, I was seeing old friends, sniffing around the galleries, trying to get back into an ex-girlfriend's good graces.

Even with the crashing of dishes behind him, I could tell he was relieved. He gave me an abbreviated account of the latest gossip. Lulu the model had been hospitalized for exhaustion, but everyone knew it was a drug overdose; Beata had left for Prague to see if she could help her family get out of Czechoslovakia; Margaux was cheating on Leo with his arch rival, Brodov; I had missed a hell of a goodbye party for Sawyer, who was on a ship steaming towards the colonies.

It was good to hear his voice. I felt a surprising pang of homesickness.

He was getting off now. "All right, Sinclair. Sartre is glaring at me, he wants to use the phone. Sounds like you're in good spirits. I was just a bit worried. Wanted to check on you. Big day and all."

I frowned, though he couldn't see it. "What big day?"

There was crackling from the international connection. Then he said dubiously, "You do know, old boy. Sofia's getting married today."

The world began to spin. Just in time, I put my hand out and caught the wall, steadied myself.

"Oh yes," I said. "That big day. Well, thanks for calling, Colby. Good to hear your voice. Do look me up whenever you get back to London, we'll go out for a drink." And I rang off.

I don't know how I got back to my room. I don't remember dressing or stumbling down the stairs of my father's house. I don't remember how I got there, or how many places I stopped in first, but the next thing I remember I was bellied up to the bar at a tiny pub down a stinking alleyway off Covent Garden, drinking great quantities of alcohol.

By then, I had formulated a plan. First, I was going to get completely bladdered. Then, I was going to go home with the prettiest girl I could find.

After the first few drinks, the pictures on the walls seemed homier, the other blokes more convivial, the girls more lovely.

I smiled at the lovelies. A promising bit of fluff flirted with me, I bought a round for the bar. I was playing some kind of truth-or-dare drinking game that I was willingly losing when the bit of fluff asked whether I had a sweetheart. A vision of Sofia in a white wedding gown, the veil over her face, rose up before my eyes. Then the vision blurred, turning to smoke in the unhealthy air.

Behind me, a cold breeze gusted in. The hairs on the back of my neck rose. I heard the door bang shut. A rustle of fabric. Someone coming in after the theater. Whoever it was parked themselves at the bar to my left, jostled my elbow. I turned, nearly falling off my barstool. She was a tall, bosomy woman in a black silk satin evening gown sheathed in black net, embroidered with swooping, sequined black birds. Plunging neckline, bare arms, under a thin wrap. Dark hair, dark eyes, lips painted a deep alizarin crimson. My lucky night after all.

She had come in with someone, a man even taller than she was, dressed for the theater. They conferred in low, urgent tones, her big round eyes focused avidly on him. She seemed to be breathlessly devouring his every word. Suddenly, she threw her head back and laughed. He rose to his feet and paid the tab, then glided out the front door, leaving her alone at the bar.

She looked familiar. I squinted at her through the smoke, and then it came to me; friend of Leo's, did something in fashion.

We chatted for a moment about Paris, people we knew. "What are you doing here?" she asked, putting a cigarette between her lips. I lit it for her, taking the opportunity to ogle her breasts.

"Financial matters," I lied. "And you? Business or pleasure?"

"Always pleasure."

She leaned over me, whispered in my ear. Too many people knew her here. She knew of a place nearby, somewhere more private. Could I follow her? I watched her shimmering bottom swish out the door; the winking sequins made her look like a mermaid. I threw money on the bar, and we headed down Maiden Lane.

The scent of roses and honeysuckle wafted through the air from a flowerseller's booth in Covent Garden, faraway stars glittered faintly in a velvety black sky. There must have been a restaurant nearby; the smell of roasting meat hung in the air, and as my stomach grumbled, I realized I hadn't eaten since the day before.

A third of the way up Garrick Street, the parade of storefronts gave way to a street I'd never noticed before, narrow and poorly lit, paved over with ancient-looking cobblestones. She glided into it. I hesitated.

"What is it?" she asked softly.

"A bit dark," I conceded. "Good place for robbers to hide."

She laughed, her bright eyes shining. "I will protect you from them," she promised, and drew my arm under hers.

A few lengths further and the street crooked to the right, widened briefly into a shadowy court, then disappeared under a dark, covered passageway. This twisted square of broken paving stones was surrounded on all sides by the backs of other buildings facing larger, more traveled thoroughfares. The few visible windows were dark and unshuttered, like the eyes of the blind. The place she spoke of came suddenly into view, a rough looking bar called The Lamb and Jackal. Though the night was warm, I remember suppressing a shiver.

She took my hand and pulled me into the passageway, barely wide enough to allow two people to pass. My senses were assailed with the stench of piss and decay. There, she shoved me hard against the dank wall and began her assault.

She ripped open my shirt—I remember the tiny click of the buttons bouncing on the flagstone—and moved her mouth down my throat, my chest, my belly, making little sounds of pleasure, tweaking me with her teeth as she worked her way down. I pressed my hands against the slimy bricks, barely able to hold myself upright, shivering with the damp and the sheer pornographic thrill of it. It was all I could do to keep myself from coming right then and there as she undid my trousers, like a present she was taking her time unwrapping.

And then she hiked up her skirts and leapt at me, and I wrapped my arms around her hips and heaved her onto myself, and in one raw, annihilating, apocalyptic moment, disgorged into her all the rage and loss and vengeance brewing in my soul.

When it was over, I could barely stand upright. "Sorry," I panted as she kissed the base of my throat. "That took every last ounce of my strength. I'm done in."

·"Oh, you were *merveilleux,* my darling," she assured me. *"Fantastique.* Everything I dreamed you'd be. Now, look at me."

She took my face in her long fingers, transfixed me with her gaze. I noticed a strange red light dancing and leaping inside her eyes, like a flame. So seductive. So hypnotic. "Beautiful," she whispered. "So sad. Like a priest."

She put her lips behind my ear, then continued lightly, tenderly, back down my neck. Her arms tightened around me like steel cables, and the world exploded in pain as she drove her teeth into my throat.

I think I got out one strangled exclamation, but she was inhumanly strong, and I was drunk and anyway helpless under her thrall.

She began to feed. She sucked voraciously, long and hard. It made a horrible wet noise, a grotesque parody of passion. Completely sober now, I resisted, tried to push her away, my hands falling on soft but unyielding flesh. In response she bit down harder.

"Don't fight it, my darling." she coaxed. "It only hurts more when you fight."

Her eyes glittered with arousal and excitement. Paralyzed with horror, I saw her fangs glinting in the dim yellow light of the single gas lamp. I didn't think it was possible, but the pain was a hundred times worse when she buried her teeth in my throat a second time.

I had been wrong all along; I wanted very much to live. I should never have come to this godforsaken place. I should have stayed in Paris, broken a few dozen hearts, made some impenetrable angst-filled art, maybe joined the Foreign Legion, done some good. With terrible regret, I flashed on all the things I would never do; the brilliant career I would never have, the drawings in my sketchbook that would never materialize into paintings. Fall in love. Marry. Have children. Grow old.

I couldn't breathe, she was crushing my larynx. Something warm and wet was running down the inside of my throat. I realized that I was going to die now.

Only six liters of blood run through the human body. A physician I knew once told me that a person cannot recover from a loss of more than three. I don't know how long it went on for, but it seemed like forever, and I think she took it all.

Finally she was done. I felt her slowly but surely letting me down to the wet pavement, like a mother putting a tired child to bed.

"Shhh, shhh," she said in a soothing voice. "Mother will take care of you."

She put her hand under my head and raised it a little, leaned over me. I tasted blood in my mouth, not my own. Then she laid me back down on the cobblestones.

Though I could no longer move or speak, I was still capable of tears, and I could feel them streaking down the sides of my face. I gazed up at her, kneeling on the mossy paving stones in her couture gown embroidered over with a murder of crows. Her skin was suffused with color; her lips were full and red. A coquettish little smile played over them now, like the Mona Lisa. She bent over and kissed me one last time, my blood on her lips.

"Goodnight, lover," she whispered. "Hurry, now." And with that, she rose to her feet and evanesced into the night.

I was alone now. As consciousness began to leave me, the pain receded. I was cold now, really cold. My chest labored up and down with the struggle to breathe. My eyelids were so heavy, I closed them; it was becoming too much effort to keep them open.

From somewhere I heard a thunderous *THUMP thump, THUMP thump, THUMP thump,* growing louder and louder while the noise from the street faded into the distance. The sound of my failing heart, beating slower and slower.

Something stirred the air like the flapping of wings. My chest rose and fell one more time. And that was all.

Tessa was crying. He squatted down beside her, rested his hands on her knees. "Sweet girl. I'm sorry. Don't cry, Tessa, I'm right here."

She flung her arms around him. Whatever grief-filled thing she was saying was lost in the wilds of her hair, in the place where her lips met his throat. Her tears felt warm against his skin.

"What was it like...being dead?"

He pushed tendrils of wet hair away from her face. "I was floating in this...vast, benevolent black ocean. I was warm. I wasn't sad. And though I couldn't see them, I could sense them, the others, millions and billions of souls, flowing peacefully along beside me."

Her arms tightened around him. For a precious moment, he allowed himself to feel loved, taking refuge in the shelter of her embrace. Then slowly, reluctantly, he withdrew from her, returning to his perch on the armchair.

My eyes opened to utter darkness.

I reached up to touch my face, and as I did, my knuckles scraped against a rough stone surface. Slowly, I became conscious of a cold, mildewy smell. I slid my fingers forward, trying to feel around for something familiar, but everything I touched was solid rock. When I tried to sit up, I thunked my head.

The events of the previous night came flooding back to me. Where was I? Had I been buried alive? Ferociously, I pounded on the walls, called out into the nothingness. All I heard was the sound of my own panicked voice, echoing back at me.

I heaved at the lid of my prison, whaled against it with all my might. This time I was rewarded with a sharp crack. Dirt fell on my face. The slab seemed to be giving way. I pushed harder. With a horrible scraping sound it moved, then crashed over the side and smashed to pieces.

Slowly, I raised myself up. I could just barely make out my surroundings. Low ceiling. Dying flowers. More sarcophagi, tucked into the other walls. A single candle in a niche, dribbling wax. The woman from the alleyway.

"Hello, my darling," she said brightly.

I cringed back into the box.

Today she was wearing a blush-colored satin ball gown with voluminous skirts, and long opera gloves that went almost to her shoulders. She looked like a visiting queen.

"It's all right," she said soothingly. "All done. Why don't you come out of there?"

"What are you going to do to me now?" I asked her. My voice actually quavered.

She laughed, brought her face close to mine. "Whatever you like," she answered, her eyes merry.

I seized a broken chunk of marble, brandished it at her. "Don't come any nearer." I warned her.

"You won't need that," she said, amused. "You're stronger than I am, now. All right. I'll stay over here. I know. It's confusing."

I climbed out of the sarcophagus, brushed myself off, staying as far away from her as I could in the confined space. "Where are we?"

"In the crypt under your family's tomb." she said patiently. "We met Tuesday night. You remember that, don't you? Our little rendezvous? May I say, my darling, you were delectable, in every possible way. You lay in the morgue for a couple of days until your father thought to look for you. You were laid to rest this morning. It was a small funeral. Your father didn't contact any of your friends."

Oh, good, she was insane. "He doesn't know any of my friends. What day is this?"

"It is a week later. Near midnight."

"This must be some kind of mistake," I said, mostly to myself. "I must have been in a coma or something, and they buried me alive."

"Oh, no, *mon petit artiste,*" she corrected me. "You were quite dead. And now you are undead."

I was looking for stairs. This episode had been a real wake-up call. I had to get back to Paris.

"All right, then." I replied, backing slowly away. "Thanks for the information, you've been really helpful. And now, I've got to be going."

"Not before I give you a little lesson."

"What kind of lesson?" I humored her. I had found the stairs.

"There are only a few rules you must follow. But they are unforgiving." She was following me. "Listen, my darling, this is important. Never go into the light of day. If you do, you will burst into flames like a torch and burn until you are dust."

"Light of day," I said. "Flames. Dust. Got it." I threw open the trapdoor, climbed up into the mausoleum. It was lighter up here. Marble benches. A wreath. Dying flowers. Inspirational words circling the top of a neo-classical dome. My name, freshly carved into a marble plaque.

Disbelieving, I traced my fingers over the letters. The epitaph was something instructive in Latin about time fleeting. "There must be some mistake," I whispered weakly.

"I told you," she said sympathetically. "No mistake."

I turned on her. "You're mad! Go on, get away from me, before I call the police. My father's a knight, you know."

As I stepped down from the family tomb, my legs were curiously wobbly. I tottered off down a wide lane towards the sanctuary, and, I hoped, the way out.

A new moon cast its greenish light over the overgrown gravestones and Victorian statuary. I was barely past the entrance gate when I faltered, pitching clumsily forward. I grabbed at the wrought iron bars to keep myself from falling down.

The woman from the alleyway was right behind me. Her thin eyebrows drew together in concern. "You must be starving," she said. "Let's take care of that first."

Footsteps echoed toward us in the darkness. There must have been a short in the streetlight; the bulb blinked on and off, revealing a reckless young toff making his way home after blowing his week's allowance on drinks. It was after eleven, the pubs were closed.

She drew herself up to her full height, rearranged her magnificent dress, smoothed a hand over her hair. "How do I look?" she said to me, then wafted out to greet him.

"*Excusez-moi,*" she said as he approached, turning her great dark eyes on him. "Do you have the time?"

He stopped, looked at his watch. He had on little round wire-rimmed glasses, like Sawyer Ballard. "Sure," he agreed, eyeing the white globes of her breasts, just visible over the neckline of her dress. "I'll give you the time. But not if he's watching."

"Run," I urged him. "Run away while you still can. She's a monster."

"Look in my eyes," she commanded. He tore himself away from admiring her breasts, met her gaze. His chin was smooth and hairless; he was barely old enough to shave. "Lovely." she murmured. "Just lovely." And then her hands were pinning him to the brick wall, her long fingers loosening his tie, undoing his shirt collar.

It was all gruesomely familiar. Her lips gaped wide in a smile, and then she was upon him. He wrenched himself upright, tried to work her fingers off of his shoulders, but she was relentless. In another moment, his legs buckled under him.

I could have saved him. At any time I could have stopped her, hauled her off of him. But I stood and watched. Hypnotized. Mesmerized. *Salivating.*

She lifted her head. Blood stained her lips a glossy red. "Go on," she said solicitously, gesturing at the poor boy shuddering on the paving stones.

"Good God!" I said. "I'm going to get the police." But I didn't move. I was staring at the pool of blood widening under his head. Staring at his torn throat. Licking my lips.

Something strange was happening to me; I could feel muscles in my face working. My mouth felt swollen, distended. Puzzled, I raised my hand, touched my fingertips to my teeth.

Fangs. The strange swollen feeling came from sharp triangular fangs, descending from the top of my gums.

I choked on the words. "What have you done to me?"

"I made you *better.*" she whispered, with a secret smile.

I stumbled away, away from the terrible sight, away from the impossible, hallucinatory truth. I didn't get far; the world began to spin, and I went down, whacking my head on the pavement.

She was there at once, sympathetically tsk-tsking. She took a handkerchief out of a little satin bag, dabbed it on my forehead.

"Raphael Sinclair." she said firmly. "You can be angry at me later. But now, you really must drink. We can't have you fainting all over town." She got her arms under me, lifted me to my feet. I was too weak to resist. She deposited me on my knees before the dying boy.

His eyes were open; he was breathing very quickly, short shallow breaths. He had lost his glasses. They lay near his hand where they had fallen, the lenses cracked. Fiercely, I shook my head no.

"Why not?" she said. "Of course. You are squeamish. You would prefer a steak. Well, my dear. The time for steak is over. Right now, we must hurry. You may be immortal, but it is still possible to starve to death."

He was weeping now. A terrible price to pay for choosing the wrong way home. In a daze, I watched his life gushing out of him into the cracks between the cobblestones. The coppery smell of blood filled the air. Insatiable hunger expanded in my chest, taking over my brain like an electrical storm. Revolted, desperate, I crouched over, touched my tongue to the blood coating the paving stones.

The taste hit me like a thunderbolt.

Rich, velvety, winey, briny, delicious blood. It filled my stomach and slaked my thirst; it banished the cold and made me hungry for more.

I took his head in my hands as if he were a lover, turned his face away from me. And then I put my lips to his throat.

I sucked and I sucked and I sucked. I drained the life out of him and into myself, until my hands were warm and his body was cold. And when I was done—when there was no more—I sat back on my knees and heaved a sigh of relief.

The days after that are dark and filled with half-memories.

At nightfall, I would wake up cursing Anastasia—for it was Anastasia, if you haven't guessed by now—for making me a monster, swearing I'd rather die than live this way. By morning, I had my fangs in some frightened shopgirl who'd stopped to give me the time. Remarkable what a human being is capable of in the struggle to survive.

She was in London for business, not pleasure. The man I had seen her with was Rudolph von Theissen, a wealthy German attaché with corrupt tastes who was her sometime lover, as well as the financial backer of her fashion enterprise.

She'd been biding her time, waiting for me, ever since that first time we met in La Coupole all those months ago. When I asked her why, she laughed, lolling over on the cream-colored satin sheets. "Of course, you are beautiful," she said. "Also, you were embracing tragedy with both arms, like a man who lies down in front of a speeding train. The way you followed around that Jewish girl, knowing you never had a chance! Let's face it, my darling. It was only a matter of time. All I did was give you a push."

I moved in with my ancestors at the mausoleum in Highgate. It felt appropriate, somehow, and it offered a certain amount of privacy that was lacking in the center of London. There was allegedly a Highgate vampire roaming the grounds, but I never saw him. For a short while, I filled his undead shoes.

Through the long, hot end-of-summer days I slept in the cool stone sarcophagus that had served as my coffin. I rose at sundown to stalk the sad, the lost, the lonely, unfortunate enough to stray across my path. Though the gates were closed and locked at night, there was always someone foolish enough, or grieving enough, to slip through.

The pale young widow who couldn't bear to part with her new husband's company, though he lay in his grave. An old pensioner with leaking eyes who couldn't believe his wife of forty-seven years had predeceased him. A sylph-like creature who returned night after night to weep at the crypt of a boy who fell in the Great War. A twelve-year-old orphan who wanted only to be reunited with her mother in heaven. A hollow-eyed mother dressed all in black who had sat by a sick child's bed and would not leave that child's side now, though he slept in the ground.

I became a connoisseur of death. I found that if I stared into my victims' eyes long enough, they would surrender themselves up to me with little or no struggle. I found that I could draw life from different places on the human body; the blue artery on the underside of a wrist, the chalice of a soft belly, the inside of a silky thigh. By trial and error, I found that I could take just enough so that my benefactor lived to walk out the gate the next morning. I found that some girls rather liked it. To make love in a graveyard is to shake a fist at death.

Eventually, I lost track of time. Every day was like the next, distinguished only by who I consumed and how. The leaves turned yellow and red and brown, then fell. The air grew brisk, then bracing, then cold. Snow dusted the Victorian angels and winged cherubs, frosted the roofs of the mausoleums as if they were gingerbread houses. A white mist clung to the ground, like ghosts filtering through the trees. I could never get warm, unless I had just fed. I chose one fellow for the size of his coat.

One night, long after dark, I heard footsteps. I halted in what I was doing, finding a final resting place for a furtive-eyed fellow with a shovel and a bag—God knows what he was looking for, but I found him first—lifted my head, and listened. It seemed to be coming from a close, circular path overhung by beech and hornbeam trees that wound its way through a city of Gothic tombs, part of the old Western section.

There were no signs of stealth, no hushed whispers, just the slow click-clack of stiletto heels and the papery swishing of many yards of silk. With the wind moaning and the bare black branches crooked like witches' fingers, even I was a bit leery.

I made out a tall, regal, dark-haired woman in an orange silk sari. No hat, no gloves, no fear. Anastasia.

I resisted the urge to duck into the nearest doorway and hide until she passed. But I brushed myself off—I had become rather disheveled during my tenure in Highgate, what with the one suit of clothes and no bathing and all—ran my fingers through my hair in a futile attempt at grooming and stepped through the squealing metal grille.

She halted, put her hand to her heart and gasped. Then she broke into laughter. "*Ça va,* Monsieur Sinclair?" she said warmly, taking in my dishabille.

"What do you want?" I growled. I pushed open a sarcophagus. Inside was a skeleton dressed in wispy Victorian weeds, the long hair still rich and red, bony fingers clamped around a posy of dried black violets tied with a black ribbon.

"I wanted to meet this Highgate vampire that I've been hearing so much about," she replied vivaciously. "It looks like you have gotten over your bourgeois squeamishness, *n'est-ce pas?*"

"Couldn't have done it without you." I snarled, dumping body and bag atop the skeleton. The bones made a rattling sound like dice being thrown across a gaming table.

Anastasia rolled her eyes. "So much *sturm und drang.* Well, my darling. I came to see how you are doing because tomorrow I am leaving."

I replaced the sarcophagus cover, a heavy stone thing that weighed hundreds of pounds. If that was so, I would be truly alone. "What about your boyfriend?"

She looked reflective. "Rudi was called back to Berlin. That's the *coup de grâce* for my little fashion house." She looked at me more closely. "Can it be you do not know? You haven't seen the papers? Hitler sent his tanks into Poland. Britain and France declared war. It has begun."

Poland. *Sofia, my Sofia.* I felt a sharp, familiar pain.

"There's nothing like a war," Anastasia went on mistily. "Buildings on fire. Bombs falling from the sky. Smoke filling the air. Confusion everywhere." Her eyes glimmered with the kind of expression usually reserved for acts of passion. "Women and children left to manage on their own. Girls sent out to do a man's job. Bodies scattered across the countryside. Chaos. And everywhere, everywhere, soldiers in adorable uniforms."

"I don't know," I said. "I've got a pretty nice place here." By this I meant that I had stolen an oriental rug from a clothesline in Hampstead and also a nice feather quilt.

Her big round eyes fastened on mine. "Come with me, Raphael." she said, extending her hand to me. It gleamed white as bone in the moonlight. "I'll show you the world like you've never seen it." And after a moment, I acquiesced, abandoning the cemetery to the absent vampire and the creeping vines forever.

We drifted around for a while after that. There was no rush for Anastasia to return to Paris; the fashion houses were all closing up shop or moving in anticipation of war.

We did as rich people do; while ordinary Londoners tearfully evacuated their children to the country to keep them safe from the brutal, take-no-prisoners warfare Hitler had perfected in the medieval town squares of Poland, we went touring.

We headed south, warming ourselves on Greek islands, the fabled Côte d'Azure, the Dalmatian coast. By day we slept in rooms shuttered from the sun. By night we walked the streets, feeding on easy pickings from the service industry that always revolved like satellites around the idle rich.

On June 3, 1940, bombs began to fall on France. Three weeks later, Hitler was posing for snaps in front of the Eiffel Tower. We were in Antibes when Anastasia got the telegram from Rudi. His *frau* and four stocky children were staying firmly put in the castle on the Rhine. For the duration of the war, he installed Anastasia at the Ritz.

I wasn't ready to return to Paris. The memories were too new, too raw. It was like watching the movie of my life story playing out around me, but all the major actors had left for other projects, and there was nothing left but the sets.

So I journeyed to London, taking over my father's house. When the neighbors commented that they hadn't seen the old boy for some time, I told them he'd been called upon to invent something for the war effort, very big, very hush hush. They nodded wisely, say no more, say no more.

The Germans started bombing in August.

Anastasia was right; war is beautiful, especially at night. The wail of the air raid siren. The deafening drone of bombers flying low overhead, grouped so tightly that they blocked out the moon. Searchlights crossing and crisscrossing the sky. Entire blocks of eighteenth-century Georgian townhouses erupting into giant fireballs, shivering and splintering down into the street. The continual thunderous thud-thud-*boom* of exploding shells approaching, reverberating off the buildings, the earth shaking beneath my feet. Unidentified glowy things floating through the blackness and then incandescing into a rain of fire. Crackling orange firepits of burning rubble that used to be a grocer, or a school, or a cathedral.

This was my Blitz. Smoke limiting visibility, making it very easy for a fellow to find a meal. Helpless lovelies trapped in the ruins of collapsed buildings waiting for a bloke to pull them out. Solitary men clutching binoculars, perched atop buildings, hoping to be the first to spot the airplanes. Tasty tidbits sheltering in the shadowy recesses of the Tube. Armies of the newly displaced, heading for the outskirts of the city, or camping out in the split-open ruins of their homes. In wartime, people disappear all the time.

"You said you took over your father's house," said Tessa. "Where did he go?"

"I, ah," he looked uncomfortable, lapsed into silence.

She paled. "Did you...um, did you..."

"Did I drink his blood? No. Don't be silly. Seems a bit like incest, doesn't it? I let Anastasia do that."

She cringed. She was trying to hide it, but he was looking right at her, she definitely cringed.

Still love me now, sweet girl? Time to change the subject. "Did I ever tell you where I got that one?" He was gazing at the Rembrandt.

"I thought all the Rembrandts were in museums."

"Not this one." Lovingly, he admired the fleshy feminine figure, the fili-gree brushwork, the crabbed little men hidden in the shadows, before going on. "Anastasia phoned me in London. She was accompanying Rudi to the East, would I like to come along. This would be late in the spring of 1941."

"This Rudi. Was he a Nazi?"

"Yes. I don't remember his title exactly. Reich Commissioner of the Department for Raping Countries of Their Natural Resources, something like that."

"And you two were...friends?" She had to prod herself to get the word out, as if it tasted bad on her tongue.

"Friends?" His eyebrows came together. "Not exactly. We shared a lover. He could be useful."

Tessa didn't say anything, but he knew what she was thinking. It was occurring to her for the first time that someone she loved, someone she trusted, might have been on the wrong side of World War II. What could he say? He was guilty, incredibly guilty. As if this were the worst thing he'd admit to tonight.

With a sibilant hiss, the logs in the fireplace lapsed into ashes. How much should he tell her? he wondered. His stories were part of Tessa's history, she had as much a right to them as he did. But knowledge was a double-edged sword. What dreadful images might he set free to pursue her, night after night, through her dreams? What was necessary, and what was dangerous?

He'd lost the thread of the conversation. "What was I saying?"

"Anastasia. The East. Rembrandt."

Her voice anchored him in the present. He adjusted the painting a fraction of an inch. "Right then."

Rudi had promised Anastasia a pleasure trip to see the ruins of a cas-tle she used to live in, belonging to the bloke who'd changed her. Well. Belonged to him before he was staked, beheaded, and burned, that is.

But first, he had the Reich's interests to look out for. The places we would visit produced oil, coal, chemicals, copper, zinc and wheat, essential resources Hitler required to continue making war. He rolled his eyes in telling us this information, as if we were children and he was dragging us to a boring grownup chore before going to the park.

We traveled by night, stopping by day in the grandest hotels Old Europe had to offer. After dark we emerged to dine on clean, safe streets, in well-manicured parks, on well-fed, gainfully employed citizens of the Third Reich.

At a cocktail party in Amsterdam, Rudi introduced me to someone who mentioned that he was holding something especially nice, for a real connoisseur, very confidential, a real bargain. The next evening, there was a soft knock at the door of my room. A nervous little man was selling a painting for a friend who needed the cash, a small Rembrandt, Susannah bathing. I would be doing him a favor, actually. American dollars only, *bitte.*

This is when I began to acquire art in a serious way.

In Amsterdam, there were the Michelangelo drawings, a sweet Madonna, a playful child, the pencil lines as fresh and spontaneous as the moment he'd finished it. In Vienna, I came into possession of the Klimt, also a set of Art Nouveau silver, place settings for forty-eight, in a glossy Rococo wooden box. In Budapest, I picked up the Botticelli and a castle-sized Persian rug, the one in my Great Room. In Prague, I met a man on the old Charles Bridge, under the sculpture of a crucified Christ ringed with golden letters in an exotic alphabet that I recognized from the storefronts in Le Marais. It was a misty night, the great domes of the Old City swam in and out of view in the distance. I was offered a Vermeer, a servant girl pouring milk in the light of the sun streaming in through a window. The seller looked hunted, distracted. He needed to leave the country, he said.

Of course I knew that the Jews were being persecuted. Everyone knew. You couldn't walk past a restaurant, a movie theater, or a park bench without coming across those idiotic signs shouting that Jews were unwelcome. What did I care? I was beyond that. In my worldview, the living were all equally delicious.

All around me, people were disappearing. Somewhere not far away, young men were dying. Just over the border, airplanes flew overhead, raining death from the sky.

It was open season in Europe, a moveable feast. But I never saw another vampire. I don't know why. I read somewhere that Hitler believed in the supernatural. Perhaps the undead were frightened too, staying undercover until it all blew over. They alone had all the time in the world.

It was the middle of June by the time we turned south toward Romania. For the trip, Rudi had thoughtfully procured for us a diplomatic touring car, a Mercedes with darkened windows. With Anastasia at the wheel, we drove through mile after mile of wheat fields, past tight little groupings of red-tiled rooftops overshadowed by ruined fortifications. Narrow, pointed haystacks dotted the landscape, Queen Anne's lace and purple wildflowers grew wild over the softly sloping terrain.

Soon we were winding up the steeply rolling hills at the base of the Carpathians. As we came upon the medieval walls of Sighisoara, birthplace of the great Romanian warrior Vlad Dracul, the sun was setting behind mountain peaks as sharp and menacing as jackals' teeth.

It must have been market day. In the main square, farmers were loading willow crates filled with flapping chickens, mud-caked potatoes, and wormy cabbages back onto crude wagons drawn by shaggy horses. The men wore colorful embroidered vests over white shirts, the women were draped in long black shawls. They stopped working and stared as we drove by. A tall, strong-looking fellow crossed himself when he caught my eye.

"Don't look at them," she admonished me softly. "They know what we are." A smile played at the corners of her red lips.

At the top of the tallest peak, Anastasia stopped the car. I could hear the bass string twang of frogs croaking, and leaves rustling together like the souls of the damned. Peering forward into the trees, I could make out the ruins of a thick stone wall.

"Careful where you step," she said as we climbed out. "There used to be a moat here."

She had dressed for the occasion in a gold lamé Vionnet gown. It shimmered and sparkled in the headlights. "Welcome to *Luceafarul De Dimineata,*" she said. "Morning Star. When it was built in the fifteenth century, it was the strongest citadel in all of Transylvania. You used to be able to see the flags flying on the towers from five miles away. It withstood Turkish and Tartar invasions. But it could not withstand the onslaught of an angry mob of villagers armed with torches and buckets of burning pitch."

I knew the story. In life, Anastasia had been a lacemaker, straining her eyes for fourteen hours a day in a poorly-lit cellar under a shop. At forty her eyes gave out. The foreman of the lace shop was sorry to see her go, but that was business. She was returning home late that night, wondering how she was going to pay the bills, when fate intervened in the person of Constantin Mondragon. Training his dark-rimmed eyes on her as she walked slowly down Rue du Faubourg St. Honoré, too preoccupied with her troubles to notice, he folded her into the black wings of his coat on the night of October 31, 1869.

Constantin swept her back to Transylvania, traveling in a dirt-filled box on the back of a wagon, made her the mistress of his castle. He took her with him on his travels, introducing her to leaders of society and heads of state, artists and musicians, gypsies and debased religious figures, bomb makers and anarchists. She smiled prettily and listened, absorbing lessons from them all, while her natural curiosity grew into a ferocious intelligence. She was his constant companion until 1899, when he was staked, beheaded, and set on fire. His castle and everything in it burned to the ground.

"I watched it all from behind that rock over there," she said. Her eyes were opaque and remote. "I've never seen such brutality in my life."

From the boot of the car, she took a dusty green bottle and three wine glasses. She handed the bottle to Rudi, who uncorked it and filled our glasses. The liquid was a deep red-brown, the consistency almost viscous.

"This, my darlings, is the very last bottle of wine from Constantin's vineyard, bottled just before the phylloxera virus killed all the grapevines. *Vizuina Dragon,* Dragon's Lair. I tracked it down in Budapest." She poured the rest of the bottle on the stony ground. "To Constantin, who gave me the world, then nurtured my spirit as if I were a cherished child. I miss you every day. *Noroc,* my darling. *Te iubesc.*"

We heard it at the same time; twigs snapping, the crackling of last year's leaves, the noises of purposeful movement through the trees. A loose cadre of men bore down upon us, carrying torches. At their head was some kind of a religious authority in a white and saffron robe emblazoned with golden crosses. An old man, at least seventy, with a gaunt face and a long scraggly beard, a figure out of an El Greco painting. He held before him an enormous painted cross bearing a hapless Jesus, suffering under a crown of thorns, his wounds raw and bleeding.

They came to a halt a short distance away from us. By the firelight I could see there were seven of them including the priest, wearing the clothes of the village. They wore the obligatory cross around their necks, garlands of garlic bulbs, and wreathes of garlic flowers in their hair. They came equipped for a fight, each man wielding the tool of his trade; scythes, pitchforks, hoes and spades.

The man in front had the smoldering eyes of a true believer. His gaze was fixed firmly on Anastasia. In a deep voice, he was declaiming something long and canonical in Romanian, making the sign of the cross in the air in front of him with two fingers over and over again. "Oh, he can't be serious." I heard Rudi mutter.

"Grigorii? Is that you?" Anastasia said playfully. "An Archbishop! You've done very well for yourself. You were just a monk back when I used to visit town."

"And you, Anastasia Bonheur," he changed over to sonorous French. "Forty years have passed, but you are unchanged. We are here to return your immortal soul to God, so that you may finally rest in peace."

"Am I dreaming?" I whispered to Anastasia. "Nobody says this stuff."

His gaze turned slowly to me. He handed the cross to the man behind him. "You were made only recently," he said, his voice gentle. "I can still see traces of a soul behind your eyes."

He stretched out his hand, beckoning me closer. Fierce, dark-rimmed eyes bored into mine. "My son. You are still a child of God. You die a little each time you take a life, don't you. Come to me and together we can rescue your tormented soul."

I took a step forward into the clearing, then another one, till I was standing directly in front of him. Behind me, I could hear Anastasia hissing. "What are you doing?" in English.

From a pocket in his robe he took a small vial of oil and anointed my forehead, my chin, my cheeks, my hands, my nostrils. He indicated that I unbutton my shirt, and when I did, he dabbed oil on my chest. As he did these things, he intoned something liturgical in Romanian, stopping once to ask me my name. He smelled of garlic and patchouli.

"He's giving you extreme unction, you idiot." Anastasia informed me.

He finished with a flourish of unfamiliar saints' names. Out of his vestments, he produced a sharpened wooden stake and a mallet, and planted it over my heart, where he had painted my chest with oil.

The point dug into my bare skin. When his eyes met mine again, they burned with religious fervor.

"The pain is your penance, my son," he said.

"Wait," I said. "Padre. Before we start."

The men from the town muttered uneasily, shuffling their feet, gripping their tools. He shushed them, then turned back to me.

"You've known other vampires."

"Yes." He crossed himself.

"Do I have a purpose? Am I part of God's design?"

Thoughtfully, he stroked his stringy beard. "Of course," he said. "Every creature on God's earth has a reason for being. You punish the headstrong, the questioning, the wandering, the weak, the ones who stray. You exist to hammer home the lessons of teachers, parents, the God-fearing. Even evil has a purpose.

"Take his arms," he said to his men.

I opened my fangs wide and struck, crushing his larynx and windpipe with my jaws. He was a wily old vampire hunter, and he got in one good stroke with the mallet before he went down. I felt the point of the stake wedge between my ribs. His blood ran down my throat, hot and garlicky.

The men around me shouted in panic and raised their weapons. Blows rained down upon my back, my shoulders. The man holding the cross wielded it like a baseball bat, striking me in the side, and I felt something break.

From behind came a sharp crack, like the snapping of a bough. The man with the cross looked concerned; and then he slumped forward and collapsed. I whipped around, and there was Rudi, holding a pistol.

"This man is under the protection of the Third Reich," he announced in German. The villagers were terrified now, staring aghast at their dead leader. "Stay where you are. I want all your names."

There was a moment of silence, a stalemate. Then one of the men flung his torch at Rudi, who dodged away, firing wildly. They dropped their tools and melted into the woods. Rudi emptied his pistol into the trees.

And then Anastasia began to laugh. Somewhere nearby, a chorus of wolves warbled along with her. "Brilliant, my darling!" she said when she could finally speak. "I really thought you were going to let him do it. Oh, you were magnificent!"

"You are one crazy bastard, Sinclair." Rudi agreed, shaking his head. "Excuse me, please. I have to make a call." He disappeared behind the car, where he kept a field telephone in the boot.

Anastasia leaned over, ran her warm tongue in a long line up my chest, lapping up the blood. Then she kissed me, deeply and fervently. "Thank you," she said, smiling. "That was a better tribute to Constantin than I could have planned." She buttoned my shirt back up and straightened my tie. "Now let's get out of here. You could really use a bath."

Rudi came hurrying up. His whole affect had changed. "Let's go."

"Where?" Anastasia said.

"The front," he said. "We are at war with Russia."

It was still nighttime when we got back to Sighisoara, Anastasia was asleep with her head on my shoulder. Rudi pulled up outside Gestapo Headquarters, formerly the town hall. "Better if you stay inside," he advised us. "I'll be back in a few minutes."

I was too restless to sleep, and besides, I was still hungry. I got out of the car and quietly shut the door. I wasn't about to start letting Anastasia's boyfriends tell me what to do.

I prowled through streets just wide enough for a horse-cart, over broken cobblestones, past stooped, darkened hovels, hoping to run into a rebellious teenager, a married someone on the way back from a tryst. I lingered outside one storey cottages with high, miserly windows, I lurked in a covered passageway completely overgrown with vines. But the streets were deserted, the shutters battened down tight against the likes of me.

Ascending a set of stairs cut into the mountain, I found myself before the massive wooden doors of a basilica. I pushed them open, waiting to be struck by lightning, or for the earth to open up under my feet. When neither of these things happened, I removed my hat and found a bench, surrounded by painted scenes from the lives of the saints.

At the moment that I stepped forward to meet the old man, I had every intention of letting him drive that stake through my heart.

He was right. Every time I dug my teeth into another innocent throat, I receded farther away from the man I used to be. I had been a vampire for almost two years now. I'd lost track of how many people I had killed long ago.

Was I evil? Yes, I killed people, many people. The savage things I did in the dead of night to keep myself alive were certainly evil. If the old man was right, I deserved to die, and sooner better than later.

Was there any good left in me at all? Could it be that my sole purpose in this world was to punish unhappy housewives and wayward teenagers? Was that the sum of me? Maybe the old man was wrong. Maybe it was still in my hands to shape my own destiny.

I dropped my head into my hands. I didn't feel evil. I felt lost. And then, Sofia's lovely face appeared before my mind's eye, as she had looked in the dance hall, listening to me go on about my hopes and dreams, her eyes half-closed as she basked in the sound of my voice. I felt anger throbbing dully behind my temples. *Sofia, Sofia. Look at what's become of me.*

The sun was coming up, illuminating the stained glass windows. Time to go.

I hurried back the way I had come, anxiously watching the lightening sky, sinking back into the soft leather of the Mercedes seat just as the sun burst in a red-orange ball over the Carpathians. As the morning light feebly touched the plaza with its first rays, I could just make out something new in the main square where yesterday the market tables had stood. With a shock, I realized I was looking at the skeletal framework of a gallows.

Seven bodies swung from it, necks stretched too long, twisting slowly back and forth. Stripped of his white and saffron robes, the Archbishop was just a scrawny old man, meeting the first few stunned parishioners in a sad gray suit of oft-mended long underwear.

Just then, Rudi returned, accompanied by a man in a black uniform with silver lightning slashes on his collar. They conferred briefly, and then Rudi raised his arm in a Nazi salute and got in. He put the car in gear, rolling us past the corpses slowly rotating in the morning breeze and out of the gates of the city, heading east into the sunrise.

The next day, I boarded a train that would take me to another train that would connect with a third train that would take me away from this place. I returned to Paris, the City of Light, from Eastern Europe, the cradle of darkness. It was June, 1941.

Outside the Gare de l'Est, I flagged down a cab and asked him to take me home. It took me a moment to remember the exact address; I'd last seen it two years ago.

Everything was exactly the way I had left it. Clothing heaped on a chair, a few unwashed dishes on the kitchen counter. A toothbrush on the sink. A dingy white shirt on the floor where I had dropped it, a souvenir of my haste to leave town. My table laid with neat rows of paint. My brushes, waiting for my return, standing bristle-end-up in a coffee can. I stroked their sable tips across my open palm, as if I were a canvas.

I gazed at the paintings in various stages of completion propped up against the walls, where they would remain forever unfinished. The young man who had started them was dead.

I was cold. I was always cold. I built a fire and huddled in front of the fireplace, bundled up to my neck in an eiderdown quilt. Then I unwrapped one of my new paintings—the Rembrandt—and hung it up over the fireplace. Stepping back to admire it, I bumped into the armchair. With a soft thump, something slid onto the floor at my feet.

It was my sketchbook, covered with a light layer of dust. I picked it up, brushing it off, and flipped idly through it. Quick drawings of old men in the Tuileries, unfinished baguettes and wine bottles, studies of an open hand or the way a skirt draped around a body. Endless doodles of people in cafés. Painfully bad poetry. Hastily scribbled appointments to meet friends at a gallery, a nightclub, a theater. Mysterious jottings, their meanings lost to time.

A paper fell out, glided to the floor. I stooped down to pick it up. I turned it over slowly, knowing what it was. An Exquisite Corpse drawing, from the night I found Sofia alone at a table in La Coupole, the same night she drew my head onto the body of a god with the wings of an angel. I leaned against the fireplace, traced my fingers lightly over her strong black lines.

The night she told me her story. The night I fell in love with her. The night she ruined my life.

And then, finally, I allowed myself to turn my head and rest my eyes on Sofia's artworks, rescued from her flat along with her paints and brushes, leaning against the wall in the corner where the porter had deposited them.

Now I leafed through her copies of nudes and holy families, holier to me because they were done by her hand. I ran my fingers over her female figures as if by doing so, I could touch her.

I was finally angry. Outraged. Consumed with fury.

Had she only stayed with me, none of this would have happened. We would have made our own happily-ever-after in Paris, or London, or New York, or whatever sodding place she wanted to live. I would not be a parasitical blood-sucking incubus, and she would not be a phony housewife going to gardening club meetings with a fake smile pasted on her face in Toledo-fucking-Ohio.

These are the words I told myself as I fed her drawings, one by one by one, into the hungry jaws of the fire.

Some of the images were visible for a few moments, backlit by firelight, before flames caught the edges. Two models in bloomers drawn in willow charcoal and sanguine. A Del Sarto Madonna. And then the paper would brown and curl into ash. With each drawing, my hatred grew.

I didn't stop there. I was possessed. I scoured the flat of my own artwork, throwing armloads of laid paper from the finest mills of Europe onto the blaze. Tongues of flame jetted forth into the room. The paintings went next; the stretchers took up too much space in the fireplace, so I took my knife to them and flayed them out of their frames.

A lifetime of work went up the chimney. The fire roared like a furnace. I held my hands up to its blaze. Oh, I was warm now.

As I was about to throw in the last of the lot, a canvas, I caught a glimpse of the image, and turned it around.

A couple swathed in white sheets, locked in embrace. The man raised himself over his partner, supported by sinewy arms. The woman spread ecstatically beneath him, her lips a red smudge in the heart-shaped face, her hair falling in blue-black streaks around the pillow. Unmistakably Sofia, her skin almost as white as the sheets. The man—well, it was me.

I'd never seen it before, she must have done it right before she left. I made to throw it in the fire, too; but at the last moment I lost my courage. Carefully, I wrapped it up in the old bedcovering I had used to transport the Rembrandt, and stashed it in the maid's room behind the kitchen.

Smoking with rage, I swept forth into the night.

So, I resumed the life I'd left behind, in a fashion. I went to clubs and bars and theaters, seeking out slummy places least likely to be frequented by the society I used to know, searching among the individuals least likely to be missed. I traded *bon mots* with the Free French, émigré spies, SS officers. I flirted with French prostitutes and lonely German girls in drab gray uniforms. I even acquired a notoriety of sorts; the papers wrote breathlessly of the Reich's tireless efforts to bring down the Montmartre Ripper.

As for all those shortages you might have heard about, well, I didn't suffer any. If a fellow had money, he had brandy, cigars, fine suits, and all the pretty girls he could eat; I didn't need ration coupons for *them*. I drank and smoked and whored and debauched and made clever conversation, just as I used to, only now the evening was likely to end with me taking a girl down the street to a darkened doorway and stealing more than just a couple of kisses.

Through it all, Sofia was my dark muse, my twisted inspiration. If I made a girl squirm, if I made a girl scream, she was still the motivation that gave my actions shape. My new life was a circus freak-show doppelganger for my old life.

December, 1942. It was late, maybe two or three in the morning. The setting was a filthy, piss-smelling alleyway alongside a theater in Montmartre, the walls running iridescent blue-green with mold. I was just finishing up with a showgirl from the naughty revue around the corner. Full, satisfied, I was just letting her down on the pavement when I heard a sound behind me.

Let it be rats, I prayed. *Please God, let it be rats.*

I wheeled around. Someone was standing between me and the street.

"Sinclair?" The voice was English, with an upper crust accent, familiar. "Raphael *Sinclair?*"

Now I could see his face. A tall Englishman with dark, wavy hair. He was gaping at the showgirl, at the blood commingling with the sequins and the bedraggled feathers on her costume. He stared at me, stared at the girl, stared back at me again. Someone was with him, a boy with eyeshadow and lipstick, who took one look at me, crossed himself and disappeared.

"Oh, my God, Sinclair," he whispered. "Oh, dear God. So it's true."

"What's true, Colby?" I said, walking slowly towards him, heartsick. *Colby, Colby, why did it have to be you?*

He was licking his lips nervously, backing away. "Leo was very funny about it...he said...it was the damndest thing, utterly mad..."

He was wearing a white dinner jacket with a red carnation under a black overcoat. I fingered the lapels of his coat. "Nice," I said. "Cashmere?"

He nodded. "Found this tailor on the Row. Brilliant work."

I asked him if he had a smoke. He reached into his pocket, produced a silver case. I put a cigarette between my lips. He leaned forward to light it, then lit one for himself. We both blew smoke into the cold air.

I named a dozen people we both knew. He'd just had a letter from Sawyer, who had married and taken up residence in Rhode Island, where his family had a cottage. Beata never returned from visiting her family in Czechoslovakia, Erlichmann was lost without her. Most of the others had emigrated to New York, except for Lulu the model, who had taken up with a German soldier.

I left Leo and Margaux for last. His eyebrows jigged up, and he gave me an impenetrable look. "Oh, well, you know. They're all right. They never seem to suffer shortages the rest of us do. They're leaving for New York in a few days."

There was a moment of silence as he drew on his cigarette. Then he said, "She's still here, you know."

Something in my head started pounding. Deep in my pockets, I balled my hands into fists. "Who?" I made myself say.

"Sofia. She's still in Poland."

My face must have registered shock, though it felt like it was made of stone. "I thought...they would have left for America by now."

"Last I heard, she was living with her parents." His face was a blur of blue smoke. "Skip seems to have arrived in Mother Europe with his own agenda. Perhaps he, like the rest of us, found the taste of liberation irresistible."

He exhaled, stubbed out his cigarette, screwed his eyebrows together and scrutinized me. "Now, what about you?" He whipped off my hat, then handed it back to me. "Smashing haircut," he said, admiringly. "When did you start wearing bespoke suits? And those shoes! Handmade as well, if I'm not mistaken. Hold on. Do I detect *cologne?* On the great Raphael-art-is-all-that-matters-Sinclair? Good God."

We touched on news of the war, the Russians beating back Hitler at Stalingrad, Rommel being trounced in North Africa, tide was turning, etc., etc. I asked him if he was working on anything new. He gave me a quirky grin. "Well...with the war and all, the market for lovely little landscapes dried up. I'm painting forgeries now. Germans can't get enough Bouguereau shepherd girls."

I laughed at that. He gave me a warm smile and said, "God, it's good to hear your voice." And then his face flooded with concern, and he said, "What happened to you, Sinclair?"

For a brief moment I considered confiding in him, letting him in on it. What a relief it would be, for a single human being to know what I was, and to accept me anyway. What would be the harm in it? Anastasia had Rudi, didn't she?

But then Colby's eyes fell on the mottled body of the girl behind me in the alleyway, and I saw his eyes fill with revulsion and fear. It was then that I understood the difference. Colby was a decent man.

"Dear God," he said. "You're the Montmartre Ripper, aren't you."

"It's not what it looks like," I said helplessly.

He was backing away. My nostrils filled with the odor of his panic. "Got to tell somebody," he said thickly.

"Can't let you do that, old man." I said. He was almost at the mouth of the alleyway now.

"Don't come any nearer," he warned me in a shaky voice. "Or I'll..."

"Colby," I said. He was already in my thrall as I walked steadily towards him. I was close to him now, so close that I could feel him breathing. I stood there for a long time, looking into his kind, familiar face, desperately not wanting to do the thing I was about to do; and then I put my hands around his neck and pulled him down towards me.

I felt a tremor pass through his body; it might have been the cold or fear or desire. I could feel his carotid artery pulsing against my cheek. I gashed it open with my fangs and clamped my jaws around his trachea.

He fought like a lion. He pushed and pulled and kneed and kicked and rolled and struggled and made horrible voiceless noises. He was a big man, and I almost lost my nerve, but my arms were coiled around him like a boa constrictor, and after only a few terrible minutes he weakened and began to sink to the pavement.

I held my friend until he was gone, feeling his heartbeat slow and stop, watching with sorrow and shame as the light in his eyes died down to a spark, then blinked out. I took his wallet, so that it would look like a robbery, but first I folded his identity papers neatly and tucked them into the breast pocket of his dinner jacket.

I left him there in a filthy alleyway, with only the body of a dead whore to keep him company. And then I went into Sacré-Coeur and lit a candle for his soul.

At sunset on the evening of January 13, 1943, I stepped out onto the platform at the eastern border town of Wlodawa. The terrain outside my window was perfectly flat, gray and lifeless savannahs rolling on into infinity under the frosty Polish stars. I refreshed myself on a reasonably clean-looking guard slumbering outside the station and went to acquaint myself with the town.

I knew exactly what I was going to do. Destroy Sofia's life the way she had destroyed mine.

I had practiced it a million times over in my imagination. She would be surprised, of course, to find me at her door. She would invite me in, glad to see an old friend, and when the door closed behind her, when she was greeting me with a polite kiss on both cheeks in the continental manner, I would sink my fangs into her lily-white throat and suck on her vital fluids until there was nothing left. As she was expiring, she would cry, "Why, Raphael, why?" and I would snarl, "Just my way of saying thanks for making me the man I am today."

I found the Wizotsky estate almost immediately, a white Baroque villa set among trees and gardens, just as she'd described it. But the family was no longer there. The local Gestapo overlord had commandeered it for his headquarters, and no one seemed to be able to tell me where they had gone.

I didn't speak Polish, and nobody spoke English. But my innkeeper knew a bit of French, and the cabdriver a bit of German, and by breakfast the following morning, I knew which part of town she lived in. By noon, I knew the name of the street. By sunset, I had her address.

It was raining as I stalked across the square. Dirty weather for a dirty deed. I found the house by the blue light of a stuttering streetlamp and knocked on the door.

When no one answered, I moved closer and inhaled. Beyond the street smells of horse dung, outhouses and fermented cabbage, I thought I detected a whiff of lilac. I knocked again, more insistently this time. I heard cautious footsteps, and then the bolt slid back, and the door creaked slowly open.

Sofia, unmistakably Sofia. Love of my life, architect to my passion, muse to my irredeemable afterlife. There was a black shawl wrapped around her head and what looked like rags tied around her hands. Her hair had grown longer, and it fell in soft, fluttering waves around her face. But her eyes, her eyes...they were just as I remembered them, dark and wild and beautiful, oracles of tragedy.

She didn't say a word. In my fedora and overcoat, she must have taken me for the Gestapo. I drew closer, stared down into her eyes. I wanted her to recognize me before I took her in my arms, then took her life.

Suddenly, her eyebrows, as expressive as exclamation points, drew together and danced apart again, and her features melted and blurred and changed shape like a watercolor. Tears came to her eyes, though they did not fall, and her lips trembled as if she were trying to remember how to speak. And then she took a single step forward and threw her arms around my neck.

My arms opened wide to encompass her, and I clasped her slight body to mine and buried my face in her hair, choking with emotion. My lurid plans dissolved like mist in sunlight, and suddenly, I understood with perfect clarity that it was I who had been in her thrall all along.

"Raphael, Raphael," she breathed. "My angel of healing."

She looked furtively to the right and to the left, to see if anybody had observed us. Taking both of my hands, she said, "Why don't you come in." Then she drew me in and bolted the door behind me.

The room is memorable only for its squalor, with stained, peeling walls, as cold inside as it was outside. A blanket concealed the windows, a single naked bulb provided the only light. In the middle of the room, a battered wooden table displayed two chipped teacups, a teaspoon, paper and a pencil. Off to one side, a bed was laid with a rumpled quilt. A door at the far end of the room opened into a small, dingy kitchen.

But I was holding her, holding my beloved Sofia in my arms, Sofia, whom I had never let go, not in life, not in death, and nothing else mattered. I kissed her hair with lips that had sucked the life from countless struggling victims, I held her with arms that had pinned them down as they died.

She stepped back and held me at arms length, taking me in, my smart handmade suit, the perfect Windsor knot in my tie, the buffed and shiny shoes. A look of admiration flitted over her features; then puzzlement, then ineffable sadness.

She offered me tea. I accepted. She seemed to need something to do to occupy her hands, they were shaking. She brought the tea in delicate porcelain cups trimmed in gold and painted with pink almond blossoms. Even with my dulled sense of taste, I could tell it was thin, horrible stuff. I choked down a swallow and carefully set the teacup back down on the saucer. I picked up the tin, printed in crimson and gold. The name *Wizotsky* ran in regal letters in a banner across the front of the box. Embarrassed, she apologized, explaining that she had been using the same dusty bits from the bottom of the tin for two weeks, the last tea leaves ever to be packaged under the Wizotsky label.

There were some sheets of writing paper in the middle of table, and I picked them up and pretended to scan them, as a way to justify the awkward silence. Heavy black lines embossed the paper; drawings of starving children, anxious mothers, soldiers menacing old women. A parade of bowed people and wooden carts filled with household possessions straggled past a row of wooden houses, pelted by rain.

My eyes strayed from the paper back to Sofia, seated across from me at the table. Now I noticed how perilously thin she was.

There was a sound from the bed, a cry. She leaped to her feet and hurried into the dark nook at the back of the room. I heard a soft muttering, a lullaby in a foreign language, and then she was back. To my infinite astonishment, she was holding a child bundled in a shawl, a dark head against her shoulder. It had never occurred to me that she might have become a mother in all this time.

"Yeshaya," she said softly. "There is someone I would like you to meet."

I saw a small pale face, rosebud lips. Sleepy eyes, half-open. Two up-and-down slashes for eyebrows, unmistakably Sofia's.

The small face turned away from me, hiding in her shoulder. I heard her hum an unfamiliar lullaby. When he had fallen asleep again, she returned him to the bed, making sure he was well covered.

I could see uncertainty in her eyes, in her fleeting tentative smile. I knew what was going on in her head; she was thinking that I had been cured of my infatuation for once and for all. Nothing could have been further from the truth. I was more in love with her than ever. She no longer looked like the girl she had been, it was true. Care had worn into her face, tracing new paths, altering her virginal prettiness into transcendent beauty. She had become one of the Madonnas she had always been copying.

"Ye-*sha*-ya," I said, the unfamiliar syllables strange on my lips. "What is that in English?"

"Isaiah," she replied.

Her hand was resting on the table next to the teacup. I knew I shouldn't—she was another man's wife, after all—but I reached across the table to take it. And then I said, "For God's sake, Sofia. What have they done to you this time?"

When her parents wrote with the news of her engagement, Sofia didn't know how to feel. She knew she was in love with me. She also knew she could never have me. I was a *shaygetz,* a *goy.* I was as forbidden to her as the snails they served at Brasserie Lipp.

The first time she saw Skip, he was standing at the bottom of the staircase off the courtyard that led up to her apartment. The shadows were deep inside the stairway, and for a fleeting moment, as she looked down at him, she thought he was me.

But then she heard him speak. From his flat Midwestern accent she gathered that he was the man her parents had arranged for her to meet. As she came slowly down the stairs, and he came forward into the light, she saw that he was remarkably handsome. A movie star, just like her mother said. And as he looked up at her, clutching a street map, she realized that he was surprised, too. He was as nervous as she was.

God had finally smiled on her. All the waiting had been worth it. She had feared her parents, desperate in these last few minutes before all hell broke loose, would pawn her off on a misfit, a cripple, a freak. All her worrying was for nothing.

There was one hitch in the plan. She loved me. There was no question, no doubt. She had felt the pull between us as immediately and as fervently as I did. But she was an Orthodox Jewish girl. And though religion played no part in my life, I was still a follower of Christ. Some years ago, a girl from Wlodawa had gone off to the study at the University of Warsaw, where she met and married a non-Jew. Her family had rent their clothes and mourned her for seven days, after which time they never spoke of her again.

This was so easy. Skip fit right into the slot in her life that was marked *Husband.* Her family was crazy about him. Of course she said yes.

The wedding was held at her parents' house. She walked down the aisle in a white silk confection copied from the dress Mainboucher had designed for Wallis Simpson, Duchess of Windsor, her face covered with a heavy lace veil. Skip was already under the *chuppah,* next to the rabbi, dressed in a white linen robe. As he slipped the ring onto her forefinger, she thought of me. Suddenly, she experienced a rush of dizziness, a heaviness weighing on her heart. She forced herself to focus on the happy life she would lead with her handsome new husband in the United States. She would leave tragedy behind her, in tired old Europe.

The newlyweds were led to the guest cottage, where they would be alone for the first time as man and wife. Skip kissed her, undressed her, took her. Only after he fell asleep did she fold the covers down, study him. In her mind, she was painting his lovely body swathed in sheets, noting the contrast of his golden skin against the brilliant white of the goosedown comforter.

After a week of parties, each more magnificent than the next, she expected to hear about arrangements for leaving Poland. However, Skip didn't seem to be in any kind of a hurry. He liked Poland, he told her, liked the relaxed atmosphere, a welcome change from the hustle bustle of the big city. People were making such a fuss about the war. There was plenty of time.

She didn't contradict him. He was her husband. She was sure he knew what he was doing.

The Holocaust came to the town of Wlodawa in exactly the same way it came to other towns in Poland. When the first German appeared in the middle of September, it was almost anticlimactic. A helmeted soldier putt-putted into the center of the market square on his motorcycle, revved his motor a few times, then stopped at the pump for a drink.

Immediately, the Nazis seized all Jewish businesses. Sofia's father was forced to hand over the Wizotsky Tea Company, which had brought the family wealth and respect for more than a hundred years, to a smirking stranger. *It's nothing,* he told his wife and children. *As long as we have a roof over our heads and each other.*

The next day, the Germans turned the Jews out of their homes. Sofia's family moved to a dilapidated house in the ghetto in the smaller, shabbier section of town. Her parents took the parlor apartment, giving Yechezkel and his family the top floor. Sofia and Skip were allotted two dark rooms on the ground level.

Swiftly, they issued a flurry of anti-Jewish laws. Jews could no longer serve as doctors, lawyers, or teachers. Jewish children were expelled from schools. Jews were to wear an armband, white with a blue Jewish star. Jews were forbidden to purchase anything from farmers, from the stores, or to trade in the marketplace. Being out after dark was punishable by death. Leaving town was punishable by death. Baking bread, punishable by death. Sofia's neighbor, blind old Mrs. Bronshtein, was executed for caning herself along the sidewalk as an SS *Unterscharführer* passed by; Jews had to walk in the gutter.

For a while, things were almost tolerable. A skinny German named Falkenberg ran a land drainage operation, a handsome German named Selinger collected the artisans. They paid their workers *bupkis,* but they seemed like decent men. Doctors, professors, musicians, businessmen went to work in the woods, draining swamps and felling trees, or to nearby towns to build roads and bridges.

This was how she found out that Skip had a mistress. Her brother Yechezkel watched him walk by with his Polish girlfriend as he worked laying bricks in a nearby village. Skip barely gave the slave laborers a glance. At that point, Sofia had been pregnant for six months.

Her father wrote angrily to the connections in New York who had suggested the match in the first place. Now the truth was revealed. Skip had been involved with all sorts of strange women back in Toledo; girls who sold cigarettes in nightclubs, girls he met at seedy bars in the seamier parts of town. A stripper, once. His father had threatened to write him out of the will unless he married a Jew. He agreed to a girl they found for him in Poland. A beautiful girl. An educated girl. A girl who knew nothing about him.

The Wizotskys accepted this news with grim stoicism. There were just too many other things going on, matters of survival.

With no jobs and no income, tradesmen who lived from hand to mouth began to starve. Seven months pregnant, Sofia stood on line in the cold, in the rain, in the snow, for half a loaf of bread, or sometimes, rotten, blackened potatoes. Sofia, who had never had to so much as boil a pot of water, learned to haul buckets of water from the pump at the corner, to peel potatoes, to wash her own clothing.

Six weeks early, she went into labor. On February 14, 1940, Yeshaya Refuel Weiss was welcomed into the covenant of Israel. He had a shock of black hair and eyes the color of a river at midnight. As if he knew they were in danger, he gave one cry and was still. For a moment, he regarded his mother with his wise baby eyes, and then he yawned and went to sleep.

As infants do, Shaya went from sleeping to sitting to crawling to walking to talking in the blink of an eye. He was the sunniest of children, with shining eyes and a sweet disposition, a laughing smile for everyone. Sofia never knew she was capable of feeling so much love. When he turned his gaze on her, those midnight eyes with those long feathery lashes, when he took her finger and gurgled out giggles, she could feel her heart expand with joy.

Splashing her as she bathed him in the tin tub, he would let loose strings of silvery laughter, like sleigh bells jingling on the horses harnesses in winter. Holding his little hand in hers, she traced circles around his soft baby palm with her finger and chanted a children's rhyme about a crow feeding kasha to her chicks. On the last line, her fingers would skip up his arm and tickle him under his delicious little neck, all wrinkles and folds, and he would squirm and burst into giggles. *Ah faygala, faygala, faygala, kitch kitch kitch keree!*

Rafe was standing by the fireplace, with his back to her. Darkness clung to him, a darkness that had nothing to do with the rumors they whispered about him at school.

"What's the matter?" said Tessa.

"Nothing," he muttered. "A little tired, is all. It's been a long time since I thought about any of this."

He swung his head up to look at her, the sad, colorless eyes searching through her as if she were completely transparent, and hidden inside her were the answers he sought. He looked as he always did, trousers pressed to knife-edge perfection, sleeves rolled up to the elbow, his hair falling in a soft peak at his forehead just so, but under his eyes there were gray shadows that hadn't been there before. Something was changing inside of him, she realized, and she wasn't sure it was for the good.

"Let's stop this," she said abruptly. "It's hurting you."

The strange eyes coalesced into an ordinary gray. "I'm fine," he said brightly. "Really I am. Let's go on."

He was lying, she knew it, and he knew she knew it. Plainly, this was disturbing him more than he'd expected. As the flames churned and danced, a rhythm of light and shadow chased each other across his face. It was so quiet that she could hear the tick of the grandfather clock upstairs.

"By the time you found her," she began tentatively, groping for the right words.

Restless, he roved over to the window. He could hear the thoughts in her head as clearly as if she was shouting them. "By the time I found her, she was alone."

"Where were her parents?"

"Gone. Transported in the first wave. May, 1942."

Her body reacted as if she'd been punched in the gut. The family she'd never known had taken on flesh, come alive. "What about my grandfather? Sarah Tessa? His children?"

"They went in the next *Aktzia*," he said to the windowpane. Outside, a plastic grocery bag went skipping down the middle of the street, carried by the wind. "The SS found their hiding place. Sofia never saw them again."

The last *Aktzia*, the big one, came in the middle of October.

A man ran past the house cursing, then two more, running in the opposite direction. She pushed open the front door, recognizing Yosha Grinstein, the pharmacist. "Haven't you heard?" he shouted to her, barely breaking his stride. "The Lords and Masters want us to assemble in the sports field by the high school. They say they're going to distribute new work papers." He seemed startled to see Shaya playing, building a house out of matchsticks. "Why are you still here?" he called back incredulously.

The screams of women, the barking of dogs, and the tread of marching boots assaulted her ears. Soldiers and SS men were blockading one end of Seminowa Street, flushing people out of their homes, beating them with sticks and truncheons, herding them through the market square in the direction of the school. German Shepherds lunged at screaming children, ripping their clothes, as officers in leather trench coats chuckled. Sofia slammed the door shut and ran to the back room, gathered Shaya up in her arms. Now she knew real terror, the cold knot of dread at the pit of her stomach.

Holding her breath, she opened the door that led to the yard behind the buildings. Surely the soldiers would already be there. Sofia imagined the feel of bullets slamming into her body, the darkness that would swell and overtake her.

Where there is no choice, there is no fear, she thought. A Yiddish proverb. She ducked through an archway that let out on Blotna Street. Miraculously, it was deserted. She scurried the three blocks to Kozia Street, her head down, Shaya wrapped in her shawl, fighting the flow of the citizens of Wlodawa being driven towards the sports field, where Sofia used to watch her brother and his friends play soccer.

She rounded the corner past the shoemaker's shop and came to a dead stop. A corpse lay across the narrow road, one side of his head a bloody pulp, blocking her path. His shoes were missing; some desperate soul had taken them.

There was no way around it, she would have to step over him. To her everlasting horror, he stirred and clutched her ankle. *"Oh, mein Gott,"* he whispered. *"Meine shicher, meine shicher."*

She pulled her leg free, and ran the rest of the way to Wishniak Street. With each step she prayed, asking only for a miracle. Since August, Wishniak was in the Jew-free zone, where she could be killed for the unforgivable crime of being a Jew on a sidewalk. Three years living under Nazi rule had changed her. She no longer stopped to consider the lunacy of this decree.

It was raining, a cold, steady bone-chilling drizzle. Shaya was wet, he wanted to walk, he wanted bread and butter. Holding his little hand as she dragged herself along, Sofia broke down and began to sob.

Then, the miracle happened.

A man with a walrus mustache and a checked workman's cap was leaning against a wall, smoking. He followed her with his eyes as she passed by. "Wizotsky?" he inquired in Polish. "Family Wizotsky?"

Brushing at tears with the back of her hand, she nodded.

"Stefan Zukowski," he said, introducing himself. "I was the foreman in the tea warehouse. I remember you. You're the artist." He shifted his cigarette to the other side of his mouth. "My brother is also an artist. He studied at the Art Institute in Krakow." The sound of soldiers breaking doors open was getting closer, the wailing louder. "Damned Germans fired me when they took over, gave my job to a Ukrainian. Now I'm a porter." He crushed out his cigarette. "You shouldn't be on the streets. Do you have a place to hide?"

She shook her head no.

"Come with me," he said. Taking a key from a circle of keys he wore on his belt, he inserted it into the door of the rundown house behind him and led them into a dingy ground floor apartment. In the kitchen, he threw back a trapdoor that concealed a root cellar, gesturing at the darkness below. "In here," he said. "I'll roll the rug over the opening and put the table on the rug."

Sofia hesitated. She had never seen this man before, and now she was placing her life in his hands. Seeing her doubt, he smiled. His blue eyes crinkled, but his great mustache looked sad. "Don't worry," he told her. "I have children, too. We will only get through these times if we help one other."

She climbed down a creaky wooden ladder into the darkness. It smelled of damp, mold and earth. He handed Shaya into her arms and closed the trapdoor, returning a few minutes later with a loaf of bread and a glass of butter. "Here," he whispered. "For the little one."

He closed the door for the last time. Dirt rained down on their heads as he arranged the carpet over their hiding place. She heard the table scraping across the floor, thumping into place. Finally she heard the squeak of the floorboards as he crossed to the door, the ratcheting sound of the key turning the tumblers in the lock, leaving her in utter blackness.

The pounding of soldiers' fists on doors drew closer, house by house, until it was right on top of them. The sound of many boots booming up the stairs, the crunch of breaking glass and splintering wood, the high-pitched shrieks of frightened children and screaming women grew louder, louder still, until it was over their heads and all around them.

The ground shook, the lock rattled. Now she could hear the steady tramp tramp tramp of hundreds of feet, walking, running, shuffling past the front door, towards the marketplace.

She heard the soft pleading of an old woman, and the sound of blows landing on unprotected flesh. She heard the sound of bodies being dragged across the pavement and the sound of wagon wheels on cobblestones. She could hear the curses of the SS men, the crazed barking of the dogs, the frantic cries of mothers calling for lost children. She recognized the laughing babble of poor Mendel the barber's son, who had never been right in the head. She could hear Gittel Danielsohn, who'd lost her mind after her husband was killed and her children taken in the first *Aktzia,* singing the beautiful Danube Waltz and begging the soldiers to dance with her, and the laughter of the soldiers as they encouraged her.

The sounds multiplied, echoing and ricocheting and resounding off the walls of the buildings surrounding the quaint old market square, roiling together into a thunderous whirlwind of noise that rose like one long mourner's prayer for the Jews of the city of Wlodawa, ascending into the leaden sky.

At the close of the second day, the dim light grew dimmer, slouching toward evening. And in that blue hour when it is dark but not yet night, Sofia heard someone fiddle with the lock, then smash it open.

Heavy footsteps entered the room, leather squeaking. A soldier's boots. Sofia hardly dared to breathe. Though she couldn't see Shaya, she could feel him, a warm bundle in her lap, and she shut her eyes and prayed that he wouldn't choose this moment to speak up in his adorable singsong.

The boots circled the room, opening and closing cupboards, banging on walls to search for concealed openings. They stopped not two feet from her head, stomped on the floor to listen for the echo of hollow spaces. Dust sifted down onto her face. She could feel Shaya stir against her, and her fingers crept across his cheeks and covered his mouth.

Whatever her visitor heard, or didn't hear, must have satisfied him, because suddenly the boots squeaked purposefully towards the door. She heard it bang shut.

Gradually the babel of noises sounded like it was coming from farther away, then ceased altogether. An unnatural silence fell over the town, a sound more terrible than all the sounds that had preceded it.

That night, she heard the door creak open, heard footsteps enter the apartment, stealthily this time. The table was moved, the carpet rolled away, and there was Zukowski, extending a hand to help her up out of the hole in the ground.

It was horrible, horrible, he said, wiping the corners of his eyes. Soldiers tearing children from the arms of mothers who fought like wild animals. Policemen beating old men over the head to move them along at a smart pace. Fresh bursts of grief as people recognized brothers, sisters, parents, children they thought had been hidden away.

Trains came and went for two days. In the end, there were not enough cars for all the people assembled; and so the last remnant of the Jews of Wlodawa were shot and beaten to death at the train plaza, the pretense of civility at an end. Their bodies were carted off into the forest by a few strong men reserved for this purpose, who performed their duties while whispering the prayer for the dead, slipping in puddles of mud and blood, before taking their turn in front of the guns.

Zukowski had visited the site himself. He knew the little children were in the lap of the Holy Mother, he told her. He took off his hat and wiped his face on his sleeve. "The ground," he whispered unsteadily. "I was there today. The ground is moving."

Shaya was asleep. Sofia laid the baby in the strange, abandoned bed, tucked him under the covers, then did a curious thing; she opened and closed drawers until she found a pen and paper. Relief flooded through her body. She sat at the table, smoothed her fingers over the sheet of paper, snowy white. "Can we stay here?" she said, her eyes on the paper as she began to sketch him, his kind eyes.

Now he shifted his weight from one foot to the other. "My wife," he murmured uneasily. "My children. If they find you..." He didn't have to finish the sentence. If she was caught, they would all die.

And then, just like that, his shoulders straightened with resolve. "Of course you can stay here," he said firmly. "But you can't leave these rooms, you understand. I'll bring you food."

She gave him her engagement ring. From her apartment, she asked him to bring clothes, some family pictures, her books, her pens and paper, her silver Shabbos candlesticks. Within a month, she had to tell him that she had nothing left to trade. He lifted his hands, palms up, and shrugged. "So it goes with my family, so it will go with yours," he said. "Don't worry about the money."

A week ago, he'd disappeared. Knowing that his wife wasn't pleased with the arrangement, she wondered if he'd finally given in to her pleading. Or worse, that he'd been arrested, tortured, killed.

This morning, the cupboard had been completely empty. As the day waned into twilight, she took a chance. She threw a shawl over her head and left the apartment, locking Shaya in with a warning to stay quiet. Keeping her head down, she hugged the corners of the marketplace, coming at last to the booth where she knew the woman behind the mound of potatoes.

"Please," she whispered to her husband's lover. "Please."

The pretty mouth dropped open, as if she had seen a ghost. "You should not be here," she hissed, but she let Sofia take two potatoes. "Now, *go.*" she said, her eyes darting around to see if anybody was watching, "and don't ever come back." And then her voice turned low, vicious. "Or I'll *tell* on you."

By the time she reached her apartment, it was almost dark. Sofia boiled the potatoes and they had a feast. When the knock on the door finally came, she was almost relieved. Whatever happened next, at least her baby had a full stomach.

She was done. In all her words there had been not a trace of self-pity.

We were sitting on the couch now, turned towards one other, our hips barely touching through all our clothing. She was resting her head on the palm of her hand and gazing up at me through half-closed lids. The white curve of her neck called to me.

I reached out and stroked her hair, dark and smooth like a rook's wing. "Sleep, my darling girl," I told her. "You've been so brave, for so long. Your angel of healing is here. I'll take care of everything. Go to sleep now."

I could spend the whole night detailing the pageant of horror, tragedy and missed opportunities that has been my life. It's the parts that are happy for which there are too few words.

Mostly, I remember little things. Sofia stealing glances at me from under long black lashes when she thought I wasn't looking. The feel of her hip against my hand as she brushed past me between the table and the cupboard. Her hands tracing circles in the air as she lit her Shabbos candles. The accidental touch of her fingertips when we both reached for a game of Exquisite Corpse at the same time.

Isaiah's tinkling laugh, like the sound of sleighbells. His small pink foot in the washtub during a bath. Down on my knees, crawling around the carpet with him on my back, pretending to be his brave steed. The sweet sound of his voice laughing with delight as I whizzed him around my head spitting out propeller sounds. His hand sliding into mine.

Isaiah cuddled in Sofia's lap, his head against her shoulder as she drew him a fish, a horse, a rocket ship, the moon and stars, the letters of his name. Sofia's pointed chin resting on the top of his head, moving to give him a soft kiss, her red lips lost in the black curls.

Sofia drawing me again and again, her hands flying over the paper, her eyes darting back and forth from her sketch back to me. Sofia directing me, with all the authority of a general in the field. Hands in my pockets. Smoking a cigarette. Hat on. Hat off. Standing. Sitting. Reclining on the couch. Looking off in this direction. With my legs apart. With my legs crossed just so. With my jacket off. With my shirt-sleeves rolled up. With my shirt open. In my undershirt. No shirt at all, my braces hanging down to my knees. A slight smile playing across her pillowy lips as she squinted to reduce me down to big lights and big shadows, to shut out unnecessary details, getting the large relationships down first.

One night towards the end I brought her a wireless radio. This was a specialty item, fraught with peril. Just to have one in your possession was punishable by death, a threat which understandably did not hold much sway with me.

Shyly, Isaiah asked me to draw him a horse. My fingers could no longer create the intricacies of the human face, but I could still manage a car, an airplane, a dog, a horse, the sort of things that a ten-year-old boy might draw.

While he scribbled ecstatic circles over it at the table, I threaded the antenna out the window in the kitchen. Sofia and I sat on the floor, head to head, as I fiddled the dial, crossing a universe of static until we found the BBC. A posh British voice declared that the Soviets had Germany's elite Sixth Army completely surrounded in Stalingrad. It sounded like a turning point.

Isaiah had fallen asleep with his head on the table, softly breathing, the pencil still in his hand. I gathered him up and carried him to the bed. His hair stuck up in damp clumps all around his face, smelling of the French milled bath soap I had brought the day before. I tucked the feather quilt around his little body.

He opened sleepy eyes. "Wafie," he said.

I crouched down beside him. "Go back to sleep, little man. Maybe tomorrow I'll bring you a toy racing car."

He smiled joyously, showing me a glimpse of pearly teeth between bowed pink lips before his eyes fell closed again. On impulse, I kissed the top of his head.

Sofia played with the dial until she found some music. She leaned her head close to listen.

A bittersweet little waltz began to play, with words I didn't understand. "I know this song," she said with wonder. "I haven't heard it since..."

Paper is white, and ink is black, she said. He is at a wedding. There are many beautiful girls, but none hold a candle to his love. Her face, her figure. Her beautiful black eyes, her beautiful black hair.

"In my heart burns a fire," she translated, looking directly into my eyes. "No one can know the burning in my heart. *Der Tod und dir Leben ist by Gott in dir hend.* Life and death are both in God's hand."

I stood and pulled her to her feet, slipped my fingers around her waist. *One two three, one two three, one two three.* I waltzed her around the room, dancing her around the table and the chairs to the melody, sweet and rueful and filled with longing. We danced for what we had lost, and for things that could never be.

Sofia in the circle of my arms. It was all I'd ever wanted. The smell of her hair. The pressure of her fingers on the back of my neck. I spirited her backwards; she drove me forward.

I never wanted the plaintive little tune to end. But it was a brief song, a poem, almost, and it was a memory nearly as soon as it had begun.

When it was over, the station went off the air, leaving only static. I didn't want to let her go, so I made a joke out of it, dipped her down to the floor. When I pulled her back up, she was breathing hard, her lips parted.

For a moment we just stood there, looking into each other's eyes, my hands around her waist. Her fingers, resting lightly on the back of my neck, slid up to the side of my face. I kissed the palm of her hand.

"Raphael," she said hesitantly.

"Don't," I said, laying my finger over her lips. "I know. Please don't say it."

There was nothing remarkable about the first hours of that day, the one that was the beginning of the end.

In the late afternoon, there was a soft knock at my door. My innkeeper with a telegram. It was from Anastasia. Rudi was stationed in nearby Krakow, capital of Nazi-occupied Poland. She was delighted to find me well, I must phone her right away. I folded the cable in quarters, tucked it away in the inside pocket of my jacket.

After sunset, I went to the black market to pick up a few things. Merchants smiled to me, waved me over. Money made for good friends.

I passed through the market square as it was shutting down. I had located Skip's lady friend, the one who sold potatoes, on my second day in Wlodawa. She looked up at me as I went by, and as I did every day, I considered luring her into a dark passageway and sucking the life out of her. It was already dark. A pretty girl in a maid's uniform was dumping dirty water out into the gutter. She had high pink cheeks, round like apples. I followed her around the back, had my dinner. Picking up my parcels, I continued on my way.

My blood racing, I hurried through the busy streets to the house, ducked through an unlit passageway to the inner yard, and knocked softly. As I waited, I laid my hand on the rough wood, imagining it would take on her warmth. She opened the door, already smiling.

"What is that scent you always wear?" she asked. The basket held a roasted chicken, potatoes, hard-boiled eggs, an orange, real coffee. As she took it, she held on a moment longer than was necessary, her fingertips touching mine.

"Sandalwood."

"*Sahn*-dahl-vood," she repeated in her lush voice. "Always, it will make me think of you."

She may as well have said, "I love you." She looked shyly away. Then, with new boldness, she stared into my eyes. That was when I saw it, the image of a man in a fedora, floating in the depths of her pupils. Understanding dawned on me slowly.

"Good God," I whispered. "I can see myself in your eyes."

She smiled, not understanding the significance. It was the first time I'd seen my own face in over three years.

I reached out and grasped her arms. Yes, I would tell her. There was no one else in all the world that I cared about more. She would understand. "Sofia," I said, softly, urgently.

There was a knock on the front door. Three sharp raps.

The color drained from her face. On the floor, playing with his new toy racing car, Isaiah froze in place.

We waited in silence, a moment that lasted for a hundred years. The knock came again, more insistent this time, accompanied by a harsh command in German to "*Aufmachen die Tür!*" Open the door.

I called, "Just a moment!" as I vaulted past the table and raced into the kitchen. Throwing back the bit of carpet, I yanked open the trapdoor in the floor. Sofia clambered down the ladder as I scooped up Isaiah and his car and handed them down to her. I looked down at them, my little family, their eyes wide with terror, then shut the trapdoor over their frightened faces.

I could hear the men outside making ready to force the door. Smoothing my hair, straightening my tie, I hastened to greet them.

There were two of them, an officer in a black leather coat, and a tall soldier carrying a semiautomatic rifle, bayonet fixed. "Hello, gentlemen," I said politely. "What seems to be the problem?"

They seemed surprised to see me. The officer addressed me in German. I didn't understand his rapid delivery, but he seemed to want to come in.

"No one here but me," I replied, smiling pleasantly. He had a little brushy mustache and the flinty eyes of a playground bully. Putting his gloved hand on the door, he barred it open, the threat implicit.

I burrowed deep inside myself, summoning all the hocus-pocus hypno-power at my disposal, then stared hard into their eyes. "There's no one here," I suggested smoothly. "No need to come inside."

It seemed to work. I could see their faces go slack, inert. Nodding their agreement, they muttered something that sounded apologetic, and turned to go. Though I had no breath, I could still heave a sigh of relief, and I did so as I closed the door behind them.

I got halfway across the room before there was another knock at the door. Cursing to myself, I opened it again.

This time, there were no pleasantries. The soldier leveled his rifle, squeezed off two rounds into the center of my chest.

The impact knocked me off my feet. I flew into the air, crash-landing on top of the table. It toppled and fell under my weight. The world receded into a tiny pinprick of light. Next thing I remember, I was on the floor, propped up by the overturned table. There was a frightening ache under my ribs.

The soldier's face swam into view, advancing toward me. Seeing that I was not quite finished, he ran the point of his bayonet into my heart and waited for me to die.

A groan. A fierce pain, cold and burning, all at once. Time stopped for a minute. But I did not die.

Wrapping my hands around the muzzle of the gun, I wrenched it out and slammed it backward, pulverizing his nose with the stock of the rifle. He sagged back, covering his face, making sounds like an injured dog, blood pouring out from under his fingers. I seized him by the helmet and smashed his forehead into the upturned edge of the table, once, twice. He fell to the floor, wriggled a little, then lay still.

I turned my head. The officer was in the kitchen, pistol in hand, his finger in the ring that opened the trapdoor.

With a single leap across the room, I was upon him. He had time for one look of horrified incredulity, one disbelieving *"Was?"* before I ripped his throat out.

He dropped the gun as his hands went to his neck. A great arterial spray fanned across the pictures on the wall. He fell to his knees, pitched forward onto the floor. His body thrummed across the trapdoor for a moment, then relaxed.

Covered in blood, I stood alone, triumphantly regarding the body of my enemy. And then I aimed a vicious kick at his head.

I dumped their corpses in the sewers.

"Olly olly oxen free," I said, opening up the trap door.

Sofia was a hazy white shape floating in the dark. "There were gunshots," she whispered, her voice trembling. "I thought you were dead."

I reached down, pulled her up. She threw her arms around my neck, held me tight.

The apartment had grown cold. I took Isaiah from her, made him comfortable on the couch, tucked my overcoat around him. Kissed his cheek. Held him for a moment.

"You're bleeding," she said.

I looked down at my shirt. It was covered in blood, mine mostly, and torn in three places. Now I ached. Pain radiated up into my arms, my neck, the back of my head. It felt like my chest was on fire.

"I'm all right. Really. If I could just rest for a minute," I said lightly. I wavered, lost my balance. She caught me, eased me onto the bed. I lacked the strength to even lift my legs onto the mattress.

I put my head back onto the pillow. It felt so good that I dozed off for a moment. I opened my eyes to see Sofia crying, tears falling down her cheeks. I smiled reassuringly at her, wanting her to know that it was all right, I was fine, but I passed out again before I could say anything. I could feel light fingers undoing the buttons on my shirt, a rush of cool air hitting my bare skin, the hiss of an indrawn breath.

It was nighttime in London. A building to our right shivered and collapsed into a mound of fiery rubble. She was walking ahead, going too fast for me, and I was shouting at her to slow down, afraid I was going to lose her in the smoke, but with all the noise and confusion, she couldn't hear me. I caught sight of the hem of her coat disappearing into La Coupole, and I followed her in. Here, it was warm, bright. I could smell the cigarette smoke and women's perfume. I sat down next to Leo, who for reasons of his own was accompanied by a dancing bear. He offered me a cigarette from a silver case, and said, "She's still here, you know."

Suddenly, a thick fog rolled in. La Coupole disappeared, and I was in a foul alleyway alongside the Élysée Montmartre. Colby lay twisted in an unnatural position on the fluorescent blue-green cobblestones, gray and lifeless next to a skinny prostitute in sequins and bedraggled feathers. "Sorry about all this," I said apologetically. "Have you seen Sofia? I really must find her. There's no time to lose."

Colby's eyes snapped open. He pulled himself up, dusted off his suit, and helped the prostitute to her feet. He offered her his arm and they drifted out of the alleyway. Just as he was about to step out onto the street, he turned and said, "Well, are you coming or not?"

I followed, and emerged from the alleyway into the Carpathians, where the rocks jutted up out of the landscape like broken teeth. Colby had misled me, she was nowhere to be seen. Suddenly, Archbishop Grigorii appeared out of the mist, his saffron vestments spattered with blood. He was accompanied by a circle of villagers that included Erlichmann and Beata, toting pitchforks and scythes. His deep-set eyes fell on me. "Even evil has a purpose," he reminded me kindly as he passed.

Now I was getting desperate. They had been no help at all. Where was she? It was late. I needed to be getting back.

Back through the corridors of my boarding school, the desks bursting into flames. Back through the hallways of my father's house, the people in the portraits applauding politely as they burned in their frames. Back through the lanes of Highgate Cemetery, the angels dusted with snow. Back through a crooked court beside a shuttered tavern, where Anastasia came gliding out of a darkened passageway. "Let's face it, my darling," she breathed, blood on her lips. "I made you *better.*"

There was a skittering sound at the mouth of the court and I hurried towards it, late for class. Sofia was already there, her attention focused on Lulu the model, brush raised in the air. She turned to look at me and smiled. I took my place behind my easel, relieved. She was safe. The monitor raised the windowshade, she was bathed in light. Now I could rest.

It was pitch black. I didn't know whether I was awake or asleep, dead or alive. Something warm and wet was trickling over my skin, dribbling down my sides. It came to me that I was being bathed, gentle hands sponging away the blood and gore, washing me clean.

Someone was bending over me, a silhouette against the rectangle of light coming from the kitchen door. My throat was parched, as dry as a brush fire, but I had something terribly important to say, something that could not wait.

I caught hold of a slim wrist. "Tell Sofia I've changed my mind," I said urgently. "Tell her Raphael said yes." Then I babbled out a dire imprecation to stay away from the burning buildings, and drifted down again into deep, dreamless sleep.

I awakened before dawn. No pain. Everything worked. Sofia must have been up for hours, scrubbing the walls and washing my clothes. It was as if last night had never happened.

Except for one thing. The miracle of Sofia in bed with me, wearing nothing but a thin slip, breathing softly in sleep.

I sat up, inspected my wounds. Three scars, new pink skin already growing over them. As I gazed down, it came to me that she had seen me completely naked. A warm sensation tingled between my legs. I forced it away. There was nothing I could do about it.

She was stirring. I dressed quickly, went back to sit on the edge of the bed.

"I have to go," I whispered, stroking her hair.

She struggled up out of a dream, rubbing her eyes. "Where?"

I looked at her lying there, half undressed and half asleep, and thought how good it would be to see her like that every day of my life. "To meet with some people I know in Krakow. I'm going to get you out of here. I'll be back tomorrow night."

I knelt beside Isaiah, asleep on the couch. "Goodbye, little man," I said. He rubbed his eyes with his little fists, then his nose. "You're the man of the house, now. Take care of your mum." He looked very serious. I fluffed his hair, kissed the top of his head.

I opened the door, squinted up at the lightening sky. Like a small, furious tornado, she was beside me, her body melting into mine.

"Don't go," she said sorrowfully. "You're hurt. You should be resting."

My hands slid up her round white arms. I could feel her ribs under the slip, her soft breasts as she pressed against me.

Sofia Wizotsky's eyes. I stared down into their wild tragic depths one more time. I did not tell her I loved her, though I think she knew. She was a married woman, after all. "I'll see you tomorrow night," I said, and slipped out the door.

I went straight to my hotel, packed a small overnight bag. My mission was simple and clear. I wanted to get Sofia and Isaiah out of Poland. I had plenty of cash and a powerful connection. I just needed to know who to pay.

My innkeeper booked a phone call for me to Krakow. Two hours later, Anastasia was on the line, purring with delight, and I had a meeting with Rudi scheduled for just after sunset.

The trip took all day, longer than I expected. There were countless stops and starts as we were shunted aside for troop movements, supply trains, more passengers. When I finally reached Krakow, it was nighttime. There was a car waiting for me, a long black Daimler coach with shaded windows and a young driver in a Nazi uniform who rushed out to open the door for me.

There was no problem getting into Wawel Castle, a formidable Gothic pastiche of cathedral, fortress, administrative offices, and prison. Getting out was the trick. A young guard at the booth directed me to a nearby building, then a junior SS man appeared and led me through a fifteenth-century courtyard surrounded by graceful arcaded galleries. He showed me into an office, then clicked himself out.

The room was empty. There was a desk, unoccupied, the secretary gone for the day. Behind the desk was a door, and now and then, I could hear sounds issuing from it. Too nervous to sit, I took inventory of the items on the desk, doubtlessly identical to items found on desks on the Allied side. A typewriter. A telephone. Rubber stamps. A stack of forms. An in box. An out box. Pictures of a smiling family.

The door to the inner sanctum opened, and there was Rudi. He had put on weight, and his skin looked thick and pasty.

"Well, well, well. Our lost Englishman, wandering the enemy countryside. I'm surprised you haven't been shot for a spy." He went to a rosewood cabinet, poured himself a drink. "So. What have you been doing with yourself, Sinclair? How do you find the hunting here? Any of our boys give you a hard time?"

"Not as long as I steer clear of German pussy," I said.

Rudi guffawed. "You've come a long way since your days as a polite English schoolboy. You must stay a while, Sinclair. I have missed your honesty."

There was a long moment where I equivocated. Was I giving Sofia away? Probably. Could he be trusted? Probably not. Where there is no choice, there is no fear. Hat in hand, I leaned forward in my seat. "I need a favor," I said.

Of course I did. He pressed his fingers together, leaned back in his chair. "I don't know what I can do," he murmured.

"I need to get someone out."

He nodded absently, rubbing a place over his eye. I had forgotten how marked his skin was, from a childhood disease, or an adolescent bout with acne, I never found out. "Who is it?" he asked with some interest.

I explained, keeping it brief. Old girlfriend from before I was, ahem, changed. I thought she had married and gone off to America. Turned out she hadn't.

"Jewish, I presume," he added languidly. "Otherwise you would not be here."

"Yes." I said. "And another thing. There's a child."

"Ah," he said. "Yours?"

Should have been mine. "No," I said.

"About the Jews, Hitler is intractable." With one swallow, he finished his schnapps. Then he leaned forward, picked up the phone, said something in German, waited. A tall, capable-looking SS man knocked lightly, entered. Rudi gestured him towards the inner door. From inside the other room, I heard his voice, abrupt, direct, and then the door opened again. A pretty woman emerged, olive-skinned, dark-haired. She was trailed by a younger version of herself, eleven or twelve, with just the beginnings of hips, breasts. The girl turned on me a helpless stare, eyes large and liquid and frightened, like a fawn. Rudi smiled encouragingly. They were guided into the hallway, where the guard quietly shut the door behind them.

"Mother and daughter," he explained, with an upward flick of the eyebrows, a sound of satisfaction. He rummaged through some papers on the desk, extracted a cigarette from a gold case.

"What is her name?" he asked.

"Sofia," I said. "Sofia Wizotsky."

"Like the tea?"

"The family business."

"Ah." He took a measured drag on the cigarette. "And where are they now, the Wizotskys?"

"She's the only one left."

Rudi turned out the desk lamp, moved fluidly to the window, pushed the blackout curtain to one side. Stars winked overhead in a moonless sky. The tip of his cigarette glowed red in the dark.

"I have money," I said. "Swiss francs, American dollars. Whatever it takes." I took a chance now, bared my soul. "I love her, Rudi. The boy, too. More than my own life. I was out trying to forget her the night Anastasia found me. She's all I've ever wanted."

This seemed to stir him. He turned towards me; only one side of his pocked face was visible in the dim light. "You love her, this Jewish woman?" he said.

"With all my heart." I said fervently.

A sharp report cut through my words, coming from the direction of the courtyard. A gunshot. Then another. The sound rang off the hard stone surfaces of the surrounding buildings.

He took a deep draw on his cigarette, let smoke drift slowly out of his mouth. "Because if you care for her," he said, staring down at the courtyard. "Really care for her; go back to her. And kill her yourself."

There were loud bumps and grinds, fitful starts and stops, as we crept through towns invisible in the dark. At various times, I woke as we were shunted right or left, wheels and couplings whining with the effort, to let other, more urgent transports pass. Once, I stared blearily at a train lurching slowly westward to find human eyes peering back at me from between the wooden slats of a cattle car.

By the time I arrived in Wlodawa, it was late in the afternoon. It had snowed. Ice covered the ground, slowing me down. It was bitterly cold. Head down into the wind, I didn't notice at first that something was wrong. It wasn't until I reached her corner that I realized it was too quiet.

The sounds of dogs barking, pots and pans rattling on the hob. The shouts of children playing, mothers raising their voices, husbands arguing with wives. The syncopation of wagon wheels clattering over cobblestones, the steady tread of footsteps on pavement. The background noises that accompany everyday life.

There weren't any.

Panic rose into the back of my throat like acid. Now I broke into a run, my footsteps deafening in the unnatural silence.

Wishniak Street was dark, deserted. Doors yawed open on their hinges, outlines of cold chimneys pierced the sky. Black and lightless windows accused me from every building. The only sound was the sobbing of the wind, periodically joined by a loose shutter banging disconsolately against the side of a building.

It looked as if I had just missed some kind of demented jumble sale. Dress shirts and dishes were strewn haphazardly along the pavement, keeping company with someone's embossed leather wedding album and a cast iron frying pan. A baby doll in a pink dress lay near my shoe.

I picked my way through ghostly piles of abandoned belongings. A Victrola sat on a stoop, alongside a stack of fragile lacquer records. A bundle of letters tied with a satin ribbon rested on top of a child's English grammar book. There were opera hats and feather quilts and hairbrushes and stamp collections and teapots. Silver candlesticks lay toppled on their sides like so many defeated kings on a chessboard. A crinoline petticoat lent a certain air of gaiety. A grandfather clock was laid out across a doorway like a coffin.

Halfway down the block, I stopped. The corpse of a young man was sprawled in the snow on the steps to her building, the cap fallen off his head. Sofia's drawings lay scattered in the gutter. As I stood there, the wind stiffened and picked up, blowing them around in a lazy spiral.

One thing was clear. They had left in a hurry.

Drawers were pulled open and dumped out, discarded clothes were heaped in drifts on the bed. Drawings and photographs papered the floor; stern bearded ancestors mingled with charcoal sketches of children begging for bread.

Near the furnace, I found Isaiah's toy car. I picked it up, warming it in my hands. I felt like I was in a dream, the one I used to have at school, where I am chased through my father's townhouse by a man without a face. But it was cold in the apartment. No dream could be that cold.

I made myself walk slowly to the back of her rooms, to the kitchen. The oriental carpet was still in place, the trapdoor was closed. I knocked softly.

"Sofia," I whispered into the blackness. "Sofia, my love. I should have been here, I know. But I'm back. I'm home. You can come out now."

I knew they were gone. Had they been there, I would have felt their presence long before I saw them. But the human heart has an infinite capacity for hope. I eased the trapdoor open, then, half-expecting to see their white faces looking up at me in the dark. A cold draft rushed up to caress my face. It was empty.

Now I bolted for the train station. Behind the ticket counter was a prim little man with a mustache that curled up at the ends, wearing a coat with a fur collar and a high peaked cap.

"Where's the train?" I asked him. I tried French, German, English. He lifted his shoulders, shook his head.

"Train," I said impatiently. "Choo, choo."

His blue eyes lit up with understanding. He nodded, pointed me towards the schedule board.

My temper flared. I wanted to lean into his booth, grab him by his skinny neck and shake him till he spoke English. Instead, I pointed to the mountain of suitcases left behind on the plaza.

"*That* train. Where did it go?"

He stared into my eyes, finally comprehending the nature of my question. He tilted his head, as if he couldn't believe what an idiot I was. He made a slashing motion across his neck with his thumb, a *kkkhhhhhht* noise deep in his throat. Then he reached up over his head, and with a bang, rolled down the metal shutter in front of his booth.

I know I've omitted a certain fact overshadowing the arc of this story, the one fact you already know. That Sofia and Isaiah were on a train that would only unlock its doors when it had reached the fiery gates of hell. That they would be freed only to join the long lines of men, women and children shifting on their feet, patiently waiting their turns to enter the gas chambers, to climb into the sky as a pillar of smoke.

For decades afterwards, I punished myself with images of Sofia standing naked in the snow, shivering, clutching a chunk of cement that a guard had told her was soap, in the worst winter Poland has ever known. But as I stared at the empty train tracks and thought of the stationmaster making the schoolyard slash across his throat, I had no idea what he was talking about.

I could not have conjured up the kind of man who would be willing to design an oven that would be economically fueled by the fat of the men, women and children it was burning. I would not have believed that these same engineers would find other men willing to carry out their monstrous plans. I, too, would have dismissed it as propaganda, that one kind of human being could industriously collect and kill six million of another kind of human being. Somewhere along the line, there would have to be someone who said no.

Forgive me, Sofia. Forgive me, Isaiah. I did not know.

After the war, I returned to Paris, to my flat in the Rue Fleurus. I found the painting Sofia had made of us in 1939, buried in the maid's room behind the kitchen. Holding it with as much care as I would have held her body, I unwrapped it, watching her come slowly to life.

My Sofia. Face shaped like a heart, her lips a smudge of scarlet, eyebrows two up-and-down slashes of bluish black, skin the translucent white of skim milk. Me, arching over her, protecting her forever.

When the end came, was it quick? Was it a bullet or the gas? Was she frightened? Did she suffer? Did she think of me, and wonder where I was?

Could she ever forgive me? I ran my fingers over the strokes and crevices her brush had left in the paint, kissed her painted lips. There was a painful ache where the bullets had lodged in my heart.

My sketchbook was still there, a reminder of someone I used to be, sitting on a side table next to the armchair. Under the seat, I saw the corner of a sheet of drawing paper.

I leaned over, slid it out. One drawing, one final gift from the artist Sofia Wizotsky, who, for a short while in 1939, lived and worked in Paris. Somehow, it had found refuge under my armchair as I threw the others on the fire. You know the one. It hangs in my foyer, over the fireplace.

A Madonna and Child, in pen and ink, after Raphael. I blew off the accumulated dust, smoothed out the creases. As I gazed upon it, the loving mother, the capering child, visions of Sofia cradling a laughing Isaiah came crowding into my memory.

My hands began to shake. I fell to my knees as tears came spattering down through my fingers.

I don't know how long I wept. When I could, I put her artworks in a blanket, wound it gently around them as if it were a shroud.

Sofia Wizotsky was an artist of rare talent and heart. She was also courageous, loving and compassionate. When she entered a room, the air stirred around her, whether that room was a café in Paris or a hovel in Poland. People seemed wittier, the occasion had more weight. You wanted to make her smile. You wanted to change the world.

She was my ray of light, my compass rose, my morning star. I had been mistaken; she was my angel of healing, not the other way around. With her, I was climbing the rungs of a ladder back to humanity. When they took her away, the last shreds of my soul went with her.

Talent and heart. That was Sofia Wizotsky. That is your legacy.

I thought you should know.

He turned his head away from her, brushing the back of his hand across his eyes. He was at the window, hands in his pockets, gazing over the rooftops of the city. The clock said six a.m. Dawn. Soon he would have to draw the curtains.

He took a chance, glanced her way. He couldn't see her face, it was buried in her hands. All that was visible was the tumble of bright hair cascading onto her knees.

"I'll understand if you want to leave," he said to the window.

She straightened up, swung her legs off of the couch. Getting to her feet, she came up behind him, silent as a ghost, bare feet padding across the oriental carpet.

He felt her arms slide around his waist, her warm cheek against his back. With that, everything flowed out of him, as if a door had opened inside. He was exhausted. He bowed his head, resting it against the cold glass of the windowpane.

"How can you," he said wearily. "After everything you've just heard. How can you."

She took his hand, led him upstairs. She unbuttoned his shirt and slid it down his arms, undressing him as if he were a child. She made him sit, pushing his shoulders down onto the pillow, then lifted his legs onto the bed and took his shoes off one by one. He let his eyes close then, his features lined with fatigue, drained of color in the gray light of early morning.

Then she withdrew. His eyes fluttered open to see her walking away. But she was only closing the drapes; they came together with a silky swish. Then she folded back the covers and got into bed, fitting herself around him, protecting him with her small, warm body for what was left of the night.

"Sleep, Angel of Healing," he heard her murmur as he drifted off. "You've been so brave for so long. Go to sleep."

Part Three

1

*T*essa rode up the elevator with a model who had a smooth, blank face and a ripple of straight hair the color of autumn wheat. At the twenty-second floor, the doors schussed noiselessly open, and they both got out. A tall thin girl in a black turtleneck came out to retrieve the model, while a receptionist with a helmet of blond hair whispered at Tessa to wait on the couch.

She gazed out of the picture window in the undistinguished reception area. An orange sun was setting in a fiery ball over the city. She had nothing suitable to wear for an interview at the world's premiere women's magazine; all her clothes were, to varying degrees, speckled with paint. In the end, she'd had to settle for the least soiled of her sweaters and jeans. Trying not to look as nervous as she felt, she picked up the February issue of *Anastasia* sitting on the Noguchi coffee table and flipped through it. The perfume ads made her sneeze.

"Anastasia will see you now," snapped a severe little woman with a British accent. Tessa followed obediently behind her as she wheeled around and scurried up the bright white hallway.

Her first impression was that she had landed on a planet populated only by women. Short women, tall women, medium height women, all on the thin side, all with straight hair, all in a tightly regulated uniform of black skirt, black tights, black flats.

A long-haired girl hurried down the hallway in the opposite direction, carrying an armful of layouts, colorful collages of xeroxed photographs and headlines. Another lingered outside an office, waiting till someone within finished a phone call. A third girl, thinner than the rest, trotted alongside a rolling rack of Easter-egg-colored clothing swinging on hangers. But the majority of the populace was parked behind low-walled cubicles, staring unblinkingly into monitors, assistants to other, more senior editors occupying the offices behind them. And everywhere, the insistent chime of phones ringing, ringing, ringing.

They reached the end of the floor. "You can go right in, she's expecting you," said the severe little woman, disapprovingly indicating the door with her chin, already deeply absorbed in some papers on her desk.

Tessa took a deep breath, knocked lightly on the plain wooden door marked *Anastasia deCroix, Editor in Chief.* The door swung slowly open.

Anastasia was seated behind a massive desk in the corner of the room, angled so it would face the entry. In startling contrast to the sea of black outside her office door, she wore a fitted wool suit of cinnabar red shot through at wide intervals with thin yellow lines of windowpane plaid. Mutton-chop sleeves came down almost to her knuckles; a ruffed collar stood at attention around her white neck, rising from a plunging décolletage. The short peplum jacket clasped her waist like a pair of hands.

Tessa couldn't stop looking at her. The perfect skin, unlined, white as milk. Enormous dark eyes, prominent and round, their intelligence hooded behind drowsy eyelids. Her gleaming hair, styled to seem carelessly chic. Full lips, as red as blood, even without lipstick. The trademark dark glasses had been put aside for the time being, resting on a pile of manuscripts.

She was on the phone. She motioned with one long arm for Tessa to sit, indicating one of the silky red chairs in front of her desk. Tessa glanced around the office. There was a brushed aluminum conference table scattered with layouts, many pots of cattleya orchids. Heavily shuttered windows, making the room dark and cocoon-like. A door marked *Private.* Meanwhile, Anastasia chattered on in rapid French, switching midsentence to German. She finished with a cheerful flourish of Italian, and hung up the phone.

"Hello, my darling," Anastasia said. In her voice remained a trace of a French accent. "So nice to see you again. Between what I've heard from our friend Lucian, and from our dear Raphael, I feel like I know you."

Tessa tried a smile. Anastasia's eyes glowed like the caldera inside a volcano.

"What do you hear from our honeymooners? Are you in touch?" Tessa recoiled as from a blow. "No? But why not? Don't you want to know how it all turns out?" She leaned forward, smiled her rapacious smile. The fire in her eyes banked to a crimson red. "I find that old lovers make the best of friends."

At a loss for words, Tessa didn't answer.

"So. How is our boy? He is so enraptured with you, he has no time for old friends. *Et, voila.* Down to business. You are looking for a job. We have a temporary opening in the art department. One of our designers is taking a computer class. We need someone to cover for her in the late afternoons for the next eight weeks. It takes someone with good organizational skills. Have you ever worked at a magazine?"

Tessa shook her head no.

"Well. Lucian couldn't organize breakfast. If you could organize him, you can organize anything."

There was a soft knock at the door. An elderly man in a gray suit entered the room, shuffling slowly forward, a sheaf of black-and-white photos in his hand. Though he was advanced in years, his eyes were sharp, he was freshly shaven, his nails were filed and buffed, and each silver hair on his head was pomaded and combed sleekly into place.

A change came over Anastasia. She leapt from behind the desk, coy, girlish, chattering animatedly in French. The old man looked at Tessa, a light like dawn breaking over his face. When he replied to Anastasia, also in French, his voice stammered with amazement.

Tessa rose to her feet. He took her hand, held it in both of his, fastened his watery blue eyes on hers. Tessa couldn't help but notice that his hands shook, slight but constant.

"Tessa," Anastasia said quickly in English. "This is Leo Lubitsch."

With a little shock of recognition, Tessa realized who he was. She took an involuntary step back.

"Hello, my dear," he said. She had never heard a voice like his; smooth, courtly, aristocratic, continental. "Anastasia tells me you'll be joining us for a while."

There was a flicker of something sad behind his eyes. She offered him a sympathetic smile. The gray mustache trembled.

"Sofia Wizotsky," he said. "To hear her name again, after all these years. Who would have thought." He patted her hand, let it go. "Welcome, my dear. Welcome to *Anastasia*. Do give my regards to Sinclair." With a little wave, he shuffled slowly back out of the room. The door closed silently behind him.

Tessa turned to Anastasia, who looked thoughtful. "You should have known him when he was young," she said reflectively. "He was a lion."

The severe little woman poked her head in the door. "Ram is here, with the *69 Ways to Better Sex* layout."

"Good. Send him in." she said. The interview was over. She was already poring over something on her desk. *"Bon soir,* my dear," she said in dismissal. "Monday at five."

The door opened for her. Only when she was sure it had closed firmly behind her did she take a deep breath, slowly exhale. Relieved, she headed for the elevators. As she stabbed the down button, she realized that she not spoken a single word the entire time she was there.

Thursday evening at six p.m., Portia Ballard approached Tessa's studio on her way back from class. Portia bowed her head as she hurried past; she felt partly responsible somehow, as if she should have known, should have been there. The office wouldn't give her Raphael Sinclair's phone number, no matter how reasonable she seemed. And when she finally summoned up the courage to ring his doorbell, no one answered.

Portia and Gracie had spent hours sorting through the shambles of Tessa's belongings, stapling her butchered canvases back onto the jumble of stretchers, pinning the mosaic of scattered postcards back up on the wall. Wild rumors were circulating. Tessa was carrying Raphael Sinclair's vampire baby, and it was slowly sucking the life out of her; Tessa was already dead, buried in Gramercy Park, while Rafe waited for her to rise from the dead to join him as a creature of the night. As the owner of a townhouse facing the park, he would surely be a key holder.

But worst of all was the last rumor, more frightening than the others because it was the most plausible; Tessa had cracked under the pressure.

Graham, who had overheard snatches of the conversation with Whit on Sunday evening, reported hearing about two C's, a lost scholarship. For

Portia, recreating Tessa's wall of inspiration became an act of almost religious belief; some higher power would see to it that she returned.

Something stirred the air behind the curtain; it was drawn aside, and there she was, in a t-shirt and faded jeans, whole, healthy, smiling. Startled, Portia dropped her paint box with a bang.

"Did I miss anything?" said Tessa.

"Oh, not much," said Portia. "The founder of the school disappeared off the face of the earth with one of the students. But that was days ago."

Gracie came in, whooped ecstatically, hugged them both, jounced off to tell the sculptors.

"It's true, isn't it," said Portia. "He really is a vampire."

Tessa looked as if she were going to say something, and then the sculptors were cramming into the small space, filling it with their big voices and their big bodies, knocking pencils and drawing pads and canvases off of the tables and onto the floor.

"Hey, Tessa," David said casually, but concern tightened his face, his voice. "Good to have you back."

Abruptly, the atmosphere in the room changed. Goosebumps prickled, hairs stood on end as if there were an electric charge sizzling the air. The art students turned as one. Raphael Sinclair stood framed in the doorway. He was staring at Tessa with his extraordinary eyes as if they were alone, as if the nearest living being was a thousand miles away.

Something was happening to Tessa. It was as if a furnace had whooshed to life inside of her, burning just under the surface of her skin. Standing next to her, Portia thought she could feel the temperature in the room rise several degrees.

"Hello, Tessa," he said, a world of tender knowledge conveyed in the two words.

"Hello, Mr. Sinclair," she replied, with a long, slow smile.

For a long moment, they regarded each other from across the room in a way that made the others feel first like they were intruding, and then as if they needed a shower. Raphael Sinclair glided forward. Stopping scant inches away, he gazed down at her. His lips parted slightly, as if he were going to kiss her.

"How are you?" he said.

"It's good to be back," she said.

He reached forward for her. Suddenly he came to himself, remembered the gaggle of open-mouthed observers, glancing around at them as if he had just woken up.

"Well then. Good luck with your thesis project. All of you." He took a reluctant step back, then another. The curtain swooshed closed behind him.

This performance was followed by a moment of unbroken, unbelieving silence.

Portia glanced at Tessa. The fiery heat had banked with his departure; still, she glowed like an ember. Tessa met her gaze, shrugged ruefully.

"Come for Shabbos dinner tomorrow night," she said. "It's a long story."

The following Monday, Tessa reported for work. An assistant in a short black skirt pointed the way to a door just past the reception area.

The art department was a large square room, painted bright white like everything else at the magazine, designed around an enormous black-topped table at its heart.

Two women faced each other around the table, staring fixedly down at the work in front of her. The first was thin, birdlike, barely wider than a child; her otter-brown hair was cropped short, standing up like a little boy's. She wore a short black and white leather skirt that looked like it had been sewed together from the skins of soccer balls, and over that, a long, fitted navy jacket. Long red and white striped ruffles poured out of the sleeves. Tessa watched as the designer deftly sliced photographs and bits of xeroxed type with an exacto knife, slid them through the rollers of an adhesive wax machine, always managing to keep her ruffled cuffs out of harms way.

The second woman was equally startling. She was dressed as if it was still morning in the 1960s, a neat cotton blouse with a Peter Pan collar in a tiny flowered print, a pleated skirt, black Mary Janes. But her face was pure club kid; flawless white skin, Chanel red lipstick. Deep kohl eyeliner stroked around her eyes, angling up at the corners. She wore her hair cut high on the back of her neck and swinging low in the front, like a China doll.

At one end of the room was a small office, a series of long black countertops augmented by a phone and some cabinets, connected to the art department by a large interior window. At the far end hung a large bulletin board. Painstakingly ruled in black were many rows of carefully spaced numbered rectangles. Tiny layouts, reduced to a few inches in width, were accumulating over many of the rectangles. At the top of the bulletin board was pinned the word *May*.

In front of this board stood Anastasia, deeply absorbed, contemplating the miniaturized layouts. She was accompanied by a young man in a brick-colored suit, pleated trousers pegged at the ankles and pinstriped in cream. Butter yellow pleats spilled out between the lapels of his jacket. He wore his hair shorn very close to his head, the top of it dyed almost yellow. Long, sharp sideburns pierced his cheeks, stopping at the corners of his mouth. Tessa stared. She had never seen anyone so artfully composed in her entire life. It was like he had stepped out of a Toulouse-Lautrec painting.

Anastasia seemed to sense Tessa's presence; she turned to face her, a smile painted across her red lips. "Right on time," she said. "You can put your things down on that desk. Ram," The young man looked up from the mini-board. "This is Tessa Moss. She will be taking Elle's place. And be nice. She is Raphael's special friend. One of his art students."

"Oh, sure," he said. "Hi." He turned to Anastasia, addressing her confidentially. "Does she know that he's just a great big homo?"

"Ram," Anastasia chided him, but then she broke into a laugh.

Wordlessly, Ram looked her up and down, assessing her clothes, her dusty Western boots, her hair. Suddenly, Tessa felt shy, self-conscious, embarrassed. At school, she fit in with the rest of the painters. Next to these exotic creatures, she was as plain as a sparrow.

"So you're Raphael Sinclair's little bit of crumpet," he said. She flushed pink. He smiled, his eyes crinkled merrily, inviting her to laugh along with him. "Welcome to *Anastasia*. We can really use your help."

They put her to work immediately, xeroxing the fashion photos, headlines, and copy for half a dozen different stories. *It's a Wrap!* was the food story. *The New Nudes* was about lipstick. *Hillary for President* was an interview with the wife of the Democratic Presidential candidate. *We Rate the Lubricants* was self-explanatory.

The work was eye-glazingly dull, but it did take a certain amount of organization to keep the stories separate from each other, and as a bonus, she got to eavesdrop on other conversations as she punched buttons on the copy machine.

She learned that Gabriela, the small one with the dark hair, had known Ram since middle school. That Thea's mother was an artist, one of Warhol's crowd in the Sixties. That one editor's father was a respected television news reporter, and that another editor's mother was a former Miss America. That a certain fashion editor ate a big lunch and regurgitated it every day at two-thirty, so regularly you could set your watch by it. That the absent Elle was very likely going to be fired.

At six-thirty, Gabriela put on her coat. "Go home," she addressed Tessa cheerfully. "Don't worry. We'll have lots more xeroxing for you tomorrow."

Behind her, Leo glided into the art department. An electrifying change came over Gabriela's exquisite face. She tore off her coat, hurled down her bag. "Get Anastasia!" she snapped at Tessa over her shoulder as she bolted for the office. Tessa hurried down the long hallway, spooked by the quiet; the phones had stopped ringing, the editors had all gone home.

The stern assistant was on the phone. Tessa waited. The conversation ended. She flipped the pages of a date book, filled something in. Tessa waited some more. Eventually, Anthea glanced impatiently up at her.

"What is it?"

"Gabriela asked me to get Anastasia."

"Well, you can tell Gaby that Anastasia is very busy."

Tessa shifted from one foot to the other. "Um. I think it had something to do with Mr. Lubitsch. He's in the art department."

As it had with Gabriela, an electrifying change transformed Anastasia's dry little assistant. She leapt out from behind her desk. "Leo? Why didn't you say so?" She pounded a button on her phone set, barked, *"Leo is in the art department!"*

Before she'd finished the sentence, Anastasia was charging through the door and down the hallway. Tessa had a hard time keeping up with her stride. At the end of the corridor, Anastasia made a beeline into Ram's office and shut the door behind her.

Through the interior window, Tessa could see the editorial director, the editor-in-chief, and the art director deep in discussion. Only Gaby moved, bustling around them, taking scissors, colored paper, and what looked like a sheet of white oak tag out of various drawers. A moment later, Ram opened the door a crack and hissed *"Lubricant!"*

Tessa tiptoed through the door, discreetly slipped the folder with the photographs and headlines to Gaby. Leo smiled warmly at her. Tessa smiled shyly back, turned to go. Anastasia's wise eyes went back and forth from the old man to the girl.

"Why don't you stay, my dear," she suggested. "Stand over here, next to me. You can see how we do things."

A flimsy white cardboard sheet lay flat on the counter. A long rectangle was ruled across it in cyan blue. A line down the middle divided the rectangle in two. Left page, right page. A single magazine spread.

Leo sorted through the various photographs, selected a large black-and-white xerox of a man and a woman in the throes of passion. This, he laid it down on the left. On the right, he put down a block of copy three columns wide; took it away, tried it in a different typeface, smiled in satisfaction. Now he scanned the headlines, spread across the counter in various fonts and sizes.

"This head. *We Rate the Lubricants.* It's not very clever. Can we do better?"

"How about Slip and Slide?" suggested Anastasia.

Leo shook his head no.

"Gentle glide," said Gaby.

Anastasia dismissed it. "Sounds like an advertisement for a new brand of tampon."

"Jiffy Lube?" suggested Ram.

Leo raised his eyebrows. He turned to Tessa. "How about you, my dear?" he said courteously. "Any thoughts?"

"Um...Smooth moves?"

He nodded, smiled. "Very good. *Smooth Moves* it is."

Leo took up one of the lines of type Tessa had xeroxed, tore off the extra words to approximate the length of the new title, laid them across the photograph. Stood back to view his work.

"Yes," said Anastasia nodding. "Perfect. Frame," she said. Gaby took a flat black plastic frame from a drawer, set it down around Leo's layout. Without the distraction of the extra lengths of paper fluttering off the edges, the intelligence of the design sprang forth.

"Tape," said Ram.

Gaby held up her hands. A piece of scotch tape was stuck to the end of each of her ten fingers. Ram peeled off the pieces one by one, taped down the collage of paper and photographs while Leo and Anastasia chatted amiably in French. When it was all secured, he handed it to Gaby, who whisked it away to the production department, where the fake copy would be replaced with real words.

"Thank you all for staying so late to indulge an old man," said Leo self-deprecatingly, inclining his head. "Now go home! There is always tomorrow." He directed a particular smile at Tessa, then floated back out of the art department like a gray ghost.

The moment he was gone, the electricity seemed to go out of the air. Tessa was surprised to find that her heart had been racing. Watching Leo lay down a magazine page had been akin to the magic of watching Lucian paint.

"You are right," said Anastasia, as if she could hear her thoughts, her dark eyes fastened on Tessa. "He is extraordinary. There is no one else like him. A genius, a legend in his time." She sighed. "But now, that time is passing. I don't know how much longer he has left. The shaking is new."

Then she smiled. "Did you know? He had a little crush on Sofia. Nothing like our Raphael—that was the stuff of epic romance—but still, enough to give Margaux some restless nights."

She was quiet for a moment, almost sad, recollecting something in their shared past; and then she brusquely shook it off, smiled in a way that was friendly and condescending all at the same time, and said, "But I despise nostalgia; that was all a long time ago."

"You were marvelous, my dear," she added. "He is quite impressed with you."

"Me? What did I do?"

"The way you came up with that title," she said. "You are a natural."

"Jiffy Lube would have made a *fierce* headline," grumbled Ram. "I even had a subhead. When a quickie just isn't quick enough." Anastasia burst into laughter. "Smooth moves. Crumpet, you little slut. Oh, don't look at me like that. I know all about you. You're a big slut. You even have slut hair."

Tessa froze, stupefied. For her part, Anastasia was delighted. "Ram, you are shocking her," she admonished him, in a reprimand that wasn't really a reprimand. "Sweet little Tessa," she cooed persuasively. "We are just having some fun. Let us make it up to you. Why don't you join us for dinner tonight?"

She was moving forward now, a crimson light leaping and dancing in her eyes. The hairs prickled up on the back of Tessa's neck.

"I have to get to my studio," she said guardedly, taking a step backwards, out of the narrow office. "Lot of catching up to do."

To her immense relief, Anastasia halted at the doorway. "Just like Raphael," she said, bemused. "Always running off to his little *atelier.*" A Gallic shrug. "All right, my dear. This time we will let you get away. But next time, you are ours. Tory!" she snapped. Behind Tessa, an assistant editor hurrying by on her way to the elevator stopped dead. "A double cappuccino, please. Tell them it's for me. They know how I like it. *Vite, vite!*" she snapped. Tessa forgotten, she turned on her Manolo Blahnik heel and shut the door behind her.

2

"What the *fuck*, man," said Levon, and that was just for openers. Rafe tensed, bracing for the rest of it. God knows, he deserved it. "Is it possible you just didn't hear me all the times I told you to stay away from her? There weren't enough women in New York City?"

"She needed me," he said. They were in Levon's office. It was early in the evening; the remains of a red sunset seethed on the horizon.

"Your *school* needs you, Rafe. *She* needed a *doctor.*"

Levon turned his back on him, stared out the window, his hands shoved deep into his pockets. Rafe had never seen him angry before. Feeling chastised, he slipped lower into his chair, wrapped defensively in his overcoat.

"I mean, what the fuck," he said again.

"It's not what you think," Rafe said mildly.

"We can talk about what *I* think, later. That board meeting you missed last night? Whit told them all about you and Tessa, starting with your sexy little Tango on Halloween and ending with your heroic performance on Monday morning. He strongly recommended that your fool ass be kicked off the board."

Wearily, Rafe put his head in his hands. The meeting. He had forgotten about the bloody meeting.

"You know, I'm not the criminal here," he said irritably. "What about Whit? Telling a student to clear out, on a Sunday night at the end of vacation when he knew nobody else would be around. Why isn't *he* on trial?"

Levon put his hands flat on the desk. "Is he an asshole? Absolutely. But there's no law against what he did; the Chairman of the Painting Department can't be dismissed for giving a student bad news." He sighed, sat down heavily. He looked thinner, harried. "It's not just about you and Tessa, Rafe. The staff needs you. The *students* need you."

"You're right. I'm sorry. I'll do better."

"You've got to end it with her."

"I can't. I love her, Levon."

"Don't tell me that. I don't want to hear it."

"You know, I haven't...we haven't...she's still, ah..." He lapsed into uncomfortable silence.

"It doesn't matter, Rafe. Everyone knows you're together." Then, curiously, "Really?"

"Really."

"Wow." Levon massaged the back of his neck. He sighed. "When I saw her like that Monday morning...I thought we were going to have to call Bellevue."

"Have you met with her yet?"

Levon lifted his cap, ran his hand over his shining bald pate. "Yes. Her sketches look great. Now all she has to do is get it all done in time."

Rafe sighed, drummed his fingers on the arm of his chair. "Okay. Tell me where we go from here."

He stared glumly out the window at the oncoming night as Levon told him how to repair the damage. Show up at meetings, seduce the board, remind them of why they got involved in the first place. Be cool and clever and charming at every ball, soiree and charity function from now until the end of the year. Bring in more celebrities and socialites, the money would follow. Giselle was going to a thing at the Guggenheim tonight. He could start there.

Rafe's attention wandered. What was Tessa doing right now? What was she wearing? He was thinking of a particular satin bustier he had seen in the window of a pocket-sized lingerie shop in the Village, and how she might look in it as he undressed her, hook by hook, ribbon by ribbon. He thought of her doe-soft eyes, starry with love. Her arms around him, creating a safe haven. The drama of her expressions as she listened to the story of his day. He could still feel the impression of her warm body where it had dovetailed with his, a few hours earlier.

There had been a single blip, one solitary bad moment to mar his happiness. Together in her apartment, both of them shirtless, the desire for

blood had suddenly reared up and overwhelmed him. There was no warning. The muscles in his jaw began to swell, his eyes to change, and suddenly
the predator was already there, taking over his brain. Rather than risk hurting her, he'd grabbed his coat and stumbled out into the night.

But he could handle it. Perhaps he couldn't have managed a relationship with an ordinary girl when he was still new at this vampire thing, but
he was older now, he had more control, more resources. There were other
ways to get what he needed.

Levon was winding down. Rafe knew the drill. Meet the people, shake
out the money. He stood up to leave, apologized for his appalling error in
judgment, promised he would get right back on track. Levon smiled in
relief, apologized sheepishly for calling him out, clapped him on the back,
shook his hand like a friend.

Alone in the hallway, he looked at his watch. Seven o'clock. An excited
tingling in the pit of his belly. Tessa would be in her studio. He took the
stairs two at a time.

"Superpowers," said Clayton.

"How many?"

"Just one."

Harker licked the rolling paper, gave a final twist to the end of a skinny
little cigarette. "Flying. No question. What about you?"

"Mind control," said Clayton, without hesitation. "Over the ladies. For
obvious reasons."

Ben blew smoke over his head in a long, steady stream. "Today?" he
said. "Super speed. Then there would be a remote possibility that I might
finish my thesis project in time for the show."

"What about you, Graham?"

"Shapeshifting," he said, squinting moodily into his empty wineglass.
"I like the idea of being able to eat whatever I want and still look like
Richard Gere."

Tessa had coerced her friends into posing for the third of her three
paintings, the whirlwind of bodies rising up into the sky, offering free wine
and a shot at immortality. They were sitting wherever there was space; piled
together on the couch, more on the cracked Danish modern chairs. The

Moroccan table stood at the center of the room, bearing an open bottle of wine, a little wooden crate of clementines, a half-empty pan of brownies Harker had brought in. A ribbon of sweet-smelling smoke wafted up into the air; Clayton had anchored an incense stick in the pliable greenish buttocks of Tessa's écorché sculpture.

"These brownies have kind of an interesting aftertaste," Portia remarked.

"Katie has a new job," said Harker. He hefted his guitar higher up on his lap. "She's working at Magikal Childe, you know, the witchcraft store over on Nineteenth Street. She put in this herb that's supposed to boost creativity."

"Tastes like basil," said Portia, putting down what was left of her brownie.

"Basil that's been shat out of a skunk," said Graham.

Tessa leaned over her work table, gazed at the photos she had taken for her project. The odd-tasting brownie lay forgotten on a paper plate.

Her friends' reactions to the revelation that Rafe was a vampire had been mixed. Clayton had leapt up from his seat at the Shabbos table, pounded Ben on the back, howling, "What'd I tell you. Ah *knew* it. Ah *knew* it." Ben, on the other hand, paled and pushed his seat back from the table, stunned into shocked silence. Harker had slowly nodded his head up and down, firing off the opening riff to *Don't Fear the Reaper.* Gracie had arched her eyebrows and tossed back her glossy bronze curls, breathlessly admitting that she actually found it kind of sexy. Graham simply shrugged and reached for another brownie.

But Portia, decent, right-thinking Portia, had a stiff, scared look on her face, just as Tessa knew she would. Guiltily, she wondered if Portia would ever feel safe on the streets of New York City again. And David...well, David.

He had been the last one to leave. As she was closing the door behind him, he wheeled sharply around, blocking it open. "Tessa," he said levelly. "It's sad, I know. And I understand your connection to him, and why you feel responsible. But Tessa, ask yourself this question. If what he says is true, this guy was a killing machine. Do you feel safe with him?"

She frowned at her photos. The model had posed in a vintage 1940s dress Tessa had purchased at a thrift shop. In the photos, she looked believably frightened as she hung onto a squirmy toddler. It was exactly what Tessa had asked of her. Still, the picture didn't sing; something was missing. What was it?

"Can we turn off the fucking music, please?"

Donna Summers was sobbing that someone had left her cake out in the rain. Tessa looked up. "Sure."

Harker popped the tape out of the boom box, read the label out loud. *"Please Mister Please,* Olivia Newton John. *Could It Be Magic,* Barry Manilow. *Le Freak,* by Chic. Where did you get this?" he said, not without awe.

"Guy on Astor Place sells mix tapes for a dollar," replied Tessa. "He looks like he needs the money."

"Don't buy stuff from those guys," said Clayton. "They just use the money to buy drugs."

"He said he was hungry," Tessa said absently.

"Why are you dressed like that?" said David.

She was in a short black skirt, an elaborately starched white blouse, black ballet flats, black stockings that stopped somewhere around mid-thigh. She'd found the clothing folded neatly on her desk at *Anastasia* yesterday. The directions had been implicit.

"Standard issue magazine-girl uniform. I came straight from work."

"How's that going, anyway?" The men were passing around one of Harker's handmade cigarettes.

"I've learned lots of new ways to work the word 'fabulous' into a sentence."

"Have you met any models?" said Graham.

"I see them around."

"Are they as gorgeous in real life as they are in photographs?"

"If you find skinny teenage girls with flat chests and tiny heads gorgeous, sure."

"I was talking about the boys."

The curtain was drawn aside, admitting Raphael Sinclair. He stood within the pool of light from the reflector lamp, regarding Tessa at her work table. Where it touched her, the light turned her tawny hair into a river of gold. Rafe moved forward as if no one else was in the room, brushed his fingertips across her shoulder. Absorbed in her photographs, it took a moment before she turned her head. When she saw who it was, she smiled in a way that made the other men a little envious, even the ones who had girlfriends.

"Mr. Sinclair, sir." said Harker, picking out the first ten notes of *Moonlight on Bleecker Street.*

"Thanks for lending me the Balthus book, Mr. Sinclair," said Portia cautiously. She was visibly uncomfortable around him. "It's perfect."

"Please, call me Rafe," he said. A small, self-deprecating smile. "I saw it on my bookshelf and thought of you. I hope it's helpful."

Clayton got to his feet. "Got something for you, Mister Sinclair," he said. He held the curtain open for him. "If you would just come this way, sir, please."

With a questioning look at Tessa, Rafe left the warmth of the studio. A few minutes later, the curtain was lifted open. A stranger stood in the doorway, just another art-student-slash-musician in torn jeans and a faded Pink Floyd concert t-shirt, his hair chunky and mussed, as if he had just rolled out of bed after a hard night of rocking. On his feet, a pair of scuffed Doc Martens.

There was a collective gasp as the students recognized him. Then Harker patted the seat beside him. "Take a load off, Mister Sinclair."

He squeezed in between Gracie and Harker's electric guitar. Gracie wiggled her tush, gave a sensuous laugh. Someone with a sense of humor passed him the brownies. Wisely, he declined.

Harker appeared to be returning to a conversation begun earlier. "So. Dude. You've never gotten stoned and listened to *Dark Side of the Moon.*"

"No."

"No Stones. No Clapton. No Dylan. No Doors."

Rafe shook his head. "I don't know much about modern music. Though I think Mick Jagger and I were dating the same model at some point during the Summer of Love."

"No Beatles. No *Elvis.* You're like a virgin. Christ in a barrel, I'm tingling. I'm gonna make you a rock history mix tape." He whipped out his sketchbook, scribbled furious notes to himself.

"Say, Mr. Sinclair, sir," said Clayton eagerly, leaning forward. "If I might ask you, sir...I have this little bet going with Ben. Exactly how many Nazis did you kill during the war? Did you keep count?"

Rafe's eyebrows shot up. He might have answered, but suddenly the curtain was drawn aside, admitting Whit Turner's square head. The students fell silent before the Chairman of the Painting Department.

"I have to cancel our meeting tonight," he told Graham. "Tomorrow good?" Graham nodded his assent. Now Whit regarded the students squashed together on the couch. Seeing Rafe, he frowned, as if he knew him from somewhere but couldn't quite place the face.

"This is my friend Udo," Graham said offhandedly. "Visiting from Lithuania. He's thinking about transferring here next year. He's heard good things."

"Oh," said Whit. He addressed Rafe, slowly and loudly. "Do you speak English?"

"No," Graham said. "We're working on it."

"Well. Tell him there are going to be a lot of changes around here." Whit said. The curtain swished closed behind him.

The students collapsed on top of one another, helpless with suppressed laughter. Clayton had to clap his hand over Gracie's mouth to keep her from giggling out loud and giving them all away.

Seeing him dressed like this, legs stretched out lazily before him, lounging on the couch with her friends, brought an unexpected tightness to Tessa's throat. He looked heartbreakingly young. She realized she was being given a glimpse of what he must have been like fifty years ago, before Sofia, before Anastasia, before the war. He noticed she was watching him, and smiled. His eyes were very fair and blue today.

"Mr. Sinclair," said Graham.

"It's Udo," he said, taking the cigarette Harker passed to him.

"Is the school really in trouble? Should we be worried?"

"No business," he mumbled, sinking deeper into the couch. "Not tonight."

"It's our school, too," said Ben. "We want to help. Is there anything we can do?"

"You can help by doing the best work you possibly can, then going out into the world and spreading the word."

"Say," said Portia. "What about a Goods and Services auction?" In response to the blank stares she received, she explained further. "My church has one every year. There's a parishioner who is a psychiatrist, he donates a session, it's auctioned off to the highest bidder. A parishioner who is a lawyer donates an hour. A woman who works for a television talk show donates tickets...you get the idea. Last year, I offered to paint a portrait in the style of Velasquez. It went for *thousands.*"

"What about Wylie Slaughter?" said Graham. "He really likes what we're doing here. We could ask him to donate a painting. And if he likes the school so much, maybe some of his groovy artist friends will donate something, too."

"Before the auction, a really great party. Like the Naked Masquerade," Portia planned. "Only this time, everything is white...white lights, white walls, white food...like a blank canvas."

"The students could contribute works, too," said Ben. "Original compositions, copies from old masters...It's a great chance to show the world what we do here."

"We need a catchy name. What would we call it?"

"Old Masters and New Masters."

"Still Life with Vampire."

"Nudes and Naked Ladies," said Tessa.

Rafe was sitting up, listening intently. "I like it," he said thoughtfully. "We could do it in the spring, maybe the end of April. Sort of a bookend to the Naked Masquerade. I'll get Giselle on it tomorrow. She loves a good party."

"To the Nudes and Naked Ladies Benefit and Auction," said Harker, raising his plastic cup.

"Udo doesn't have any wine," said Graham.

Hastily, Tessa filled a glass and handed it to Rafe. They smiled at each other through the forest of arms as the others raised their voices and their glasses.

"To art that matters."

Much later that evening. The studio floor was empty, the lights lowered. "Do you like me better this way?" he whispered as he unbuttoned her blouse.

"I don't know," she whispered back, pulling the faded black t-shirt up over his head. He was bare-chested underneath. "I kind of like the overcoat and fedora thing."

"Where did you get these clothes?" he said, unzipping the short leather skirt, slipping it down her legs.

"Ram left them for me. What do you think? Do I look like I belong at *Anastasia?*"

She sat back against the dark wooden slats of the chair, wearing only a lacy black bra, a pair of panties, stockings.

Rafe knelt between her knees. "Oh, yes. But I think I like you better..." He began to carefully roll one black stocking down her thigh. "...like this."

3

*R*afe woke with a start. Two-thirty, said the numbers on the dial. Tessa slept on beside him. He sat up in bed, trying to figure out what had awakened him, when he heard a noise on the landing outside his door. Pulling on his robe, he went to investigate.

At the top of the stairs, he paused. The lower level was almost entirely dark, save for a soft glow from the clock in the kitchen. A tremor of fear passed through him. And then a shadowy figure darted out ahead of him on the floor below.

The figure was the size of a small child. Gripping the banister, Rafe made his way down the stairs.

"Who are you?" he said into the dark. "Are you lost?"

The shadowy child was a master of camouflage; it hid behind curtains, behind furniture, going from nook to nook and room to room, hopscotching its way across the main level.

He found the door that led to the cellar opened wide; after a moment of trepidation, he followed it down. Despite the fact that he was an actual monster, his heart knocked against his chest; he was unreasonably frightened.

The basement was dark and lined with pipes. Suddenly, the furnace whooshed on, an evil orange glare crackling and snapping behind the grate. The dim firelight revealed the ghostly outlines of unused furniture stored along the walls, shrouded in white; it revealed the small figure, standing in the middle of the floor.

"Don't be afraid," he said gently. "I want to help you."

The small figure shifted from one foot to the other.

From the shadows along the walls, a figure emerged. Man-sized, this time. Another materialized between the shrouded furniture. Then another. And another. And another. With every passing moment the shadowy figures multiplied. Dozens of them, then hundreds, advancing on him, their mouths gaping wide with broken, jagged teeth.

Terrified, his knees buckling under him, he backed away towards the main staircase, but they were waiting for him there, too. The first one leaped upon him, screaming. He was almost overwhelmed by a powerful stench, the smell of the grave. He smashed it howling against the wall with one blow of his arm, the second one, too. The third one came from behind, crushing him to the ground. The rest of the ghostly figures followed, throwing themselves upon him until he was buried under a churning mountain slide of cold, bony bodies.

"You were shouting," Janina said.

Rafe touched his face, found it slick with sweat. His body ached, as if he had been running.

She yawned. "Bad dream?" She walked her fingers up his thigh. "You know, I have a degree in chasing away bad dreams."

His mouth was dry, he was shaking, his heart was full of dread. He wanted a drink, he wanted a cigarette, he wanted Tessa.

Rafe leapt out of bed, stalked to the bureau, found his wallet in his trousers. "Here," he said, pushing three crisp bills into her hands. "Go home."

Her eyebrows went up, her mouth made a round O. "You want me to leave? Now? It's the middle of the night."

"Yes, please. I'll call your agency. If you wouldn't mind waiting downstairs."

Ever the gentleman, he saw her to the door. Then he bolted the iron gate behind her, went upstairs, and crawled back into bed, where he lay awake for the rest of the night.

4

*T*hat evening, after closing the April issue, Anastasia took the staff to Odeon. Vintage 1920s fans hung from the pressed-tin ceilings, rotating slowly through the thick air, perfumed heavily with the smells of classic French bistro cooking. The walls were washed a tobacco-stained yellow. Old-fashioned venetian blinds with tapes and wide wooden slats shielded the celebrities dining inside from the stares of passersby.

The wait staff all seemed to know Anastasia, fawning over her while leading them to a large round table in the middle of the room. She ordered a round of Bellinis for everyone, champagne cocktails with a jolt of peach puree at the bottom. And that was before they sat down.

A waiter came, made suggestions, took orders. After the Bellinis, there were appetizers, little plates with exotic baby lettuces swimming in balsamic vinegar, smoked octopus, red slices of beef or duck, more drinks. Ram was sitting happily before a deep dish with nine cupped indentations in it, blissfully inhaling the aromatics of garlic and brown butter. As Tessa watched, he speared up something wiggly with a special fork, gobbled it down. He presented one to her, twinkled winningly. "Here, honey. Want to try one?"

"Escargot," advised Gaby. "Snails. Definitely not kosher."

Tessa leaned far back into her seat, as far away from the garlicky smell as she could get. Tried hard not to look as grossed out as she felt.

"I know," he said. "I can't believe I eat them, either. Say, Crumpet. I've been wondering. Does Raphael Sinclair mind that you're a great big *slut?*"

She sighed. "Ram," she began.

But he'd already turned his attention to Anastasia and the beauty editor, who were discussing the impending reshoot of the lipsticks for *The New Nudes.* "I thought we were done with this," the editor was saying, sounding faintly exasperated. "There's no time to get it reshot."

"Nothing is done until Leo says it is," said Anastasia dismissively. "And Leo thinks that picture is *boring."* To be called boring was the most heinous crime imaginable at *Anastasia* magazine. Boring made the numbers go down. Boring got your big story demoted to a paragraph in the front of the book. Boring got you fired.

Ram was smiling politely. When he noticed Tessa watching, he tied an imaginary noose and pretended to hang himself.

Tessa liked Ram. Despite his fierce appearance and his outrageous declamations, he turned out to be surprisingly, well, normal. She'd never met an art director before, as a matter of fact, she still wasn't sure exactly what they did, but it was clear that whatever it was, he was very good at it.

Gaby sat before an exuberantly ornate Versace dessert plate, contemplating an undersized cylinder of chocolate cake. With a certain kind of awe, Tessa had already witnessed the diminutive designer demolish a blackened hunk of hanger steak that would satisfy a heavyweight boxer.

"How long have you known Ram?" said Tessa.

"Since junior high," she replied. She sank her fork into the cake, releasing a volcanic gush of molten chocolate.

"What was he like?"

Now Gaby looked at her. "Do you mean, was he gay in the ninth grade? Then the answer is yes."

"No, I mean," Tessa hesitated, wondering how much she knew. "Was he different before he was, he was..."

"Before Anastasia turned him into a vampire?"

Tessa nodded, relieved. Gaby turned her attention back to her cake. "Maybe he was a little shy. But he was always this good." Under her breath. *"She* just didn't take the time to notice."

Anastasia sat at the head of the table; it wasn't that her seat was different, or faced a particular direction; wherever she sat would have been the head of the table. All attention was turned to her, all decisions deferred naturally to her. Seated between Thea and Ram, she was pushing some frisée and monkfish in a veal and balsamic vinegar reduction sauce around her dinner plate, sunglasses firmly in place.

"Tessa, my dear," she exclaimed, leaning towards her across the table. "I have heard from Lucian. They went to the Greek Islands for their honeymoon. Did you know?"

Tessa felt a small, buried part of herself curl up and die a little. Anastasia, sensing her pain, luxuriated in it. "There is already trouble," she promised. "They are seeing a therapist."

Then she moved on, asking Ram about a layout that had gone to the printer. Tessa let out a deep breath; she hadn't realized she was holding it in.

"What is the craziest thing you have ever done to a lover?" Anastasia was now demanding of the table.

The beauty editor, whose name was Poppy, answered first. "I was having this big fight with my boyfriend," she said. "We were at my place. While he was in the bathroom, I threw his pants out the window. And then I left for work."

Thea held a cigarette in a long black holder clenched between her teeth. "I was living with a musician," she said languorously. "When I found out he was cheating on me, I dragged all his stuff to the club and threw it at him." She expelled a cloud of smoke. "Including his stereo and his record collection." Another puff of smoke. "I waited until his big drum solo."

"Tell them, Gaby," said Ram.

"Oh, all right." She rolled her eyes. "Benno was supposed to drive my parents to the city. They had this big doctor's appointment. And he came home from work and said he couldn't do it, he was too tired. I got so mad, I went outside and slashed his tires." She smiled sheepishly. "Twenty minutes later, he said he felt better, and he could take them now. So then I had to explain to him about his tires."

"What about you?" Gaby asked Anastasia. "You're French. You've got to have some good stories."

Anastasia smiled, her teeth gleaming. "Oh, you know all about me," she said self-deprecatingly. "The worst thing I ever do is leave them thirsty for more." There were hoots of laughter. She trained her attention on Tessa. "But, my friends, all our stories pale in comparison to what our little *jeune fille* has done, only a few weeks ago."

Bewildered, Tessa turned to Anastasia. A smile was spreading across her scarlet lips. "Do I have your permission?" She leaned forward. "There is something you may not know about our little assistant. Up until recently, she was deeply involved with Lucian Swain." All heads turned to look at her in surprise. "Behind her back, he was seeing April Huffman. Who just so happened to be one of her teachers at art school. I know. It is fabulous. So. Our girl happens upon a nude picture of Lucian's new girlfriend that he is using in a painting. She steals this picture. She and her little classmates make hundreds and hundreds of copies, in every color of the rainbow. And paste them up all over school."

The table exploded into incredulous laughter. Tessa, feeling pleasantly buzzed under the influence of the Bellini, blushed furiously, dropped her head into her hands, found she was laughing too. Gaby actually fell off her chair. Ram turned lipstick red, wheezing. Gaby pounded him on the back until he could speak again, whereupon he burst into laughter all over again. "Oh my God, Crumpet," he kept repeating. "Oh my God. Oh my God."

She didn't get home until midnight. As she put the key into the lock, a dark figure materialized beside her.

"You're late," said Rafe.

"And drunk," she said, leaning sleepily against him. "Anastasia took us all out to dinner."

He put his arms around her to steady her. "Portia said you weren't in school this morning."

"Busy at work. Closing the April issue. Anastasia asked if I could give them the whole day."

Tessa plopped down on her bed, pulled off her cowboy boots one by one, let them drop on the floor.

"Have you started on your next canvas?" he asked.

"No. Too busy."

"Tessa," he said, his lovely voice chiding her in reprimand. "You should be well along by now."

"I know, I know." She yawned charmingly, covered her mouth, giggled. "I'll start tomorrow."

He hung his coat on her easel, came to sit next to her.

"You look different," he said, passing his fingers through her hair. It was long, lustrous, the same glorious shade of red-gold-brown one might find on a Madonna in a Titian painting, but infinitely changed; it lay perfectly flat, an untroubled river flowing from the top of her head to her waist.

She was having some trouble rolling down her tights. He used it as an excuse to kneel between her knees and roll them down for her.

"There was this stylist, shooting a story about some new Japanese hair straightening techniques. Anastasia had him experiment on me. I'm the only one in the whole building with curly hair. Do you like it?"

Sitting on her single bed, she was barefoot, adorable. "Of course," he said, but the truth was, it made him feel a little uncertain, as if she were someone else dressed up in a Tessa suit.

"S'temporary," she mumbled. "Wash out when I shower. Is the world spinning," she said, "or is it me?" and she settled onto her side. After a moment, he pulled his shirt up over his head, lay down beside her.

"I love you," he whispered, his lips in her hair, familiar yet unfamiliar.

"Mm," she said, seeking his lap with her bottom. He folded himself into her angles, gave himself over to the peaceful oasis that was her body.

"Gotta get up early," she exhaled, her eyes closed. "Meeting Anastasia downtown. Photo shoot for the cover."

"But class, Tessa," he said, feeling a twinge of concern. "What about class?"

She was already asleep, her chest rising and falling with the guileless rhythm of sleep. With a queasy jolt, he wondered if Anastasia was intentionally leading her astray.

It was silent but for the steady tick tick of her clock. They were alone in the apartment, the alleged roommate was staying uptown with the alleged boyfriend. In the long, still hours of the winter night, Rafe closed his eyes.

Ahead of us stands an ordinary yellow brick building, rather long, with a gabled roof. The only thing that sets it apart is a tall chimney, a smokestack, really, embedded in the stars. The smoke belching out of the top is red against the moonless black sky. She puts her arms around me, rests her head on my shoulder. Reflected in her eyes, I can see the chimney, the smoke, the stars. Holding his precious little body close, dressed in the warm coat I bought for him, I fall out of line.

He threw the covers off and got out of bed. Pulling on his coat, he came to look at Tessa one more time before grabbing his hat and stalking back out into the cold February night.

5

*T*he students were all well along in their thesis projects by now. Harker had several finished portraits glowering on his wall, denizens of the East Village, calling to mind Toulouse-Lautrec's *fin-de-siècle* singers, dancers and prostitutes. Gracie's column of women had acquired a silvery coating of underpaint; even at this early stage, it had a lazy, sensual feel to it. David's *nature morte* had an otherworldly stillness to it, the light filtering tenderly over objects he had found in the streets of New York; a silk opera hat in a velvet-lined hatbox, a school clock from the 1930s, a brass watering can, a dressmaker's dummy, an old Barbie doll. Graham was almost finished with St. Sebastian, his beautifully articulated body pierced through with arrows, his eyes lifted heavenward, suffering sexily. Shaded in black, Portia's paintings of children had an eerie, Diane Arbus-like quality to them; the Balthus book Rafe loaned her was exactly the inspiration she needed.

Clayton's centaur was gorgeous. Other students, even teachers, would stop by to ooh and ahh over the anatomy and the musculature. The mythical creature, half-man, half-horse, stood on three legs, the right foreleg raised and curled close to the chest. The human half of the torso rocked back, the hands fumbling at an arrow embedded deep in its clay breast.

It was nearly complete, breathtaking, filled with pathos, or it would have been, had it possessed a head. Originally, Clayton had used himself as a model. The following morning he had come in to find a doobie clenched between its gray teeth. Daily, he would come in to find it had sprouted wings, flippers, a martini glass, a jet pack, an enormous phallus, fangs.

Since then, he had tried David's head, Ben's head, the dual heads of the Olsen twins. In a fit of frustration, he had sculpted the head of the custodian's cat and grafted it onto the torso, and this was how it remained. Harvey was after him to hurry up and choose so that he could go on and cast it in plaster already.

Tessa stood before a large white canvas, gazing at the drawing she had made. Following Levon's suggestions, she had come in tighter on the figures, cropping the mother at the knee for a three-quarters view. She had also scrapped the clothing from the Forties, deciding instead to leave them nude. The changes had certainly helped, dramatically increasing the emotional impact of the image. Still, something just wasn't right.

She put her pencil down and rubbed her eyes. Working at the magazine was more consuming than she had thought it would be. And last night, Anastasia had taken the whole staff out to a private screening of a new movie, then to dinner at 150 Wooster, where there had been drinks, a meal, coffee, fancy desserts, more drinks. She had fallen into bed after two. It was only noon, but she was already exhausted.

When someone knocked outside her door, her heart fluttered. Perhaps it was Rafe. But it was only Levon, there for her advisory meeting. He came to stand behind her, filling up the space with his big ex-athlete's body, viewing her progress.

Since the end of Intersession, her paintings had acquired a new depth, greater clarity and richness. He was startled by the speed of her progress. She had begun as a good painter. She was becoming a great artist.

"That's right," he said approvingly. "That's what I'm talking about. Look at how the whole thing just snaps into focus now."

"It still isn't right. Something's missing...I don't know." She yawned, stretched. "Sorry. Late night."

"Have you started on your other canvases yet?"

Guiltily, she shook her head. "Work is taking a lot out of me," she confessed.

"You've got to get your priorities straight," he said, admonishing her. "You have the whole rest of your life to work. You'd better get a jump on this if you're going to finish all three canvases in time for the show."

Rafe had said the same thing. She nodded her assent. He didn't even mention that she was jeopardizing her chance for the coveted Prix de Paris. Probably, he didn't think she had a shot.

Levon shoved his hands deep into his pockets, gazed up at Gracie's tapestry of female figures.

"Got a minute?" he said.

Touched by a sense of foreboding, she perched lightly on the edge of the velvet couch. Removing his golf cap, Levon passed his hand over his shining head. Turned around. Looked at her earnestly. Burst into laughter.

"I can't talk to you seriously when you're sitting on that whorehouse sofa," he said.

"This is going to be about Rafe, isn't it," she said.

"Yes," he said.

She was looking at him warily, like a tiger in a cage at the zoo. "I won't give him up," she said, quiet but resolute. "I need him, Levon."

He sat down at the edge of her swivel chair, leaned forward. "I've been working for Raphael Sinclair for four years, now. In that time, I have seen his name connected with at least a dozen gorgeous, accomplished women. Now, I like Rafe. I like him a lot. I consider him a friend. But tell me, Tessa. How is this not going to be Lucian Swain, all over again?"

Her eyes turned a malevolent, crackling black. Levon was startled backwards into his seat. He'd never seen her express that kind of intensity of emotion, didn't known she was capable of it. She seemed so sweet, so suggestible, so *nice.*

"There are things you don't know," she said.

Levon sighed. "Look, Tessa. Rafe was nearly thrown off the board a couple of weeks ago. Did he tell you that?"

The shock in her eyes told him he hadn't. "Why?"

"Turner told them that the two of you have been having an affair."

She sat quietly for a moment, absorbing the seriousness of the situation. "We haven't. I mean, we don't...we, uh..." She lapsed into silence.

"There's going to be a vote," he said. "On the future of this school. Whether it stays classical or goes modern. Or whether it ceases to exist, altogether." He leaned forward. "The board members love Rafe. Every time he opens his mouth, every time he bats his pretty eyelashes at them, they fall in love with the idea of a classical art school all over again.

"But Rafe hasn't been around much lately. So I'm asking for your cooperation. Matter of fact, I need you to be seen around town with someone else, to throw Turner and his minions off the scent. David, maybe. He already has the hots for you."

The quirky eyebrows drew together, the dark eyes marked and measured. She turned away from him, towards the window, surveying the water tanks and rooftops of the East Village. There was a look on her face that was too wise for her years, as old as the forests, as old as time. Levon watched the play of love and loyalty chasing each other across her face. It was no wonder Rafe wouldn't give her up; if she were his, he wouldn't give her up, either.

"Look, Tessa," he went on, his deep voice compassionate. "I know you've had a rough year. And I'm glad you've found yourself this little patch of happiness, even though I'm worried about how it's all going to end. I'm not saying forever. Just till graduation. What is that, three and a half months away? Three and a half months to save the school."

He gripped her shoulder as he got to his feet, and she was struck by the odd sensation that it was more for his support than for her comfort. He paused at the door. "Look at the bright side," he said affably. "Think of what all that frustrated sexual energy will do for your paintings."

Tessa pressed her cheek against the cool surface of the table, folded her arms over her head. She wondered how she would begin each morning without the promise that Rafe was her reward at the end of the day, how she would pick up a brush without the shivery certainty that each stroke was for him.

The hairs on the back of her neck prickled to attention. She lifted her head to find Rafe watching her, his strange eyes full of sorrow. "How long have you been here?" she asked miserably.

"Long enough," he said.

"So you heard?"

He nodded, came slowly forward. Put a hand out to touch her, jerked it back, buried both hands in his pockets. "This is all my fault," he muttered. "If I had been more careful. If I hadn't missed all those bloody meetings. This never would happened."

"I'll quit school," she said suddenly. "The heck with my stupid thesis project."

"Absolutely not," he said. "You are the reason I created this school in the first place."

"Who wrote that stupid law, anyway?"

"I did," he asserted glumly. "Board members were always hanging around, trying to talk pretty girls into bed. Seemed like a good idea at the time."

Everywhere, the cheerful noises of the art studio. Hammering from the sculptors' grotto. REM wailing on the radio in Graham's nook across the way. First-year students slamming locker doors, shouting to each other, laughing. But in Tessa's studio, there was a painful silence, growing like a bubble, taking up all the air in the room.

"So I guess..." Tessa was going to say, *this is goodbye,* but the words stuck in her throat. She hid her face in her hands.

Swiftly, Rafe went to her, went down on his knees, kissed her wet eyes. "No, no, sweet girl," he whispered passionately. "Never goodbye." He kissed the palm of her hand, held it to his cheek. "I've been reckless, it's true; visiting your studio in the middle of the day, all those meetings and galas I missed...we can't afford to give Turner any more ammunition."

He sighed, interweaving his fingers with hers. "So we're going to do exactly what Levon said we should. I'm going to show up at every last gig with some prattling debutante on my arm. You're going to work very hard on your painting and be seen all around town with that damned David." For a moment, his eyes took on a pale, frosty hue. It faded. "I'll come when I can, after midnight. I'll knock on your window."

She climbed into his lap and rested her heated forehead in the cool curve between his shoulder and his neck. He put his arms around her.

"I can't do this," she said miserably. "How am I going to get through the next three months without you?"

"My sweet girl." He smoothed the hair out of her eyes. "Everywhere you look, you'll see me. Everywhere you go, I'll already be there. You won't be able to get rid of me." He took her hand, slipped it under his jacket, held it over his heart. There was a radiant blue light in his eyes. "What's three months," he said, "when we have a lifetime ahead of us?"

She slid her arms into his coat, leaned her bright head against his shirtfront. He inhaled deeply, memorizing the blackberry fragrance of her. "I love you," he whispered into the untamed depths of her curls. *Love you, love you, love you.*

Outside, he strode purposefully down Lafayette Street. Halfway down the block, he slowed to a stop in the middle of the sidewalk. His body was wracked by a single dry sob; he covered his mouth and leaned against a building, overcome with grief.

All his courage had been for her. Inside, he was dying. How he was going to get by without the constant reassuring touch of her hand, the steadying comfort of her softly rounded body, he could not begin to imagine.

6

*R*eady?" said David. Tessa pushed away the uneaten half of her bean and cheese burrito and nodded.

It had been almost a month since Rafe and Tessa agreed to separate. Portia had been kind, sympathetic, but Tessa knew she was secretly relieved. The other artists showed remarkable understanding, pledging to look in on Rafe from time to time. Harker went right to work on a rock history mix tape, delivering it to the townhouse with his own Walkman in case the founder of the school didn't own a tape deck.

Levon was right, all that sexual frustration made for better art. She was already finished with the painting of the mother and child, and had already drawn the outlines for the other two paintings onto the canvas.

Ram had taken her out for drinks down the street at the Royalton, nodding understandingly through the entire story. The next day, there was an enormous box of Godiva chocolate and a bottle of Cristal champagne sitting on her desk.

"The chocolate is for now," he explained. "The champagne is for your first night back together again. *Ay, Mamacita!*" he cried, heedless of the passing editors' incredulous stares. "Ay! Ay! *Aieeeeeeeee!*"

David stepped seamlessly into his role as Tessa's boyfriend, without so much as a hiccup of hesitation. "But what about Sara?" she asked cautiously. "Won't she be jealous?"

"I broke up with Sara over winter vacation," he answered.

In truth, it hadn't been as onerous as she'd thought it would be. Classes kept her busy in the morning, the magazine kept her busy in the afternoons, and the rest of the time was spent hard at work on her thesis project.

It was not exactly a chore to meet David for dinner, or a movie, or a visit to a museum. He was smart and funny, easy to be with. It was no secret that he thought he had a chance with her if he just stuck around long enough. The other students already treated them like they were a couple.

She learned that he had a married sister living in Brooklyn Heights, a dog named Roxy, a niece and nephew he liked to babysit. That his favorite book was *Catcher in the Rye*. That his favorite artist was Rembrandt. That he could play piano. That he still listened to Cat Stevens.

That he always held the door open for her. That he liked to rest his hand lightly on her elbow, guiding her out of a movie, out of a restaurant, walking her home. That when he stood back from his easel, he always crossed his arms and tilted his head a certain way. That when the light fell on him in the late afternoon, he was really very handsome. Sometimes she enjoyed herself so much she felt a little guilty.

True to his word, Rafe was everywhere. Never had his presence been more felt in the hallways of the school. He would catch Tessa's eye while conversing with Levon near the office, while querying teachers about student progress outside their classrooms, taking donors on tours of the studio floor.

As he said he would, he came to her when he could, only twice so far, long after midnight. Their meetings were brief and intense. There were few words; mostly, they clung to one other.

Tonight, after dinner, Tessa and David were attending the opening of a new exhibition at the Met. Tessa knew very little about Lucian Freud, only that he was the celebrated grandson of *that* Freud. The instructors all seemed to be very excited. The whole school was going.

"Tell me, Tess," said David, bringing her back to the present, his hands—nice brown hands, the fingers well-shaped, she noticed once again—wrapped around a cup of *café con leche*. "How is it that you're so careful to keep kosher, but you're dating a goy?"

Tessa raised one eyebrow, stirred her coffee. "A goy who also happens to be a vampire." He was wearing that chambray shirt that made his eyes look very blue, and the way he looked at her, she knew he would be hers if she just gave him a sign. "I think it would be a problem if he were actually alive. I don't know what the rabbis say about dating the undead."

He leaned back in his chair, signaled the waitress for the check, leaned forward again. "I'm not just saying this because I'm jealous. Truth is, I'm jealous as all hell. Of course you're in love with him. Who wouldn't be? He's rich, he's gorgeous, he's got the great suits, that great accent..." He'd been drawing her face in his sketchbook. Now he slapped it shut with more force than he'd intended, making them both jump. "Look. I don't believe in all this supernatural crap. To me, it looks like an eccentric British rich guy way to score babes. But if he really was a vampire, I'd be asking myself these questions."

"Like what?"

"Like this. What kind of future can you have with him? Are you going to marry him? Have his vampire babies?"

Tessa sighed. "I'm not thinking about the future right now, David. I'm so behind on my painting that I can't think past next week."

"Then you won't want to think about this, either. Does he love you? Or are you just a convenient replacement for Sofia?"

She scowled at him, irritated. But David wasn't done yet. He spread his fingers on the table, leaned closer.

"One last thing. What does he eat?"

"He's a wealthy man," she muttered, defending him. "He can buy anything he wants."

But her eyes were clouded with doubt. David entertained a small thrill of victory. "Ask yourself this, Tess," he said, slipping the tip under a water glass. "What does he buy? Does it come in a can? Or does it come from a real live girl?"

They paid the waitress, took the subway uptown to the Met. Ascending the wide white limestone stairway, Tessa was overcome by a feeling of almost religious awe. Lit up like a Greek temple, the pillars and pediments stood out in yellow relief against the black New York night.

"I should bring you on a Saturday night," he said. "There's live classical music playing as you go through the galleries."

The show was in the American Wing. They passed a table selling books, calendars and posters, went through the double doors.

"Oh my God," she whispered, and stopped there.

All around them, average, lumpy bodies sat heavily on chairs, lay draped across beds, sofas, and lovers. Ordinary faces stared back at her from monumental canvases, freighted with believable life. A man lay on a couch, his face turned away, touchingly vulnerable in his nakedness. A sleeping baby was dressed all in white, with cheeks so full and round that Tessa wanted to touch them. A blond woman leaned ecstatically into a mountain of discarded painting rags, the pinks and ochres of her skin contrasting with the gray folds. Two sisters, dressed warmly against the London chill, gazed at her as if they were in possession of a nasty little secret.

She'd never seen anything like it, the living humanity in the expressions, the broken rainbow of pigments making up the fleshtones. The texture of the oil paint, thick with lead, ropy, twisted, clotted.

They made their way slowly through the gallery, passing other Academy students, similarly bedazzled. In the next room, they joined Portia and Graham in staring up at a painting of the monolithic back of the performance artist Leigh Bowery, almost bursting from its frame.

"He's made figurative art relevant again," Graham said in awe.

Across the room, Rafe stood with Anastasia before a painting of a woman with a greyhound, holding a forgotten glass of red wine.

"This is very good," said Anastasia, looking at the painting. She sounded surprised.

His heart in turmoil, Rafe didn't reply, preoccupied with Tessa's progress around the gallery.

The past month had been a misery to him. He was trying, he really was. He went to the meetings, he went to the parties, he smiled at the pretties, he charmed the donors.

But everything was different now. Before Tessa, women had all been the same to him. Oh, he would appreciate a pair of pretty eyes, another girl's lissome figure. He would remember a pair of voluptuous lips, or a spectacular set of legs. But that's all they were to him, almost indistinguishable from one another; seduce one, seduce them all.

Now all he could think of was her. Dressed or undressed, in her studio, on her couch, across the room, across his lap, in his bedroom, in the moonlight. He longed for the touch of her hand, the steady warmth of her presence in the night.

Seeing her with David drove him nearly mad. Hidden in the doorway of a nearby building, Rafe tormented himself watching another man buy her dinner, another man making her laugh, another man walking her home.

They looked so natural together, it made his heart ache. Some part of him whispered *let her go.* What was he doing with a girl like Tessa Moss, anyway? What could he possibly bring her besides sorrow, degradation, an untimely death at his own hands? In the deepest, darkest recesses of the night, as he watched over her from the steps of St. Xavier, the voice whispered on.

"Hi, Mr. Sinclair," said a voice to his left. He tore his gaze away from Tessa and looked down.

"Oh, yes, hello, ah—"*Andy? Amy? Alice? Annie?*

"Allison," she said. Ah, yes. Long dark hair, sad shapeless mouth. She had been thin at the New Students party. She had lost weight since then. Her desperation sang to him.

"Right." He said. "Sorry. Allison, Anastasia deCroix."

Reading the gargantuan neediness that lay just beneath the surface of the girl's skin, Anastasia's lips stretched out in a greedy smile.

"One of my students," he reminded her.

"D'accord," she said graciously, putting out her hand. "Nice to meet you. That pin," she said, reaching forward to examine a large, bejeweled cross on the girl's sweater. "Where did you get it?"

"I made it," she said.

"Really," said Anastasia, interested now.

Tessa and David had joined Portia and Graham, and here were Clayton and Ben, all of them clustered together before a painting of a man in a tan raincoat, holding a cigarette and standing near a potted palm. Someone must have said something funny, they were all laughing. It wasn't fair, he thought. He should be with them.

Anastasia was writing Allison's phone number down. "My assistant will be calling you," she promised.

Now the group of students were joined by Levon and Turner. Whit was gesturing at the potted palm and explaining something, maybe about the composition, maybe about the meaning of the cigarette. David, playing the role of Tessa's boyfriend to the hilt, slid his arm around her waist.

Feeling sick, Rafe turned away. Weaving through the crowd of enthusiastic opening night guests, he made for the far end of the gallery, positioning himself in front of a painting as if he were carefully scrutinizing it, when in reality, he was just getting as far away from the swarm of art students as he possibly could.

"What did I tell you? Blows the lid off of modern painting." Sawyer Ballard came to stand beside him.

"Nice show," Rafe said politely, though the truth was, he had barely noticed the art.

"Nice? There's nothing nice about Lucian Freud. Everyone should see this. He's what the twentieth century has been waiting for. "

A tall blond woman in a Chanel suit came to claim him. "Your father would have loved it," he called over his shoulder as she piloted him away.

He studied the painting before him. A man and a woman, side by side in a single bed. Behind them, the vertical pipes of an old-fashioned radiator. The man snuggled cozily around his partner, his arm draped around her waist. There was a look of bliss upon their sleeping faces.

A fierce throb in his heart; and then he was surrounded by his students.

"Hey, there, Mr. Sinclair," said Clayton. "Looked like you could use some company."

Ben and Clayton, Harker and Portia, Gracie and Graham, all circled around him, forming a wall, and a hand came seeking his in the crush of bodies.

Tessa stood beside him, shielded from view by the barrier of burly sculptors. Something tightened in his chest; he could feel his eyes stinging with tears. His fingers curled around hers and squeezed.

As quickly as it had begun, it was over. She melted back into the pack of art students, and they lounged on to the next painting.

"So sweet," said Anastasia, coming to stand beside him. She had felt his anguish two rooms over. "Leo adores her. He calls her his *petite jeune fille.* They have a little crush on each other. Just last week she presented him with a little watercolor portrait. He was enchanted." She reached out and smoothed his lapel. "Did I tell you how she nearly gave her life rescuing the *69 Ways to Better Sex* layout from a ledge outside the twentieth floor?"

She frowned, pursed her lips. "Then again, perhaps there are some things it is better you do not know."

"She needs to spend more time working on her paintings," he said grimly. "And less time with you."

"My dear Raphael," Anastasia said firmly. "In a few months, she will graduate. And this dream of being a painter will have to face the reality of the market. She will need a job. Why shouldn't she work at my magazine?"

Rafe felt his lip lifting in a snarl. They watched Tessa drift from painting to painting, David in tow. "They are so cute together," Anastasia said affably.

Her words brought an accusatory flash to his eyes, an arrow of pain to his heart. "Oh, come on, my darling, such an orgy of *tristesse*," she teased. "Always so much *sturm und drang*. You are doing the right thing here. Letting her go, letting her have a chance at a normal life." She waited for a moment before giving him the *coup de grâce*. "It's what Sofia would have wanted, don't you think?"

Shooting her a look of pure hatred, Rafe plunged into the crowd.

It was wrong, it was stupid, it was reckless, he knew it, and still he charged forward. Snapshots of David Atwood with his arm around her waist replicated in his brain like a virus. What else did they do together, in the name of saving his school?

"Rafe," said Levon. Rafe barely acknowledged him, plowing through the throng of downtown artists and Upper East Side elite. Giselle loomed before him, in a pair of brown stirrup pants and a tweed jacket. She must have come directly from riding, he smelled polished leather; she kept a Tennessee Walking horse at Claremont Stables over on Eighty-ninth Street. She was accompanied by a well-preserved dowager, also in horsey dress. As he passed, she put her hand on his arm.

"Rafe," she chortled in her throaty voice. "There you are! I'd like to introduce you to—"

With a sinking feeling, Levon watched him pull away from her.

"What is it?" said Turner.

"Nothing," he replied. "Someone I used to know."

Tessa and David were stopped in front of a painting of a rather grotty-looking studio sink.

"It's obscene," he said. "And I'm not even talking about the genitalia."

"Don't you see it?" she said, incredulous. "The unconventional way he uses space? The way he uses paint?"

He shrugged. "It's all just another way of saying ugly. Like Van Gogh before he got to Paris. All these soupy grays and browns and lumpy paint and bad drawing."

Tessa felt a kind of turbulence disturb the rarefied air in the gallery, tipped like chimes into motion around her. She turned to see Rafe slicing towards her through the crowd.

Their eyes met; he looked as if he had something important to tell her, something that couldn't wait. With ten feet left between them, he slowed to a stop.

He was wearing her favorite suit, a double-breasted chalk-striped gray with baggy pants and peaked lapels, lined in crimson, all very 1940s, and she smiled at him, understanding that he had donned it as a signal, a kind of discreet love letter. But his face, his beautiful face...he was pale and ashen, as if there were a shadow moving under the surface of his skin. Some crisis was happening inside him, some private agony she did not know about and did not share. His eyes fastened on her as if he were drowning and she was a faraway shore; his lips parted, as if he were going to speak; and then he changed direction and stalked out the front door of the gallery.

Tessa had already taken an automatic step forward when a hand locked around her wrist. "Don't," David said quietly. "Turner's over there, watching."

Tessa turned her head. David was right. She closed her eyes, took deep breaths, counted to ten, put on a smile and took his hand.

Outside in the corridor, Rafe slammed open the door marked Emergency Exit. Shaking, he leaned against the wall of a decidedly unglamorous cinder-block stairwell and put his head between his hands. The bright lights were hurting his eyes. He reached out and snapped off the light switch, waited for the madness to go away.

The steel fire door yawned open, admitting two more people. Hidden in the shadows halfway up to the next landing, they didn't notice him.

For one ghastly moment, he thought it was David and Tessa. There followed the sounds of giggling, the papery rustle of clothing being removed. A girl's voice saying, *no, no, no,* giggling louder.

Not Tessa, thank God. He rolled his eyes, trapped. What was the best way to escape? He could head up the stairwell, which exited on the second floor, or he could wait quietly until it was over and they left.

No, no, no, the girl was squealing, but her voice had changed, the giggling was nervous now, the *no no nos* evolving into frantic protest.

He reached out and flipped on the light switch.

A man in a tight iridescent suit was grinding himself against a waif of a girl he had pushed up against the wall. Allison, half-dressed, red lipstick smeared across her pale face.

"Are you all right, Allison?" he asked.

"Oh, hi Mr. Sinclair," she said in a tiny voice. She was very frightened, he could feel it coming off of her in great wide waves.

"Do you need help?" he said, his eyes meeting hers.

"Yes," she said, and began to cry.

He started down the stairs. "Let her go," he said. "Find someone else who wants to do all those naughty things you've been dreaming up since you were ten."

"I have another idea," the young man said in a bored Teutonic voice. "Why don't you fuck off."

"Let her go," Rafe said.

The young man turned to face him, then tilted his head in recognition. "I know you. I was at your Halloween Party. What was it? The Naked Masquerade? You're the vampire. The Phantom of the Art School. Look here, Mr. Vampire. You just fly away now, and tomorrow morning I'll send you a big fat check so that all the little artists in your school can go on making potholders and leather wallets for the rest of the year. All right? Now, *fuck off.*"

Rafe grabbed him by the throat and hurled him up the flight of stairs. There was a horrible clang as his head hit the metal railing. His body slumped into an awkward pile on the landing.

Allison stared at Rafe as he came down the stairs. He smiled reassuringly as his fangs receded into his mouth, his eyes returned to their usual smoky gray. "You might want to fix your lipstick," he reminded her. Then he opened the door and stepped back out into the corridor.

7

"re they going to sue us?" asked the baby powder magnate. The board was furious. One man, the heir to a pharmaceutical fortune, implied that it would have been best for all parties involved if the girl had just kept quiet and taken it like a man. There was a silence in the room as the other members contemplated the implications of the mixed metaphors.

Rafe hadn't said a word in his own defense. As a matter of fact, he hadn't said anything at all, sitting on a folding chair in the Cast Hall, still wearing his coat, toying with the brim of his hat.

"I think it's been withdrawn, now that we have Allison's story." said Levon. "This wasn't his first time, either. Last year, his family paid a girl a million dollars over something that happened at the Limelight."

"Well, that's a relief," said the heir to the cough drop fortune. "Bernard, will this present any foreseeable problem with the Corning Institute?"

Blesser made a rueful face. "We'll see. They haven't called. I've got my fingers crossed." He consulted his notes. "They did want to know if we'd made any progress towards hiring someone who could head up our video art program."

"Tell them we're working on it," Turner instructed him.

Levon looked at Rafe; had the words "our video art program" really just come out of Bernard Blesser's mouth? *Say something,* he urged him silently. *Just smile at them.* But Rafe said nothing, continuing to stare out the window at the rain.

"Anything you want to add, Rafe?" he prodded, bewildered. The board members were looking to him for guidance. Giselle was staring at him, too.

"I'm sorry," said Rafe, stirring himself. "Were you talking to me?"

Levon looked at him strangely. There was a moment of awkward silence, and then the meeting adjourned. There was coffee in a silver pot and lovely little cakes and petits fours from a new catering place in Tribeca. While the members of the board rose from their chairs and made their way towards the refreshments, Blesser found Rafe and took him aside.

"There's a problem," he said.

The dream was coming every night now. The shadowy child, the fiery furnace, the host of demons chasing him through the house, sinking their teeth into his flesh. Today there had been a frightening twist; he woke to find himself outside on the balcony, scant minutes before the sun would have risen and turned him into a heap of ashes.

Pay attention. He trained his eyes on Blesser, willed himself to listen. Smiled politely. "What is it, Bernard?"

Blesser dropped his gaze. "It's the new ventilation system. Turns out it cost twice what they quoted us. We can't meet payroll this week."

"Oh." He tried to think of what to do, but now the only thing that came to mind were pictures of Tessa and David on a sunny beach, rolling around in the surf while U2 wailed *With Or Without You.* Soundtrack courtesy of Harker's rock history mix tape.

He couldn't process this right now. Patting his pockets, he found a business card, jotted something down. "Here. Call my banker at Barclays. Give him these numbers. Tell him what you need, he'll take care of you."

Blesser took the card, then whispered, "I think you did the right thing with that Austrian fellow. So what if his father's a diplomat. Anyone with an ounce of decency would have done the same."

Rafe smiled at him. "Thank you, Bernard. I appreciate that."

He could see Levon was working his way over to him, holding a little glass plate bearing a pink petit four, laughing at something the cough drop magnate had said. Rafe could see what was coming. First, Levon would ask if he could see him in his office. Then he would lash into him.

Rafe almost growled. He was not feeling very fond of Levon lately. Turning on his heel, he skulked off through the back door of the Cast Hall.

In the stairwell, he thought, *I wonder what Tessa is doing right now?* He was already on his way up to the studio floor when he remembered that it was off limits. In a rage, he grabbed the pay phone and smashed it against the metal receiver. It made a deafening clamor before shattering in his hand.

He paused on the sidewalk outside the building to collect himself. It was evening, the lights had twinkled on. New York was magical at this hour. People leaving work, their glad footsteps echoing down the streets. Friends meeting friends for a drink, or dinner, a club, the movies. Lovers hurrying towards each other in a heightened state of anticipation under a deepening blue sky. But Raphael Sinclair had nothing to do, nowhere to go, and no one who was waiting for him. He might as well go home.

He cut through Washington Square Park, his footsteps echoing on the pavement. The sulphur lamps bathed the benches and the sidewalks and the dead grass in a yellow glare. There was not another living being as far as the eye could see. Except for a girl with dull brown hair, making slow, aimless circles on the swing.

He stopped in front of her. "Hello," he said.

"Spare any change?" she said in a flat, colorless voice.

"How old are you?"

"Old enough."

Her pupils were fully dilated, like black holes. She was seventeen, maybe eighteen, he guessed. The girl put her arms around herself and shivered, her teeth rattling, though it was not a cold night. Something in his chest began to swell and thicken, his eyes began to change, his fangs to lower.

"Come with me," he said. His voice shimmered with every color of the rainbow, an angel's song. "Let me take you somewhere warm."

8

"Hello, my dear," Leo greeted her warmly as he glided through the art department into Ram's office.

Tessa looked up from the layout she was working on. Ram thought she should try her hand at designing. On the table before her were three columns of type and a few photographs. Under Gaby's deft fingers, it would already have been a witty front-of-book page juggling a story about blush, a hot new diet trend, and a Swiss anti-aging treatment. In Tessa's hands, it looked like the bottom of a birdcage.

"Tessa!"

Gaby was beckoning her towards the office. She had to find Ram and Anastasia, she didn't want to leave Leo by himself. Could Tessa babysit him for a few minutes? Gladly, she left the layout on her desk.

Leo was at the window, fiddling with the blinds. Afterwards, he leaned back against the wall, his eyes closed, basking in the weak winter sunbeams that filtered in between the slats. In the light, his thinning hair was as white as snow.

"I have something for you, my dear," he said. From under his arm he produced a manila envelope. His hands under the command of a slight but perpetual tremor, he undid the clasp and pulled out a black-and-white photo. Tessa watched him struggle, understanding that she must not offer to help him with it.

When he had it out, he gazed at it fondly, then placed it in her hands. *Saint Valentine's Day, Paris, 1939,* it said in a small neat script at the bottom.

She gazed at the characters from Rafe's story, seeing them take on contours, come to life. A woman with serious gray eyes who must be Beata.

A tall man with blond hair and telltale round glasses who must be Sawyer Ballard. Leo himself, neat, dapper, suave. Next to him must be Margaux, in a tight chignon, something a little pitiless in her expression. Colby, identifiable by his warm smile. Rafe, or rather, the eager, driven young man he used to be, staring forever at the woman in the center of the photograph, a slender, dark-haired sylph with a heart-shaped face. She wore a black dress with white polka dots, her white-gloved hands folded in her lap. The tragic beauty of her eyes marked her clearly as Sofia.

"Her beauty extended to the inside, as well." Leo remarked quietly.

Tessa looked at him, this man who knew her grandfather's sister when they were both young, his fragile skin marked with age spots, his trembling hands. It was hard to connect him with the self-assured young man in the photograph, poised to take over the world.

He was pensive, communing with his ghosts. "You may have that one. I made you a copy."

"Thank you, Mr. Lubitsch," she said.

"Thank *you*, my dear." he said with a small bow and a courtly smile. "You have given me great pleasure during your time here."

Gaby came into the room, peremptorily closed the blinds, shutting out the sun. Leo gave out a little sigh, almost imperceptible.

Together, Tessa and Gaby opened and closed drawers, quickly laying out the tools he would need to design. His special Swiss scissors, the blades long and light. The headline and subhead to each story, cut into long strips. Sheets of body copy, color xeroxes of the photographs, all neatly trimmed and clipped together.

Leo was on a roll, they finished three new stories as the afternoon waned into evening. Deftly, Tessa and Gaby taped down the bits of typography and illustration and photos and charts and whisked them off to Production. Leo chatted to Anastasia in French as he stood at the counter, sedately laying down type, frowning at it, moving it elsewhere.

At seven o'clock, the sun long gone, Leo gave them a small wave and glided out the door. Thea left first, then Gaby. Ram was effortlessly wrapping an orange scarf around his neck in a way that made him look like he was ready for a *GQ* photo shoot. If Tessa tried to tie it that way, the scarf would just end up looking messy.

"Elle was fired," he said. "I bet Anastasia asks you to stay on."

"I can't," she said. "I am so behind on my thesis project. I should be in my studio right now, as a matter of fact."

"You'll have to do better than that. She can be very, um, convincing." He was wearing a voluminous dark coat with a high collar, a white kerchief bound artfully around his head. Now he was pulling on a pair of leather gauntlets. "I'm doing the clubs tonight. Someone may not make it into work tomorrow. How do I look?"

She smiled. "Like a character in a Toulouse–Lautrec painting." When he raised an eyebrow, she corrected herself. "I meant, you look fabulous."

"Thank you, honey," he said. "That means a lot, coming from a big slut like you."

The way he pronounced it, there were two syllables; sssss-*lut*. She sighed in exasperation. "Were you born talking that way," she said, "or did you have to take a class?"

His eyes crinkled in a smile. At the door, he hesitated, turned back. He had recently grown a caterpillar's worth of hair under his lower lip, and now it twisted in a frown. "Crumpet," he said, a look of concern crossing his marvelously styled face. "If that's what you really want, to spend more time painting, you should tell her. You're too nice. You have to do what's best for you."

"Tessa!" The hairs prickled up at the back of her neck. Anastasia was still in Ram's office.

"She won't hurt you," he promised. "Much." He turned and then he was gone.

Reluctantly, Tessa poked her head around the door. The lights were off, it took her a moment to acclimate to the dark. Anastasia had raised the blinds, and she was sitting at Ram's desk, her feet up, gazing out at the skyline. Upon seeing Tessa, she fluffed her hair and smiled.

"Join me." she said, gesturing at a chair. Tessa slunk in and took a seat. "Why are you still here? Raphael will kill me, he says you need to spend more time on your homework."

"Gaby needed the raw food story for tomorrow morning," she muttered.

Anastasia smiled again. "Very dedicated." She turned towards the window. "Beautiful, isn't it. I love the city at night."

Tessa studied her dramatic profile, nodded.

"I'm sure Ram told you. Elle found another job." She slipped off her shoes, wiggled her painted toes. "You could stay on with us, you know. Everyone here loves you."

Tessa said. "I should get back to my thesis project."

Anastasia chuckled. "Yes, of course you should. But you still have to eat, my darling. Sometimes I think our Raphael has his head in the clouds, so irresponsible, letting his beloved students think they have a future in art. This dream he has of recreating a world that appreciates his kind of painting...that's all it is. A dream. He does not seem to know that painting is already dead. They held the funeral the day the camera was invented."

Without warning, she snatched off her glasses. Tessa gazed into the dark eyes, captivated by their lava-lamp glow.

"My *petite jeune fille,*" she said, almost tenderly. "You really love him." She leaned back in her seat, sighed. "Of course you do. He is like a puppy dog with you. I am thrilled for both of you. Really I am."

Then she smiled convivially, lowered her voice in a playful, just-us-girls sort of way. "All right, I admit it. I have to know. Has he ever...*tasted* you?"

Taken aback, Tessa shook her head.

"Incroyable! It was hard to believe with Lucian Swain. It is even harder to believe with Raphael Sinclair. Well, my dear. I am impressed. He can be very persuasive." The red light danced joyously in her eyes. She sighed expressively. "I feel so comfortable with you...like you are my niece. Should I tell you a story? I shouldn't. So, I will. Of course, this was many years ago, in a very different world. Lisbon, before the war. We were bringing this girl back to our hotel room. I think she was Jewish—we had promised to help her with papers to get out." Anastasia's large brown eyes assumed a serious expression. "It seems so wrong now, but back then, who knew how badly it would all turn out? *De tout façon.* Back to our Raphael. So beautiful, so charming, such a gentleman. With that voice, those eyes...I don't have to tell you. This girl turned around as we entered the elevator, just in time to see his eyes change, to witness as the fangs broke through his gums, and she began to scream.

"I thought we were done for. He moved so quickly, and with such grace; I have never seen anybody move like that. With one hand, he reached out and took her elbow. Not with force, anyone can use force; he held her with the strength of his compassion. I saw her look into his face, knowing what he was, and she quieted down like an obedient child, moved into the circle of his arms, offered him her neck, knowing she would, in all likelihood, die.

"He made her *want* it. I have never seen anyone do a thing like that in my life." She sighed. "Of course, that was all a very long time ago."

And you miss it, don't you. Tessa found she was trembling.

"Does it disturb you, hearing that story?" When Anastasia smiled, Tessa could see the tips of her fangs. Her voice dropped lower, became a sultry purr. "A girl from your background, with someone like Raphael Sinclair...I can imagine there must be something of a disconnect. So many differences...perhaps it is not of concern to you right now, but later on, they may come to haunt you, when these differences have grown from a minor inconvenience to a monster with nine heads. In my experience, it is always best to be honest and upfront from the beginning."

She shifted in her seat, reaching for a sheaf of manuscripts. Weak with relief, Tessa thought she was being dismissed. But no, Anastasia was merely switching the subject. "So," she said, flipping through a story titled, *Break Up or Make Up? 25 Signs That It's Time to Cut Him Loose.* "What is happening with our boy?"

"I don't know. We're not supposed to be seeing each other."

Anastasia nodded sagely. "He is so lost without you, so sad. I am getting worried. I haven't seen him in this kind of distress since...oh, since he lost Sofia and the little boy." She stared out the window. "He was never the same after Auschwitz. Something broke inside of him."

"Auschwitz?" Tessa repeated. Anastasia must be mistaken. She corrected her. "But he wasn't in Auschwitz. The train had already left."

Anastasia turned to look at her. "Of course he was in Auschwitz. Didn't he tell you?" The truth dawned on her in a slow, steady stream. An incredulous smile snaked up the sides of her red mouth.

Tessa paled. She shook her head in denial, kept shaking it. Anastasia was still talking, but it fell on deaf ears. She hadn't heard a word after *didn't he tell you?*

"Go home, my dear." Anastasia was saying, with a wave of her long, French-manicured fingernails. "You look tired. Don't worry. There will be plenty more xeroxing left for you tomorrow. And when you have a chance, do ask Raphael about the Angel of Healing."

Tessa felt sick; she went back to her desk and retrieved her coat, stood by the elevator and punched the buttons. After a moment, she decided to take the stairs. It was twenty-two flights to the ground level. But she had to get out of there before Anastasia came out of the office and started telling her more things she didn't want to hear.

The knock on the window came long after midnight. She thought she had dreamt it at first; she waited a moment, and there it was again.

Flinging the covers aside, she flew to the window. Rafe smiled when he saw her, laying his gloved hand flat on the windowpane. She spread her fingers over his on the cold glass. They both smiled, and then she went to the front door and buzzed him in.

There were no pleasantries this time. He strode into the apartment and swept her up in his arms, burying his face in her hair, holding her so tightly she couldn't breathe. She leapt on him like a cat, wrapping her legs tightly around his waist. He carried her to her room, as she covered his face in kisses and he struggled to free himself from his coat.

He kicked the door shut behind them, laid her down on the bed. With a single movement, he stripped her of her nightgown, and she lay there like a nude by Modigliani, blue in the moonlight, looking up at him.

"I've missed you so much," he said.

"Me too." she said.

"You heard what happened."

"Yes."

He sank onto the edge of the bed. "I'm falling apart, Tessa," he said. She couldn't see his face, hidden in shadow. "I think about you all the time. Whether I'm at a party flirting with strangers, or at a meeting with those wankers on the board, whoever it is, whoever I'm with, it's always you." To her astonishment, he was wiping his eyes with the back of his hand. "Every girl on Fifth Avenue carrying a portfolio, I think it's you. A girl laughs outside my window, and I think it's you. Each leaf I hear skittering across the pavement, I think it's you. Every barking dog, every creak in the floor, every ring of the phone, it's you, it's you, it's always you. Last night, when I saw that damned David with his arm around you..." his voice was breaking. "I'm afraid I'm losing you."

"Never," she said fiercely. She took him by the lapels, pulled him closer. "Do you hear me? *Never.*"

She rose to her knees, took off his hat, kissed his soft, sad mouth. At first he didn't respond, and then his hands moved, slipped down her sides. She unknotted his tie, pulled it free of his shirt. Quickly, she undid the buttons, pulled his shirt over his head. He fumbled with his trousers and let them slide to the floor.

For a moment he stood before her, nearly naked by the light of the moon. It picked out the rise and fall of his chest, the ripple of abdominal muscles, the tops of his hipbones; and then he was next to her under the blankets, drawing her close, and he could feel the sustaining touch of her heated body against his bare skin. When she raised her face to him for a kiss, he knew he had been wrong in ever doubting her. The inside of his head filled with warmth and light, and he began to move against her, and she against him, and the world was filled with their sounds, the rustle of sheets, the silky friction of skin against skin as their bodies came together.

She climbed on top, straddling him. She had never done that before, it was just like in his dream, her upturned breasts, the moonlight on her skin, the tips of her hair brushing his face, nothing between them but a pair of white satin shorts. He dug his fingers into her hips, slid his hands to her bottom, shaped like an upside-down heart.

"I want you," she whispered. "I'm ready."

With his thumbs, he smoothed the tumbled hair out of her face. "Are you sure?" he whispered back.

She nodded. With one continuous motion, as graceful as a ballet dancer, he rolled her over, and then he was kneeling between her knees. Her soft eyes held his, he could see that she meant it, he could smell the commingled scents of her desire and her fear. He brought his lips to her throat, kissed the place where her pulse pounded at the surface. Between them, the yellow ring revolved slowly on the chain around his neck.

A long time ago, another pale face, upturned in the dark.

With a strangled sound, he thrashed back the sheets and swung his legs over the side of the bed, bare feet thudding heavily against the floor.

"I have no right," he said, a cry of torment. "I have no right."

She rolled onto her side, placed a warm hand in the small of his back. He shuddered away from her touch.

"Is this about yesterday?" she asked, bewildered. "About what happened at the Met?"

He was pressing the heels of his hands into his eyes, as if he wanted to block something from his sight. "Not just yesterday," he said, his voice strung tight. "All my yesterdays."

She wanted desperately to help. "Does this have anything to do with..." she drew a shaky breath, "...something that happened in Auschwitz?"

He froze; then he turned slowly to face her.

"Who told you that?" he said. His eyes had changed, iced over, hard and pale. "Anastasia?"

She nodded.

"What else did she tell you?" His voice shifted now, ominous and low.

Now she felt fear. "She told me to ask you about the Angel of Healing," she whispered weakly.

He got out of bed, dressing hurriedly.

"What?" she said, panic tearing a new edge in her voice. "What happened? Where are you going?"

He stopped for a moment, gazed at her. Poor Tessa, sweet, lovely Tessa, sitting there in the dark, her hair wild around her face, blankets fallen around her waist, her eyes mirroring his anguish. He couldn't answer her, he could never answer her. The past had caught up with the present, and he couldn't stay here anymore.

He grabbed his coat and he was gone. She heard the door slam shut behind him, listened to the sound of his footsteps running down the empty street.

Across the street at St. Xavier's, one of the huddled shadows on the steps stirred, straightened up, and hailed a taxi going north up Sixth Avenue.

9

$\mathcal{T}$he rumors started the following morning. Geoff had been sacked, Tony had been sacked, Josephine had been sacked, Randy was on his way out. April was seen strutting around the hallway at Whit's side, dictating as he scribbled away on his clipboard.

"What's going on?" Tessa asked Portia. They were in the Anatomy room, waiting for Life Drawing to start, the animal skeletons encased in antique wood cabinets looking dolefully on the proceedings. Portia thought she looked tired. The skin under her eyes was a smudgy blue.

"Are you all right?"

Tessa grimaced. "I'm fine. But Rafe is coming apart."

"Rafe's been taking care of himself for a long time. It's you I'm worried about."

Graham came in, dropped his art box on the work table next to Portia. They both jumped. "Well, that's it, then."

"What?"

"Turner's set a date to vote on the future of the school. It's going to take place here, in the Cast Hall, at the end of the week. The board and the faculty all have a vote."

"What about us?" said David, puzzled. "The students? Don't we have a say? It's our school, too."

"Apparently not," said Graham.

"What about Rafe?" asked Ben, sanding his pencil to a fine point. "Where is he? Why is he letting this happen?"

"Well," said Graham, bending a look at Tessa. "As of this morning, it seems our Mr. Sinclair has been booted off the board for fraternizing with a student."

Tessa blushed a furious scarlet. "That can't be," she stuttered. "We broke up. We did exactly what Levon told us to do."

Graham looked more than a little pained. "Sorry, Tessa. Turner has pictures. Blesser knew this private investigator. Very artistic, incidentally, lots of atmospheric low lighting and grainy black-and-white."

Her blood ran cold. "How long?" She gripped the side of her work table to steady herself. "How long was he watching us?"

"According to the date stamps on the pictures," he said, "since the end of Winter Break."

"What does this mean?" Ben interrupted.

"Rafe's out," Graham said glumly. "Our quaint little *atelier* will cease to exist as we know it. The board has lost their faith in Rafe's ability to run the school. Without him, Whit has a free hand in hiring and firing. Seems like he's going to let go most of the teachers and replace them with April's emerging artist buddies. Starting next fall, we're going to be a groovy new boutique art school, something like Art Center in Pasadena. And the grant money will start rolling in. Or so says the word on the street."

"So it's over." David said incredulously.

Ben sighed. "It was always too good to be true."

"This isn't right." Harker struck the pick across his guitar strings, a harsh, discordant sound that bounced off the walls and echoed through the room. "There must be something we can do."

"This is outrageous," said Clayton indignantly. "I'd like to examine the evidence for myself. Now, where exactly are they keeping these pictures?"

No one wanted to look directly at Tessa, no one wanted to make her feel responsible, but as the conduit to the founder of the school, it was unavoidable. They turned to her for hope, for help, for an explanation.

Portia tried to draw attention away from her friend. She clearly had enough on her mind.

"Let's go talk to Levon," she said.

The call came at eight a.m. Rafe was in a deep sleep. It took him a moment to realize that the shrill ringing wasn't part of his dream.

"You'd better get down here," said Levon.

"It's been a rotten night, Levon," he said. "Can't it wait?" Then, with a sudden stab of dread. "It's not Tessa, is it?"

"No," said Levon. "It's not Tessa."

The hallways were deserted that time of day; the first class started at nine. Rafe found Levon's door wide open, his office oddly shrunken without his outsize presence.

Two doors further down was Whit's office. Rafe pushed open the door. The walls were neatly hung with Whit's paintings; sterile architectural renditions of plazas in Italy, or Spain, eerily devoid of human life. Painstakingly plotted landscapes, where nothing in nature seemed natural.

Whit was posed in front of his desk, legs crossed casually, humming to himself as he marked something off on his clipboard. Rafe was reminded of a patient spider at the center of an intricate web.

"I tried, Rafe," he said weightily, shaking his head. "I really tried."

Rafe looked to Levon for an explanation, but Levon seemed to be preoccupied with looking out the window at the wet gray morning.

With a look of grim satisfaction, Whit pushed a large manila envelope across the desktop. Rafe opened the flap and slid out the contents.

Grainy black-and-white photos, ten in all. Tessa getting out of the car in front of his house. Tessa kneeling between Rafe's knees as he sat on the bordello couch in her studio. Tessa's lovely bottom astride Rafe in her bedroom late last night, his hands around her waist, the photograph shot through a chink in her blinds. Rafe arched like a ballet dancer over her body, her hair flowing over the pillows. Rafe fleeing Tessa's building last night, the photo time-stamped 5:00 a.m.

It struck him that Whit had already seen the pictures, salivated over them, God knows what else. Rafe slid the photos back into the envelope.

"Sorry, Rafe," said Whit. A smile was breaking through his professionally somber expression. "As of now, you're out. I know what you're thinking; don't bother. The other board members have already seen the pictures. And let me tell you, they are very disappointed. They want you out with as little fuss as possible."

Rafe's head pulsed, ached. "Who's going to pay the teachers?" he demanded harshly. "Who's going to pay for the ventilation system? And the new boiler? Do you have any idea how much all those things cost?"

"It's not your business anymore, Rafe," Whit said smoothly. For the record, he assembled a look of bland sympathy. "Look. No one wanted this to work more than I did. All I wanted was for you to meet me halfway."

"No you didn't," said Rafe, gliding slowly towards him. "That's what you want everyone to believe. We were struggling along very nicely before Blesser filled your head with pictures of dancing grant checks he could procure if only we hired these teachers, or filled these ridiculous require-ments, or changed our program to fit whatever p.c. nonsense is being sold under the name of art this year. The minute Bernard promised fame and fatter paychecks, you were ready to sell your soul."

Whit crossed his arms, smiled blithely. He could afford to be gra-cious now, he was the victor. But something mean in him wanted to hold the cool, aristocratic founder's nose to the dirt and rub hard. "Look at the bright side, Rafe. You have no more obligations to meet. No more parties, no more galas, no more meetings. You have all the time in the world." He turned back to his desk to arrange some papers. "I hope she was worth it."

Levon didn't know how he did it, Rafe seemed to fly over the desk. He seized Turner by the neck, punched him full in the throat, once, twice. Then he let him sag to the floor and stood over him.

Turner curled into a ball, gagging, lying helplessly between Rafe's legs. Levon stared. Rafe's eyes shone white, like an icy pond. He had never seen anyone look like that before.

"Rafe," he said quietly. "Let him go."

The wolfish eyes turned to stare at him.

"Get out of here," said Levon.

The icy eyes flickered, went back to their usual cloudy, indistinct gray. With a swish of his coattails, he stepped over Turner's body and was gone.

Despite the sleet falling from the sky, Rafe strode forward, driven into the wind. He should never have started with Tessa, he saw that now. It had promised heartache and ruin from the beginning, and yet he had pursued it, grasped for it with both hands.

People brushed past him, leaving an unwelcome smear of their pas-sions across his soul. This one was in fear for his job. That one was lying to her lover. A third had let credit card debt pile up with no way of paying it down. Another had a lump that needed further testing.

As the afternoon slouched towards an equally dreary evening, he placed a call to the agency from a last anachronistic phone booth in Cooper Square. Janina was already waiting at his door by the time he got home, the hairs on her fox coat flattened by the wind. She stamped her stiletto-heeled feet on the pavement as he found his keys and opened the door.

There was no coy conversation. His fangs were bared, his irises were wide and glacial white as he flung her onto the carpet in front of the dead fireplace.

She laughed a little breathlessly, excited. She was wearing almost nothing beneath her fur, breasts nearly bursting from a ludicrously tiny bra. Sheer black stockings stopped halfway up her long lean thighs, attached to the skinny black straps of a barely-there garter belt. Laying back on the rich pile of her coat, knees apart, she waited for him.

"Ooh," she whispered, smiling. "Feisty."

With a roar, he was upon her. Crushing her under his weight, his teeth ripped into her throat, drawing great drafts from the taut artery beneath her jaw. She cried out, first with professional sounds of passion, and then in terror. She bucked her hips into the air, trying to throw him off, but he had the strength of ten men. When she slashed at his cheek with her teeth, clawed at him with her nails, he pinned her wrists over her head as easily if she were a little girl.

The wet sucking sounds went on for a long time. Long past the time that she had stopped moving.

Finally satiated, he raised his head. "God," he said, wiping his mouth. "Sorry about that, old girl. Been a rough week."

There was no response. He rolled her face towards him. The eyes were closed, the skin mottled and gray. "Oh, no," he whispered. "Oh, no no no." Frantically, he patted her face, her wrists, trying to restore circulation, trying to wake her. Panicking, he put his ear to her chest, over her heart. He was rewarded with a thin, thready heartbeat.

There was a phone on the table between the chairs. He leapt to his feet, dialed 911. When the operator answered, he hastily hung up the phone. He was Raphael Sinclair, millionaire philanthropist, for God's sake. How would it look to have a half-dead vampire hooker in his foyer? Ashamed of himself, he picked up the phone again. Suddenly he remembered something, opened his wallet, took out a card. *Drohobych Import Export,* it read. Underneath the regular number was an emergency number, and he dialed it now.

"Drohobych Import," droned the bored Russian voice.

"I need help," he said. He could hear his voice shaking. "My, ah, friend, is not waking up."

The voice was no longer bored. Within minutes, there was a cautious knock at his door. He opened it to two men in blue uniforms. They could have been plumbers, electricians, dishwasher repairmen. Behind them, idling on the street, was an unmarked van.

Together, the two men moved her onto a stretcher. One of them took her blood pressure, looked inside her eyelids, while the other slipped an oxygen mask onto her face and hooked her up to a tube that dripped a clear liquid into her arm.

Immensely sorry, Rafe touched Janina's cheek. Cold, colder than any live human being's cheek should be. "Is she going to be all right?"

The man administering the cuff wore glasses with black plastic frames. "We see this all the time," he said reassuringly. "Don't worry, she'll be fine." He glanced up from the dial. "You might want to change," he added, almost apologetically.

Rafe glanced down at his shirt. It was striped with blood.

They carried her down the steps to the unmarked van. The man with the glasses climbed into the back and shut the door, the other went into the passenger seat. The van pulled away from the curb, and zoomed off, heading northwest. A prickle of fear touched him, like a breeze. Rafe wondered where it was going; it was navigating away from both nearby Beth Israel and the emergency room at St. Vincent's.

The gaslights in front of the graceful nineteenth-century townhouses were just flickering on. Fuzzy catkins swelled on the magnolia trees in the gated park. Early snowdrops pushed their bowed heads up through the cracked crusts of ice holding out under the rhododendrons. Somewhere in the bushes, a bird twittered. Gramercy Park was beginning to wake from its bleak winter slumber.

Alone in his glorious mansion, Raphael Sinclair was afraid of sleep, afraid of dreaming again that he was being pursued through every floor of his lovely home before being torn to bloody bits and devoured by the shadowy child and his malevolent companions.

He knew of only one cure. Rafe threw on his overcoat, pulled the fedora low over his forehead and slipped off into the night.

"Wow," said Blesser. "Were there any witnesses?"

Slumped on a chair in Bernard's office, Whit was applying a bag of ice to a purplish mark swelling on his Adam's apple. "Levon says he was looking out the window when it happened," he replied hoarsely.

Blesser peered closer at the hematoma. "If he hit you any harder, he would have killed you."

Whit grimaced. "Maybe I should get a police order to keep him out of the building. He's dangerous."

"I don't think you can do that. He actually owns the building."

Whit looked gloomy. Blesser went to the door, peered up and down the hallway before quietly closing it and turning the lock. When he returned, he drew his chair close to the Chairman of the Painting Department.

"Look, Whit," he said. "The vote is in four days. What if Rafe shows up at the meeting to rally the troops? Most of the teachers are on his side. Geoff, Tony, Harvey, Ted, Randy, just to name a few. And though a lot of the board members claim to support us, it's not a lock. You know how it goes. When Raphael Sinclair speaks, people listen. By the time he's done giving his side of the story, I'll probably stand up and applaud, too."

"Maybe I should look into that police order."

"That'll end up in the papers." Blesser shook his head. "I don't think we want that kind of publicity."

There was something perpetually apologetic about Bernard Blesser. Meek, with thinning hair and a slight sloping belly, he had been with a small technical college in Maine before answering an ad the Academy had placed in the *New York Times*. Despite his mousy demeanor—he was partial to wearing nondescript brown suits set off by unfashionably wide blue ties—Whit found him to be a dogged ally in the battle to free the school of its dependence on its charismatic founder.

Bernard pulled his chair closer. "Look, Whit," he said cautiously. There was an undertone of something like apology in his voice. "We've all heard the rumors."

"What rumors?" Turner put his hand to his Adam's apple; it was feeling a little better now.

"You know. The vampire thing."

"Oh. That."

"You know, the way he looks at you...sometimes, even I believe it," said Blesser. "What if we..." He cleared his throat; he was playing with a coin, twiddling it back and forth between his fingers like a magician. "There's this store called Magikal Childe. Maybe you know it, Nineteenth Street between Fifth and Sixth. Full of skulls and jars and crystal balls and whatnot...I pass it every day on my way from the train. Today, I stopped in there on my way to work, told them I had a..." and here he paused out of sheer embarrassment, "...vampire situation. They mixed up some kind of potion." He held out a small brown glass bottle.

The bottle seemed to absorb all the light in the room. Whit offered a fleeting incredulous smile. "You can't be serious."

Bernard sighed, drummed his fingers on the desk. "I know. It's crazy. It's ridiculous. It's idiotic. It's laughable. But look at it this way; if he's not a vampire, all it will do is keep him in the bathroom for a few days. But if he really is a vampire, then..." he didn't finish the sentence.

Whit felt a whiff of unease. "This doesn't feel right, Bernard."

Blesser raised his hands. "You know, you're right. I don't even know why I stepped into that store. It probably wouldn't work anyway. Never mind. We'll just go to the meeting and hope for the best. Maybe Rafe will be feeling too humiliated to show up."

"No," said Turner glumly. "This school is his baby. He's not going to give it up without a fight, even if he has been thrown off the board. He'll be there."

For a moment, Turner thought about how good it felt to be walking through the hallways of the school with the glamorous April Huffman at his side, warmed by the thrilling possibility that he might exhibit his paintings alongside her celebrated artist friends. April had told him she liked his work; she said his canvases had a surreal, de Chirico-esque quality to them.

"Forget I said anything," said Bernard, getting up to leave. "It's probably just Ex-Lax, anyway."

Whit looked down at the bag of ice melting in his lap. It hurt to swallow. "All right," he said. "Go ahead. I just don't want to know anything about it."

10

At seven forty-five the following evening, they closed the May issue. To celebrate, Anastasia took the entire staff out for dinner. "Make reservations at Florent," she told Tessa. "I have heard so much about it."

At dinner, Tessa sat between Gaby and Ram. There were the usual Bellinis, appetizers, entrees, wine, molten chocolate cakes and cappuccinos, all paid for by the generosity of Agha Publishing. Tessa toyed with her food, pushed it around her plate. She had no appetite tonight.

Three more teachers had been given notice on Tuesday. The first-year students were panicking; the school they had signed up for was dissolving before their eyes, and it was already late to apply anywhere else for the following year.

When the students went see Levon, they found him sitting in his office, gazing absently out his window.

"You haven't been let go, have you?" Ben asked, worried.

He shook his head. "No, they made it very clear they want me to stay. Only black guy on the staff and all."

"What can we do to help?" Portia got right to the point.

"I'm not going to lie to you," said Levon evenly. "Raphael Sinclair is our only hope. If he shows up at the meeting, gives one of those rousing St. Crispin's Day speeches like the one he gave at the new student party, well...they stuck with him this far, I think they'll give him another chance."

He had turned to Tessa. "Is he up to it, Moss? What do you think?"

A waiter wearing a blond beehive wig and large breasts set a plate with rounded indentations in front of Ram. "I'll be right back with your salmon," he promised Tessa before scurrying off again.

Ram leaned forward, closed his eyes and inhaled.

"Snails again?"

"Oysters, honey. Want some?"

"No, thank you. If I was going to eat *traif,* it would have to be really special. A great big slab of Kobe beef at the Old Homestead Steakhouse, maybe. Followed by the cheesecake."

"Mmm," said Ram, twinkling at her. "Ever notice how Rafe rhymes with *traif?*" He leaned closer, his eyes twinkling. "Say, Crumpet. As long as we're in the neighborhood, let's hit the gay bars after dinner. I'll tell them you've just discovered you're a great big lesbian. We'll start with the Anvil. Then, maybe, the Glory Hole, the Spike. Followed by the Vault. We'll end the evening at the Mineshaft. Come on. It'll be fun."

"You're such a liar," said Gaby. To Tessa. "He's never been to those places. He's been with the same guy since high school."

"Really?" said Tessa, surprised and intrigued. "Is he a vampire too?"

Gaby paused in coaxing a mussel in her bouillabaisse out of its shell to stare at her like she was an idiot. "Of course not. He does window displays for Barney's."

"But...how can that be? Ram's a..." she lowered her voice, whispered. "...you know. Isn't he afraid that Ram will...um...hurt him?"

Gaby's short hair was lavender this week. Today it stood up in stiff spikes. She observed Tessa with wise brown eyes. "Ruben has stayed with him through all of it. You don't just leave someone you love because something bad happens to them."

At eleven, the cappuccinos drained, the wine drunk down to the dregs, the staff of *Anastasia* began to call for limos. As a temporary employee, Tessa was not eligible for a car.

"Walk with me," said Anastasia to Tessa. It was not a request. "It's lovely out."

Tessa had had a Bellini, a Kir Royal, and not much else; she was a little unsteady on her feet as they left the restaurant. Anastasia observed her gait, and smiled in amusement. *"Ma petite jeune fille.* Let me put you in a taxi." But the cobbled street was deserted. Looking around, Anastasia frowned. "Perhaps we should try Fourteenth Street."

Tessa could barely see the other woman's face in the dim light of the nineteenth-century streetlamps. The drinks had dulled her senses; it occurred to her that she should probably be frightened. An old townhouse stood sentry on the corner, the peeling brick facade almost hidden behind iron grillwork and skeletal wisteria vines. Blue light from a television set flickered behind closed shutters.

Tessa shuddered. "Who would want to live here?"

Anastasia smiled. "It's become quite popular among photographers. You see, there are no high buildings to block the light."

They came to a stop at the poorly lit heart of the Meatpacking District, where the arteries of Gansevoort, Little West Twelfth Street and Ninth Avenue intersected in a wide and crooked hub. The slush and sleet that had fallen from the sky earlier had moved eastward, leaving the old square Belgian blocks, laid in great arcing fan patterns, shining with a lacy pattern of frost. Transparent veils of clouds lingered overhead in a muzzy aura around a crescent moon.

Simultaneously, they both heard it; a cry, a tussle, the sound of a wooden crate being kicked aside. It seemed to be coming from an alleyway behind the restaurant.

"What was that?" said Anastasia, startled.

The alleyway was dark and enclosed on three sides, slasher-movie-scary in the stuttering light of a bare bulb fixed over a black metal door. A couple was embracing against a leprous brick wall, surrounded by overflowing dumpsters and empty wooden fruit crates. The woman was young, with long clean hair and a fine-boned profile that suggested a Connecticut upbringing and an Ivy League education.

"Is that Poppy?" Anastasia wondered. The beauty editor. She was moving and making sounds that could have been pleasure or a struggle, it was hard to tell which.

"Maybe she needs help," whispered Tessa doubtfully. There was no answer. When she turned around, she discovered that Anastasia was gone. Gathering up her courage, she edged forward.

The man was tall, well built, under his long overcoat. He wore a wide-brimmed felt hat over his light-colored hair. Tessa could not see his face, hidden as it was between Poppy's jaw and her neck, but when he raised his arm to pin the girl's hands against the wall, she could see a telltale flash of crimson silk from inside the jacket of his suit.

"Rafe?" she said.

He lifted his head, turned towards her. In the yellow light, the face was cruel, the cheekbones as sharp as edged weapons. His pupils telescoped down to pinpoints, then flared out again like the rays of the sun. Two triangular fangs gleamed, limned in blood. Frozen with horror, she watched him pass his sleeve across his mouth, wiping it clean. The whites of his eyes flamed a bloody red.

Quickly, she backed away. Rafe launched himself through the air like a leopard, landing on top of her, crushing her to the ground.

She lay perfectly still, paralyzed with fear. Underneath, she could feel the shattered wooden slats of a smashed orange crate poking into her sides and the wet cobblestones slowly soaking through her coat. She could smell the scent of the other woman's perfume on his clothes, and the rank coppery tang of blood on his mouth.

He crouched on top of her, his fingers digging into the flesh of her arms. Inches from her face, the ice-blue eyes bored into her as if she were a stranger. He lowered his head, sniffed at her as if he were a dog, inhaled sharply.

Suddenly, the face changed; the fangs receded up into the bloody mouth, the cold, wolfish eyes morphed back to their familiar shape and color. "Tessa?" he said in his lovely, lulling voice. "What are you doing here?"

"Anastasia," she managed to say. "Dinner. Florent."

Rafe pushed himself up off of her, helped her to her feet. There was a long moment where neither of them spoke. Then he glanced at the girl collapsed in a heap behind him. When he turned back to Tessa, she saw that his eyes had flamed red again.

"For God's sake, Tessa," he said. "Get out of here."

11

*A*t precisely twelve o'clock midnight, alone in her bedroom in the apartment on Sixteenth Street, the hairs on the back of Tessa Moss's neck began to tingle, then stood on end.

There was pounding at the door, *boom, boom, boom, boom, boom.* She hesitated for only a moment before flinging off the covers and going to answer it.

Rafe stood before her in his fedora and overcoat, penitent, sorrowful, beautiful.

"Tessa," he said, before running completely out of words.

He had waited a full fifteen minutes before mustering up the courage to knock, trying out different scenarios in his head. Tessa hurt. Tessa scared. Tessa angry. Tessa crying. And then the door swung open, and there she was, small, vulnerable, her hair in whorls around her face, wearing a floaty white nightgown thingy that made him sick with desire.

I'm sorry, he wanted to say, *Can you ever forgive me, you should never have seen that, I will never allow this to happen again, let's put this all behind us, let me make it up to you in a thousand ways, let me start here, now, like this, and this, and how do you like this,* and as he took a step forward into her apartment, he was bounced violently back, as if he had walked straight into a wall. His hat was knocked off with the force of it; it rolled to a stop at her feet.

"I've been to Magikal Childe," she said. "They told me what to say. You can't come in anymore."

"Magikal Childe?" he said, baffled. "On Nineteenth Street? I've passed that place a million times. What is it, anyway?"

"A witchcraft store," she said.

"Oh, come on, Tessa," he said. "You don't believe in that stuff."

"They sold me this," she said.

In her right hand, the small white hand that drew such beautiful pictures, the same hand that touched him with so much love, she held out a gnarled and twisted splint of wood. Foreign words were inscribed around the handle. At one end, it was engraved with a diamond pattern for a better grip. The other end tapered down to a sharp point. A stake.

"Tessa," he said again, hurt and bewilderment coloring his voice.

"Also, this," she said, showing him the small gun she held in her other hand.

"That won't do you much good against a vampire," he said.

"It has a silver bullet in it," she said. "In case you travel with a werewolf." She looked a little abashed. "Is Levon a werewolf?"

"No."

She set it down on the table. "Well. I'm out twenty-five dollars, then."

Minutes of silence stretched interminably on as they faced each other across the threshold, at a loss for what to say.

"So, they sell stakes at Magikal Childe?" he said, mainly to break the awful yawning silence.

"Oh, yeah, they had a whole boxful. It's made from some tree that only grows in the Carpathian Mountains."

"That makes sense," he said. "I bet you can get one in every souvenir shop in Romania."

"What do you think the words mean?"

"Um...my parents went to Transylvania and all I got was this lousy stake?"

She smiled. His heart lifted a little. "Tessa," he said. His voice was soft and yearning, suffused with apology. "Any chance I could come in? Can we at least talk about this?"

She shook her head no.

He sighed. "Well then. I guess I'd better be going." He passed his hand over his head. "Would you mind?"

Tessa stooped down, picked up his hat and gave it to him. As her arm crossed the threshold, he seized her wrist, yanking her through the doorway. She bounced against the opposite wall with the force of it, and then he had her, pinned against the cheap wooden paneling in the hallway.

"I believe this is the fellow with whom you have issues," he growled.

The angles of his cheekbones seemed higher and sharper in the light of the hallway. With growing horror, she stared up into his eyes, watched the whites turn a bloody red, the irises clear to a hue the color of ice. She realized she was still holding the stake, and she raised it now in a half-hearted attempt at self-defense. He bent his head, directed his attention towards it. When he spoke again, she could plainly see fangs.

"Of course, a weapon isn't going to do you any good unless you use it properly," he said harshly. He grabbed her wrist, flexed her arm up and positioned the stake so that it was pointing at his chest. "And, in all fairness, it doesn't actually work unless you put a little pressure on it." Savagely, he hauled at his tie, tore open his shirt. Tessa tried to squirm away, tried to let go, but he was relentless. "No no," he said firmly, training the tip of the stake against the scar over his heart. "You may as well kill me. I won't survive losing you."

He gritted his teeth and thrust himself onto the sharp point.

Explosive, blinding pain. It was as if a fire had erupted inside his chest. *The pain is your penance,* the old Archbishop had said.

"Oh," he said. His eyes flew wide; blood welled up, skidded down his chest. He swayed. Hastily dropping the stake, Tessa's arms went around him for support. Rafe keeled over, his hands over his heart.

"Are you all right?" she said, worried.

"God, that hurt," he said. "Let's never do that again."

She got him a wet dishtowel. While he pressed it to what should have been a minor puncture wound but was instead a wicked, star-shaped burn, she stood a safe distance away, watching; however, he noticed that she did not retreat to the sanctuary of her apartment.

The door of the building opened and closed, admitting another resident. In true New York fashion, he barely glanced at them as he passed between them, intent on reaching his own place down the hall. Tessa said nothing, let him pass without a word, and Rafe noticed that, too.

He handed her back the dishtowel, tried to button up his shirt, but it was useless, the buttons were missing. He gave up in frustration.

"So," he said. "Where do we go from here?"

"I don't know," she said.

He saw anger in her face, shock, and disappointment. Love, betrayal and hurt. What she had seen him do behind the restaurant had shattered something finite inside of her, and he saw now that it might not be possible to make whatever it had been whole again.

"What did you think I do at night, Tessa?" he said, suddenly bitter. "I'm a vampire. I live on blood."

"I knew that," she said. "I guess I thought you bought it or something."

"I do," he said. "I always pay for it. In one way or another. Or I take it from the willing; there are plenty of them, too. Those women mean nothing to me, Tessa. They're dinner, that's all."

She winced, turned her face sharply away from him. The wrong words. She put her hand to her forehead as if it ached. "Have you ever...um...tried anything else?"

"Like what? It's not like I can become a vegetarian."

"I don't know...animal blood? You can probably get that at a butcher, right?"

"I don't know," he said. "I've never really had to think about it before."

She sighed. Her shoulders slumped in defeat. "I don't think..." The angled eyebrows, so much like Sofia's that it hurt, danced together, danced apart. "I don't think I can do this anymore." She pulled herself away from the wall, retreating back towards the safety of her doorway.

Her words pierced his heart. Without her, he was lost. "Please, Tessa," he said. He opened his arms wide, pleading. "I wish I could take it all back, make it like it was before. But I can't. We can only go on from here. You can shut me out and find yourself another Lucian, or you can stay here, with me, and we figure this damned crazy thing out together." He saw her back stiffen; he had struck a nerve. His voice grew husky with longing. "Come on, sweet girl. Give me a chance to make this right. I'll do whatever it takes."

She turned on him, her eyes flashing with anger. "All right, then. Bite me."

He recoiled. "What?"

"Bite me," she said vehemently. "I'm a woman too, just like Poppy, just like all those other women. I want to know what it feels like. Bite me."

He shook his head, backing away from her. "No. No, that's not...that's not love, Tessa, it's something else..." he trailed off. He was thinking of

Janina on the stretcher, thinking of the endless parade of others he had left gray and mottled and lifeless in countless alleyways and doorways and piazzas and passages and courtyards all over Europe, a gray parade that stretched far beyond the horizon, and he involuntarily slid away from her, his back against the wall. "I might hurt you...no, Tessa, anything but that."

She strode purposefully across the corridor, unbuttoning the white floaty nightgown until it opened up, slipped down her shoulder, and she took his face in both of her hands and pulled it to her neck.

"Go on," she said fiercely. "You bite everyone else."

The blackberry scent of her perfume. The touch of his mouth against her soft white throat. The feel of her pulse beating beneath his lips.

In his ears, there was a roaring sound, like a hurricane, an avalanche, a forest fire. Shaking with desire, he pushed the hair from her neck. Grasping her shoulders, he pressed his fangs into a soft, throbbing place below her jaw, just breaking the skin. Blood welled up in two tiny puncture wounds. He put out his tongue, tasting the sweet, salty richness of her, and knew he had never loved anyone more.

Her body, moving in the circle of his arms. Her hands, moving over his chest. But something was wrong; she was pushing him off, wriggling away from him. Crying out in horror.

Rafe blinked, his reverie broken. No, it couldn't be. She couldn't judge him on that, it was too soon, she hadn't given it a fair chance. In an instant, his eyes switched back to normal, his fangs receded back into his jaw.

"Tessa?" he said, reaching out to touch her, to reassure himself.

But she stood just beyond his reach, her lovely breasts rising and falling under the nightgown with each breath. The look she bent on him was filled with disgust, not desire; he had miscalculated, it had been a terrible mistake.

She was so beautiful standing there, he thought reflectively, her face grave and pale, her wild hair a river of life, adjusting the nightgown that was falling so fetchingly down one shoulder. She was so beautiful to him as he was losing her forever.

In desperation, he tried once more. "Please, Tessa. Let's just go inside. I'll swear I'll make it up to you. I swear I'll—"

He faltered when he saw her stoop to pick up the stake. Pinching it gingerly between thumb and forefinger, she carried it to a chromed trashcan between the elevators, popped open the dome, and dropped it inside.

With that done, she returned to her doorway. "Please don't come back here anymore," she said. The door closed softly behind her. He could hear the tumblers click as she turned the key in the lock.

Midtown. The slumbering guard never noticed as Rafe slid past him and took the elevator up to the twenty-second floor.

At two in the morning, the lights were all off in the offices of *Anastasia* magazine. Rafe was guided down the corridor by the blue light of the computer monitors.

She sensed him long before she heard him. *"Quelle surprise!"* he heard her call cheerfully when he was still well outside her office. "Come in, my darling,"

Rafe swept in, shut the door behind him with a bang.

Seated behind her desk, she could smell his grief roiling the air before he entered the room. She came forward to greet him the French way, a controlled peck on each cheek, taller than him in her heels. She had dressed for the occasion in a floor-length strapless gown made from a raw silver silk that looked well in the light of the moon; her breasts rose round and full over the bodice that barely constrained them.

"She saw me," he said, his voice breaking. "Tessa saw me while I was… when I was in the middle of…" he couldn't finish the sentence. He threw himself into one of the chairs in front of her desk, covered his eyes with shaking hands.

She leaned over further, bringing her breasts that much closer to his face. The flames in her eyes leapt higher. "Tell me, my dear," she said confidentially. Her words poured over him like warm syrup. "Does she still love you, your little art student, now that she has seen what you really are?"

"I think I've lost her," he said, wiping his eyes with the heel of his hand. He heaved a ragged sigh, a deep, wet, painful sound. She laid long white fingers on his shoulder, glistening like bone.

"Why," he burst out. "Why did you take her there? You know I'm there all the time."

"So much *sturm und drang*," she cooed, sitting on the edge of her desk. "Why don't you just make her one of us and be done with it?"

He looked at her with real amazement. "We're damned, Anastasia, and it's got nothing to do with God, or hell, there's something wrong with us, something missing, something elemental. Something human. Look at you, your bloody magazine. You prey on women's insecurities, telling them they're not young enough, not pretty enough, not smart enough, not sexy enough for their man. Certainly not rich enough to buy the clothes in your fashion layouts.

"We don't create, we destroy. We stalk innocent human beings, sometimes for fun, sometimes to stay alive. Tell me, Anastasia, what is so fucking superior about that? Why on *earth* would I bequeath an eternity of that on anyone I loved?"

"And what is it about being mortal that is so damned noble?" she retorted. "Left to the fates, your little girlfriend will squeeze out a few paintings, marry that cute boy whom you hate so much, discover she does not have the *cojones* to make a living in art, move to the suburbs, surrender her freedom to a couple of squalling progeny. She will spend her days driving the squalling progeny back and forth from doctor appointments and soccer practices and obsess about what the neighbors think and whether the curtains match the couch. He will cheat on her with his students. She will worry about getting old and fat and gray and ordinary. And who knows what silent killers are lurking in her gene pool, just waiting for the right time to strike?

"We live above it all, above the strife and doubt and chaos of humanity, taking the best it has to offer in every generation." She smiled at him seductively. "Tell me, my darling. What could be better than that?"

Rafe looked out the window for a moment before answering. Blue and white and yellow lights from the building across the street spilled across his face, coloring it with regret.

"I would have liked the chance to drive my squalling progeny to soccer practice," he said wistfully. "And in her later years, if she asked me if I still loved her, even though she might be older and grayer and softer, this is what I would say: 'My own sweet girl, you are exactly the same today as you were the day I fell in love with you.'"

Anastasia stiffened, glided back behind her desk. She looked out her window at the skyscrapers, sparkling like jewels in the night.

"I took her to Florent," she said. "I sent Poppy to the back of the restaurant where I told her a car would be waiting, I directed our *petite jeune fille* to that little alleyway where I knew she would see you together."

Rafe stared at her in disbelief.

"I am so tired of all these lies. If you had been honest with each other from the start, none of this would have happened."

She leaned across her desk. Her big, round eyes bored into him.

"And let me tell you something else, my dear Raphael. As long as we are on the subject of honesty. If you hadn't been so busy playing house, you might have saved your precious Sofia. If you were so bent on getting her out of Poland, you should have started as soon as you found her. Why did you wait so long, anyway? Were you afraid she would leave you once she found out what you really were?"

With a roar, Rafe leapt to his feet, grabbed her around the throat with both hands, driving her backwards until she smacked against the window with an audible crack.

Behind her, the magnificent light show that was New York City after dark. Tall buildings lit up like Christmas trees, the great red and gold arteries that flowed from the South Street Seaport up past the George Washington Bridge, the bridges that joined Manhattan to the rest of the country. Stealing a glance at the pavement twenty-two stories below, Anastasia appeared to be frightened for a moment; then she opened her mouth and managed a merry laugh.

"What are you going to do, my dear?" she said, amused. "Throw me through a window? Imagine *that* splashed across the cover of the *New York Post!* How will that help your little art school?"

His eyes, gone glacial with fury, faded slowly back to a despondent gray. With a snarl, Rafe flung her down on the chaise lounge and stood over her. His hands balled slowly into fists.

Under the scrutiny of those eyes, the same beautiful eyes that had first attracted her attention so long ago, Anastasia felt triumphant. Right now, he looked like he wanted to kill her, and she liked that, she liked it very much. On the lounge, she propped herself up on her elbows, her knees parted, yards of raw silk hiked up around her hips. The fire in her eyes leapt higher. Her magnificent breasts trembled with excitement. The tip of her tongue moved in a greedy circle around her red lips.

"You're still sucking the life out of me," he said, as he stalked out of her office for the last time.

Driven, the wind lashing at his coattails, Raphael Sinclair made his solitary way towards Gramercy Park. An orange and white smokestack loomed up from the middle of the tarmac, spewing clouds of sewer steam into the air, obscuring the street. He could have taken one of the numerous yellow cabs trolling down Fifth Avenue, but he couldn't wait, he couldn't sit still, he had to keep moving.

With one broad brushstroke, he'd lost all the things that mattered to him most. His beloved school, his nicely ordered life. Tessa. As his mind raced over the details again and again, he thought of how little effort it would have taken to do things right; made the time to get to this meeting; stroked that donor's ego; made a discreet donation to a patron's favorite charity; taken a certain well-heeled dowager out for dinner. Listened to Giselle. Heeded Levon's warnings, one by one.

The only thing he wouldn't have changed was the girl. She made his long and empty life worth living again, for a little while.

He turned down Twenty-first Street, past the fence standing sentry over Gramercy Park. Home was right ahead of him now, a home filled with masterpieces, with burnished woodwork, original fireplaces, fretwork and moldings. A spectacular showpiece of a home, but hollow at its heart, with a hollow man holed up inside.

As he drew closer, he noticed that someone was waiting for him under the portico, a girl, thin, with long hair, and his heart gave a little leap.

"Tessa?" he called hopefully.

The girl poked her head between the columns of the portico. "Hi, Mr. Sinclair," she said.

His heart fell. He trudged up the stairs to the entryway, took the key out of his pocket. "Hello, Allison," he said, struggling at polite conversation. "Isn't it a bit late for you to be out?" He glanced at his watch. It was just turning four o'clock.

"Oh...I've been having a hard time sleeping," she said. She was thinner and paler than he remembered, her eyes sadder, her shapeless mouth more desperate. She looked more like a vampire than he did.

"Are you feeling all right?" he asked her.

"I hate my life, Mr. Sinclair," she said, the words tumbling out of her. "I don't have any friends here. I'm always behind with my schoolwork. I can't seem to catch up. And I just found out I'm failing two classes."

He put the key in the wrought iron grill, turned the knob. Tried to summon up the proper things to say. "You do have a lot going on. Have you tried talking to your parents?"

"My parents are divorced. I can't reach my mom. She's on a cruise with her boyfriend in the Galapagos Islands."

"What about Levon?"

She looked gloomy. "He says I should work harder and stop going to clubs every night."

The grill was open. He inserted the key in the inner door, turned the tumblers in the old brass lock. "Sounds like good advice."

"Do you remember my boyfriend? You might have seen him at the Naked Masquerade."

Rafe tried to remember back to Halloween night. Allison, coming to tell him that Giselle was looking for him. Behind her, a first-year student, from Germany, maybe. Tessa, in a black crinoline skirt and a lacy black camisole.

"Yes, I remember," he said, rubbing at a place between his eyes.

"He dumped me," she said. Tears were brimming in her helpless brown eyes.

"Look, Allison, it's very late," he said gently, patting her arm. "Everything seems worse at night. Why don't you go home. You'll see. It will all look better in the morning."

"I want to be like you, Mr. Sinclair," she said. Suddenly, words were pouring out of her. "I saw what you did to that guy at the Met. I saw you change. I know what you are. Please. Make me like you."

"No," he said, but it was late, he was tired, he had nothing left to give, he said it without conviction. "You don't know what you're saying. You don't want to be like me, Allison."

"I do," she said fervently, drawing closer.

Her desperation swirled patterns in the air around him. Her coat was open, exposing a length of white neck. She was wearing a velvet lace-up camisole she must have gotten at one of the stores that sold Goth clothing on St. Mark's Place. She looked up at him, her eyes wide and wet and imploring. "I don't want to feel these bad feelings anymore, ever again," she said, her shapeless mouth contorting with sorrow, tears running down her face.

The hour was late, he was sick at heart, and what he really wanted to do was get into bed, pull the covers over his head and sleep forever. He knew exactly how she felt. He was overcome by a strange pity; why not just give the girl what she wanted?

Rafe put his hands around her small waist, leaned over. She stood on her tiptoes, stretching out her neck, long, longer. He pushed her hair aside, feeling for the artery, and then he put his mouth to her throat and bit down.

He felt her nails dig into his arms, and she jerked, just a little. He bore down harder, and blood rose into his mouth. If he closed his eyes, she could be anyone.

There was a bitter, herbal aftertaste. Suddenly, he was revolted. *For God's sake, one of my students. What the hell am I doing?*

He stepped back, releasing her. Startled, she looked at him for an explanation.

"Go home, Allison," he said, looking down into her eyes. "This is not the solution to your problems."

She protested, she wept, she swore it was all she ever wanted, but she came around to his way of thinking once he had her safely under his thrall. He put her in a taxi, waited at the curb until it rounded the corner on its way to some address in the East Village.

There was a stiff breeze blowing across the park. Rafe shivered. Alone, he turned to mount the stone steps of his palatial mansion.

He felt queasy, as if something he'd eaten disagreed with him. He frowned, put a hand to his stomach. In all his years as a vampire, this had never happened before. A wave of nausea followed, stronger this time. Then came the pain.

A passerby might have noticed an elegant, well-dressed man in an overcoat and a fedora pause at the curb, a look of concern creasing his handsome face. Perhaps the passerby would have seen him lay a gloved hand across his abdomen and fold neatly in half, almost apologetic at the scene he was making.

Something was terribly wrong; inside him, something vital was oozing, putrefying, slipping. Right away, he knew that he had very little time. *Not going to die in the street this time.*

Already weakening, he gripped the balustrade and hauled himself up the stone steps. He just made it through the front door.

Great, gushing fountains of blood erupted from his mouth, splattering the Venice plaster walls of the entryway. Blood spattered the cherubs flanking the fireplace, the graceful columns, the leather Morris chairs. He retched again and blood sprayed the quartersawn oak table, a vase of apple blossoms, the lamp with the mica shade made by a famous Arts and Crafts coppersmith. Blood jetted forth in a slippery river across the veined marble floor. A fine pattern of scarlet spots dotted the framed drawing of the mother and child.

His vision fogged with pain, Rafe stumbled forward, scrabbling at the walls and furniture for support. His stomach heaved again and again, washing the foyer in fresh bursts of gore. In a brief moment of clarity, he wondered at the quantity; he didn't think he'd drunk that much blood in his entire life.

He made it as far as the sculptured angel, her arms open wide in welcome, before collapsing at her cold marble feet.

12

*T*essa didn't go to school the next day, or the day after that. She stayed in bed, her arms wrapped around her knees, fearful of leaving the apartment, fearful she would find him waiting for her.

Ram called, wanting to know where she was. Anastasia was concerned, Leo was snappish and irritable without her. She told him she had class, she had to work on her thesis project, she had a bad cold, anything to get him off the phone. There was a silence at the other end of the line, and then Ram said cautiously, "Is this about Rafe?"

She fell asleep shortly before dawn.

By the time she awoke, it was nearly noon. Tessa peered through the blinds to find a day that was bright and cold. She stole a peek at the steps of St. Xavier, half-expecting to find Rafe sitting there holding vigil, but today they were just steps, polished by the shoe leather of decades of the church-going penitent, shining in the late-winter sun. She was beginning to feel a little better. Perhaps she would go in to her studio today.

The doorbell rang. Frantic, she clutched at the blankets. Footsteps echoed through the hallway, followed by a knock at her door. She was embarrassed to find that her voice quavered when she asked who was there.

"Tessa?"

Portia's voice, sounding concerned. Relieved, Tessa opened the latch and let them in. Behind her, Graham, Harker, Gracie, Clayton, Ben and David stomped in like elephants. They helped themselves to her cereal while she pulled on her jeans.

"Where have you been, girlfriend? We haven't seen you in days. We were starting to worry."

"She was worried," said Clayton, tipping the last of Tessa's box of Life cereal into a bowl. "Me and some of the boys here kinda figured that you and Mr. Sinclair were hooked up somewhere, riding each other like wild pink ponies."

"Clayton," said Ben sternly, glaring at him. "We hate to bother you with this, Tessa," he said mildly.

A flutter of fear. "If it's about Rafe, I can't help you."

"Why?" said Portia, narrowing her eyes. She put her hands on her hips, looking suspicious. "I had a feeling. What happened?"

"Let's just say, it's over."

The students glanced at each other. "Well," said Harker. "We're screwed, then."

Graham popped a handful of Captain Crunch into his mouth. "You remember what Levon said, Rafe's our only hope. Well. No one can reach him. He isn't answering his phone, he's not calling into the office. This is the time to rant and rave and conspire. And no one's seen or heard from him in three days."

"We were kind of hoping we would find him here," said Gracie sheepishly. "Now that he's not on the board anymore, we thought, you know, maybe you two..."

"What happened, Tess?" David finally spoke.

Involuntarily, Tessa's hand rose to her neck. She forced it back down, trapping her hands between her knees. "I caught him...I saw him..." Unwelcome visions of Rafe embracing Poppy in the alleyway, of Rafe lying on top of her with fangs bared, his eyes fierce and bloody, unrecognizable. Tears teetered at the edge of her lashes. She dashed them angrily away. "It doesn't matter. You were right about some things, okay? Let's leave it at that."

The students looked warily at each other. Ben spoke first. "We need your help, Tess." he said, spreading his broad sculptor's hands wide. "We need you to talk to him. If he doesn't address the assembly tomorrow, the school as we know it will cease to exist, except as a footnote along the way to the death of art."

"Look," said Graham. "I don't know what happened between the two of you. And, for the record, I don't give a damn. If he's just sulking, we need you to work some magic on him. He's got to be at that meeting."

"You don't have to do it alone," said Harker. "We'll go with you."

Tessa, wanting very much to say no, looked to Portia for support. But her chin was up, she was pulling her hair back into a tight bun, fighting mode. This was beyond hurt feelings, beyond petty emotion. She was a Ballard, after all.

"In every city in all the world," said Portia, slowly but firmly, "there is someone like us, someone who doesn't quite fit in. Someone who sees things a little differently than everyone around them. Someone who has the ability to do things that other people don't understand.

"This school is the only place on the planet where those people can come together; to become the next da Vinci, to become the next Michelangelo, to become the next Lucian Freud.

"It's not just about us, it's not just about now," she said. "It's about the future of art."

Tessa was pale, as silent as death, her hands still trapped between her knees. Suddenly she rose, went to her art box, rummaged around till she found a yellow number 2 pencil. From the table, she took a pad of paper. With the tools of her trade in her hands, she could think.

"Where there is no choice," she said. "There is no fear."

13

$\mathcal{T}$hey walked. Though in reality, Gramercy Park was a scant fifteen minutes from her apartment, it felt like forever. As they drew closer to his home, as it took up more and more space in her field of vision, Tessa trembled. Never had the townhouse seemed more imposing, the brownstone darker, the knotted and gnarled wisteria vines more threatening. The gray and skeletal branches of the bare, mottled trees seemed to be reaching for her.

Ben mounted to the top of the steps while the others remained clustered on the sidewalk. Mail stuck out of the slot, more was piled up on the landing. A couple of forlorn copies of the *New York Times* lay on the welcome mat, yesterday's news, unopened.

"Maybe he's away," suggested Tessa hopefully.

He rang the doorbell. She could hear it chime faintly within, and her heart beat faster. But there was no electronic buzz from the speaker box, no answering footsteps. Apparently, no one was home.

"Maybe it's open," said Gracie.

Ben pushed the handle of the wrought iron gate. It clicked open at his touch. Turning around, he raised his eyebrows.

"Try the door," Portia called up to him.

He put his hand on the doorknob; the heavy wooden door swung open.

They saw him take a step forward, calling out, "Mr. Sinclair?" And then he stopped cold, involuntarily putting his hand to his mouth.

"What?" said Portia. "What is it?"

Ben turned slowly around. Looked directly at Tessa.

"Tessa," he said. "Stay there. I don't think you want to see this."

She bolted up the stairs.

The lights were off; something dark stained the walls in great brown fan patterns. There was a pungent odor, like the rank stink given off by a package of hamburger she had left too long in the back of the refrigerator once.

David found the light switch and turned it on. There was a collective gasp. The pattern writhing across the walls was painted in blood.

Only Tessa moved, picking her way through the long entryway, avoiding the pools of gore checkering the marble floor. She noted the blood drying on the chairs grouped before the fireplace, blood spotting the lampshades, freckling the petals of the flowers in a vase. Glancing up, she saw that there was blood on the ceiling. "Oh, God," someone was repeating behind her. "Oh, God. Oh, God. Oh, God."

At the far end of the room, before the curved double stairs, a heap of bloodied clothing lay near the pedestal of the sculptured angel.

"Don't, Tessa," said Ben.

"Please, Tess," said David, catching her arm. "Come back outside. Let's just call the police."

Tessa shook herself free, moved deeper into the hall. As she drew closer to it, the heap of clothing began to assume the shape of a man. She stopped. At her feet was a gray fedora, upside down in a crimson puddle. Her heart began to knock painfully against her chest.

Rafe lay curled in a fetal position on the floor, painted in blood from his head down to his shoes. His eyes were closed. He had obviously been there for some time.

"Oh, God," she whispered, a sob, a prayer, as she went down on her knees.

He was cold to the touch. Taking hold of his arms, she turned him on his back. Gently, she stroked the hair off his forehead. It was stiff with congealed blood.

"Come away, Tessa," said Portia, touching her on the shoulder.

She opened his coat, his jacket, looking for she knew not what, a stake, a wound, anything that would explain the carnage around her. But she could find nothing amiss; she cradled his head in her lap, took his face in her hands, and kissed the cold lips.

He stirred, mumbled something, turned on his side. She drew back in shock. A clear red liquid dribbled out of the side of his mouth, and then he rolled over and retched, splattering her with gore.

His eyes flickered open, focused on her. She tried to wipe his face with a corner of her shirt.

"What happened?" she asked urgently. "Who did this to you?"

"Tessa?" he said. He blinked once, twice, and then his eyes slowly closed again. "Thank God," he whispered. "Thank God."

The sculptors carried him up the stairs, Ben taking his arms, Clayton his legs. They laid him gently in the guestroom bathtub on the main floor. As the old fashioned claw-footed tub filled with warm water, they undressed him, using scissors to cut off his shirt, his trousers, looking for telltale wounds, signs of a struggle. Finding none, they withdrew, leaving her alone with him.

As she washed him, the clear greenish water turned a brackish red. Blood had seeped everywhere; into his armpits, the hair on his chest, in his eyelashes, between his toes. At the sight of the star-shaped scar over his heart, the hand holding the washcloth faltered. Once or twice his eyes cracked open, and he smiled at her like a sleepy child before falling unconscious again.

They lifted him out, dried him off, put him in bed. He was as pale as the sheets he lay on. Instead of burning with fever, like an ordinary human being, his temperature plummeted, grew colder.

He must have been in pain; he moaned in his sleep. He couldn't bear to have clothing touching his skin. After he ripped pajamas from his body for a third time, they gave up trying to dress him. In his dream, the shadowy child and his compatriots had their teeth in him, and they were tearing him to pieces.

The art students tiptoed around them. Tessa didn't stir from his bedside, her eyes fixed on him as if she could will his recovery, pressing his cold fingers between both of her hands. Occasionally, she would lean forward to touch his face; he would open his eyes to reassure himself that she was really there.

Portia came in, put a hand on her shoulder. "Why don't you take a minute to clean yourself up a bit," she said softly.

Tessa glanced uncomprehendingly at her shirt. She looked like an extra from *The Texas Chainsaw Massacre.*

In the bathroom, she pulled her sweater up over her head. Catching a glimpse of herself in the mirror, she leaned closer. The scared little girl who had crawled out of bed at noon to peer fearfully through the venetian blinds had vanished. In the crucible of the past few hours, some element in her had changed, hardened. That girl was gone.

At the sound of her footsteps, his eyes flew open. She took his hand, conjured up a smile. "You're looking better. How do you feel?"

"I think I'm dying."

Her bravado crumpled. It was a moment before she could speak again. "All those things I said to you..."

He shook his head, impatient with her apology. A shock of pain accompanied his movements. He shut his eyes until it passed.

"Where did you go after you left my apartment?"

"Anastasia's office. Almost sent her flying through those great bloody windows. She set the whole thing up, you know; she wanted you to see me like that."

"She thinks we should be more honest with each other."

"She did say something to that effect."

Shakily, he pushed himself up, bending over the side of the bed. She held the bucket for him. When he was done, he fell back onto the pillows.

"I went home. Someone was waiting for me. I thought it was you." He closed his eyes. "First-year student. Allison something."

Tessa frowned. "What did she want?"

"She hates her life. She wants to be a vampire."

"What did you do?"

He opened his eyes, looked directly at her. "I bit her," he said. "And then I came to my senses and put her in a taxi."

Tessa sighed, put a weary hand to her forehead. His hand crept over the blankets, seeking hers. She took it, laced her fingers through his. They were as cold as ice.

"Go home, Tessa." His voice was growing thin, beginning to fail. "Haven't you heard? You'll be better off without me."

"My place," she said, "Is here. With you." Her words crackled with fierce energy. "We need you. I need you. Your *school* needs you."

He turned his face to the wall. "It's not my school anymore," he breathed, and then his eyelids fluttered closed again.

Tessa slumped down on one of the Stickley couches in the Great Room. "How is he?" Portia said.

"He's dying." she replied.

"We should be dialing 911," said David.

"And tell them what?" Graham drawled. "Send an ambulance quick, we have a sick vampire?"

Goosebumps prickled up and down Tessa's arms, raced along her spine. Anastasia swept through the doorway, magisterial in the orange silk domino she had worn to April's gallery opening.

Ignoring the art students gaping at her from the couch, she addressed Tessa. "What has happened to our Raphael?" she said, whipping off the dark glasses.

She couldn't bring herself to say the words. It didn't matter, anyhow; Anastasia had tasted the measure of her fear before she'd walked through the door. Tessa saw her steel herself, straighten her shoulders; with a rustle of fine fabric, she glided past her into the guest room, volumes of silk ballooning out behind her.

"How are you, *mon ami?*" she said brightly, bending over him.

At the sound of her voice, his eyes sprang open. "I've been better," he replied, with a trace of boyish pugnacity.

"Get well soon," she warned him. "Or Ram will rob you blind. He has an eye on your pie safe."

"That poser," he mumbled. His eyes closed again.

Dropping the light-hearted facade, she turned to Tessa. "Who did this to him?" she said. In her expression was anger blended with curiosity.

"We don't know," she replied.

Anastasia bent over and kissed the point where his hair met his forehead, held his face in her black-gloved hands, pressed her cheek against his. *"Bon nuit, mon petit artiste,"* she heard her murmur as she stroked the hair back from his forehead. "I hope they are kind to you, wherever you are going."

"He's not going anywhere," said Tessa flatly, her arms folded defiantly over her chest.

Anastasia focused her attention on her now, drawing closer. With the hood framing her dramatic face, she had never seemed taller or more imposing. The flames in her eyes leapt and churned. "So. Now you have seen what he really is. And you still love him."

"Yes," she said. "Now I know what he struggles with, every day. If anything, I love him more."

She pursed her dragon-red lips. "Well! Who would have thought. You seemed like such an ordinary sort of girl. I thought for sure you would run from it. I don't suppose you are coming back to work."

Tessa shook her head no. Anastasia shrugged, one Gallic lift of the shoulders. *"Bonne chance,* then, *ma petite jeune fille.* If you ever need anything, you know where to find us." With a flutter of orange silk, she was gone.

She found the artists in the kitchen. They were going through the cabinets, the refrigerator, searching for something to eat. Graham had discovered that there were only two items in the refrigerator, a carton of Tropicana that had just passed the sell-by date and a desiccated lime. So far, Clayton was the big winner, with a box of Carr's water crackers; then Gracie hit the jackpot, finding an unopened package of Chips Ahoy in a drawer.

"Say, is she a—" Graham left the end of the sentence dangling.

"Yes." Tessa said shortly.

"We've been cleaning up the entryway," said Ben, sounding distant, removed. "We filled ten of those big black leaf-and-garden bags with bloody paper towels. Bounty really is the quicker picker upper."

"That was the worst thing I've ever seen," said Harker. "And I've worked in a slaughterhouse." As he rolled another one of his cigarettes. Tessa could see that his hands were shaking.

"Who would hate him enough to do this?" Portia wondered.

"A lot of people, I'll bet," said David.

"Angry ex-girlfriend?" suggested Gracie.

"Vampire hunters?" Clayton guessed.

"Someone who really doesn't want him at that meeting," said Graham.

Tessa shook her head wearily, massaged her forehead. Every time she closed her eyes, pictures flashed on the back of her retina, pictures she'd rather forget. Rafe, poised over Poppy behind the restaurant. Rafe, his fangs bared, crushing her to the pavement. Rafe, drenched in blood, motionless beneath the white marble angel. Rafe, his arms open wide, begging for another chance.

Harker prowled through the Great Room, looking for something, opening and closing the highly polished cabinet doors. Hidden inside a handsome Arts and Crafts hutch, he found a state-of-the art stereo system.

He punched a few buttons. The house seemed to levitate off its foundations; their hearts reverberated with the ominous cartwheeling synthesizer chords of Pink Floyd's *Comfortably Numb*, pounding through the speakers.

"Hey," said Harker. "He's been listening to my mix tape."

They all felt it at once, an electric sizzle in the air. Rafe was standing in the entryway, wearing only a pair of striped pajama bottoms. His eyes had gone that frightening hue, like scratched glass, burning, feverish.

"What are you doing out here?" he shouted, his voice raspy and raw. "Get back into the cellar! *They'll see you!*"

He bounded towards her, moving like a jungle cat; they had never in their lives seen anyone move that fast. Launching himself through the air, he tackled her to the ground before Ben and Clayton were able to get to their feet. Crouching over her, he stared at them with frightened, smoky eyes; and then he passed out.

They decided to move him to a couch in the Great Room. He seemed to be more comfortable there, nearer to them, to the artifacts of his life. The light bothered him; they dimmed the chandeliers and the Tiffany lamps while Tessa shielded his eyes with her hand. Shadows danced. Gloom gathered in every corner.

"What the hell was that," said Ben.

"Okay, I believe," said David.

Preoccupied with tucking the covers around his shivering body, Tessa heard nothing but the rattle of Rafe's chattering teeth.

"There's gotta be something we can do," Clayton struck his knee with a meaty fist. "This can't be the way it all goes down."

"Hey," said Harker. "How about Magikal Childe? Katie says her boss has millions of books on the occult, a whole library. There's got to be something there about sick vampires."

"They can't possibly be open this late," said David.

Harker shrugged his thin shoulders. "Katie says they keep crazy hours. A lot of their clientele is only up at night."

"I'm out," said Clayton. "I'm not going anywhere that caters to the dark arts after midnight. I admit it. I'm just flat-out scared."

"I'll go," said Harker. "I gotta get rocking, anyway. Death Monkeys got a late gig at CBGB's."

"I'll go with you," said Portia. "Tessa, you stay here in case Rafe wakes up."

"No, " said Tessa. "I can't sit still. If there's anything we can do, I want to be the first to know."

She pulled on her coat, slung her knapsack over her shoulder. At the door, she looked wistfully back at the others. She was afraid of what she might find when she returned.

"Don't worry," said Portia, reading her thoughts. "I know where to find you if there's any change. Now *go.* "

The storefront was nondescript. *Magikal Childe,* the sign said in medieval script. The display window featured a dusty signed copy of *Lord of the Rings,* Viking runes inscribed on ivory tablets spilling out of a wine-colored velvet bag, a crystal gazing ball, a kitschy cut-glass dragon, a mug with a wizard's face on it.

Tessa pushed open the door, passed a bulletin board hung with flyers. *Wiccan picnic scheduled for April 11 at Strawberry Fields. Rain date, April 18,* said one. *New Necromancy Group forming,* said another. *If interested, call Todd at 718-867-5309 after 5 p.m. No Weirdos!*

Harker was already inside, conferring with a balding man in round rimless glasses behind the counter. Tessa made her way through the rabbit warren of glass display cases filled with jeweled skulls and magic wands.

The walls were painted black and lined with shelves from floor to ceiling, a very high ceiling, also painted black. Crowding the shelves were wide-mouthed apothecary jars, exhibiting various quantities of many-colored powders. A rolling ladder stood ready to assist with the items on the higher shelves.

Some sounded harmless; white sage, yarrow, chamomile, lavender, hibiscus, frankincense and myrrh. Then there were the others, labeled *Croatian Mugwort, Carpathian Wormwood, Bat's Head Root, Midnight Mandrake Root, Cat's Eye, Calf Hoof, St. John's Wort.* Passing a half-empty jar with a metal scoop inside, Tessa saw that it contained dried newts.

"Arnie, you remember Tessa," Harker was saying to the middle-aged man behind the counter.

"Sure, I remember," he said. "Vampire situation. Man, look at all that hair! Are you sure you're not Wiccan?"

"Orthodox Jew, actually," said Harker.

"No way," said Arnie, perking up. "My grandparents were orthodox. Anyway. How'd the vampire thing go for you?"

"The hex worked," she said. "He couldn't come in."

"Cool," he said.

"That's kind of why we're here," said Harker. "We've got a sick vampire."

"Really," said Arnie. "And you came here instead of taking him to, say, a doctor?"

"I don't think a doctor can do much for him," said Harker. "He's, well, you know, undead."

Arnie had a particular expression, one he reserved for dilettantes and weepy college girls, and he was directing it towards them now. "There are a lot of people in New York who call themselves vampires. How do you know he's for real?"

"Harker said you have a lot of books on the occult," said Tessa. "Look up 'The Angel of Healing.'"

Arnie disappeared into the back, returned with a large and dusty volume bound in stained brown leather. He cracked it open, ran a bony forefinger down a long column of words while muttering to himself.

Suddenly he stopped, tilted his head. The light reflected off his glasses, turning them opaque. "The Angel of Healing? You're kidding. He's your vampire?" She nodded. His eyebrows shot up. He looked back down at the book. "Wow."

"What's it say?"

He put his finger on the text, read out loud. "Angel of Healing. Born Raphael Sinclair, UK, 1909. Active since 1939. Known to have operated in Auschwitz, Poland, from 1943-1944. Possibly resurfaced in Marrakech in 1945. Last known whereabouts, New York City."

"Whoa," said Harker. Even his tattoos paled a little.

He put the book down. "The same Raphael Sinclair who's always on Page Six?"

"That's him."

"Huh," said Arnie. "Just goes to show you. You never know. Sick, how?"

Glancing at Tessa, Harker related the details. Arnie frowned. "Hm. Let me ask Laurie."

Laurie was a girl with a plain oval face and long brown hair, not the sort of person you'd associate with a store catering to the occult. She was presently with a customer, scooping powders out of jars and shaking them into small plastic bags. When she was finished, she joined them in the back, holding a ledger.

"You know, I mixed up something for a guy earlier this week," she said. "He said he was having some kind of vampire trouble. I offered him a stake, but he wasn't interested."

The words struck at Tessa's heart. "What was in it?" she said.

"Ex-Lax," said Laurie. "Also, tincture of wormwood. It's not harmful to humans, aids in the digestion, actually, but it's deadly to vampires."

Harker frowned. "How would you get a vampire to drink a solution of Ex-Lax and wormwood?"

"Well," said Laurie. "I guess you could slip it into his drink while he wasn't looking."

Arnie bent a scornful look at her. "What, like when you're standing next to him at the bar at CBGB's?" He turned to the art students. "You get some pretty girl to drink it. And then you get your vampire to drink from the pretty girl."

"What did this guy look like?"

The girl shrugged. "I don't know. Short. Tubby. Losing his hair. I couldn't pick him out in a lineup."

"Well, that only describes half the men in New York City," said Arnie. "Including me."

"Is there any cure?" Tessa said quickly. "An antidote?"

Arnie rolled the ladder to a shelf high above the counter. Climbing to the top, he reached into a bookcase, pulled out a book with a red leather cover. He thumbed through the yellowing pages, then ran his forefinger along a paragraph printed in tiny type. And stopped.

"You really care for this vampire?" he said to her, pushing his glasses down the bridge of his nose and looking at her.

"Yes," said Tessa fervently.

"Then go home," said Arnie. "Spend some time with him."

"What do you mean?" she said wildly. "What does it say?"

"It says," he said, "that the only cure for a vampire poisoned with wormwood is the heart's blood of a virgin."

He shut the book with a bang. Dust rose from its yellow pages. "Heart's blood of a dragon, I can get," he said. "But where are you going to find a virgin in New York City?"

"Oh, good, you're back," said Portia. She looked exhausted. Three blots of blood the size of a quarter stained her blue chambray shirtfront. "He was asking for you."

Tessa threw her bag and coat down on a chair, went to him.

He lay on his back, his eyes closed. His hands were outside the blankets, waxy and still. At Tessa's approach, he struggled to sit up, and failed. She gave him some water; he drank it gratefully, only to retch it back up a few minutes later. He lay back on the pillow, drained. Turning his head to look out the window took everything he had.

"What day is it?"

"Thursday," she said. "The big vote is tomorrow morning. Eight sharp."

He nodded, but his mind was elsewhere.

"Look," she said firmly. "You've got to get better. Turner has been letting all the teachers go and replacing them with April's friends. We need you to address the assembly. They'll listen to you. You're our only hope."

"All right," he said, to make her happy, but it was clear to both of them that he would be dead by morning.

She sat on the edge of the bed, trying not to notice that even this slight motion made him wince. "I have news. There's a cure."

"Oh," he said, curiously disinterested. "What is it?"

"It's me," she said. "Heart's blood of a virgin."

"Heart's blood of a virgin? What does that mean?" he said, puzzled.

"Um...I don't know, exactly. But it's our only chance."

"No," he said. "I can't. I won't."

"You have to," she said. "We have to try."

"*No!*" he thundered, and began to cough. He doubled over with the force of it, helpless against the explosions that convulsed his body.

"Okay," she said, frightened. There were flecks of blood on his lips. "Never mind. It was just an idea. Rest, now."

His lovely, almond-shaped eyes stayed closed until it passed. When they opened again, she was amazed to see that they had changed; the shifting colors, the opaline opacity, were gone. The irises had returned to an ordinary human gray.

And something else. The covers. They were moving up and down.

Unbelieving, Tessa leaned over, rested her head on his chest. Heard the steady *thump thump thump* of a beating heart.

"Rafe," she whispered urgently, wanting to tell him. "Rafe..." But his eyes were closed, shut off from the world.

The students had built a fire in the giant fireplace, settled themselves around a comfortable leather couch and a matching set of club chairs from the 1930s. They fell silent at her approach.

"Is he any better?" said Portia.

"He's breathing," she said grimly, throwing herself into a chair. "He has a heartbeat. Probably not a good sign."

"What did they say at Magikal Childe?" said Graham. "And, as an aside, I can't believe I just asked you that."

Tessa heaved a sigh. "Heart's blood of a virgin."

They stared at her.

"What the hell does that mean?" said Ben.

"I think we all know what it means," said Graham.

"I don't know about this," said Clayton uneasily. "What if it means *all* of your blood?"

"It doesn't matter," she said dully. "He already said no."

"Hello," said David incredulously. "Why are we even considering this? Medical advice from Magikal Childe, for God's sake. It's *insane*. You don't even know if it'll work."

He gripped Tessa by the elbows. She had the impression that he wished he could shake some sense into her. "Did you ever think that maybe this is just the way it's supposed to go? I know you have feelings for him, Tess. We all do. But let's just look at this for a minute. He's done some pretty god-awful things in his life. Maybe this is just his time."

Ben leaned forward. His face radiated pity. "Tess," he said gently. "He's gone downhill since you left. He can't keep a sip of water down. Every move is agony. He wants to go, Tess. He's ready."

"So we just give up on him?" she said desperately. "What about the school? I thought he was our only hope."

"So, we lose the vote," said Graham. "We'll start our own school. The Sinclair School of Art."

"Yeah," said Gracie. "This time, no one can take it away from us."

"You're looking at the faculty," said Clayton.

"We're the lucky ones," said Ben. "He's already given us all the skills we need."

She stared at them long and hard; and then she covered her face with her hands, her shoulders curved inwards and shook with grief. Ben put one of his big sculptor's arms around her, held it there.

A log whooshed into ash. In the long, heavy silence that followed, Gracie yawned, then glanced guiltily at the clock. Tessa noticed the time.

"It's late," she said. "Go home. All of you. You must be exhausted. I'll call you when...I'll call you if anything changes."

The students looked at each other.

"I'll stay," said Portia.

"No, I'll stay." David said, and rose to his feet.

Tessa raised her head and looked at him. Her look was not unkind, and it was not without gratitude. Though no words were spoken, the meaning was clear. His hands dropped to his sides, and he took a step back.

Now she straightened up, squared her shoulders. Her voice rang with a raw, determined authority. "It's three a.m. The vote is tomorrow morning. Rafe may not be able to speak for us, but you can, Portia, you've been speaking to these people all your life. And you, David. You want to be a teacher? Teach *them*. Ben. Dazzle them with your *Gates of Hell*. You're going to be the next Rodin. Gracie, you draw like an angel. Bring your *Ages of Woman*. And wear your shortest skirt. Graham. They're going to love your St. Sebastian. It doesn't get more classical than that. Clayton, show them your centaur. It's a showstopper, even without a head."

She looked at each of them in turn. Her eyes were rimmed with red, but her voice was calm and strong. "Each one of you has it within yourself to save this school. So, go home. Get a good night's sleep. Tomorrow's going to be a hell of a day."

There were murmured protests, but in the end, they respected her wishes. As they filed out, Portia hung back to hand her a thick, cream-colored envelope.

"He was up for a little while when you were gone," she said. "He asked me to take this out of his desk. He wanted you to have it."

Tessa smiled brightly, stood on her tiptoes to give her friend a hug. She held on tight, then stepped back, releasing her.

"Call me if you need anything," said Portia. "Anything at all." And then she joined the others at the bottom of the flight of stone steps.

Later, they would recall how she looked as she stood under the portico, dressed only in jeans and a camisole, a small brave figure waving at them as they turned down Fifth Avenue, the whorls of her hair tossing in the March wind.

Tessa closed the well-oiled door, walked alone through the entryway. The art students had been thorough; with the lights lowered, she could barely see the pattern of bloodstains on the wall.

It was quiet; the only sounds she could hear were the tick of a long-case clock on the stairs and the boom of her boots across the empty floor.

She drew a chair up next to the couch. In the envelope, she found the deed to the house, blue-backed books for several bank accounts in several different countries. She flipped through them. Unintentionally corroborating the impossible facts of his saga, the dates spanned a period of fifty-four years. She shook out several keys, inscribed with the names and numbers of various banks, the entry to safe deposit boxes scattered between here and Switzerland.

The last thing she drew out was a letter, folded in three. She turned it over in her hands. It was written on heavy, cream-colored stationery, his monogram, the S twined through the R like a snake, watermarked into the paper.

My sweet Tessa, it said at the top, in his graceful old-fashioned long-hand. *This is the rest of the story. I cannot bear to let the words pass my lips. Still, I find I cannot hide from the pain, can no longer run from the truth, nor can I live with the burden of my guilt any longer. Someday, I hope you may find it in your heart to understand. I do not hope for forgiveness.*

Experiencing an oncoming wash of dread, she refolded it, put it in her lap. She gazed at his face on the pillow, his skin the color of candle wax. So helpless. So harmless. She stroked his long fingers. They were as cold as the frost on the windowpane.

Expelling a long sigh, Tessa willed herself to open the letter again, smoothed out the folds, and began to read.

14

$\mathcal{E}$verything I told you is true. Except this. I did not return from Krakow after seeing Rudi that evening. I went to the Hotel Europa where Anastasia was waiting for me, soaked myself in scented bath water, luxuriated in clean sheets on soft mattresses, took advantage of the carnal comforts always lurking behind her sly smile. I slept through the next day, departing the following evening on the train for Wlodawa. Upon my return, I found her street empty and bereft, just as I described.

When I reached the train plaza that night, I found an enormous crowd of people packed in a tight circle in front of the platform. Villagers clutching suitcases and children's hands, being pushed, whipped, beaten, and cursed at by SS men in greatcoats holding semiautomatic rifles, in the service of jamming them into slatted wooden train cars. I remember noticing how snow lay in the open spaces between the slats.

I forged my way through the melee, frantically calling out in English. To my immense relief, I heard a voice call back.

There she was, crushed between a family of eight and an elderly couple. She was holding tightly onto Isaiah with one hand, and a brown valise with the other.

Her old caution was gone. She threw her arms around me. I kissed her, stroked her hair. "When did this happen?"

"The day after you left, there was a knock on the door. Dogs found the bodies of two missing SS men in the sewers. Mangled beyond recognition, they said...I had twenty minutes to pack a bag. We have been sitting here since yesterday. This morning, there were corpses. An old couple, sitting against a wall...a baby..." Now she pulled away. "What are you doing here? They don't want you. You can still get away."

"My place," I said to her, "is here, with you." I hefted up Isaiah, held him in the crook of my arm. "Look," I said, taking his toy car out of my pocket. "You left this."

He smiled in delight, patted my face with his small hand. "Going on a train!" he said.

"Where are we headed?" I asked, as Isaiah drove the car over my shoulders, the crown of my hat.

"Resettlement," said Sofia. There was a struggle going on in her tense face. She could barely make the words leave her stiff lips.

Finally, it was our turn. We were lucky; we were among the first to be herded onto an empty train car. Shocked and dismayed, I hesitated at the entrance; there were no seats. It was bare, unlit, unheated, the walls slatted to let in the cold air. A voice behind me barked, *"Schnell, schnell!"* strong arms encouraging me along with several enthusiastic applications of a truncheon to my back and shoulders.

After depositing Sofia's suitcase against the wall, we turned to face the door. When no more bodies could be levered into our car, the door slid closed with a sickening metallic shriek, bolted from the outside. There was shouting in German. We could hear the sounds of more doors as they were slammed and secured. From outside our car, from the cars beside us, and all down the line, soldiers called to one another. The train shuddered and jerked. With a high-pitched metallic whine, we began to move.

I looked down at Sofia. Her eyes sparkled in the darkness, her face incandescent in an errant beam of light that found its way between the slats.

"We'll get through this," I whispered encouragement. "As long as we're together."

Her eyes fastened on me as if I were the giver of life, the answer to all her prayers. "Yes, yes," she repeated. "As long as we're together."

It was brutally cold. I fashioned a bed for Isaiah with my overcoat. Sofia protested when I tucked the fine fabric around him. I assured her that it would take more than a little cold to kill me.

There was wailing, and snatches of prayer. The complaints of children, cold, tired, hungry, afraid of the dark. A bearded man in a rusty black coat sustained a mournful chant. Sofia rested her dark head on my chest and closed her eyes. After a moment, I dared to lean my head on hers, my heart bursting with love for her, for Isaiah, for us.

"We are headed west," she said.

"Yes," I agreed, stroking the hair out of her eyes.

"Raphael," she spoke in a low, hurried voice. "I'm sorry about...you know, back in Paris..."

I laid my gloved fingers over her lips. "No, my love," I replied softly. "I was wrong. I have been paying for it, every day, ever since."

The train went clickety clack, clickety clack, clickety clack. I remembered I had cigarettes. I took them out, lit one for her. Even in these circumstances, I thrilled to the sight of her profile illuminated by strike of the match. In the dim orange glow from the cigarette, I could see the curve of her breast, I could see her breath rise.

Suddenly, she turned her face up to me, lips parted and trembling, red, red, red in the darkness of the cattle car. She reached for me then, her hands sliding under my jacket, over my chest, tugging at my shirt, pulling it free of my trousers. My arms went swiftly around her, and I bent my head to meet her eager mouth.

Hand over hand, I hiked up fistfuls of her skirt. She made small catlike noises as I pinned her against the wall, pressing my lips to her mouth, her eyes, her throat, the cleft between her breasts.

Kissing. What an inadequate word. Savoring. Sanctifying. Worshiping. Exalting. These begin to describe the actions I took with my mouth, and the emotions they encompassed.

Her lips, everywhere, as if I were a continent she wanted to explore all at once. The hiss of her breath, rising through the air in white plumes. The neat curve of her waist. My fingers, sinking into the flesh of her hips.

Hurriedly, I unbuckled my trousers while she undid my buttons with shaky hands; and then I hoisted her up against the rough wooden wall, and with a single culminating thrust, we two, separated for so long and for so many reasons, became one.

Sofia was innocent when I met her, and though she had known one man and delivered his child, she was innocent to me still, and this was our wedding night, and the cattle car our marriage bed. I took my cues from the gentle rocking rhythm of the train, slowing as it took a curve, then speeding up to a headlong gallop on an unobstructed straightaway across the frozen Polish plain.

I could not hold out for long. I came inside of her with the pent-up force of a hundred lifetimes, and as I came, so did she, with a single escaped cry of rapture, or maybe it was something else.

We whispered our love for one another, and that was when she slipped the wedding band from her left hand and pushed it onto my little finger. When I attempted to return it, she said simply, "It has always belonged to you, anyway."

We held onto each other all through that long cold night.

By the first frozen light of dawn, we could see that some of our companions had perished overnight, too young, too old, too sick, too fragile to resist the frigid temperatures. Sofia gave Isaiah the last of the bread and told him tales of a town called Chelm where all the inhabitants were fools. I put him on my knee and told him every nursery rhyme I could remember. He rode a rock horse to Banbury Cross, he went to market, to market, to buy a fat pig; he twinkle, twinkled like a star.

Night returned, and with it, the frigid temperatures. A punishing wind blew down from the Soviet steppes and battened its way through the chinks in the car. Someone to my left drew harsh, rattling breaths. By midnight, the sound had ceased.

Suddenly, the train slowed into a turn, jerked, stopped. Harsh lights thrust through the spaces between the slats. There was a clanking sound, shouting in German, and then the doors slid open.

It was snowing. There was a long building with an arch in it big enough for the train to pass through, and a sign that read *Auschwitz-Birkenau* in big black letters. Uniformed officers paced back and forth beside the steaming engine. Soldiers with machine guns and barking dogs rousted us out onto the frozen landscape. Spectral figures dressed in outsized striped uniforms that flapped in the wind were dragging bodies out of our car.

You've seen the pictures. You know where we were.

I took in the barbed wire fences, the wooden guard towers, flood-lights. A strange, indefinable smell permeated everything. We were herded towards a line of people waiting to register at a table near the tracks. A long wide trench was burning to the left of us, flames climbing high into the night.

I saw your drawing come to life. Sofia, frozen with fear. Her hand covering Isaiah's eyes. The flames leaping and dancing in her terrified eyes.

The trench was full of burning bodies.

"Don't worry," I said firmly, capturing her gaze, but my voice was unsteady. "Everything will be all right."

We came before a young soldier with a large ledger, backed up by an officer holding a baton. The officer wore a black uniform, and had shiny black hair that came down in a widow's peak. He looked at Sofia and smiled, clearly taken by her beauty. Then, with a flick of his stick, he directed her towards the left; with another flick of his stick, he sent me to the right.

Damned if I was going to let anyone take Sofia from me now. I left my line to join hers. A guard lifted his weapon, but I glowered at him with all the thrall in my power. His eyes glazed, and I slipped over to my little family.

When I took Isaiah from her, he smiled at me, holding fast to his toy car. With that marvelous ability children have, he settled into my arms and fell asleep, a small rebellion. I teased the car from his hand, tucked it into his pocket.

Ahead of us stood an ordinary yellow brick building, rather long, with a gabled roof. The only thing that set it apart was a tall chimney, a smoke-stack, really, embedded in the stars. The smoke belching out of the top was red against the moonless black sky.

Sofia was pale and frightened. She turned round and round, mutter-ing to herself rapidly in Yiddish, her breath coming in great gusts of vapor. Finally she nodded, as if she were confirming something she had always known.

She whipped around to face me. "I know what you are," she said.

"What?" I stuttered. "What do you mean?"

The words poured out of her. The day after her wedding, she'd had a call from Colby. As gently as he could, he'd broken the news to her that I was dead. So when I showed up at her door on that cold January night, she already knew that I was not among the living. At the time, she didn't know whether I was to be a punishment or a gift. Whichever it was, she had embraced me, taken me by the hands, welcomed me in.

The night I killed those two Nazis, the night she cared for me as I lingered between worlds, she had been fully aware that these were injuries that no human being survives. She cringed as, in my delirium, I shouted out terrible, unbelievable things. Sofia had known all along.

"Raphael, Raphael," she said now. "My Angel of Healing. You have watched over me, even after death. There is something more I must ask of you." She trained her gaze on me, then Isaiah. "You could not love him more if he was your own son," she said, in a voice that called down all the sorrow in the world. "I know. It is because of this, that I ask you to take him."

"Take him?" I said stupidly. "Take him where?"

"Far away from here. To a place only you have been."

I pulled away from her, croaked, "What?"

She took my arm then, a grip like steel. A year ago, the Germans had selected a group of a hundred men for a special project near a town called Sobibor. Three months later, two of them had showed up at her father's house in the middle of the night, stark naked, and proceeded to tell him about what they'd been working on, so deep in the forest. A factory for killing, they said. A building with rooms large enough to fit a thousand people at a time.

No one believed them, of course. It was impossible. Ridiculous! Her father had given them clothing, told them to stop scaring people.

This line we were waiting on ended in a cloakroom. First, we would undress. Then, we would be herded into a long, bare room with cement walls. The lights would go out. The gas would hiss. People would begin to scream. The biggest and strongest would fight the hardest, scratching and clawing their way to the top, where they might steal a last few lungfuls of air. The small and weak would end up at the bottom of the pile, terrified, in the dark, crushed under a mountain of bodies.

Is that how I wanted Isaiah to spend his last moments on earth.

She'd lost her mind. This could not be true. None of this could be true. "No," I sputtered ferociously. "It's a lie. I won't do it. There's got to be a way out of here."

Desperately, I scanned our surroundings for an escape route. I would use my thrall; there had to be a weakness somewhere. But the Germans were thorough and well prepared; there was a row of soldiers with dogs, double fences of electrified barbed wire, bright lights, and in the many guard towers, men with machine guns. Though bullets might have no effect on me, they would surely cut down anyone I was trying to protect.

I'd been lying to myself. It was completely hopeless.

She put her arms around me, rested her head on my shoulder. Reflected in her eyes, I could see the chimney, the smoke, the stars.

Holding his precious little body close, dressed in the warm coat I had bought him, I fell out of line.

I pressed my face to his. His soft round cheek, so warm against mine. And then I did the unspeakable thing Sofia asked of me.

When it was done; when he had grown heavy in my arms, the soft, downy cheek grown cool; I carried him to the great, flaming pit and set him down inside, unmindful of the fire licking at my face, as gently as if I were putting him to bed.

For just a moment, he looked as though he were sleeping. And then he was surrounded by light, like the sun.

I returned to Sofia where she stood in line. When she saw me with my arms empty, a terrible choking sound escaped her. Her eyes, those wild and tragic eyes I had fallen in love with the very first time I gazed into them, spilled over with tears. I wanted to say I was sorry, but the words stuck in my throat. I had placed myself beyond the pale of humanity. Something inside me cracked, then broke.

I was standing a small distance apart from her, my hands like weights at my sides. She came close, took my face in her hands and pulled it down to the delectable swan's curve of her white neck.

"There is one more," she murmured.

"No." I pushed her away, resolutely shaking my head. She almost lost her footing in the sticky mud underfoot. "I won't do it! Don't ask me!"

"Raphael, please," she said softly.

"*No!*" I roared. Backing away, I went crashing into a babushka-ed group of women behind me, scattering them like bowling pins. People in line muttered, craned their necks to see. Soldiers with submachine guns turned their heads to pinpoint the source of the ruckus.

In my last memory of Sofia, she is staring at me. No, not at me, behind me. Her great black eyes are filled with horror.

I turned to look. Something struck the back of my head. And then everything went black.

I was being dragged. As I swam back to consciousness, I became aware that someone was trying to get my shoe off my foot.

"Hey!" I yelled. "Stop that!" And yelped with pain; it felt like the roof of my head was coming off.

With a frightened look, two inmates, dressed in the striped uniforms I had seen earlier, dropped my legs and scattered.

In the east, the sky was beginning to lighten. Lucky for me, I thought. Any closer to morning, and I would have been burnt to cinders.

I had lost my hat. I hauled myself up into a sitting position, cradling the top of my head. It felt like someone was hammering at it with a pickaxe. Cautiously poking around, I found a small, round hole at the base of my skull. I had been shot. My fingers were slippery with blood. Perhaps that was what Sofia had seen.

Sofia.

I leapt to my feet.

The line of people was gone. It was as if they had never been there at all. Above me, a churning pillar of smoke billowed from the smokestack, drifting high into the atmosphere. Swiftly, I turned around in a circle. I was completely alone.

Fluffy traces of ash, like gray snowflakes, drifted down from the red sky. One fell on my cheek.

O, Sofia.

O, Isaiah.

I howled, then. And howled again.

A guard in a tower trained his rifle on me. It was early in the morning; he must have been tired. I heard the bullet whistle past my head. I lumbered forward, started to run. Dodging among the buildings, I dived into the first one with an open door.

It seemed to be some kind of a warehouse. Suitcases filled the room. Thousands of them. Suitcases stood open on tables, their contents splayed promiscuously for the taking; suitcases were stacked high against the walls.

On the table closest to me, a brown leather valise perched on top of two others, waiting for attention. Painted upon it in white was the name Wizotsky.

I stayed on for a time in Auschwitz. I never saw her body, you see; and as I told you, the human heart has an infinite capacity for hope.

When night fell, I crept forth, hugging the shadows. My plan was to search for Sofia, but I didn't know where to start. The camp was enormous, hundreds of low wooden buildings, with signs in German that I didn't understand.

As I stood there, pondering what to do, a woman crossed my path.

She shambled forward in a loose, jerky manner, slowing only to drag her ill-fitting wooden clogs out of the sucking mud. On this frigid night, she was dressed in layers of thin cotton rags, a kerchief tied around her bald head. She was wretchedly thin. I wondered where she was going, all alone, this late at night. As I watched, she reached forward to take hold of the electrified fence.

I lunged forward, pulled her back into the shadows with me, just in the nick of time.

"No," I said, shaking my head, looking into her eyes. "You don't want to go that way."

When she returned my gaze, I shuddered. I knew those grave gray eyes.

Beata Grunzweig, respected journalist, stationed in Paris in the years leading up to World War II. Beata Grunzweig, the lover and companion of well-known German newspaper photographer, Willie Erlichmann. Beata Grunzweig, who had disappeared off the face of the earth in 1941.

"Beata?" I said. "It's Raphael Sinclair. We knew each other in Paris. Remember?"

But the mechanism was broken, the eyes smudged and blown, like burnt-out bulbs. There was no recognition in her hollow, starved face. The body was still moving, but there was no one left inside.

"Don't do it, Beata," I begged her, with all the supernatural persuasiveness at my command. "Don't you want to know how it all turns out?"

She jerked her hands out of mine to resume her agonizing, bent gait towards the electric fence and the five thousand liberating volts of electricity that it carried.

I seized her then, unable to watch. She struggled, reaching for the wire. And then, wishing for a kinder, gentler end to her life, for my old friend's lover, I drew her close and put my teeth to her throat.

There was so little life left in her; it was like blowing out a candle. When it was done, I laid her gently on the ground. And then I got down on my knees and prayed to God for both our souls.

The other inmates had a name for people like Beata. They called them *muselmen*. They came to the electric fence every night; the ones who had seen too much, or eaten too little; the ones who were the sole survivors of an entire village, the ones who had lost all their children. The ones who could not bear to see the light of another dawn.

Night after night, I asked them the same question. "Don't you want to know how it all turns out?"

Sometimes, it worked; something would click on behind the eyes; a woman would stare at me as though she had never thought of it in exactly that way, then vanish back into the night.

But for most of them, it was too late. They would look past me with those smudged, blown-fuse eyes and reach for the wire. Gently, I would take them into my arms, and gently I would send them on to the next world. It was the last act of kindness I was capable of performing for anyone in that place.

A woman, still sentient enough to wonder who I was, responded with, "Raphael? Like the Angel of Healing?" when she heard my name. One of those who chose to live another day, she must have told somebody.

The next night, a poor, shivering, ragged creature looked up at me from shadowed, sunken eyes, and asked me in perfect Parisian French if I was the Angel of Healing. And if I was, could I please heal her of this miserable life. It happened again the next night. And the next night. And the night after that. And the night after that.

For six months, I glided through the different barracks, gazing hopefully into the poor, starved, sleeping faces. Eventually, I faced the truth. She wasn't there. Clinging to one last illusion, I persuaded myself that she had been transported to another camp.

So I left Auschwitz. In the end, it was as simple as peering into the open window of a car, putting the driver under my thrall, and asking for a lift. I would leave the hell that was Hitler's Poland behind me. But first I planned a quick trip to a small town on the Ukrainian border, near the city of Wlodawa, where I asked around until I found the isolated, out-of-the-way farmhouse in which an American bloke known as Skip lived with his pretty Polish potato-farming mistress.

I left their bodies to the animals.

So, sweet girl. You asked me about the Angel of Healing. Now you know.

Sofia said she would haunt me, and now she did. Safe in my bed in London, I would jolt awake in a cold sweat, convinced that I had locked Sofia into the root cellar and forgotten to let her out. Dozing on the train, I would leap to my feet, crying Isaiah's name, certain that I had left him at the last stop. Passing children at play in a park, I would turn my head and break into tears. It happened again and again. People stared.

I couldn't stay there. I couldn't stay anywhere. It wasn't long before I was walking down a gangplank into New York City.

For a long time now, I have been successfully going through the motions. I talk, I smile, I joke, I charm, I screw the pretties that come my way. It makes me feel alive for a little while. Up until this year, I have been, like it says in the song, comfortably numb.

I'm not sorry I told you; it needed to be told, and you needed to hear it; but in the telling, my demons have awakened, opened sleepy, malevolent yellow eyes, and I find I cannot outrun them any longer.

I am haunted. The only peace I have ever found has been with you.

There was a bit more, something to do with lawyers, something to do with where to lay his body to rest, but she had read enough; she laid the letter down in her lap and covered her face, for she was crying, tears coursing down her cheeks.

Rising from her seat, she went to the window, pushed aside the heavy velvet curtain. A cotton-candy-colored glow suffused the eastern horizon. It was dawn.

She turned to find him awake. He had changed considerably overnight. Death was stealing color from his face and replacing it with lines of gray. He was looking at her. No, not at her. At the letter she was holding in her hand.

She sat down beside him. The letter lay open between them like a small corpse.

"But what else could you have done?" she said.

His eyes, the color of smoke, the color of shadows, flared with the fiery brilliance of a gemstone.

This time, when she put a cup of water to his lips, it dribbled out the side of his mouth. Unquestionably, he was at the end of his struggle. A soft pink sunbeam crept towards him from a crack between the curtains, lighting a path that fell across the carpet, across the covers, across his face. Tessa put her arms around him, rested her head over his heart. He summoned what was left of his strength, put his hands in her hair.

"Please, Rafe," she begged him, one more time.

"No," he breathed.

She sighed and climbed to her feet. Her knapsack was sitting next to the couch, and she went to it now, fished around inside until she found what she was looking for. When she returned, she was holding at arms length the silly little gun with the silver bullet they had sold her at Magikal Childe.

"I thought you would say that," she said. "Can you reach the phone?"

They both glanced at the alcove near the stairway. It was a good thirty feet away. Not a chance. He could barely lift his head.

"Because you're going to need to dial 911."

He tried to start up off the couch, found he couldn't. She went on. "I took Anatomy. I know where to shoot myself so that I don't hit any major organs. But I'm still going to need a doctor. If you're going to help me, you're going to have to save yourself first."

He tried to reach a hand out to stop her, found he couldn't do that, either. "Don't," he croaked desperately. "Don't do this, Tessa. Bullets are funny things. You never know what they're going to do."

She stood before him, a pre-Raphaelite Joan of Arc in a camisole and blue jeans, her untamed hair in a halo around her face. She put the muzzle of the gun to her side.

"Save me," she said, and pulled the trigger. There was a loud pop. She jerked back and fell down.

Tessa lay on her back on the Persian carpet, stunned. A small red dot appeared, then began to bloom across the front of her camisole.

"Wow," she said. "That really hurt."

With great effort, he slid off the couch and knelt beside her. "Oh, you stupid girl," he said. "You stupid, stupid girl."

She actually smiled at him, her eyes shining with faith and trust. And then the pain set in. She squeezed out a moan, her eyes clamped shut. "Damn," she said. "This *was* a stupid idea."

Uselessly, she cupped a hand over the wound. Blood puddled up between her fingers, crept out on the floor beneath her, spreading out in a circle on the carpet.

She had left him no choice. Rafe dropped over her, his arms barely able to support his own weight. The world was spinning; he rested his forehead in the soft curve between her neck and her shoulder until it passed. His mouth moved to the place on her throat where her pulse throbbed at the surface of the skin.

Inhaling deeply, he took in her summery blackberry scent and the salty musk of her blood. His fangs dimpled the surface of the white skin of her throat.

"I love you," he whispered.

And then he bit down.

Blood spilled into his mouth, sweet and salty and rich. She cried out, arching her body into the air. He loosened his grip, afraid she was trying to get away, afraid she had changed her mind. Fiercely, she wound her arms around his neck, pulling his face back down.

He lapped tentatively. Swallowed. Waited fearfully to be sick again. Instead, he tingled all over, a prickly warmth returning to the surface of his skin. Something was definitely happening.

He lowered himself over her. Sucked harder. Stronger. Faster.

Strength came surging through his fingers, his arms, his legs. Electrical impulses arced and sparked and blew and vibrated, blasting their way along neural pathways and nerve endings to his brain. His arms went around her, and he clutched her small, fragile figure to his bare chest so that he could feel her heart beating against his, faster and faster, as he drew life from her body. It felt so good, it felt so right, his soft full lips against the curve of her neck. He had never been this close to anyone before. She lived inside of him, for now and forever.

Let go, a voice said inside his head. *You've had enough.*

Something else, something dark and grotesque whispered to him from the burnt, shadowy edges of his history. *Look at her,* it urged him. *She wants it. Come on. Just a little while longer. Heart's blood of a virgin. What is that, anyway?*

But wait, there was something he was supposed to do, something he had to remember. Something important. Something about Tessa. What was it? He closed his eyes, gave himself up to it.

Save me.

His fangs retracted, he released her. Gasping, he pushed himself off of her. He hovered between her knees for another moment to cup the side of her face, to kiss her lips, before springing to his feet.

He vaulted over the couch to the phone, dialed 911. Told them his address. Told them to hurry.

He grabbed a dishtowel from the kitchen, pressed it to the hole in her side. Were you supposed to press on a gunshot wound? He didn't know.

"They're coming, you little idiot," he said.

She was gazing at him as if she wanted to take the memory of him into the next world. The flecks of green in her eyes sparkled like stars. Though he was trying to keep it to himself, he was frightened; she looked like she might pass out at any minute. His considerable experience with death told him she needed to stay awake.

He took her hand in both of his. "I never told you this...I first noticed you back in September. You didn't see me. I was passing by your studio. There was a sliver of space between the curtain and your doorway. You were bending over, putting away the heaters. I had an uninterrupted view of your sweet bottom. And then you straightened up...and your hair tumbled down to your waist..." he smiled at her. "I created the student liaison committee and put Graciela on it just so I could ask her about you."

She smiled drowsily at him. "What about you?" he prodded. "When did you know?"

Her eyes closed and opened, closed and opened. Closed. He was beginning to panic, when they flew open again. "That time on the pier," she said. "I knew I loved you. In the middle of a crisis, in the middle of the night, in the middle of the Hudson. I knew."

He bent over, rested his cheek on her forehead.

"What's going to happen?"

"They'll take you to the hospital," he told her. "Fish out the nasty bits. Sew you up. Let you rest up a bit. Then you've got to get back to work on your thesis project. You're behind, you know."

"I know," she said. Then, "Is it cold in here?"

Her voice was shaking. Now he noticed that she was shivering. Her skin was pale, clammy. He moved his thumb across her wrist. He could feel her pulse galloping as her heart worked harder to make up for the quantities of missing blood. Her lips were turning from pink to purple. She was exhibiting all the classical signs of shock.

He wrapped her in a blanket, pulled her close for warmth. Tessa's sweet face, smiling up at him adoringly. Her eyelids were growing heavy. *Where are they, where are they, where are they?* "You're going to be fine," he said firmly.

"Mmmm," she said. She loved the sound of his voice, like a lullaby. She wanted him to go on talking forever. "Tell me a story."

"Hmmm, a story, a story...let's see. Once upon a time there was this girl. Let's call her, Little Red Riding Hood. Her mother packs her a basket to take to the Seven Dwarfs' house, because one of the dwarfs isn't feeling very well."

"There aren't any dwarfs in that story," said Tessa.

"Well, there are in my story," said Rafe. "Anyway. It's getting near dark. The way to the Dwarfs' house runs through the woods. 'Just one thing,' her mother tells her, as she leaves the confines of her cozy cottage. 'Whatever you do, don't stray off the path.'

"So Little Red Riding Hood skips off into the woods. The path is bright and clear. She trots along, making good time. However, soon enough, she slows down, starts looking around, noticing just how pretty it is in the woods.

"Then it happens. The most beautiful flowers she's ever seen, growing just off the side of the path. 'Just the thing to cheer up a sick dwarf,' she tells herself. She stands there for another minute, just looking at those flowers, thinking about how nice they must smell, how much the dwarfs would like them. Finally, she comes to a decision. 'Come on,' she tells herself. 'What harm can there be in one teeny-tiny step off the path?'

"So. She takes just one teeny-tiny step off the path. And there, standing right in front of her, is the Big Bad Wolf. 'What's in your basket, little girl?' he growls."

"That's a loaded question," said Tessa.

"You are a very naughty girl." he said sternly. "This is just your standard, G-rated fairy tale. Now, hush." He continued. "She opens up her basket, and it's full of, oh, all kinds of yummy things you people like to eat. But that's not all; there's paper, and paints, and brushes, and pencils, and everything else a girl might need to make great art.

'I have to get these to the Seven Dwarfs,' says Red. 'Portia's waiting for this tube of Naples yellow.'

'Stay here in the woods with me,' says the Wolf.

'Why?' says Red.

'Because...'" and here, his voice grew shaky. "'Because I'm in love with you,' he says."

Tessa smiled up at him, reached up to touch his cheek with cold fingertips. He leaned over, rested his forehead on hers. "Hang in there, sweet girl," he whispered. "Stay with me."

"Okay," she said obediently. And closed her eyes.

Startled, he called her name, patted her cheeks, but it was useless; she had slipped away from him into unconsciousness. He strained to hear the cry of an approaching ambulance siren, but the streets were strangely tranquil this morning.

He was already on his knees. He clasped his hands together, bowed his head and prayed.

Dear God. You know what I am. Your archbishop once told me that my purpose on this earth was to punish the wayward, the reckless, those who ask questions, the ones who stray. I don't know if You hear the prayers of a creature like me, but I need Your help, Lord. I am wicked, and she is good. But here I stand healed, and here she lies, dying. I will do whatever You ask of me, give her up, if that is the price. Please, Lord. Give her another chance. Bring back my Tessa, who fills Your world with light.

He waited. The dear eyes stayed closed, the lashes long and black against pale cheeks.

Frantic, he clutched his forehead. He could lift her, run with her to the emergency room at nearby Beth Israel, but it was risky; he didn't know where the bullet was lodged, if it was in one piece or many, it was possible he could do more damage by moving her.

He held her face, pressed his cheek to hers. Choked back a sob. *Tessa, don't leave me here. I don't want to walk through this world without you.*

There was one last thing he could try.

If he could get her to drink his blood, she might still die, but she would return in a day or two as a vampire. She wouldn't be the same; Tessa with an unquenchable thirst, Tessa with a pitiless hunger, Tessa without a soul, but he was desperate; he couldn't bear to lose her.

He ran to the kitchen, rummaged through drawers till he found a knife. Kneeling at her side, he made a slash across his chest, over his heart. Blood welled up. A single drop spilled down his ribs. He lifted her into his lap, holding her as gently as he could. Then he turned her face towards his chest and leaned over her.

"What have you done to Crumpet?" came an outraged voice from behind him.

Ram was in the doorway. He was glaring accusingly at Tessa's limp body, the pool of blood on the carpet. His hands were curled into fists.

Taken by surprise, words tumbled out of him. "They told her at Magikal Childe, heart's blood of a virgin...this morning there's this crucial vote, future of the school. She kept telling me they needed me, they needed me...drinking her blood was the only way."Tears were stinging his eyes. "I wouldn't do it, so the little idiot shot herself. I think she's..." He choked, bent over her again. "I don't have time for this. What are you doing here, anyway? Go away."

"Anastasia said you were dying. I wanted to get to that pie safe before anybody else did." He came closer. "Did you call 911?"

"Ten minutes ago."

"The President's in town. He's at the UN this morning. The whole East Side's a parking lot."

Ram came into the room. Narrowing his eyes, he saw the slash on Rafe's chest, looked into Tessa's pale face, realized immediately what he was about to do.

"Don't," he said, without hesitation. "Don't do it."

"I have to," Rafe said. "I can't live without her."

"If that's the only choice," he said, his voice hushed with compassion, "turning her into one of us...then let her go."

Rafe stared at him. Suddenly, he leapt to his feet, ran to the credenza. Opened and closed drawers until he found his wallet, stowed safely away after the students recovered it from his bloody clothing. He pulled out a card, stabbed numbers into the phone.

"Drohobych Import Export," drawled the bored Russian voice.

"I have an emergency," said Rafe hurriedly. "A civilian. I've already called 911, the ambulance can't get through."

She took down his information, then severed the connection. Rafe turned around to look at Ram. The doorbell rang.

Two men in blue jumpsuits were at the door; the one with black plastic glasses, and a second one Rafe didn't recognize. In moments, they had moved her to a stretcher, hooked her up to a bag of clear liquid, bandaged the hole in her side, strapped an oxygen mask over her face.

"What happened here?" said the man with the black plastic frames, holding a pen and a clipboard.

"She shot herself," said Rafe. "and then I..." he glanced at her, his voice faltered, he lost his train of thought. He didn't recognize her anymore, tubes everywhere, her face covered by the mask. He swiped at his eyes. "Her name is Tessa Moss. She's lost a lot of blood. Please, please help her."

The man looked Rafe up and down, taking in the blood on his hands, the reddened eyes, the wedding band hanging from the chain around his neck, the slash across his chest. "Why don't you come along in the ambulance," he suggested.

Stashing the clipboard, he turned to his partner. On the count of three, they lifted the stretcher.

Ram put his hand on Rafe's arm, stopping him.

"I'll go," he said hurriedly. "She did this so you could be at that meeting. It must be important. Get showered, change into one of your fabulous suits, slap on some cologne. And for God's sake, get some product in your hair. No one's going to listen to you looking like that. I'll stay with Crumpet."

Rafe yanked his arm away. "The *meeting?* Are you out of your *fucking mind?"*

Ram had been gripping him very tightly; it left a mark. Surprised, he rubbed his bruised forearm, stared at the other man. Ram was Anastasia's creature; he didn't even know his last name. Ram, with his pierced tongue, his carefully sculpted goatee, his pencil thin sideburns, his yellow hair, his ridiculous ruffles and 1940s zoot suits. Ram, who was never serious about anything, was dead serious about this.

"You're not the only one who cares about her, you know," he said.

"You know what? Take the pie safe. Then *bugger off."*

"You'll come later. After your meeting."

The EMTs were waiting. Rafe cursed, then caved. Ram was right; she would want him to go to the sodding meeting.

Flexing and unflexing his fists, he looked at her. The life in her hair wouldn't be confined; long, bright curls trailed off the sides of the stretcher, stirred by the breeze coming up the stairs.

"I *hate* you for this, you right ruddy bastard," he said through gritted teeth. "If anything happens to her, and I'm not there, I'll *kill* you."

He accompanied them as far as the door, gripping the small white hand tightly all the way down the stairs. He watched as they slid her carefully into the back of the unmarked blue van, watched Ram fold himself in behind her, watched the man with the black plastic frames close the doors, shutting his darling girl away from his sight.

The van pulled away from the curb, heading towards Fifth Avenue. He waited until he couldn't see it any more.

He turned around and bolted up the stairs. He had exactly one hour to shower, shave, dress, and get across town; one hour left in which to save the school.

15

It wasn't going well. Though the board members, all thirty of them, had exclaimed over Ben's *Gates of Hell,* though they had murmured in pleasure over Gracie's prowess with a pencil and pretended they weren't gawking at her bosomy beauty, though Portia had given a speech that was reasonable, resonant, and glowed with promise, though Clayton had told them some wonderful stories as he showed off his centaur, they remained unconvinced. Oh, they clapped, they oohed and ahhed, they smiled politely and nodded their heads, they were impressed by everything they saw, somebody offered to buy Clayton's sculpture on the spot, even without a head, but fundamentally, they remained unconvinced.

First Whit spoke, then Blesser. There were charts, spreadsheets, an overhead projector, a PowerPoint presentation. Letters from various foundations to prove they were just waiting with bated breath for word that the Academy had added the twentieth century to its archaic curriculum.

Then it was Giselle's turn. She argued eloquently for keeping the school classical, reminding them of the shivers up their spines they'd experienced the first time they'd walked into the Louvre or the Uffizi, or upon confronting Michelangelo's *David* in the flesh. She was followed by the Chairman of the Department of Sculpture, the Chairman of the Drawing Department, and the Chairman of Anatomy, all of whom spoke in defense of keeping the school exactly as it was.

Initially, Whit had said no to the students' request for equal time, but a man whose family had made a fortune in disposable diapers wanted to hear them out. By the time Clayton's last story had rambled to a close, the room was growing restless. Just outside, the student body seethed, wanting in, wanting a say in the matter, but Turner had posted guards at the door to the Cast Hall.

Giselle and Levon looked grimly at each other.

"How could he do this to us?" she wondered quietly. She meant Turner. She had given up on Rafe. "I never would have believed it. This school was his baby, too."

They both heard it, the sound of a hundred voices joyfully raised at the same time, coming from the corridor outside. Then came the metallic squeal of a steel door, opening and closing. Levon felt the hairs on the back of his neck begin to rise. And smiled.

Rafe was striding down the aisle between the folding chairs, fedora in place, coattails billowing out behind him.

"Sorry I'm late," he said breezily.

Turner's jaw dropped open. He turned to stare at Blesser, who looked as though he'd seen a ghost. It took him a moment to find his voice. "You're not on the board anymore," he said, scrambling to recover his confidence. "You don't have a vote."

"But I am still the founder of this school," he replied with a friendly smile, staring directly into Whit's eyes. "And though you are entirely correct, I cannot vote, I believe I am still permitted to speak. May I?"

Whit dropped his gaze.

All eyes were on Rafe as he glided around the room, stopping in front of the replica of the *Pietà*. He took off his hat and smoothed his hair, smiled gorgeously. There was a sudden crossing and uncrossing of many legs.

Uh oh, thought Whit. His heart sank.

Rafe's eyes roamed the crowd, searching for allies, smiling at old friends. Imported fabrics stretched and rustled as the thirty members of the board sat forward. Unexpectedly, a picture of Tessa rose before his eyes, her eyes closed, her face hidden behind an oxygen mask, and his courage faltered.

How would he even begin? What could he possibly say to undo the damage he had wrought?

For some reason, he thought of the New Students Party. It felt like a hundred years ago. Fights had broken out after Whit had announced that April would be the new painting teacher. Tessa, wearing that cream-colored macramé shirt, the coffee-colored glass bead like a sucking candy on a tether around her neck. Tessa, her fingers running over the watery green sculpture in the alcove. Tessa, on her knees before him.

"Many months ago," he began. "A student asked me a question. 'What's a board member?' she said."

They tittered. He smiled as if it were a joke. "I explained how we were responsible for keeping the lights on, for keeping the boiler lit. If it means we have to throw fabulous parties and invite lots of friends and celebrities to get it done, well then, so be it."

He was warmed by a wave of laughter. He had them.

"Veronique," he said to a woman in a pink and black Chanel suit who had created her own cosmetics line. "Remember when we met? Always the same tired gallery openings, the endless excruciating merry-go-round of oddly-shaped canvases and impenetrable videos." She nodded her coiffed helmet of brown hair.

"Holland." He turned to the right, addressing a man in his fifties who had made a fortune in designer jeans. "Collages made from trash. Rooms filled with mud. Manifestos on the walls to tell us what to feel." Holland rolled his eyes.

He began to pace, weaving in and out of the masterpieces along the walls of the Cast Hall. His voice was as smooth as the caress of his fingers along the polished surfaces. At Rodin's *Kiss,* he reached out to pass his hand along the female figure's thigh. The women in the room sighed.

"Five years ago, the people in this room came together to see that the secrets of the Old Masters live on. Thanks to you and your efforts, they do live on. In our students. Through the prism of their training, our artists can turn an ordinary model posing in an ordinary classroom into a painting that sears the soul, or a figure that might have been sculpted by God. Thanks to you, these techniques, these recipes, these skills, are being passed from our teachers, to our students, to their students. That is how a revolution begins."

He stopped to face them. "But perhaps you're thinking this. Sure, Rafe is charming. Fun at a party. Knows all the pretty girls. But recently, he's not the same fellow. He's erratic. Undependable. Distracted." He waited a beat. "Gotten involved with a student." Another beat. "You've all seen the pictures."

There was a murmured undertone of agreement from one quadrant of the room, but he faced it down, his eyes calm and clear.

"On a personal level," he continued, "This has been a difficult year for me. I'd like to apologize. First, for any damage I may have inflicted on my beloved school. And second, for any pain I may have caused the people I work with. People whose opinions I treasure. People I care about deeply." He glanced at Giselle. At Levon, who rewarded him with a warm grin.

"I am not asking to be reinstated to the board. What I did was wrong, and I accept the consequences of my actions. All I ask is for your vote. That you choose to keep this school in peak running condition for the next da Vinci, the next Rembrandt, the next Raphael, the next Michelangelo.

"Because he is already out there, my friends, sitting in a dreary, underfunded public school in some dusty little town where they just cut the art program, doodling in his textbooks instead of listening to the teacher, waiting for that blessed day that he moves to New York and finds a place where they will understand him and nurture his God-given talent."

His voice was like a beautiful song you strained to remember, because once, a long time ago, it was playing on the radio the first time you were falling in love.

"It is we who are responsible for the soul of the school," he said, coming to a passionate crescendo. "What is a board member? It is this, ladies and gentlemen. *You* are the beating heart of the American Academy of Classical Art."

For a moment, the room was still. He had failed to move them, he thought in despair. Acknowledging defeat, he bowed his head, took a step back.

Someone began to clap. The thirty members of the board burst into thunderous applause. Giselle leapt to her feet, followed by the heir to the cough drop fortune, the baby powder magnate, and then the rest of the people in the room. The sound was deafening, echoing through the vastness of the Cast Hall, bouncing off the vaulted ceiling, reverberating wildly off the mute statues and down the eggplant-colored halls. The students gathered outside behind the steel doors heard it, and began to applaud too, hooting and whistling and stomping their feet. Profoundly moved, Rafe spread his arms wide, the sides of his voluminous coat opening like wings, as if by doing so, he could embrace them all. And smiled.

In the end, it was close. With the faculty and board members all counted, it was nineteen to twenty-one. The Classicists nearly won.

Rafe had guessed correctly. He had been too unstable, too unpredictable, and the improvements that could be made with the promised grant money, too irresistible. Whit gloated with triumph. It had all been for nothing.

He slipped out the back door, avoiding her friends. In the stairway, he dropped a quarter in the new payphone, called the emergency number on the card. The operator knew nothing about Tessa, nothing about a van or men in blue jumpsuits.

He hung up, dialed his answering service. A young man with a Southern accent told him a man named Ram had left a message; Tessa was in surgery, he would try again later.

He hurried home through a cold drizzle, just in time for Ram's next call.

She nearly died on the table, he told him. By the time she got to the hospital, she'd lost close to a third of her blood. Feeling faint, Rafe leaned his forehead against the cold surface of the wall. The surgeons recovered two pieces of the silver bullet that perforated her small intestine. The third lay close to her spine, in a nook so risky to penetrate that it was considered safer just to leave it in place.

She was at St. Vincent's, in the Village. Rafe slammed down the phone, headed back out into the drizzle, realized he had forgotten his wallet, went back home, went back out in the rain, remembered all over again that it was impossible to catch a taxi in this weather. When he finally reached the hospital, rain dripping off of the brim of his hat, he was told that only immediate family members were being allowed in to see her.

"But I *am* immediate family," he said, without hesitation. The guard looked him up and down, exhibiting a certain amount of disbelief. "I'm her..." and there he stopped. Yes, what was he? Lover. Patron. Muse. "I'm her boyfriend," he said, wincing at the inadequacy of the word.

The guard shook his head. Not good enough. Rafe slammed his fists on the desk in rage, splintering the surface of the wood. A police officer started towards him. He put up his hands, palms facing out, backing away. *See, I'm not crazy.* He would have to find another way.

He never did get to see her. In the end, her family chose to have her flown back to Chicago. They had warned her that New York was a jungle. They wanted her in a hospital nearby, one where they knew the doctors.

At home, he found the blanket in which he had wrapped her, strewn across the tiles of the entryway. He gathered it up and held it to his face. It still smelled of her.

Rain streaked the windowpanes of his enormous, empty house like tears. Raphael Sinclair climbed the stairs to his room, tiredly stripping off his coat, his hat, his tie, his impeccably tailored Savile Row suit. He left each item where it fell, a trail of wrinkled bespoke clothing stretching behind him, as far as the front door.

He crawled into bed, between cold sheets. *Come and get me,* he thought tiredly, addressing the shadowy dream child and his teammates.

Under the covers, he wondered briefly if he had locked the doors. He was surprised to find that he didn't care anymore.

16

wo weeks later, Levon Penfield climbed heavily up the steps to the townhouse at the edge of Gramercy Park and rang the doorbell.

It was the evening of a perfect day, the skies a deep cobalt blue overhead. As he waited, he admired Spring's first pleasures in the gated park; white and purple swaths of crocuses undulated along the raked gravel paths. Above them, jonquils nodded their stately heads. Forsythia burst into sunny drifts of yellow.

Music played from somewhere inside the house. Levon thought he recognized the tune, something by Roy Orbison. The voice sobbed and sighed, rising to a crescendo of sheer, unadulterated woe. When the song ended, there was a moment of silence, and then it started over again.

He rang one more time, but the house showed no sign of life. Just as he turned to shuffle back down the stairs, he heard a bolt turn, and the door opened a crack to display Rafe's unshaven face.

Levon followed him through the entry hall. The place was a mess; the walls were being re-plastered, in a burnt orange color you saw sometimes on old houses in Rome.

But the real transformation was in his appearance. The sartorially splendid Raphael Sinclair was turned out today in a robe, pajamas, and a pair of slippers, and by the looks of it, had been wearing them since the last time Levon had seen him two weeks ago. He had lost weight; his cheekbones angled sharply out of his handsome face. His hair stood up in tufts around his head, as if it hadn't seen a comb, or possibly, shampoo, for a similar length of time.

Upstairs, Levon eased himself onto a sage-colored velvet couch, looking around. He frowned. "Something's different. You got rid of the carpet."

Rafe rubbed his eyes. They were bloodshot, rimmed with red. "Yes. I was tired of it."

"You know, you look like hell."

"Thank you."

His robe was open, he wasn't wearing a shirt. Levon took note of the star-shaped scar over his heart, the gold ring on a chain around his neck.

"You might want to think about changing your clothes, shaving, maybe taking a shower once in a while."

"Why? I have nothing to do, nowhere to go." He turned his head towards the window. He looked as if he hadn't slept in weeks. His skin was pasty, there were shadows under his eyes. Suddenly, he leaned forward. "Have you had any news of Tessa?" he asked urgently, the strange eyes boring desperately into him. "I can't seem to get through."

Levon shook his head. "Her family doesn't want to have anything to do with us. Apparently, they didn't want her to go to art school in the first place. They're saying they're not going to let her finish the year."

With that, the air seemed to go out of him. He sank back into the couch.

"But Clayton managed to speak to her. He pretended he was from the records department at St. Vincent's."

Life entered his face again. "What did she say?"

"She's back on her feet. She misses us. Her family is driving her crazy. She's worried about her thesis project. She wishes she was here."

Rafe expelled a great sigh, caved over, buried his face in his hands. Levon stared at him curiously.

"So it's true, all those things they said about you. You really are a vampire."

"Yes. Who told you?"

"Everybody."

The unkempt head nodded understanding.

"So, you actually drink blood."

The melodious voice was muffled. "Yes."

"And you really are immortal."

He nodded again.

"Wow."

"It's not all it's cracked up to be," he replied. There was a wineglass on the Mission coffee table, filled with some viscous liquid. Levon looked at it now. The color was somewhere between a deep alizarin crimson and a brownish umber.

"Is that..."

"Blood? Yes." He gestured sardonically towards the glass. "May I offer you a drink? It's not so bad if you add a bit of sea salt and a splash of grenadine."

"So, you don't have to feed off of a live human being? You can buy it?"

"Apparently." He grimaced. "Comes in a bag. Falls off a truck in Staten Island or something. Cheers."

Levon nodded, then picked a piece of imaginary lint off of his jacket. "Rafe," he said. "This is not strictly a social call." He took his cap off, rubbed his shining head. "How do I say this." He placed the cap back on his head. "Bernard Blesser never wrote any letters to grants or foundations. He never made a single call to an institution on our behalf. He was never in touch with any of the places he talked about."

Rafe slowly raised his head.

Levon rested his hands on his cane. "And the reason I know is because the bank called. Our checks are bouncing all over town. Blesser's gone. With all our money." He paused, then added, "With all *your* money, I should say."

Rafe stared at him, remembering. "He came up to me after the last meeting, said the ventilation system cost double what they quoted us, we couldn't make payroll." The color of his eyes was swirling and shifting like fog. "I gave him my banker's number. My passwords."

"According to the police, his name's not even Blesser. It's Gerritsen. He set up this conflict between you and Whit, and kept escalating it, to distract us from what he was doing with the books. We're not the first school he's cooked. The police said there was some place in Florida, a couple of years ago, and another one in Maryland before that."

He leaned forward on his cane. "Rafe. I'm here, representing the board, in formally asking you to come back on as a full-time member."

"Yes," said Rafe, trying not to sound astonished. "Of course I will. Yes."

"Good." Levon was relieved. He had been a little uncertain of the form Rafe's reply might take. "On another, personal matter. You're going to have to find yourself a new Dean of Students for next year."

"Oh," he said, surprised. He tried to keep disappointment from coloring his voice. "Of course. I understand."

Levon was bemused. "You understand what?"

"You're quitting because of me. Because of what I've done. Because of what I am."

Levon smiled. "No, that's not why I'm leaving. I admit, it kind of freaked me out when I heard, but no, it's not about you." He massaged the back of his neck. "That old sports injury I told you about. It wasn't an old sports injury, after all."

"What do you mean?" said Rafe, puzzled. A chill went through him. "What is it?"

"Bone cancer," he said.

"Oh." Stunned, Rafe scrambled for words. "How long have you known?"

"Since Winter Break," he said. "Maybe that's why I was so rough with you. This school is my legacy, too. I want to know it will go on after I'm gone."

"Come on, Levon." he said lightly. "Don't talk like that. Years from now, you'll still be calling me into your office, trying to get me to behave."

"Listen. Let me save you a bunch of awkward questions. It's pretty far advanced. I've tried everything. Nothing has worked. The doctors give me till the end of the summer."

Rafe sat back on the couch, shocked into silence. Levon looked around the Great Room, admiring the high red walls, the art, the polished oak trim, the antiquities, the vintage Mission furniture. "I've always liked your place," he said affably. "It must have taken you years to collect all this stuff."

"Half a century," he said absentmindedly. "I started in 1940."

"I bet a museum-quality Rembrandt was a lot more affordable back then."

"You don't know the half of it."

"You know," Levon said pensively. "If I was going to live forever, I'd do exactly the same things you've done. Buy a house. Collect art. Start my own art school. Find a nice girl." He scratched his beard. "Maybe I'd learn how to play the saxophone."

Rafe's eyebrows drew together; hesitantly, he leaned forward. "Levon," he said carefully. "If you're asking me to...if you're asking if I'll...Levon, I can't. I won't do that to you."

Levon frowned at him, confused. And then rocked back in his chair and guffawed.

"You think I want you to make me a vampire?"

Rafe nodded.

"No, man. I just wanted you to know," he said, with a wry smile. "You're a friend."

He stood up to leave, leaning heavily on his cane. Rafe rose to his feet. "Let me call you a car."

"That's all right. I've got one waiting downstairs."

He accompanied him through the Great Room, down the double stairs. Now Rafe noticed how gaunt Levon's face had grown, how much gray had entered the grizzle of beard, how his clothing swam loosely around his limbs when he moved.

Levon paused at the door. "You love her, don't you," he said. It was a statement, not a question.

"More than my own life," said Rafe. "You're going to tell me to give her up."

Levon, gazing up at the drawing of the Madonna and Child over the fireplace, didn't answer right away.

"Is that a real Raphael?" he said, turning to Rafe.

"No," he said. "It's a copy. Made by my beloved, Sofia Wizotsky, when we were both art students in Paris. She probably died in Auschwitz." He jammed his hands into the pockets of his robe. "Tessa's grandmother."

Levon's eyebrows lifted. He turned to look up at the drawing. The serene, loving mother. The capering child.

"I believe that life is short," he said finally, his deep brown eyes meeting Rafe's. "And that we must cherish love, whoever we are, however we find it."

They shook hands. "There's a strategy meeting tonight," Levon said over his shoulder as he treaded carefully down the stone steps. "Eight o'clock in the Cast Hall. See you then. And Rafe. Don't forget that shower."

17

As it turned out, a museum-quality Rembrandt brought considerably more in 1993 than it would have in 1940.

Rafe had to sell the Vermeer as well to get the school back on its feet. And then he disappeared.

A week later, he was back, no explanation forthcoming. Not long after that, there was a story in some of the papers about the body of a Queens man that had been dragged out of a river in Uruguay. It was eventually identified as that of Eldon Bernhard Gerritsen, known con artist, most recently sought for bilking the American Academy of Classical Art out of millions of dollars. The article went on to say that the police down there were baffled. Though there were no gunshot or stab wounds, the body had been completely drained of blood.

The arrangements were almost finished for the Nudes and Naked Ladies Benefit and Auction. It was scheduled to take place at the end of April, after Spring Break. Wylie Slaughter had been surprisingly helpful, coaxing many of his artist friends into donating something, a drawing, a sketch, a painting, to be auctioned off to benefit the Academy. Giselle was in her element, calling caterers, florists, scenic designers.

The school hired a new chief financial officer. This one came with excellent references. Levon called every single one.

The first time Rafe encountered Turner in the hallway, he pretended not to see him. Carrying a Styrofoam cup of coffee, he was staring at his clipboard and scurrying along close to the wall, on his way to his office.

Rafe stepped in front of him. Forced to stop, he looked up at him with fear in his eyes.

"You're going to fire me, aren't you." he said miserably. *Or worse.*

"No," said Rafe.

Whit's mouth dropped open.

"I know you tried to steal the school from me," he continued levelly. "I'm not an idiot. But it's hard to find people who can do the things we do. You're a good teacher, Whit," he said.

Then he had drawn close to him, so close he could feel Turner's breath on his face. To Whit's eternal horror, the irises of his eyes morphed to a clear, icy blue. The whites flamed a bloody red.

"Just don't do it again." he whispered in his ear. And smiled.

Life returned to something like normal. Rafe went to parties with Giselle. He went to meetings with Levon. He chatted up the board members. He flirted with the lovelies. He even made a visit to the offices of *Anastasia*. But late at night, he sat on the steps of St. Xavier, gazing at the darkened ground floor windows of a certain apartment building, waiting for the lights to come on.

The second-year art students of the American Academy of Classical Art were hard at work. Most of them stayed on through Spring Break as they struggled to complete their thesis projects in time for the Graduate Exhibition. Simultaneously, they were putting their hearts and souls into creating masterworks for the auction.

Tessa's side of the studio remained empty, her mosaic of postcards and sketches an increasingly ghostly reminder of someone who wasn't there anymore. The jars of linseed oil and painting mediums, the coffee cans bristling with pencils, the mason jars of up-ended brushes, remained undisturbed on her table, gradually becoming coated with a fine layer of plaster dust. The painting of the grandmother standing before a table full of memorial candles stood half-finished on her lyre-shaped easel. The completed painting of the mother and child waited against the wall. All that existed of the cyclone of bodies whirling apart into ashes was a pencil drawing.

With her return still in doubt, Gracie stacked Tessa's things into a corner. She needed the extra room.

The date set for the Nudes and Naked Ladies Benefit and Auction was a Thursday at the end of April. It was a mild evening. As Rafe stepped down the stone stairs to the street, the sky overhead was deepening to a rich royal blue. The pink double tulips and white narcissus nodded their stately heads over pools of purple grape hyacinths in the gated park. A serious little boy in a navy blue coat stared at him from between the bars, a uniformed nanny hovering suspiciously behind him. The little boy smiled at him. Rafe smiled back.

The party's theme was the color white. The color of a fresh sheet of drawing paper, the color of a blank canvas. The *fin-de-siècle* chandeliers were swathed in white tulle. Through the netting, tiny white lights twinkled like stars. Candles, tucked into gold mesh votives that twisted upwards like flames, were tucked into nooks and crannies wherever there was room. White cotton fabric, hundreds and hundreds of yards of it, was gathered and draped across the ceiling, the walls, and the fluted Doric columns. Battalions of framed artwork hung in neat rows from floor to ceiling around the room.

It was Gracie's idea to paint the waiters gold. Gilded leaves were arranged in their gold-painted hair. Their bikini tops and loincloths were gold. Even their skin was painted gold.

The story of how the Academy had been bilked out of millions had been covered exhaustively in the news, had made the front section of all the papers. It made for great free publicity.

The invitation called the party for six o'clock. Even at $150 per couple, hundreds of guests poured through the doors. They wandered through the Cast Hall like tourists, awed by the art hung salon-style almost all the way to the ceiling; they stopped to gape in front of a copy of a Leonardo *Holy Family,* unable to believe that a modern artist had the skills to recreate it; they stood in front of a first-year student's version of Raphael Sanzio's *Leda and the Swan,* sketched with a crow quill pen, arguing over which one of them would be taking it home; no one could pass David's exquisitely rendered charcoal drawing of a reclining Sivan without stopping and sighing.

Raphael Sinclair moved through the crowd, his progress slowed by the numbers of people who recognized him from one place or another stopping to congratulate him on the beauty of the room, on the glorious art, on his students' prodigious abilities, on coming up with the idea of a classical art school in this day and age.

Wylie Slaughter was there, with a group of his supercool postmodern artist friends. There was a smattering of local celebrities from the worlds of stage and screen. Art critics from the *Times.* Sawyer Ballard came to see what all the fuss was about. Anastasia attended on Leo Lubitsch's arm, Ram and Gaby trailing in their wake.

During a rare moment when he wasn't being besieged by well-wishers, Rafe saw Tessa's legation of friends lounging through the hall. The Seven Dwarfs, he had called them. He averted his gaze. It was too painful to look upon them, knowing what he had done, knowing what they must think of him, knowing she wasn't there.

The auction began an hour later, with Giselle holding the gavel.

The resulting tumult was astounding. Bids escalated quickly into the thousands. And they bid on *everything.* From paintings contributed by famous artists, to a pen and ink sketch made by the rawest new student. A fight broke out over the charcoal drawing of Sivan. One of the writhing figurines Ben sculpted for his *Gates of Hell* sold for five figures. Two people were under the impression that they had purchased the same sketch that Gracie had drawn of the voluptuous model Rachel playing languorously with her hair. Every piece sold, down to the bare walls.

Near *Dawn,* Sawyer Ballard stepped closer to the sensitively drawn portrait of a child to read the name of the artist, and saw his granddaughter's name on the plaque. He put his hand on Rafe's shoulder, smiled tearily, told him how proud his father would have been, and that he could expect the Ballard Foundation's support from now on.

The school was saved.

Rafe felt a kind of peace flow through his body, knowing that this place, this sanctuary for artists that he had created, could continue on without him. He wasn't exactly happy; happy would have entailed different circumstances, and Tessa by his side; but he allowed himself a smile of satisfaction.

A pretty, dark-haired woman was looking at him a certain way, he noticed. Then, just beyond her, he caught a glimpse of a small, familiar figure with a cascade of unruly hair, not red, not blond, not brown, falling down her back.

Then he lost her; there were so many people, she was swallowed up by the crowd. Or he might have been mistaken.

He sought out her friends. There they were, massed in front of a large painting of fancy layer cakes, contributed by the painter Wayne Thiebaud. Something was going on. Portia was grinning with delight, while luscious Gracie was elatedly jouncing someone in a hug, blocking his view. In the dull roar reverberating through the high-ceilinged room, it was impossible to hear what they were saying.

And then, there she was, her bright head emerging in the middle of the circle. She wore a sleeveless dress with a low, round neck, printed all over with old-fashioned cabbage roses. The dress had a full skirt that swished and swirled when she moved. When she walked, she may have been favoring her left side.

There was a fire burning in his chest now. Though he longed to be at her side, he contined to smile, to shake hands, to endure the myriads of well-wishers, clapping his shoulder in congratulation.

He circled the room, trying to catch her eye. Every time he thought he had it, she glanced off in another direction. After half an hour of this cat-and-mouse game, the realization that she was avoiding him came stealing over him, and his heart sank.

"How are you, my friend?" Anastasia was beside him.

Now Ram was in her circle, wearing that stupid aqua cocktail jacket with the ridiculously wide lapels, hugging her, goosing her with a pelvic thrust or two, doubtlessly saying something outrageous.

"Ah," said Anastasia. "Our *petite jeune femme* is back."

"It looks that way," he said.

Her eyebrows rose. She looked at him, and the way he looked yearningly at the girl in the middle of the circle. "You know," she said lightly. "Perhaps it was wrong of me to do what I did to you. I thought I could make you happy. I see now. I should have let you go."

He turned to look at her. The big round eyes were just barely visible behind her dark glasses. Anastasia deCroix. She had been many things to him over the decades; mother, sister, teacher, lover. His fellow traveler. His partner in crime. His murderer. His friend.

He smiled. "Then I wouldn't be here with you," he said. He took her arm, put it through his. "Come on. Let me get you a glass of terrible white wine. I'm buying."

At nine-thirty, Tessa separated from her phalanx of friends. Rafe, chatting up a feminine hygiene products heiress, felt his heart give a little leap. She went to the bar, asked for and received a wine glass filled with something red. Still on her own, she dawdled over to the statue of the *Pietà*. He saw her stand back from it, tilting her head, taking in the dolorous beauty to be found in the body of the young man cradled in the young woman's lap. Surreptitiously, she reached out a hand to caress the cold fingers.

No one was watching. He swept her into the niche behind the large sculpture.

She didn't say anything. He gazed down at her, trying to read her expression. The memories of what had transpired in these past weeks came swarming over him. The look on Tessa's face when she saw him with that woman behind the restaurant. Tessa terrified, as he crouched over her in the filthy alleyway. Tessa holding up a stake, however reluctantly, to defend herself. Tessa, telling him to leave her alone. True, she had almost given her life for him, but then again, she had been trying to save the school.

He realized that he still had his hands around her waist; he released her and stepped back.

"Sorry about that," he said, reflexively raising his arm to smooth his hair. Not knowing what else to do with his hands, he let them drop to his sides. "This was a mistake. You can get back to your friends now."

He was even more beautiful than she remembered, she was thinking. He was wearing a dinner jacket with a shawl collar that showed off his wide shoulders and his narrow hips, and as he ran his fingers over his gleaming hair, she was remembering what those hands felt like as they ran down her sides.

"How are you?" he said awkwardly.

"Fine," she said. "Those doctors. They exaggerate everything."

"I tried to see you," he said. "They wouldn't let me in."

"I don't remember," she said. "I was kind of in and out. You were telling me a story. Then I was on an airplane. I woke up in a hospital bed in Chicago."

He took her hand, turned it so that it was facing up. Kissed the soft pink palm.

"You know, I never heard the end of that story."

"Oh...something about Grandma's house. A huntsman. Doesn't end well for the wolf."

"Hmm. I thought I remembered something about Seven Dwarfs. And a tube of Naples yellow." She was smiling. "What do you think Little Red Riding Hood wears under that cloak, anyway?"

She launched herself at him then, throwing her arms around his neck, her pink lips seeking his mouth. His arms went around her as he staggered back against the enormous sculpture.

"I've missed you so much," she panted, and then her mouth was on him again, and his hands were in her hair drawing her closer, and her fingers were tunneling under his tuxedo jacket, as if she wanted to climb inside him.

"I tried to call you. No one would put me through. They said you were too sick."

"I thought you didn't want to see me anymore."

"God, no. I missed you desperately. I was a wreck. I wore the same pair of pajama bottoms for two weeks. Why wouldn't you look at me? I kept trying to catch your eye in there."

"I didn't want to get you into trouble," she said.

At that, they both exploded into laughter. Afterward, they smiled at each other before he touched his fingertips to her face, bowed his head, spent a long time savoring her berry-colored mouth. For a moment, he moved his lips to the small scar on her throat. He felt her suck in her breath, then exhale.

"Levon said you weren't coming back."

"My family wanted me to stay in Chicago," she said. "The ambulance driver told the ER that I had been the victim of a drive-by shooting. Get this! It's illegal to own an unregistered handgun in New York City."

"Really. Even if it's only to be used against werewolves?"

She put her arms around him, laid her cheek against his chest. "I told my father Sofia's story."

Sender. Tessa's father, Sofia's son. "How? What did you say?"

"I told him that I'd been in touch with Holocaust researchers. That they found Zukowski, who'd hidden Sofia and her little boy for a few months during the war. As far as my dad knows, the story came from him."

"How did he react?"

"He was very quiet," she said. "The next day, he said, 'Go to New York, my *shayna maidel*. Be an artist.'"

His arms went tighter around her. He felt her flinch, and he released her, frightened that he had hurt her. She touched her side.

"I'm all right," she said quickly.

"Does it hurt?"

"No. A little. Sometimes."

"You *idiot.*"

"I know, I know."

"Thank God you're back," he said fervently. He burrowed his face into her hair, tickled a place just behind her ear with his lips. "You saved me a lot of trouble. I was just about to start an art school in Chicago."

"Rafe," she said hesitantly. She loosened her arms and stepped away from him. "While I was home, I spoke with some researchers. I really have been in touch with Zukowski. He's still alive, still living in Wlodawa. He remembers everything. My great-grandparents. My cousins. The tea warehouse. The villa. Sofia, Isaiah. Skip, believe it or not. Zukowski didn't abandon Sofia. The Germans shanghaied him into a work detail at one of the camps. He was very excited to hear from me, happy that some part of the Wizotsky family had survived."

She took a deep breath. "Why didn't you tell me Sofia was my grandmother?"

So she knew. "I always meant to tell you."

"How long have you known?"

"Since Winter Break. I've been in touch with researchers too, you see."

He'd gotten the call the week she lay in his bed, sick with fever, fleeting in and out of consciousness. Crouched by her side for hour after hour, he'd been captivated by every breath, every sigh, alternately exultant and filled with dread, marveling at how this small piece of his life had been returned to him.

Cautiously, he asked, "What did they say?"

"In October of 1942, a workman named Zukowski brought a baby boy to the orphanage in Chelm. He told the nuns that the mother, Sofia Wizotsky, of the famous tea company Wizotskys, was going into hiding with an older child, and she was worried that the baby's cries might give them away. The father, an American, had deserted them to move in with his Polish girlfriend. Apparently, Zukowski used some very colorful words to describe Skip—colorful enough so that one of the nuns still remembered the incident, fifty years later.

"After the war ended, the nuns gave the baby to the Red Cross. That's how my grandfather—um...I guess he's not my grandfather anymore—found my dad. Yechezkel was already married again, to a distant cousin. It was easier to adopt the baby without telling him about his real parents than to go into a lot of complicated explanations."

Rafe nodded. That was the story he'd heard, too. "I was going to tell you. A week went by, then two...I couldn't, Tessa. I just couldn't. Can you forgive me?"

In reply, she put her arms around his waist, leaned into his shirtfront. After a moment, she said, "There's something else."

Even in the dark, something in her expression made him fearful.

"Zukowski knew about you," she went on gently. "He'd heard that Sofia had lost a lover before the war. He remembered how sad she was."

He was surprised to find that this could still make him cry. He turned from her, receding further into the niche behind the statue. She followed slowly behind him. He could hear her dress swishing in the darkness.

"I keep coming back to this one thing. Why didn't she tell you about the baby?"

He thrust his hands into his pockets, gazed into her dear, sweet face. He already knew why.

"I've had a lot of time to think about this. When Sofia went into hiding, Germany was still winning the war. For all she knew, there really would be a thousand year Reich. Maybe she was afraid that you would try to do something foolish and heroic. Go after Sender yourself, something like that. Both of you might have been killed. I think she was trying to protect you."

He came very close to her, then, because he wanted her to hear everything he was about to say. "Tessa," he said. "She didn't tell me for one simple reason. Because of what I am. A vampire. And she knew it from the moment she opened the door and invited me in." His eyes sparked a frosty blue, then faded back to their familiar shadowy gray. "She knew me at my worst, and she loved me anyway."

She was shaking her head, disagreeing, but in his heart, he knew he was right. He felt a certain lightness. This was the answer. Knowing she had loved him was enough.

"Raphael," she said hesitantly. "There was one more thing the researchers helped me find."

Something new roiled the darkness in the niche, filling him with fear. The sleeping demons stirred. He took an involuntary step back.

"When the Berlin Wall fell, all these records became available. I have a xerox of a page in a ledger. From Auschwitz. With Sofia's name on it."

She said the next words so quietly he could barely hear her. "And a date."

He turned from her, braced himself against the wall, slid to his knees. A harsh and guttural cry escaped him.

"I'm sorry," she whispered. There were tears in her eyes. "Do you want me to go?"

He reached for her, pulled her against him, buried his face in the folds of her dress. His words were inaudible, lost in the swelling noise of the crowd.

If anyone had been looking, they would have seen a girl in a flowered dress emerge from behind the *Pietà,* combing her fingers through her long, curly hair in a vain attempt to impose some order on it, straightening her skirt. A few minutes later they would have seen a man buttoning his tuxedo emerge from this same spot, a man with a face so handsome it was almost a sin.

At some point, as the crowds began to thin, these two people glanced at each other across the room. She was with a group of friends. He was with a striking woman in a couture dress. They shared an unusual, intimate look. And then the girl left with her friends, and the man smiled politely to a coquettish dark-haired woman who said she was dying to meet him.

18

$\mathcal{T}$here were three weeks left until the end of school. Tessa had two paintings to finish. If she was going to graduate along with her class, she would have to work twice as hard.

They agreed to observe the ban that Rafe himself had written. But that didn't preclude long, heated looks when they passed each other in the hallway, or the brush of their fingertips if they met accidentally on the landings between floors.

She asked him not to visit her studio. He understood; she had to concentrate fully on her work, without fear of distraction. That was all right, he was busy, too. By day, he slept alone, warmed by the knowledge of her love for him. In the evenings, there were gallery openings with Giselle, galas to attend with Anastasia. And late at night, he could still sit on the steps of St. Xavier, watching over her after the lights went out. There were no rules against that.

Upon returning to her studio after class, she would find souvenirs of his love for her; a bowl of chicken soup in a footed porcelain bowl; Earl Grey steaming away in a Hall teapot; pastrami on rye wrapped in wax paper on a white china plate from Wolfman-Gold; Romanian tenderloin from the Second Avenue Deli, still warm on a covered silver tray.

The lights on the studio floor burned day and night. The sculptors, having already cast their pieces in plaster, were deeply engaged in the process of sanding down the blips and edges as a prelude to gilding them with paint. Footprints marred the layer of fine white plaster dust that settled on the floors.

Models posed behind drawn curtains. Tempers grew short, then exploded. Sudden bursts of inspiration occurred, changing the entire focus of certain paintings. Late at night, under pressure, people made strange, irreversible decisions. Early one morning, Tessa walked into Graham's studio to find sexy St. Sebastian suffering without a head. "Don't say anything," Graham had growled at her between gritted teeth, pinching a place between his eyes as if he had a hangover. "Just. Don't. Say. *Anything.*"

As the days counted down to the show, students passed ever more frequently in and out of each others' studios, called in for frantic final consultations, clutching the day's tenth cup of coffee. Is this dark enough? Bright enough? The right size? The right color? Too colorful? Should it be more in the light, or more in the shadow? Will this win me the Prix de Paris? Do I have any talent at all? Should I go back to Ohio? Should I go back to law school?

One by one, the artists began to finish their thesis paintings. Those who did began building frames. Sawdust joined the light coating of plaster that seemed to be everywhere. Harker was done, then Graham. Gracie followed Portia.

David was still working on his lone still life, two studios down. The last time Tessa had seen it, it was magnificent, nearly finished. The colors and composition were exquisite; the light seemed to be sifting in from another world.

"It's perfect," she said. "Step away."

"I told him the same thing," said Portia.

"It's almost done," he said, squinting at it. In the past week, he'd repainted the background, the hat, the face of the clock. The Barbie doll twice, the watering can three times. Personally, Tessa thought he was being a little obsessive.

"What's left to do?" she asked.

He looked at her speculatively, his china blue eyes cool and veiled. "The light's not right yet," he said. He no longer visited her studio. While she was away, he'd gotten back together with Sara. They would be married at the end of the summer. Though she was swamped with work, and deeply in love with another man, Tessa couldn't help but feel a twinge of regret.

Eat. Sleep. Drink coffee. Mix colors. Paint. Sleep. Do it again.

Slowly, her visions came to life; in a darkened room, the babushka-ed grandmother's face glowed in the amber light of a hundred *yahrtzeit* candles.

"Great," Levon told her. "Now finish the other one."

The twisted vortex of human beings climbing towards the sky took on dimension, the faces, expression. At the bottom of the canvas, where the whirlwind sprang from a still green savannah, the figures were in full color, dressed in fashions from the 1930s; overcoats, suits, hats, round glasses. By the time the eye of the viewer reached the top of the canvas, the figures had lost everything, evolving into gray ghosts. The arms of a child dissolved into smoke; a woman's long, drifting hair melted into a passing cloud.

The night before the exhibition, Tessa laid the last stroke of paint on the last figure on the last canvas. She lowered her brush and stepped back.

She should have been happy.

It was a warm evening in Manhattan at the end of May, the kind that promises that summer will break out at any moment. Orange streaks could still be seen in the western skies over the chimneys and water towers.

She went to the window, felt the soft breeze on her face. She closed her eyes. Rafe would be waking up right about now. She imagined him getting up out of bed, raking his fingers through his tousled hair, the breathtaking beauty of his body as he glided across his room to the shower.

Across the street, people were gathering for the eight o'clock performance of Blue Man Group. Someone was practicing the violin with the windows open. An opera singer was warming up in the acting school that occupied the top floors of the building. She could hear the excited chatter of NYU students, or perhaps they were from Cooper Union, walking by on the sidewalk below. She smelled lilacs, and remembered that they were in bloom this time of year. Perhaps there was one flowering in one of the impromptu gardens that peppered the roofs of the nearby buildings.

With a sigh, she turned back to her studio. The mother and child painting peered reproachfully at her from the wall. She frowned at it. Though it had been completed weeks ago, she had never been satisfied. Something was still missing.

Tessa crossed her arms, leaned against the radiator. She thought about the girl she had been when she had started classes last September, unformed, naive. She had been a blank canvas then, unaware of her own singularity, hunting for an identity among other people's lives.

Her thoughts traveled further back now, into the past; she thought of a girl who'd gone to art school in the long ago winter of 1939, a girl just like her, blazing with talent, burning with a passion she did not dare reveal.

She thought about Yechezkel and his first wife, Sara Tessa. About their children, and the millions more just like them. She thought about her father, growing up under his uncle's watchful, unloving eye. She thought about her family, fifty years later still shackled to the catastrophic damage Hitler had wreaked upon the human psyche. She thought about Isaiah, sentenced to death for the unpardonable crime of being a Jewish child on the continent of Europe in 1943. About Sofia, whose last independent act as a human being was to be a choice between the unspeakable and the unthinkable. She thought about Rafe, who'd witnessed it all.

Taking a clementine from the little wooden crate on the octagonal Moroccan table, she stood before her wall, as she had a thousand times before, looking to the postcards of famous artworks for inspiration. As she peeled the clementine, her gaze roamed across the playing field of art history. Hopper's *Nighthawks,* the loneliest painting in the world. The rich reds, blues and browns in Titian's palette. The fierce bravado in Velasquez's brushwork. The tenderness in a Raphael Madonna. The densely muscled back of a Sibyl in the Sistine Chapel ceiling. The pink-cheeked innocence of a Bouguereau angel.

Finally, her eye fell on the photograph Leo had given her, the one titled *Saint Valentine's Day, Paris, 1939.*

Studying it again, Tessa felt excitement bloom inside of her. She looked at her watch. It was eight o'clock. Perhaps...if she worked all night.

Lifting the heavy canvas back onto the easel, she began to paint.

At three in the morning, she was finished. Which was good, because the porters were coming at eight to move the paintings to the Cast Hall for the show.

It was too late to go home. She collapsed onto Gracie's couch, falling promptly and deeply asleep.

When she awoke, it was already morning. Sunlight streamed in through the window. Her side ached. For a moment, she was confused, and then she remembered the night before, and swung her feet onto the floor.

Something was going on. There was a babel of noise from one of the other studios, growing louder as she sat there. She boosted herself up, feeling a little wobbly, then pushed aside the curtain that opened onto the aisle.

A crowd of people was gathering around Portia and David's doorway. Two first-year students ran by, nearly knocking her over. "Can you believe it?" One of them said to the other. "I never thought it would be—" and then they were past her; she didn't catch the name. With growing unease, Tessa pushed her way through the throng of students.

The sight that greeted her was so strange she thought she might be dreaming it. Sunlight filtered in over Portia's neat wall of postcards and sketches. There were art books and sketchbooks, a teapot with a matching teacup, a box of Celestial Seasonings herbal tea. Her crock of brushes, her can of turpentine. The usual stack of paintings against the radiator.

David's side of the studio was empty, stripped down to the bare walls. Everything was gone. Even the floor had been swept clean.

The only thing left behind was his easel. The crossbeam supported a large canvas, newly coated with a thick layer of white paint. His thesis painting.

Ben and Clayton were huddled together with Portia. They glanced up at her as she came in, as stricken as if they had discovered his body.

"What?" she said, bewildered, fumbling for words. "When?"

Portia was shaking her head. "It must have happened some time during the night. I came in this morning and found it like this."

"I was up painting until three. I didn't hear anything."

"Us too," said Ben, nodding towards Clayton. "I crashed at around three-thirty."

"The last time I saw him was around two o'clock, heading down to the deli for a cup of coffee," offered Clayton. He was in a daze, from the shock, or from the exhaustion, Tessa didn't know which. "He was going on about how he couldn't get the transition of light right on the watering can. It looked fine to me."

"Did he tell anybody?" said Tessa, bewildered. The sculptors glanced at each other, shook their heads. "Leave a note?"

Portia looked haunted. "No."

Clayton was still shaking his head. "He seemed so...*normal.*" he said, summing it up for all of them.

Suddenly the porters were there. Slowly, reluctantly, the artists parted from one another, returning to their studios to oversee the safe transit of their thesis paintings, most of them still wet, down the freight elevator to the first floor.

19

he Graduation Exhibition took place, as did all other events of importance at the Academy, in the Cast Hall. It had been painted white for the occasion, the wooden floors sanded and polished to a high gloss. Special full-spectrum lamps were installed overhead, positioned so that they would cast light, but not glare, onto the varnished paintings. The skeleton from the anatomy room had been wheeled in, a diploma clutched in the bony metacarpals of its right hand, dressed formally for today's occasion in a cape, gown and mortarboard.

No decorators had been called in, no fancy hors d'ouevres from Glorious Food, no candles or smoke or waiters or special effects. There was a discreetly skirted table bearing glasses of white wine, some platters with cheese and fruit, a tasteful floral arrangement. Tonight was about the art.

Rafe ran his hand through his hair, checked his clothing yet again for lint, for invisible traces of plaster dust. He was nervous. Had he still been in possession of a heartbeat, it would have been racing.

The Exhibition was what the Academy held instead of a traditional graduation ceremony. Engraved invitations had gone out weeks ago to family members, to galleries, collectors, curators and the press, as well as to the board members and the faculty. At the end of the evening, Giselle would announce the winner of the Academy's prestigious Prix de Paris, awarding a single lucky student an all-expenses-paid year of study in Paris. And then the second-year students formally became Masters of Fine Arts.

Portia's family was coming, and so was Ben's. Harker's family was driving up from Texas. Clayton's father was flying in from Mississippi. Graham's parents were making the trip in from the Midwest. If there were a prize to win for traveling the shortest distance, Gracie's parents would win; they just had to traverse the few blocks from Mulberry Street to Lafayette.

Tessa would be on her own. She had already graduated once, her parents had seen it, they were not flying out to New York to see an art show. Besides, they were invited to a bar mitzvah on Shabbos, and Cilla had delivered a baby boy, his *bris* falling, by coincidence, on the same day as the show. His name was Isaiah.

Rafe glided into the Cast Hall. Allison was poised near the door, handing out programs. She looked healthier; perhaps she had put on a little weight.

"I'm sorry, Mr. Sinclair," she said hurriedly, before he could speak. "I was failing two classes. Mr. Turner told me he'd change my grades if I just..." she looked down at the floor, then determinedly met his eye. "It was all true, though. Everything I said. I wanted to die." She looked helpless again, remembering. "That night was kind of a bottom for me. I got help the next day."

"It was a bad time for me, too, Allison," he said.

"Thanks for not taking advantage of me," she said, and handed him a program.

He smiled at her and went in.

He was late; the Cast Hall was already packed with graduates and their families. He himself had not yet seen the show; Giselle and a team of board members had overseen the hanging of the paintings, holding long heated discussions about which paintings should go next to which, and where. Temporary walls had been constructed so that each artwork could be viewed separately, without being crowded together or hung atop one another. He set off through the aisles searching for Tessa.

A critic from *ArtForum* was staring at him. So was someone from the Marlborough gallery. Rafe was used to being looked at, it was nothing new for him, he was looking particularly sharp tonight, and he knew it. After tonight, Tessa was no longer a student at the American Academy of Classical Art.

A critic he knew vaguely from the *Times* regarded him with interest. Wylie Slaughter and his group of supercool artist friends glanced at him and whispered furiously.

Self-consciously, he checked his suit, smoothed his hair. Nothing seemed to be out of place. He shrugged it off.

Rounding a corner, he saw a large crowd gathered at the far wall. A student he didn't know noticed him, then whispered to his friend. The friend elbowed a third boy, who turned around, too. Two first-year students glanced at him, then returned to staring at whatever was on the wall.

Rafe shouldered his way to the front of the throng, and found himself face-to-face with Tessa's painting of the mother and child, the one that had affected him so deeply when it was just a pencil sketch, that long ago day in September.

Only now, it was Sofia.

Once again, the look of horror dawned across the face shaped like a heart, a wall of flames leapt in her wild and tragic eyes. Once again, she held tight to a sweet and pink-cheeked little boy, her fingers covering his eyes.

A grieving young man wrapped his arms protectively around them, his head turned away, as if he couldn't bear to watch. Great black feathered wings rose from his shoulders. Raphael Sinclair, the Angel of Healing. He clapped his hand over his eyes, shutting out the sight.

Someone took his hand. "I'm sorry," he heard Tessa whisper beside him. "Is it all right? I didn't know how to tell you. I'm so sorry."

Tessa's painting was only the beginning. The gallery was filled with tributes to the embattled founder of the school. Graham had painted him as St. Sebastian, looking to the heavens, his body pierced with arrows. Harker had included him in his portrait gallery of downtown denizens, his collar pulled up, the brim of his hat pulled low over his eyes. In her tower of edenic female nudes, Gracie had found room for just one perfect man. Portia had painted two children holding hands in a green and threatening landscape, children who looked suspiciously like Rafe and Tessa. Ben had sculpted him struggling to free himself from the Devil's grip, alongside small tortured figures of Harker, Portia, Gracie, Clayton, and, of course, himself.

But the biggest surprise was the centaur. Displayed on a pedestal in the middle of the Cast Hall, grafted onto the body of a horse, was the muscular torso of Raphael Sinclair.

"There was this eureka moment," Clayton was explaining in his juiciest Southern twang to a plump journalist who was scribbling away in a notebook and nodding vigorously. "Artists. Half human, half something untamed that the rest of the world doesn't understand."

"Historic," the journalist was muttering ecstatically. "This is his-*tor*-ic."

Anastasia materialized from the crowd to take his arm, "Well, my dear," she said. "You have succeeded. Your students are quite gifted. Really, I am impressed."

He turned to her and smiled. "They are, aren't they."

She was dressed in a little blue cocktail dress with insets of lace and studs, tiny pleats set all around the skirt. Between her breasts hung a large bejeweled cross, perhaps four inches in length, made from black metal and burgundy stones. "Made by one of your children," she said, holding it in her palm. "That Allison girl. We are featuring it in the September issue. My last."

Rafe wasn't listening. He was watching Leo Lubitsch converse animatedly with Tessa Moss, part of a circle of people that included Ram, Portia, Giselle, and Sawyer Ballard.

And as he looked upon them, his contemporaries, aged and wrinkled, spotted and stooped and shuffling and gray, he thought back to a time when they were all young and wealthy and ambitious and talented together, sitting around a table at a bistro in Paris, each of them half in-love with the same mysterious dark-haired girl, completely unprepared for the monumental changes history was assembling to wreak upon them. It seemed like only yesterday. It seemed like a hundred years ago.

Portia leaned over to say something to Tessa, resting a hand on her shoulder. Whatever she said made Tessa laugh. And as he looked upon the easy friendship between the granddaughter of Sofia Wizotsky, and the granddaughter of Sawyer Ballard, he realized that time had its own way of meting out punishment, making restitution, healing old wounds.

"I don't know if you heard," said Anastasia. "Margaux died two weeks ago."

He turned to her. "I'm sorry. I know how close you two were."

She sighed moodily. "There is more. Leo is retiring. I have met his replacement, some hot new boy from L.A. I am being kicked upstairs."

"How can that be? You've been the editor of *Anastasia* since...what was it, 1975?"

"1976," she said. "It was the Bicentennial." She smiled, remembering. "My first issue, I had to marry patriotism with fashion and sex. The lingerie shoot almost got me lynched."

"What does it mean, you're being kicked upstairs?"

"They've given me a fancy title, Vice President in charge of New Media, they'll find me an office somewhere, but I am being quietly, politely, fired. The new boy wants to bring in his own people, shake everything up."

"What will you do?"

"I will do as I have always done, my dear Raphael. Move on. Perhaps I'll go to Eastern Europe. Prague seems to be very exciting right now."

Rafe went to work, circling the Cast Hall. He shook hands with magazine editors and critics and curators and gallery owners, and charmed an old school chum of Giselle's who had married an Italian Count. Several board members told him this was the best graduate show they had ever hung. He spotted April Huffman in a corner of the room, looking haunted. Word had it that Lucian Swain was already cheating on her.

All night long, he watched as people approached Tessa. Wylie Slaughter and his friends bent her ear for a while. Rafe recognized a magazine editor, a collector or two, someone from a gallery in Soho, someone from a gallery in Williamsburg. One woman in particular seemed very excited, she kept gesturing at the paintings as she talked. He saw her hand Tessa a business card.

In the middle of a sentence, he would feel her eyes on him, and he would glance furtively at her and smile. Immersed in explaining her paintings to yet another curator, she would feel the hairs prickle up on the back of her neck, and just for a moment, her eyes would search him out across the room.

Finally, at seven-thirty, Giselle took the microphone, and an excited burst of murmuring filled the hall. "That's right guys," she said, nodding her sleek blond head, "It's time to announce the winner of the Prix de Paris."

"You are all talented," she continued, looking fondly at the graduates. "If I could afford it, I'd send you all to Paris. But there can be only one winner."

Rafe smiled politely, waiting with the rest of them. Deep in his heart, he prayed; *Not Tessa. Not Tessa. Not Tessa. Not Tessa.*

"This year's winner surprised us all. Not for lack of talent—she always had that—but for the many obstacles she had to overcome to complete her project."

Giselle continued, her voice throaty and strong. "Halfway through the year, our winner lost her job, her scholarship and her adviser. Not once, but twice, it looked as though she wouldn't be able to finish at all. And when she did complete her thesis project, not only was it a showstopper, a shining example of everything we teach at this school, but it made us look at something we thought we already knew, in a completely different way."

"The winner of this year's Prix de Paris is...Tessa Moss!"

Just for a moment, Tessa was overwhelmed. Blinking back tears, she wished that her family had come, she would have liked them to witness this, to share in this part of her life.

A few feet away, Rafe smiled at her, his beautiful face filled with light, so proud. Portia threw her long arms around her in a hug. Clayton grabbed her, bouncing her up and down and whooping with joy.

Suddenly, she understood. Portia was family to her now, and so was Ben. Clayton was family, and so was Graham. Gracie was, and Ram, and Gaby, and Harker, and Leo, and Anastasia, and even David, wherever he was. Rafe, of course. It went without saying.

It was all very clear to her now. She could not change the family she came from, but she could create a new one. A family that accepted her for who she was, not what they thought she should be. So in a sense, her family was there, after all.

She stepped forward to accept her prize.

The graduates posed together for a group photo under the *Pietà*. The camera flashed. The class of '93 hugged each other and promised to stay in touch.

By all standards, the show had been a smashing success. A collector had bought Clayton's centaur on the spot. Harker was going to have a one-man show in a new gallery opening on the Lower East Side. Ben's *Gates of Hell* had so awed one of the board members that he had offered then and there to become his patron. A well-known restaurateur commissioned Gracie to paint a mural for the hip new place he was opening in Tribeca. A handsome young curator from the Jewish Museum had given Tessa his card and asked if she would be part of an upcoming exhibition showcasing art of the Holocaust.

The party began to thin out. People had made reservations weeks in advance for New York's best-known restaurants; the graduates and their guests began to drift away, to dinner, to Broadway shows, to see the sights.

"Come with us," said Portia earnestly. Auden nodded his agreement. Portia leaned over, put her hands together in prayer, hissed. *"Please."*

Sawyer Ballard's spare frame towered over them. "Yes, do come!" he exhorted enthusiastically. Portia had introduced Tessa to her grandfather as Sofia Wizotsky's long lost granddaughter. He looked a little dazed. She tried to visualize him as a young man, flirting with her grandmother.

"Another time," she said.

The Ballards moved off, tall and languid and graceful, like a herd of gazelles through long grass.

As the evening drew to a close, and the crowds ebbed away, Rafe and Tessa began to make their way towards each other. They met in the middle of the room, near Clayton's centaur.

"Hello, Tessa."

"Hello, Mr. Sinclair."

They smiled at each other. And then he took her hand.

They sauntered at a leisurely pace through the Cast Hall. First-year work-study students moved efficiently around them, ferreting out glass plates and empty wine glasses stashed in corners and behind sculptures. When they reached the stairs, Rafe held the door open for her. Tessa took one last look around the room, inhaling deeply of the turpentine-scented air. Together, they stepped out onto Lafayette Street.

At the corner of Gramercy Square, the plane trees had leafed out, shading the south side of the house. Morning glories and moonflowers twined green stems around the lamppost. The wisteria vines that grew in gnarled clusters over the mullioned windows were in full bloom, long trusses of lavender blossoms cascading down the chiseled face of the old brownstone mansion.

At the top of the steps, Rafe leaned over and lifted Tessa off of her feet. He carried her past the drawing of the mother and child, past the sculpture of the welcoming angel. Up the carved Gothic stairs, through the Great Room, up a second stairway to the loft. He paused before stepping over the threshold to his room.

The first thing she noticed was the bed. It was covered in rose petals.

Pillar candles of many different heights and widths cast their shimmering light from every surface and corner. Smoke from a filigreed incense burner curled lazily skyward, perfuming the air with jasmine and vanilla. An opened bottle of champagne waited on the dresser alongside two crystal flutes, the slender bowls engraved with wings.

With the greatest of care, he laid her down and gazed at her, at her miraculous hair spilling out over his pillow, at the filmy black dress that settled over his bedspread, at the seraphic smile playing across her lips.

"They reminded me of you," he said. "They were just exactly the color of your skin."

Handfuls of creamy rose petals fell through her fingers. "Turn around," she murmured.

He went to the window, pushed open the fringed velvet drapes. Unlatching the French doors, he stepped out onto the terrace.

Outside, a full moon was visible over the park, shrouded in a gauzy haze. Gramercy Park was particularly beautiful tonight, the overgrown trees casting intricate patterns of light and shadow on the sidewalk, the fanlights above the doors beckoning to passersby with a friendly yellow glow. The gaslight lamps raised the specter of the nineteenth century with a ghostly luminescence, the wrought iron galleries brought to mind old black-and-white photos of Paris. Under the dogwood trees, the azaleas in the park blazed with cerise, with salmon, with violet, with pink. The raked gravel paths glistened an unearthly white.

When he turned around again, she was laying naked on the bed. Moonlight slanted in long parallelograms across her bare skin. He ran trembling fingers over her rounded bottom, finding the sweet dimples at the base of her back. He skimmed the flat of his hand along the muscles that rose alongside her spine, the level plane between her shoulders.

He stripped off his clothes; they lay discarded at the foot of the bed in a crumpled heap. He leaned over to kiss the pink lips. Tessa's eyes were wide and full of wonder. She had never seen him completely naked. He was as beautifully made as one of the Michelangelo sculptures in the Cast Hall.

The contours of her body emerged from the rose petals like Cabanel's *Venus* from the sea. Her fingers furrowed through his hair, she pulled his face to hers. She knew him now, had tasted what he was capable of, and still, she drew him closer.

He took his time, wanting to prolong the moment; to take hold of the firm curve of a hip, to rest his cheek upon the mound of her belly. To dwell upon the swell of her breasts, the lick of golden orange hair between her thighs.

His hands went around her waist, his fingers sinking into the flesh as he pulled her against him. His eyes fluoresced an extraordinary blue.

"I love you," he told her. In the perfect stillness of the room, his voice was a rapturous melody that only she would ever hear. "I love you now. I will love you always. I love you more than I can ever love anyone, ever again."

She didn't say anything. She looked up into his eyes, and he found his answer there. His own reflection. Faith and trust. The only peace he'd ever known.

He braced himself over her. The commingled scents of sandalwood and blackberries rose from their heated bodies. The lovers gazed into one another's eyes. With a single fluid movement, he was inside of her, making them one.

A gasp, a stifled cry, a rattling intake of breath.

"Oh, God," he whispered in awe. "I've come home. Finally, I'm home."

He was in Highgate again. It was the middle of winter, snow dusted the wings of the angels watching over the dead. Looking down, he noted that he was dressed entirely in white. London in January; he shivered, and not because of the cold.

Once again, the branches of trees reached out like bony fingers to pluck at him, his shirt, his pants, his hair. Rafe realized that he was barefoot, he was leaving bloody tracks in the snow.

Up ahead, the shadowy child ran lightly over the frost-whitened path, disappearing just where it curved into a lane of mausoleums. Now he slowed, afraid that his confederates with the jagged teeth and cadaverous breath were waiting there, just out of sight.

"Come back!" he called. A cemetery at night was no place for a child.

He could see him now, skipping far ahead, balancing on the bricks that edged the sides of the path. Reluctantly, he followed, glancing fearfully at the monuments. He expected the arrival of the child's shadowy compatriots at any moment.

Rafe found him sitting on a bench in an Egyptian-style tomb, swinging his legs back and forth. He approached slowly, afraid he would start running again.

"Are you alone?" he said cautiously. "You don't have to be afraid of me. I want to help you. What's your name?"

The boy looked up at him. A pretty child, dressed in short pants, a cap, old-fashioned clothing. In the moonlight, it was impossible to tell what color his eyes were. Something about him seemed familiar.

Tired of the chase, Rafe sat down beside him. The little boy smiled. When he smiled, his eyes weren't so sad. Where was his mother, anyway? Such a sweet child. Who would leave a child like this, on a night like this, in a place like this?

The boy reached out and took his hand. Rafe shivered. The little fingers were as cold as bone, as cold as a headstone in January.

"You're nice," he said.

"No I'm not," he said. "I'm a very bad man."

"No," said the little boy. He smiled a crooked smile, much too old for his years. "You're not. I would know."

"What do you want from me?" he said.

"I have to tell you something."

The chilly little hand was pulling him now, pulling him down so that he could put his lips close to his ear. Fear beat its wings in his heart. Suddenly, he didn't want to know what the shadow child had to say.

The boy cupped his hand over his mouth so that only Rafe could hear. "She forgives you," he whispered in his ear. "She forgave you a long time ago. She wishes you could forgive yourself."

The boy jumped down from the bench and continued on his way down the path. Rafe began to follow. The little boy stopped and shook his head. "No," he said. "It's not time yet."

Then, as if someone was calling him, he cocked his head, listening to a voice beyond Rafe's hearing. "I have to go now," he said. And then he turned around and went tripping off down the lane. His outline shimmered, then disappeared into the thin cold air, leaving Rafe alone in the snowy graveyard.

She found him in the garden. She stepped out the French doors, looking up at the sky. It was a deep Prussian blue; she could see Venus twinkling overhead. He was dressed in gray trousers and a soft black crew-neck sweater. It was as casual as she had ever seen him. His hands were in his pockets; he was staring absently up at the stars. This late in spring, the Japanese cherry was already weeping its petals to the ground. Moonflowers turned their pale, open faces to the night sky, weaving themselves through a white clematis vine that trailed up and around an arched wooden arbor. A fountain of white roses clambered enthusiastically up the wall of the next building. Hanging pots of night-blooming jasmine perfumed the air. He turned at the sound of her padding down the steps.

"Your ring," she said. "I noticed you weren't wearing it anymore."

"Yes," he said. "I've put it somewhere safe." Before the Graduate Exhibition, he had lifted it off from around his neck, held it in the palm of his hand. He had bent his head and kissed it goodbye before shutting it carefully away in a velvet box in a drawer in his bedroom.

Her hair was wet, falling to her waist. She smelled of the lily-of-the-valley shower gel that was in his bathroom. He pulled her up onto her toes, pressed his lips to hers. Pushed the robe down around her shoulders and nibbled kisses down her throat.

There was something she wasn't telling him, an unspoken air of regret. He pulled away, looked gravely into her eyes.

"What is it, sweet girl?" He was hesitant with her, awkward, almost shy. "Did you...was it...was I all right?"

She put her arms around him, whispered into his chest. "It's just that... well, I can never save you again."

He pushed aside her hair, cupped her face in his hands. "You're wrong about that," he told her earnestly. "You do save me. Every day."

He went down on his knees before her, bowed his head to kiss her belly, the muscles of her abdomen reminding him of the body of a violin. A memory teased at the edge of his consciousness. Something about Clayton's centaur. It had been a little too accurate.

"Tessa," he frowned. "Did Clayton see me naked?"

"Um. He might have."

He grimaced. "Anyone else I should know about?"

She lifted her shoulders, dropped them. "Ah—maybe Ben."

He sighed.

"It really helped him with his sculpture," she enthused. "Did you see?"

Art students. The robe spilled to the ground with a silky splash. He made love to her amidst the clouds of white flox creeping across the earth at their feet.

She dabbed a jot of raspberry jam onto her croissant, poured them both a cup of coffee. He preferred his black; she took both cream and sugar.

"When we're in Paris," she said dreamily. "It will be like this every day." She was sleepy and radiant, her hair tumbled in tawny ringlets around her face.

His heart filled with love for her. Inside, he was already grieving. He couldn't go back to Paris. Sorrow was etched on every building and streetlamp in the City of Light. Turning a corner in le Marais, in St. Germain, in Montparnasse, in Montmartre, each vista would bring renewed feelings of tragedy and loss.

He busied himself with stirring cream and sugar into her second cup of coffee. "It's going to be brilliant," he said courageously, trying to work up some enthusiasm. "I want you to do everything I did...take classes, sit in cafés, paint in the Louvre. You won't want to come back." His smile was a ruse to conceal his grief. "You can even stay in my old rooms. I think I'm still paying rent on them. Then again, you might prefer the Marais. It's gotten very hip."

The first cloud of doubt crossed her face. "You're not coming with me, are you."

Slowly, he shook his head no.

"You can take a year off, the school is in the black now," she said quickly. "You can fly back whenever they need you."

He dropped his gaze. "I can't go back to Paris, Tessa. Too many memories."

"We'll make new ones." She reached across the table, took his hand. He rubbed his thumb over hers. From the look on his face, the lengthening silence between them, she knew he meant it.

She looked down at the table, heaved a sigh. "Then I won't go, either." she said decisively.

He looked up at her in alarm. "What do you mean? This is a once-in-a-lifetime experience, Tessa. You *must* go."

She shook her head resolutely. "I'm not leaving you. If you're not going, I'm not going."

He sighed, covered her hand with his, wished he had a cigarette. "Tessa," he said quietly. "I want you to have the life that was stolen from us. From Sofia and me. I owe it to her."

"I have that life," she said. "With you."

"I nearly killed you, Tessa. That's the life you have with me."

He couldn't meet her startled gaze. "I never told you. The night you saved me...The night you did that brave and foolish thing..."

"Anyone would have done it."

"No. No one but you." He squeezed her hand. "You were in shock. Dying. The ambulance wasn't coming. I almost..." He looked away for a minute, remembering her unconscious in his arms, her life bleeding away into the oriental carpet. "I almost made you...one of us." He sounded tired, even to himself. "I'd already made the slash across my chest. If you had swallowed even a drop of my blood, that would have been enough. Ram stopped me."

She leaned both elbows on the table, took her head in her hands.

"I would do anything to keep you here with me. *Anything.* Understand? Even that."

He'd crossed some kind of a border, he knew. But he had to shock her to her senses; she had to be made to understand. She was a sweet and lovely girl, and he was a Beast. Her purpose was to live in the light. His was to punish the wayward, the ones that ask questions, the ones who stray. They could have no future together.

She got to her feet. *This is it,* he thought dully. *I've really done it this time. This is goodbye.* He tried to steel himself, found that he couldn't. He had used up all his defenses.

She sank to her knees in front of him, unbuttoned his shirt. The air was perfumed with the scent of sandalwood. She stared at the star-shaped scar she had made over his heart, then kissed it. He made some kind of a sound, bowed his head.

She reached into the shirt to put her arms around him, laid her head on his chest. "I love you, Raphael Sinclair," she whispered. "And I am not going to Paris."

So he lied to her. He told her he would join her in September. Now she was excited; there were flights to arrange, boxes to pack.

She'd spent the entire day moving her studio equipment back to her apartment while he slept on, insisting that she could do it all by herself. Now she was asleep in his bed, exhausted. Barefoot, he went downstairs. Alone among his trophies and his possessions, dressed only in a pair of striped pajama pants, he stood before Sofia's drawing and tried to think.

He would not repeat the agonies of this past winter, when he laid waste to his carefully cultivated reputation and almost destroyed the school. It was the only legacy he had to leave this world. He would die first.

Rafe put a disc into his new CD player, recommended by the lethargic heroin addict with a pierced lower lip working the counter at Tower Records. Lotte Lenya's throaty vibrato hissed out of the speakers.

He had caused so much pain to so many people over the span of his long life. This time, before the demons took over, while he would still be remembered as the founder of the American Academy of Classical Art, and not for whatever atrocities he might commit after madness robbed him of his higher faculties, his thoughts turned toward taking his own life.

Better to die now, while his mind was clear and his conscience at peace. While he was still a man, and not a monster. Tessa would be taken care of, he had seen to that; she would get the house, the art, whatever he had recovered from Blesser before he paid so dearly for his crimes. She would never have to think about money again.

He had worried that she would find another lover. But that had never been the real issue. She loved him completely, he knew that now, she would never leave him. But to keep her for himself meant to steal her away from the light, forcing her to exchange it for an eternity of darkness. With him there would be no family, no car pools, no cheerful holiday feasts with aunts, uncles and cousins. No soccer practice. No shambling house in the suburbs. No children. And always, always, the lurking possibility that she might come to harm at his hands. Taking himself out of the equation seemed like the logical solution to all of his problems.

She would be devastated, there was no way around it. Simple logic dictated that he wait until she was far away in Paris, settled in, entrenched in her new life. But he would be lost by then, cutting a bloody swath through the boroughs of New York City. If he did it now, while her friends were still close enough to lend support, while Levon was still here to see her through, while that damned David was still in love with her, she could mourn him over the summer and then fly off to Paris to get on with the life he had planned for her.

He went to the window, pushed aside the fringed velvet curtain. It was still dark out. He cranked open the casement window, inhaling the crisp night air, scoured clean by a passing shower. New York City was very dear to him, now that he was leaving her. He could hear the lonesome tinkle of wind chimes drifting in from a neighbor's deck, the sibilant whoosh–*sssss* of a bus braking at Third Avenue. He could smell the vinegary odor of mulch rising up from the park below, of new life breaking through the clods of damp earth to the surface. The acrid scratch of a lit match, the sweet perfume of tobacco. The smell of lilacs floating up to him from someone else's garden.

The way he saw it, there were two possibilities. One, he could turn himself in to the Romanian Orthodox Church, see if they were still in the business of sending vampires back to God. It might be painful, but it would be quick. The second choice was easier, but would take some courage; he could simply walk outside and wait to greet the sunrise.

As if in response, a harried rustling began in the plane trees below, like the wings of a thousand birds taking flight; it came to a tumultuous crescendo, then died slowly away.

There must be a God, he thought, otherwise, how else to explain the existence of a creature such as himself? And if he had been, as the old Archbishop had said, part of His design, perhaps there would also be forgiveness.

He would have liked very much to believe this; he did not, however, hold much confidence in the quality of His mercy. Isaiah had died and he had lived, where was the justice in that? If there were indeed a heaven and a hell, he was sure to be sent straight to the latter. He entertained no vain hopes of a heavenly reunion with Sofia. She had died a martyr's death, she was a shining star; he had been an agent of the Other.

The long-case clock bonged softly, told him it was five a.m. It was almost dawn. Suddenly, he felt a deep longing to hear Tessa's voice. He took the stairs two at a time. He climbed into bed, slid his arms around her waist.

"Mm," she said. There was a silky commotion of sheets as she rolled over to face him, nestling back into the quilts. Her scent, blackberry and musk, trapped in the tangle of sheets and blankets, escaped lazily into the air.

"Hello, sweet girl," he said. A feeling of peace washed over him. He pushed the twists of her hair, not blond, not brown, not red, away from her face. "I just wanted to say good night."

Her eyes cracked open, eased closed again. "Come to bed," she sighed.

He put his mouth very close to her ear. "I love you," he told her, wanting to be sure she heard it.

"Love you," she repeated drowsily, tucking herself into the hollow of his chest.

He held on to her, reluctant to let go of her soft, warm body. Then he pulled the covers up around her chin, pressed his lips to her raspberry mouth. She smiled in her sleep.

Sitting down to his desk, he took out a sheet of monogrammed note-paper, scratched out a letter of explanation. The thought of her searching the house for him, calling his name, was unbearable. By the time she awoke, there would be nothing left of him but a handful of ashes.

He didn't want to die. Far from it; he wanted to live forever with his darling Tessa, just the two of them, playing house forever in the brownstone at the edge of Gramercy Park. But he couldn't do it to her, couldn't do it to Sofia.

A quiet voice arose within him, presenting itself for consideration. *Go back to bed,* it suggested. *Everything looks worse at night. Just go to Paris, memories be damned.*

I can't, he answered sadly. Sofia's face is imprinted on every Rue and Boulevard. And not just Sofia. All those living, breathing human beings that I transformed into lifeless corpses. I can never go back.

All right then, the voice argued reasonably. *Just tell her the truth, that you'll die without her. Ask her to stay.*

Was it that simple, then? Just forget all this sacrifice and nobility, live happily ever after, like in the fairy tales, Little Red Riding Hood with the Big Bad Wolf?

"No," he said out loud. "I can't. It's wrong."

He was shivering, and not from the cold. Still wearing only pajama bottoms, he unlatched the French doors, stepped out onto the balcony.

There was a haze hiding the face of the moon, a fresh breeze blowing down from Canada. He closed his eyes, felt it caress the hair off of his forehead. His mind wandered back through the years, over all the accidents of chance and the choices he had made, that had brought him to this place, to this moment. The lonely boy at school, finding salvation in Art. The broken-hearted young man, letting his lover walk away into the blue of a Paris evening. The angry young man, foolishly entering the cracked and cobbled courtyard with a beautiful stranger, his life bleeding away into the cracks between the paving stones. The murderous young man, waiting for unfortunate stragglers amidst the billowing smoke and the crackling fire pits of the Blitz. The same young man, hapless witness to a modern massacre of the innocents. A changed young man, his head filled with plans to save his lover and her child, unaware that they had already been claimed by the jaws of history no matter what he did.

The monster. The philanthropist. The lover. The unlikely founder of an arcane and necessary art school. The Angel of Healing.

Do I have a purpose? he had asked the old Archbishop. *Am I part of God's plan?*

Raphael Sinclair, no longer young, no longer angry or hapless or murderous or monstrous, suddenly understood that he had been given the answer to his long-ago question. It had come to him in the form of another girl who needed saving, and who had, to his infinite surprise, saved him right back. The circle was complete; perhaps that had been God's plan all along.

Tessa was the best of both of them, he realized. She had inherited Sofia's exquisite sensitivity, yes. Her artistic gifts, her beauty, also yes. But under the fragile girlish surface lay a natural self-reliance, a stubborn streak of independence, an insouciant, easygoing embrace of life that Sofia could never have known. Those had been qualities of his, when he was still a man.

He had loved Sofia Wizotsky without reservation or condition, with all his heart and all his soul. But he had also wanted to own her, to possess her, to control her destiny. He had been entirely prepared to kill her rather than see her with another man. Fifty years later, with his heart breaking inside of him, he just wanted his darling girl to be happy.

Birds were twittering in the trees below, it was almost dawn. The sky turned from a velvety black to a celestial blue. His hands were shaking; he clung to the wrought iron bars for courage. The first pink streaks appeared on the horizon. He closed his eyes, waiting for the sunrise.

Epilogue

"*T*essa," said Portia Ballard in surprise. "Come on in." It was nine-thirty on a steamy May night, and she had been strapping duct tape around her last box of books when she thought she heard a knock at the door.

The cozy ground floor studio apartment she had occupied for the past nine months seemed remote and anonymous now, her belongings stowed away in boxes and bags except for some old furniture.

"Have a seat," she said, indicating an empty chair with a round back and a threadbare needlepointed cushion that had belonged to her great-grandmother. "Can I get you some tea?"

"No thanks," she said. "I'm kind of in a hurry." She shifted from one foot to the other, glanced over her shoulder, then came in anyway. "I tried to call. Your phone just kept ringing."

"It's already disconnected. Auden's been driving around the neighborhood for half an hour, looking for a place to park the van. We're leaving in the morning."

On the streets of New York City, girls were already showing off their new tans in camisoles with skinny straps, their skin burnished brown by the late spring sun. By contrast, Tessa seemed paler than ever, dreamy, ethereal. She handed Portia a package wrapped in butcher paper.

"But I didn't get you anything." Curiously, she peeled off the paper, revealing the dustcover of the Balthus book. She looked at her questioningly.

"Rafe wants you to have it. He says you'll make better use of it."

"Wow. Tell him thank you." She ran her hand lovingly over the book's smooth surface, then narrowed her eyes, looked at her friend. "Okay, let's hear it. What's going on?"

Tessa's hair was like a barometer; some days curly, some days fluffy, some days waving around her head like Medusa's snakes. Tonight it hung down her back in loose ringlets, casting her as a da Vinci angel, or a Titian Magdalene. She sighed, glanced at her feet. Took a long deep breath, blurted it out. "I'm not going to Paris."

Portia blanched. "What do you mean? Why not?"

"We're going away for a while. Rafe has some places he wants to show me in Eastern Europe."

She was stunned. "Tessa. You *can't.*" The words gushed out of her before she could think. "Sure, he loves you now, but for how long? He'll be young and beautiful forever, while you get older and older." Desperate to save her friend from making an irrevocable mistake, she abandoned all gestures at diplomacy. "He's a *vampire,* Tess. He killed your *grandfather.* He killed *Isaiah.* He almost killed *you.*"

Tessa said nothing. In the wake of the news, Portia had forgotten to close the door behind her. Just beyond the stoop, past the moths batting themselves against the single neo-Gothic lamp at the entrance to the building, darkness reigned, the dim yellow glare from the streetlights breaking only intermittently through the heavy canopy of trees.

Goosebumps lifted the hairs on the back of her neck, the backs of her arms. Something moved in the shadows under the tree by the curb, something dark and immeasurably powerful. Portia saw the end of a cigarette glow suddenly red, silhouetting for a moment the figure of a man in an overcoat and a fedora.

Tessa smiled at the shadows. Something whooshed on inside of her, like a furnace coming suddenly to life. Her cheeks flushed pink, her lips grew red, even the hairs on her head seemed to stand up and quiver.

"You know," she said, without rancor. "Everyone's always so sure they know what's best for me. My grandfather, my family...David, Levon, Anastasia...you...even Rafe. So I packed up my studio. I made ticket reservations. I made all these arrangements. Today, at five in the morning, it came to me. *I'm already here.*"

Portia shook her head, not understanding.

"This is my Paris," Tessa said, spreading her arms wide. "This is where I belong." She smiled. "In New York, you can be anyone you want to be."

Portia was perspiring. It was warm in the small, airless room. "Tessa. Let's say I'm wrong. Let's say nothing happens. What about the future? Can you picture Rafe at your Shabbos table? With your parents? At a piano recital? At a playground?"

"What about *children, Tessa*?" She was almost shouting. Wiry blond hairs were springing free of her tightly wrapped bun. "A family? A *normal life?*"

"David was normal," said Tessa.

Portia put her head wearily into her hands. Tessa perched on the edge of the bed, regarding her with sympathetic brown eyes. It wasn't that she wanted Portia's approval; she just wanted her to understand.

"I'm not saying I don't want those things," she said. "Maybe someday I will. But not now. Not for a long while. Right now, we're taking it one day at a time."

This was a terrible idea, Portia was thinking. What could she possibly say to talk her out of it? And then she had it.

"Tessa," she said. "What would Sofia say?"

Immediately, she wished she could take the words back. With that one statement, she had gone vaulting over the boundaries of their friendship, of history, of civilized behavior.

But there was no reproach in the soft voice. "What would Sofia say," she mused, almost to herself. "When I woke up this morning, I just knew. What I really want to do was stay in New York City. Of course, I wanted to tell Rafe right away, but he wasn't there. So I went to look for him."

She was massaging her fingers in slow circles across her forehead, a gesture Portia realized she had picked up from Rafe. "His coat was still in the closet, his hat was on the dresser where he left it...a breeze was blowing the curtains in and out. That was when I noticed. The doors leading to the balcony were open."

"He was outside?" said Portia, puzzled. "At sunrise? But if he's a vampire, isn't that...wouldn't he..." she stared at her, aghast.

"He needs me, Portia," Tessa said simply. "And I need him. He makes me a better person. He makes me a better artist. Everything in my life is better, in every way, because of him. Can you understand that?"

Portia sat down heavily in her great-grandmother's chair, bowed by the impending sense of doom she felt hovering just overhead.

"To answer your question. I don't know what Sofia would say. But if she was here, if she could speak for herself, I think she would say this. If you are fortunate enough to have someone to love, treasure them for as long as you can. Because you don't know what tomorrow will bring."

There was an expression on her face that Portia had never seen before on a living human being, only in certain paintings by da Vinci, by Titian, by Raphael. It spoke of peace, of consolation. Of redemption. Of love beyond understanding. Of a forgiveness beyond earthly comprehension.

Tessa got up to go, shouldering her knapsack. She seemed very small and vulnerable in her thin cotton summer dress, framed against the black backdrop of night. Tendrils of tawny hair fell around her shoulders, backlit by the streetlamp like a halo.

Portia relented. "Send me a postcard from Prague," she said.

Relieved, Tessa broke into a smile. "I will."

"And call me. So I know you haven't been turned into the evil undead, over there in Romania, or Transylvania, or wherever the heck you're going."

She laughed. "They might not have phones, some of the places we're going. I'll write."

An early cicada rattled and whirred at the top of a linden tree. Moments later, it was answered by another cicada from a tree down the block. Portia saw Tessa's gaze wander out the door, to the shadow waiting for her in the impenetrable gloom under the tree.

Suddenly she smiled. Something seemed to stir the air around her face, lofting and fanning the intricate loops and whirls of her hair like a warm wind. Tessa was alight, glowing with an inner fire, and Portia knew she had never seen her friend happier, or more beautiful.

She sighed. "So go to him already," she said.

Tessa beamed at her one last time. Then she turned, running lightly down the stairs on sandaled feet. Knee-deep in moving boxes, Portia watched as she disappeared into the shadows just beyond the stoop.

She heard the tender whisper of a girl's voice in the dark. She heard another voice rumble in response, rich and impassioned, touching the heart like a sad and beautiful love song.

Portia Ballard, engaged to be married to a handsome and socially appropriate young man with whom she was deeply in love, experienced an unexpected stab of envy. Wrong or right, what they had was the kind of love the great poets wrote about. A glamorous aura surrounded them, Tessa Moss and Raphael Sinclair, the artist and her muse. Together, they *were* Art.

She went to close the door. As she stood there, she saw two shadows come together under the tree by the curb, embrace. Holding hands, the shadows flitted across the street. She watched until they turned the corner, vanishing into the vast, sheltering darkness of the New York City night.

Acknowledgements

$\mathcal{T}$his book couldn't have happened without the extraordinary support of many extraordinary people.

My heartfelt gratitude to my agent, Jean Naggar, whose efforts on behalf of this story has been nothing short of Herculean. Her unshakable faith in this manuscript has gotten me through a lot of dark nights of the soul. Her wisdom and her grace are a constant inspiration.

I am indebted to my team at JVNLA; Jennifer Weltz, who is always there for me with insight, patience and guidance, Laura Biagi, whose skill with editing made the story better than it was before, Tara Hart, who made my cover art sing. Thank you, too, to the many others at the agency who helped bring this book to life.

My eternal thanks to David Naggar, my first beta reader, who called me from a vacation in Paris to suggest that I get a copy of the manuscript to his mother.

Myriam Auslander, Leora Fineberg, Olivia Fischer Fox, my friends, my first readers. Thank you for plowing through those early versions, and for being brave enough to tell me what worked and what didn't. Your friendship has kept me more or less sane through births, deaths, rejections, homework, car pools and three-day *yontifs*. Thanks also to Jessica Raab and Bluma Katz Uzan, who made me feel that I'd written something special.

For the World War II section of the book, I turned to *The Yizkor Book of Wlodawa,* available online at the Nizkor Project. Philip Soroka, Chaim Melzcer, and Dieter Schlüter shared their wartime experiences with me, confirming and filling out my mother's war stories.

My gratitude to Siu Wong and Rivkie Greenland, whose suggestions made the cover more beautiful than I could have made it on my own.

Many thanks to my fellow masters from the New York Academy of Art class of 1993, Doug Blanchard, Conrad Cooper, Cessna Decosimo, Ken Hochberg, Sean Leong, Terry Marks, Alissa Siegal, Patrizia Vignola, with whom, thanks to Facebook, I still share a virtual studio.

Sometimes, when you put up a flyer in a student union building advertising for a new roommate, you get a wonderful surprise, someone who becomes part of your family. Big hugs to Karen Benchetrit Naggar, my dear French roommate, who always makes me feel like I'm family.

To all Maryleses, Sorokas and Shankmans, thanks for your unending support. Life is a journey, and it is a better journey when I travel it with you.

From the moment I landed in New York, Daisy Maryles welcomed me into her home, made me laugh, and showered me with free books. I can never thank you enough.

Gabriella, Raphael, Ayden and Jude, who grow tall and brilliant and beautiful on pizza, hot dogs and chicken nuggets while I punch obsessively away on the computer, thank you for putting up with me. You are my greatest creations.

This book would not have existed without my mother, Brenda Soroka Maryles. With her immigrant English, she read to me when I was little, took me to classes at the Chicago Art Institute, and reported her Holocaust experiences with pitiless accuracy. My dad, Barry Maryles, told me family stories of blinding courage and incomprehensible horror. I pass them on the only way I know how.

To my sister Bernice, thank you for your faith in me, your boundless encouragement and unwavering support, in a thousand different ways large and small. To my brother Chaim, who introduced me to rock music and science fiction and runs the Maryles family cafeteria, I owe you many thanks. Sam—sorry I left when you were nine and missed your childhood. It's a good thing you moved to New York so that we could share the rest of our lives. Thank you for advising me on the emergency medicine aspects of the story.

And lastly, to my sweet Jon, the first face I see in the morning and the last face I see at night; my ray of light, my compass rose, my morning star. You are the greatest thing that has ever happened to me.

Q&A With Author Helen Maryles Shankman

"Barbecues are a leap of faith." This is what I told my sister, many years ago, as I held a match under the little pile of coal in my Weber Smokey Joe kettle grill, located on the crummy, tar-covered rooftop of my crummy building, thirteen flights above downtown Manhattan. Eying the anemic wisp of smoke dribbling from the briquettes, she seemed unconvinced. Despite all evidence to the contrary, I insisted it would be burning brightly by the time we returned with the food. We left the grill and went to wait for the elevator.

By the time we climbed back up to the roof, the little pile of coals was glowing red and coated with ash. As the sun slipped down over the city, we tore into our steaks, Fourth of July fireworks bursting overhead, lighting up the skyline.

Writing is a leap of faith. Let's face it; without readers, an author is just a lone crazy person, making up stuff inside her head and writing it down, sometimes on paper, sometimes on index cards, sometimes on the envelope the electric bill came in, or the backs of PTA flyers. Buying a book by a no-name first-time author is a leap of faith, too. I extend my deepest thanks to every one of you for taking the leap with me.

Q. But wait! You can't just leave me like this! What happens to Rafe and Tessa? Is that all there is?

A. Oh, no. I just told you, Rafe is taking Tessa to Eastern Europe, to show her where her family lived and perished. And after that, well, it's back to New York City! Don't forget, Tessa's a starving artist. She needs a job.

And a place to paint. And a new roommate. (Rafe wants her to move in with him, but she won't do it. She's too proud.) Meanwhile, back at the American Academy of Art, there's a whole new lineup of students and board members...And you can bet Anastasia is up to something...hey, what ever happened to David, anyway?

Q. I want to live in your book! Can I tell you how much I loved it?

A. Are you kidding? Yes, please! I want to know every last thing that moved you, made you think, made you laugh, made you cry! The best way to do this is with reviews. I'll be trolling the internet, reading every last one I find. If you loved Rafe and Tessa, and you want other readers to love them too, write a review! Two places where reviews really matter are in Amazon and Goodreads, but anywhere is good. That way, readers can keep on finding the book. This is the single nicest thing you can do for me or any author.

Q. This sure was a long book.

A. That wasn't really a question, but that's okay. Some of my favorite novels are long reads. *The Historian* is actually fifty thousand words longer, *American Gods* just a few thousand words shorter. Rafe has seen a good many things, some of them remarkable, some of them terrible, and they just kept spilling out of him. (We're saving some for the next book.)

Q. Is it true that you painted a portrait of Hillary Clinton that is hanging in the White House?

A. Well, it's mostly true. Shortly after I graduated the New York Academy of Art, Second Genesis, an innovative drug rehabilitation program in the Washington, D.C. area, commissioned me to paint a portrait of Hillary Clinton. It was presented to the First Lady as a gift for her support. I don't know if it's actually hanging anywhere. I'm pretty sure it's decorating the eaves of the White House attic.

Q. How will I know when you've written something new? I want to stay connected!

A. Wow! Who's feeding you these great questions? Here are some ways you can keep up with what I'm doing.

You can follow me on Twitter: @hmshankman

You can friend me at Goodreads: www.goodreads.com

Check out my Pinterest boards: www.pinterest.com/hmshankman

You can visit my blog: helenmarylesshankman.com

And I love getting emails! Write to me at helenmarylesshankman@gmail.com.

Made in the USA
Lexington, KY
25 February 2014